THE NETRON ORIGINS

NETRO TWO

THE NETRON

-ORIGINS-

NETRO TWO

M.V. MENDEZ

THE COSMOS

A formation of potent beings who simply wanted to entertain themselves through their own establishments, sit back and observe like watching a film that's recorded millions of years long. These potent beings were called the Pinnacle, the creators of galaxies harnessing the *Crystal of Zenith* for assistance and constructing galaxies for epochs until they were finally stultified. It's the identical routine repeatedly ever since they were originated. Their bodies never aged, they kept the same figure ever since they were formed, and no one knows how their existence came about or where they originally arose from—not even themselves. The Pinnacle was an assemblage of four—Jhankunelle, Zelantabo, O-Neuton and Pezabull who all resided on interstellar clouds also known as *space clouds*. Jhankunelle is the being that creates the planets and everything that comes with it. Zelantabo creates the moons, Pezabull creates the suns and O-Neuton creates an entire galaxy and everything in a galaxy combined. Well, they all have the capability of creating an entire galaxy, it's just that his siblings were too lazy to be like him so they each give themselves different roles to accomplish.

"Generating new life is now of the essence in a universe which is quite large and filling the voids would be most admirable." Pezabull speaking in the *Zenith language*.

"What should this new life be? The species amongst the galaxies that we created before are truly remarkable but now something more ideal is waiting to be born." Jhankunelle deemed.

"Yes, it's challenging to bring forth beings who are most impressive as the others." Zelantabo said.

"Let us directly change the methods on how we create galaxies and the species residing in them. A new circle of life." O-Neuton proposed.

"Splendid idea. . .. But how so?" Zelantabo asked.

"We should leave this to you O-Neuton, you're the one with the propositions." Jhankunelle implied.

"Well, let's uh, create… bigger planets. Yes, this time with lots of moons and suns." O-Neuton suggested.

"Right, planets that are superior to the galaxies we usually make." Jhankunelle said.

"The suns are all mines to create." Zelantabo said.

"And you know I got the moons." Pezabull added.

"Ok my brothers, let's begin." O-Neuton confirming their innovative diplomacies.

The Pinnacle found an empty void in the universe, immense enough to fit bigger planets than they usually make. It was the ideal capacity for them to customize their natural abilities and create two large planets which had precisely the same size, but they couldn't create anymore because there wasn't enough space to put another one.

"Two planets will have to do." Jhankunelle said.

"Now it's time we create the beautiful features these two planets will own." O-Neuton said.

Zelantabo molded twenty suns surrounding both planets while Pezabull molded twenty moons surrounding both planets.

"Do you all remember, that one galaxy with the Homo sapiens?" O-Neuton asked.

"Yes, it has a planet called Earth with nine other planets with one sun and moon residing in it." Jhankunelle replied.

"Yes, well; we certainly didn't create that extraordinary galaxy, but we can create something similar." O-Neuton added.

"I say, an abundant proposal that's well obtainable." Pezabull said.

On one planet, the Pinnacle used the Crystal of Zenith to create life forms comparable to humans with similar skin colors, eyes, hairs, height and more. Only major differences are that they don't have belly buttons, their hearts are in the exact middle of their chests and their abilities are a lot different from what humans can perform. The second planet had life forms that resembled Dragons, the mythical creatures from fiction stories created by humans. The Pinnacle decided to form more than a trillion species living on each of the two planets which resulted in both planet sizes to possibly be quadruple the size or more of Earth and this is a galaxy far beyond Earth.

The Dragoons have different body types as such as every kind of species, but they're considered beasts and their sizes depend on the genes and genders. Dragoon royals portray figures that stood up right with scales, horns, claws, wings and etcetera. The ordinary male Dragoons are usually smaller but physically stronger than female Dragoons which makes them more in control of physical aggression. The ordinary female Dragoons being much larger about eighty to a hundred feet tall than the ordinary male Dragoons which is about thirty feet tall, this is because the female needs a large body to sustain and convey their offspring. They can lay up to three hundred eggs as female Netrons can only birth up to four at a time though they are much more sexually active.

"What should we call the first planet?" Zelantabo asked.

"Netron! The first one is called planet Netron with species entitled the Netrons." O-Neuton said.

"And the second one?" Pezabull asked.

"Planet Dragoon! With species that's entitled the Dragoons." O-Neuton said.

Both planets began with a ruler, Prince Netro One who later became a king, King Netro One of Netron and Prince Larthgon who later became a king, King Larthgon of Dragoon. They were best of friends, sometimes one would visit the other and help rule each other's life forms. The kings of both planets began their phases as children molding themselves with highly developed intelligence and relying on the Crystal of Zenith to accomplish many great establishments. The Crystal of Zenith, also known as the *Zenith Crystal,* which possesses unspeakable infinite deity power that they have never witnessed before granted by the Pinnacle. More crystals were discovered on both planets which claimed ownership for each. Both kings decided to create more crystals with the help of the Crystal of Zenith then they later divided them across the universe. They also carried out an extended inventory of enhancement, assisting with everyday life as Netrons and Dragoons don't rely on technology or machinery in which they have never considered to create. They mostly rely on the crystals and their phenomenal abilities.

After living an ordinary childhood, they finally had found their queens—Queen Tella of Netron and Queen Kelligon of Dragoon. Both kings had chosen their queens from their female life forms and crowned them with assistance from their council which had used books for guidance. With the help of the Crystal of Zenith, both kings made these books like human made books with the English language granted by the Pinnacle which is the only language that the Netrons and Dragoons knew except for the two kings because they both also speak the Zenith language.

These books were built with diamonds and impenetrable glass that acted as pages used like a touch screen. These books contributed their life forms to understand more about their own special abilities, limits and overall truth about their existence. These books also contained rules, laws and regulations of their planets and the key to solving almost anything past, current and future.

"They are just outstandingly beautiful."

"Yes, I enjoy the peace and love propelling through the ambience to the very core beneath the surface of my planet."

"It's unfortunate my brothers didn't meet you up close yet."

"Where are they anyway?"

"Resting somewhere, ever since they finished their fraction of the labor, they left me to do the residuum… lazy bastards."

"Well, you did a fine job, a total masterpiece. You all have an amazing gift."

"Thank you. Where is Larthgon? He's usually here with you."

"We had a slight disagreement and I haven't seen him since."

"A disagreement now? Over what?"

An undeviating dispute erupted because Netro One didn't agree with the way Larthgon treated his life forms. He confronted Larthgon and his oppressive sovereign only resulting an upsetting exchange of words telling Netro One to worry about his own planet and he'll worry about his. Larthgon's behaviors seemed malicious but Netro One doesn't know exactly what it was. All that he knew was Larthgon's habits were the opposite of the deeds of Netro One's life form which was absolute goodness.

O-Neuton was stunned to hear his creations doing such evil things when Netro One explained to him about the previous dispute. O-Neuton then clarified to Netro One that Larthgon has been performing unspeakable evil acts and explained the absolute true meaning of evil.

"Be careful my creation, I fear he's plotting on something, I just have that gut feeling that this might turn left... Two planets with very similar structures but still opposite features combining with the positives and negatives. This just... this just makes us look naïve."

"No, I doubt Larthgon will do anything foul... he's been my companion for thirty-three years now. He's more than a friend, he's like a brother to me."

"Hmm, let's just hope so."

As planet Dragoon gets darker and darker each day Netro One gets concerned, Netro One visited Dragoon once more to speak with Larthgon and Larthgon wasn't too pleased to see him. "What!? What do you want?—Filthy Netron!"

"Is this your humor or do you really think pure goodness is filthy?"

"Gaagh'... you and your petty soft kindness is unbearable."

"I thought we were friends Larthgon . . . brothers."

"Those words . . .friends . . . brothers . . . Is that what we truly are?"

"What do you mean? Of course, we are? Have you lost your mind?"

"Oh, but my mind is still intact."

"Then you have truly reshaped your image . . . the Pinnacle, they were right."

"Ha, the Pinnacle?! They need to be executed!"

"What? Executed? That's not like you."

"Oh, Netro. It's a lot like me, more than you think . . . I'm just bored Netro residing next to your boring necessities of goodness . . . So, to enlighten my interests... I'm going to murder all your species and destroy your disgusting planet called Netron. Then, I'm going to do the same with the rest of the planets in the universe. Yes, my profession will be to cause total demolition."

"No... No, you wouldn't!"

"Hmm, ever since I was a child Netro, I felt a different feeling than you do. You loved beauty and I loved ugly. I wanted to figure out what are these feelings. So, I dug deep, then deeper and I found out that its genocide, war, demolition, absolute and utter darkness! I never liked what you wanted for your planet it wasn't the same vision I see."

"No, we negotiated about so many positive things, we gathered ideas for a great era, and we spoke about love and beauty for both of our species!"

"No, not positive, I want negative. I'm not for love—I never was and never will. It's about time I show who I really am . . . Now get off my planet!" Larthgon ranted.

"Ugh..." Netro One stammered while being dramatically interfered.

"I said, get off! You're not worthy on my royal grounds." Larthgon blurted in a severe manner then Netro One shook his head showing dissatisfaction then turned his back towards him.

Netro One began to walk as Larthgon smiled then added—

"Or else you want me to slaughter you right here and have your planet destroyed. No... I want your species to suffer slowly so I can enjoy every bit of it.. . . Yes! Prepare for war Netro!"

Netro One couldn't resist replying to him, he turned his body back around facing him once more.

"War? No need for war Larthgon! But if you and your species try to do anything to my planet, we will defend it with honor and proceed with force!"

Harsh devious laughter came from Larthgon then he gave a devious look behind Netro One's back as he ascended away traveling light speeds.

Larthgon had become a tyrant resulting in his species existence rendering pure evil, playful, reckless and rowdy. The Dragoons have no motive, no honor, they will murder their own species for sport, ingesting, raping and enslaving each other while an elevated majority of the Netrons have virtue ethics of an ethical system. The Netrons are the embodiment of righteousness, carrying an endless nature of purity with soft hearts that can be easily broken from the shackles of deviousness. Once a Netron snaps subsequently from a crumbled core, their rage sometimes opens their true limits. Although most Netrons are very sympathetic, they are still resilient, courageous and they will never give up in the face of adversity.

Larthgon ordered teams to different planets causing destruction, useless warfare and spreading his ruthless tyranny just like he said he would. The Pinnacle were disgusted and had enough of it after they had seen what he'd done. Consequently, all four of them took it upon themselves to visit Dragoon, Netro One followed secretly behind the Pinnacle only to see that the conversion wasn't so pleasant and Larthgon destroyed all four of them with ease. The authority to be the new Pinnacle and the power to create galaxies could now be in the hands of Netro One and Larthgon but both don't see eye to eye which caused clutter in the universe.

The time zone on planet Netron and Dragoon stirred partially like Earth's but have different moons and suns. A few days later a miniature team of ten powerful Dragoons attacked one of Netron's regions and murdered three hundred and eighty-six Netrons, a hemorrhage of prominent species. Some of them fought back and two of the Dragoons were defeated but the Netrons in that region just wasn't powerful enough. When Netro One heard the report from one of the ambassadors of the Netron Council, 'Keluncarr'—about his life forms being slaughtered, he was outraged.

In the highest Sanctuary of Royalty, a place of refuge, Netro One's spouse Queen Tella was trying to calm him down.

"Demonic forces had their way into our homes, now the Dragoons had betrayed us."

"I fear the Dragoons are now a bigger threat than our demons. Evil spirits are presumed to be on every planet, no matter how pure of heart we may be, these demons can possibly take control of our souls... The Dragoons however are far more dangerous, I see now."

"They absolutely are my king…"

"Then I'm going to build an army… with powerful soldiers, soldiers that not only Dragoons would fear but the evil that surges across the entire universe . . . There's one thing these Dragoons don't know is that we can be more powerful than they are in many ways. We need to use this advantage and bring them to permanent exile for their wrongdoing!"

"How my king? Only ten managed to destroy over three hundred of our own within my embassy with only two of them left dead from the region's self-defense attacks." Keluncarr mentioned.

"How you say? . . . Hmm, you haven't seen my true power unfold, haven't you? I could wipe out the entire Dragoon race, but their king is in the way. Therefore, we fight as one…"

"Wait, this is not right—my love, you have to go back to planet Dragoon and make peace." Queen Tella interrupted him.

"My Queen, we have to defend ourselves.... the Dragoons... they said that they will return. My king, we need justice, they need punishment and to be neutralized."

"Yes, I saw it in his eyes, the look he had given me . . ."

He paused and shook his head then continued—

"Keluncarr is right, I'm going to create a powerful army with help of the Zenith Crystal—an army that will have skill, loyalty, honor, respect and ready to fight for our planet. I will not let this go on any longer!"

"There has to be another way—many will die."

"Trust me my love, I try to reconcile with Larthgon, but his mind is somewhere else, far beyond of what I could see . . . The way I'm going to create my soldiers will make the Dragoons think twice the next time they decide to attack us again!"

"What about the Pinnacle? Why don't you just ask them to deal with the Dragoons?"

"No, they aren't of any use for us anymore."

"What do you mean?"

"What I mean is, that Larthgon murdered them right in front of my eyes, leaving me and him the creators to be. The power of the Pinnacle became a stray but as you can see the way things are, only one must carry out this power. The Pinnacle was a species of only four who were perhaps created by the Zenith, but they act as one. Not just acquaintances but brothers . . . Hm, . . . this chaos must be stopped, no more!"

"But my love..."

"As King of Netrons . . . the first abiding Netron and highest guardian of the pure of heart—I'm building a militia and hereby declare war amongst the Dragoons . . . Larthgon and his planet will be banished—and that's final."

Moments later, he molded his species into soldiers in every region on the planet by using the abilities that the Crystal of Zenith possesses to create the *Netron Suits*. The

Netron Suit is a type of body armor and power enhancer, the suit has supremacies that Netrons cannot perform when they are without the suit. These suits became a natural ability which only beings with Netron DNA can access at any given time.

A Netron could be at any age to join the Netron Army, first becoming Cadets, then they will be trained until they meet the requirements of a qualified soldier. Netrons go through brute screening to be placed under a high rank such as "Elite Soldiers, Captains and Generals". Netrons cannot enter warfare without a Netron Suit and if they don't meet the requirements of a high rank, they become a methodical soldier such as "Netron Battle Officers". Although Netrons can train themselves to be powerful without these suits, the Netron Army still restricts it. Permitted to allegiance and service, the first ever ready army which contained just over a thousand soldiers with only two generals were developed in three days while the Dragoons haven't returned ever since their first attack. Nevertheless, the Netrons rebelled against the Dragoons as orders were placed to travel to Dragoon and capture the ones that slaughtered the three hundred and eighty-six Netrons and any Dragoon that stood in their way. The Netron Army arrived, and the Dragoons refused to turn over the murderers which later resulted in combat. The Netrons were winning the battle with only twenty Netrons dead and over five thousand Dragoons dead. The Netrons had made a retreat after a miraculous increase of Dragoons stepped forward and returned fire. The Dragoons didn't round up an army as yet, but they came in large packs. Larthgon realized Netro One is a force to be reckon with and later made an army of Dragoons called the Dragoon Army. Both kings decided to advance their warfare on a large meteorite half the size of their planets.

Eleven years went by and the war remained unrelenting with catastrophic sufferings. Leverages were built and the Dragoons figured out how to be more resilient by obtaining duplicated Netron Suits with evolved abilities. When the darkness had seemed whole, a pint of light appeared. Within the years, King Netro One then became a father as Queen Tella had conceived a baby boy named Nealo in which they entitled him the "Royal Son of Netro One" or simply the "Royal Son".

When Nealo was born he became the start of the Netron Cycle and must carry out the royal eternal prophecy. Carrying out this prophecy means two life stages must be fulfilled passing the adolescence stage which is twenty years of age in order for the next prince or princess to be announced as the highest leader. The Pinnacle generated the royal prophecy in this way because Netrons and Dragoons have a long-life span.

Netro One finally had a face to face physical conflict with Larthgon in which both fought for days to only recognize that they were evenly matched. With assistance from the Zenith Crystal, Netro One had created a Confinement Crystal before the fight which he later used to trap both himself and Larthgon. The strategy that he carried out was successful and the only way to be free of the crystal is if one dies.

Seeking a place of better well-being, Queen Tella sent her son Nealo to Earth in the year 2264, the 23rd Century with a beautiful Netron female companion named Raenia and a duplicated book of the original Netron Book of Edu, so that they could learn and understand how to perpetuate the Netron cycle.

Traveling light speeds through hyperspace to Earth's solar system in year 2262 Earth years, Queen Tella and her squadron of soldiers encountered a few of the Grainians. A species from planet Grain that are known for being bandits amongst the universe. They are microscopic compared to other beings, as small as a *Dicopomorpha echmepterygis*, a parasitic wasp in the family of Mymaridae—which is one of the smallest insect in the world. They can also naturally increase their size up to forty feet tall. Queen Tella discovered that they pose a violent threat to her, her soldiers and her son. Her squadron easily destroyed them, but little did they know the Grainians were mainly interested in humans. The Grainians anonymously resided on Earth ever since the year 2233, slowly harvesting on humans, obtaining intellect and overall habits of incarnation until they invaded Earth for three years after year 2261.

The Grainians or as humans sometimes nicknamed them the *Brain Suckers* who had peculiar flushed bodies with large antennas, razor sharp teeth that bites deep, cords that drilled through the temple passing through the skull then proceeded to siphon the brain particles ensuing increased strength and improved intelligence—sometimes they even eat the brains. The Grainians then utilized their victims as hosts, using the carcasses for many duties. Sometimes they would consume their meal without using the carcasses which led humans to subsequently turn into the brainless living dead that will devour flesh, including the Grainians. Yes, the irony of the piece of food you once ate wants to eat you.

In year 2264, Earth was up against a formidable force, but humans finally came together as one and found a way to defeat the Grainians by using their technology. They had special assistance from Jahzin Yoko who wielded the *Twin Swords of Ketsueki*. Jahzin Yoko was the first *Death Angel* that can utilize Tektonian enchantment abilities which is operated solely with the Tektonian Crystals. These enchantment abilities were originally used by the Tektonians, a peculiar race from planet Tektonia who are now extinct.

With an ideal strategy, Jahzin successfully executed Bullbourne, the Emperor of the Grainians but perished along with him. His bravery was respected which occasioned him to hold the title as a legendary hero of the Grainians vs. Humans War along with the many valiant soldiers that fought and died for a better world. Earth was badly damaged, and countries were left in ruins, but humans came together once more and later reconstructed after the brutal warfare with the new technology they developed from the Grainians. The alienated technology was recycled to construct the continent named *Gigantica*, which is a combination of Canada, the United States of America, Mexico, the Caribbean islands and many more countries within the northern hemisphere. Gigantica is not often but still mentioned as North America because of history and since global warming occurred over the years, the lands shift apart and shaped differently over time.

Gigantica almost resembles a large donut on the map which comprises name changes to countries to cities to towns to villages to street names. Gigantica had famous cities that brought a lot of attention to tourists such as Gigantica City which is the largest city in the world located in the middle of Gigantica. Atlantis, which is under water and many more that are still around since the 21ˢᵗ century. There are three major cities floating in the sky which are owned by Gigantica, they are simply called *sky cities*— Empyrean City, Azure Region City and the Great Welkin City. There are many more sky cities and other marvelous locations that humans vested in and yes, if you guessed it, the planets in our solar system. Humans wanted to expand as much as possible especially after the high volume of deaths from the war. Thanks to NASA, SpaceX and many other aerospace companies, humans extended with increased population and built new habitation on other planets outer space such as Mars, Venus, Saturn and more.

Mars is the first planet to obtain residency in the early 22nd century. Humans transported animals and nurtured crops that were merrily confined inside large shelters and time capsules that had certain temperatures for different species. Most of the animals were at the brink of extinction but luckily, they had a successful resurgence. Many farmlands were also established along with many lakes to rivers to seas to oceans in every planet.

Space-ways were built to connect from Earth to the different planets in Earth's solar system creating unlimited entry. All the planets in Earth's solar system are covered with shields around them filled with oxygen produced by photosynthesis which is the process of agriculture. Humans generated a more polished Earth and solar system, this was called *the New World Order* with new laws, higher level technology, humans with enhanced capabilities, and overall a successful evolution. These times are more about peace with an easier life to live, the 21st Century's ultimate "dream life".

Formal ways of living with less murder, rape, drugs, racism, illegal trades and lowered overall crime rate. Even after the New World Order, devious minds continued to implement the worst acts. The wicked roams in the midst of the peaceful and new phenomenon are amongst the cosmos. Although Earth constantly had heroes who perished or disappeared, there's still life which means there's still hope.

EVOLUTION

Everyone deserves a family living with great energy and inordinate care for one another. Family is most important, and we shall cherish our loved ones, especially if we're surrounded by cruelty. Year 2322, the 24th century proclaiming the face of a nearly pale decaying corpse looking down on his sworn enemy. It seemed as if the underworld has reached the skies which captured smoke and ashes from the poisoned ground. Everything is so dark, and the nearest light was never to be found. The stakes were high but now it's time to perform the final strike to end him and build a better life from the rigid and violent harm that the enemy had caused.

No mercy, it's time to fulfill his duty with such anger boiling. He knew being in battle would be insufferable, but he never knew it would succumb to this.

"From this day forward . . . I will never forgive you!"

TWO MONTHS AGO...

⊕NE

Firmness of purpose, restrained impulses, every movement and every fiber in his body must correspond with his path to victory. Three years had passed since the untraceable abduction of the first born which simultaneously caused nothing but anxiety and distress within the Kafmora family. The family now has their mind-set to be more cautious of any hazardous future event, under any circumstances should another blameless child be jeopardized. The remaining children constantly thought about the endless grieving from their mother's love torn in half, a piece of her everything gone with only fragments of what's left to remember him by. A mother's precious children—certainly, they aren't as normal as other humans but ever since the abduction, it's clear things could swivel for the worst. They aren't just beings, they are simply part of a family that loves each other dearly.

Some may not know what or who is truly around them, what's beneath the skin, the flesh, the bones, the spirit and the overall being. Unordinary species residing amongst unordinary species, any breed that possess the particular senses and in general just an unfamiliar complex.

Displaying frustration while standing still, closing his eyes and clenching his fists. —**Ki-Yale Kafmora**, at age thirteen with a scrawny body, brown skin, five feet-three inches tall and a low tapered dark haircut with the sides faded.

A noise rattled his attention in front of him and as he slightly opened his eyes.

"Yo, Grandpa! I'm not getting this flying thing right. Like what am I supposed to do just float?!"

"Hmm… you've been at it for almost three hours now Ki-Yale."

"Yeah, I'm getting tired now. I should just go home and try again another time."

"Hmm…"

A chiseled old man approached him being at age seventy-two looks to be in his late thirties, six feet tall with fair skin wearing a simple all black extra high-grade neoprene training outfit, used for fighting sports. He has a full gray thrown back hairstyle, strong facial structure and a few wrinkles.

"It's all about focus my grandson, utilize your core until you feel yourself about to take flight. It's a very basic Zeal ability, like how you shot the 'Loose Cannon' out of your fists."—**Nealo Kafmora** lecturing his grandson.

Nealo is in good shape mostly because Netrons can age up to five hundred years and can keep a younger look once they go through puberty, usually passing age twenty-five.

"Hmm, you told me this already, I thought about it and…"—More frustration from his voice then his grandfather interceded him with a stern voice—"I said focus!"

"Ok, ok . . . here goes…"

Ki-Yale straightened his white tank top and grey fitted sweatpants then closed his eyes once more. A few seconds after, his body began to slowly float from the ground.

"Hey! Kid, look around you."

"Woaah'! GRANDDAD! YO, I'M FLOATING!"

He ignored his default airborne posture, wobbling and loosing balance, witnessing the beauty above Little Tree Ville as he slowly elevated forty feet in the air.

Little Tree Ville, a charming village which is about six hundred square miles and rests in a large island named Gel Hev. Gel Hev about two hundred thousand square miles, south of the Atlantic Ocean and it's a systematic system ever since it's been declared ownership by the Gigantica government. It has a compact economy with well-built houses chiefly in tremendous architecture, interior design and some outstanding farmlands. Usual weather changes instantaneously experiencing all seasons, from below twenty with snow to ninety degrees with most days being windy and habitual rain from time to time. Some tourists say, *this village is a paradise* and some others say, *it's only for the rich folks*. The village has all sorts of trees and they are most appealing because they are peculiarly diminutive compared to the usual heights from different trees. They are about four feet up to twenty feet tall and up to five feet wide depending on the variety—hence the name of the village.

The cause for these threes being little came from a man of style and creativity named Benson Langard III. He brought upon the idea to create a village accompanied by infinitesimal trees using the M.N.S.C, meaning *Mother Nature Standard Chemicals*. Benson had a certain position under the government which allows him to perform his art on nature. At first people thought it was wrong to interfere with nature's natural abilities but when they saw the beauty and the outstanding wonders, they thought otherwise. It's not just the trees that are focused on by tourists that comes from all over the world to visit but the fact that it's on an island that links to the deep underwater City of Atlantis.

The air pressed against Ki-Yale's face as he elevates higher. He moved forward ten miles per hour, then thirty miles per hour and just like that, Ki-Yale is flying. A little shaky at first but he's getting the hang of it. Now moving sixty miles per hour, then eighty miles per hour.

"WOO HOO!"

He then flies lower, about seven feet and swerving around the little trees going about fifty miles per hour. He clenched his fists then shoots yellow blasts out his right hand called the *Loose Cannon* onto random trees with his arms being pushed back a little from the it's recoil.

Lethal particles of the blast which becomes the size of a shotgun slug, will scatter when fired and when the particles hit their targets they explode, hence why it's called the Loose Cannon. This attack emits radiation that could be deadly, but the effects of this attack depends on how powerful the user is and varies when the user charges it as if it's a battery. The more it charges the more powerful it gets which is more solid and the faster it shoots. An example of a very futile and slow blast, would be moving at eighty kilometers per hour and an example of a very robust and hasty blast, is moving at light speeds.

Ki-Yale twisted his body around causing him to face the sky glaring at the birds fluttering and the clouds shading him from the sun. Entering a pathway, slowing down traveling twenty miles per hour and not watching his direction with his arms pinned behind his head as if he's lying on a bed. Instead, he daydreamed about his brother **Narrken Kafmora** who was abducted at age twelve.

As Ki-Yale continued to lose focus, he unexpectedly collided into an *American sycamore* tree.

"Wha'... What!? Ki-Yale?" **Tajaymae Kafmora** alarmed. Ki-Yale's sister at twelve years old, five feet tall, a slender body and dark brown skinned. Her outfit is a simple—grey fitted t-shirt, black pants and white sneakers.

Adopted style from the 21st Century corresponding with her natural purple Afrocentric hair being in a ponytail.

"Huh? Oh Tajaaay'—wadduup'? What are you doing here?"

"Uh, youuu'!!"

"Naaah', I don't wanna' know what you doing anymore." He said then lightly chuckled while she looked at him like he had twelve heads.

"Sis, check this out—see, check this out. I was flying and I wasn't paying attention then I crashed into this tree. By the way, I just learned how to fly, like finally! Isn't that awesome!? I can freaking fly!. . . Now I don't have to take an airbus or a regular bus or ride in Mommy's car to school, although sometimes I walk... Walk?! Who the hell does that anymore? I don't! Yo, flying is freaking dope! Despite the hovercars… it feels so different to be the actual person flying. Talk about that special commute! WOO!"

Ki-Yale jabbered then continued to ramble quickly with enjoyment—

"But wait, I think Granddad doesn't want me to fly around so much cause' people might see me, hmm'... Ok, ok, I can just fly occasionally at certain hours of the day. Definitely not flying at nighttime, too dark. This is like super freaking awesome!"

"Ki-Yale!! . . . SHUT UP!!"

"Oouuu', someone is upset."

"You have no idea what you just did. Don't you!?"

"Ummm', no."

"Look behind you."

He scarcely peeked behind him, then turned back around quickly and looked at his fists.

"Did I do…?" He whispered then continued—"I mean, whoa'! What is that? Looks like a history project on a mechanical board . . . all destroyed."

"YES, DESTROYED! A HUGE HOLE IN-BETWEEN MY PROJECT! . . . KI-YALE, IT TOOK ME A MONTH TO GET THIS DONE! GRAAAGH! YOU ASSHOLE!"

Tajaymae's history project not only took her a month to get it done, it's also due the next day. She had sleepless nights researching history about the government and her topic was *Feminism* and the first female P.O.T.W, abbreviation for *President of the World*—which was President Lynda Valerie Polara in the years 2265 to 2300. She was the 2nd P.O.T.W. Now, currently the 3rd P.O.T.W is President Blane Nixon Moore Jr. and the first ever P.O.T.W was named Mario Troy Silva in year 2258 to year 2265. Being President of the World also means you can be in office for as long as you like but this position has the most stress in government history thus carrying a lot of power over the human race.

Tajaymae gave a serious mean mug as her round shaped amber eyes began forming into purple lusters. Ki-Yale puts on an innocent face and tried to play it off to escape his faulty actions.

"WHEN FINALLY FINISHING MY PROJECT, YOU COME IN AND DESTROYED IT! YOU UGLY GOOFY PIECE OF… AAAGH!"

"Listen, sis, I didn't see it… Okay? I was so focused on the fact I can fly now you know…."

"GRRAAAAAAAA!" She yelled while charging at her brother and clenching her fists as he vibrantly ran away.

His teeth gritted while his prominent shaped hazel eyes goggled, realizing his sister isn't down for any more talking.

"Alright, it's time for me to gooo' airborne!"

Ki-Yale took off seven feet in the air flying back to his grandpa.

"COME BACK HERE, YOU STUPID GOOFY ASS LIL' BOY!"

Two young ladies in their early twenties kissing each other and being fully naked while one is getting oral sex from another lady. Another couple, man and woman partaking in sexual activities, doggy style position, half naked in the middle of the café on a table while customers sit and watch. People come to this twenty-four-hour café originally to have sex with someone and hoping people throw money at them almost like a strip club but this time the entertainment is actual sex. Food and drinks from many different cultures could be served in the naughty area where the performances are kept or the regular dining area where no sexual activities are visible just subtle music for the variety. Some are neutrally drinking big bottles of liquor, big jugs of beer, coffee and some are just _vaping_ through electronic vapor cigarettes, cigars and smoking finely cut and rolled cannabis cigarettes from high end marijuana companies. This diverse café is called the _"Never too Early Café"_.

The door slammed open, a nineteen-year-old with dark spiky hair, full face tattoo of an endless maze down to his entire neck with ink surrounding his eyelids. Piercing of a bull nose ring and earrings. He has an ectomorph body type wearing black boots, black jeans, black tech gloves and a black long sleeve fitted Kevlar shirt with a black bandana wrapped around his neck.

The unconscious bouncer lying on the floor as he sashayed through the entrance hallway.

The bald-headed bouncer alarmed and racing towards his co-worker. "What the...? Benny!"

The teen approached the lady bartender and presented to her a holographic picture from one of his devices then spoke with a strong Irish accent—"Where the fuck is this kid?!"

"Um… Excuse me?!"

"Oy'! I said…!"

"Look, I don't know who that is. Alright? Now go bug someone else with that nasty attitude of yours."

"Hm… Does anyone—in this shit whole, know where I can find this fucking kid?!!"

His device made the holographic picture become larger displaying to everyone, then the android DJ stopped the music and half the café went quiet.

"See, if I knew where he is and you would've asked nicely, I would've told you."—**Neecho Kafmora**, Ki-Yale's father, at age thirty-eight, six feet, three inches tall with medium skin like Nealo and wearing regular mechanical clothing on his muscular body. He has marginally brown hair buzz cut, almond shaped hazel eyes with a strong jaw line and sharp cheek bones in lined with his medium size nose.

"Hm…" The teenaged boy murmured as he strolled towards Neecho then asked—"Do you know where I can find him—please… sir?"

"Now that's more like it…"

The teen beheld with determination and wanted a glorified answer. "No . . . no, I don't know where that kid is. Never seen him before."

The teenaged boy eyeballed Neecho up and down with a mean mug then said—"Hm… okay, thank you."

He looked around the cafe then strolled to the exit. The music started playing again and the second bouncer stopped him in the hallway—"Hey kid…" Said the bouncer touching the teen forcing him to turn around.

The teen shoved his hand out as if he wanted to shake hands for a greeting then abruptly, a glass katana appeared from the center of his palm as if a tiny projector was in his tech gloves. Without hesitation, he stabbed the bouncer in his stomach as blood vigorously oozed on the glass sword halfway through his body.

"You don't ever, touch me."

"Haagh'!"

He pulled the sword out of his stomach as he fell to the floor then the teen dropped his glass katana causing it to shatter before walking away leaving the Café.

Steadily and feeling relaxed, Neecho continued to drink his coffee then said—"Some kids out here, they need better manners."

"You're damn right they do!" Said one of his old friends.

"You ok? You look like you did something that you regret doing." Nealo worries while he used his right hand to caress his painter brush mustache down to his circle full gray beard and wrapped his left forearm around the top area of his belly.

"Naah'. I'm all good over here. Aaall' good. Now let's get back to this training."

"You sure?I know that look Ki."

"Yeah, yeah I'm good."—Ki-Yale said then flashed a large smile trying to hide the guilt on his face as soon as Nealo raised his left flat eyebrow and slightly tilting his head to the right.

"Ok, let's proceed. Now that you know how to fly, it's time you expand your abilities my grandson, can't risk another grandchild being abducted."

"I thought I was already expanding."

"Yes, and it's still a lot to learn my grandson. You must learn the Netron abilities, perfect them then get more powerful."

"Hmm."—He said with a puzzled face, his left cheek lifted, squeezing his left eyelid and scratching his head as if he is trying to figure out difficult mathematics.

"I want you to hit me with the Loose Cannon. You can be airborne if you like, I don't mind flying around a bit."

"Hm, okay Granddad, I'll try to shoot softly."

"No, no, no, no, no… no need to shoot softly my grandson, your hardest shot is like a tingle in my armpits."

"Oh… Your armpits huh?"—"There's no rules Ki, just hit me with a beam and here's a twist. I'll be shooting back my Loose Cannon beams in which I will use only fifteen percent of power. That's a little more than what your full power Loose Cannon shoots… This is training my grandson and you'll get the best from me." He said while Ki-Yale bared apprehension then continued—"Now let's begin!"

Ki-Yale's veins appeared through his skin and in the process of changing into a burnt orange color that glows. He clenched fists and his veins appeared yellow which is revealed when charging his Loose Cannon then the color drastically changes to a pale-yellow beam when fired.

Nealo started doing the same, he fired the first shot with his right arm which at first seemed like a horizontal punch to Ki-Yale's left foot. He moved his left foot in time for the beam to dodge it then returned fire the same way as his grandpa, but this time Ki-Yale used his left arm. Nealo dodges the shot that was aimed for his chest by twisting his body sideways while still airborne. Ki-Yale kept on firing about six more shots while Nealo was too fast and dodged them all.

"Hm, this is harder than I thought."

"C'mon my grandson. Hit me!"

Nealo soaring in front of Ki-Yale while he's getting shot at—

"Woah, Granddad is fast! I just—can't—hit him…"

Nealo went at a lower level in the air and instantly stopped while Ki-Yale couldn't control his breaking. Nealo now behind Ki-Yale and immediately shoots his 'Loose Cannon' towards his buttocks.

"Aah my ass!"

"Haahaha', look at that. You need to control your breaking my grandson—Bwahahaha'... I can't..."—He laughed excessively.

"Hmmm', not funny…"

"You need to also watch your back. Get it? 'Watch your back'."—Nealo trying to convey a joke.

"Hmm, it's not funny! It's more gay than funny!"

While Nealo continued cackling with laughter, Ki-Yale saw an opportunity to strike then shot a Loose Cannon blast towards him. Nealo opened his eyes then instantly vanished, allowing the beam to hit the ground.

"I'm right here." Nealo miraculously behind Ki-Yale. "How did you?!"

"It's my speed my grandson, I'm fast as a speeding bullet. I'll go faster if I want, you know."

"Ok, I quit!"

"Quit?! No, you don't quit my grandson. That's not the Netron way. What happen to your heart? Hmm? Where's your slogan you always use?"

"I got the heart—of a lion..."

"Yes, my grandson, that one, the slogan that boosts your confidence. Hmm—remember, your greatest enemy is yourself. You must face and prevail against any enemy." Nealo said hovering towards him.

Ki-Yale in his off-guard position not knowing that his grandfather would hit him, then Nealo punched him in the face and kneed him in the stomach.

"Aaaggh'."—Ki-Yale in a fetal position enduring pain while Nealo constantly hits him.

"You—never—give—up! No—matter—the situation!"

"Agh, agh, agh!"

Relentlessly, Nealo swiftly hits Ki-Yale in the face and body as each impacted him from his knuckles puncturing his flesh and bones.

"You must—persevere!!"

TW⊕

It's a Friday morning around 5:30am, the birds chirped to the bright maroon and orange sky that's been uttered by the hues of the burning yellow sphere. Ki-Yale began performing his regular morning routine which consisted of pushups with loud music, playing Hip Hop from the 21st century. "91, 92, 93, 94, 95, 96, 97, 98, 99—100."

With a muffled voice from his broken jaw. "One hundred pushups to start my day."—He added to himself as he puts on his mechanical clothes using his housing tech built inside the walls of his room while carefully brushing his teeth and freshening up. He turned on his holographic TV just by saying—"TV on." and proceeded to watch the Gel Hev news channel.

"In today's news law enforcement is making the world a safer place every day, every hour, every minute with new upgraded suits that put criminals in fear. These suits are specially designed for officers ready to serve and protect. They are now the biggest crime fighting success ever since they were launched two weeks ago and it's already affecting the strategies of criminals across the globe, even our solar system."

Ki-Yale is evidently aware of the world with the remaining corruption that roams, and most people would like to get rid of it all. He believes that evil will always be there no matter how many times you go up against it and defeating it—Evil always seem to step back in the house like an annoying buzzing fly. When his brother got kidnaped that's when he started to look at the world differently. Although his older brother is part Netron, he's still stronger than most humans and would've put up a serious fight eventually but you may ask... 'Was there any self-defense skills involved?' Well, his father didn't want any violence getting involved with his children at first until it paid the price of one of his sons, ever since that night, Neecho's ways are profound. Timeless dedication, keeping the light of hope, vigorous training at mid-night for an hour then went out searching for his son.

He puts on his black and gray pattern sneakers that he usually wears and proceeded down the hallway with a mechanical book in his hand towards his pet lion Titus that is four years old. He's an evolved lion equipped with an enhanced Mega Animal serum being 5.2 feet tall standing on his four legs and about 8.4 feet long. He sits inside a large cage with enough space to walk around and do indoor activities. Ki-Yale walks to the cage to hold his hand out to pet him.

"Hey, what's up Titus?!"

He roared and rushed towards Ki-Yale and brings his head down for him to pet his hair while he stood sideways.

"I have a new book for you... since you love to read..."

Ki-Yale handed him the mechanical book on the cage floor in front of him. Titus crouched down and stared at the book as it opened on Ki-Yale's command with holographic frames emitted from it.

"Aw, you're such a good boy... Sorry, I have to keep you in here. My mom won't allow me to have you roam around the house too much . . . Hey, later we can play when I get back from school."

After watching over Titus for a few minutes, he carried on down inside the elevator to the first floor of their three-story house to eat his mamma's cooking—bacon, egg and cheese sandwiches. He saw his scrawny little brother **Oji Kafmora** eating breakfast. Oji has a medium beige skin tone with hazel eyes like his brother and brown curly hair. Almost every morning they clown each other until one quits. — "Punk ass."

"Morning butt hole." Oji taunted then smiled showing his bucked teeth.

"Little rat dick." He responded.

"Hippo doo-doo stain."

"Hairy silverback gorilla vagina."

"Looking like my dirty underwear that I haven't washed in several weeks."

He squeezed his eyelids at his little brother in response to what he said.

"Good morning Ki-Yale, you're up early."—Ki-Yale's mother, **Demi Kafmora** said appearing from the living room. She's at age thirty-six and two years younger than her husband Neecho. Very Afrocentric because of her roots with her luscious dark skin. Her natural dark medium length dreadlocks brought out her amber eyes and oblong shaped face with a straight forehead. She's six foot-one inches tall with a curvy body, wearing a simple house garment with an apron and furry house slides on her feet.

"Yes, hmm, big day, hmm, today." Ki-Yale jabbered while eating his sandwich.

"Hey. What did I tell you about food in your mouth while talking?"

"I know, I know Ma! I'm just so excited, because today is the day I pass my final exam with the rest of the Super Geniuses!"

"Well now, that's good... I'm proud of you son."

"So nervous though." Ki-Yale continued talking while eating.

"Hmm, look at all those bruises, I feel like I'm the only mother that would accept my son getting beat up by his granddad." Demi peered while grabbing Ki-Yale's chin and looked closely at his bruised face.

"Yeah it's hard for me to chew with a broken jaw."

"Hmm', broken jaw huh? How was your training with Granddad yesterday?"— "You got messed up." Oji added and whispered.

"Yeah, it was intense as you can see with the bruises Mom— 'You just need to expand your abilities and perfect them my grandson'." Ki-Yale mocked his grandfather with a bad impression of his voice.

"Good! You need to be able to defend yourself out there in the world and gain some meat on your bones." Demi giving her son encouragement.

"Yes, I know Mom, I got the heart of a lion. Remember?" Ki-Yale quoting the slogan he always uses.

"Yes, and I wouldn't want to lose another half alien son so that training is for the best… Remember to inform those social workers that your granddad is with the Gigantica Military Training System and he's training you. That's why you have bruises, which is true he has the papers. Just in case they ask."

"Yes, I know Ma."

"Ok, hmm', um… Ki-Yale?"

"Yes Ma."

"What happened with you and your sister yesterday? I heard you destroyed her project then flew away?" Demi scrutinizing him while folding her arms.

Ki-Yale fleetingly looked at Oji as he paid no mind to the conversation and watching holographic TV.

"Who me Mom? I can't fly remember?"

"Hm, hope you aren't lying to me boy!"

"Ok, ok I just learned how to fly, Granddad taught me; then I accidentally crashed into Tajaymae's history project, well I think I blasted it... Hm, I don't remember exactly."

"Did you at least say sorry?"

"Um, ah... No—I didn't but she called me stupid, ugly and an asshole!"

"So, she was upset, not that I agree with her calling you stupid and all but that's your sister not your enemy. Plus, she puts so much work into that project. Boy, you have to apologize."

"Yeah, ok, sure Ma."

"Tajay should be waking up at any minute."

"Aah... maybe later." He said then levitated a couple inches off the floor, then kissed his mother on her cheek.

"Bye Ma! Goodbye Oji!"

Ki-Yale quickly walked through the hallway that leads to the exit of the house while Demi is left with a smirk on her face.

"Hey Ki-Yale!" Oji hollered.

"What?!"

"Which came first the chicken or the egg?"

"I'm not going to have this conversation with you anymore Oji!" He said then exited the house.

"You know it's the chicken . . . Hey, don't play yourself for a fool!"

"It's the egg Oji."

"Moooom'! You supposed to be on my side!"

Jolene Lucio Elementary School—

"Tajaymae Kafmora, please present your project to the class." Said the history teacher.

"Oh, that project looks old school with all that cardboard and shit... What happened to using modern technology?" One student whispering as she stood up to bring her project to the front for everyone to see.

"Ok... hold on—I just have to bring this up here . . . Ok, so... ahemm'... ok umm'..."—Feeling a bit of apprehension from the tension of her quiet fellow classmates as they gazed deep into Tajaymae's nervous soul. Her confidence had perished as her eyes bounced left and right.

"Speak bitch!" Said one of the male students as the rest of them instigated.

"Wallace! Say another word like that again and its detention."

"Detention my asshole and ball sacks..."

"What was that?!"

"Nothing, nothing!"

"Tajaymae, please now proceed..."

"Ok um', so my project is aah' called 'The First Female P.O.T.W' . . ." She paused with a tense look on her face.

"Lynda Valerie Polara demanded equality between the genders and as you know, with the previous war against the Grainians, humans wanted to prepare for another possible attack by combining all nations with one supreme leader after knowing there's life beyond our solar system..."

She paused again as she rocked her hand and accidentally broke a piece of cardboard connected to a five-inch globe which was glued onto her project. Complete silence around the classroom as the globe fell and rolled all the way to the teacher's desk then the class immediately laughed at her blunder.

"She's a clumsy little hoe!"

"Wallace! Detention!"

"Well then, I quit!"

"This is not a job idiot." Said a girl student named Vivian.

The school bell rang, and students got out of their chairs as if there was great danger amongst them. "Leave the project here, I'll grade it later... tomorrow you will present it first thing in the morning." As they head to the next class Tajaymae gathered her things and exit to the classroom onto the hallway then Vivian bumped her shoulder.

"Watch where you're going you purple haired weirdo—you got my brother in detention! I should..."

"You should what?" Tajaymae intervened her speech.

"Hmm. Why do you even keep your hair dyed purple anyway? It's the same style ever since you started this class, shaking my head. Change it already!"

"I have natural purple hair!"

"It's dyed you idiot! There's no such thing as natural purple hair!"

"Idiot huh?"

"Yeah, ummm', you're a dumb ass. An ugly, delusional, dumb ass and you ain't slayin' with that stupid hair." Vivian puts her hands on her hips strutting closer to her.

"Ok. You know what? Your mother! Yeah, she looks like she has a gaping vagina! Yeeaah—yeah, now I remember. I heard all her work friends use to "DP" her. No—matter of fact, "QP" that stupid hoe! Yeeaah!"

"What!?" Vivian gasped as Tajaymae continued to pummel her with harsh words—

"You probably don't even know what those abbreviations stand for, you senseless daughter of a penis hopping thot! She eats tons of grown men's sweaty booty holes every morning then kisses you on the cheek before you come to school! 'Oh, bye Vivian, I'll pick you up later Vivian... yeah, I'm going to do more blowjobs all day and forget cleaning my mouth because I gotta' pick you up on time!' Aagh! Just imagine what else she does before she picks you up—aagh! That's so unsanitary..."

Vivian immediately whimpered as her face seemed as if it's about to melt.

"Aaagh! Not true! Don't talk about my mother like that! She only did it once in porn! Ok?!"

"Oh… I'll talk how I want! . . . What?! What you going to do, thot?!"

More tears from Vivian as she stood still like she's trapped in an invisible steel box with no space to move around. Her face began to puff then she dashed to the staircase.

"Well Ms. Kafmora, those are some monumentally fine words you just said there."

She turned around quickly responding to a familiar voice. "Oh… Principal Hanes... How… How are you today?"

Little Tree Ville High School—

A school filled with teenagers and young Super Geniuses originally at ages ten and up. Four years ago, Ki-Yale at age ten was pushed forward by school officials after exhibiting fascinating grades and now he's near graduation.

"Nack, I'm so nervous bro. I'm so nervous… I don't know if I can do this."

"What you mean Ki? I thought you're prepared to dominate this easy test man! This is like elementary for us man. This is like *Homer Simpson* teaching us 'how to strangle a kid'."

Nack Yaldara, Ki-Yale's best friend. He's a fifteen-year-old boy with fair skin and a slender body wearing regular high-tech clothing. He has natural blonde hair with light blue eyes with a slightly sharp nose.

Nack is a 'Super Genius', born with a Super Genius serum or Intellectual Enhancement serum injected into his body as a newborn consented by his parents. Now he seems to be one of the quite a few young Super Geniuses in Little Tree Ville with the IQ of 118 and up. Nack is one year older than Ki-Yale and two inches shorter than Ki-Yale. Netrons are naturally more intelligent than humans, since Neecho and Demi's children are Netron royalty they are slightly more enhanced than most Netrons. Even at age two, Netrons could be smarter than an average thirteen-year-old human adolescent.

"Just relaaax'… You always seem to exponentially keep up with me in class, it's like we have the same intellect." Nack continued as he scratches his head with his fingertips.

"True but I'm not a Super Genius like you, I'm a little different."

"Yeah, you mention that a lot Ki."

"Yes, and I'm going to show you what I'm really talking about after school."

Ki-Yale uses his two hands to pick up his test sheets and neatly puts then together.

"Alright Ki. I'm ok with that—for now, let's keep our minds focused on these tests… What supposedly happened to your face by the way? It's your grandpa again, right?"

"Yeah, he's part of my explanation too."

—Four hours later Ki-Yale and Nack received their tests results in envelopes. They exited the school yard and the eagerness had already built up as their lives would change from this day, this very moment.

"Wow, don't you love it when the test results originate in on the same day you take the tests!" Nack raved.

"Hell yeah! Let's both open them at the same time."

"*STRRRAAAP! STRRRAAAP!*"

Both ripped open their envelopes. Nack examined his results then peeked at Ki-Yale's results.

"SEE? I KNEW YOU WOULD PASS THIS EAAASY TEST!! Well, easy for us because of our intellect."

"Yeah... you passed too right? Of course, you did... I shouldn't even be asking..." He said as he got interjected.

"Yo, Ki, we're going to college man!"

"Nah, college isn't for me. I'll just take the Central IQ test, twelve hours straight!"

"Oh shit, you got approved for that?"

"Yeah bro, I got the email saying I would be the first Super Genius to take it, so I said why not."

"Ah... that's wonderful man, if only I was a year younger. We would initially be the first ones."

"Now, Ki, what was it you were trying to show me?"

"You promise not to tell no one bro?"

"Listen, I'm your best friend... I promise bro, just tell me." Nack spoke with emphasis on *best friend*.

"Remember I'm always telling you that I'm a different kind of Super Genius, well it's not cause' I'm being cocky—it's cause' I actually never took the Super Genius serum the day I was born and never did. I'm naturally more intelligent than most humans. What I'm saying is... I'm actually . . .." He paused then looked around to see if anyone is watching then whispered—

"A different species... I'm half alien, half human...."

Nack stood in front of him with a blank stare and remained quiet for about twenty seconds then vaguely said—

"Ha. What? You're an alien? Well ok, I guess I'm outta' this world too."

"No, no, I'm really an alien... half alien.... I'm a Netron and a human."

Nack's leveled eyebrows lifted as Ki-Yale expressed seriousness in his speech wondering why his best friend is explaining this peculiar statement to him.

"Ummm..."

"I'm also a prince."

"And I'm also the Terminator heading back to the past to assassinate Sarah Connor."

"Aagh', I'm being for real here Nack… I have all sorts of powers; I can lift things that humans can't and I'm getting stronger each day."

"Really? So why do you look so humanlike? Even if you are half alien and half human. You should be looking like, I don't know—green or something. You know, like a different form. Unless your true form is in this counterfeit body that you have here…" Nack being confused and playing along to what seems to be a joke to him.

"No, this is my true self. Netrons were created based on humans and my mom gave birth to me through a crystal called the Netron Crystal of Birth… Check out my stomach…" He said while lifting his shirt.

"Ok, um'… you have . . . no belly button."

"Yeah, I didn't extract it or anything like that, it's just that we don't have any, even if we're half breeds. I was born differently through a crystal—which doesn't need an umbilical cord and technically the crystal acts as a placenta in the womb providing whatever it does to maintain the fetus. The crystal also provided a cocoon for me to reside in while I'm being born."

"So… ok. Let's get rational here and take it waaayyy' back. How were you so called Netrons came about?"

"The Pinnacle, the creators of galaxies."

"The Pinnacle, hm,'… doesn't ring a bell."

"Ok, you're still thinking this is bullshit, aren't you?"

"Extreeeme' bullshit. Not to exaggerate or anything but I'm going to exaggerate and everything. You know what I'm saying Ki?"

"Yeah uh, yeah, I think I know what you're saying…"

"Ok, I need you to clarify this some more."

"Ok. You see me as a very skinny kid, right? Now, check this shit out."

Ki-Yale walked towards a junkyard that they usually pass by before arriving home. He stopped with his feet planted firmly on the ground as he uses his two hands to lift and turn a large eighteen-wheeler truck on its side then he lifts the semi-trailer with both hands without a struggle as the tractor unit hangs down a bit.

Immediately Nack is lost for words as Ki-Yale balanced the truck with just one hand causing it to lean back and forth.

"Woahh!! Holy shiii'… zzznit'!!" Nack tremendously amazed and trying not to say 'holy' with a curse word together as he gazed at the truck above him.

"Dude, you weren't lying about that strength. You are like a Sila Human but... without the muscles and blue veins!"

Not to be confused with *steroids*, Sila Humans who were injected with microchips constructed from the "Grainian Tech" surplus salvaged by the government from the *Grainians vs. Humans war*. Through their growth process and rigorous training, they can evolve to a higher rank which is called Prime Human which is a descendant from a Mega Human, they are usually quadruple times the power and 'Mega Human Prime' is a descendant of a Prime Human which is quadruple that power. This form is usually harnessed in the military and hard to accomplish. They consist of having more than one special ability and it's a very insufficient amount of Mega Human Primes living amongst human society.

"That's not all I can do bro, I can fly, and shoot blasts out from my fists!"" Ki-Yale bragged as he floated for him to see. Nack stood motionless and stared at him, speechless for a minute.

"Woah! I can't believe my eyes right now… You got to be wearing floating shoes, right?!"

"No, no. No floating shoes Nack, this is me really floating... Let me show you."

Ki-Yale began to fly around in circles while doing full body twists and flips, almost as if he's figure-skating for the Olympics.

"Ok, you reveal this pretty freaking well... Still hard to believe but I guess I'm gonna' have to for now... There's no hover device on you either?"

"No, no hover device." He said then landed next to him.

"Hm, so, you're a prince of another planet? How intriguing..."

"Yes, I'm Netro Two. I'm not a king yet because I need to be crowned on my planet in front of the Netrons but I have the highest authority right now because the first king trapped himself in a crystal with his enemy."

"He imprisoned himself with his enemy?"

"Yeah that's what my granddad said... to be free one has to die."

"Ok, very intense..."

"Sorry I didn't tell you earlier in life, my parents told me not to tell anyone but you're someone I can trust."

"Don't sweat it bro, I kind of understand. I ain't mad, just surprised. So, you're sort of inferior to humans and your intellect is of a Super Genius like me. Hmm, you should be like a freaking superhero bro! That would be so dope!" Nack encouraged him then sat on the ground next to a tree.

"Yeeaah, my grandpa said I have powers like those heroes in the comics, so I just have to learn and master all of my powers." He said as he sat next to him.

Nack with his left hand folded around his upper stomach and his right hand on his chin.

"Very fascinating... all this is so difficult to grasp right now. Your mom... she isn't an alien I suppose?"

"Naah, my mama… she's fully human and is the only one without powers in the family."

"Yeah, it figures. She never struck me as an odd person, well, being odd doesn't always necessarily mean you're an alien… no offense this is just something you don't witness very often."

"None taken bro, compared to what's around already, I'm still close enough to the odd side of things."

"Hmm, interesting, I mean, they were extraterrestrial beings invading before and tried to dismantle the Earth but now there is one right in front of me!"

"I'm not here to invade bro but the Dragoons are the ones that humans should be worried about. They will do much worse than just invade… They want absolute destruction!"

"The Dragoons who?"

"Another alien nation, an evil one. We call them the Opposites or sometimes we call them Dragons and I believe they're the ones that took my brother Narrken when I was six! Well, I didn't see who exactly took him, but my guess, it's one of them!" He said with an irritated tone, punching a tree next to him leaving a knuckle print on it.

"Hmm, alien Dragons, possibly had taken your brother… These aren't the magical Dragons of the medieval times, right?"

"No, but they were created based on those mythical creatures from that time by the Pinnacle and these Dragons aren't magical either."

"The Pinnacle? You mentioned that earlier. Aren't they the most powerful? I can tell just by the name."

"Yes and no, they are also an alien species that has the power to create galaxies, but they aren't the strongest. My grandpa said the first King of Dragoons, Larthgon, destroyed them like it's nothing. So, they're like dead now but man just imagine the power to create a whole galaxy."

"They did a good job creating you guys, but they also created those awful creatures you speak of which makes me wonder, if they're on the good or bad side."

"I wonder the same too."

"Hmm… you mention that you have a one-year older brother that was abducted, did he have powers too?"

"Yes,   and even though he had powers, the abductor seemed to be stronger… now we still don't know where he is. Dad and Grandpa searched for days and even today, they would still search thinking he's alive, but we all know… he's… he's gone, all because I wasn't strong enough to save him."

His brother's abduction created a volume of sadness and loss of hope as Ki-Yale gazed down at the tree across from him.

"Hey, it wasn't your fault…"

"No, it is, ever since the day I was announced as Netro Two things just fell apart…"

"Hmm'. You know what I say? I say he's still out there! You might not see him since that day, but I believe he's out there, alive and you should believe that too. Whoever took him is in for a world of pain because you're extremely strong from what I've seen."

"Hmm… I don't think my strength is good enough, especially if I'm in training. If I was already strong enough, I wouldn't be training as much but you're right bro. I should keep believing in him and I'm going to see him again someday."

"Yeah… now that's the spirit! So, should I call you Netro or is it still Ki-Yale?"

"I would love it for everyone to call me Netro… but, for now just call me Ki-Yale. My parents nor my granddad never call me that anyway. They said… 'Ki-Yale is your earth name and you're on earth, so you should be called by your earth name!"" He said mocking his parents and grandfather.

"Hmm', I'm still trying to wrap my head around this alien stuff."

"Ha'… yeah I know… C'mon let's go home, I'll tell you more."

<u>Machida Bar & Lounge</u>—

Later that night at 10pm, customers were already arm wrestling while androids serve the small audience. A regular activity orchestrated by the Machida family and mainly by **Fang Machida**.

"Oh, I'm bout' to end your streak!"

"Oh yeah? Have a seat then."

Neecho Kafmora and three mutual trainees had just finished their training on becoming Pharmacist managers. Neecho has been away from family for two weeks because of company regulations and training, now he's finally finished and doing a brief celebration over drinks. His three mutual trainees were doing most of the talking while he sat silently and listening to their conversation.

"Hey, I'm about to make a move on that chick over there. She's hot as fuck man."

"You ain't making no moves you pussy."

"Aye man, watch me." Said the one to the fight from Neecho, as he stood up and instantly wobbled.

"Hey, be vigilant man, the girl should be the one falling, not you."— "Ha! Don't worry about me Neecho. I… I got this." He said continuously wobbling over the woman he likes.

"Ha', he so doesn't."

Neecho remained quiet again as the two mutual trainees continued to talk.

"Ah man this is the only bar I see with such wildness."

"It's one of the wildest bars in the village, I'm still surprised we all agreed in coming here."

"Well, it ain't wild enough for me man. These guys are chumps . . . weaklings."

"Oh, you trying to test your strength now?"

"Trust me these guys are bozos."

As the other trainee companion took his last gulp of *Brandy* and gets up from the table, he strode along to the arm wrestler with absolute confidence. The look in his eyes immediately signifying that he isn't a match for him. The arm wrestler was buffed as if working out was a religion to him. "Oh, have a seat."

"Oh, I will! You think you're tough cause' you're all big? Those are fake muscles! You ain't shit!"

"You still haven't sat yet sir... Have a seat."

As he wobbled a little, he sat on the chair across from the arm wrestler. The Pharmacist trainee slams his hand in the table as the audience got drastically silent.

"Damn, he's about to get smoked." Neecho said.

"Let him do his thing, he got this."

The arm wrestler placed his arm on the table with a light smirk and looked in his eyes with determination to win. The Pharmacist trainee does the same then the referee placed both of his hands on theirs as they both gripped each other's hands. The referee lets go and launched the contest then instantly, the mutual trainee's arm is twisted to the right as he leaned his body in the same direction.

"Oouu'... I knew that was gonna' happen."

"Does he always do this?" Neecho asked.

"Yeah, it's one of those nights."

He stood in the same position lying down sideways on the chair as the audience laughed at him then the arm wrestler said— "Hey asshole, get up, I didn't even use my full strength."

He wobbled back up then glared at him.

"Asshole?" He inquired then he tumbled his body over to the right, landing on his knees and puked on the floor.

The audience were disgusted by what he did then Neecho stood up from his seat feeling the need to speak— "Guess he had a little too much."

He walked straight over to the mutual trainee with a slight wobble then grabbed him by his shirt collar— "C'mon, you embarrassed yourself enough."

"Hey, that's one of your hoes, right? . . . Be a good pimp and take care of your hoes." The arm wrestler jeered.

"Sure, then I'll take care of you right after."

"Trying to be smart with the lame come backs huh?"

"Only thing lame I see in this room… is you looking like a crackhead, had sex with a juice-head, then they had you."

"Have a seat."

"Have a seat?"

"Yes, have a fucking seat..."

The anger in his face was reflected towards Neecho as he sat on the chair across from him. With a little quiver, he placed his arm on the table then his opponent did the same. The referee did his routine then launched the contest giving Neecho time to speak—

"Do your worst. I dare you." He spoke sluggishly from the effects of the alcohol.

As soon as the referee lets go of their hands gripping each other firmly, utter struggle came from the arm wrestler as Neecho's arm didn't move an inch.

<u>Later at Gel Hev Mini-Mart</u>—

A convenience store that is currently the number one on the stock market amongst the Gel Hev communities. Neecho and his three co-workers decided to take a stop at the Mini-Mart to pick up a few things pertaining food. As the store is close to being empty of clientele, Neecho picked out exactly what he wants. His favorite snack called *Doritos*, a popular American brand of flavored tortilla chips, produced from the 21st century.

"Oh man that guy's face when you heaved his arm. Man, it almost looked like his entire body was about to get thrown off his chair."

"Yeah that guy looked like he eats booty holes with a spoon."

"You're the shit Neecho!"

"How are you even stronger than that juice-head? I mean you're chiseled yourself, but that dude was like huge and you don't even eat much too, just this old school snack you always get."

"I don't know man sometimes it's not the size that counts…"

"I guess you're right."

"Yo I'm still stoked that I got that chick's number man. She's like twenty-three, apparently she works there."

"Oh, look at you."— "Oh yeah, I'm getting some ass!"

"Man, I just can't wait to get home and it's been two freaking weeks since I fucked my girl."

"Oh yes some fucking would be good right now. Nasty, slushy, gushy, fucking . . . yeeahhh'."

"What about you Neecho? You said you gotta' wife at home, right?"

"Yeah, I'm married. I needa' call her before it gets to midnight though. Especially after I didn't for the whole week."— "Oh yeah, you gotta' call her or else you ain't getting nothing when you get home."

He opened the Doritos bag then ate a few chips as the rest of the trainees walked to the checkout. He walked down the aisle by himself to pick up a soda and ogled at it in front of him as the corner of his left eye noticed a familiar figure. He turned his head to the left and it was a boy with his back turned. The boy was standing at the end of the aisle as Neecho stared at him with a dumbfounded expression. He could hear his own heart beating faster while he wonders and tries to figure out who could that really be, until the boy turned around. His skin began to tingle, and his muscles became rigid with a stiffening posture.

"It's . . ."

He was actually a spitting image of his abducted son in plain sight.

"Na… NARRKEN!" He shrieked and ran towards him.

He lost sight of the boy as he walked to the next aisle on the left then as soon as he reached the end and turned his body, he gawked at the empty floor ahead of him. Without giving up, he quickly walked forward looking through every aisle and still not a trace of him as if his mind is playing tricks on him. He used his enchanted eyesight looking through the entire market as his trainee companions caught him in a strange trance and still, not even a figure that matches his son's height.

"No, I could've sworn I saw him... It was so real. . .. What the fuck… I couldn't have been that drunk…"

He beheld the entire store while turning his body around doing a three-sixty then ran to the exit.

"Yo! You good Neecho?!"

"What's wrong with him?"— "He's on that nut shit man."

He ogled out in the woods looking and looking but still not a soul exposed to be his son.

"Don't worry about me… I'm good guys, I'm good."

Neecho's mind had grown into a clouded mass of desolation and because of this, he forgets to call his wife.

THREE

Your life could parish at any given moment. It could be the next day, next hour, the next minute, or the next second. Especially by a blood thirsty young man probing to end a life for any reason they can discover.

"Hmm, this kid is hard to find." **Push Monaghan** mumbled to himself.

The same nineteen-year-old boy that attended the *Never Too Early Café* searching for a young man on the holographic poster that emits from a device.

It's close to midnight and the relentlessness of Push prowled through Little Tree Ville, still on the hunt. Anyone that stepped close to him he would question, he even asked police officers if they saw him, but no one seem to have a clue. Push became fed up and started asking more vulgarly than before with his strong Irish accent, until these three older men weren't having it—

"Hm, kid, you need to learn some manners!" The middleman said.

"Listen, I don't have time for fucking manners. Alright? You know who Xack is and I would like to find him… nooww'."

"Yeah, I know him. He comes to the shop that I work at and buy knives all the time. He collects them but it doesn't mean I know where he is." Said the man on the left facing Push.

"Hm', some knives aye? . . . Oh yeah, that's something an Apaki Warrior would do." Push noted.

"He's one of them Apaki Warriors huh? Aah fucking Mega Humans." Said the man on the right facing him. — "Yeah and I need to find him now you fat fuck!"

"Listen here boy! If you don't keep your trap shut with that stupid tattoo on your face, I'll teach you a quick lesson!" Said the middleman.

"Ah Shiite'! A lesson? What am I in school?! Hmm', if you lames don't tell me where he's located, I'm going to have to kill you all."

"Kill what!? I just dare you to try it! You delinquent!"—"Who are you working for kid?"

"Obviously, the boss is a fool, using such a disrespectful piece of shit to do his work."

"The man I'm working for . . . is Dr. Sagan!" Push assured with pride.

"Doctor… Dr. Sagan huh? That guy ain't something you want to mess around with kid. He's the real deal!"

"That's' why I'm fucking working for him, he's the real deal."

"Kid, you're rude and stupid… Just rude and stupid! That's a wrong combination and it ain't going to get you far—especially if you're working for someone like Sagan."

"Ok, since you bitches don't want to tell me, then the edges of my glass blade are what I'm going to give you!"

Push used his tech gloves and released a glass katana out of his left hand.

"Oh yeah kid, just try it! Just fucking try it!" Said the middleman as he revealed an illegal Fed gun.

His illegal weapon was somehow recently obtained on this same day and LTV law enforcement hasn't detect the firearm yet, especially when the woods being the factor of short detection rang. The gun is a half bullet firing and half heat ray firing gun. He ran towards the three men as the man in the middle shot at Push twice while the other two behind him stood in boxing stances. These men were stocky and well-built while Push is a little smaller and skinny. Push rapidly hit both bullets with his glass katana as the bullets didn't break the glass and he didn't even get a scratch. He got closer to the front man and quickly sliced his left hand off—the one hand that had the gun.

"AAAAGGGH!! YOU MOTHER FUCKER!!"

A clean slice of the man's left hand hits the ground as he screamed loudly constructing fear from his friends witnessing such a horror happing so fast.

"Oh, shit! Oh shit! You fucking bastard! Oh shit!" The man on the left panicking and wailing behind the middleman.

Push sneered at them while the man with the severed hand was on his knees.

"It's time to die bitches!"

Push ran past the middleman then stabbed the man who's standing on the left in the heart while the other tried to grab Push but he released another glass shaped katana out of his right hand. Within seconds, a red-hot thermal energy appeared around the glass katana as he cuts the man in his neck about five inches deep.

"Aagh!"—The man's breathing interrupted by the deep cut.

His neck splits open with steam erupting, as the middleman began to quiet down a bit while gazing at his friend on the ground with a blurry vision. Merely gasping for air and near sighting the blood bursting rapidly leading him with little time to think, he reaches with his right hand for his gun that's still in his left hand that got severed. As soon as he touched his firearm, Push twisted his body with one sword in each hand causing the middleman's head to be sliced off clean from his torso.

"Hmm'. You idiots didn't wanna' give me shit? Now you eat shit."

The Kafmora residence—

The next day, which is a Saturday. Ki-Yale woke up around 5am then does his stretches, hundred pushups and sit-ups. He eats his breakfast then heads out around 6am to Nack's place to hang out for the whole day. He wore a Burgundy, Navy & Charcoal Flannel long sleeve shirt with black pants and blue and black sneakers as he faced the fifty-degree weather. He walked through his usual pathway and an old former drug addict is walking towards Ki-Yale.

"Ah man, Mr. Turd is walking this way."

"Hey, good morning Ki-Yale!" Hollered **Dunkin Turd** a.k.a Mr. Turd who allegedly abused heroin and crack cocaine when he was younger. He then later attended rehabilitation, counseling and anti-drug classes. Eventually, he became fully sober and free from all drugs, but he occasionally drinks and when he does, he drinks lightly. He is a Caucasian man with a large stomach, a bald head and a four-inch dark beard with a walrus mustache covering his upper lip.

"What's up Mr. Turd…?"

"Nothing much Ki, just heading to the bar. How's grandpa doing?"

"Grandpa is fine I think he's at his place meditating. You know he loves bettering the mind."

"Well in fact it is sonny, you see many years ago…"

"Man, this guy is gonna' have me here talking for another two hours. I ain't got time for this…" He thought.

Mr. Turd prattled about history of meditation then suddenly, a screaming Japanese eighteen-year-old boy with long black hair that's tied into knot and wearing a simple blue and black Kevlar garment seems to have randomly launched himself fifty feet from behind the trees that mushroomed over a boulder.

"What the... You ok Ki-Yale?" Mr. Turd alarmed as the boy landed on Ki-Yale.

"Yeah, I'm ok, good thing he landed headfirst onto me instead of the ground."

As Ki-Yale held him by his armpits, he leaned over and noticed that the teen has a sign on his garment along with the familiar technology.

"*Ok... I know this inscription, it's one of those Apaki Warrior symbols and those gloves—they're Apaki Tech gloves.*" Ki-Yale thought.

"You know that young man Ki-Yale?"

"Nah, this is my first time ever seeing this dude."

"He's not getting up! Is he dead!?"

Ki-Yale unexpectedly heard a footstep landing on some dead leaves from behind causing him to turn around halfway.

"Step away from him, now! Don't let me have to hurt you little kid!"

Mr. Turd immediately turned around reacting to the voice.

"You know him Ki?"

"Nope." He replied as he laid the Japanese teen by the large boulder and at that moment, the teen woke up.

"I said—get—the fuck—away—now!"

It was the same nineteen-year-old boy with a full-face tattoo.

"I should cut you little punk! —Get away!"

"Um... Why? Who are you?" Ki-Yale queried.

"My name is Push... Push Monaghan."

The eighteen-year-old boy interrupted Push with a dainty Japanese accent and taunted him— "Ha, Push? That's your name? Ha, more like, more like... Puss!"

Ki-Yale faced the Japanese teen and saw that he's standing with his fist clenched.

"Hmm and you're **Xack Machida**, the little wanker I'm going to capture, sadly, alive! Hmmm... Requested from Dr. Rogue Sagan."

"Oh no . . . not Dr. Sagan." Ki-Yale thought.

"Whoa... Who the hell is Dr. Rogue Sagan?" Whispered Mr. Turd while Ki-Yale looked strangely at him then explained.

"Wow. What world do you live in? He's a fugitive and one of the most notorious mass murderers of all time."

"I see you're an Apaki Warrior like me." Xack said walking closer to his new foe.

"Yes, I am." Push responded.

"Well, besides the bitch ass off guard hit you just did... Let's see what you got."

"Let's."

"You guys need to step all the way back . . . Don't want you guys getting hurt." Xack warned them.

"You heard him Ki! Let's goooo'!!" Mr. Turd shouted while struggling to pull Ki-Yale away.

"Wow kid . . . you're like freaking heavy..."

"C'mon little fuck boy!"

Push opened his right hand revealing an orb of generated glass hovering over his palm, clanking and moving around in a circle. One glass katana emerged out of it like previously when he killed the three men that didn't want to inform him about Xack's location. The glass katana then ignites the red-hot thermal energy that surges through it.

At that exact moment, a glass katana emerged out of Xack's right hand then it ignites, like Push's sword.

—Brmm' . . . *Brmm'* . . . *Mmrrrr'*...

The indistinct sounds of the buzzing idle of the two swords drawn, as it lagged then it went on repeatedly.

Ki-Yale and Mr. Turd stepped back a few feet away from the duel.

"Yeah—Ki-Yale, let's move away from these freaks."

Push charging at Xack then they both swung their heated glass katanas.

Both heated glass katanas collided and both fighters immensely holding their own. Push released another glass sword from out of his left hand while still operating with his other sword against Xack.

Push utilized his vastly sharp glass sword on his left hand and cuts Xack's left bicep. He felt a sting of pain and walked backwards about four feet then Push's glass sword in his right hand cracked itself. He opened his palm causing the cracked sword to levitate facing Xack. Without hesitating he released the cracked pieces out onto Xack's chest.

Apaki Warriors can detach pieces from their glass sword with their minds then shoot the escaping pieces of extremely sharp heated glass and shoot them directly from their gloves as well. This alternated attack can usually go up to fifteen hundred miles per hour or even more depending on the technology.

Xack fell back about ten feet on his back then slid next to Ki-Yale as his Kevlar garment decelerated the pieces from penetrating his chest entirely.

"Woah..." Ki-Yale astonished.

Push gripped his remaining heated glass sword as the radiance shined brighter than before then ran towards his adversary ready to cut him.

Suddenly... a flash of lightning illuminated the area with an electrical discharge emitting a loud thunder sound. Xack turned around and it was from Ki-Yale's eyes striking Push in the stomach. Even though Push wore protective gear the powerful attack struck him with rigid sufficient force for him to fall back ten feet onto a red maple tree. He landed on his buttocks and held his stomach with an astounded look on his face.

"Blaaaghh'!!" Push vomited a bit of his food then coughed as if he's a diseased patient.

"Woah... Did I?. . . Did I just do that?!"

"Who the hell are you boy?" Mr. Turd talking to Ki-Yale.

Ki-Yale stared at Mr. Turd with a confused look on his face.

Xack was baffled by what had just happen as he slowly got up from the hit he took from Push.

"What the... what the hell was that?"

Push expressed lassitude, kneeling with his eyes closed, holding his stomach and making a groaning noise. With no further reluctance, Xack walked closer to his new enemy releasing another glass katana and aimed it towards Push.

"No, wait."

Xack concocting his next move as he lifted his glass katana to wedge Push's head in half.

"Wait, No!" Ki-Yale continued, raising his voice then began to express his moral character—"Killing him is not proper justice!!"

"Trust me... It's proper justice! He's working for a heartless mass murderer and probably killed people too! Ain't that right Push?" Xack opposed him.

"Ok, it looks like you guys just met so you don't know for sure that he killed anyone and even if he did—it's not our say or to make such judgment!"

Push tilted his head up looking at Xack with a grin then said—"Hey, if you really want to kill me, come see me at the 'Crouton Village Tournament'. . .In Crouton Village of course… You know where that is right? Hmm?"

Push chuckled then continued to talk—"There, we will have the ok to murder our opponents or just knock em' out but killing is more of my style."

Xack looked at Push with a vengeance and then disarmed his katana by radiating about 2,900 degrees Fahrenheit heat temperatures from the center of the glass, causing it to disintegrate.

"Ok, that sounds like a better idea, as long as I get to stab your throat and not get the law involved."

Push stood up slowly with a grin on his face then said—"I'll be seeing you again fresh meat and I hope to see that lightning shooting freak too."

"Yeah, make sure you tell your boss that your mission was unsuccessful."

"No worries chum, he's gonna' love this news right here." Push replied to Xack while holding his stomach then turned around and walked the opposite direction.

While he's walking away, he used his wrist tablet and ordered his flying mini transport scooter that has no seats, it's only designed for standing up and steering.

"See you all at the tournament lads." Push said then he smirked.

After about ten seconds the transport scooter arrived, and Push sauntered onto it then it flew with him forty-five feet in the air. Xack turned around and looked at Ki-Yale looking at his hands and saying—"What the..."

"Thanks for helping me back there and I guess you're right about me killing that asshole. It's not my call but I'm tired of these goons murdering the innocent, especially if they're working for Sagan..."

"Um, who the hell are you? Where is Ki-Yale!?" Mr. Turd utterly confused.

"You're looking at him, right here..." Ki-Yale felt hindered as he squints his eyes and pursed his lips.

"Hmm, nah you can't fool me. You got the same hair style but you're definitely not Ki-Yale."

Ki-Yale squinted at Mr. Turd some more and thought— *"Is the drugs getting to him again or is this guy just getting weirder and weirder?"*

"Well, I saw another kid before you showed up. Yeah— I landed on him, poor kid, then out of nowhere you blasted Push with your lightning but with the same hairstyle just not that black and white suit."

Ki-Yale realized Xack couldn't recognize him as well then thought—*"Him too? This has to be a joke, right?"* He looked down at his attire then continued while touching his face with his right hand—

"I didn't have this black and white suit on before though but isn't my face the same?"

"Well, freaks... again… my name is Xack Machida and it's been nice meeting you all. Hopefully you guys will be at the tournament in Crouton Village... Especially you kid, with that gift and the other kid wherever he's at. He seemed brave as well."

Ki-Yale looked at Xack with a lightly puzzled look. Xack then summoned a mini transport bike from his wrist device and rode off in midair, about forty-five feet.

"Alright Xack, sure… I'll see you when I see you."

"Are you really gonna' show up to that wild tournament? Cause it sounds like you faked what you said."

"Yeah, I lied."

"Well, I need to go find Ki-Yale."

"Ok good luck with that Sir..." He said sarcastically then thought— *"This dude is always wilding out."*

Mr. Turd began to walk away while Ki-Yale began to stare at his new peculiar outfit some more. He's wearing dark chrome gloves that seems to be fitted firmly on his hands. Boots, shoulder pads and black pants with a black belt that has a two-inch chrome "N" symbol as the belt buckle. The rest of the suit is pearl white with black crystalized lining and a four-inch chrome "N" symbol on Ki-Yale's chest.

"Maan'. How did this thing get on me?"

"I need to head to Nack's place... Hopefully he recognizes me." He continued speaking to himself.

—Five minutes later Ki-Yale knocked on Nack's door.

"Yo Nack! Open up!" He hollered while knocking on the backdoor on the second floor of the dorm room.

Nack was granted with his own high school dormitory room. He resides there by himself while his parents are living in Gigantica City. Some might say this is ridiculous to have a fifteen-year-old living on his own. Well, Super Geniuses have the authority to live in dorms granted by the Gigantica Government. Majority of Super Geniuses under eighteen possess an outstanding level of intellect so much that they can perform the simple responsibilities such as living on their own. This is only optional, and the school officials provides whatever is needed.

"Yeah hold on!"

Nack opened the door then asked while being perplexed—

"Hey. How can I help you?"

Ki-Yale looked at Nack portraying a similar delirium then said—

"So... so, you don't recognize me?"

"No... Who are you?"

"Don't tell me this is happening to you too. It's me Ki-Yale."

"Ok, give me a second, stay here, I'll be right back."

"Oook'."

Nack went back inside, shuts the door leaving Ki-Yale outside. A few seconds later Nack opened the door with a registered hyper beam shotgun.

"You better have a microchip inside you… Don't play me kid, I asked who are you? Why are you impersonating my best friend!?" Defensively Nack questioned Ki-Yale pointing his shotgun that his father allowed him to buy for his birthday towards him.

"Woah!! Nack, chill!! What are you doing? It's me Ki-Yale!"

"You think I'm a dickhead? Do I look like a dickhead to you? Huh? Does it look like my head is a penis to you?"

"No, no you're pretty smart man, you're a Super Genius but right now… you seem to be acting like Mr. Turd."

"What?! Mr. Turd? So, you're saying I'm a dickhead?"

"Yes—No wait—no . . . bro, it's probably this suit I got on."

"Who sent you here?"

"No one. It's me Ki-Yale! Just chill man."

"Hmm… get out—of here now—before I call the authorities…" Nack warned him with a low tone as his hyper beam shotgun is charged up to shoot.

"This is not like you Nack... You know who I am and I'm going to get to the bottom of this."

"Nah I don't, I know who my friend Ki is and it's not you. And I don't know how you know my name but you gotta' leave."

"Alright I'll leave, I'll leave."—Ki-Yale tramped away backwards. "See I'm leaving…"

Nack confused but still defensive with his shotgun pointing at him as Ki-Yale turned around then flew away going fifty miles per hour.

"What the...? He even flies just like Ki."

His eyes then slightly tolerated a burning sensation. "What the…? My eyes!"

"This is just weird. Why aren't people recognizing me?" Ki-Yale queried in his head.

Ki-Yale arrived back at the Kafmora residence. He opened the front door and saw his little sister.

She observed him as he stared at her.

"Nice outfit shit brain!"

"Yo, that language! —Wait... You can recognize me?"

"Yeah unfortunately, I see your ugly ass every day."

"Well if you can recognize me... So why Nack and Mr. Turd couldn't? I can understand Mr. Turd but Nack, my best friend? He was acting all defensive, Nack was all like 'Why are you impersonating my best friend!?' and I was all like 'It's me Ki-Yale!'"

—He gasped.

"He was about to shoot me Tajay."

"Ha! I don't blame em'. It's that ugly face of yours. Dude, you need surgery ASAP!" Tajaymae joked.

"Hmm, it's probably this suit. Humans don't recognize me when I have it on. Man, I don't even know how to take it off, it feels like its super glued onto my skin . . . or maybe... it is my skin!"

"Let's go talk to Grandpa, maybe he knows what's up."

"He's in the training room?"

"Yeah as usual, let's go."

Ki-Yale and Tajaymae heading down to the large training room in the elevator as they heard noises.

"Graah'! Grrraaah'! Haah'! Grrraaah'!"—Grunting, inhaling and exhaling, the sounds of Nealo pushing 15,000lb weight made for Mega Human Prime Sila Humans.

"He's been at it all day, since 4am in the morning."

"Granddad!" Ki-Yale shouted.

"Uh, it's my grandchildren... What's shaking?"

"Turn around Granddad and check out Ki's new outfit."

Nealo turned around then instantly being surprised as he lifted his flat eyebrows.

"Well—it's about time!"

FOUR

Nealo Kafmora was just fifteen years of age when he was sent to earth in the year 2264 along with his partner Raenia who is the same age as him. Nealo and Raenia needed to adapt to the societies and their ways of living on Earth; therefore, they built their own home in Little Tree Ville. Nealo generated the Gigantican surname, "Kafmora" and Raenia created the surname, "Love". Nealo and Raenia provided an excuse to the ID department which is held by the government claiming that they got their identity erased from the system during the Grainians vs. Humans War and they were the last of their family. They both had a SS microchip inserted but first, it was difficult with the general practitioners because Netron skin is tougher than human skin therefore Nealo and Raenia both reduced the thickness of their skin and got the chips inserted after two tries of a failed bent knives and broken needles.

That's just the least of their problems to blend in, the ID department did a full body check, although Netrons look exactly like humans both Nealo and Raenia were originated with no belly buttons, their hearts are in the exact middle of their chests. Eventually Nealo came up with an idea to use their Netron Suits to camouflage themselves as humans with belly buttons, heart shaped as a human heart and being slightly to the left side instead of the exact middle. They even mimicked blood types, cells, hair and all human organism traits hoping that the machines don't recognize that they are aliens. Results were in and surprisingly, they passed the checkup then moved on. They both lived a normal earthly life, going to school, having a job and then five years later they got married.

Fifteen years later Nealo at age thirty-five and Raenia at age thirty-five had a son named Neecho Kafmora in year 2284. Neecho later met a young lady who goes by the name Demi Okeke, they fell in love and later got married. Neecho and Demi birthed their first-born son named Narrken. The second born son named Ki-Yale, Ki pronounced as *Kee* or *Key*, *Kee-Yale*. Additionally, Neecho and Demi birthed two more children, a girl named Tajaymae pronounced *Tah-Jay-May* and a third son named Oji, pronounced *Oh-G*.

Neecho had informed Demi about him being an unearthly life form before their love affairs and even up the fact that he cannot ejaculate inside of her because his sperm cells can be lethal to her. It's vice versa for Netron females as well, their ovum or egg cells are too acidic for the human male gametes. Human's sex cells aren't strong enough to face these cells, so they rapidly eat away the bodily fluids then attacks further inside for five to thirty minutes. With the help of the Netron Book of Edu, Neecho discovered the *Crystal of Birth* which Demi can consume in order for Neecho to partake in successful intercourse with her, for as long as they like.

In order for a Netron or any other species to successfully give birth to a child with another species they need to use a Crystal of Birth. Although this is so, one crystal could still possibly be fatal for her because humans are not as physically strong as other beings that can contain the crystal, but Demi wanted children with Neecho despite the risks on how she will conceive them and later consumed it otherwise. The crystal is as small as a tablet and the undertaking was very straightforward. She simply drunk it with water then the crystal became infused with her body, then had intercourse with Neecho and later obtained a fruitful pregnancy.

Demi began to do her stretches in her room with her dreadlocks tied up in a bun. She's wearing a black shirt, training shorts that revealed her upper thighs that had a bit of her stretch marks along with sneakers and a strap that has pockets holding a small metal framed picture of her son Narrken. She reached to touch her toes as the small metal frame began to dangle. Abruptly, it fell on the floor as her reflexes failed her, but it was still being intact and unbroken.

She bends down then went on her knees to pick up the metal framed picture. She wiped the smear from the glass as the picture of her son is staring right at her. Her first born resembled his father the most with his playboy smile. Tear drops hung from her right full thick lashes then she blinked repeatedly. Demi wiped her tears with the lower side of her palm then she puts her head up then puts the framed picture to her chest and closed her eyes. She then puts the picture back in her pocket slowly then unexpectedly—

"Daamn' girl—you're hot!" Neecho with his clean shaved face, flirted as he walked in on Demi.

She turned around drastically then paused and scowled at him then said—

"Well… I'm only hot for you but you wanna' be missing in action . . . No call within five days, no what's up, hello, no location!"

"The pharmaceutical training was an overload hun'."

Demi continued to grimace at him for ten seconds then he asked—

"What?"— "Nothing, I just I hope it doesn't involve other ladies."

"Other ladies?"

"Yeah don't act like you didn't hear me." Demi argued while she stood up.

"C'mon Demi…" He said as he smiled.

"This is serious Neecho."

"Aaah'… Why are you talking like this Demi?"

"It's time I get to the bottom of things."

"Get to the bottom of…? Baaaby'—don't get like this."

"Hm', someone told me…"

"Someone told youuuu'?"

"Yeah, I got eyes and ears everywhere… someone told meee', you were at this Café that does sex for freaking money and entertainment!"

"Oh c'mon, I was just hanging with my co-workers from the training—you know—bond. I don't wanna' be too anti-social and I didn't wanna' go at first but they kept pushing me to go, so I just went."

"Peer pressure huh? Don't you know it's a violation to our marriage to see other naked women?"

"I'm sorry Demi… Look, I won't do it again, I swear to you!"

"Hmm—well—I'm going to ask you this one important question. Did you bang any females there? Or anyone for that matter?"

Neecho kept quiet and being confused—

"What do you mean by anyone?" He asked.

"You're an alien, so maybe you're into that homosexual shit too."

Neecho tilted his head back, lifted his left curved eyebrow showing a baffled facial expression then said—

"C'mon Demi you know I don't swing that way…"

"Well. Did you?" Demi in an aggressive tone while ambling towards Neecho.

"Hey, my fluids can't get in contact . . . it's like acid."

"Unless you don't explode! Or use a condom! So that point is invalid."

"No."

"No what?"

"No, I did not participate in any sexual activities with anyone that day and that's the honest truth!"

"Hmmmm'... ok."

"Ok? Um, s-s-soooo'... now what?"

"There's a lot we need to catch up on... Ki-Yale just learned how to fly, and he passed his exam...." Demi said and being discontinued by Neecho—

"I know, I know. My father told me all about it. Now, now. What can I do to cure my wife's anger?" He said while he slowly approached her.

Demi glared at her husband while he gets even closer to her. She reminded herself that he always strives to please her and learn from his mistakes as she puts her arms around his neck then they locked lips.

"Just put me to sleep baby."

He lifted his left eyebrow then instantly puts his hands-on Demi's waist. She bit her bottom bow-shaped lip with an ongoing smile. She flicked one lock that was untied to the back of her head. He slowly lifted her shirt as she helped him remove it ultimately exposing her breasts.

"What about your little workout? Don't you wanna'...?" Neecho concerned as he got interjected.

"Finish? —I'll finish that later—"

"But are you sure you wanna' do this? We hadn't had sex in so long especially with Narr..."

"Sshh... It's ok... I need this right now."

Her sudden seductive ways made Neecho electrified as he began kissing Demi gradually then aggressively while she moved backwards to the dresser. She savored his brimful succulent lips kissing her neck as he gently rubbed his hands from her back to her waist. She caressed the back of his head as he slapped her firm pear-shaped ass then persistently rubbed his hands down her thighs. The passion bloomed as he lifted Demi and puts her on top of the table while he's still making out with her. Demi pushed her essential products away as she smiled illuminating her dimples and lifting her petite nose.

Neecho gave her a smile back and took her shorts off. That is when he recognized she had worn no underwear.

"Hmm, you're prepared huh?"

"I've been waiting for you for two weeks—hoping you still love me." She spoke sarcastically.

"I will always love you baby. Don't ever forget that."

Neecho kissed her again while he undresses his pants then she said—

"I'll never forget."

At that moment, he thrusted slowly as Demi began to release her breath lightly and firmly hugging Neecho.

In the Kafmora family training room—

"Ah... the Netron Suit—so that's what this thing is called." Ki-Yale said as if he just solved a *'Final Jeopardy'* question.

Tajaymae is behind her brother with her mouth completely shut but seemed eager to hear about the suit.

"Let's hear about this Netron Suit granddad!" Ki-Yale spoke with excitement.

"The Netron Suit or Netron Armor… it's like a cheat code my grandson."

"A cheat code?"

"Yes… this is the suit that enhances your abilities, it gives you more special powers that your regular form can't do and didn't learn as yet, like shooting lightning out of your eyes."

"Yoooo', that's what I did today! I shot lightning out of my eyes!"

"Hmm'." Nealo muttered.

"How did you know?"

"I didn't know, that was just me giving an example and shooting lightning was the first ability that your father first discovered when his Netron Suit came alive. That attack is called 'The Lightning KO'. It's one of the Zeal powers and it's not just us Netron royalty that can use this power—normal Netrons can as well. The only ones that won't be able to use this power is another Zeal Netron solely capable of doing only one Zeal power like Tajaymae over here who was born with Zeal powers implanted with the Crystal of Birth."

"Hey, but… I'm Netron royalty!" Tajaymae argued.

"Yes, that is true but since you only possess one Zeal power which is Netron Plasma—you only can perform abilities relevant to Netron Plasma. These supremacies were created from Zeal Crystals and these crystals produce genetics that will dominate the regular Netron gene."

"Hmm'… the Lightning KO huh? But I didn't knock out the person I shot."

"Ha! Well, you didn't put enough energy to K.O whoever you shot and hopefully he thinks that you're just using gadgets."

"Naah', I doubt it he even knew I was part alien."

"Hmm' . . . now your suit, consists of the Intercosmic Crystals which has two things, the *light* and *darkness*. The chrome 'N' symbol on your belt and on your chest in the lower middle stands for Netron, it is the sacred Netron symbol and has both light and darkness. You as Prince Netro Two, your ancestor King Netro One, the imminent

Netro Three, Four, Five and so forth are the only ones that will always have the chrome 'N' symbol on their suits..."

"I see, it's shaped like an *Asscher cut diamond* . . . so instead of the symbol being black it's actually chrome for me—hmm', I see—and the one in the middle of my chest... that's where my heart is."—Ki-Yale interrupting his granddad.

"Yes, and a regular Netron symbol would just be chrome black and pearl white. The suit is also weatherproof, it can handle any temperature no matter how low or high the temperature may be, and it regenerates... Now, do you remember what can penetrate any Netron's heart completely?"

"The Dragon's Blood." Tajaymae answered.

"Exactly, a powerful enough *Dragoon's Blood* or as they call it... Dragon's Blood. Their blood can do serious damage to our suits, especially to your heart."

"Dragon's Blood, well of course... but, I can heal myself rapidly?"

"Yes, you can rapidly regrow or regenerate any part of your body that gets damaged—ANY PART! The Dragon's Blood though, is our reverse blood which the Pinnacle made it so that our species blood types become sort of like lethal contaminants. Our blood is essentially their weakness because of unmatched DNA but the way they generate their blood from their body is an ability no Netrons could barely do... unless we get creative with our suits. The blood will first penetrate the suit then enter your bloodstreams and decomposing the cells away, replacing it with their blood causing your suit to give in. Our blood can regenerate while the Dragon's Blood takes its course, but it all depends on how powerful that Dragoon is..."

"Very unusual stuff... I was still a little sore from my jaw earlier until I had this suit on now the pain is gone but I guess the soreness will be back when I take this off..."

"Yes, you can't heal rapidly in regular form and when you're hurt in regular form then utilize your Netron Suit you are in good shape but when you transform back, your injuries on your regular form is still there. It also has the ability to shape shift into everything or anyone..."

"Except Dragon's Blood."

"Yes except for Dragon's Blood... The Netron Suit is compatible with matter, atoms, subatomic particles and all sorts of particles. I'm talking about protons, neutrons and electrons—literally everything you feel, touch, hear—your Netron Suit is my Netron Suit. Your Netron Suit is life itself and so is any other Netron or half breed ones wearing a suit."

"Basically, it's part of everything, everyone, every creation, space, time—the whole universe, multi-universe and beyond that. Even all of reality . . . Essentially, the Netron Suit is omnipresent and omnifarious in its own way."

"Yes, you are absolutely correct my grandson . . . You know the saying 'beaten to a pulp'. Well, literally if you were beaten into a tiny molecule or atom or even smaller... the suit will redevelop you from existence, it will comply even before the deadly attack and then it molds itself as the universe, or universes, or literally anything around us or anyone—even after getting hit with the attack, it simply reforms you back to your form."

"Woah..."

"Nice..." Tajaymae said.

"You get your form back and can transfer yourself far away from whatever threat attacked you. Traveling within a picosecond or even faster, faster than hyperspace, through the space time continuum—the suit can place yourself anywhere in the universe, another universe, another realm, the multiverse and so forth... If there is anything pass the universe—oorr... you can just remain and fight like a warrior. It's been so many years of fighting the Opposites, the suit could never comply to defend itself against their blood but as long as you and your suit is strong enough you can be successful."

Ki-Yale paying attention to detail and said—

"Wow… this suit is superbly powerful, even when you don't have enough power to end your enemy you will still be alive… unless that enemy is a Dragoon."

"Yep, this is why you need to get stronger my grandson cause if you were to die then Tajaymae or Oji will get the crown and if all of you die the whole Netron race will be destroyed."

"Hm... so I can regenerate any part huh?" Ki-Yale still amazed about the regeneration.

"Yeah even your small wiener and your big ass head that emits all that power!" Tajaymae joked.

"Granddaaad'… Didn't you hear what she just said?!"

"Tajaymae, stop it."

"I mean she is really nice when Mom and Dad is around but when they're not around, it's a different Tajaymae. Mmrrrr'."

Tajaymae smiled at her brother then asked him—

"So, what about Nack and Mr. Turd being retards earlier and they said they couldn't recognize you?!"

"Yeeaah'." Ki-Yale said with his annoyed face raising his left soft arched eyebrow then said—"Hey. Nack isn't a retard and Mr. Turd is just you know…"

"A freaking retard!"

"Tajaymae." Nealo sternly said.

"Hm… earlier Nack was about to shoot me, he was all paranoid and saying I'm impersonating myself! I never seen him act like that—I can understand Mr. Turd with a scene like that... But Nack?!"

"The Netron Suit has a way of manipulating the mind, especially humans. If another species knows you without the suit and seen your regular form before with a photographic memory, the Netron Suit manipulates the other species minds to think otherwise like schizophrenia. It's a defense mechanism. The only way to get him to know you through the suit is if you transform back to your regular form in front of him. We Netrons recognize you regardless."

"Ok, then I need to go back and transform in front of him ASAP before he loses it some more."

"Don't worry about it Ki, once you are gone and out of range, he will forget everything that happened earlier."

"Oh really?"

"Yes, my grandson."

"Hmm. What about Mom? I need to transform in front of her too."

"Yes, you will have to do as I and your father did."—Nealo smiled then he recommenced his speech—

"I'm proud of you, you got your Netron Suit at an early age and I didn't even have to teach you. It's soon time for you to step the game up."

"I hope my suit looks better than his."

"I never seen a Plasma Netron's suit because well, you are the first one ever born. But since plasma on Netron is typically purple. So, my guess is that it should be purple."

"Dope—purple! I like it..." Tajaymae satisfied and slowly nodding her head with a huge smirk on her face.

"Ok now how do I transform back Granddad?"

"It's easy, just like how you walk, talk and fly. It's all in the mind, just command your Netron Suit to transform you back just like how you command your legs to walk. It's pretty easy, it's no pass code."

"Oook."

"Ok, let me show you my transformation with my Netron Suit, so you can see and get an image through your head."—Nealo's entire body started to fade, within seconds his suit appeared on his body.

"Nice." Tajaymae said.

"Woah..." Ki-Yale slightly gasped.

"Yep this is my suit. Now you try it."

"Alright."—Ki-Yale closed his eyes and began to think of changing back. His suit started to fade—then, he opened his eyes and saw his regular clothes again. In a second, Ki-Yale transformed back to his regular form. He looked at his hands and body then said—

"Ok, that was easy!"

"It only took you less than a second to transform like Granddad."

"Told you, now transform back."

"Hm, ok."—He didn't close his eyes this time and had complete confidence. Suddenly his suit started to fade back on his body.

"Now you're ready for some real intense training my Grandson."

"Blaaah'... like the previous training wasn't intense enough."

"Hello Mini Machida!! Where have you been all this time?! Why you look so shitty?!"—Xack's father Fang Machida delved with a strong Japanese accent.

Xack immediately fell to the floor after he opened the doors into his father's bar. There is only two customers and they were alarmed along with Fang. All the attention is on Xack and everyone wondered why he's beaten up.

"XACK!" Fang shouted.

Xack started panting then spoke—

"I've been out all-night Father and now—now—I'm tired..."

His father helped him up on his feet and brought his son to a chair then probed—"Out all night doing what?"

"Looking for Dr. Sagan but one of his men discovered me, his name was Push...."

"Push? That name sounds familiar... and Dr. Sagan? What did I tell you about looking for him? It's not the right time yet!!"

"Father, I'm tired. Alright? I'm tired of waiting! I'm ready to murder that piece of shit!"

"No!"

"Yes! He is responsible for the deaths of our people in Crouton Village, the children... Our friends. Mom?! I won't stand for this much longer!"—Xack blustered then continued—

"Crouton Village Tournament?! Where people could kill without getting the law involved?! Sagan secretly enforced with the Mayor of the Crouton Village. The Crouton Village law enforcement allowed it knowing that if they refuse Dr. Sagan will apply pressure to their families or even worse..."

As Xack is seated on the chair, Fang looked at him as if he was dull-witted. He couldn't withstand the sudden pressure from his son as he slapped him across the left side of his face in a jarring way. "Don't talk like that around me boy!"

With his head turned to the right resulted from the impact. Xack turned his head back and stared at this father while he breathes heavily knowing that his cheek hurts.

"I'm leaving Father... I'm going to fight back in my real home. The home that he took from us! You want to stay here and think life's good? Then fine. Do that! I'll be avenging my mother!!—I never killed anyone but the first one I would love it to be, is Sagan or his disgusting looking henchman Push."

"You're blinded by anger . . . have patience Xack."

"My patient days are over! Bye Father."

He stood up and proceeded to walk to the exit.

"Wait! Let's get you fixed up!"

"Dad, I didn't come here for relaxation. I come to you to tell you what my next move is."

"Hmmph', stupid child!" Fang spoke with emphasis in Japanese.

Xack held the door with only his head turned sideways squinting his left eyes at this father, then exits the bar and leaving his father in despair.

"The kid is going to get himself killed." Said one of Fang's customers speaking in Japanese.

<u>*Quentin Valar High School of Educational Careers*</u>—

Loud talkative teenagers across the hallway with advanced lockers on the walls. High tech automated lunch machines and vending machines with touch screen and holograms.

"What's up loser?" Liam Paterson hailed, a seventeen-year-old boy approaching and speaking to another seventeen years old boy named Tony Torbino walking out of class.

"Hey, what's up moron?"

"How's that travel from here to the City of Atlantis every day?"

"It's not so bad actually—the commute—it's harmless."

"Of course, because it's owned by Gigantica. What's it like over there with all that water?"

"Its beautiful man, the city is covered by a large barrier near the bottom of the Atlantic Ocean. You can see all sorts of different water creatures pass by."

"Yeah because they wanna' eat you fuckers . . . As long as that barrier doesn't break"

"The barrier is absolutely indisputable and indestructible according to the *Wikipedia*. It's made from the strongest glass in our galaxy—silicon dioxide mixed with minerals of 'Tektonium' the Grainian metal which is the strongest metal yet. So that barrier isn't breaking anytime soon and if it does, it has a backup invisible barrier that will cover the city which is strictly Tektonium."

"Aaah I see, well one day, I'm going to crack open a large hole in those barriers and let everyone drown. Hahahaha'!"

"Yeah, yeah, fuck you."

"I'm just messing with you man. You're a real brave son of a bitch living there though."

"Yep . . . Oh—there goes your crush man."

"Oh dude, she's so beautiful."

"Ha', I bet she heard that already."

"So, what should I say Tony?"

"Call her an ugly bitch... You gotta' put the word 'bitch' in there because they love that, the aggressiveness and the dominance. It shows you're the man, the boss! Ya' know what I'm saying Liam? They want a man that takes charge! Say it like this. — 'Damn bitch! You're so freaking ugly with that wide ol' gap tooth!'—trust me it works all the time."

"You, you serious man?"

"Yeeaah', yeah bro. Think about it—you tell her something new that she never heard before and BAM! You get a kiss and a hug. You gotta' give things a try man—say that shit with your chest too."

"You know what? That sounds slick man... Yeah, I'll give it a try... alright, here goes."

In the hallway entrance, Nicole Torbino at age thirty-six and her husband Fabian Torbino at age thirty-eight, holding their youngest son Dorimzy Torbino at age four patiently waiting on their son Tony. The Torbino family is Caucasian, Fabian has an average build body and height while Nicole is slightly shorter and slim. Nicole has brunette hair around her diamond shaped face, thin lips, snub nose, with hazel eyes while Fabian has dark hair, square face, bumpy nose and brown eyes.

Dorimzy Torbino was born with *tetra-amelia* without fully formed limbs. Both his legs are tiny and deformed feet, he has one deformed arm which is the left arm and his right arm was regularly developed. He is usually in a wheelchair, but his mother decided to keep him on her chest carrier while he sleeps.

"Enough of the carrying… let him walk, let him be a big boy already."

"What? He can't walk Fabian! I swear your jokes are so stupid."

"Aah', you never know maybe he can walk without legs and prove to the world that you don't need those things. Watch, when he gets older and he'll be a man with lots of hair, a handsome face, fit body. Ya' know what I'm saying Nicole? I want him to fuck all the bitches and not be like this fool Tony."

"You want him to… fuck all the bitches?"

"Yes, he's a Torbino and a Torbino can get anyone they want."

"Umm… whatever."

Liam received a vicious smack to the face by the girl he likes then Tony spoke under his breath—

"Such a gullible idiot."

"Hey. Why did she do that to your friend?"

"I don't know Dad, let's go."

Later at the Torbino residence—

Tony and Dorimzy has a nineteen-year-old sister named Chloe Torbino. She has a chunky body wearing a simple outfit with her natural brunette hair. She enters the living room while her parents stepped in the house. Tony goes straight to the kitchen to grab something to eat then Nicole said—.

"Oh, Chloe is home."

"I didn't ditch school Mom."

"Didn't say you did now, didn't I? —Hm', sometimes the guilt speaks for itself."

"Mom?"

"I'm just saying."

Nicole then walked inside Dorimzy's room as Fabian sat on the couch in the living room.

"How was school today?" Fabian asked.

"Great." Chloe answered.

"Great? That's it? C'mon now!"

"It was good. I did my regular things I always do, not much to say here."

"C'mon now don't give me that bullshit Chloe—talk to me—have a fucking conversation!"

"Stop it Fabian!" Nicole shouted from Dorimzy's room.

"Are you drunk Dad?" Tony probed.

"No son I'm not drunk. Ok? —I'm just tired of the bullshit ya' know."

Dorimzy woke up, he fiddled as his eyes slowly opened and the first thing, he saw was his mother hovering over his shoulders.

"Hey buddy. You hungry?"

No response from him as he just stared at her with no emotion.

"Of course, you are baby."

Dorimzy is strapped tightly down to his bed with leather straps. His mother pulled out a needle and as soon as he saw the needle, he twisted his body, wiggling and squirming around but that doesn't help from escaping the straps clamped onto his bed railings.

"Here you go son. Just relax baby."—Nicole jammed the needle into his left armpit, under his deformed arm, injecting serum into his system.

"How long are you going to keep this illegal shit up Mom?" Tony approached the bedroom entrance being concerned.

"Until he's one of the strongest Mega Humans in history! He will consume as much Mega Human serums, then, in the future he will consume Death Angel DNA and even learn Apaki Jermayin."

"Don't you think it's just a little too much? I mean all this injection can kill him."

"No, no, no he needs this. My boy will be the best there is. A force so powerful that nothing can end him."

Complete silence in the air for thirty seconds as Dorimzy moved around aggressively but no screaming coming from him, just silent agony with his mouth shut. He finally stopped moving as he breathes heavily then calmed down by the minute.

"Now, leave us."

Tony squeezed his eyelids for five seconds then walked away.

<u>*Gravy Hunt Restaurant Gigantica City*</u>—

This multicultural restaurant is for the clientele who desire the many sounds of opera or jazz music, chills vibes, upscale environment with nothing but peace and tranquility. **Henry Luciano**, an Italian fifty-six-year-old man with strong facial structures and a few wrinkles. He has dark hair with a few shades of grey, slightly jagged nose and slightly sunk in cheeks. A formal attire for him is his signature look, sitting at a table for two and gradually looking at the menu then seconds later an android waitress approached him to take his order.

"May I get the dynamite rolls with the shrimp and white rice combo? And aah… A slice of avocado on the side?"

"*Any sauce sir?*"

"Yes, Duck sauce please. Also, another order of the half snapper with guacamole and chips."

"*Any drink sir?*"

"Yes, may I get the Royal Dragon? The bottle with two glasses please."

"*Ok, be right up in fifteen to twenty minutes.*"

"Ok thank you."

A minute had passed by and a teenage boy randomly sat around the same table across from him and spoke with an Irish accent.

"Hello Mr. Luciano. Lovely evening isn't it?"

Henry kept silent for twenty seconds then the teenager said—

"Ok, you don't have to say hi, that's cool."

"What happen to your stomach? Why do you have it wrapped up like that?"

"Ah nothing just a minor accident."

"Accident? Looks more like an attack."

"Don't worry about it. I feel like you worry too much."

"I'm just a curious guy."

"Hm, I see. Now the reason I'm here…"

"The Motogon." He interrupted.

"Yes, the first thing and most important thing on the agenda."

"Does he like it?"

"Oh yeah, he loves it. He reeaaly' loves it, it's a fascinating technology to say the least."

"Good, it's perfect for the Mad Doctor."

"Yes, I agree on that."

"I'm still surprised you're still alive. Looting any Luka Shale Tech isn't a walk in the park."

"Well, of… of course you would know that." He said with emphasis on *you.*

"I know a lot of things."

"Which makes me wonder, if I should continue to trust you."

"You? Or do you mean your boss? Isn't he running things and should be the one that, you should be distressed about?"

"Well, he is the 24th century's most vile criminal."

"That answered my questions very well."

"Whatever man. He wants to work with you further more."

"Good, I knew he wouldn't resist."

"Hm, he's already working on projects just in case the end comes earlier than expected… Well, with his tactical shrewdness, he never moved this hastily before."

"'Time is of the essence… someday he will have to leave this earth and passing down his reign of trepidation and bloodlust amongst the human race is what he truly wants."

"Indeed Mr. Luciano."

"Hm', this is my third time meeting with you and still you never said your name."

"It's Push Monaghan."

"Push? Hm, ok Push . . . Your half snapper is coming up."

"Hm, it's about time."

The android waitress arrived with the two meals and placed them on the table—

"This meal… It represents you."

"Hm, I guess it does and your aah'—sushi rolls?"

"Yes… It represents me in many ways Push… Many ways."

"Like your true self?"

"Oh, he must have mentioned that to you… You don't wanna' see my true self Push."

"Oh… Why is that?"

"Well, let's just say I'm more of an atrocity when it comes to my true self."

"Hmm', I see."

FIVE

<u>Nack Yaldara's residence</u>

Ki-Yale stood at the entrance with a slight nervous feeling after his best friend that he known for two years pointed a real weapon at him. He contemplated about what will happen next although his grandfather told him the details about his suit, he still thinks something may go wrong. As he waits for the security system to recognize him, he puts both hands in front of him and holds them together then he quickly turned his body left then turned to the right.

"Ki-Yale is at your door! Ki-Yale is at your door!" Said the security system recognizing him.

"Oh, look who decided to finally show up! What's up man, I thought you was coming over this morning bro. You forgot about me and overslept, didn't you?"

"No bro. I found out a new ability, so I could do more abilities." He said as he walked inside Nack's room.

"Nice, so aah'... What do you mean bro? Like, you developed an ability to do more abilities?"

"Let me demonstrate, now look closely." He said then he began to fade into his Netron Suit.

"Who the hell are you?"

"It's me… uh' hold on."

He quickly changed back to his regular clothes.

"Wha-what? Woah... bro… this is like a serious mind fuck! I mean you were just in a black and white suit then… but aagh'—my head!"

"Yeah… this must be what Granddad was talking about. Ok, ok now I'll change back."—Ki-Yale changing back to his Netron Suit.

"Wow! Why is my head hurting?"

"Well, you're not going to believe what happen earlier this morning."

"All this weird shit you told me before, I'm pretty sure I can handle it now." Nack said while holding his head.

"Well, you were pointing your shotgun at me earlier, thinking I was impersonating myself."

"What?! I… I don't remember doing that..."

"Now your brain is going to sting a little more thinking about it and trying to remember."

"Aaaagghhh! Yeah... ok I feel it... Aaaggh', my head! What the hell Ki!"

"Just let the pain run through, it'll go away soon, well at least that's what my granddad told me." He said while Nack bawled in pain.

"Ok—ok it's going away now. This is some serious mind fuck man! Ok, now I think I'm good."

"Good, you're good now."

"Hmm', a little woozy but I think now it's gone… Wow! Now I remember the whole thing bro! I was telling you to leave while I was waving my shotgun at you... Woops, my bad man, I thought that someone... Well, that you were impersonating yourself!"

"Hmm, it's cool, the reason why you couldn't recognize and remember because the suit tapped into your mind as a defense mechanism. To make you think otherwise."

"I see, so the suit manipulated me, got me thinking it wasn't you, but it was really you. Hmm', weird man."

"Yeah, weird stuff man."

"Strange." Nack added.

"Yeah."

"Well—problem solved, and I apologize for acting like that earlier bro."

"Its aaall' gooood' maan', no worries."

"So, you're stronger than regular now huh?"

"Yeah, only two times my strength—when a Netron first ever transforms into their suit it increases overtime, my granddad said. Also, this suit can handle any weather, I can heal fast, I can change the style of the suit, change into any form, thing, clothing with any color, pattern—I can grow my hair faster! I can set a hairstyle that I used on my regular form into the suit when transformed and keep that same hairstyle for as long as I like…" He said as he picked up Nack's basketball then threw it in a spinning like motion to the ceiling.

"Umm ok… almost like a camouflage thing going on here… Real soldier like I guess."

"It's considered a war suit or you can just call it an armor, when I transform, the suit thinks I'm in a battle—it can download any power or ability from any living species then instantly perfects them and perform them to its full potential. Well, except for the Dragoons, I can't imitate Dragoon powers of course because they're the opposites of us and Netrons as well because, well, I already have Netron powers. I just have to perfect them myself and be more powerful."

Nack sat inaudibly and stared at him as he prattled even more—

"I can even copy powers from weaponry and even robotics since my suit becomes a part of everything!"

"Remarkable… and you babbling this much just shows that this stuff is legit."

"Yes, sometimes I talk a lot when I'm excited… but, it's so many other things I could do with this suit too,

Granddad said he's going to have more training sessions to improve my suit and learn more about it!"

"I see . . ."

"I can duplicate the power and abilities of this basketball too."

"Man, you're like unstoppable… you can freaking do like Mega Human capabilities if you wanted to. You already have a keen intellectual mind and your strength is already similar to a Sila Human or even stronger . . . Does your parents and your granddad have these suits too? What about Tajay and Oji?"

"Granddad and my dad are equipped with one, but my mom can't because she is human. Remember?"

"Oh yeah, I forgot your mom is pure human."

"Oji... he's only seven and Granddad told me Tajay is close to developing her suit, but I don't think she would develop it anytime soon, because the way I did it was when someone was in danger. I felt like I had to retaliate when these Apaki Warriors was about to kill each other."

"Wait? An Apaki Warrior fight?"

"Well there was this older kid with tattoos on his face named Push and another one named Xack. I guess Xack was the victim and the other were the aggressor . . ."

"A dude named Push with tattoos on his face… He already sounds like a douche bag…"

"The tat wasn't so bad actually, it was impressively inked but Xack, man he came out of nowhere and landed right on me. If he would have hit the ground, he probably would have broken his neck."

"Hmm, sound like you saved him."

"Yeah, he thanked me after my eyes... well, they started fighting for a minute then the Asian guy looked like he was about to get murdered... then all of a sudden, freaking lightning came out of my eyes bro!"

"Lightning came out of your eyes? What the...? Broooo'!"

"Yeah bro, I can shoot lightning out of my eyes!!"

"Now that's some shit."

"I know, it's freaking awesome."

"Can you shoot the lightning now?"

"Well, it just happened out of the blue... Unexpectedly... I don't know how to do it willingly yet."

Silence for about thirty seconds then Nack looked at the time then said—

"Hmm, we should get going."

"Wait? Where are we going?"

"To do some sports bro. Come on! I'll show you."

Ki-Yale constantly playing with his basketball then throws it to the window putting a hole in it as it shatters to pieces.

"I'll fix that . . . no worries bro, I got you." He said as Nack became annoyed at what he did.

Machida Bar & Lounge—

"It's 11:30am... so yeah, let me get a Mimosa." Dunkin Turd ordered.

"Ok, one mimosa coming up." Said the lady bartender.

"Yes gotta' love a drink to start my day. Yes, I woke up late today but it's my day off from work you know, although working at home sometimes feels like a day off to me."

The bartender hands him his drink then he said—

"Thank you, I'm an agent by the way—like secret agent or like those spies you know. Ha! Nah, I'm just an agent for the public holographic telephone lines."

Mr. Turd took his first gulp then continued—

"It's a great work experience you know—possibly the best I must add. Awesome benefits but I feel like college kids would love this more especially the ones that got the home schooling and all that. You in college hun'? Hmm', you look like you are in school."

"Yeah."

"Great… that's terrific. You're on your way to fantastic things. Poppa always told me— 'Great things come to those who wait'. You ever heard that saying?"

"Yeah, I heard it plenty of times." The lady bartender dragged her voice.

Mr. Turd took another gulp then looked at the lady bartender then whispered—

"How's about you and I do something later? Huh? I could fulfill your wildest dreams; I could make you do things that you never in your life would ever think of doing."

She peered at him then a male bartender came by and intervened—

"Hello sir. Would you like any more drinks?"

"Freaking guy—freaking—interrupts. What a damn cock block…" Mr. Turd slurred under his breath.

"You say something sir?"

"Oh… you probably didn't hear over the music. Sorry, I said... no thanks man, I'm fine."

<u>*Little Tree Ville Train Station*</u>—

Its sundown and the weather dropped below the fifties, Xack Machida is on the platform for the next train going to the Eastside of LTV. He took off his black sleeves exposing his tattoo he recently inked on his right arm. He observed it with an admiring look on his face and relieved to comprehend that there isn't a wound over it.

A slim but toned teenage girl walking seven feet towards Xack. She has long straightened brown hair with her favorite burgundy headband that displays the Crouton

Village Apaki Warrior symbol. She wore a red high-tech polar fleece with blue workwear fabric fitted pants and black sneakers.

"Don't tell me you are regretting that already." She said.

"Naah. I'm loving it the more I look at it. It gives me the courage to move on."

"Ha', good answer I guess."

"Back in the 21st century—this would be considered foolish."

"I actually agree with that, but our love never seemed to cease, and we been together long enough for that."

Xack's Caucasian eighteen-year-old girlfriend, Adelia Woods expressed their companionship. She never wears makeup but Xack still thinks she's very attractive, nevertheless. Adelia has freckles on her round cheeks, hooded grey eyes and diamond shaped face. They have known each other throughout their childhood and being best friends initially before being partners. Her parents adopted her but later moved out to finish her Apaki Jermayin training at aged sixteen in Crouton Village in which she resided at the dojo. Despite going through countless troubles and being an Apaki Warrior herself, Adelia would always support him and he would do the same for her.

As the air shifted, wind blew along Adelia's face. She sat next to him as they ogled at each other, then Xack smiled, ready to make his first move. He pecked on her thin lips then they made out aggressively. A passionate clash of two tongues and lips with her left hand on his shoulder while he caresses her hip with his right hand. Xack displayed a bit of aggression shoving his body forward then she snickered and said— "Nooo', mmm… we should get a—mmm… a room Xack."

"You know I don't care where we do it."

"I know but a room is better." She said then giggled as she stood. She grabs his left hand and slightly began pulling him up.

"Ok, let's gets out of here but… agh'." He paused as he stood up.

"But what? What's wrong?"

"I'm wounded."

"Again Xack!? Where?"

"My upper left arm and chest, its ok I patched it earlier…"

Adelia lifted his sleeve to observe his injuries then said—

"You've been grazed by glass attacks. What happened?"

"It was another Apaki Warrior. He was trying to capture me."

"Well you're here that means he failed… Why didn't you tell me before I came?"

"I didn't want you to worry. I'm fine though I'm all patched up—my clothes were technically a shield."

"Well, it is Kevlar that's adequately manufactured for us …"

She attentively looked around then said—

"We should get going."

"Yes, yes, let's go"

A few minutes later they both walked off the train after arriving at their stop.

"Crouton Village Tournament… We haven't been there since—."

"Yeah but it's time I avenge our people and most importantly my mother's death."

"Or maybe we can still sit this one out. I mean, I know you are upset about it and so am I but fighting in that tournament isn't going to bring them back."

"Can't just sit around and do nothing Adelia. I must fight with honor for my mother and my people… our people. What Sagan did was—was by far the worst thing to ever happen to us . . . He must be held accountable for his actions. He's a coward at best, sending his men, his beasts and his machines to do his dirty work while he concealed himself..."

"Yes, all of that is true, however, he's very crafty using his clever mind to outsmart anyone, even the Gigantica Army."

Xack goggled at her and slowly shook his head up and down then said—

"It's blatantly obvious that he is dangerous, and it's seen for years now that he's unbeatable, but I must..."

Adelia immediately rolled her eyes and began to walk in another direction before he could finish his sentence.

"Where are you going? Abi... hey Abi..."—Xack followed her while she tromped angrily.

"I just want you to be alive Xack ok?"

Her back still turned to him with her arms folded as he looked down to her A-shaped ass then he said—"I know but..."

"I don't want to lose you. Do you understand what I'm telling you?"

"Yeah. I do—I..."—Xack hesitated swiftly noticing the bushes were shaking and heard a growling noise. He casually pushed his girlfriend out of the way then a muscular male coyote with several strands of white hair in the middle of its head appeared out of the bushes following three more.

"Oh shit..."

"Draw your sword Adel."

She promptly drew her glass katana then ignites it and stood in defense form while another three more muscular coyotes appeared out of the bushes.

After utilizing several equipment to prevent extinction of most animals, the 24th century has many evolved animals and some are equipped with the Mega Animal serum which has portion of human DNA, strictly for military or Law enforcement. This serum not only enhances them, it makes them more vicious in battle than ever before. They become larger, stronger and faster. Their minds become smarter with better hunting abilities and amplified senses. Depending on if they're cold blooded or warm-blooded animals, they also adapt to the temperatures a lot faster than usual.

The seven coyotes seemed belligerent as they revealed their sharp teeth ready to strike as they growled. Their teeth are also enhanced to be sharper than usual, sharp enough to graze metal. They all snarled with bloodlust in their piercing eyes, legs apart and their heads were downward preparing to attack.

"If they jump—shoot em'. If they get close stab em'!" Xack said.

The coyotes ran toward them and pounced ten feet in the air as Adelia instantly let's go of her sword letting it gravitate in front of her palm. The pouncing coyote received her heated glass sword in its mouth which went deep down the critter's esophagus while another coyote landed on her and bit her arm.

Three coyotes dashed towards Xack while he swung at them slicing one in the left eye and halfway blinding the coyote. The half-blinded coyote squealed while the other two jumped ten feet in the air. Xack stabbed one on the right side from him in the stomach while the other landed on him. With quick thinking, he lets go of the sword that he stabbed the other with and swiftly formed another glass katana from his left hand in front of the coyote's mouth. The coyote bit the heated glass sword as blood from its tongue and lips were bleeding with bits of oozing saliva.

Adelia on the ground wrestling with the coyote then molded another glass katana from her right hand again then decapitated the coyote's head.

The two residual coyotes were fathomed that their companions were defeated so quickly. The male coyote with the white strands in the front of his head and a female coyote succumbed to the unexpected outcome of this battle which resulted in retreat, immediately running away.

The glass katana that was left inside the coyotes turned into burnt glass and cooled down as smoke ascended from their wounds.

"Are you alright Adel?"

"Yeah… hmmph'… now we're both hurt."

"We must go, this is a felony."

"But they attacked us, and these aren't regular animals."

"True but the system will try their best to criminalize us Apaki Warriors... C'mon let's go."

"Oh, so you wanna' get smoked Nack?"—He challenged him as they looked up at a basketball court hovering forty feet in the air. This court is the same size as an NBA court, same rules apply but the players are using air technology sneakers to fly around with the court. A player can still dribble on the court surface then jump up to twenty feet in the air. A player could be a dwarf and do amazing dunks and sir tricks. Different rules apply depending on what type of match they play.

"Yeah I just got into playing and I want to perfect my craft you know."

"You're doing sports… I never knew I'll see the day."

"It's a first time for everything Ki."

"Well, my dad and I ball all the time." He said then he looked up underneath the see-through court surface and saw two young boys playing one on one.

"Good so you know some moves…"

"Yeah I'm Ok."

"So, help me school these fools, you know, embarrass them like how they did me."

"Ha! You got scraped huh Nack?"

"Yes, and I want their asses handed to them!"

Ki-Yale burst out laughing then said—

"Ah man. I can just imagine you getting crossed. 'Oh, oh. What just happened? Oh wait, oh'."

Ki-Yale imitating basketball cross moves around Nack and mocked his voice.

"It's not funny Ki!"

"Ok, ok I'll chill. Let's work em' and see what they truly got."

Nack, Ki-Yale and the two young boys who appeared to be twin brothers who were fifteen started a two on two game of twenty-one points. The twins had made their nineteenth shot while Ki-Yale made most of the points with Nack only making three causing them to have seventeen points.

Nack had the ball dribbling on the court surface while the twin is on defense.

"You ain't got the juice! Wassup'!" Said the boy on defense.

"Right here Nack!" He hollered being open and signaling Nack to pass the ball.

He passed the ball to Ki-Yale, he caught it then dribbled. The other brother progressed his defense against Ki-Yale as he backed up about five feet then crosses the boy while Nack *sets up a pick* for him to run around. Ki-Yale gets an open shot then shoots it from half court.

"Oooh' shii'…" Nack said while Ki-Yale made it in the basket gaining two points and tying the game then one of the brothers said—

"Dude made it from half court like it's nothing."

"It's the protein baby, makes you get muscles on my muscles!"

"Dude. What muscles? You're made of bones. Come on, I'll check it up!"

"Don't let my scrawny body fool you." Ki-Yale said with a smile.

"Hmmph'." Said the boy as he roughly checked the ball to Nack.

Nack bounced the ball then immediately passes it to Ki-Yale. He dribbled it while Nack tried to get open for a shot. With his Basketball air sneakers, he levitated about four feet and one brother also levitated then got closer to him and got on defense.

Ki-Yale dribbling fast and being too fast for the boy as Nack struggled to get open

"C'mon Nack get open…"

He finally got open and Ki-Yale threw the ball at him. Nack hesitated consequently permitting the defender to catch it.

"Damn it Nack."

The twin dribbled back behind to the line and acquired the consent to shoot the ball but instead, he passed it to his brother then immediately Ki-Yale guarded him. The twin couldn't get past him because he is unusually too fast and stronger.

"How am I not getting past this dude?"

"Told you not to let my size fool you."

The twin slipped the ball out of his hands then it bounced towards Nack and the other brother.

Nack chased after the ball and so is the twin brother. Nack caught it and with little experience of the game, he hesitated then the boy snatched it out of his hands.

"C'mon Nack."

Its game point and the twin dribbled as if he's putting on a show.

"Defense Nack! Defense!"

The boy slipped pass Nack, hurdled towards the basket and dunked it over him.

"I sort of seen this coming."

"Game over losers." Said the twin brother next to Ki-Yale.

A few minutes later…—

Ki-Yale and Nack both sat down on the sidelines of the Basketball court while they observe other players during a game.

"You choked Nack. That's probably why you lost last time. You choked like six times in the game man!"

"I didn't choke…"

"Yes, you did… Hesitating the whole game with your face looking confused."

"Whatever."

"We'll get em' next time, no sweat."

"Yeah, I guess… I guess I need more practice."

"A lot of practice then together we could be an unstoppable team. They wouldn't know what hit em'."

"Unstoppable team indeed. Hm', I need to show you something Ki."

"Ok. I hope it don't involve you losing again. If so, I want no parts in it."

"Ha! No, this time it's more serious."

Later, in an abandon warehouse—

Garrett Lynch, wearing an LTV upgraded police outfit with illegal Fed weapons equipped which consisted of guns, grenades and two long knives. Another man next to him with a suit and tie sitting on a chair named Kojack Thompson smoking a nicely rolled cigarillo cannabis cigarette, a 'blunt' so to speak. All around Garrett and Kojack—are about six men standing in a half a circle behind them. Across from these men stood another eight men dressed in regular clothes as if they were going out to the movies with friends. The one in the front that does the talking for them also known as their leader, is named Rojohn Bibbon. They all don't look so pleased to see each other but only pleased to see what's inside the three feet high, five feet long tech box that Kojack is sitting next to.

"What's this stare down all about fam'? —I want this money." Kojack said.

"Well, how about we open up that contraption first and pass me a little bit of that smoke." Rojohn said amongst the eight-armed men across from Kojack.

"Nah—you get your own weed bruh' . . . Punk ass fuck boy! . . . You want to see what's inside this bitch!? Well, come closer."

"Hmm', we all know you full of shit Kojack, so how about you bring it over here."

The look on Kojack's face after he said that made it seem as if he wanted to murder Rojohn and his crew.

"Who are these guys?" Ki-Yale whispered standing behind a trailer with Nack.

"They stole my dad's police uniform a couple days ago. It's the new model edition police suit, capable of enhancing strength, one hundred percent bullet proof, heat ray proof, water resistant, ninety percent electricity resistant and it comes with a helmet that reads human backgrounds by just looking at the face."

"Similar features like the old model but just updated with a newer look."

"Yes, pretty much."

Ki-Yale in his Netron Suit, used his Netron vision and said—

"Hmm, I see police suits, weaponry and some weird tanks filled with some sort of gas inside that box—it's probably dangerous."

"Woah, you can see inside the box?"

"Yeah, the suit enhanced my vision. It's called Netron Vision."

"Awe man that ability could be of so much good use."

"We need to call the authorities."

"Yeah after you kick their asses..." Nack encouraged Ki-Yale.

He looked at his hands for five seconds then made two fists indicating a drastic boost in his confidence.

"Yeah. You know what Nack? That sounds like a good idea."

Ki-Yale stepped out of the shadows from behind the trailer and knocked it with his left knuckles, leaving a small dent in the metallic material. The noise startled some of the men standing across from Kojack as Rojohn and his men turned around.

"What the hell?!" Rojohn alarmed.

Nack stood behind the trailer while Ki-Yale stood out in the open for everyone to see.

"That police suit doesn't belong to you."

"Who the hell are you fam'? And how the fuck you got in here?" Kojack perturbingly asked.

He clenched both fists with his chest out slightly ready to speak with pure confidence.

"My name is Netro and I see that you are breaking the law!"

"Ha'. Netro!? Kid… You know who I am? I ain't the nice man that lives next door."

"So aah'… What are you exactly…?"

"Ha! What am I? I'm worse than the fucking bully that bullies you in school! I'm worse than the boogeyman that hides under your bed at night! I'm worse than the creepy old guy that stares at you in the morning!" Kojack babbled.

"Hmm'. Nah, never heard of you."

"The little boy's name is Netro huh? You got balls stepping up to armed men, but you really shouldn't have come here. Now we have to waste you." Rojohn said pulling out an illegal Federal gun, Beretta 92FS Semi-Auto pistol and pointed it at Ki-Yale.

"Yeah… well… I do have balls and I got the heart of a lion too."

Complete silence from everyone as they bared serious faces and ogled at him for twenty seconds after he said his slogan.

"Heart of a ha…! Heart of a… What the fuck he just said? Heart of a hahaha…! Heart of a fucking lion? Haha! You're killing me kid."—Rojohn cackled along his crew. "Lil' man thinks this shit is a joke."

Ki-Yale became the laughingstock as everyone's chuckling made him seem chastised and a little embarrassed.

"Garrett. Can you get a background on him?" Kojack asked.

"No, this police suit isn't picking anything up for him." Garrett said with a deep muffle voice.

"You shouldn't have been here, you witnessed what we're doing and now you're about to get handled boy."

"Rojohn, you ain't doing shit!"

"None of you guys ain't doing nothing." Ki-Yale provoked everyone.

"Hm, yeah? Here's something for you!"

Rojohn unloaded five bullets at Ki-Yale while Nack with his eyelids wide open peeking from behind the trailer in fear. Rojohn stopped shooting as he stood there without a single scratch on him, no bullet holes in his body, no blood whatsoever.

"What the hell?! This dumb ass missed all five shots. C'mon Rojohn!" Kojack uttered.

"Naaaah! What are you talking about? I shot right at him! His clothes must be bullet proof!"

"So, shoot that shit properly fam'! Shoot at his head!"

Ki-Yale just stood there with a little smirk but in his mind, he thought—*'Wow this is freaking intense, shooting at me like that, I'm only thirteen and I never got shot before…! Until today… Hmph', I'm pretty sure I can take bullets to the head with this suit, no problem… bring it.*"

Rojohn, walked up to Ki-Yale then questioned him while gnashing his teeth—"What's the smirk for kid?"

He removed the smirk then said— "I'm sorry... go ahead, shoot me."

"You here this kid man? He's crazy." One of the goons said.

"The lil' motha' fucka' wanna' die! So I'ma' give it to em'! Yeah, I'ma give it to em' real good!"

Rojohn got closer to Ki-Yale and stopped about two feet from him—then he fired a shot at his head... *BAAMM!* —Complete silence from everyone for ten seconds as the echoes from the gunshot hurled through the abandon warehouse. Ki-Yale stood motionless with no gunshot wound to his head.

The bullet astonishingly bounced off him and ricocheted upward into a window.

"What . . . the . . . fuck?" Kojack flabbergasted.

"What kind of technology is this kid using?" Rojohn queried.

"No technology, I'm just different!"

Ki-Yale gradually walked up to Rojohn who now displays a frightened persona then comfortably snatched his gun and punched him in the face. He stumbled back about five feet as Ki-Yale crushed the pistol with his hands while Rojohn's thugs shoot their guns at him. This time these guns were heat ray guns, one had a Fed Raven LKG-32 while three other goons had heat ray machine gun called the Assassin Ready J6 and three others had an illegal Fed Stinger Beam 300 heat ray gun.

Ki-Yale took all the heat ray shots like it's a walk in the park then sprinted towards them while dodging the rest of the heat ray shots then he jump-kicked the front man in the chin.

The man hits the floor with his gun doing the same out of his right hand in which fired a shot towards one of his companions and hit him on the arm. One guy reached for him at the right side, but Ki-Yale elbowed him causing him to fall back about six feet, another goon tried to make a move but instead got knocked out. The thugs fell back while Rojohn tried to get up, then Ki-Yale bashed Rojohn back down to the floor with his left fist.

He moved so precisely, so smoothly and unbothered that his ways convinced Kojack to take an exit.

"Hey, Garrett, forget this shit, let's get out of here! A little kid beating up grown ass men? I've seen enough!"

"Yes, agreed."

Garrett, Kojack and his goons proceeded to the back doors carrying the tech box full of weapons and chemical tanks then fled in air vehicles. The goons kept trying to fight Ki-Yale as he displayed little effort but seconds later, he finished the rest of them off with punches then went outside to check which direction they went, and it was the Eastern direction where Crouton Village is being held.

He went back inside and saw Nack next to the beaten goons knocked out cold.

"Wow, you put a beating on em'! It's a shame you didn't get to use your lightning."

"Well, it wasn't really necessary... We should tie them up and call authorities!"

"Yeah, great idea bro."

After they tied up the unconscious thugs along with Rojohn, Nack wrote large 'N' markings on Rojohn's four head and the rest of his goons with a marker then Ki-Yale asked—

"Why are you writing that on their four heads bro?"

"To signify . . . That there's a new hero in the village!"

<u>At the Salon</u>—

Demi Kafmora sits on a hover chair while robotics work on her hair robotics performing pedicure, skin care and all sorts of beauty desires.

"So, how's school lately?"

"It's doing fine Mom, the usual stuff." Tajaymae said sitting beside her on a separate hover chair with her right fist on her chin.

"Oh no getting into trouble, right?"

"Yeah, of course. Why would I be getting into trouble?"

"Oh, just asking you know, lately it's been quiet with your school calling my phone…"

"Yeah…"

"How did you manage to get the destroyed project all done in five hours?"

"I used cardboard, glue and picked up the pieces then put them back together and just did whatever—I got an eighty-three on it."

"Hm, not bad, at least you passed."

"Yeah but I could have gotten a hundred the way I did it at first Mom…. Hmmm', Ki-Yale and his stupid habits, sometimes I just want to... Aagh!"

"It was an accident baby; c'mon you have to cut your brother some slack. He does his usual blunders here and there but he's training for the best—he's to become a king and according the code he must be the strongest . . . Hm, it could be very exhilarating."

"I guess…"

"It's amazing how you did that all by yourself though. You had no friends to help you?"

"No Mom, I have no friends."

"C'mon Tajay. It's time you make friends and get to know new people." Demi said then recommenced with a whisper— "You are part human too you know."

"The kids in my class—are douchebags…"

"Well ah—just—be a douchebag too…"

"Wow… that was horrible advice and I don't want to make friends Mom. I'm good by myself."

"You're not always by yourself hun', you got me, your dad, your granddad, your brothers… Well…"

"Yeah."

Tajaymae looked away from her mother for five seconds then Demi said—

"Hey, I miss him a lot too."

"Why did he have to run away? I know it's because he isn't Netro Two but c'mon is it really worth it?"

"Being Netro Two was all he ever wanted. I just wish he accepted it how it is."

"I think he did a little bitch move."

"Tajay."

"Hm', sorry Mom."

"Look, I know what he did wasn't right and I'm sure he didn't want to get taken by whoever or whatever took him. It wasn't his fault that he was problematic, it was truly… It was truly us being such bad parents and it sucks. Now we must pay the price . . . but, what we need to be angry about the most is the kidnapper that abducted a part of our family." Demi said then revealed a bit of sorrow in her face.

"Nooo. You're not a bad parent Mom and Dad isn't either, don't blame yourself." She accredited her mother as she hugged her stomach.

Demi smiled and puts her daughter's arm around her back.

Training room—

Nealo and Neecho are in the training room at home sparring and decided to start talking about their family situation. As they hit each other, things began to heat up while Nealo held his own against his son. Neecho seemed to be the predicted triumphant, hitting his father hard against his guarded arms causing him to back up to the ropes.

"I know you are feeling a lot of anger in you my son; I've seen it in you ever since they slaughtered your mother Raenia! I miss my love every day of my life but remember what I told you, each day that I want you to keep in mind . . . Let this anger be a weapon when you find that asshole who took Narrken from you . . . From us!"

Rawzogon at age fifty-nine, the son of Larthgon and one of the many children, discovered what Queen Tella did with sending her son to Earth so that the royal eternal prophecy stood fruitfully continuous. In spite of that, Rawzogon sent his thirty-five-year-old son Deathogon to Earth.

Deathogon encountered Nealo and Raenia in outer space slightly away from Earth. They fought but Raenia didn't stand a chance and got executed resulting Nealo to carry out the slaying of Deathogon. Though Deathogon traded bloodshed with Nealo in outer space, a baby Dragoon was born and being the heartless beings, they are,

Terrorgon, who is Larthgon's royal liege, disposed of the female Dragoon then firmly ensued with protecting the only child.

Although the Dragoons found the Netrons on Earth, the Netrons decided to stay on Earth discreetly and proceeded to complete the cycle.

Neecho dramatically shrieked in a barbaric tone as he hits his father uncontrollably then paused and said—

"Yes, I never forgot that advice, but it's been about three years now and still nothing, no traces of blood, footprints! Nothing!"

Nealo created a path for him to circle his son while he followed in the opposite direction and said—"Hmm, the abductor knew what he was doing. It could be the Opposites, but our suits haven't sensed any of them here since we defeated Deathogon. I'm pretty sure they all left the earth; I know they are coming back to try and kill us using Deathogon's offsprings."

"But what if it truly was the Opposites? No, they aren't the strategy type like us, just straight destruction for the fun of it... Maybe it was one of the offsprings. But why hide? Why don't they just—pull up?!—What? Are they too afraid of the fight?!!"

"It's possible that they were smart enough to actually strategize and wait for the right opportunity to strike my son. We still don't know for sure that the Opposites took him because of the lack of trace but I just know my grandson is still alive out there somewhere. I have that feeling in my gut, maybe whoever or whatever took him figured out a way to suppress his abilities so he can't escape but we will find them and get our Narrken back!"

"You think it's Sagan? Although we never crossed each other..." Neecho speculated as he withdrew his hands and stopped moving.

Nealo did the same then said—

"Back in my military days, I had conflict with him . . . I was victorious stopping most of his plans, but it is possible that he figured us out and decided to make a move. We never stepped to each other face to face—he was always hiding which makes this situation even more questionable."

Neecho returned to his orthodox boxing form then leisurely circled him. Nealo did the same moving in the opposite direction.

"Nah, Dr. Sagan taking Narrken doesn't make any sense and even if he did... What would he do to him?"

Nealo saw that Neecho won't give up even after three years of searching for his son. All Nealo really can do is support Neecho and articulate to him about the right things to do.

"The determination in Ki-Yale's heart led him to learn faster each day... he already developed his armor. Ki-Yale is what we need to focus on the most right now, it may sound erroneous but searching for Narrken needs to put on hold now because Ki-Yale is our chance of survival."

"The worst is coming for us isn't it?"

"Yes, my son . . . I believe so."

Eastside LTV—

The moon is fully exposed, striking its luminescence amongst the village as the pole lights lead the pathway. With deft motions of the nimble police vehicles flying overhead towards whatever crime scene, Xack ceased along with Adelia. He remembered his medical procedures from his Apaki Jermayin training trying to use his hands very gently, wrapping his fresh bandage that he carried with him around Adelia's bite wound on her left arm. She acknowledged the petite treatment he had to offer and blushed then proceeded to saunter down the pathway.

"You're a tough girl. You know that?"

"Hm, well I am an Apaki Warrior… Ouch! Too tight"

"Hmmph', I remember saying that two nights ago."

Adelia smiled as she lightly slapped him on his head then Xack smiled back and said—

"Hmm, looks like you're good to go now."

"Those coyotes. Where the hell did, they come from?"

"I don't know but they weren't normal ones, they looked like Mega Animals. Hm, especially the first one with the little strands of white hair looking at me as if it was about to speak to me."

"Talking coyotes? Hmm, the only actual talking animals were the Apes and the military are keeping them somewhere right now—and also you know… Azuma."

"Adel, I really don't like it when you mention his name…"

"Sorry..."

"It's ok… Well, I believe it could be possible overall."

"Yeah . . . We need to keep a low profile, first it was that Apaki Warrior attacking you then these coyotes. This has to be all Sagan's doing."

Xack kept silent after what she just said and thought—

"*Yeah… let him bring whatever and whoever he wants. I will fight all of them and as long as I'm still alive I won't stop moving until he's dead.*"

SIX

Gigantica, one of the most marvelous accomplishments ever established with a more combined government. Extremely large land on behalf of over billions of people to reside on and prolong the aspects of everyday life. Buildings floating in the sky with barriers around them connected to the pavements provided and the barriers contain anti tilt plates linked from the surfaces. Emergency anti-gravity plates on the ground that will hold it up in case the buildings fail to remain in place and protective shields surrounding them equipped with fail safe systems. Highways and freeways in the air with vehicles going over a hundred miles per hour or more without an accident. These vehicles are equipped with a self-driving system that has not failed since they were made in year 2273.

Some civilians would sleep inside their vehicles while it carries them to their destination, minibuses, trailer houses and more. Automated roadways that are operated by satellite frequency corresponding with the vehicles ordering them to drive on its own by choice. Before they launched this, the Grainian Tech companies contracted an assurance that no failure would occur but there were a few known incidents triggered by hackers that took control of the motherboards inside of main power plants throughout different cities. Other highways and freeways don't have vehicles with the self-driving system, so they separate these highways and freeways. The regular roadways are only for regular driving vehicles with wheels or air driving technology with low boosted thrusters.

Safer ways to live were also taken into play such as the *Social Security microchip* which is placed in all humans immediately when birthed. The SS chips are shock resistant, water resistant and heat resistant with the help of Tektonium Metal. This was launched in the beginning of the 23rd century after the Grainians vs. Humans War and is still forced upon. If a human does not have this microchip there will be consequences such as prison time or even death by a bullet or a heat ray beam by an assailant. The SS microchip is not only for identity and tracking system, but it is also designed to prevent a stray bullet or heat ray beam from a regular gun—these chips are the size of a rice grain or sometimes even smaller.

The SS microchip which is equivalent to a force field that's five feet around the human body, prevents a regular gun with bullets or heat ray from firing up close and from a distance depending from how far the firearm can shoot. Firearms are now equipped with chips inside called the *Assassination Prevention microchip*, these chips are impossible to extract from the firearm with the benefit of the Grainian technology surplus and it is required by law that certain guns must have these chips. These regular guns with AP microchips cease fire when interacting with a SS microchip through an interstellar network. Scientists believed that these specific alienated technologies are similar to the internet but is operated and linked through all the stars amongst the universe. These guns are also recorded whenever they're fired and where it's fired. Guns without an AP microchip which are manufactured through authorized factories are called federal guns or military guns which are registered. Once a military/Fed gun is missing or not reported back to base or any police facility they are marked as stolen and called illegal Fed guns or illegal military guns.

Although leaders had been pugnacious of banning weapons of mass destruction and even just relinquishing weapons in general, they were consistently made because of the fears of drastic decreases within the business world and conquering lands with act of violence to locals. Society then demanded protection with concealed carry and in their homes from illegal Fed guns and governments from all nations agreed that it's needed. Criminals with these stolen guns usually remove the SS chip from their bodies so that they wouldn't be tracked, depending on what part of the body it was placed. However, when criminals remove them, this allows citizens who own registered AP firearms to defend themselves. Police officers or military officers also have equipment on their uniforms, vehicles, drones that fly around cities and in the facilities in which they operate to track down many illegal technologies and mostly firearms that does not have an AP microchip, which is why criminals tend to use illegal Fed guns quickly as possible and ditch them before authorities arrive.

The tracking or detecting devices which has either automatic or manual coordination, uses advanced sonar technology in the biosphere that is typically constructed with computerized technology. These devices can operate on its own without sonar in non-computerized areas such as the woods—also with various distances it relies on detecting and tracking down gun powder, lead, red brass, explosives, Tektonium metal and any other features in which a non-AP gun holds along with high quality radiograph machinery. Citizens who live in certain areas do not have the right to own a non-AP gun unless they possess the proper license to do so.Legally owning a non-AP firearm or firearms are only to be kept in a locked and secured safe and can also be used for home defense in certain areas.

Gigantica City, year 2270—

A beautiful Caucasian, Irish and Russian four-month-old baby boy waiting for adoption at any moment. The baby boy gazed up at an African American couple named Ralph Roland and Gina Roland. The couple was so amused by him and decided the boy was meant to be a Roland. They named him Kevin Roland and Kevin were the couple's first child due to Gina's abnormal inability to conceive. She didn't give up though—three years later Gina finally got pregnant and had a son named Tyson Roland. This gave Kevin the opportunity to share a childhood with a little brother.

In year 2288—

Kevin and Tyson are now teenagers, Kevin is eighteen and Tyson is fifteen. Kevin has a high bald fade with cropped fringe haircut while Tyson has short hair, high top skin fade. They both have slender bodies and wearing automated clothing. After school, they met up then began walking through a mall on the 36th floor, a building which hovers around 1,089ft in the air. Kevin looked to the side and saw two men kissing, he squeezed his eyelids then walked up to the large window as his brother followed then looked over the city. This is a routine for these two brothers, reminding themselves how beautiful the world is when humans come together and create marvelous possessions.

Moments later they both were heading home on the transport train in Gigantica City. Kevin reading his book on *Clinical Epidemiology* and Tyson noticed a man staring at him and Kevin. They both got off the train, but the man didn't follow then Tyson said—

"Hey, that guy was looking right at us. It's every time we ride this train there is like always weird looking people staring at us."

"Yea I know, this is why I read my books on the train, so I won't look at their ugly faces."

"Well, that's not always smart. They could come up from behind without you paying attention."

"That's why I have this little brother." Kevin said as he pulled out a knife and started slicing his book.

"Oh shit, that knife is pretty sharp!"

"Yes, it is." He said as he gazed at his knife.

"Don't you need that book?" Tyson puzzled.

"Nah I read that thing over five times already. I'll get a new one." Kevin said as Tyson looked at him with a confused face.

"No worries, I'm good to go." Kevin continued.

"Whatever, you're so predictable brother."

"Ha', I kind of wish I could use it in an actual situation."

"Well, for starters you can't bring it at school, and I don't know how you got that in school with all that security."

"I simply place the knife somewhere else and that somewhere else no one knows about."

"The river near Bleak Street! You always walk through there and say that you have to piss. Which you shouldn't be pissing in public—that's a serious offense Kevin."

"Ah man you figured it out so easily." He said sarcastically then continued—

"Now, these offenses I don't care about Tyson. I'm a visionary kind of person. I see things differently and I never see me getting caught slipping."

"Ok, said the one that's going for a doctor's degree."

"When you get to my age, you'll understand brother."

"I understand a lot already."

"Yeah? And what's that do you truly understand?"

"Well, for one, I think people now will never accommodate to imperfections..."

"Now I'm going to stop you right there little brother... society everywhere are prone to generate the thought of being perfect as opposed to being unhappy with themselves. Living in fear plays a big factor in this against the ego driven also. For example, the famous Luka Shale. This guy wanted to freakishly remodel the Earth's shape for climate control like what the fuck! After basically obtaining ownership for expanding the overall complex of the planetary rings of Saturn."

"I agree on that, but Luka Shale actually had key points to his theories."

"Yeah but from what I observed; Luka is still just another ordinary man with ideas hoping for more wealth but sometimes I feel not everyone should live under today's order. Well we'll see how well his progeny succeeds . . . Hm, the basic way of living now... I think its bullshit."

As they kept on walking home through their neighborhood and prolonged a conversation, precipitously an air vehicle drove by them in high speed causing them to eat some strong wind.

"Freaking asshole!" Kevin complained.

"Aagh, I absolutely agree."

"It's like people buy cars just to be an asshole. No decency."

"Hey, Kevin."

Kevin looked at his younger brother as an answer to him.

"You ever thought at every move we make is a move connected to our last move?"

"Yeah, sometimes but thinking like that isn't good you know."

"I know… I think about it every day for some reason—it's like my mind is leading me to the end."

"What's your preference Tyson? To enjoy your life? Or to live in the fear for the rest of your life? That shouldn't be in your head at all brother, you're too young to be thinking like that. Be thankful you're still alive today and every move you make is a move towards greatness. You should be thinking about the future and the success you will have. Don't let unfortunate events lead you to give up. Especially the events you live through."

"Hm, —ok. Hopefully I keep that mentality."

"You should, it's a way you should abide by while finishing your growth into a man."

It's 8:15pm, they finally arrived at their home entrance and saw a suspicious vehicle by the drive way. It could just be one of Dad's friends they thought.

Kevin and Tyson went inside and barely witnessed the slight darkness of the living room trashed then yelled at the top of their lungs calling for their parents but no answer. Some evenings they would be out at the same time but something just doesn't seem right.

"Kevin, the seniors should've known we stepped in the house and the lights should've turned on by now."

"Yeah, that means the electricity has been tampered with."

This is when they truly suspected a home invasion as Tyson picked up his metal baseball bat that's been sitting on the massage chair. Kevin pulled out his knife and started walking towards the kitchen leaving Tyson behind him. The kitchen was clear, no one and no sign of their parents. The paranoia hits Tyson as he turned his head left and right, ambling towards his room.

"Drop the knife and the bat." Calmly said a man just three feet away from them, wearing an all-black outfit from head to toe including gloves and a mask.

The darkness made him look even more frightening to them.

He quickly seized Tyson with his left arm around his neck and an illegal Fed pistol with a silencer in his right hand pointing at his head. Kevin trembled in fear with loss for words beholding his brother being scared shitless and continued holding the bat.

"I said drop it! Both of you!"

Tyson unhanded his bat and Kevin unhanded the knife knowing his brother would get his head blown off if he doesn't listen.

"I want you to walk upstairs and go into your parent's room—no questions."

Kevin turned to the stairs then quietly and gradually sauntered up.

"C'mon boy. Hurry the fuck up!"

He walked a little faster until he reached the top then opened his parent's room door. Kevin was the first to see his mother and father being comatose, badly beaten and tied up siting on a chair. He witnessed them being motionless and completely naked, nothing but bare skin as blood oozed down their bodies from the open wounds.

"No Mom! —Dad! No!" Kevin vividly screamed out to his parents.

Tyson observed his parents and started tearing up and loudly grieved until his voice cracked.

"What do you want from us?!"

"Oh! Nothing major! I just want you to know the truth Kevin!"

"What truth?!"

The man in all black took out some papers with the gun still in his right hand out of his side jacket pocket while holding on to Tyson.

"Read that... but first… take a look at this." He said as he pulled out a picture.

The picture had a young man and a young lady in it. The young man strongly resembled Kevin and even had reddish hair like Kevin. He seemed to have similar skin color and similar facial structure.

"Who are these people?!"

"That's your real parents Kevin."

"Real parents?!" He queried.

"Yeah, the ones you see beaten up is your adopted parents. How do you not know this? You're like eighteen now you suppose to know a long time ago."

"I don't believe you!"

Tyson stopped weeping and stood quiet staring at his brother.

"But you have to believe me. I mean look at them they're black and you're... you're Russian and Irish!"

"I know this already. I know I'm adopted but, I just don't believe these people in the picture are my parents! I need more proof!"

"This proof is clear as day Kevin!! Now, I want you to read these papers."

Kevin began to read the papers while Tyson gazed at his parents fretting about what the invader would do next.

"Is this some kind of sick joke?"

"No. I'm gonna' put this bluntly Kevin... they are your real mother and father! Bobby Sagan and Jennifer Kozlov . . . They want you back . . . I want you back son."

"What?"

The man took his mask off using his left hand while the gun is still in his right hand pointing at Tyson. Kevin revealed more tears as the man he just saw in all black now looked exactly like the man in the picture.

"I'm Bobby Sagan and you're my son. They've been lying to you son, you're all grown up now and they still didn't tell you the truth about who your real parents are! They never... they never wanted to because they figured out what family you truly came from. A family of crime and extortion but looked past the beauty of family. Hm… you know what they told me when I asked for you back? Hmm? They said 'You can't have him back he is ours. You need to… you need to leave! Before we alert the authorities. It was my first time coming to get you. They couldn't even let me see you!" Bobby said as he vulgarly pushed Tyson on the floor.

Kevin remained inaudible and couldn't think of anything to say while Bobby pointed his suppressed pistol at Ralph.

"Yes, I put you up for adoption because I had nothing to take care of you with…"

"All of this… All of this isn't true!"

"YES, IT IS!"

At this very moment, he shot Ralph three times putting two rounds in his chest and one in the neck.

"NAAAOO!" Tyson hooted louder than he ever did.

Kevin beheld his non-biological father, eyebrows raised and shaking his head with tears quickly coming down his cheeks.

"YOU'RE A SAGAN! YOU MUST EMBRACE YOUR TRUE FAMILY NAME!"

Bobby had no remorse in his face as he pointed his illegal Fed gun at Gina. "Wait, wait, look, she's… she's only seventeen weeks… please… have some mercy! Please!"—Kevin struggled to speak as he begged.

"Man! Fuck that hoe! Alright?!—I already drugged the cunt… Yeah—I raped her too… Yeeahh'… the bitch was bleeding! Aagh! IT WAS A FUCKING MASSACRE!! . . . Hmmph, I don't think this info really matters now. Does it?"

Kevin hastily went in front of his mom protecting her and not caring about the gun pointing his way.

"Get away from that bitch or I blow this kid's brains out!" Bobby demanded, holding his gun at Tyson's head once more.

"No, please don't. No more!"

"I said move!"

"Plea'..."

"DON'T LET ME HAVE TO SAY IT AGAIN!"

Held against his will, Kevin shook his head then looked at the floor and strolled back to where he was standing before. "Ok, ok I'm moving, just please don't..."

As soon as Kevin ceased his stroll, Bobby pulls the trigger twice making Kevin jump in fear. He kept his jitters, trembling and slowly looked behind him.

Two bullets had already entered Gina's stomach killing the baby and Gina.

Kevin was speechless with wide open eyelids and in utter shock. Tears dripping down his cheeks, a young man's heart shattered to pieces because of one man, a man who is now his worst enemy.

Bobby then shot his brother's left leg. Tyson instantaneously fell to the floor as Kevin sobbed.

"Hm'.... now let's go son. I'll leave Tyson alive so he can soak in what I did here... Then he will burn to death." Bobby said pointing his gun at Kevin.

They both went into the car that Bobby was driving in earlier.is in the driver seat while Bobby is in the back with his gun keeping authority and compelling him to drive.

Bobby lit the house on fire before he left while Tyson, his dead father and dead pregnant mother remained inside the house.

He looked at the rear-view mirror as it revealed his house with despair on his face then ultimately reminisced about his parents.

SEVEN

<u>*Year 2281—*</u>

At the Countrywide Shooting Park in the main intersection, where the Roland family had reserved an area for target practice. Ralph Roland is teaching Kevin how to shoot and Tyson is with his mother Gina. Ralph had set up targets, timers and shooting tech that kept track of each shot that hits the targets. These devices will let the shooter know detail by detail what he or she is doing wrong for missing the targets.

"Always remember when you hold a gun, you treat it with absolute caution!"

"Yes, I know Dad." Kevin said being eleven years old while Tyson is eight years old.

"I'm glad you know but what I don't know is why you hold the rifle so timidly. The stock is way too out on your shoulder which makes your body lean like a one-hundred-and-thirty-degree angle. You should look like a seventy-degree angel from helicopter's view. Now, keep your body straight and have the rifle a little more towards your chest. Now remember that recoil, it's no joke."

"Like so."

"Yes, yes… ok, now fire!"

"I wanna' shoot a rifle Mom!" Tyson said.

"Rifles are for children at age ten and up, that's Gigantica's laws. How many times I have to tell you?"

"I know Mom, but no one has to know."

"Hey. You have two more years to go and I'm sure Dad will save up for some more rifles and even better ones with all that tactical stuff."

"Wow, I'm hitting the target a lot easier."

"See? Now aim the rifle towards something you don't wanna' shoot and act as if it's always loaded even though you checked the chamber... Now reload, put another mag in."

Gina with Tyson behind her walked up to Ralph then kissed him. "This boy here wants to shoot a rifle."

"He shot a pistol already now he wants rifles..." Ralph said then chuckled.

"Looks like you're hitting targets Kevin."

"Watch out, this is for big boys, little brother."

"Whatever."

"Hey Tyson, no rifles yet and stop asking.... Here, linger with a 9-millimeter." Said Ralph as he handed him a pistol.

"Hey, no worries Tyson, Mom's attempting to get another brother or maybe a sister and you ain't gonna' be the youngest anymore."

"Yes, but our attempts fail again Kevin... Looks like we won't be having another one."

"No Mom don't give up. Someday we will have an additional family member."

The different ways of living, some are enjoying the fascinating commodities of life and some are vulnerable to agitation, going through difficult times.

Funeral honors were bestowed on the remains by the Roland family and friends for Tyson, Gina and Ralph. The service was held at the burnt down home of which they use to reside in. Kevin didn't attend because he believed that there was nothing for him to look at, everything and everyone was burnt down to nonentity. Kevin wouldn't speak to anyone, not even cousins, friends, he just stayed in a mental facility for four months then went on to counseling. His mind was still set on being a medical doctor and nothing is going to sojourn him from becoming one.

The human race, decades of evolvement taking on new heights each year and divulging an abyss of progression and fulfilment. This is the century where a larger majority work together with ambitions, plotting for success and being strong enough to defend themselves against another threat. The Grainians vs. Humans War left many in anguish but arose with new beginnings causing substantial occurrence just like any other war on Earth. Although the hearts of men with the thirst for conflict revealed that senseless war could never end, no matter how much they run away from it.

The New World Order birthed outstanding technology, inflicting stricter laws that are more focused on safety rather than inflicting corruption. New actions such as elimination of segregation and elimination of poverty. There is no such thing as 'minorities' everyone is treated as equal, diversity at its best and money wasn't an issue. Yes, there is employment but if you don't want to work, the government provide their citizens many choices that would benefit themselves and society. Some people would still work out of courtesy, interest, boredom or inspiration. Now, androids have toppled the many diverse employment aspects around the solar system, even machines were built by humans to create more machines that are programed for services.

It's Welfare on a new level. About ninety five percent of the entire population throughout the solar system has a home to live in. The other five percent is just the people that simply doesn't desire a home to reside in. Even treatment and prevention of diseases is supported in the best way possible in terms of financial issues within medical health fields. Doctors found the impossible cures to be possible and providing considerable immunity for previous illnesses and new ones. Human's understood that the more they expand through the universe and finding new discoveries, the more the beneficial survival of life.

—Two months later a French twenty-eight-year-old Detective Tyler Delancey born in France but raised in Gigantica. He dealt with the Bobby Sagan case and now stumbled upon it in his office once more, then reviewed the case. Thanks to the illegal fed gun tracking implements, he was captured right after he fled the Roland residence and is now incarcerated while the case remains a mystery why Bobby killed Kevin's non-biological parents and his brother Tyson. Kevin wasn't so productive after he blamed the system for the lack of accuracy and technology that day allowing an illegal Federal gun to surface amongst his neighborhood which made detective jobs a little harder to interpret the rationality for the murders.

Detective Rana Saleen, wearing a black wool cashmere-blend trench coat covering her body walked in Tyler's private office. The clacking of her high heeled pumps triggered his attention beholding her assertiveness. She is a twenty-two-year-old very attractive Latin woman with dark curly hair, cute face and tan skin. She's the new partner for Tyler ever since the Bobby case opened for him. It's her day off and she just wanted to stop by to check up on her partner.

"Rana… you're here fast."

"Aren't I always?"

"Kevin claims he's not related but DNA says otherwise."

"Well, I say this case is over and we got this dude in lockup. He has a history of mental illness and he's just a psychopath. He planned the entire thing, even sabotaging the home's anti-fire system and the home's federal fire fighter system." Rana said as she locked the door.

"This whole set up sounds complex even for a guy like him… Hmm, I just think this case isn't finished yet."

"Hm… you really speak like you have a mind of a detective." She said while dropping her trench coat uncovering her sexy outfit as she walked up to him.

The tone has drastically changed as she exposed her petite hourglass body wearing all white denim high waist cutoff shorts revealing her toned legs and a silk half top over her large breasts.

"Well yes, I am a detective after all…" He said then paused as Rana pierced her soft dulcet lips together.

He loosened his tie then continued. "And a sexy ass detective."

"And you know you love that shit daddy." Rana flirts as she undressed her top.

"Oouuu', those words are gonna' get you in trouble Rana."

"Trouble is what I'm addicted to . . . Hhaaah', the uncontrollable rush… ain't nothing better than that."

She threw her top on the desk with her body sideways towards him, showing off her round ass and revealing that she's wearing a black transparent bra. He bit his bottom lip as she leaned over to him then kissed him as he sat motionless on his chair. He's now completely shirtless as he fondled her left arm with his right hand then held her neck gently bringing her down and kissed the right side of her neck.

Despite her bra being transparent, he still wanted to see her fully naked. Tyler used his left hand to unclip her bra resulting her breasts to be exposed. He acknowledged her measurements while unbuckling his belt then pulled down his pants.

"Oh, those fucking titties are awesome . . ."

Rana smirked deviously as he steadily removed her thong with his teeth then gradually tickles her up to her stomach with his tongue. He stood up and grabbed both of her large side set breasts then kissed her on her lips again, then made his way to her juice box using his middle finger in a circular motion and gradually fingered her. She rolled her eyes and faintly lifted her head up exposing how stimulated she was. His confidence boosted as the moisture dripped down his fingers. Tyler adores teasing her as he went down on his knees then kissed her stomach while she moaned and held the back of his head. He then lifted her right leg onto the table then slightly licked her clitoris.

"I love that sweet, scrumptious beautiful pussy."

Her arousal state bounded, moaning louder and fueling the lust as Tyler worked his tongue until she has an orgasm. He pulled her down slowly with her to be on top of him. She caressed his chest, smirking and being flattered by the hardiness of his skin, then leaned over and kissed him on his lips.

"Now let me feel that fat cock." She said then he made his way inside her.

Rana faintly titled her head up while she rode him slowly enjoying the erotic affections. She tried to whisper her moans using a monotone voice as she picked up the pace. Rana looked up to ceiling and lightly blaring preventing others from hearing any noise. She stood up palming her clitoris then he turned her around and bend her over then slowly inserts his tip in while pulling her hair. After moving in a paced motion, he batters Rana with his hips meeting her butt cheeks.

He pulled her off as he is about climax and stood up then she gets on her knees and opened her mouth wide, stroking his shaft. The sensation rushing to his head as she trundled her mouth on his tip. She glowered up at him targeting his weakness then he finished his load in her mouth. She squinted then puckered her lips and smiled at yet another quick one in his private office.

Later at the Delancey Residence—

Tyler sat on his hover chair feeling quite comfortable wearing a robe putting away copies of his completed cases in a storage box. The room's mechanical sliding door opened then he pushed the lever on the armrest which turned the hover chair around slowly.

"You're always so focused on your work." Cindy Delancey said, Tyler's wife.

"This one is worth the overtime."

"Overtime without pay. C'mon give that a break and come down to eat."

"I'm coming. I'm coming."

She looked at him then walked closer behind him and puts her arms around his neck then said— "Oh I remember that, I seen that on the news before. It's so—so messed up."

"Tell me about it. Cases like this I thought I would never get but here we are handling a man that was lucky with an illegal Fed gun."

"Well, his luck ran out."

"Yes, thanks to us participating in teamwork."

"It's all part of your evolution . . . you'll continue to succeed. I know it."

"This success, it's my destiny, right?"

"Yes, and you can't fulfill it on an empty stomach though... Get the food while it's hot." She said as she kissed him on the cheek.

Moments later the Delancey family in the dining room eating while the Holographic TV is on.

Tyler has one son and one daughter, and they are mischievous as he used to be when he was their age— "Look at Dad, all focused on soap operas." His daughter Felicia said.

"He's about to tear up! Boohoo!" His son Nate jested.

"Hey Dad. Want a paper towel?"

Tyler stared at the TV and seemed to be ignoring his daughter asking him a question.

"He's too into it. Hey Dad, cheating happens all the time in these shows."

He slowly turned his head then looked at his daughter and raised his left eyebrow.

Year 2294—

Six years later, Kevin graduated and got his master's degree in the medical field attending Forecastle University located in Gigantica City. Right after he graduated, he got hired to work in a hospital as a doctor's assistant. Kevin decided he wanted to get away from the madness and did a transfer to another Hospital which was in Gel Hev Prison. This is when he became an official doctor with much more experience. This prison is also where Bobby Sagan is spending his life sentence ever since he got prosecuted for his crimes.

Hotel room—

It was a Saturday and Kevin in a hotel room lying in bed with another man. He slowly looked to the left and saw that he's sleeping. He puts his hand on his chest and leans over then kisses him on the cheek. Kevin then got up out of the bed only wearing boxers then walked to the bathroom. He looked in the mirror for about twenty seconds then closed his eyes. He returned to the bedroom and grabbed the keycard then walked out through the high-tech sliding door. As he walked down a street a few blocks from the hotel he stopped and saw holographic TVs displayed in a store. He sat down and watched it next an elderly lady. "Hey."

"Oh… Hello there young man."

"I guess this is your free cable huh?" He joked.

She chuckled then said—

"No, I'm just waiting for my son, he's buying out some nifty electronics. You know, he doesn't want me with him—he should keep me around more often though, you never know, I could just 'poof' the next day."

"That's very true ma'am."

"I know he doesn't like to be the momma's boy type but hey—maybe he's buying a gift for me, it's Christmas around the corner you know." She paused then asked— "What's your name son?"

"Kevin, Kevin Roland."

"Oh Kevin . . . I had an uncle named Kevin. He was a bright man, smarter than all his friends. My name is Maria Stone, nice to meet you."

"Ah… nice to meet you too… So, what was he studying?"

"Forensic science, he wanted to be a detective and things made him turn another path . . . He became a musician, totally different career right after he went through college and all that studying. It's amazing how one's mind changes."

"In today's news an armed robbery took place at the Gigantica City National Bank. The Gigantica City police executed a successful strategy in which left no one being deceased and only minor injuries. Yes, another success for the Gigantica City PD and their androids. Here is the brief interview of the convicted felon as they took him into custody— 'I loved every minute of it! It was the adrenaline rush and the chance of gaining billions! Better lock me the #### up for years cause I would ###### do it again!'— 'When will they ever learn Chuck?'— 'Yes, you can't stop the Gigantica City PD. They are the best in the solar system.'

"Look at that Kevin. These criminals will never learn huh? All this money they could get from the government and they do these crimes. Uugh', they must think that prison is a paradise. That man could be enjoying life instead doing stupid stuff like that."

"Hm, I agree."

"Well, word of advice to you and I say this to all of my grandsons all the time... 'Its better you stay out in the world and screw as many bitches as you like than to stay in prison and be one of the bitches'."

"Aah' ook', thanks for the advice—I guess..." He said as he beamed then chuckled.

"You're welcome handsome."

Maria gave him a wink as he began to walk away then said— "I'll see you around Maria."

"Hm,'. Bye sweetie."

<u>*Gel Hev Prison*</u>—

A large prison with only just under two hundred inmates due to the low percent of crime throughout Gel Hev. Inmates that needed treatment are relocated in the hospitalized section. Bobby Sagan was being moved to treat his bronchitis. Bobby is strapped to a reclining chair sitting inside the blinds and no one is assisting his company for fifteen minutes. The blinds started to open and there he was. Dr. Kevin Roland and Bobby Sagan intensely glaring at each other.

"Woah, you . . . you look... You..." He stuttered then Kevin interrupted him— "I look familiar?"

"No, wait... No!" He panicked while Kevin had the thirst for blood in his eyes walking closer to him.

Bobby's hands trembling and sweat trickling down his cheeks.

"Why are you scared? . . . Why?" He paused then said—

"You weren't scared when you... when you put several bullets..." He paused again then said—

"You fucking piece of shit!! You knew what was coming. You thought you was safe in here but you're wrong. You're dead wrong!! What you did was unspeakable. Don't be all disappointed though, you wanted me to be about my true family, the Sagan family. Well, so be it—I will pay my true family a visit, introduce myself. Have a sit down and build a strong relationship then get situated with a new life." He paused and waved his syringe needle as Bobby sat down and being frightened by his appearance then he continued—

"The bloodshed you caused made it clear what my purpose in life was and that is—to . . . wreak . . . havoc!"

"Listen, killing me, your own father, it won't bring good fortune son. I had to send you away because I was on a budget. You know as grown men we go through—we go through a lot man... When I... When I found out where you were... You're... You're the only one I had left that truly brought hope in my life... Those people you say you call family? C'mon they weren't your family... I was trying to be there for you my son!"

"Is that what your final words will be?" Kevin asked as he tilted his head to the left.

Bobby gulped then opened his mouth to speak then instantly Kevin jammed his needle into Bobby's left eye. He screeched in immense pain for twenty seconds while strongly vibrating back and forth losing air and lifted his arms. His skin turned pale while his eye sockets began to bleed as Kevin watched, overcoming the horrors of the ghastly spectacle. He punctured him with another needle in the mouth through his tongue, feeding him a virus that contains many deadly contaminants combined. He foamed through his mouth as his skin began to decay rapidly revealing his bones through his severed flesh and pus bubbled throughout his body.

Kevin managed to get away from his murder that he successfully committed and in no time proceeded to go on a one-way trip to see the Sagan family in South Gigantica City. Apparently, there is a family reunion for the Sagans and it's a warm and idyllic moment.

It's 10pm and Kevin arrived at the reunion where it took place at a house that Sir Peter Sagan and wife Megan Sagan owns. He walked up to the doorstep then wrung the bell. Seconds later, Peter opened the door.

"Hello sir. How are you?"

"Hi, my name is Kevin and I would like to join the reunion. I'm family."

"Ook', uh Kevin. I'm Peter… Are you one of my daughter's boyfriends because she has one already in here?"

"Oh, she does? I don't really care for that. I'm just here to join the family. I was adopted and found out my real family is the Sagans"

"Ooh ok, uh hm', come on in I guess."

Peter surprisingly allowed Kevin in although Kevin said that he's adopted flew right over his head that it could be just a complete stranger, but he's drunk and already focused on having fun—plus, he doesn't mind a little more company. Kevin saw that everyone is at a large table eating dinner. Everyone is looking at Kevin wondering who he is and why he's here.

Kevin looks around the dining room then a baby wrapped in between a woman's arms caught his immediate attention.

"Ok guys, this is Kevin!"

"One of your friends I don't know about?" Megan asked.

"Nah, I just met the guy. He said he was adopted by another family and now realized that he's a Sagan."

"You're my cousin's son, Bobby's son that he had given away for adoption, right?" Jacob asked.

"Yes, I'm his son."

"Well then a bite of our food won't hurt, have a seat. Welcome to the family... Dig in, eat up!" Said Cory Sagan, Peter's father.

Peter got an extra chair for him to sit at the large table. "What would you like to eat Kevin?" He offered.

"Oh, I like everything on the table... So, a little of everything would be nice."

Peter's youngest daughter who is eight years old picked up a plate then gathered every little piece of nourishment and place it on the plate.

"Hey Jeff. Can I speak to you real quick? In private?" Jacob asked Jeff Sagan, his brother.

"Yeah I think that would be good."

Half the table wondered and looked at them acting secretively. Jeff and Jacob entered in the hallway next to the living room.

"Ok this doesn't add up. Why is he here and how did he find this address?" Jacob probed.

"That's the same question I would ask you. Bobby, you know... He murdered his parents, his brother and a freaking unborn child. I don't think he would want to hang with his real family."

"Well, it's been six years since the incident. Maybe he got over it."

"Hm, what's that awful smell?" Jeff asked after he sniffed the air then started to cough.

The baby in between the woman's arms bawled uncontrollably.

"Yeah. What the hell is that smell?! . . .It's coming from the dining room!" Jacob panicked.

Both rushed in the dining room then saw their family all on the floor fidgeting and chairs knocked over. In the air, it appeared to be some sort of gas surfacing as Jacob and Jeff started choking while the gas gets darker and Kevin appeared out of the corner wearing a gas mask.

"Once inhaled, you will feel the particles entering your body, blistering. The gas effects your system, damaging your inner organs. This gas allows you to mutate—putting your body parts out of line, then... Hm,—then the real fun part comes in!" Kevin spoke with a muffled voice as he sat back in the chair that Peter gave him and watched the Sagan family challenge the effects of the lethal mutation gas.

A few minutes later he exited the house and saw a reflection of himself through the window. He beheld deeper past the reflection and saw an image of his dead parents tied up to a chair naked and unresponsive. No remorse in his flesh, pondering and overlooking the gritty carnage he just undertook with feelings of regret of not preventing his parent's passing. With clenched fists quivering, his rage boiled then he squinted his upturned eyes.

<u>Three hours later at midnight</u>—

At the Countrywide Shooting Park where his parents use to take him almost every weekend. No one around, just a quiet scenery with the wideness and vegetation. He sat back on a *Fagus grandifolia* tree trunk watching the only things that gave him light in the darkness, the Moon and the stars hovering above him. The chilled wind blew against his face as he inhaled the fresh air.

Kevin didn't plan the aftermath of what he had done. He doesn't even know what to expect now after he left the house with possible DNA presented. Even thinking that the authorities are on their way to get him now but he's sure of it that they wouldn't find him. Now all that's left for him to do is plan for a way out. He began to consider his next move but yet another memory as haunted him, remembering the precious moments he had while closing his eyes.

<u>Year 2281—</u>

On the expressway above the buildings, Ralph Roland driving from the grocery store while Kevin is in the back seat. A beeping noise came from the dash indicating he needed to recharge his electrical car.

"Shit…"

"What's wrong Dad?"

"It looks like I need to recharge… Could have sworn I had enough to get back home, but it seems like we're taking a trip to the charging station instead."

"Mmmmrrr'…"

"Hey, this will take like five minutes…"

They arrived at a local charging station for electrical cars, but the station doesn't allow self-service.

"I hope these androids aren't slow." Kevin said.

"Nah they shouldn't be."

Androids are machines that display a humanoid figure and this one resembled a brawny man. It's encoded to simply charge electronic vehicles, collect the payments and deal with any additional circumstances. "How much would you like sir?" The android asked.

"Full charge please."

"Ok, coming up."

"Hmm, androids…" Kevin scorned.

"Their built to make our lives easier."

"Sir. I need you to step out of the vehicle."

"Step out of… the vehicle?"

"Yes, it is a new protocol that we perform at this station."

"Oook? That's an odd new protocol."

"Just do what he says Dad. I don't wanna' hear any arguments."

Kevin opened the door and stepped out then Ralph said— "Get back in the car son. Someone must have programed it to do some other shit." The android's mechanical eyes turned red staring at Ralph as he squeezed his eyelids. Kevin lifted his left eyebrow wondering what's wrong with the machine.

Instantly, the android formed five ten-inch sharp nailed fingers then grabbed the metal driver door then ripped it off with its substantial strength. Ralph terrified of its ferociousness as Kevin screamed—

"Dad!!"

The android grabbed him by his shirt and deeply scratched his chest them threw him to the right side of it behind Ralph's vehicle.

Ralph landed on his side then Kevin immediately ran towards him as the android walked closer to them.

"Aagh... stay back son."

"What? But Dad..."

"I'll... I'll give my life for you Kevin!" He preached while pushing Kevin behind him.

"What? No... I'm not even your real son..."

"Kevin... you may not be blood but you're still my son and I love you always. Don't you ever forget that!"

He gazed at him witnessing the first time his father ever said those words.

"I'll try and hold him off, which will give you enough time for you get out of range."

The android lifted his right arm ready to strike him. "Kevin run!!"

Within seconds an electrical 50-caliber bullet impaled the android's skull causing it to malfunction. The bullet emitted an electric charge overloading the circuits then fried the entire mechanical system.

With nothing but tremor and astonishment in their faces near sighting a miracle. Ralph looked at the direction were the shot came from and it was police officers responding to a local android attack which is picked up on their detectors at will. They ogled at each other, then Ralph hugged him tightly. "I love you too Dad... always."

<u>The next morning at the Crime scene</u>—

"Hm', security cameras were down, no prints, no DNA left around… Hm... Looks like he was injected with a needle. Not much to work with here—the only person we ask now is Dr. Kevin Roland." Rana said.

"Remember, Kevin was the victim of Bobby's little melt down six years ago." Tyler said.

"Yes, I'm thinking the victim got his little revenge."

"Yeah, that's one suspect already but let's not be too hasty on that one. I'm sure the Sagan family has countless enemies waiting for this moment."

Tyler's phone rang then he answered it revealing a hologram of the South Gigantica City Commissioner. *"Detective Tyler, Detective Rana. How are you two?"*

"Hello Commissioner."

"Commissioner Sir. I'm great. How are you? Haven't seen you in weeks" Tyler said.

"I've been around, I'm just busy is all and I'm sure you're busy these days too."

"Yes very…"

"You worked on the Bobby Sagan case, correct?"

"Yes, we were on the Bobby Sagan case, we then terminated it on August 16th 2288 after we captured him and all the charges went into play."

"Ok, you might have to reopen that case and check on something. I found the Sagan family dead at their reunion. Apparently, it was everyone that's in the Sagan family including friends got killed. The cause seemed to be some sort of mutation gas inflicted by someone. This could be tied to Bobby and I'm digging into every scenario as in to why someone would murder the whole family with this monstrosity."

"Ok, thank you for sharing this with us sir. I will reopen the case and look at it for you. This is very important to us as it is to you."

Tyler hung up his communication device and looked at Rana then said—.

"The Sagan family, all of them, contaminated with some sort of mutation gas. I mean the entire family . . . It was a family reunion."

"It was definitely planned. Hm, you think Bobby ordered a hit?"

"On his own family? Yeah, that fits his profile... then maybe he offed himself."

"Hm... let's check with the old partner then check with Kevin."

Tyler and Rana used their tech to locate the possible suspects and only one rang on their radar.

Detective Tyler and Detective Rana rang the doorbell then a lady with a thick Russian accent inside the apartment spoke— "Who is it?"

"It's Gigantica City PD. We would like to talk to you. It's about Bobby." Tyler said.

The lady opened the door then permitted Tyler and Rana in her apartment.

"I'm blind, so obviously I can't see who you are. My security system said you are legit so I'll take the chance I guess."

"Hmm, your name is Jennifer Kozlov? Am I Right?" Tyler asked.

"Yes. What's wrong now officers?" She said, Bobby Sagan's ex-girlfriend the biological mother of Kevin Roland.

She slowly sat down on a Nordvalla grey armchair fixing her robe then sipped her tea.

"My name is Detective Tyler and this is Detective Rana."

"Hi Jennifer."

"We came by you before about six years ago. We are the same detectives and surprisingly still partners." He said then sat down on a sofa across from her.

Rana glared at him responding to his comment due to the previous affair throughout their career despite that they were both married and surprisingly didn't get caught.

"Oh, yes I remember you two. Well, you guys were the only detectives that came by. What did Bobby do now? I thought you guys put him away?"

"Well, Bobby, he recently got killed in his treatment room. The killer injected him with a needle."

"Whah-what? Oh no… Bobby."

"I'm sorry Jennifer but we are looking for the killer now. That's why we are here to ask you some questions." Rana said.

"Oh my... to be honest with you... I never visited him in prison, ever since I dumped him, I never got in contact with him. I told you this before we had our differences. Our child was a mistake. I met him at a night club, he brought me to his place. We had sex then exchanged numbers… It was great sex, I mean I did it with him over and over ever since that night but it was just sex… no love. I later got pregnant and he didn't believe it was his like what do you expect! I told him 'I will not get an abortion! It's wrong! I… I begged him to be a father to his son but not even the decency to buy some freaking diapers . . . I thought about raising him on my own, but I just wasn't cut out for it."

"Hm, what help are you going to get with a guy that you're just screwing?"

"Yeah." Rana hazily added as Tyler squinted at her.

"I was young I didn't think that through. My parents kicked me out because of my pregnancy and lies. Bobby convinced me to put our child up for adoption and then later maybe I could see him in the future. I agree that was the best thing at the time. Bobby later regretting it and he just went… He just went mad.”

“Hmm, Bobby tried to renew his life after sending your child for adoption wishing he could have done better.” Tyler said.

“No, he’s done worse he went around getting other women pregnant and doing the same thing he did to me.”

“So, there’s other children out there?” Rana asked.

“Yeah, I guess. I mean I don’t know but he’s a mess.”

“Is he so much of a mess that he would order a hit on his own family?” Tyler inquired.

“Yeah that sounds like him.” Jennifer said then continued— “A young man also came by me today.”

“Hm, what young man?” Tyler asked.

“He said his name was Rogue Sagan. He told me it's nice to finally meet you. I’m guessing it's one of Bobby’s cousins. He didn't say but it was so weird he kept quiet in our half hour convo. I thought he was going to take something since I’m blind but… nothing was taken.”

“Rogue Sagan?” Rana puzzled while her probing processor constructed within her wristband searches the name of the possible suspect.

“Yeah, he said his name was Dr. Rogue Sagan. It's an awkward name to be honest.”

“Hm.” Tyler muttered and looking at Rana. “Ok, that’s probably one of Bobby’s relatives but I don’t remember that name being found while conducting research on them.”

Tyler looked back at Jennifer with a wondering facial expression, both analyzing the meaning of a random man visiting this apartment with a last name connected to their case. Without any awareness of what’s to happen next, a massive explosion detonated from Jennifer’s body emitting enough C-4 to destroy the entire apartment room and impacting neighbors in the building.

"The ways of life comprehensible now…"

"Number 105!"

"First there's love and then there's hate."

"Number 105!"

"There's commitment and then there's disloyalty…"

"105… number 105!"

"Sir wake up… I think that's you." Said a man sitting next to Kevin.

"Oh yeah, yeah. I'm coming." He said as he quickly stood up then walked to the clerk.

"How may I help you today sir?"

"I would like to change my name and I filled out the application they gave me back there." He said showing the clerk the application.

"Ok, yes you filled out the important parts, good. Now sir, just to let you know you have to get a new microchip inserted and you went through the process of taking out your old one correct?"

"Yes, it was on the ninth floor. I was there since 7am—I know the cops ain't finding me for a few hours." He said then chuckled indicating his comment was a joke.

"Yes um—haha… Now. What would you like to change your name to?"

"I would like to change my name to Rogue Sagan, Dr. Rogue Sagan."

"Ok, aah'… Rogue Sagan it is Doctor."

EIGHT

Luka Shale Jr., a billionaire, philanthropist and CEO of Luka Shale Tech & Co. sitting in his luxury limousine furnished with all sorts of advanced features. He is a fair skinned man, six feet tall with a mesomorph body type and a bald head. He has mysterious brown eyes, a strong facial structure with natural flaxen stubble medium beard wearing a formal attire which is a grey suit, white buttoned-down shirt with a violet and black silk tie. Marvin Dalton, the Shale family's British butler sits in the driver seat while his youngest daughter Melissa Shale at age sixteen walked towards his limousine. She is five feet and two inches tall, long curly blonde hair wearing her school uniform, a simple blue cardigan over her white shirt with a red tie, plaid grey skirt, white socks and polished shoes. As soon as she entered the limousine, she greeted her father with a simple hello while he held an important conversation on the phone which led him to be unresponsive to her. Her rounded left eyebrow lifted, waiting for an answer from him as Marvin began to drive.

"Sorry about that baby, just some things I had to clear up with a partner of mine. So, what's up? How was school?"

"It was wack as usual. I had to take three quizzes today and I almost sprained my ankle."

"Sprained your ankle?"— "Yeah it was in P.E class today, playing volleyball and I landed on the side of my right foot. It was hurting for a little then the pain stopped after a while."

"Yeah, I saw that you were walking fine coming over to the limo. Hey, at least you're ok..."

"Yes, and now I have a ton of homework to do. Hmm', being in the eleventh-grade sucks."

"Hm', you were all pumped up the first time you elevated to a new grade now you hate it."

"Yes, and I can't wait till it's over."

"You say that now but once you finish school, you're gonna miss the good times."

They ceased talking for one minute then Melissa said—

"Dad... let's go ice skating at the Ice Amity."

"Ice skating? Ok, we can do that someday."— "No, not someday, I meant today, like now."

"Now? We were just heading home and you sprained your ankle."

"Yes, now and I'll be fine Dad. We don't need to change our clothes either..."

"No Melissa, I got some important things to do."

"C'mon Dad, I've been bored all day and I never been ice skating before. It's on my bucket list."

"You can go tonight, with your friends."— "I don't have any real friends Dad... well, I guess the only true friend I have is Bucky..."

"Hm, . . . ok, ok, we'll go."— "Yes, let's forget about your business matters for a change and have a little fun!"

"Hm'... Marvin, I decided on a change of route. Let us journey to the Ice Amity."

"As you wish sir."

Luka smirked at his daughter while she looked through the tinted window with her arms folded. He contemplated on how she's growing up and he'll do the most to make her happy.

The Ice Amity Ice Skating Rink—

A large skating rink with robotics teaching first time skaters how to skate. Within minutes Melissa is skating like a pro while her father still isn't getting the hang of it.

"Wow, I thought you said this wasn't your first time!"

"It's not, I'm just a fast learner and you're so slow." She taunted.

"Ha, whatever, I'll get this."— "Let's see you catch up." She said then giggled as she spun around like a ballerina. "Wow, such choreography and panache!"

An hour later, they sat down to eat a few slices of pepperoni pizza.

"That was fun Dad, I'm so doing this again."

"Yeah, it took me a while to skate without holding a robot."

"Ha, you almost fell like twenty times already, you're so clumsy."

"Hm,'." He muttered. — "Oh shit." She slurred hiding her face with her hands.

"What's the matter baby?" He asked looking around.

"It's Jace Terry… and he's looking this way."— "Jace Terry?"

"Yes, is he coming over?"

"Um, yeah it appears that he is indeed coming over here… Do you like him or something?"

"Yeah… he's my crush."— "Crush huh?"

"Oh, he's coming, Dad please don't embarrass me."

"Pardon me for interrupting but, haven't I seen you from somewhere?" Jace asked, a seventeen-year-old boy with an athletic body, strong facial features and an overall mature appearance.

"Yes, well, no but we have the same P.E class together. You're always playing basketball."

"Oh yes I remember now, you're a volleyball player that really knows how to kick some ass."

"Woah… I kick ass?" She surprisingly asked while scrutinizing him. — "Yeah you're awesome."

"Oh, well thank you." She blushed and acknowledged him.

"Whoop', sorry, you must be her father. My name is Jace Terry." He said reaching out to shake Luka's hand.

"How do you know that I'm her father? Do I look old to you?" He said while shaking his hand.

"No, no I didn't mean it like that…"— "Ha, I'm just messing with you kid. I'm Luka Shale Jr. and my daughter here is Melissa Shale."

"Luka Shale... I've heard that name before . . . Oh yes, you're the billionaire Luka Shale Jr. of Shale Tech! Oh my God, it's a pleasure to meet you."

"Likewise, son and its Luka Shale Tech." He said putting emphasis on *Luka*.

"Wow, this is so cool. I guess you're taking your daughter out to spend time with her. You're a wonderful father… very inspiring."— "Oh, thank you young man."

"Well, I would love to take her out myself and provide many joyful and abundant moments. That's exactly what a gorgeous girl like you deserve."

"Oh really?" She asked blissfully as she blushed. "Yes, I would love to be around with such a cool and athletic girl like you."

Melissa looked at her father hoping for an approval.

"Go ahead give him your number."

"Really? Oh my gosh. Are you sure you're my dad?"

"Yees', I'm your dad Melissa, now go ahead."

The next morning at the Kafmora Residence—

"Be quiet Tajay... you know he can hear us, we don't want to wake him up."

"Hey, just make sure the visionary contraption is working."

Oji and Tajaymae decided to surprise Ki-Yale on his 10th birthday, May 9th.

They both had organized undetectable holographic frames all around his room while he was out with Nack the day before. It's around 6:30am and he's not planning on waking up until 9am.

"HAPPY BIRTHDAY KI-YALE!!" Oji and Tajaymae yelled at the same time.

Electrical illumination all around emitting from the apparatus constructed into the walls with holographic frames. Downstairs, Demi squinted her eyes and moved her head towards the sound coming from Ki-Yale's room. The noise was so loud even Nealo who was outside the front yard payed attention to the voices coming from Ki-Yale's room. After all that noise he's still lying in his bed sleeping. The only way to wake him up now is doing the extreme.

"Wow, you got to be kidding me. After all this noise he's still knocked out!" She said.

"Hm', let's push him off the bed."

"Nah, I know what we should do."

Tajaymae held on to a computer device that produces electrical current. The pupil and iris within both of her eyes glowed purple as she gained energy from it then created what is called Netron Plasma. This plasma is contained inside a purple sludge, which is called Netron Plasma Sludge. If her victim is hit or even touched slightly by this sludge, it drains the victim's electrical energy and can also electrocute them. She gains energy from human life forms because they produce electrical signals from the brain and any static that roams around the body. This sludge digs deep down to the potassium and sodium ions and perhaps even equivalent to matter.

Yes, that's just some of Tajaymae's powers. She can't fly, she's not naturally super strong and naturally super intelligent but the more energy she takes from electricity the stronger, faster, smarter she gets in every way. Ki-Yale can shoot lightning out of his eyes and that's a lot of electricity, now just imagine the power Tajaymae can obtain with just one touch.

Tajaymae has a slimy, gooey purple sludge moving around her right hand. She glanced at the purple sludge then touches her brother's face.

"Aaaah'! Aaaggh'!" He shouted.

"Whooah'." Oji said as he watched his sister shock his brother and woke him up.

"Yo what the...!" He said with plasma on his face.

"HAPPY BIRTHDAY KI-YALE!"

He glared at his siblings showing big smiles.

"You don't feel any different right?!" She asked.

"No, I don't." Ki-Yale irritated.

"He ain't a man yet, of course he won't feel different." Oji said.

Heavy laughter from Tajaymae then Ki-Yale puts up the middle finger being annoyed. "Thank you but I hate—both of you…"

Minutes later, he got ready then went downstairs and saw his mother with a large breakfast plate.

"Happy Birthday son!" Demi said as she grinned.

Ki-Yale gasped.

"Woah."

Machida Bar & Lounge—

"Good morning Mister Machida Sir!"

"Good morning Pickle Dick'ems!" Fang Machida hollered as he walked hastily to his office, he closed his door and looked up to the ceiling then walked to the window. He saw an imaginary vision of four young Apaki Warriors around ten years of age practicing with their Apaki Katanas. One was his son Xack and the rest of them resembled three of his best students back when he owned his Apaki Warrior dojo.

Someone knocked on the door startling him then he commanded the mechanical sliding door to open by pressing a button on his shirt.

A lady employee entered then said— "I got stopped by police yesterday evening. They said they were looking for you and your son."

"Yes, I know they stopped me earlier on my way here. I don't know what for but I'm guessing it has to do with that triple homicide by an unknown Apaki Warrior."

"You think it was Xack?"

"I know my own son… and I know it wasn't him."

"But the way how he spoke to you…"

"I KNOW HOW HE SPOKE TO ME!"

Intense silence as Fang's lady employee scarcely looking at him then turned her head away with her lips pursed.

"Sorry… I do remember how he was, and I can't shake the feeling that he's already in danger. He doesn't know what he's getting himself into, but he's grown up into a man now and I can't stop him."

"The memories of when you brought him back to the dojo in the Crouton Village. Those images will always be in his head… Xack can't ever forgive Sagan."

"So, can't I but laying low and defending whatever we have now is our best option—a roof over our heads, this bar, this village…"

The lady employee nods her head then said—

"I guess the best offense is good defense in this situation."

"Should be the other way around but yes, you can say that."

"Hm', the police are going to be up our asses now."

"So be it, we got nothing to hide."

"Well, whoever did that crime is giving Apaki Warriors a bad name around LTV and soon you have to really fight again."

"I haven't drawn my sword in a long time—I really don't wish to anymore. Over the years of all that bloodshed and violence… I just want peace no more fighting. No retribution, no more grieving and being angry all the time."

"Yeah… Peace—peace is what we all want Machida sensei."

Adelia Woods's apartment room—

Aggressively French kissing each other as Xack remained on top of Adelia caressing her left cheek with his right hand while his left arm is around her abdomen. Both completely nude with the sheltered wounds excluding the bed sheets and enduring the room temperature combined with the warmth of their sexual encounter. His scars bared all around his body and his tattoos are linked to them. After every battle he chooses a scar and gets inked.

This is their second round inducing the endless love and passion. He softly bit her bottom lip while gazing into her eyes. She squeezed her eyelids teasing him with an intense sexual expression.

Xack then lifted his body up with his left hand on her stomach as she arched her back and his other hand on her crotch spreading two fingers around her clitoris. Adelia stroked his man wood and massaged his genitals making him adore the sensation.

He pinned her down with her legs on his shoulders penetrating her slowly thrusting his hips back and forth. Faint sounds coming from the moist friction as she puts her two hands on his ass and moaned then puts her head back feeling the hard penetration from Xack. He enthralled both of her round breasts as he thrusted faster spanking her lower end with his front hips. Seconds away from climax, he went closer to her face again as if it's the only face he wants to gaze at, then French kissed once more.

Moments later, Xack sits on a hover chair viewing some videos on a website on Adelia's holographic computer after he turned on the Wi-Fi. He moved the holographic items in which revealed behind the scenes of the videos. She wrapped her burgundy headband around her head as he focused on her computer then she approached from behind. After seeing his scars countless times, it reminded her of how determined he is of attaining vengeance.

"You still want to join that tournament, don't you?" She asked while caressing his hair.

"Yeah . . . but maybe, maybe you're right, I should hold off on it and stay low."

"Hm, . . . good, getting killed, isn't going to do any justice."

"I believe the tournament is too risky, but we still can actually plot our way to him without tumbling into deception…"

"So, let's join the Military, together we could become Mega Human troopers. I'm sure they have missions that would get you out to him."

"Hmm', we are Apaki Warriors from Crouton Village… not the entire Gigantica. We fight for Gel Hev—the Mad Doctor's current location is unknown according to the broadcasts, but you know the government is probably working with him." He said after he turned his head and rotated his body towards her.

"You don't trust the government, don't you?"

"No, I don't, and no ordinary citizen should. They constantly hide things; it's shown throughout history. Especially with alien activity and that 'Heaven Bolt' of mass nuclear destruction that orbits the Earth. They can turn on us at any minute."

"Hmm', you do have a point."

"A few days ago, I found a kid that looks to be about thirteen or maybe younger the same time I met Push, the one that injured me."

"So, there's more to the story?"

"Yes, I didn't tell you the full details... I figured you wouldn't believe me."

Adelia looked at him with a slightly annoyed face then he continued— "Ok, there was a man with him too. I landed on the boy first then I fought with Push, then suddenly, a lightning bolt came out of nowhere... I turned around and there he is, another boy who looks like the boy I first saw."

"Hm, like a twin?"

"Agh', I guess... agh', I don't know but he slightly looked different, same hairstyle but different. I just can't explain it. Thinking about it just messes with my head right now . . . But the first boy I saw, was gone."

Adelia raised her left angled eyebrow then Xack gasped— "The lightning came out from the boy's eyes Adelia! I never seen anything so powerful in my life. First, I couldn't believe it, but it was right in front of me... A human that possesses such power... He can do a lot of damage."

"The lightening came out of his actual eyes? You sure this isn't some military tech?"

"I don't know, maybe it was invisible weaponry around his eyes that shoots lightning. But I strongly believe that's not the way it was shot out."

"Hmm'… that's interestingly strange . . . We should go find this boy."

<u>Crime scene</u>—

Gel Hev Police arrived at the scene in the abandon warehouse the night that Ki-Yale and Nack called the authorities as an anonymous caller and when they arrived, they didn't show-face. It's now 7am and the chief of Little Tree Ville Police Department, a deputy, two detectives along with other forensics teams and a few rookie officers were at the scene. Rojohn recently woke up after being knocked out by Ki-Yale's hits and now sees that cops are around him.

"Hm, mmmm'! Hggmm'!" The struggle from Rojohn and his goons all tied up with duct tape around their mouths and "N" marks marked all around their foreheads, shirts and all over.

"Hey, give me some mints man." Said a rookie officer walking around the warehouse with his partner.

"Sorry dude, I'm a little sleepy from last night being at the café."

"You been making moves on Patty lately huh? That bitch will have you up in many ways."

"Oh no. I can't get with a lady that's been slobbering on Blake's knob on the low."

"She slobbed on Blake's knob? Hffm', that means there's a chance she'll slob on your knob too."

"Yeah, she must've certainly lost her self-esteem after that one, cause' that guy is a total loser."

"Hmmm! Hmmm!" Rojohn muttered.

"These 'N' marks are all over these guys. What the hell does this mean?" Chief Jorge Leon baffled.

"I need to analyze this place again." Said the African American detective, Detective Cane Holloway.

"Hm… nothing was stolen, no drugs, just formerly active illegal Fed guns lying around. Looks like a crime was stopped." Deputy Michael Sharks said.

"This could be someone against Sagan and how he makes his profits." Jorge said.

"Hmmmmm! Hmmmmm!!"

"Think this has to do with that triple homicide and the coyotes?" Deputy Michael inquired.

"Nah, that's work from an Apaki Warrior. I already have my guys check on every Apaki Warrior in the village. This right here is something different, some vigilante shit." Cane said.

"It looks like someone big did this, like a Sila Human." Jorge implied.

"Yeah, I bet there's a couple Sila Humans heading for Sagan's neck." Deputy Michael said.

"There's a lot of people out there heading for his neck, well the ones that has the guts but just too blinded by anger and don't care of the consequences or what they're getting into." Cane said.

"Hmmmm! Hmmmm!"

"Quiet! Menace!" Deputy Michael blurted.

<u>*Little Tree Ville Center Mall*</u>—

Later in the mid-day after Ki-Yale got a good wakeup call from Tajaymae and Oji—Ki-Yale and Tajaymae went shopping for his birthday while Oji is at school. Tajaymae is supposed to be at school as well but skipped school just so she could hang with her brother.

"You shouldn't have skipped school Tajaymae. Mom said we will be going out to eat later at Raider Playhouse." He said while walking down the mall and window shopping.

"Yeah, Mom says that every year since the embarrassing incident but now she never brings us there anymore."

"She probably thinks that we still can't handle going out without wrecking the place."

"Well. What can I say? We get excited on birthdays."

"You should go to school sis before you get in trouble. I'll convince Mom to let us all go to the Playhouse later."

"Nah, I want to spend time with my big bro."

Ki-Yale looked at his sister knowing she wouldn't listen to him and kept walking.

"Well, let's go do some damage sis!"

"I'm hoping the rain stops when we get out."

She said as they both looked out of the large window observing the thunder appearing in the clouds with loud thunderclaps. "The weather guy in the morning needs to be fired." He said as the sky got darker and rain began to fall.

"Yeah, we're definitely not prepared for that rain... eh', I'll just buy an umbrella."

An hour and a half later after buying tons of merchandise, Ki-Yale and Tajaymae are now walking through a pathway in the village. Ki-Yale being the stronger one with both hands full carried all the weight while Tajaymae... well, she carried nothing, except for a drink in her hand and an umbrella.

"Ok, good thing you got the bag covers for this pouring rain and now I see why you came out with me, so I can carry all this load." He said while being completely soaked from the rain.

"Hm, yeah sort of. At least I bought it with my money."

"And most of the stuff in here is for you. Again... I hate you..."

"Aww' I love you too broth..." Unfinished utterance from Tajaymae while immediately dropping her drink.

"TAJAYMAE!!" Ki-Yale yelled his sister's name while she crouched down with bits of blood bursting from her stomach.

NINE

His heart was racing as he stood motionless being in utter disbelief of what had just happened.

His little sister got shot with a metal arrow right through her stomach and the pointed tip went through her back. Ki-Yale dropped the bags with the covers still on them then rushed to her looking at the damage.

"Aaggh'... Uuhh'." She said staring directly at the metal arrow that's rammed through her inner organs while bleeding heavily.

He looked around and oddly doesn't see anyone.

"Who did this?!" He yelled with anger as his voice echoed through the village.

"Aagh'... Ok this hurts a lot..."

"No... Tajay..."

He placed his left arm around her back preparing to lift her.

"Hm, I'm the one that shot her! Now, run all of your merchandise or you too will get an arrow!" Said a man in his muffled voice beneath his helmet, stepping up out from behind a red maple tree as the vibrant scarlet leaves fell off a branch.

"Huh? Oh... I remember you." He spoke under his breath.

Within a millisecond, he changed into his Netron Suit while the man was staring right at him, but his mind froze while he was changing.

"Hm? Where is that kid… that I was jacking?"

"I got him out of the way. You do remember me, right? …Garrett."

This is the same man wearing the enhance police suit with illegal Federal weaponry and gear that was stolen and partook in arms trade back at the abandon warehouse.

"How'd you know my name kid? And yes, I do remember you, but I don't remember mentioning my name to you."

"I heard you when you and your boss Kojack was talking."

"Ok, so you planted some microphones on us..."

"Nah, I just got enhance hearing."

"Ok, ok, whatever…How the hell did you pull the kid out of here without me looking? This is freaky man!"

"I'm just very fast, so fast you can't see me!" He said with a smirk giving Garrett a jokingly excuse.

"I don't believe this. Aagh, you kind of look like him too!" Garrett said in his muffled voice being confused and his mind getting effected by the Netron Suit.

"Don't think about it too much, your brain will get fried."

Unknown Area—

Dr. Rogue Sagan, at age 52, natural red hair, with a slightly built toned body, dressed in all black heavy Kevlar fitted shirt with a neck guard that fits snugged, black pants with leg pads, brown shoes with a large grey fur coat. He now has a scar along his face, the scar is connected to his left eye down to his upper lip, which made him half blind and almost looks like he has a third lip.

Playing with an anti-stress device, he sat across from Kojack while looking at his paintings of cadavers made from actual corpses. He squints his eyes, revealing his crow's feet, admiring the work he had done and being proud of his brilliance of using human remains to make paint. There's still frustration existing and speaking with a grunt.

"Hm', I need results."

"Push is here sir, I'm sending him up now." Said an android.

The room became a strict library the way Push quietly walked in with a serous face.

"What you got for me Push?"

"I went to Little Tree Ville like you said and hunt down Xack Machida and bring him in to you but— I found new results."

"Oh really? And what's that?"—He asked anxiously.

"Well, some kid with a black and white suit shot lightning out of his eyes..." Push said showing Dr. Sagan the wound on his stomach and being interrupted at the end of his sentence.

"Black and white suit huh?"

"Yes sir, I offered both to see me at the 'Crouton Village Tournament' the one that you are taking control of. I will murder both, this time it's legal!"

"I don't know if you can slay that kid in the black and white suit Push." He sarcastically said and moving away from Kojack then he continued— "I mean my boy here Kojack is telling me that Rojohn and his goons shot at him. The bullets and heated rays didn't even faze him. Isn't that right Kojack?"

"Yes, sir that must be the same kid and I forgot to mention; his name is Netro. The kid took all shots and he took it like it was pebbles being thrown at him."

"Hmm, so you saw that kid too and his name is Netro...? Hm… I guess that's what that chrome 'N' in the middle of his chest stands for. Almost sounds like airspace military type shit!"

"Nah, sounds like alien to me." Kojack said.

"Yeah alien could be right… Damn. So, he's bulletproofed and shit?!"

"Yeah, to put it in retrospect, he's a little boy that can take bullets and shit." Dr. Sagan sarcastically said with some aggression.

"You don't believe us. Don't you sir?" Kojack asked.

"No, I don't… I mean, both of you fucked up my plans and came back here with a bullshit excuse."

Sagan ceased playing with his stress device then picked up his firearm, a bioweapon that he calls "Ronda". Ever since he created it, no Fed tracking devices could trace or detect the weapon. The gun is made from Grainian glass, the same glass that Apaki Warriors used and is nearly indestructible. Instead of bullets for ammunition it is filled with small insulin syringes that contains the "Genchi" virus. Genchi in Japanese meaning "actual place, actual thing" Sagan used this name because the virus can travel and survive in the air, wind, soil and even water for up to two weeks without a living host. This virus has tendencies to make living things mutate until the point of ultimate death and it doesn't just contaminate a person but also trees, plants and other life forms rapidly. Although it impacts different life forms, some living things may mutate without dying but humans are the most vulnerable to the virus.

"Well Push, it's not a bad idea bringing Xack to the tournament. I mean, you could have brought him here so I could let him join the tournament my way but I'm pretty sure that, you're pretty sure that, he is pretty sure that… he will join."

"Yeah, I seen it in him, he wants to kill me."

"Well, this info saves you from getting your balls chopped off Push. I want that kid to be in the entertainment of Crouton. The people… they love to see Apaki Warriors fight to a futile death."

Kojack's eyes are wide open watching Sagan and knowing that he's upset with him.

"Well, now my boy Kojack over here didn't get the job done not even a similar scenario. Like at least bring the freaking money! Simple task… Simple task was, to make the deal with Rojohn and spread the virus amongst Little Tree Ville."

"I'm sorry sir, I was frightened."

"You were frightened?! That means I don't need you. I need people with brave hearts! People that will get the job done!"—Sagan blurted then pointed his bio-weapon at him.

"Wait! This won't happen again!"

As soon as Kojack finished his plead, Sagan shot him in his neck as he stood stationary and barely breathing. The needle injected his throat rapidly with the Genchi surging through his body and head allowing him to foam through the mouth. Kojack's eyes turned blood shot red and his veins started to spring up as he juddered his entire body then fell to the floor and died instantly.

"Pfft." Push uttered.

"Now, I already sent Garrett to run some errands for me and go after this kid in the black and white suit…"

"What you need me to do?"

"I want you to introduce my creation on Little Tree Ville and make sure you come back with positive results!" He demandingly said then Push nods his head.

Meanwhile—

"I was going to rob that kid and this little girl with all that merchandise they're carrying but you came out of nowhere… Well, I was looking for you anyway."

He ran towards Ki-Yale as he stood seven feet in front of his sister and started landing punches to his head.

Ki-Yale withstanding the punches like its nothing, like two very soft pillows hitting him then he grabbed Garrett's hand then swung him around and threw him against a tree.

"Agh, this kid's strength." He thought.

As he hits the tree, he fired rapid red Heat ray beams from the tech in his arms at Ki-Yale. He took the hits while he ambled towards him. Garrett kept firing while a miniature tech gun that shoots bullet sized flash bangs, released out from his left arm. He fired the tech gun and the bullet stopped in midair then flashed Ki-Yale in his eyes. He covered his eyes with both hands, irritated as he crouched down a bit then Garrett kept firing.

"I'm going to end you boy!" He said sauntering towards him.

Tajaymae is still hurt from the metal arrow that Garrett shot her in the stomach with. While being in pain, she reached for her communication device as her mother was trying to contact her but Tajaymae didn't pick up.

"Not right now Mom, aaghh'."

"Hm,'… It's funny how she's still alive… She should be dead by now, from the poison in the arrow…"

She touched the device with her right hand then gained electrical energy from the device and a purple sludge came from her right hand. She dropped the device then pulled the arrow out of her stomach.

"Aaaaggh'!" She then puts her right hand that holds the plasma on to her stab wound then the purple sludge filled in her wound and gradually began to heal it.

"Impossible!"

"What did you do to my eyes?!"

"Ha, no more sightseeing for you! This flash is permanent, it'll blind you for life kid."

"Brother…"

Ki-Yale smirked causing Garrett to wonder. "Huh? Why are you smiling kid?"

"You may have blinded me but I'll still eat your shots."

"Ok, you can eat my shots but let's see if the girl can do the same."

He opened his eyes barley looking at Garrett with a blur pointing his right hand equipped with the heat ray gun at Tajaymae. She stood up with a slight staggered look in her face. A thunderclap impending from Ki-Yale's direction as he fired a low powered lightning strike out of his right eye at Garrett's hand that's equipped with the heat ray gun. The lightning shocked his arm immediately and damaging the tech gun.

"Aaahhh'!" Garrett screamed.

"I guess I can shoot lightning on command now."

"Let's see if you can eat my shots." Tajaymae said while she threw her plasma sludge at Garrett's helmet.

The plasma sludge thrown from Tajaymae traveled about one hundred miles per hour. Due to Garrett's slow reaction, the plasma sludge landed on his helmet and went inside then shocked his face. Smoke came out from the four-inch hole in his helmet as he fell.

"Woah, Tajay…"

"I didn't mean to…" She said while running towards Garrett.

She stopped and crouched down holding her stomach four feet away from Garrett.

"Don't worry… your plasma just drained some of the electrolytes in his brain." Ki-Yale said while his vision became clear thanks to the Netron Suit healing them.

"Ok. So, he's like brain dead but not dead right?"

"Yea something like that, hopefully you didn't drain a lot."

"I'm pretty sure I didn't throw a powerful sludge."

"I'll bring him to the hospital and have the authorities on this." He said while he picks up Garrett and puts him on his back.

"You will be fine right Tajay?"

"Yeah, the plasma is finishing up the healing process on my wound."

"Ok, good. I figured it'll do that."

"Are your eyes ok now?"

"Yeah my eyes are clearing up now. It may be permanent, but the Netron Suit is doing its job." He said while he picks up Garrett.

"Where are you taking him?"

"To the hospital."

<u>Meanwhile—</u>

The rain continued to pour, the sky became dark with thunder rumbling in the clouds, strong winds blew from different direction causing the temperature to drop to fifty degrees.

Push Monaghan is back in Little Tree Ville with two coyotes next to him, the same remaining ones that attacked Xack and Adelia then fled. Ryker, the male coyote with the several strands of white hair from the middle of its head stood next to the female coyote named Beatrix.

The rain slowed down into drizzling rain and he's in a full body plague suit riding in a hybrid air cargo vehicle in which he carried the box filled with chemicals and viruses in some minuscule glassed containers.

"It's about time this village fall to its knees."

He landed in a secluded area then hooked up the containers to his puncture machine then pointed it at the ground near a tree. He then injected the bottom of the tree with the containers that's secured to his puncture machine allowing the liquid viruses that's in the containers to drain unto the bottom of the tree. Push completed the drain process then kept on doing his work by releasing the rest of the containers. Every half a mile he injected the virus all around the village. In total he had fifteen minuscule glassed containers filled with the virus and he emptied them all. Once the virus is infected into the trees it exposes itself to the open air and ordering the trees to grow exponentially. As long as the trees are there the virus will continue to take its course to unknown various distances.

"This is a beautiful day in Little Tree Ville… The sky is falling, the wind is calling." He quoted the legendary *Kendrick Lamar* as he laughed deviously.

"Woah." She said being behind a tree looking at Push.

Push got back into his hybrid air cargo vehicle where the coyotes stood in then he took off to another location in the village. Tajaymae recognized that the trees are slowly rising unusually. Elongated branches, roots below the ground appearing above the surface, trunks getting wider, stems growing higher, leaves and grass are getting bigger even flowers are getting bigger. The threes growth in height, went up to three hundred feet tall while Tajaymae appeared as if she's frightened out of her mind.

Nack's residence—

"The police are at your door! The police are at your door!" Said the security system implanted inside the door noticing policemen and detectives.

Nack heard the automated door and thought— *"The authorities couldn't be here because of the warehouse incident… Right?"* Nack made sure no evidence was around for detectives to find but it seemed as if they found something.

"Can I help you officers?" Nack asking the officers after he opens the door.

"May I speak with Nack Yaldara" Detective Cane Holloway said in a high-tech rain suit.

"That's me sir." "Nack, nice to meet you. My name is Detective Cane Holloway." Cane said and being interrupted.

"Nice to meet you Cane. How may I help you?"

"I've found evidence linked to an incident that happened yesterday at the abandoned warehouse. The incident involved Rojohn and his crew, most likely it could have been an illegal arms deal. This deal could also be linked to Sagan, we found Rojohn and his crew tied up with the letter "N" marked all around them, we do believe it could be a vigilante move…" Cane said as he raised his eyebrows and stared at Nack then said—

"We're not sure yet that you are the culprit. Hmm, but we still like you to come with us for some questioning."

"No warrant?"

"Ah no but…" Cane said as Nack interjected him—

"It's cool detective, let's go." Nack said without nervousness and an easy-going attitude.

Little Tree Ville Hospital—

Ki-Yale informed the hospital front desk that Garrett got hit with electrical current then they called the emergency team and got him into the ER. One of the doctors looked at Garrett's attire and realized it's a stolen police suit from which he saw from the news. The doctor quickly called the authorities while Ki-Yale left the premises.

Ki-Yale in his Netron Suit went outside the hospital. He keeps his arms close to his body while flying about three hundred miles per hour back to Tajaymae then he slowed down and realized the trees are growing bigger than usual.

As he noticed the trees changing, he shouted his sister's name and looked through the woods with his Netron Vision as far as three miles.

"I'm right here!"

Ki-Yale spotted her then landed softly on the ground next to his sister with a lady that looked as if she's in her twenties lying on the ground and appeared to be sick coughing up blood with her eyes red. Her skin turned pale and in the process of decaying as he gasped— "Who's this?"

"I don't know but she's very sick though. I heard her coughing and throwing up so I went to check it out. Loads of blood was coming out her mouth, ever since these trees started growing."

"Hmm, these trees could be poisoned or infectious. I never seen them grow like this before." He said while looking at the trees that were once little turned into rainforest trees with up to 30,000 cubic feet of girth.

"I think I saw who did this . . . It was some boy injecting some sort of chemical or something into the trees."

"Really? Who is this boy?"

"I don't know who it was but—he had a helmet that revealed his face and it looked like he had tattoos all over it."

"Tattoos on his face? This could be…"

"Could be what? You know who it is?"

"Maybe but there are plenty of people with tattoos on their faces."

"Well, we can't focus on that much longer Ki-Yale, we need to get her to the hospital."

"Ok. You're right sis." He said while he picked up the lady with both arms and Tajaymae climbed on his back.

The rain finally cleared up as he slowly took off into the air then went on his way to the hospital again.

After the "New World Order" in year 2264, things became different for viruses, diseases, bacterial infections, poison and all sorts of illnesses. The previous President of the Word Lynda Valerie Polara in year 2268 decided to exploit wealth solely towards the impurities and created the G.N.I.C. Gigantica National Infection Control and represents cleanliness and saving lives. Without citizens needing millions and low income being an acceptation, the G.N.I.C provides vaccines, cures and absolute wipe out for any contamination throughout the world. One major cure was the cure for HIV/AIDs using Death Angel blood sample that was somehow extracted from Jahzin Yoko and the Tektonian Crystals which were left behind before he died. The Tektonian Crystals cleanses any individual with Death Angel DNA from many bodily pollutions such as viruses and other related contaminants. Doctors would operate blood transfusion on infected patients which later would result in the cleansing of the blood. Doctors understood that these operations took a toll on patients making them Death Angels as well with the thirst to kill any life form. So, they ceased the operations for a while and then they eventually came to a conclusion on only providing the operations to certain patients, preferably young ones who would later participate in taking the life of animals only for nourishments, or even convicted felons who are charged with the death penalty.

Sagan wanted to raise the crime rate, prolonging illegal oil trades being the first one to ever do contraband with illegal Fed weaponry overseas and other planets in year 2296 to which he made outstanding profit. With help from unknown sources, he bypassed police and military equipment uniquely for contraband. He is also the first to bypass anti-virus and disease control in everyday life. He spent nights studying from stolen confidential information from the G.N.I.C in how they operate to keep away all contaminants. Since Sagan is now in control of all these contaminants, he seeks catastrophic proceedings making it checkmate for all humanity.

. . .

Ki-Yale arrived at the hospital with Tajaymae and the sick lady. As soon as he brought her in, doctors noticed that she needs medical assistance and took her along with other victims in the hospital lobby. Androids putting sick victims into tube launchers that proceeded unto the ER where doctors can work on them quickly. The sickness indeed came from the Genchi that Push injected into the air, the ground and the trees, allowing them to grow to an extended height.

Netrons are resistant to this virus, in fact, they are resistant to any Earthly viruses and even the Grainian contaminants. Viruses from other planets though could affect them unless they are wearing Netron Armor. Despite Ki-Yale, Tajaymae and Oji being half human, their Netron anatomy conquers the human anatomy which gives them a better chance against the Genchi.

Tajaymae went along with the lady unto the Emergency Room while Ki-Yale stood in one spot looking around and saw what's happening on the news—

"Just not too long-ago Little Tree Ville's little trees started growing oddly and they seem to be spreading some sort of virus among us." Said the news anchor wearing a gas mask while solders help the EMT carry patients' aboard ambulances.

Ki-Yale saw the sick victims on the floor and the benches inside the lobby which for him was very overwhelming.

Children screaming, throwing up blood, shaking and foaming from the mouth. Parents crying loudly and grieving for their children to get better. Some didn't make it because the virus attacked their system faster than others.

He overlooked his surroundings, then quickly walked out the hospital.

He went airborne again, moving with instant speed at six hundred miles per hour towards the Mayor's Office.

Ki-Yale looked down and understood the villagers are struggling and in need of some assistance. He couldn't resist, he lowered his flight then decides to use his abilities to halt any collateral damage from growing trees. Most of the people were too sick to fathom the heroic actions that Ki-Yale performed. Despite the lack of notice, he doesn't care for the popularity as he is more focused on trying to reduce the dangers while the trees are still growing, causing a lot of damage and mayhem. He expressed his frustration on his face because people are still dying around him, right in front of his eyes and his whereabouts with him having these amazing abilities, it's still not enough.

<u>The Kafmora residence</u>—

Demi, the mother of fascinating children has her guard up preparing for whatever is out there. Wearing boxing gloves and gear, she circled the boxing ring and faced her husband in her boxing stance while he wore black punching mitts. He took every punch that she gives him while guiding her to express her natural human strength.

"Hugh . . . hugh . . . hugh!"

"That's good Demi, keep that form."

"It's Ki-Yale's birthday already and soon it will be Oji's birthday next month then Tajaymae in December..."

"Well, they aren't going to get younger."

"Hugh!" Demi swung one good right hook to the punching mitt then ceased.

"You wanna' take a break now?"

She lowered her guard and paused then tilted her head down a bit.

"Hm, this is the first time that I skipped Narrken's birthday in a conversation."

Neecho sighed then calmly said— "Even though he's gone, we should never separate him from us in any way."

"You're right, I shouldn't even be talking like this, but the hardest part is to move on."

"When I started the Pharmaceutical training on becoming a manager… I try to give up the search, but I just can't. Even now I have the urge to go out looking for him."

"You never brought me with you because you fear something will happen, which I understand truly but, I always feel like I'm worthless in this situation, so I go out there to look. I'm not scared anymore!"

Neecho remained silent and nods his head then she continued— "But even after, I'm just at a dead end."

"You and I both Demi, I feel the same way, worthless. Even with my abilities, I just can't…" He paused as she peered at him then he continued—

"Looking for him when you're out there is okay… Right now, it doesn't even matter. I just want our son back."

Nealo sat down on a cushion by the wall in a meditative state like a monk who performs religious asceticism by monastic living. He has his legs crossed, his knees kept below his hips, back straight, hands placed on his lap with the knuckles of the middle fingers resting on top of each other and his thumbs slightly touching.

Nealo is completely focused on the things he could only see. His eyelids twitching while being closed and his eyebrows squeezing together. He sees something, a being he has never seen before. He saw a face with severe pale decaying skin, deep cut marks on its cheeks and its lips were nothing but gashes. Its sclera was black, and its pupils were white.

Harsh murmurs of his name coming from the unknown being while Nealo began to twitch and slightly turned his head left to right.

"What is this?" He thought.

Outer darkness behind him as electricity began to flow around his face. Nealo's vision flashed repeatedly for him to recognize exactly what he's looking at.

His eyelids continued to twitch then suddenly a small cube shaped computer detached itself from the wall behind him. The computer sparked his attention and approached in front of him revealing a hologram of a news station.

"Breaking news . . . agh' damn tech interrupts, just when I was about to witness some peculiar shit."

Gel Hev, Westside LTV—

A farmland which holds a barn and pathway to a large secluded old school Mansion next to the mountains. This mansion is worth seven hundred million including the farmland in which the Shale family lives. Luka Shale Jr., carried down ownership and raising his two children with a gorgeous wife by his side. The mansion has about fifteen thousand square foot of floor space and has a large fence around it with their crops being in the backyard. The Shale family also has a large field with blue agave plants used to create Tequila.

Luka Shale Jr., wearing a red shirt and jeans with loafers stepped into the room to see his wife Pamela Shale who was born with the surname known as Taylor. She is fair skinned, six feet tall with a fit body and jet-black hair corresponding with her bright blue eyes. Sitting on a hover chair with her legs crossed staring outside of the window.

"Hm, sundress on a rainy day?" He asked walking closer to her.

"I was just about to change it; this rain came out of nowhere."

"Well, this is Gel Hev, the place known for this kind of consistent change in weather."

"It's a shame I have to waste this outfit…"

Her alluring bowlike lips triggered his exhilaration all because she wore that sexy red lipstick again.

"You know what?! If the clouds can get wet, then so can you."

"What are you implying here?"

"Hm, baby… you're about to find out."

"Wait . . . How about… you close the door."

"Aah… ok, ok."

Luka walked up to the door and his youngest daughter Melissa Shale appeared from the hallway yelling— "Hey Mom! Are you watching the news!? Oh, Dad you're here too… Don't go outside."

Her older sister Kathleen at age nineteen with a petite body and dyed sandy blonde hair followed behind her.

"Don't go outside? What's going on?" Luka asked.

"A plague, that's what's going on." Kathleen said showing a news station through a holographic screen from her right jacket sleeve— *"This is not a drill! We need for everyone to stay inside their homes and activate quarantine mode. Quarantine mode will lock up your windows, doors and any passageways that can possibly bring in a virus traveling through the air. LTVPD is working on ensuring everyone's safety."*

"Oh my God…" Pamela gasped.

"Bucky." Luka said.

"Oh no… Melissa. You locked the barn, right?"

"No Mom, I was just out there but… no, I didn't lock it."

"I'll go." Luka insisted.

"What? But the air is contaminated." Pamela said.

"I have a plague suit."

"Hey, just be-careful. Alright?"—Pamela said while grabbing his hand as he turned around and saw his wife gazing into his eyes.

He paused then said— "I got this."

He proceeded downstairs to the exit and stumbled upon his butler. Marvin glared at Luka gearing up with his plague suit and asked—

"Is this a very wise idea sir?"

"Hmph', if it was, you wouldn't have asked me that."

"True and if you would've said that it isn't a wise idea then you would just be contradicting yourself."

"Oh yes I would Marvin. My daughters love this horse very much and it's the right thing to do."

"The things we do for love sir."

Riding on a hover scooter through the field going forty miles per hour then Luka stopped in front of his barn and realized that the door is open. With the full body plague suit he jumped off his hover scooter then walked up the door.

"Buck? Buuuck? Buck—hey Buck."

He ambled towards the hay where Bucky usually sojourns.

"You alright Buck? Ah man. You're a strong stallion, aren't you?"

Bucky lying down sideways throttling and moving his head up and down. Luka went on his knees then tiled his head to the right side then touched his neck. His lips were pursed as he goggled at him then shook his head. "Ah damn…"

He pulled out a heated beam knife from his pocket with a look of dejection on his face. He quivered a bit then shook his head once more and staring at his family horse. He closed his eyes and turned his head away for ten seconds then stabbed Buck in the back of his neck, penetrating his throat. The beam was very thin which makes it easier to cover up the stab wound with the horse's hair.

"It's ok Buck, everything will be ok."

TEN

Drones began flying out from the police station, searching for conceivable illegal weaponry across the village. Detective Cane Holloway walked in the interrogation room, this interrogation room is more advanced than the ones from the 21st century. The room has optional secret lie detectors all around equipped with voice analyzed system. These detectors are based on movements, body heat, heart beat and many more. Hidden cameras, microphones and more features are installed.

Detective Holloway sits in front of Nack then glared at him.

"So, tell me Nack… Why were you at an abandoned warehouse at 11pm in the night? You should be home about to go to bed for the next day of school."

"I finished school already and I'm a well-educated Super Genius."

"Well educated Super Genius huh? I would more than likely call it a smart ass."

"Yeah that sums it up for you I guess."

"Hm, you may be a Super Genius, but I know most of the schools don't teach y'all about forensic evidence for police to find. Because they don't want y'all educated Super Geniuses, to do stupid shit." He said with emphasis on *Super Geniuses.*

"Hmm, what I did, definitely wasn't stupid."

"You sure? According to forensics—using our marvelous devices, distinguishing your DNA, the little piece of fallen hair that was found made it clear that it was something stupid you did, like you know—vigilante shit. You know how much time you can get for being a vigilante?"

"It depends if the vigilante did an additional crime but in Gel Hev, it's originally five months to a year in prison or house arrest with community service. Possibly shorter time if I was to cooperate in anything."

"Ok, you know your shit. Your father is a cop nonetheless…"

"So, you've been snooping around on my background…"

"That's what we do."

"Of course."

"If you knew the consequences. Why do it? Why go around beating up thugs and vandalizing their bodies."

"I didn't exactly say that I did that now. Did I?"

Cane leaned back on the chair and folded his arms then questioned him more—

"Ok then. Who did it?"

"You saw those "N" marks on those thugs, right? It stands for 'Netro' and he's going to be our guy that gets the job done. Stopping the evils and the criminals like Dr. Sagan, the goons, the robbers and all the illegal conspiracies out there."

"Oh yeah? And you saw this Netro character doing what the police could have done. Well not putting the "N" marks on them but you get what I'm saying. This is vigilante work interfering in what could have been an illegal weapons deal."

"Yes, it was a deal, a deal to sell illegal weapons and some sort of chemical tanks for money, the seller was some guy named Kojack with his goons."

"Kojack? Ok…"

"Yeah… I come to the warehouse every week to just, you know, chill and do my homework. Until two weeks ago these thugs were selling items in containers. It's the same routine ever since then until Netro came along…" Nack said and being interjected.

"I'm going to stop you right there. Now two weeks ago!? Why didn't you tell the authorities?"

"I was… I was scared man, plus I'm thinking maybe they will relocate over time. I don't like to get involved in things like this at all."

Cane got up from the chair and fixed his tie then said—

"Well kid—you can go now."

Nack questioned his sudden decision— "I can go now?"

"Yes, I got all my information that I needed here. I don't really care much for a vigilante crime at the moment plus no one was killed just beaten up maybe by some Netro character."

"Yes, Netro is the real deal."

"And so am I… My main objective is Dr. Sagan and apparently Kojack Thompson is working for him now. All I need was a name—you will be back with us sometime in the future but for now I'll let you go."

<u>*Subjective location in LTV*</u>—

Push in a full body plague suit with a see through transparent nearly indestructible Grainian Tech glass helmet, in the process of gathering his appliances in his hybrid air cargo vehicle to another spot elsewhere from where Tajaymae saw him.

After exiting the train station, Xack and Adelia proceed towards a certain destination to possibly find the boy that shot lightning out of his eyes. They weren't sure that he would be in the exact same spot but maybe if they search around in nearby public properties and at least obtain more details.

The area seemed unusually dim while a shroud of ghastly mist heaved around the village, this is when Xack and Adelia finally understood that the air is contaminated as they both started coughing then Xack said— "Here take this…" He took two mini gas masked that only covers the mouth and nose from his side pocket then he handed one to Adelia.

"It'll protect you from the contaminants."

"Where is it coming from? And the trees, the trees are growing higher than usual!"

"I don't know Adel, but we need to be isolated before these masked give out. Come on let's go."

Xack now wearing his *haori jacket*, sprinted following a trail while Adelia followed behind him for about one minute then abruptly, he stopped next to a shrub.

"Keep your head down…" He whispered.

"What is it?"

"It's Push." Xack located his enemy while Adelia did the same.

"That's him huh?"

"Yeah and I think he's responsible for this pollution."

"We should ambush him from both sides."

"He's about to leave, by the time you get to the other side he would be already gone."

"It's still worth a try."

Push persistently packing his air vehicle then unexpectedly, six policemen wearing level one armor arrived landing from the sky— "Halt! GHPD!"

"Woah, looks like they beat us to it."

"We should help them out."

"No—we don't have the authority for that Adel…"

"Identification. Identified as—Push Monaghan trained as an Apaki Warrior and infused nanochip." Said the automated recognition device on the police armor.

Push smiled as he released an Apaki Katana in each hand.

"Yeah, that's me baby."

"Draw down your weapons!" The police trooper in the middle demandingly said while his comrades drew their Fed pistols.

"That wouldn't be any fun now wouldn't it?"

"This is your final warning… disarm your weapons or we will shoot!"

"Hm', having my glass blades visible doesn't always mean I'm going to attack you fellow policemen. C'mon you Gel Hev cops are always frightened when it comes to Apaki Warriors. Hm, you know what? How about… you go fuck yourselves."

"Don't do it!"

Push shattered his sword into tiny pieces as the two coyotes ran towards the policemen. He then released heated glass pieces which simultaneously hits one in the helmet and one in the stomach.

"Return fire!"

Bullets fly by the coyotes as the heated glass pieces didn't harm them because of their level one armor. The policeman in the middle fired multiple shots at Push but he blocked and deflected the bullets with a second heated glass katana. The coyotes were quick and agile as they dodge bullets.

"Switch to beams!"

The officers switched their guns from bullets to heated beams as the two coyotes ran forward and quickly jumped eight feet in the air then both landed on the policeman in the middle then began biting his helmet with their metal sharp teeth. Push kept firing at the police armor began to crack then one officer got pierced in the gut.

"Aaah!"

"His Apaki Katana is strong enough to pierce through Police Armor? He even deflected bullets so smoothly."

"Yeah he's pretty skilled and the coyotes are well trained."

"Seems to be almost on par with a Mega Human Prime Apaki Warrior . . ."

"His glass swords are strong but it's only because his nanochip is different... Hm... He's distracted fighting these officers, maybe we can attack him."

"No, we're not going over there Xack, he's too skilled— let the cops handle it and we need to get out of here." She said then coughed heavily.

Gel Hev, GTC meeting room on the 19th floor. (Grainian Tech Corporation)—

Henry Luciano, six feet and two inches tall with his signature look, a formal attire, toting an invention called the 'Motogon'. The Motogon is simply a very tiny crystal inside a one-inch cubic computer drive which emits unknown power according to Henry. As he spoke with his strong Italian accent he explained and showcased the project.

"I would say this is by far my greatest discovery yet. I stumbled upon a power source no man has ever seen... This object is just as phenomenal as the Interstellar Network. Now pay attention close as I promptly display my rational explanation. First, we have the size, the size is for fitting and travel. Second, the extra features operated by a micro motherboard to perform with so many mechanical features . . . It's all about true substance everyone... and producing enough power to operate a space bus . . . or even more."

"How does this contraption work exactly? What's the mechanical engineering process?" One of the company executives wondered.

"You see now that's a secret ingredient I can't tell, all you need to do attach the Motogon to any broken machine and there you have it a fully functioning operation. This is as splendid as the Heaven Bolt."

"Demonstrate to us Mr. Luciano." Weever said.

"Hand me your holographic receiver please."

"Hm, ok. Here you go."

Henry smashes the cubic cell phone then dropped the Motogon to it. Immediately the phone is back together and fully functional. Everyone in the room is stunned while he serenely looked at them with a smirk.

"Hm, lovely… hmm, very remarkable! How much is he asking for?"

Luka Shale Jr. pushes open the meeting room door then said—

"Eight hundred million . . . Each… Sorry I'm late guys, I had family issues."

"You must be out of your fucking mind…"

"I'll take it."

"What?"

"I agree. I'll take it also."

"Same here."

. . .

"Weever?"

"Yeah—I say—yeah, I'll take it."

"Ok fine. This better put some outstanding marketing in the game…"

"C'mon now, didn't you see what it can do… You won't be disappointed, I promise." Luka said.

An hour later everyone left the conference room except for Luka and Henry— "Great presentation."

"Hey, you said you were going to be late and I cover for you. That's what friends are for Luka."

"Thanks for that man, your help is much appreciated. Hopefully this shakes off the dept."

"You live and you learn then you hustle, and you earn."

"Yes, counterfeits can do this to you"

"Haha'. I guess it can or—just being young and dumb. Your pop had it mapped out for you anyway and even so, it's always problems you have to face." Henry said as he touched Luka's shoulder.

"Yeah like this freaking plague going on out there today… I'm surprised this meeting still went down." Luka said as he walked to the large window.

"Nothing and I mean nothing, will stop anyone when its business like this involved."

"Hmm, even when the terror of Dr. Sagan reigns."

"This doesn't surprise me anymore Luka."

"One day… yes, one day I believe he's going to be stopped plus he's getting old now and he isn't immortal."

"Well, as long as he lives, he won't stop until he's deceased."

"You know Henry, a man like him can motivate you."

"Motivating people to murder?"

"Murder… yes, he is a perfect role model for the psychos. His motivation can be expressed in many ways, constructed from enthusiasm. He never stops and never gives up no matter how many agents who are coming for his neck."

"He's an inspiration indeed."

"But he's always hiding, cowering in fear while I'm getting millions added to my millions that I worked for, added to my billions that my dad passed down to me."

"Well, Mr. Shale Jr., you are the spitting image of your father. I see it all the time."

"Pfft… me and you Henry… we will continue to change this world."

"Yes, we will… starting with this madness. Those trees—just look at them. It's a total disrespect but I'm sure the M.N.S.C has the wealth to fix it."

"It was disrespectful to God in the first place, inducing chemicals and injecting them to make them smaller in size for trivial styles."

"Hm, maybe the Mad Doctor is actually doing something right."

<u>*LTV Mayor's Office*</u>—

Mayor Tyson Roland, the Mayor of Little Tree Ville stood at his window and gazed at his village seeing the drastic changes occurring right in front of his eyes. The facial expression wouldn't reveal itself thoroughly because of the severe burn marks across his right cheek which connects to his eyebrow, forehead and covering his temple. The burn marks are also seen connected to his neck which seems to be down to his body permanently scarring his dark skin.

"Ever since I met Benson Langard the Third as a child, I was amazed and inspired by his abilities and ideas." He reminisced.

The Mayor's assistant, Preston looked at him then said— "Yes I agree, these trees are so iconic, and the Mad Doctor messed it all up!"

"I need to put a stop to this . . . But how?"

"Sir, there's a fourteen your old boy who calls himself, Netro and he wants to see you." Said the front desk operator through his office phone.

"Hm, a fourteen-year-old boy? What is a fourteen-year-old doing here? Tell him to stay home with his parents. I don't know why my security is letting kids in here while there's a plague going around… Better yet, he can stay! At least he's not outside right now."

"If he doesn't let me upstairs his brains are going to get fried with electrical current coming from my eyes." Ki-Yale said with his arm tightly gripped around one of the guard's neck.

"Wow… Can you really shoot lightning from of your eyes? Or you're just bluffing?"

"You truly want to risk knowing that?"

"Hm, ok… I'll try again." Said the front desk operator pressing the button again to speak with the Mayor— "*Sir, the boy is very abnormal… he said he would fry one of your guards with electrical current from his ah… From his eyes sir…*"

"Bring him in… wait… What the fuck!? This is a fucking child… Why is a child placing my guard hostage!?" Tyson inquired then he looked at the security camera.

Ki-Yale released the guard while the elevator doors opened.

"I gotta' get stronger guards. Unbelievable… Who the fuck is you kid?" Tyson delved, being six feet tall and looking down at him.

"My name is Netro Two!"

"Ok, ok, let's get serious here kid and cut the shit… Who the hell are you?"

"I told you, my name is Netro Two."

"Ok then . . . Netro Two—tell me. What's going on? You coming up in here like you're some tough guy…"

"I would like to know why the village is under attack with these viruses."

"Why is it your concern kid? Are you on some type of drug?! Coming in here thinking you can ask me anything. Do you live in LTV?"

"Yes, I live here but that's confidential stuff and none of your concern…"

"None of my what? Hmmmmm'." He muttered.

"If it's you who's causing this plague then it needs to stop—otherwise, I'm here to help."

"Now, why would I put such a huge burden on my village? There has been devious Mayors over the years but I'm not one of them. Now… I'm presuming Sagan is the main source."

"He was the first on my speculations."

"Already forty-six casualties because of this plague and the body count is rising rapidly."

"This is why I'm here to help Mr. Mayor."

"And how are you going to help me kid?"

"*Sir, your son wants to come up.*" Said the front desk operator.

"Ok, bring him in." Tyson said while looking at the camera that's showing his eighteen-year-old son. He's five feet, seven inches tall and appeared fair skin because his late mother's genes.

"Wah'… what's up Dad? Its freh'… freaking crazy out there." He stuttered because of his autism spectrum disorder and heavy voice from the full body suit he's wearing to deflect the viruses.

"Yeah I know son. Are you ok? Did you take your medicine for your autism?"

"Ye'… yeah Dad I took my medicine and no Dad… ev'… everyone in my school was equipped with a body suit and… aaand… the cavalry you sent arrived for me." He said while taking off his helmet then undressed the entire suit.

"Well, you are special to me my son and I don't want a thing happen to you."

"So, does the other parents that were unfortunate with their children. I'm sure they felt the same way you do before they were infected."

"Hm, Netro… Two? You say your name was? Where does your origin come from and that suit?"

"I'm an extraterrestrial species from planet Netron and I've been in hiding since I was born but I seek peace with humans . . . I also have special abilities and this suit enhances them in every way." He said standing up straight slightly poking his chest out.

"Ok... ok. Suh'... so you're saying that you're an alien?"— "Yep... half alien to be exact."

"You sure you ain'... you ain't on... drugs bro?" Mike assumed while Preston stood quiet and confused.

"That's the same fucking thing I said son... Hmm, I never seen that suit before, and you gripped my security guard that's twice your size around his neck and he's the only one struggling to move... You're definitely not a Muscle Boy because your muscles don't grow."

"I possess a different level of strength far more than humans."

"Hmmm, ok Netro... Let me see those abilities you say you have, more in action."

"Ok. How do you want me to show you Mr. Mayor? I don't want to damage anything in this room."

"Follow me, we are going to the training room. I'm guessing you don't have a SS Microchip since you're an alien?"

"Aahh'..."

"It's ok, no need to lie."

"Well sir, I do obey the law..."

"Ha, yeah right kid..."

"My body has a microchip, but my suit has the power to manipulate the mind and also the equipment that tries to identify me."

"Hm... interesting suit . . . Either way my military androids would still attack you with or without a microchip because they are non-AP."

Mayor Tyson brought Ki-Yale, Mike and Preston to the training room one flight down. They entered the pitch-dark room, ten seconds before the lights turned on with androids exiting from the floor on the lower platform.

"Now these androids are level one with vast artillery and don't mind their humanoid look, they're just androids. They're used for toddler Mega Humans with advanced abilities but most likely they can't control their powers to the full extent, so these little things help them improve."

The second that Tyson finished his sentence Ki-Yale floated on ahead to the androids on the lower platform. "You're going to need more than that Mr. Mayor."

The droids blasted their heat ray guns then he shot his lightning out of his eyes. This time the lightning turned up a notch so that it pierced the android's metal skin. Ki-Yale over did it and burnt the floor and the walls.

"Woah!"—Mike and Preston both surprised.

"Didn't mean to do that…"

Tyson looked at his son then blinked a few times trying to believe what he just saw, then looked back at Ki-Yale.

"Its ok kid, aah, it's actually amazing! Let's see what you can do against a level three android.

"Wo… Woah, you jumped thuh… the gun there Dad."

"Don't worry… This kid is not even fazed from anything that's going on here." Tyson said as Preston looked at Ki-Yale with a focused face.

More machines appeared from the walls and ceiling with flying disks sharp enough cut almost anything. The disks were launched into the air and surrounding Ki-Yale, ready to attack him while he stood motionless.

"Dad! He's not moving!"

"Sir…" Preston being paranoid while the sharp disks are heading towards him.

"I'm not stopping the session." Tyson said.

Ki-Yale got hit with all the sharp disks then they blew up on him, leaving him covered in smoke. So much smoke that they couldn't see him.

"Is he dead?" Preston asked.

"Get the infrared glasses."

Mike rushed to the mini inventory station on the wall and grabbed the infrared glasses. He released the cover and picked up the rubber head support then stretched it around his head.

"Hm, I doe'… I don't see anything Dad!"

"What!? Let me see those glasses!"

"That's why the other androids aren't attacking." Preston said.

"No way!" Tyson said.

"Should have stopped it while you had the chance sir."

The smoke started to clear up a bit and Mike saw a dark figure appearing within the smoke.

"Wai'… wait… Dad, I think… I'm seeing something!"

"Oh shit! He's still alive!" Tyson said after taking off the glasses.

Ki-Yale jumped out the smoke then smashed all the floating androids in midair with his fists while the androids that's on the floor shot at him. He then went to the floor then used one of the androids to smash the rest.

"Ok, stop session! I've seen enough."

Moments later—

"I have many more abilities but I'm still learning, and I'm considered a soldier in training if I was on my planet."

"Yes, I bet you do have more but you took those blasts and lethal weapons like its nothing. That's already enough to prove that you can help... Now, my son's infrared glasses couldn't see you. Why is that?"

"Maybe it's broken Dad."

"Nah, it's not broken, my suit doesn't expose me or generate any kind of body heat. Including my head, it's almost like a stealth maneuver when I'm in a fight. Well my suit always thinks I'm in a fight when it's on."

"You tal'… You talk as if your sue'… your suit is a person."

"Yeah, it's something like that."

"You're not telling us everything kid and that's not good overtime but, I'm glad you're on our side."

"Sorry Mr. Mayor, it's just certain things I can't say right now."

"I see . . . You smoke? I got some good herbs here. Back in the 21st century, it would be just Tobacco, but the Marijuana is illegal. Now the greens are used to the fullest now a days... All legal stuff now." Tyson said as he lit a joint.

"Nah I'm good, I don't smoke."

"Good! You're too young to smoke anyway… Now I need you to join the Crouton Village Tournament which is in three or four days. That's where Dr. Sagan's whereabouts are. I want him here, unarmed and we will see to it that he answers for his crimes…." Tyson said then puffed smoke from his mouth.

"Nah . . . I'm not doing that . . ."

"Why not kid?"

"I don't kill humans…"

"Don't kill you say?"

"Putting him to work already sir."

"Yes, he wants to help, and he proved that he is capable. I never seen powers like this… so let's give it a shot."

"Killing is a no but I'll be glad to turn him in. Besides, I got the heart of a lion!" He said with confidence and slightly thrusting his chest out again with his hand folded behind his back.

"Heart of a lion huh? Ha! I like you kid!" Tyson chuckled.

"It's just something I like to say."

"That's a good one. Now, this is our preferred ultimatum, you still have to enter the tournament… this is a greater chance of getting closer to finding his whereabouts."

Ki-Yale looked to the floor showing contempt.

"You don't have to murder anyone just knock them out or get some friends and fake the funk. Make it seem like you are killing each other but you're really not, it's just an act. After you do all of that, tournament officials might even let you see him."

"Hmm."

"I… I want in!" Mike joyfully said.

"You're going to use the device that I made you?"

"Yeh'… yes sir, this kid ain'… ain't the only one with abilities."

"Naaah, I still don't want you out there. Dr. Sagan ain't someone you play with."

"C'mon Dad! —C'mon… I cah'… I can handle myself!!"

"No Mike and that's final!"

Mike's face expressed anger towards his father. He squinted and opened his mouth as if he wanted to speak then shuddered his head in a jittery like motion then walked out the room.

"Now Netro, I need you to finally confirm with me that you're up to the task."

"Yes sir. I will bring him in, so he pays for his crimes!"

"Good. I'm hoping to see you succeed!"

"Oh, I will Mr. Mayor."

ELEVEN

The woods of LTV—

The air became heavier and heavier by the minute, it appeared to be a deep fog abnormally sweeping through the village. It was not windy nor was it tremendously cold just the gas surfacing as if they were in the belly of a beast. A mini gas mask still intact with Adelia but she's barely breathing while Xack is in front holding her left hand roaming their way towards a supermarket. "You think they've got A.J Null Systems at the entrance?" Adelia asked.

"Yeah, they should, especially in Gel Hev but safety is what we need now. This gas is way too toxic for us to be out here."

A.J meaning Apaki Jermayin Null Systems are machineries built within the walls of a building that disarms the Apaki Jermayin technology in their systems once they walk through the door to prevent possible harm to civilians. Only the building attendants can deactivate the disarming system while an Apaki Warrior is in that specific building and when they exit their tech is automatically armed again. Apaki Warrior attacks are merely insignificant compared to the low-rated gun violence across the solar system. However, action against aggressors are forced upon. Outside or inside of the structures, civilians also have the choice to instantly report an attack just by the click of a button on their clothing which connects to the nanochip inside those individual warriors and the same goes for illegal firearms. This allows police officers to detect the meticulous location of that Apaki Warrior who inflicted harm.

They approached the supermarket then came to find out the doors were shut.

"Shit! It looks empty… Hello?! Is anyone there? Hello?!" Xack hollered with his strong voice.

"Maybe there's a back door." Adelia said with a hoarse voice then she coughed heavily holding her chest.

"C'mon."

They both carried on to the back only to find out that the back door is also closed.

"Ok, ok. Let me check for the nearest hospital."

"Hospital?! Hell no Xack, I hate hospitals!"

"I know, me too but you're coughing like crazy."

"I'm ok."

"No, you're not! Your mask, it has become nonfunctional."

"No, I'm…" She wheezed then paused holding her mask then she started to cough more heavily while blood leaked down her chin.

"Adelia…"

The Shale residence—

It's a little after 8pm and Kathleen is in her room lying down in her bed while her nineteen-year-old best friend Chloe Torbino the daughter of a Fabian Torbino, playing virtual reality video games. This is merely for exercise and overall fun. She wore a headset that covered her eyes and the game console is connected to one area on the mechanical floor which she stands on with a barrier around her. This gave a good amount of space for her to move around as if she's in the actual game.

"You're crazy leaving your house in these circumstances." Kathleen said.

"I promised that I would come over and I'm not letting some stupid plague stop me."

"Everything just sucks ass this week."

"I know, I was supposed to throw a party tonight now everyone is either too scared to go outside or in the hospital." Chloe said.

"They're just not prepared like you."

"No one really expects shit like this out here in LTV."

"Yeah. It costs the life of my horse."

"No way! . . . Buck is dead?! Why didn't you tell me before?" Chloe immediately stopped playing the virtual reality video game.

"My dad found him lying in the barn unresponsive earlier, at the same time that you came." Kathleen sobbed.

"I'm… I'm so sorry to hear this… aaw' come here."

Chloe scrutinized her, grasping how sorrowful she felt then attended to her with a tight hug.

"I loved him—so much—especially my sister she's taking it worse than me. I feel like this might be the end of the world."

"I know… look, everything is turning into shit right now. It may look scary outside but it's not the end. Well, maybe this is the end but I'm not leaving your side no matter what. I'll always be there to support you."

Kathleen ogled at her then Chloe continued— "Fuck this stupid plague. Ok?"

Kathleen smirked indulging what Chloe just said as she smiled back and came closer to her face. She wiped the tears off her fluffy cheeks then moved in closer to her wide lips.

"What…?"

With no more hesitation and thinking about rejection she went ahead and kissed her on the lips.

"What are you doing Chloe?"

"Sorry, I'm just…"

Kathleen with her nipples exhibiting though her compact shirt, pushed Chloe on the bed then stood in front of her. Chloe then recognized that she took it too far. "That won't happen again Kath…"

"Sshh…"

Kathleen went closer and hovered on top of her then pecked her on the lips. That was when Chloe knew that her move wasn't in vain as they kissed aggressively. Chloe smiled then slowly caressed her hips up to her belly. Kathleen gently bit her lower lip then Chloe gently took off Kathleen's compact shirt displaying her breasts without any bra. Kathleen smirked then did the same back to Chloe, also exposing her. They were both spellbound by the magnificence of each other's bosoms as Chloe placed her two hands on each one fulfilling her erotic dreams—

"These are what I always pictured them would be."

"Hm, you've been fantasizing, haven't you?"

"I knew you liked girls ever since I met you Kathleen. I just wanted this to feel right."

"Well, you picked the right time."

Chloe's face glowed while jiggling her breasts as Kathleen grinds on her as she's riding her. Kathleen chuckled then smooched her again. She then sucked on her neck slowly as Chloe undressed her leggings. Kathleen made a trail down to her waist then bit her panties and pulling it off with her teeth.

"I feel like you did this before."

"You could say I'm just freestyling."

The lust blossomed as Chloe is completely naked. Kathleen licked her stomach in a circular motion then made it around her rosebud. Heavy breathing from Chloe as she stroked her hair while Kathleen continued to tease her then made her way to her clitoris. Chloe curved her back, covered her mouth, preventing herself from shrieking too loud and adoring the pleasure she's receiving.

—Downstairs in the kitchen, Luka comes back home and saw his wife cleaning.

"What's up honey!?" Luka chortled.

"Well hello…" Pamela responded.

"Guess what?"

"Another success?"

"Oh yes baby, you know it… Eight hundred million… from each buyer."

"Added to all of our billions."

"What's better than more millions? Huh?"

"Hmm, let me see… Honesty, trust, integrity…"

"What you getting at here Pam?"

"What I'm getting at here is that… is that I know Luka…"

"Know what?"

"How Bucky died… I know exactly how he died."

His mouth was slightly open with a puzzled face thinking what to say but couldn't say anything.

"The stab wound . . . I saw it."

"What?"

"Did you do that? Please be honest with me."

"Aah—ok, yes I did it."

"Why!? Why Luka?!" She bickered.

"Look, I had to, he was already suffering. I checked his pulse too… He was infected pretty badly."

"This is fucked up man! You could have transferred him to a vet."

"I know but it was already too late from the infection… Why were you out there in the first place?"

"Because I just couldn't believe it. That's our family horse."

"Did you tell the girls?" Luka blatantly concerned.

"No but you're going to do it."

"Not right now."

Pamela shook her head as she grunted at him. He turned his back and walked to the cabinet.

"Damn it Luka… I hate it when you lie and try to keep secrets. Especially to the girls… the day isn't even over yet and shit just went left."

"I'm sorry."

"Are you really? They sincerely loved that horse. Melissa loved him the most… Damn, her heart was already broken when you told her today."

"I'll fix this…"

"Yeah? You're gonna' fix this? Look, whatever it is you're gonna' do next, just don't do it in a conniving way."

"Ok, sure Pamela…"

In the hallway, Melissa eavesdropping on the entire conversation with tears of disappointment tumbling from her eyes. Emotions clouded her, feeling frail as she sat in the fetal position. She puts her head up then looked to the left then she slowly got up with her hand on the wall. She leaned on the wall using her arms as she puts her head in between them wiping her tears then looked back once more.

Little Tree Ville Police Precinct—

"I know you're keeping me in here because of the virus spread in the air outside… I'm sure there is a plague suit somewhere in here for me. I mean, I have rights to go free you know." Said Nack, being a little paranoid and talking to the police guards while sitting next to a group of men that's most likely in custody.

Some sat down with braced arms while Nack was loose.

"The guys are working on it, just sit tight. No need to be scared." Said one of the guards.

"Ok. Can I make a couple of phone calls? Or at least one?"

"Sure. You have a cellphone equipped with your shirt, so you can make one right here."

"In a private area please."

"Hm', ok, this way..."

One of the guards escorted Nack into a private room where he can utilize his phone to make a call.

Ki-Yale flying back towards the hospital and felt his phone vibrating. Although Ki-Yale is in his Netron Suit he still can feel or hear his phone. His phone is connected and linked to his regular clothes that can be projected as a hologram when calls are made almost like iPhone FaceTime except more advanced. "Yo Ki-Yale!"

"What's up bro? You alright? I was just going to check up on you after I make this run back to the hospital and pick up my sis."

"Yeah, I'm good. What happened to Tajay?!"

"Nothing she saw a lady being sick, so she wanted to help her to the hospital."

"Oh ok, well I'm at the LTV Police Precinct and these guys are taking forever to get a plague suit for me. Can you come and get me bro?"

Ki-Yale turned around and instantly flew in a different direction.

"Yeah I got you right now. I'm on my way."

"Thank you so much bro but you can get me after you get your sis."

"Naah, she can take care of herself. I'll just come and get you then pick her up."

"Ok… then well, Happy Birthday by the way!"

"Oh, thanks bro. All of these random things happening I forgot all about it."

The stench of rotten carcass reeked along the room. A gutted deer lying on the inside of a large metal pan on top of a table. Dr. Rogue Sagan seemed unfinished as he used a large knife wearing plastic gloves cutting through the oozing flesh.

"Hmm, Garrett..." He said.

Push entered the room then immediately revealed some details.

"Sir. I have news for you."

"Hmm… Let me hear it!"

"I discovered that Garrett was apprehended by authorities. According to my tracking device he was at the hospital at first…"

"Yes, I know that he's in custody. I have a tracking device as well and I know where everyone is just in case you guys are dicking around."

"The cops ain't gonna' find out about that bug, right?"

"Well, the bug is untraceable in the human body. I invented it a while back and I still use it today as you can see. The invention is what I call an infused bug that becomes part of your body and it can be somewhat very lethal."

"Hm', ok I see."

"Now there is other news I'm looking for from you."

"Yeah, I injected the virus into the trees and it's spreading around Little Tree Ville leaving plenty of casualties… They're going to need a whole new cemetery!"

"Ha! Deprived LTV…. The Mayor must now understand I don't play around. He has a deal with me that hasn't been dealt with because he can't propose to it and he is also a person I'm willing to meet and correspond with again . . . It's been too long."

"What about this Netro kid? I think he got Garrett to the Feds."

"Ok, I'm just going to believe this Netro kid is real…"

"No, he is real. Listen to this."

Push evinced his proof to Dr. Sagan as they listened to a recording device that recorded conversations with the Mayor and his LTV council.

"Today was a tragic day. We lost a lot of innocents, children, animals and this tragic event made a powerful impact on our village. It made us vulnerable."

"Hmm'…" Dr. Sagan mumbled with a grin on his face.

"We can turn it around and get stronger and build back what we started. We must fight and protect our village.… I have a young boy that came to me today and asked me if he can help. To me I thought. Why help? You should be home with your parents, but this boy possessed abilities that I have never seen before. He proved to me that he can take on anything that Sagan dishes him. I know it sounds crazy to have a boy do the job, but it might just be the only way."

"This child of whom you speak of. What's his name?"

"It's Netro… he isn't a Mega Human either, he's much, much more and he's coming after Sagan wherever he is!"

"Hmm, so this Netro kid is coming for me huh? Hmph', let him. I'll show him what death tastes like."

Push sneered showing approval then Dr. Sagan robustly cuts off the deer's head and continued—

"Hm', as a matter of fact. I want to see for myself, what he can do."

<u>LTV Hospital</u>—

Ki-Yale went for Nack while he wore a plague suit then arrived back at the hospital in the Emergency Room—

"Thank you for bringing me here." Said the lady that Tajaymae and Ki-Yale helped.

"You're welcome." Tajaymae said with a giant smile on her face.

"I wish I helped everyone else."

"Aw, you're such a sweet boy. Whoever your parents are must be proud." Said the lady still coughing but less crudely.

"Thank you." He expressed gratitude while smirking.

"I should get some sleep..."

"Hello. How are you? Is she alright?" Asked one male doctor randomly appearing from the room entrance.

"Yeah, she's ok now." Tajaymae said.

The doctor stared at Ki-Yale then upstretched his left eyebrow.

"I know what you're going to ask. It's about why we didn't get infected without plague suits. Right?" Ki-Yale inquired.

"It's complicated to share." Tajaymae said.

"I actually had a plague suit on coming here." Nack added.

"Aaah… no, that wasn't what I was gonna' ask you."

"So, what is it?" Tajaymae asked.

"I could have sworn I saw him on the news about nine hours ago…"

"Well… aah', yes that's me."

<u>The Shale residence</u>—

Luka with his holographic computer projected by a miniature tech cube and using his communication device.

"Hmm. That's the only one?"

"Yes, express shipping from Gigantica to Asia."

"I have the money obviously, but I just prefer the cheapest just to be safe."

"Sometimes going cheap is really expensive at the end."

"True."

"Why Asia being the first anyway?"

"Hm, my dad always did shipments with Asia first. Everything I learn and picked up was from him before he died. He left these devices that I should've carried out a long time ago, but I let this money go to my head thinking it won't go away but even billions can drop rapidly."

Pamela entered the room then goggling at him with a frightened look in her face— "Luka I can't find Melissa anywhere in the house!"

"What? I'll call you back."

"She's probably outside. We have to look for her!"

Luka puts on his fully functional gas mask and let's Pamela put on the only plague suit in the house. They proceeded to search outside and the first place they search is the barn.

"Melissa!?—Melissa!?" Luka called out.

"Look over there! Oh no my baby—she's not breathing—she's not breathing." Pamela panicked.

Luka stood frozen looking at his daughter lying down and being unconscious. Melissa's insides were being mildly consumed by the Genchi as Pamela held her chest as she dropped on her knees. Terrified and confused, he went close to her and felt her pulse with his left hand while his right arm hugged Pamela.

With little time to think he touched a switch on his belt that immediately ensures an emergency call.

"Nine-one-one. What's your emergency?"

Luka stood up and spoke to the dispatcher while Pamela cried irrepressibly then notices her cube in which has an online setting. Ten-dimensional image emerged from the cube revealing a post from her social media website in front of Pamela—

"I know what Dad did—it's not fair. I love Bucky and I just wanna' be with him forever."

TWELVE

Gigantica Air Force Station, General Tirana Gale, she is the highest ranking General of the Gigantica Air Force. Thus, encountering moles impersonating comrades within her quadrant, one of her teams collected data on Sergeant Roscoe and transmitted the data to her station. After conveying the data West Great Welkin City, the team confronted a suspicious group mostly to be under Sergeant Roscoe's command. Moments later Tirana lost connection with her team and believed that they are under fire.

"Raven Six, status report! Raven Six, status report! "

"Ma'am, a message from Sergeant Keith—We have two men down in West Great Welkin City and scattered enemy forces positioned for ambush. I'll send you the Coordinates." Said Airman Steven Hall acting as dispatcher.

"Hm', ok call in Eagle Team 43, this fight is far from over."

"Ma'am, Eagle Team 43 is in a mission on Venus. Looks like we might lose this fight ma'am." Said Lieutenant General Avory West.

"Don't be pessimistic! Which teams are available now?"

"Teams 33, 34, 40, 56, 70…" Avory said as he got interrupted by General Tirana.

"Ok, send out Team 56 and 70 to these coordinates. I need more Intel on Sergeant Roscoe Scheel I think he's in on this mess. Create a randevu at Base 16 in Lexington and make sure these missions are accomplished… Roscoe needs to pay for his treacherous ways."

"Yes ma'am."

<u>Little Tree Ville</u>—

This is year 2319, the abduction of Narrken recently occurred. Neecho reported the incident to the police and instructed Ki-Yale to inform them with a different story from the real one. Although the Kafmora family allowed federal agents to help search for Narrken, Neecho and Nealo later decided to take actions into their own hands because they believed it was more than just a human that took him but since Narrken exists in the system and being a minor, this needed to be reported to the authorities. Nealo and Neecho would utilize their powers to mislead detectives with no evidence until it's a complete dead-end case especially since this remains as a higher risk of alien mysteries being revealed.

Detective Cane Holloway captivated the case, he sat in front of Ki-Yale in the interrogation room trying to gather all the evidence and try to piece the puzzle together.

"Hmm', so you were walking with your brother Narrken Kafmora… Am I saying it right? Narr—ken Kaf—mora?" Cane asked.

"Yeah, that's right…"

"Ok good. So, it's a regular evening, walking with your brother in the woods of Little Tree Ville then ya'll came across a bridge over a waterfall. Correct?"

"Yes."

"You don't know what happened for sure, but your theory was that your brother was sitting on the bridge railing then all of a sudden your brother fell into the water fall... You lost sight of him so you went looking for your

204

brother in the same trail as the waterfall but couldn't find him. Also, your parents went looking afterwards but couldn't find him. Correct?"

"Yes."

"Hmm. Is there anything else I need to know about?"

"No that's all of the story."

"Well this investigation leads with nothing Ki-Yale, it's like he vanished in thin air."

"Maybe he went under water and the water pushed him away faster than I can rush to retrieve him... I went to get my parents right away but by the time they came it was too late and nowhere to be found."

"Hm, I prefer you call the cops first."

"With what? My loud voice?"

"No. If you had a cell phone built in your clothing but I guess you didn't at the time which would've been beneficial and yes, the water could've flushed him but I'm not going to always rely on stories now Ki-Yale. I need the exact incident, which means—I'll keep on investigating and a search party will continue."

"Thank you sir."

Moments later, Ki-Yale walked out of the precinct and saw his father.

As Neecho began to drive and Ki-Yale kept quiet as a mouse next to him in the front passenger seat. Five minutes later Ki-Yale decided to speak—

"When will I get to go with you, Grandpa and the search party to look for him?"

"I told you son, leave that to us. Stay home with your mother and support her."

"Why only you guys? What? You think I can't handle myself against the world? Whoever kidnapped him didn't have the balls to even face me, because they know I would take them out!" Ki-Yale badgered, hitting the car door armrest.

"No Ki, I hope you don't mean kill when you say, 'take them out'."

"No Dad… but what if the perp wasn't human?"

"Well that's a different story if the kidnapper wasn't human… And let's get real here, Narrken was stronger than you. What makes you think you can handle whoever took him? Whoever took him, must be a lot stronger to even grab him and knock him out. That's what you said right? The masked person knocked him out with one blow, right?!"

"Yea but…!"

"But what?"

"But… I'm Netro! I should be the strongest… If I was the strongest, I would have stopped whoever that was… I guess I was too weak."

"Yeah, you are Netro, but you weren't born the strongest. You're a prince and we must keep you safe. Until your strong enough and will be strong enough to stop any foe, then I'll let you do what you want but for now you have to be smart and be patient because it's only a matter of time that you will be King of Netron."

Ki-Yale folded his arms and looked out the window feeling pestered. "Hmmmmm." He mumbled.

Neecho and Ki-Yale arrived home and saw Nealo getting dressed.

"Hey! What's up my grandson?" Despite the hello from his grandfather, he ignored him as he walked past him to the elevator. "What's eating him?" Nealo worried.

"It's noting . . . What's up? Where you going?" Neecho asked as Ki-Yale entered the elevator, heading to his room aggressively.

"The Gigantica Army called today... I'm needed for assistance with a situation."

"And what did you say?"

"I'm retired but I am a veteran recruit and eligible for volunteering." Nealo said as he walked to the door.

"Yeah but you're not obligated to go. You can say no if you want to and you know that."

"You're absolutely right—but... I choose to go..."

Nealo was ranked as General of the Gigantica Army and then later retired. His comrades were amazed of his skills, his fast movements, his strength and the fact that he never failed a mission. Individuals began to wonder about him and have Nealo undergo tests in the laboratories but Nealo hid his true self surreptitiously without any suspicion.

Neecho followed his father outside the front yard.

"It's in my nature to be a soldier, ever since I was back home on planet Netron. I started joining the military at age eight doing missions, stopping any evil that steps in my way." Nealo said.

"So, you're going to kill more humans?"

"I've learned some humans don't deserve to live especially if they are just as wicked as the Opposites."

"But that decision shouldn't be ours to make, let the humans deal with it. You're making a complete violation of the Netron code, made by your mother... our first Queen!"

"Yes, made by your grandmother the Queen of our planet. She doesn't know how it truly is on Earth, she didn't even live a day on this planet just sent me here and that's it. 'Start your mission son'..."

"Well, I say its blood lust."

"Hmm... don't worry, I won't be killing anyone."

<u>*Gigantica Hustlers Strip Club*</u>—

This strip club is more old school with just women stripping naked and dancing wildly as men throw their money at them. In a V.I.P section a group of six men all surrounding three dancers while taking over a couple drinks—

"Which is better man ass or tits?" Asked one African American man who seemed athletic.

"Hm... I don't know man, both!" Said the Caucasian heavy-set man.

"Naah bro, you only pick one."

"Damn ok, ok! Hmm… ok, I'll have to go with the ass, yeah I'm an ass man."

"You an ass man huh?"

"Damn just imagine a flat chested bitch with just ass." Said a short guy who is also African American.

"Wouldn't be so bad when you hitting it from the back bro!"

"Aye bro! What about you? What you think man?!" Asked the Caucasian man.

"Hmm, it doesn't matter to me what she got. I'm going to eat the bitch alive." Said the young Italian man in his early twenties.

"Oh, you are a savage huh?"

"Yeah you talking bout' eating her out right? Like go down on her? You know like eat her box out? Like her pussy right?! Her pussaayy?!" Jestingly asked the African American man as the Italian man shook his head in denial after every question.

"No, I'm going to eat her alive, as in chop off her limbs, her fingers, her toes, her ears. Chop her breast off, slice off her nipples then her ass cheeks. Aaah, yes I'm getting hungry just talking about it!"

"What?!"

"Hmm, I'll just snatch her organs and feast on her liver, her lung passage, then, take the cerebral hemispheres and make it look like noodle soup. Hmm, then, I'm going to chew on her eyeballs then fry the rest of her body." Said the young Italian man as he smiled and gazed at the dancer above him.

Everyone stood completely silent and awkwardly glaring at him for twenty seconds.

"This mother fucker is crazy… Where you said you met him again?"

"At this aaah'… to be honest with you… I totally forgot."

West Great Welkin City—

"Encrypt the data and confiscate the rest of the Genchi. We need to process a few transports before we head back to Crouton." Sergeant Roscoe ordered.

"Yes sir."

"And after that… saddle up. I'm going to need more muscle back at the base."

"Incoming, unknown call sir." Said one of his troops that handed him a mechanical cube that emits a ten-dimensional image of the person who calls.

"Hm?"

"Hello General."

"Oh—and who are you supposed to be?"

"My name is Luka Shale Jr."

"Luka Sha… Aah yes, the rich fucker... Luka Shale Jr. How can I forget such a face?"

"My father's face is more appealing I guess . . . Plus, I haven't made much of a big scene lately."

"What would you like Mr. Shale."

"I would like to make profit General. Whatever you can dish me, I speak stern cash and I guarantee your boss demands that you bring him some stern cash."

"Yes, it's all a cycle, you buy and sell. That's how an operation should run and he's willing to do anything to keep it alive."

"Great, I love it, business is always necessary."

"Ok good. I will inform him."

The Never Too Early Café—

Luka Shale Jr. hung up the call and took a gulp of his drink.

"Haahh… I love this place." Mr. Turd said as he walked down the seating area.

"Hmm, I bet it tastes as good as it looks." Said a random man slapping another man's ass standing at the bar.

"What the fuck!"

"Aye."

"Do that again and I'll take that hand of yours and shove it up your—"

"I—did that already man… This morning, first I put on some lube then…"

"Listen, listen man, I don't need to hear that faggot shit man. Get away from me! This is your final warning!"

Mr. Turd stood across from the bickering and just stared at the two men that are about to scuffle.

"Wild place ain't it?" Luka asked.

"This is one of the reasons why I love it." Mr. Turd responded.

"Hm, yeah I guess, entertainment everywhere."

"Heyyy. Didn't I see you from somewhere? I can't shake this feeling that you're a celebrity."

"I guess you can call it that."

"Oh, I remember now. 'Fat Bitches Take Giant Robot Cocks.'! Featuring Betsy Peaches and some guy that looks just like Luka Shale Jr.—OMG! Best porno ever… Well, one of the best."

"Aah—close—but no."

"Wait? Are you… are you the actual, factual, authentic, tangible, real Luka Shale Jr? The billionaire Luka Shale Jr.?"

"I wouldn't say billionaire right now—kind of got a little tied down and especially having my two daughters but no biggie, I'll get back up."

"Hm, well, you're still a wealthy man. I know you live in Gel Hev but this Café of all Cafés? C'mon man, this is for the low life scum like me. Dunkin Turd… that's my name—no kidding—here's my I.D."

"Hm', I've heard worst names… Not that I think it's a bad name—it's just…"

"It's cool man…. My parents were a little on the narcotic side, hard rehab changed everything fifty-two years ago though."

"Really? Hm, sorry to hear that, usually I don't condone drugs whatsoever. I'm guessing your parents were constantly under the influence."

"At least it didn't pass down. I'm stable you know…"

"Um yeah—I see it a little…"

"Well, due to the fact that this era is a high percentage of anti-illegal drugs but still the small possibility of using remains within the low percent…"

"As long as you keep being fifty-two years old and stay in places like this—you'll be absolutely dandy."

"My age… You're quite the good guesser." Mr. Turd surprised.

"It's obvious… Your parents had you then they decided to shape up fifty-two years ago. Same process when I had my first daughter."

"Ha! I still think you're up to something being here Mr. Shale Jr.—I wanna know man."

"Trust me aah… Dunkin Turd . . . Something's you don't wanna know and just, shouldn't get involved with."

Gigantica Army Main Southern Post—

It's the next day and Nealo contributes himself to a private assembly inside a conference room with other soldiers. After the New World Order, regimes wanted a more combined military. Leaders declared Gigantica Military which is a continental defense of armed forces particularly for a stronger and larger body of soldiers. This is uniquely why the Gigantica Army are the strongest army in the Solar System.

"Just got word from the air base about a new threat in West Great Welkin City. Sergeant Roscoe Scheel . . . I have gathered personalized Intel to lock him up for years to come but he is armed and dangerous. He is responsible for establishing an underground business with the Mad Doctor. The Genchi virus has been a widespread throughout the world and in certain areas, Roscoe had secretly undermined hospitals and their systems including billing anyone affected with the virus. These tragedies will not be overrun by wealth and any hospital who bills a patient affected with the virus is subjected to fines and imprisonment. He is also responsible for multiple deaths of our soldiers—full force or not, he will be held accountable for his crimes. He is also profiting his soldiers to do the dirty work. I'm having someone inform the Mayor of the city and have a few law enforcements to tag along. Although law enforcement will accompany us, this is our fight and this mission should be a walk in the park. . . This will be light work; we will not use any aerial attacks. We are going to simplify the positions and surround his base then have Roscoe surrender if he refuses then the use of force is tolerable. Captain Vixen here will give the confidential blueprints and game plans. She is very straight forward with her plans so it shouldn't be hard to understand as some of you mentioned earlier . . .We also have our veteran Nealo over there, he is our only veteran that volunteered for veteran recruit. Now please give him the utmost respect." Said General Zion William the current highest ranking General of the Gigantica Army.

"Yes sir." Said all the soldiers in the conference room.

"You are dismissed."

In orderly fashion, the soldiers gathered their belongings then left the room.

"So, you think our veteran is capable of surviving this mission?" Captain Vixen asked.

"He used to be a General and now he's volunteering. He doesn't necessarily have to be in the fight, but you have seen him in action before Vixen. He did things way better than any Mega Human Prime soldiers."

"Front and center with me, Gerbs, Maya and Kenneth. I had to cut Basin and put him in a different mission he doesn't like it because he was replaced with this veteran."

"Because this veteran, has still got it." General Zion said as Vixen squinting at him then he continued—

"Look, I was under his command back then and he was something else. The best solder in his prime, his skills were unbelievable . . . This is his passion."

"Yes sir, his prime... I remember him. I used to be under his wing as well but look at him now... he's..."

"He's what Vixen? He's old? So, what. Around fifty years in the military and look at him, he's still in good shape today. He wants to volunteer, and he's brave enough to take on any adversary... So, he's in and that's final."

"Ok sir."

Nealo and other soldiers are gearing up in the inventory room with suits and weapons.

"These uniforms are different."

"Well, times have change old man!" Private Maya Gatson said, a young lady in her early twenties with brunette hair a fit body, tattoos around her neck and arm.

"Private, you should be referring to me as General Nealo."

"Firearm ready." Said Nealo's smart automated pistol.

"Hm, all I see is an old man trying to get himself killed. You should be home relaxing, not going on a mission. If I was your daughter, I would be very upset."

"Firearm ready." Said Maya's smart automated rifle.

"I like your concern for your fellow elder's wellbeing but kid, you don't know what I'm capable of."

"Firearm ready." Said Nealo's smart automated rifle.

"Well, whatever is it that you got… Just don't get in our way. Hmm, at least you're still fit and handsome." Maya said while Nealo leered at her then she continued—

"Yeah, I've been looking at your old pictures."

"Hey, is she bothering you? She could be a little bit of a pest" Private Gerbs Ramirez said, a young man in his twenties.

"Nah, just going through a few things." Nealo responded.

"Ok good, so you are front and center with us. You're going to get to see us capture that son of a bitch. Up close and personal!"

"Hm, I admire your bravery and confidence."

Nealo wearing his army uniform, proceeded to the nearest restroom while in the hallway with the front and center of Eagle Team 5 walking towards the transport vessel that fits over sixty passengers and weapons for each one. He entered the restroom and immediately made his Netron Suit appear on his body then altered it to look meticulously like his army suit. This is like camouflage, so that humans don't get confused and get effected by Nealo's Netron Suit's defense by interfering with human's eyes and memory by seeing Nealo without the Netron Suit then changing with it. Also, this helps Nealo balance and perfect himself more in a fight against humans achieving their malevolence.

Nealo on the special aircraft with front and centers Gerbs, Maya, Kenneth, Captain Vixen and several other troops commuting to West Great Welkin City. The sounds of the engine reverberated as the aircraft burst through the clouds, Nealo and Vixen sat across each other and partaking in a stare down.

"Ah I miss my wife right now man. Sucking on her big tits and going balls deep in her. Oouu' man, I wish I was home right now . . . Fuck, I can't wait for this to be over. You know what I'm saying Nealo? I mean, General Nealo?" Kenneth Jase said, a young man also in his twenties with a built body.

Nealo looked at Kenneth with his left eyebrow up then Captain Vixen said—

"I miss my wife too."

"You like women now?" Nealo slightly surprised with undersized emotion put into the question.

"Yes. Hope you wasn't thinking about hollering at me."

"No, no. Those days are over for me. Well, it's been a while I guess—"

"Hmm'." Vixen muttered shaking her head up and down then Nealo continued—

"Uh… I'm not celebrate but I'm just focused on something else right now."

Vixen grinned at Nealo then he continued—

"Aand' ahh—being a lesbian... It's a beautiful thing, I admire it."

"That's good for you I guess, being focused on something other than affection, shows that you really want to accomplish whatever you want to accomplish, and I certainly agree on that sir."

Eagle Team 5 had arrived at Sergeant Roscoe's base in a secluded area which is guarded by an electrical barbed wire fence. The fence's electrical system became non-functional leading the team to consider that it was a trap or a strategic ambush. Wearing full body nearly impenetrable suits with helmets, proceeded inside despite the risks with dozens of teams and police officers. The teams expanded through the large field in the front area of the base with large shields guarding their lives. Vixen hailed him through his affixed speakers all around the base and said—

"Sergeant Roscoe, we have your base surrounded. We will give you till the count of ten to come out and surrender!"

Dozens of androids instantaneously came from out of Roscoe's base and then fired shots at Eagle Team 5.

"Everyone, take your positions now!" Vixen commanded then everyone including Nealo took a defense position according to Vixen's blueprint.

Abruptly, Eagle Team 5 and other soldiers are pinned down, ducking for cover as the androids kept firing. Nealo flung a few grenades that compresses onto the androids then disrupts their system causing them to malfunction. More androids came from out of Roscoe's base, twice as many than before then opened fire at six troops. The heated beams from the androids shoots up to one thousand rounds per minute and hot enough to penetrate the soldier's armor. Rapid fire beams hitting them as each of the six soldiers were grazed, about twenty-three times and easily gunned down as the rest of the shots evaded.

"Shit, take cover!!" Vixen ordered.

"You guys thought it would be easy and didn't fully prepare yourselves huh?!"

Vixen looked at Nealo then looked at the androids with sights of despair. With the courage to linger offensive attacks, she puts her rifle in aiming position, preparing to fire then snappishly, Nealo came out firing shots at every android and moving quickly towards them as they shot back uncontrollably. He went behind an empty mid-sized lorry, crouched down and waits for his automatic assault rifle to cool down as it fully reloads itself with bullets then continued firing.

"Woah." Kenneth said as Gerbs and Maya looked at Nealo strangely.

Nealo gave a quick signal to employ force.

"Ok everyone, engage!" Vixen commanded.

The soldiers were like athletes at the Olympics, moving in closer going head to head with each android as Nealo progressed himself inside the base.

"Hmm, c'mon front and center! Let's go!" Vixen said while following Nealo while Gerbs, Kenneth and Maya began to trail behind.

"Wait up! Stick to the plan, we go in with caution."

"You go ahead and do that Vixen. I'll go in my way!"

"No…"

"You saw how I handle things back there. I could take out this entire army no sweat. Now I'm still a general, you don't give me orders. You stick to your plan and I'll do my own." Nealo said as he kept walking in front.

"Hmm… former general." She muttered.

Nealo went inside an elevator that quickly brought up to a different hallway within a few seconds while Vixen stood behind.

"I need medical assistance from the transporter to the cleared battle area, south east front of the base for six wounded men stat!" Vixen said on the radio then she ordered—

"Alright, we proceed with our route."

Nealo disconnected the security cameras with his mind unplugging each one. Nealo then spotted several hostiles taking position in the next room with his Netron vision. Netrons can see four times or more from what humans originally see. Nealo's vision is like X-ray vision but more effective—Netron vision can be focused on the microscopic things such as cells, molecules or even smaller. Nealo aimed at the wall and fired his rifle shooting a hostile in the head, then he fired several more shots executing the rest, even though they moved around and stooped for cover.

Nealo proceeded to the next room then used his Netron Suit to change his entire body invisible then climbed up railings and maneuvering through tight areas. His army suit has invisibility, but the enemy would have recognized it with the devices that they've implanted on their armor. He entered the room silently as if he were a ninja and hit every guard with his fists effortlessly knocking them out one by one then heads towards the exit. He understood the structure of the base and encountered a bridge ahead. After proceeding across, he sets up a few small radioactive explosive charges on the eastern deck of the Base.

"This mission already got me amped." Gerbs said.

"I agree." Kenneth said.

"Still ain't better than the military space units." Maya said.

"Oh, and work around that Heaven Bolt? I just hope that thing don't fire at us on accident."

"It won't Gerbs, we have signals sent to us every hour by actual agents working around the clock and making sure everything is intact, which is part of our fail-safe system." Vixen said.

"Oh, I see… well I still don't trust it…"

"So, do I . . . Hm? These guards are rapidly decreasing on my radar." Vixen said.

"Maybe they found out we got radars." Gerbs said.

"No, I made sure that won't happen." Vixen said while Nealo ran towards her from down the aisle.

"Looks like you're actually useful." Vixen said.

"Why wouldn't I be?" Nealo asked as he detonated the charges blocking the entrances to the east deck.

"Really? Radiation?" Maya queried.

"Yeaahh, old man knows how to set the mood right with a little light show!" Gerbs said.

"Ok, now I believe Sergeant Roscoe is on the third floor next to the bridge. If we split and go around the bridge, we could leave him with less options. Maya go with Nealo. Gerbs and Kenneth you're with me." She ordered.

"Hm." Nealo muffled raising an eyebrow looking at Maya.

"She may have a mouth, but she is good." Vixen said.

"Hm, yeah I bet she's good with her mouth." Nealo chirped.

"Shut up! ...Dirty old man!" Maya responded but isn't really upset and took it as a joke.

He gave a smirk then began to move while Vixen shook her head.

Moments later, Nealo ran ensued through an aisle heading to the third floor while Maya portrayed a sluggish crusade.

"Hey slow down!"

"What? You can't keep up with an old man?!"

"Look, I'm sorry for what I said earlier about you being old. I now acknowledge that you truly are an amazing soldier and crazy as fuck but you need to give me a quick break here... Please."

"Hmph, ok, I'll stop."

Maya stopped with Nealo while she is out of breath.

"Hmm, you need to work on your stamina soldier... More cardio." Nealo said while Maya gave him a slouchy middle finger.

"This is a pretty large base you know." She said then they both heard a noise behind the walls.

"What was that?" She asked with perplexity.

"Sounded like a gunshot." Nealo said while he is looked through the walls and saw Roscoe.

"Let's check it out."

"Yes, let's go."

Nealo and Maya continued to run down the aisle then came across a mechanical sliding door. Nealo popped the door open with his heat ray beam pistol.

"Hmm, this place is wired." Maya said with her rifle by her shoulder aiming in the direction that she is walking, in tactical style.

"All these chemicals."

Nealo and Maya awaited an ending to the chemical station and expected none other than Sergeant Roscoe. The intensity in the air became thriving as the deceitful high ranked officer had his back turned towards them.

"Hands where I can see them!" Maya commanded and aiming her gun at Roscoe.

Roscoe had his rifle leaning on the wall next to him, he turned around and glared at Maya while Nealo pointed his gun at him.

"I said hands!"

Soon after Maya spoke, a shot came from the left direction from her and Nealo. One bullet pierced her stomach deeply. "I'm hit!" She yelled with a cracked voice. Another shot instantly punctured her neck with a splash of blood gushing out of her armor.

"Damn!" Nealo retaliated hastily firing his pistol toward the masked armored shooter on the left with precise aim and landing each of his four special shots that pierced the shooter's armor.

Roscoe crouched to the left and picked up his rifle then quickly fired a shot at Nealo but none of the shots injured him while Roscoe stood dumbfounded. "What kind of armor are you wearing?!"

Nealo firmly walking closer to him with his pistol aimed at his Roscoe's forehead. Roscoe began to panic knowing he is good as dead.

"No! Please… wait don't kill me! Don't you need me for questioning?!"

"Shut the… fuck up!!"

"Look, I can get you to work for the Mad Doctor, easy. He'll love to have his enemies on his side. It will make him stronger… please just don't ki…"

Seconds before he could finish his plea, Nealo shot him two times in the lower chest area, one directly to the heart and one shot to his head. Nealo breathing heavy with anger disclosed around his face and his finger still on the trigger as if he wanted to fire his pistol some more for the hell of it.

Nealo looked around to see if he could spot anymore shooters in the shadows but no one else was there. He turned around then walked vigorously back to Maya and realized she got hit badly in the stomach and neck with a special bullet that can impale her suit and expands when fired into the target. Her neck wound didn't expand as much as her stomach and she is presumed to be still breathing according to the indications on her suit.

Seeing a comrade down made him furious and reminded him how it was back in his younger days as a soldier. Nealo unlocked her partially glass Grainian Tech helmet and called for the support teams and medical assistance.

He heard a noise behind him. *"It couldn't be."* He thought and it was indeed Roscoe trying to slowly get up. Nealo recognized a familiar power source behind him then he leisurely turned around and there he saw Roscoe unbelievably on his two feet again.

Maya lying down flat and wouldn't move while Nealo ran towards Roscoe with fury in his eyes. His rage unwinding like a spooling turbine as he held his neck, pushing him on to the wall. A familiar life force caught his attention, he unlocked his helmet, squinting his eyes looking deeper behind the mirage of this unknown entity—

only to encounter something he would never even imagine seeing.

"Ne… Neecho?" Nealo puzzled with a faint voice.

"Your real Roscoe is over there to the right of you. The same way you shot me is the exact same way I shot him, three to the body and one to the head. You're my father I know your style."

Stuck with this awful misperception, he implored his conscious to depict this scenery as a delusion or just a dream. "But… but why?"

"Now I see the truth to what you said you wouldn't do yesterday."

Nealo lets go off his son in his disguised Roscoe body, shapeshifting ability from his Netron Suit.

"I guess this is like . . . father like son huh?" Neecho continued.

Still more questions sprinting through Nealo's mind as he looked away to the floor while Neecho morphed himself into the wall then vanished.

"Nealo! . . . Maya! Oh shit, Maya… Is that Medical assistance on its way?" Vixen asking for backup on her radio.

Vixen then used medical cloth from her first aid kit in her suit to cover both her wounds to stop the bleedings.

The real Roscoe had a trail of blood on to where he is lying down dead after Neecho allegedly shot him in the head and body, Neecho dragged Roscoe from behind his desk. This only gave the impression that Neecho planned everything just to see if his father would kill another human again which he promised him not to do again and keep it in the past with his military days. Neecho hid Roscoe's dead body from Nealo's Netron vision so he could lure him in without any suspicion.

"Oh damn… Maya…" Gerbs grieved.

"Damn, where is that medical?" Kenneth worried.

"They're coming, as soon as they're here, she'll be fine. The armor did well protecting her neck, only a partially deep graze but her stomach though is more severe but she'll live." Vixen answered.

"Good."

"All of these chemicals, it looks like Roscoe was working for Sagan after all."

"Yeah, this is Sagan written all over it."

"Hm, I have a feeling our next mission is going to be more difficult than this one."

"Well, we are prepared for it as long as we have General Nealo with us." Gerbs added.

Vixen walked over to Nealo while he is staring at Roscoe's dead body while the paramedics arrived to pick him up.

"You did a good job General... My guys and I would like you to stay."

Nealo looked at her then shook his head up and down then looked back at Roscoe's dead body while paramedics crowded over him.

"Just by looking at what I did reminds me why I resigned. It's not because I'm old it's because of what I'm capable of."

"These skills that you have is well needed in our field. Think about it." Vixen said as she walked away from him.

Nealo looked at Vixen as the paramedics took Maya then he turned his head slightly to the wall.

<u>*The Never Too Early Café*—</u>

Luka Shale Jr. is still at the café with his head down taking a quick nap. His body moved slightly reacting to a noise coming from footsteps.

"Aye! Aye! Get up 'Mister Loaded with cash'." Said a man snapping his fingers waking up Luka.

223

"Huh…"

"It's closing time, which means you're coming with us."

The man is associated with a group of seven men which seemed to be gang members with illegal fed automatic rifles in their hands.

"This place is twenty-four seven."

"We shut it down now, therefore, the rules changed."

Luka moved backwards in his chair then unexpectedly, an African American man with high tech gloves appeared behind them and said—

"You guys have got it all wrong, I'm the owner and I'm sure I made this place a twenty-four-hour spot."

"Well, we don't give a shit what you are. Business hours have changed."

"Alright, if you say so."

The man and his gang aimed their guns at the owner. The café owner quickly pulled out a device from his pocket and instantly the illegal guns were disarmed.

"What the fuck?"

"It's not fucking shooting! I swore I took it off the safety and there shouldn't be any AP chip in there!"

"So is mine."

"We all modified our firearms before we came here . . . Fuck it, let's brawl."

"Now that's more like it, slow killing with more effort, a real man's way." The café owner said.

All eight men circled the café owner while he gets into a martial art fighting stance. One man reached at the owner from behind.

The café owner leaned to the side then caught his arm then immediately snaps it in half then pushed him at full force to a table landing on it and smashing it. Two other men came from one opposite direction, then the owner quickly did a jump kick pushing the two men back.

The café owner landed on his feet as the two other men in front of him approached with knives. He grabbed one guy's arm from the bottom and uses it to stab himself in the eye. Screaming coming from the attacking man as the other gets punched in the face knocking him back.

The café owner's sclera revealed red veins as if it was diluted blood vessels affixing to his pupils. He drew three chains with baseball sized flail balls at each end out from his high-tech forearm guard on his right arm. Acting like a skillful warrior, he swung the Morning Star weapons like a windmill then tossed it at one of the man's neck wrapping the chains around. The flail ball hits the man's right cheek and the spikes went through his skin as the chains are still connected to the user's forearm guard. He pulls down, ripping the side of the man's face off revealing just a piece of flesh as his skin dangled from the metal flail. His neck bone snapped then the café owner pulled out another pair of three chains with a flail ball at each end swinging all six advanced Morning Star weapons slicing all seven attackers in every direction around him.

"Now I gotta clean this mess up, good thing my employees let the customers out… Less witnesses."

"Thanks man. I don't know what these guys were here for."

"No problem. Here's my card, my name is Joe, but you can call me 'the Kleaner' with a 'K', Gigantica's most successful and highest paid bounty hunter."

"I see . . . you're a Death Angel and that weapon is made of Tektonium steel."

"Yes… You're absolutely right and this gadget here, the gun disarmer—is made from your father."

"Hm."—Luka smiled at him.

Unknown area—

Paintings of Mayor Tyson Roland, Tyson's son Mike Roland, General Zion, Detective Cane Holloway and Nealo along with many more are hung up on the walls in a large office room.

"Real art, art that was once alive, art from actual corpses shredded down to substitute as flour. Nevertheless, beautiful I must say. Such magnificent sentiments, it's a shame not much can witness true art and creativity . . . Hmm—Sergeant Roscoe's Base has been confiscated. I'm certain this is the work of General Zion and maybe he had a little help from Nealo. Hmm, that man's skills are just not of the ordinary." Dr. Rogue Sagan said.

"I agree sir . . . that Nealo guy is something else, must be a machine. He's single-handedly taken down some of the worst men, mass murderers, terrorists..." Said one of Dr. Sagan's men getting oral sex from an android that resembled a real woman.

"Hm, a machine? No, more like extraterrestrial. The government has their little ways with secrets."

"I agree. So, what… aahh'! Damn girl! Slow down on it… yeeah'… gentle… yeeeaah'… gentle now… just like that . . . So, what are you going to do now sir?"

"Now? I'm going to continue what I've always been doing . . . Dominate and kill everyone."

"Um… Except for me, right? I mean… I'm your main man."

Sagan turned his head halfway towards his guard then sneered deviously.

"Yeah, you can say that…"

THIRTEEN

LTV Police Precinct, Luka Shale Jr. and Detective Cane Holloway is in the interrogation room trying to figure out what really happened with his daughter. Detective Holloway held his forehead and started to massage it with the tip of his fingers then rubbed his right eyelids indicating a thinking and stressful manner.

"Ok, let me get this straight—you were in your room and your wife comes in saying she can't find your daughter Melissa anywhere in the house. It's nighttime and you went searching outside in the plague, which is odd that you didn't get infected… You do know a mask isn't enough to protect you from the Genchi. Right?"

"Yeah but somehow I survived…"

"Very odd but then you found her at the barn unconscious. Your wife saw that Melissa wrote something. When she arrived at the hospital, she is already presumed dead. Now you're saying you think it wasn't suicide."

"Yes, I know my daughter very well. She was never depressed—I believe someone killed her!!"

"Ok… Well, sometimes depression is hidden in some people, this is a disorder that has many ways of showing itself."

"No! No! I don't wanna' hear that shit!"

"The autopsy report confirmed no signs of force, no stoppage of breath but that happens overtime when you are infected with Genchi."

"Hmm."

"Luka, we will investigate further but for now it's ruled a suicide—we will investigate further in the house."

"You're saying maybe one of us did it?"

"It's the procedure Luka."

Luka shook his head in renunciation then Cane got up from his seat then said—

"Now as for your horse, investigators found that he was indeed sick and dying of his last breath before you punctured him with your heated beam knife. Now technically you have the right to do so, only, if the animal was extremely ill. Regular animals and Genchi virus don't do too well so... yeah, that's sums it up."

Luka nodded his head then looked away to his left then Cane exited the room.

Cane saw Pamela Shale and Kathleen Shale in the lobby. He pursed his lips showing a bit of distress then walked pass them going seven doors down in the hallway. He entered another interrogation room and there he was, Garrett Lynch.

"There he is, the guy with the huge balls that stole police tech from us!"

Garrett had gotten seized by authorities at the hospital when Ki-Yale brought him there and he's in this unsolicited situation staring at the table and hardly blinked. Cane placed both of his fists on the table across from him.

"How did you get this suit Garrett? Hm? Maybe you discreetly worked with a few police officers then Sagan gave the waypoint by hacking satellite systems to avoid police illegal Fed gun detecting devices?"

He paused then slowly got closer to Garrett. "Who are you working for? Dr. Sagan? Hmmm? You know you're working for a man that will kill you just for looking at him wrong."

"So, you should obviously know that if I tell you who I'm working for I will get killed. Right?"

"Oh, you finally talk! . . . But yes, I am aware of that… I can put you in protective custody you know."

"Including the cops…"

"Hm, my guys are well trained Garrett, especially for Sagan… We just need to find him."

"Well, I'm just going to tell you anyway…." Garrett said then revealed a bright smile and looking at Holloway.

Holloway squinted then seconds later he reached out to cover Garrett's mouth and yelled

"Wait!!"—

Garrett had his hands cuffed but he can still push away the detective and so he did. He pushed Cane away with his legs and immediately screamed— "I'M WORKING FOR THE MAD DOCTOR!!"

Within seconds that Garrett said his name an explosive device detonated from Garrett's body. The explosion impacted all around the room as the blaze escaped through the walls thrashing a few officers in the hallway. Pamela and Kathleen drastically got up then ducked their heads. Pamela quickly grabbed her daughter then looked up and saw smoke bursting her way. She glanced at the one-way mirror and sighted Luka standing. The moment took a peculiar turn, Pamela dazed and confused while he looked right at her as if he can see her.

Little Tree Ville—

Life is precious in LTV and is still in grave danger as the Genchi virus roamed around the village. People are now mostly indoors, doctors treating patients at the hospitals and androids are visiting homes providing vaccines and medical assistance. Corruption becoming rampant as people unable to attend grocery stores for food supply. Rampage arose in the eastern side, the slums where the Apaki Warriors reside. Nothing but violence, theft and some are begging for better days all because of individuals who chooses to inflict harm.

Three men with stolen police suits similar to Garrett's suit were mobile around Little Tree Ville searching for a young boy with capabilities disrupting Sagan's devious ways. Since there isn't a certain location that was elaborated on, these men were having difficulty finding the boy, but they need to find him and execute him or else consequences will happen.

"You think this boy is really what Push said he is?" Asked one man with a muffled voice underneath his tech mask.

"I doubt it and if he is, I'm sure the kid is all flesh and bones and bleed just like us. Just another human working with the military trying to take down out our boss."

"I hope so. What if the kid is really bullet proof and heat ray proof with extended strength?"

"Dude, it's probably some military microchip that makes the anti AP bullets stop at the body making it look like it bounced off the kid or something and that strength, he's probably a trained muscle boy." Said the man in the middle.

"What about the lightning?"

"Look you pussy, there's nothing out there you need to worry about. All that shit is rigged bullshit! It's all make-believe… Just watch and see when I pull this kid's card."

"Hm,'… Yeah, he ain't shit."

"Now that's the spirit!"

LTV Hospital—

Ever since the incident of the Genchi virus spreading through the village medics performed their duties nonstop and doing the best they can to ensure that patients get the treatment they need.

"We tried everything. This patient is one of our worst ones yet, she mutated until her insides were outside. It's unbearable."

"You did everything you could Doctor."

"Now we need to notify another devastating news to family members . . . When will this tragedy end?"

One doctor and his assistant proceeded down the hallway as stretchers with screaming patients past by them. They reached to the hospital front desk and looked at the list of people that are in need of assistance next.

A few minutes later Xack rushed in the hospital holding Adelia's body with both arms. Using the little strength, he must keep his beloved in his arms. The look of absolute sickness in his face after enduring one horrendous experience.

"I need medical assistance now!!"

"Ok sir, hold on. What's the name?"

"Adelia Woods."

"Ok, just please wait over here—it's a lot that needs assistance sir. We're working as hard as we can."

"Please, just get her to the ER! *Cough—cough—cough.*"

Xack placed Adelia on a chair then coughed again. The front desk attendant recognized fatigue in Xack then precipitously he fell sideward to the floor.

"Oh no." The doctor said as security rushed to him.

City of Atlantis, the Torbino residence—

Deep in the underwater city, sheltered with a large barrier, protecting the city from water entering and sustaining the vast pressures. Fabian was outside of his home cleaning his front yard from dead leaves with a blowing machine. His wife then came out and said—

"I'm heading out, Dorimzy is in his room sleeping and he's not feeling so well."

"Yeah it's cause all of that needling you're giving him—hmm."

"No, it's just a fever."

"Yeah and you think these little serums will help?"

"Fabian... We both agreed to this... he's gonna be a Mega Human Prime but under our command... not the Military's."

"I know, we decided that we make our boy the light of the world someday, giving him some value and purpose... and not some worthless nobody."

"Yes, even if it means that we do the extreme... I will not allow such defaults turn him a stray. I will make sure to it that he fends for himself when the time comes. Near perfection has to be formed from an early age."

"Hm, I wish my parents were like this... providing this much adoration."

"I just hope he sees it like that when he gets older."

"What he's gonna' do? Kill his own parents."

She beheld at him with one eyebrow up then said—

"Considering that he will be a Death Angel, that might be an option for him."

"Do you hear yourself right now? Seeing you being so tolerant about this really scares me Nicole."

"Hmm... Tony wants you to pick him up later from school."

Fabian chuckled after she changed the subject then said—

"Ok... ok I'll pick up the young man."

"And please, no drinking."

"Yeah, yeah I don't drink and drive although I can just switch to full auto pilot."

"You can still get a ticket if you're caught."

"Yeah I know. I won't I promise."

"Whatever."

Chloe is in her room listening to the 21st century's rock music then unexpectedly, her father walked in.

"Oh shit! . . . Dad, you scared the shit out of me."

"Sorry."

"What are you doing?"

"Nothing just checking on you."

"Ok, well I'm fine."

"What's up with you lately?"

"What do you mean Dad?"

"I mean your attitude towards me... Am I doing something wrong?"

"No, you're perfectly fine…"

"C'mon now, that's a lie."

"Ok, yes, there is something wrong."

"Is this cause what we're doing to Dorimzy?"

Chloe looked at her father then turned her head away from him.

"Look, Chloe . . . He has a disorder. These freaking doctors don't even want to do anything about it. All they talk about is prosthetics, he should be walking with real legs and using a real arm. The only solution now is the serums making him perfect with unimaginable power."

"Perfect? Do you hear yourself right now? You and Mom truly changed ever since he was born. Might as well just fucking kill him while you're at it!" She seethed in white hot anger.

Fabian stood there motionless as he scowled at his daughter then she said—

"Look, Dad I'm sorry but—this is messed up. He doesn't deserve this."

He kept the same look then walked up to her then forcibly pushed her on the bed.

"Really Dad?!"

He reached over and held her down on the bed trying to subdue her as she tried to push him off her.

"WHAT ARE YOU DOING?!"

"Sshh, sshh! Shut the fuck up. Shut up . . . you're going to wake up your brother."—Fabian punched his daughter in the face repeatedly as she tried to fight back with blood dripping down her eyes resulting in a cloudy vision. He expressed no remorse, detaining her on the bed some more, being dominant with is strength.

He then unbuckled his pants then continued to hit her in the face. The unbelievable terror ascended as she shrieked at him telling him to stop but he kept going. He pulled her sweatpants and underwear down to her knees and proceeded to penetrate her aggressively. He covered her mouth with his entire hand as she moved left and right feeling the agony and utter pain. He continued to thrust as he groped her down and pressing his entire body on her.

As tears of torment ran down her round cheeks, she turned her head to the right and saw her brother Dorimzy lying on the floor watching her with a phone in his right hand, his only hand.

<u>*The Kafmora residence*</u>—

It's the next day after Ki-Yale's birthday, Ki-Yale and Tajaymae sat down in the living room while their parents Neecho and Demi were standing in front of them and staring at them intimidatingly while the LTV News broadcasted—

"People on the ground mutating and ####! Paramedics on the scene, man it was crazy, then I saw him! I swear it's a little boy flying around and ####! Man, I was like… 'Oh ####! Oh ####!'

*Then the lil' dude stopped a moving train man, it's like #######
incredible!"* Said one man in an interview.

The news reporter then walked over to a police officer
for another interview.

"What is your thoughts officer? Did you see this boy around too?"

*"Yes, my men and I saw the little boy. He helped us with that
impressive strength, his muscles didn't bulk up like a 'Sila Human'
but he lifted the car with ease out the lake."*

Demi paused the TV then said— "Ok... first, the
freaking detention about you making fun a student's
mother that I didn't even know about! And I don't even
know how they didn't call me."

"I aah'... kind of used my powers to drain the electricity
in the Principal's phone, plus I umm' collected the letter
they sent home."

"Really Tajay?!"— "I was going to tell you..."

"Yeah, after you and your brother starting fights? Or
after you skipped school? Huh? Tell me? . . . And you had
the audacity to allow this Ki? Such recklessness!" She
argued.

"He told me to go to school and not to skip but I didn't
listen Mom. We didn't start..." Tajaymae said but got
interrupted by her mother.

"Ki should have called me so I could put some senses
into you but... go on."

"I'm sorry Ma. I just wanted to spend that one whole
day with Ki on his b-day but we didn't start any fights. This
guy came out of nowhere and shot a metal arrow in my
stomach!"

"I think he was after me, but he didn't know it was me
at first because I wasn't in my Netron Suit. He was just
jacking us for the fun of it."

"Well, he came across the wrong kids, but you shouldn't
have attacked back. You should have left the scene and get
Tajay fixed up."

"Sorry, Mom but I just… I just don't go by your logic… He should be stopped before anyone else gets hurt and that's what I did… I stopped him."

"Ok, what about Tajaymae?! Your sister was hurt..."

"Yes, but she fixed herself up with her plasma. I even checked her before I decided to defend myself and my sister, if I didn't, he probably would have shot her again while we're leaving the scene."

"I like that you want to help the world son, but your mom is right. Luckily Tajaymae didn't get infected by the viruses, I guess she's immune without a suit like us but if she didn't use her plasma to heal her wound, she wouldn't be sitting next to you right now." Neecho said with his arms folded.

"I was obviously thinking rationally." Tajaymae muttered.

"Hm, now, we have to lay low… You don't want other humans to get the idea of not having us here…."

"No Dad... it shouldn't be that way." He countered. "Why? You want to be a celebrity now?"

"No Mom."

"Ok then, if I'm not mistaken it was confirmed that the Mayor of LTV ordered you to go after Dr. Sagan?"

"On the contrary Mom… I was the one that implemented that decision and its ok I..."

"Ok? I don't know how the Mayor would let a minor go on a mission against one of the most dangerous men in history."

"Ma, I showed him my powers and he approved of it. I'm not just a minor, I'm considered a Mega Human on my social security documents and I'm not even fully human."

"Yes, a Mega Human on file because you were registered as a Mega Intellectual Individual or Super Genius as they call now."

"Hm', I think he spoke to him in his Netron Suit." Neecho added.

"Yes, I did... I was going to tell you about the suit Dad, but I hardly see you, you're mostly at work..."

"I know, your grandpa tells me everything."

"Ok, so they don't know my human form, so this is good."

"Good? So now what? You gonna be a hero? You're gonna, go after Sagan and then kill him!?"—Neecho badgered.

"No Dad! I'm going to turn him in and let the authorities deal with him."

"Ki-Yale . . . I don't want you going out there fighting that man!" She demanded.

"That goes for you too Tajaymae. I know you were thinking about it!" Neecho raised his voice a bit.

"No, I've seen people die in front of me all because of that virus . . . I'm going after Sagan! I'm going after him and it's time for the world to see who we really are . . . Who I really am . . .? I'm royalty—and I won't have anyone order me around..." He scowled at his parents then walked out the living room.

"What!?" Demi blurted.

"Hmm, let him go." Neecho said.

Tajaymae still seated staring at her parent's then Demi shook her head and rolled her eyes then started walking away.

Ki-Yale now all alone walking through the woods of Little Tree Ville after leaving the house without his parents knowing. The trees are still big as forest trees, he elevated into the air then looked over the trees for a few seconds. He changed into his Netron Suit then flew towards an arbitrary location, going about three hundred miles an hour.

"No! I want my village to be restored! I have to make my own decisions from now on and no one will stop me." Ki-Yale thought then he began to daydream—

<u>Little Tree Ville, year 2319</u>—

It's the evening time, in a junkyard on their way home from school. Narrken and Ki-Yale tried to see who is currently better in terms of strength which has been a norm ever since they found out about their abilities. Ki-Yale struggled to hold up a car crusher machine while Narrken lectured him on how to lift—

"Nooo' Ki, that's not how you do it. You must lift with your legs. You have more strength in your legs than you do in your arms. Bend your hips and knees." Narrken said with a slim body and medium skin tone.

"I know bro. I'm just... Raagh'! Ok, I give up, this is way too heavy." Ki-Yale said while his body fluctuated.

"Gaagh', don't hurt yourself! Let me try now. It looks like you're shaking man, let me try..." Narrken said in a cocky tone as he smirked.

"Ok, ok."

"Stay right there don't move."

Narrken went underneath the car crusher machine that Ki-Yale is holding up and puts his one hand on the crusher.

"You can let go now."

"You sure Ken?"

"Yes, let go bro."

Ki-Yale lets go and jumped off the machine then he turned his head around in his direction and said "Woah..."

"One handed like a pro!"

"It's cool . . . I'll be stronger than you one day."

"When that day comes lil' bro—remind me to pinch you so you can wake up from your dream land."

"Whatever bro."

"C'mon we gotta' go home."

"Yeah."

Narrken jumped out of the crusher machine and let's go causing it to slam down making a loud sound, 200 tons of heavy metal hitting metal.

"Wow, Kafmora means Royal Family, this Zenith language… does it really exists?"

"C'mon Ki, after all these special abilities and you still don't believe we're part aliens? We both witnessed the Book of Edu, I've never seen such a functional book that's made out of crystals."

"Everything is just still so baffling."

"Yeah, it is a little crazy… We still have to fulfill the prophecy and tonight is the night we will find out who is the new Netro!"

"You already know that's you bro. You're stronger, smarter and you're the first-born child."

"It could be Oji too or even you Ki! It's all up to the Book of Edu."

"What if it's actually Tajaymae and we have the first Netron princess that bears the name Netro… Hmm, Princess Netro Two. Wouldn't that be something?" Ki-Yale said as he stepped over a puddle.

"Yeah but the book said it's actually a prince again, no princess."

"Yeah well, whoever is going to be Netro will have a lot of responsibilities and will have to go up against the evil ruler of the Opposites!"

"Pfft, evil don't scare me!"

"Nothing scares you Narrken…" He cooed.

"Yup! You gotta be brave! Get a slogan for yourself that pushes you."

"A slogan huh?" Ki-Yale said twisting his lips to the left side and raising his eyebrows.

"Yeah… remember sometimes I would say 'I got the heart of a lion'? That saying it gives me motivation all the time." Narrken said smiling and slightly slapping his chest three times with his fist.

"Ooh I see now. I got the heart of a lion. Yeah! I love that! It makes me feel brave already!" He exulted.

"Told you, sometimes you say things with some meaning, and it gives that extra push to have courage. Now, I want you to get one for yourself and I promise you, you'll go up against anything."

"Yeah Ken... You ain't 'lyyying'. Ha! You get it lion and lying." He grinned.

"Oooh, I knew you were going to say that... The freaking joke is like decades old."

They both continued to walk home then suddenly— "C'mon let's go down this block." Narrken said.

"Hilton Street? That's where all the mischievous older kids hang out. Mom said never go there." Ki-Yale stammered.

"And Dad never said… 'Never go there'."

"What?"

"C'mon Ki-Yale, don't be a pussy..."

"Heeey', bad word!" He hummed.

"Look, its a couple of goons' right over there…" Narrken said as he began to walk forward.

"Yeah, I see them. Ken? . . .What are you going to do?"

"I'm going to kick their lame asses."

"For what? Hey… Hey!" Ki-Yale whispered with a high-pitched voice.

"Woah. Who is this little guy?" Said one of the teen boys.

Narrken punched the teen in the genitals. "Aagh!!" The teen boy yelled.

"Oooh shit! Lil' dude decked you in the Nuts!" Said another teen boy as Narrken smirked

"This shit hurts yo! What the fuck kid? I think—I think one of my balls popped!"

Narrken continued to punch him in the face.

"Woah, kid that's enough!"

"This kid is crazy."

One of them tried to grab him but Narrken held his hand tight then hits the teen in the face knocking him out. Ki-Yale didn't participate in such behavior with his brother because he thought it was wrong as he stood behind a tree, barely beholding Narrken beating up all the teen boys.

<u>*Later at the Kafmora residence in Little Tree Ville*</u>—

"Woah! Boys, you're home early." Nealo said.

"Yes, we are Granddad. We just can't wait to get the results." Narrken said.

"Well the book has finally concluded. You boys need to come with me."

"Ok Granddad..."

"Alright, here goes." Ki-Yale nervously said as they followed Nealo to the basement then stumbled upon their father.

"Hello my sons."

"What's up Dad?!" Narrken and Ki-Yale spoke at the same time, thrilled to see their father.

"You want to do the honors Neecho?"

"Yeah. Why not...?" He chirped as he opened the Netron Book of Edu and immediately a bright light appeared from the book.

As crystals widely flew around in a spiral helix curve from the book as the Netron symbol appeared as if it's a hologram.

"Have a seat both of you . . . as you know the book has conclude that one of you will be known as 'Netro Two'. Now this is not our decision entirely, the Book of Edu also comes into play. The book simply deciphers who is the next Netro. We can argue with the book and say who it should be thinking that somehow the book will change its mind but, most likely that's not going to happen." Neecho said then he continued—

"Ok, before I announce who is the next Netro, I have to tell you the responsibilities of such a prince. Netro shall be a worrier and protect the Netron species at all costs, Netro shall not kill, rape, enslave their own species and the same goes for other species as well. Netro shall always take charge and be a prosperous leader, a prince or princess must evolve into a king or queen, granting such royalty full control and order over all Netrons. Netro must overcome all evil that

dwells amongst the Netron race and if need be… the universe. Do you understand these responsibilities?"

"Yes sir." They both said at the same time sitting on floating chairs.

"Ok now I will pronounce the new Netro and the first prince to carry that name…" Neecho said then he paused.

Ki-Yale looked at Narrken and saw that he had full confidence on his face, as if he already knew that it would be his name then unexpectedly— "Ki-Yale."

"Yes Dad?" Ki-Yale answered.

"It's you son."

"It's me what?"

Narrken glanced at everyone with a feeling of disapproval.

"It's you . . . You're the new Netro."

"No way…" Ki-Yale astonished.

"Yes, way… According to the book, it is indeed you my grandson. When the book analyzes both of you, it reads that you are the one."

"My son—you are now Netro Two."

"What?" Narrken astonished.

"Wow, I thought… I thought it would be Narrken."

"So, did I son."

Both Neecho and Nealo looked at Narrken and saw that his face is totally confused and misguided. "Narrken… you are still royalty. You have the same blood as Ki's." Neecho said.

"Hfm', but—but I'm not Netro Two! . . . I feel betrayed!"

"Betrayed?" Neecho wondered.

"I wanted this a lot. I constantly dreamed of this day father… I bet you didn't even try to change the book's choice."

Neecho gulped as he stared at his son then Narrken continued to speak— "Let me ask both of you something… Who was the original choice before you looked at the book?"

"It was… it was you Narrken." Nealo said.

Narrken immediately shook his head in disappointment then he turned away from them. "Yeah right." Narrken seethed.

"Son…" Neecho said as Narrken started to walk with aggression up the stairs.

"I don't want to heeaar'—none of that—son bullshit! I was supposed to be the one, you all were crowding over me—the first born to be Netro! Father… your exact words to me was… 'Ken, you will be the one! I promise'… Forget this, I'm out…" Narrken argued with a stormy demeanor. *"Out where?!"* Neecho disturbed. *"Bro…"*

"Don't 'bro' me Ki-Yale!" He huffed as he stomped his feet up the stairs while Ki-Yale gawked with his eyes wide open and breathing heavily enduring the intensity.

Narrken went outside the house then Ki-Yale ran upstairs to follow him, by the time he exited the house his brother disappeared. Ki-Yale then went out searching for him in the woods of LTV to see if he could cheer him up.

"Ken! Ken! Where are you going bro?!" Ki-Yale searched for an hour and a half and still no sign of him, then moments later— *"I know the book made its choice, but I thought Narrken was going to get it for sure."* Neecho said.

"Let's go talk to him, he should calm down by now." Nealo said.

"Narrrkennn!" Ki-Yale shouted his brother's name.

He ceased and turned his head— *"Woah…"* His face was bright as the sun displaying relief, beholding Narrken sitting on the bridge which is on top of a waterfall looking down at the water.

He ogled at him recognizing that he was truly unhappy with this entire outcome. With a sound mind, he decided to make his move, walking closer and prepared to speak to his brother. *"Nar…"*—the rest was just his breath as Ki-Yale noticed what it appeared to be an older person in an all-black hoodie, all black balaclava and overall black outfit quickly running up to Narrken. Narrken startled, looking to the side as the hooded person is only a few steps away but before he could react. The unknown person shot him with a beam from an illegal Fed gun and grabbed him with one arm locked around his neck.

"NO!!"

The person ran with Narrken into the woods as Ki-Yale quickly tried to follow them, but the hooded person was too fast to keep up with. Losing them in the woods as the darkness of the night consumed his abstinent sight.

"No, no, no, no bro..." He panicked as tears ran down his cheeks.

"DAAAAD!!" Ki-Yale yelled as loud as he can and standing motionless screaming. The echoes surged through the village alerting Neecho.

He gathered the sound of his son's voice then instantly flew light speed towards Ki-Yale's location as Nealo followed.

"Ki-Yale... What happen?!" Neecho worried.

"Someone... someone took Narrken!" He said with tears covering his mouth.

With no hesitation, Neecho and Nealo went searching for him but nowhere to be found.

<u>*Present time*</u>—

"Let me guess, thinking about your brother again huh?" Neecho asked creeping up about six feet behind Ki-Yale in the sky.

"I miss him a lot father." He admitted.

"So, do I son and I do believe he's still out there."— "Where could he possibly be?"

"I don't know... I just don't know..."

"Hm,'... well I believe he's still out there too and I'm going to find him one day. But first, I'm going after Sagan and turn him in." He said clasping his fists.

"Hm." Neecho uttered while floating towards his son then asked— "So you think going after Sagan will get you answers?"

Ki-Yale kept silent for a few seconds looking down to the left then said—

"Yes… I don't know, maybe…"

"Your name is imprinted in the book, which comes with many tasks."

"Yes, and I'm taking on those tasks."

"Hm, I see… I see you really want to take action now." Neecho glowered at him, then slowly blinked and instantly without any time for Ki-Yale to react, he used his right hand and smacked his son across the face.

He smacked him so hard you could hear it about two miles away. Ki-Yale's head turned to his right along with his body. He's felt nothing but being baffled while his father said—

"Yes, you are Netro Two, which has authority over every Netron including me and you will be a king someday, but you are still my son, I'm your father and Demi is your mother. So, whatever we I say you should obey . . . but since you think you're mature enough I will let you do your own thing for now . . . and we will see how that goes."

Neecho squinted at him then flew away precipitously, leaving his son touching his cheek. Ki-Yale breathing heavily and seemed generally upset, he held his jaw back in place while looking down with a slight red mark on his cheek.

FOURTEEN

The next day, 8:34am at the Roland residence—

"Hmmmm'…" The lust for boundless stimulation in the air with the stench of physical attraction reeking. "Yeah! Oh, fuck yeah…"

"Aah, aah… Oooh' shit!" His sex android Helen moaned while wearing her sexy mesh lace lingerie that was crotchless and exposed her breasts with open cups.

Androids that programmed strictly for sex, they pose as anyone eighteen and up, usually someone's favorite porn star or someone that they truly lust over. Any voice, any hair, any weight, any height, any shape and much more modifications can be done to the body. It's up to the user to buy whatever clothes for the android. They are laterally symmetrical, bipedal and built with insides like humans and private parts like humans. They are ninety percent humanoid and ten percent robotic, so humanlike you wouldn't notice the difference just by touching, hearing, looking, or smelling them. Their insides and outs are extremely realistic, so realistic people go crazy for them. You can program them for any desired sexual mood, any kinky ideas or fetishes. They produce absolute sexual sensation allowing climax for the user. These robots obviously cannot produce babies, and therefore the creator—Valentino Cruz, is making a fortune every year. This was first produced in year 2265 and only six percent of mechanical failures worldwide since then.

Tyson and his android lady friend Helen fondling in his room and getting busy, pounded Helen from the back. "Relax baby, take it like a champ."

"Yeah beat this pussy up!! Beat it up! Beat it up!!" She yelled as Tyson stroked harder.

"Oh my God! Oh my God!" He sang loudly.

Tyson's son Mike walked by his father's room and heard the sexual noises. Despite the awkward rackets, he continued to the closet down the hall. Inside this closet is the device that his father mentioned earlier when Mike wanted to go with Ki-Yale to Crouton Village. Mike opened the closet and retrieved the device. This device is not just a device it's a weapon created by Tyson registered under the Gigantica Government and only arranged for Mike just in case anything was to go down within his residence.

<u>The Kafmora residence—</u>

"I apologize for talking to you like that earlier Mom. It was wrong and…"

He paused as Demi rubbernecked at him for a moment with her eyelids low then said—

"Apology accepted son. It was the heat of the moment and the passion you have for this village won't make anyone stop you… even I can't stop you. Now, go out there and make me proud."

"Yes, Mom I will."

Ki-Yale readied his gear for the tournament which were three bags of clothes and hygiene supplies. He walked down the hallway then realized Oji's room door is open. He slightly opened it to check up on him and saw that he is fast asleep he took the elevator down to the living room then gave his mother a kiss and a hug then went outside and saw Tajaymae. She got her hair braided by her mom and is now being trained by her grandpa while Ki-Yale is walking by and saying his goodbyes. Ki-Yale also has a new hairstyle, his hair grew about six inches then he decided to do miniature twists on the top and his sides faded.

He puts his hand on his backpack while his mother stares at him. She walked up to him and gave him a hug from behind. "Be safe son, please. I love you."

"I will and I love you too Mom." He said as he clenched her arm that's wrapped around his chest.

"Hey, be careful out there, I don't want another missing brother. Ok you goof ball?" Tajaymae said with an ephemeral smile.

"I promise that won't happen sis." Ki-Yale responded giving his sister a hug.

He began to leave the property then suddenly— "Tajaymae." Demi called.

"Yes Mom."

"How about you go ahead and accompany your brother."

"What do you mean?" She queried.

"Go ahead silly! Go with your brother."

Ki-Yale stood at the front door and about to close it.

"Really Mom?! Dad?!"

"Hurry up before he goes far without you." Neecho said.

Tajaymae ran to the elevator to her room and packed her things quickly, then a few minutes later— "Thank you my beloved parents!" She expressed her gratitude as Demi reached in for a hug.

"I love you Tajay, be safe."

"I love you too Mom."

"Now go kick some ass baby girl!" Demi cheered and hugging her firmly.

Ki-Yale changed in his Netron Suit which contained all his belongings, prowled down a pathway to Nack's place. This saved him from carrying his bags and kept his hands free.

"Wait bro, I'm coming with you!" Tajaymae yelled running towards him.

"What? Are you sure sis?" He surprisingly asked.

"Yes, Mom and Dad said its ok. We just have to be vigilant that's all."

"Alright—let's go."

Neecho appeared from his room unto the kitchen to see his wife.

"Hey." He said leaning on the table chair.

"Hey." Demi replied with a paper towel in her hand.

"Well, there he goes..."

"Yep. He's only getting older not younger..."

"Hmm, I smacked him across the face yesterday."

She blatantly looked at him for five seconds then said—"Well, he must have been in his Netron Suit cause' I didn't see any bruise or a big red palm mark on his face."

"Yes, and I felt it was necessary."

"You wanted him to be disciplined for the way he talked to you yesterday and I understand... I would have done the same thing."

"Let's just hope he succeeds. It's the first time we truly showed ourselves to the world. I mean it's only Ki-Yale that did the exposure part, but people will suspect there are more among them."

"Well, I'm a human and I approve of you. I'm sure others will approve of you, Ki, Tajay, Oji and your dad." Demi said then she puts her arms around Neecho's neck and looking up at him.

"After the conflict against the Grainians, some might think otherwise."

"It's about time you get here."

"I had to ah—say my goodbyes."

"I know. What's up Tajaymae? You're coming too?"

"What's up super brain? Yes, I'm tagging along."

"You took a vaccine, right?" Ki-Yale asked Nack.

"Yeah of course."

Ki-Yale exited Nack's house along with Nack and Tajaymae. They are now walking down the pathway that is owned by the dormitory where Nack is living in.

"These trees… It's like a disrespect to the Village."

"Yeah, it's messed up." Ki-Yale said then he strode in the front leading the way out of the driveway.

As soon as Ki-Yale turned the corner, three men in police suits like what Garrett Lynch was wearing—blocking the way for them to walk by.

"Oooh' shit! Look the 'N' on his chest." Said one of the men in a muffled voice then another one asked— "Are you the boy we're looking for?"

"Must be the three musketeers… the pedophile edition." Tajaymae taunted.

"Yeah, maybe. I don't know. What do you want?"

"Your life kid."

"Well, let's see you try and take it."

The men with the stolen police armor all fired bullets at Ki-Yale as he remained in his Netron Suit taking all the bullets then Tajaymae said— "These guys are a bunch of dick heads."

"Ha, I thought ya'll learned from this already." Ki-Yale said—

"Apparently they haven't." Mike said randomly loomed about seven feet from behind the men.

"What the…" Said one of the men.

"Mike?" Ki-Yale concerned raising his soft arched eyebrows in surprise.

Mike smiled then uses his weapon that his father made him which is wrapped around his arm. This weapon is called the "Gazen Weapon". The Gazen Weapon took up Mike's entire left arm, but he could still move freely because of bending material around his elbows, wrists and upper arms. Mike simply pressed a button on the weapon then instantly a full body suit was materialized from the weapon including his head along with advanced goggles, mouth and nose protection. This suit is made specially to protect Mike from sharp glass. As soon as the suit was fully equipped, a large clear glasslike cheetah appeared around Mike's body.

"Nice, should have been a lion." Ki-Yale said.

Mike doing a cheetah growl then one of the men with the police suit said—

"You two take care of whatever he is, and I got the wimpy looking boy."

"How did he do that?" Nack asked.

"Beats me…" Tajaymae said while having her arms folded.

Mike with the projected tiger around him attacks the two men shooting at him. With only some of the bullets hitting the projected glass animal instead of hitting Mike, he jumped on one of the men brining him down and swiped his gun away with his cheetah claws then jumped on the other attacker. He grabbed the second man's gun with his cheetah mouth and tossed it fifteen feet on the ground away from him.

"Make your move so you can fail like Garrett did." Ki-Yale jeered.

"Shut up kid!" Said the man in the police suit aiming his grenade launcher at him then fired it. Within seconds, Ki-

Yale deliberately caught the grenade with his teeth then quickly swallowed it.

"What the fuck?" The man in the police suit being astounded.

Mike is hitting the second man in the chest with his cheetah claws rapidly while the first man he jumped on gets up slowly.

The grenade exploded in his stomach causing it to inflate as if there was a basketball under his shirt. His stomach instantly back to normal as smoke slowly exits his mouth then he belched intentionally. Nack showing complete utter shock on his face looking at Ki-Yale then looked at Tajaymae. "What? Don't look at me like that!" She said.

"But... ah... he just... That didn't amaze you?" Nack being confused then Tajaymae looked at her brother's direction then smiled.

"You guys really need to come up with something new." Ki-Yale said then moved towards the assailant and punched him in the face knocking him out. He raised his fist with a burnt orange color glow emitting from his veins turning yellow and imprinted through his black chrome gloves. He then shot his 'Loose Cannon' at the other assailant with the stolen police suit who is about to attack Mike from his rear. The attacker is then knocked out by one single blow from Ki-Yale while Mike roared at his assailant as he gets beaten up with hits that are hard enough to knock him out. The comatose attacker landed on the ground then Mike deactivated his weapon then said— "Thuh'... thanks for having my back."

"You're welcome bro, it's just my reflexes."

"Yeah but um it's fan'... its fancy meeting you here . . . Where are you going?"

"I'm heading to the tournament."

"Guh'... good, so am I."

"Oh, really your dad let you?"

"Well, I wouldn't sah'… say that but I have my ways."

"You talked him into it huh? Well, I had trouble with my parents too, but they changed their minds I did a little talking myself."

"Nice…"

"So that weapon makes you change into animals huh?" Ki-Yale fascinated.

"Yeah, it's… It's pretty cool."

"I agree, very cool! You made this?" Nack said as he walked up to him.

"No, mah'… my father did."

"He must be a super genius… Looks like the projector is sampled by Apaki Jermayin Tech." Nack said analyzing the technology.

"Yeah, my dah'… my dad did a little something. He's the may'… he's the Mayor of Little Ville now."

"Oh, speaking of Mayor." Ki-Yale said then he began to use a mini holographic projector cube from his wrist band that is underneath his suit. "Mister Mayor!"

"*Aye! What's going on kid? What's your status?*" Mayor Tyson asked swiftly answering his call.

"Oh… oh shit… that's my dad." Mike whispered with his eyelids wide open.

"Well, I gathered all my stuff and I'm heading out now."

"*Ok good. Remember, just turn him in and use those powers of yours for good. I have faith in you and your abilities. He's a conning one too, he's always been.*"

"I will try my best sir." Ki-Yale spoke with confidence.

"*Now I have a question for you… Have you seen my son Mike anywhere? It looks like he took off with the weapon that I designed for him.*"

"Oh Mike? Yeah, I found him sir…" Ki-Yale said seconds before Mike whispered—

"Wait…. don't tell him." Mike was too late then Tyson yelled—

"*What? Let me see him!*"

"Damn it…"

"Whoops… Sorry, didn't know you were hiding from him." He whispered to Mike.

Ki-Yale turned the holographic wrist band device the other end so Tyson could see his son. "*There you are! What the hell boy? Where have you been?!*" Tyson bickered.

"I'm going aw'… going out to fight… fight for the greater good!"

"*Fight for the what?! Boy you need to get your ass back over here!*"

"No, I'm goi… I'm going… Whether you like it or not."

"*Kid, don't let me bring a squad other there to man handle you!*"

"Oh… ok, bring em' on, I'll just use the weapon you made me."

"Ok, ok Mr. Mayor. I understand you want him to be safe but . . . He's safe with me. If he wants to go fight for his village. Then, I'd say let him."

"*What?!*"

"With all due respect sir. If you bring a squad here to take him, they would have to go through me and that goes for anyone else out there that wants to attack us."

"*Hhfm', kid…*"

"C'mon Pop. Why yo'… Why you gotta' be like that? I ca'… I can handle myself and Netro has my back."

"*Hm.*" Tyson said, then it was complete silence for thirty seconds.

"Alright I'll… I'll go back home, no ne'… need to start shit." Mike spoke with slightness of doubt in his voice.

"*Alright son, you can go with them. But… I don't want you doing stupid shit out there. Alright? Just be safe! . . . Netro, please take care of my son and bring Sagan in for me… You got this kid!*"

"Yes sir. I will and you know I got the heart of a lion!"

"Thanks Dad." Mike expressed gratitude as he smiled. Tyson grunted then hung up the holographic transmitter.

"Nuh'… now let's go in my truck."— "Well, looks like we have transportation like normal people. I was going to lift everyone and fly."

"Nope! A car is better." Tajaymae said.

"Ok so a car it is then. But first let me introduce my other identity and everyone else."

"Other identity? Ye'… you don't have a mah'… mask on."

"I don't have a mask on but when I take my suit off you won't recognize me. This is a defense mechanism against other species. When changing back to my Netron Suit it can affect your mind, your eyes and your sense of smell, all of your five senses but traditionally the mind and your eyes. But first guys—this is Mike, the Mayor of Little Tree Ville's son. Mike, this my sister Tajaymae—a little brat..."— "WHAT?!"— "And my best friend Nack, a Super Genius..."— "Nice to meet you Mayor's son." Nack said.

"Now here is me without my Netron Suit." Ki-Yale said while Tajaymae squinted her eye at him.

"Ok… ok nice to meet you guys."

"Nice to meet you too." Tajaymae said with a blush.

Within a millisecond, Mike stared at him while Ki-Yale altered back into his regular clothes.

"Woah… Who? Who are you? . . . Aagghh' my head!" Mike being confused by Ki-Yale's change of attires.

"That is very unpleasant, and I know from experience." Nack recalling the incident.

"Now let me change back." Ki-Yale quickly changed back into the Netron Suit in front of Mike.

"Ok my eyes are starting hurt along with my head… Ok! Ok! Make it stop! Make it stop!" Mike suffered the pain.

"It's ok Mike! It will go away soon, just hang in there."

"This is not good…" Nack said.

"He's good right Ki-Yale?"

"He should be fine…"

"Oh… Ok. It's com'… coming to me… It's, it's uh' ok now… I'm ok now."

"You ok man?" Ki-Yale concerned.

"Ye'… yeah, hmmm', I'm good, I'm good."

"Ok, good, you gave me a scare."

Nack contemplates on what just happened as he focused on both.

"He has autism, its mild now after serious treatment was given to him."

"Oh, I see, it's a little risky doing that with his condition though."

"I know, with the reaction but it's not permanent… now that you saw me change once and you should see me change again without a problem."

"Ok ma'… my mind was blacked out for a few seconds...na… now it's coming back and I'm recognizing you."

"Good, I guess we're all set to go." Ki-Yale said.

"Heyyy' everyone!" Said a man running towards them.

"It's your friend Ki-Yale." Tajaymae said.

"Aah no—not this guy."

"Oh, it's him…" Nack said.

"Who's that?" Mike asked.

"A previous drughead. He used to take some hard stuff, he stopped now but he can be really annoying."

"What's up my homiiieees'!? Where ya'll bout' to go today?" Mr. Turd chirped.

Unknown Area—

"You got to be fucking kidding me." Dr. Rogue Sagan said looking through the body cams and listening to the microphones on the men he sent out to kill Ki-Yale.

Some of the body cams from the police suits were facing up to the sky once the men were unconscious which their bodies were flat on the ground.

"I told you—he ain't no ordinary kid." Push said.

"Hmm, well, at least I know Mike Roland will be at the tournament also." He said as he walked up to the window then cracked a tiny smirk.

LTV Hospital—

"Xack Machida… Xack Machida? Xack Machida?" Doctor Damian trying to wake him up.

Xack slowly opened his eyes and saw the doctor over him. He woke up then leaned forward while liberating his glass Katana then placed the sword in defense position.

"I knew this was going to happen. I'm not here to hurt you son, you're at a hospital."

"Hm, I'm not your son."

"Yes, I'm sorry… You're very lucky, you came just in time before the Genchi started to take effect."

"Where is Adelia?"—Xack disarmed his sword then the doctor said.

"She's next door. I successfully cured you—your infection wasn't whole, just a minor sickness. Good thing you came here in time."

"Is she alright?"

"Yes, but she has to recover. She got infected a little worse than you did but it was curable."

"I need to see her." Xack said slowly getting out of the bed.

"I don't think you should walk just yet…"

"Let me see her!"

"Ok . . ."

The doctor assisted Xack into the next room where she is held in a coma, unresponsive. His conscious was set on the unidentified outcome of his beloved. As soon as he entered the room, he gazed at her with a feeling of trepidation then he strode towards her. Adelia's body is wrapped up with rolled gauze ceasing the blood from escaping the decayed skin caused by the mutation process that the doctors aided. He puts his hands on her arm then the doctor said—

"Let me get you a chair Xack."

Dr. Damian, retrieved the chair for him and he slowly sat down while continuously staring at her. His body trembled, thinking to himself. "*Adel... Why does this have to happen to you...? It should have been me.*"— "Please . . . Leave me."

<u>*Atlantis News at 5pm*</u>—

"*This is Selina Davis reporting to you live from the Atlantis News Station at five. In today's news, unbelievable tragic events had occurred as Chloe Torbino was raped by her own father, Fabian Torbino. Atlantis PD was on the scene and captured the father in the act. The caller was a four-year-old impaired child named Dorimzy Torbino. He has no legs and only one arm in which he used to call the police shortly after he heard a suspicious noise from his sister's room.*"

"*It sounded like a preschooler on the phone and I heard the noise in the background and we immediately got to the scene and got the job done. It's amazing, you don't hear stuff like this all the time, the boy called then he went to his sister's room, laid up on the door so he can record what he saw. The kid is very smart.*" Said a police officer conducting his response in a news interview.

"*It's messed up what he did man, that's his own daughter, it's so disgraceful! He should be ashamed and embarrassed; he deserves whatever punishment that's coming to him.*"

"Thank you, ma'am, I appreciate your say on this. Sir... What do you think about this horrific crime?" Asked the male news reporter.

"Yes, I'm a neighbor, I live a couple houses down and I don't know man, it looks like crime is getting higher each year now. It's not like how it was like back in the 2200s—there was crime but not like this. We're living in the prime era with so much to offer like what else do you want?! If this keeps up soon, things will be like the 20th and 21st century all over again."

"What do you think needs to change?"

"History does repeat itself, but I say a stricter system would be a big change. It's already strict but it seems like the system is getting soft... You know what? Lynda Valerie Polara needs to come back! She was the best in office so far."

"Ok, thank you sir. Now back to you Selina."

<u>*Atlantis PD*</u>—

Fabian was held in a jail cell until he faces trial and he was given permission to talk with his loved ones.

Nicole on the other side of the glass glowering at Fabian with repugnance, as he vaguely stared back and having a hard time keeping eye contact. Nicole took her wedding ring off of her finger then gently puts it on the counter. Complete silence and not a single word from each other, she then picked up the wedding ring then gets up as he looked at her with not even a sign of remorse. She walked to the garbage bin and drops the wedding ring in it. He lifted his head up and takes a deep breath then brings his head back down as she walked back to him.

"How could you Fabian? That was your own daughter, your own flesh and blood now you don't even show no sign of guilt. Have you been possessed by a demon? I don't even know you anymore . . . Now I have no sympathy for you... You will pay for what you've done, I swear it, on my mother's grave! Mark my words Fabian, I'm going to make sure they give you the absolute worst… I will never forgive you! I WILL NEVER!!"—Nicole articulated her bottomless antipathy then paused as she took a deep breath. Her face slightly turned red, then she spat at him ensuing the gush of saliva landing on the glass then she scowled while her tears sprung from her eyes. Still no sign of remorse, no retaliation, as he gawked into her eyes without a single blink.

FIFTEEN

<u>The Kafmora residence around 7pm</u>—

Oji bobbing his head, humming and walking down the hallway towards Titus's room. He slowly opened the door and he already knew the large cage was holding him— *"But was the beast stable?"* He thought.

He steps forward as the carpet floor made his shoes less squeaky. Titus heard him anyway and lifted his head from the cage floor.

"Woah… I haven't seen you in a while."

Titus gets up on his feet, growling and looked at him with a menacing facial expression. Oji strolled towards him. "Its ok boy, it's me, Ki-Yale's little brother."

Titus walked closer to the cage bars and growled once more.

"I wish I had powers… Ki-Yale and Tajay is out there getting all the action and I'm here stuck with homework."

Oji is now one foot away from the cage bars as he ogled at Titus. His heart pounded faster while his body shivered as he slowly reached out to touch him. Titus turned his head to the left as he stopped growling and crouched down. Oji is now playing with his hair, prolonging the friendship then seconds later. "What did I tell you about being around Titus?" Demi said standing at the entrance.

"But Mom, he's totally harmless."

"He wasn't so harmless the last time he was out of that thing. He almost bit your head off."

"Ki-Yale said he was just excited…"

"Yeah but we didn't know that for sure." Demi said as she walked closer to the cage.

"I think he should be free Mom."

Demi looked to the cage floor and realized a mechanical book that has a title.

"'How to Linger with Humans… For Mega Animals' . . . Hmm."

"That's his book… he likes to read."

"Yeah I see that…" Demi paused then said—

"C'mon, let's go."

Oji had no choice but to go with his mother. He looked back at Titus for a few seconds wishing he could stay with him more then began walking away.

In the dark skies of Little Tree Ville—

Neecho soaring through over the woods of Little Tree Ville while wearing his Netron Suit. He commanded it to make his entire body to be invisible and intangible. He lowers his flight and goes directly through the trees without any physical touch as if he was a spirit then he ceased and stared at the waterfall ahead of him. His search for Narrken didn't stop for him, he just wants to see his son at least one more time, in person and face to face.

"I could have sworn it would be you Narrken…"

Year 2319—

"I can't wait to be Netro Two… then I'll become a supreme leader of an entire planet."

262

Neecho smiled at his son as they float in the sky with their bodies facing upward and their hands clasped behind their heads.

"What if I was to overthrow the human race?"

"Overthrow the human race?"

"Yes, to be a proper leader for them, establish a new government along with planet Netron. I am half human after all."

"I think they're ok right now. There's only one crisis and that's Sagan, the man who will eventually go down."

"Yes, but time proves that conflicts would never change."

"That's true son, if you think you can manage to be the leader of Netron and humans then so be it but remember, it isn't going to be easy."

"I know..." Narrken paused then said— "I still don't understand how Ki-Yale cannot execute his flying ability yet. He's so flawed and I'm learning so fast, I'm definitely going to be Netro! A king . . . a strong ruler!"

"Hm, each and every one of us is different in some way. Your brother... he will get it eventually. It may not be soon, but he'll get it."

"Yeah, let's just see if he can catch up." Narrken said then began flying in the direction behind Neecho.

"Where are you going?"

"I don't know, anywhere! This flying thing is a new experience for me you know..."

Present time—

"I had so many chances... so many chances of informing you more about things... maybe he would've understood the ways of life better. Your abilities were more evolved, but your heart wasn't. Now I can't fail Ki-Yale like I did you."

<u>*In the woods of Gel Hev*</u>—

Just outside of Little Tree Ville, Nack opened a mechanical cube which has a built-in tent with plenty of indoor supplies. The tent is big as a mobile home and they're proceeding with overnight camping.

"You always got the tech for the right moments." Ki-Yale said in regular clothes sitting next to him and Mr. Turd while Mike is asleep.

"Well, I love to carry various tech around with me. Hopefully I maintain being a superb asset."

"You will Nack, you will."

"Hey Ki-Yale, what does your last name mean?" Mr. Turd said.

"You wanna know what Kafmora really means?"

"Yeah, what does it really mean Ki?"

"Well, my grandfather says it means royal family in the Zenith language."

"The Zenith language?" Mr. Turd asked.

"Yes, the Zenith is only spoken by the Pinnacle and also the royalties of Netron and Dragoon…" He paused with a sniff then said—

"What's that smell? Oh no…"

"Ki-Yale! Your food is burning on the grill!!" Tajaymae shouted from the corner of the tent.

"I know, I know… damn it. You're right next to it Tajay! Why didn't you stop it?" He said while rushing towards the advanced automated grill.

"I'm tired and too lazy to get up."

"Nooo! My beef patty… I put the wrong cooking code." He whined as he took a bite— "Aaah this way too hot!"

"Yo'… you put the wrong cooking code?"

"Yeah I forgot the code for the patty so I just put a random code in! Aagh'!"

"You kno'… you know you could have just looked it up on how to co'… cook a patty on a web search engi'… engine online right?"

"Oh Mike, I totally forgot about that…"

"How could you forget that Ki." Tajaymae said.

"You can call it over burnt beef patty for now on." Mr. Turd said.

"You should fry it some more with your lightning. That would be epic!"

"Tajaaaaaayyyy!!"

Dr. Rogue Sagan beside Henry Luciano facing three off duty military personnel kneeling on the floor with their heads down.

"The Motogon is an extraordinarily source of potential for humanity."

"Yes, changing humans into better entities so that they can never be bullied by outsiders ever again but first there has to be bloodshed." Henry said.

"To be honest with you, I could careless for the people of this word. I just want to see them squeal and suffer, then, everyone will realize that this New World Order that they follow isn't enough to survive against one another and whatever's out there."

"Change will come soon…" Henry paused with a light chuckle then he queried— "Hmm, you sure this is the right thing to do…? Mad Doctor?"

"Yes, I hear a young one with unbelievable abilities is coming after me."

Henry chuckled then said—

"The Mayor is so desperate to put an end to you."

"Oh, I'm sure he is… Whatever weapon that you guys built to take me down it wouldn't be enough."

"No weapon from us, it's all Tyson Roland. He claims that he stumbled upon the boy with amazing abilities." One of the military personnel replied to Sagan.

"Hm, well, Tyson is going to regret orchestrating such foolish moves."

"I'm surprised that any of their fellow operatives hasn't presented themselves here yet. General Zion isn't the one to be so sloppy."

"Oooh, I'm not worried about her. I'm glad she became the new general."

Henry chuckled then said—

"There's always a plan with you."

"Yes, and if I fail… a second option is available and that's you Henry."

"It's more than just possibilities Sagan . . . It took me a while to understand the many characteristics of this world to the point I asked myself why. Why is it so vulnerable?"

"Hmm… we just need another apocalypse, a renewal." Dr. Sagan said as he held his left arm out and palm open.

One Apaki Katana emerged from his left open palm then cuts the heads of the three soldiers off of their torsos.

"Another Android again?"

"I thought you knew this already Henry."

It was an android disguised as Dr. Rogue Sagan. The android version of Sagan began to dismantle itself and revealing mechanical organs. Henry Luciano didn't move, just staring at the android as it triggered its self-destruct mode. Within seconds the android exploded whipping away everything in the room. The windows instantly shattered, releasing the dreaded fumes and burning a few of the trees outside of the abandoned building.

In the woods of Crouton Village—

Inside a large tree hollow, a semi enclosed cavity formed in the trunk. Ryker and Beatrix, guarding what they have left. Seven young coyotes with only five left for them to raise. Two of the pups were presumed taken without a trace and Push does not know anything of it. Ryker being the father watches over Beatrix and his five children huddling around her. Mega Animals have one very impressive feature that humans adore the most, is the ability to speak like humans.

"I know you think what we're doing is wrong." Ryker said walking closer to Beatrix.

"We lost plenty of comrades in battle against the Apaki Warriors and yet we stand by one."

"Yes, but he is working for the same man we're working for."

"I guess we don't have much of a choice Ryker."

Ryker walked closer to his broods then leaned his head onto them. Expressing love and affection, one infant coyote raised its left paw touching his cheek, closing his eyes and rubbing against each other.

"We have to bring them to undergo the speeding growth process… they will be in battle real soon."

"And make them suffer?"

"Like you said Beatrix, we don't have much of a choice. He implanted the devices inside us, in case we disobeyed him. Everything is madness… I don't even want to fight but if it means having a better chance of survival with our children, then so be it."

The next day on the Charroson Bridge, Gel Hev—

A long bridge that is ninety-eight miles long from Little Tree Ville connected to Crouton Village. Mike is driving his full-size diesel engine air truck while Ki-Yale *sitting shotgun* in his Netron Suit, Tajaymae, Nack and Mr. Turd are in the back seats. Ki-Yale revealed his suit's defense mechanism of manipulating the mind when changing in front of Mr. Turd and since he knows, he gladly likes to call Ki-Yale—Netro.

"Clu'… clutch, then down shift—dow'… down shift to third gear and gas. It's all in the timing Netro."

"I see, I see… Can't wait to get my license and start driving, just two more years."

"I ha'… hate the age bullshit'… some pe'… some people my age can't even drive yet alone drive a manual. You kno'… you know whah'… what I'm saying man!? You're smart enough… you passed High School and already heading to take on college level education."

"Yeah back in the 21st century, it was like seventeen or eighteen and up to drive anything. I'm considered a Super Genius and the first semester; I'll be taking the 'Central IQ Test'. The twenty-four-hour test about what everything they teach in college all in one for a local Degree. It's a huge freaking test like two hundred pages long or more and you have to finish that in twelve hours no exceptions"

"Woah, already you're like a Mega Human on a new level." Mr. Turd said.

"Yeah, I'm going to be interviewed and announced as the ever first Super Genius to take the test at fourteen in Gel Hev." Ki-Yale said then smiled and looked at Nack in the back seat of Mike's small air truck.

"What about you Nack? Are you doing the same?" Mr. Turd asked sprinkling drops of his saliva in Nack's direction as Nack leaned back marginally.

"Umm—no, I'm actually going to college and study for engineering physics. That's the major field I'm going for."

"Ok enough of the nerdy stuff, can't wait to beat the crap out of kids." Tajaymae said pounding her right fist onto her left open palm.

"Well… I see who isn't scared you little Purple Haired Devil." Mr. Turd said.

"Purple Haired Devil?"

"No, don't like that nick name? Ok how about Purple Fire Girl! . . . Yeeaaah'."

Tajaymae glared at Mr. Turd then said—"No 'dunking in the turd!'—it's just Tajaymae and I'm the toughest one here. Mommy told me to always be tough."

"So, you're the one that's going kick the most ass huh?" Mr. Turd inquired.

"EVERYONE'S ASS!" She shouted.

"Kicking ass is cool with me but killing is a no go. Hate the idea of murder in this tournament. How can the Crouton Village superiors allow this?" Ki-Yale spluttered.

"It was taken over by Sag'... by Sagan I don't know ho'... how he did but he did and it's impossible at this point fighting for it back. Mo'... most of the population in Crouton Village is youn'... young teens and under. These teens are mostly a buh'... a bunch of runaways subjected to follow Sagan's mutiny and some actually have adults who sup'... supports them in the fights because of other adults placing bets. Sag'... Sagan would even intoxicate some of them with speh'... special drugs so that they guh'... go kill each other for entertainment or work for him. Mo'... most of the android guards are specially trained for Mega Human Primes if they get out of line. Man... It's a lot of crazy shit... wi'... with that village all because of Sagan."

"Hey. Why was your dad so protective of you? I know you are the son of the Mayor but you aren't a baby anymore..." Nack questioned.

"I over... I overlook that title everyday... I ma'... I may be the son of the Mayor but that don't mean shit! I'm just as nor'... I'm just as normal, as everyone else and I should go and fight for my village! There's one thing, he di'... didn't tell you guys, is that he is the brother of Dr. Sagan."

"Say whaaat?" Ki-Yale perplexed.

"Woah…" Nack surprised as Tajaymae eyelids were wide open and her eyebrows lifted.

"Yeah they ain'… they ain't blood brothers but they grew up together in the same house un'… until Sagan's real parents came and murdered my grandparents. As yo'… as you know or may not now, Sagan use to be named Kevin Roland tha'… then he later changed his name to Dr. Rogue Sagan."

"Ooh shiiiaaat!" Mr. Turd blurted. "The media never revealed that info out to the general public…" Nack said.

"I guess that's why your father is stressing to me about bringing Sagan in specifically to him."

"Yea an'… and my dad feels like Sagan is only his problem."

"Nah, he's everyone's problem and the way I see it, anything is possible. We will find him, take him in, then Crouton Village will be back to its own ways. No more wicked ways from Sagan—I'll make sure of it." Ki-Yale said.

"I agree—he's done for." Nack added.

"Hm." Mike muttered as he peeked at his back seats. "Looks lik'… looks like I made everyone stay up with these crazy details."

"Yes, these details are very exciting." Mr. Turd said.

"Yeah I'm surprised my sis is till up! She didn't get any sleep last night and Nack well, he has sleeping habits that's been fumbled."

"Oh yeah brother, now that you mention it…" She yawns loudly then said— "I am tired and I'm about to sleep in the next couple of seconds."

"Yo'… you should ge'… get some sleep too."

"Yeah maybe I should, I haven't slept for two days straight, I mean I don't need any sleep at the moment we Netrons can go months without sleep depending how powerful they are."

"Nuh... now that's crazy and no sleep for two days. Ev... everyone needs their sleep man." Mike said then stopped at a Deli as Tajaymae started to close her eyes and tilting her head to the left.

"True but if I knock out now you won't be able to wake me up so easily."

"Hm, I see... I'm going to geh'... I'm going to get some snacks. Ye'... you want anything?"

"Nah I'm ok, thanks. Just get some Doritos for Tajay and some Baked Crab Chips for Nack." Ki-Yale said.

"Oh, look at you, being the considerate brother."

"Wha'... what about yo'... you Mr. Turd?"

"Aaah... I don't know. Let me go with you Mike."

"Ok an'... and it's on me everyone, juh... just get some sleep everyone. It's going to be another three-hour ride tuh'... to the tournament."

"Three hours? Ok, yeah, I'm going to listen to music till I knock out." Ki-Yale said.

"Thanks Mike." Nack said.

<u>*The Kafmora residence*</u>—

Outside in the balcony Neecho glared into the sunrise as the large trees began to produce more shadows than usual across the driveway. As the wind blew past him his hair propelled to the left. "Anticipating something I suppose." Nealo revealed himself from behind.

"Yes, the troubles, they never go away father."

"Hm, Ki-Yale recently left a few hours ago and you're already worried."

"I've always been worried, every time he walks out this house."

"It's you and me both and I'm sure Demi feels the same way."

"This plague, this torment on this village shouldn't be for Ki-Yale to handle."

"He lives in this village Neecho. Does he not?"

"Yes, but I have this feeling I should be out there with him."

"No, let him and Tajay handle it. They need this and once they put a stop to Sagan humans will see us as allies."

"Still, if you couldn't find Sagan… What makes it so different that Ki-Yale can?"

"Well, I was holding back my abilities and every time I'm closer to finding him he finds a way to evade me. This time Ki-Yale is using his suit without hiding . . . That's what I should've done a long time ago."

"Yeah… and whatever is out there, at any given moment, can acquire him too."

"Hm,'. Do you believe he is after more truth to Narrken's abduction?"

"Yes, knowing my son, he would do whatever to get answers."

"Which is what we should be doing as well."

"We constantly do but we end up in a dead end."

"True but we could give up on many things but giving up on family isn't the Netron way."

"Hm,' . . . I have something to inform you about . . . I should have told you sooner but…"

"Go ahead my son…"

"The other day… I saw Narrken…"

Nealo confusingly stared at his son. "I saw him at the Gel Hev Mini-Mart, it seemed like my mind was playing tricks on me but I saw him and it looked so real… I had to see for myself but once I walked over... He vanished. For once I felt whole again, finding him but I guess the whole thing was just fantasy, a figment of my imagination."

"Hmm."— "No, I just can't believe that it wasn't real. I know I saw him."

A modified remembrance in Tajaymae's dream state projecting unknown motives as her oldest brother sat next to her on the boardwalk over the lake.

"Planet Netron, I wonder what it's like to really live there." He said.

"Grandpa said it's a very large planet in a very large galaxy."

"Yeah and it has one of the strongest gravity-pulls in the universe. This is why we are so naturally strong . . . We need the strength to handle that gravity."

"I guess that makes sense but I'm not strong like you."

"Well, I guess strength isn't your resilient feat as yet."

"Yeah... I have something to ask you Ken."

"Go ahead sis."

"I don't have my Zeal powers yet either and Granddad doesn't know what it is, like no clue at all. I just want powers already!"

"You gotta be patient Tajay, it will come in due time."

"Yeah but I want it now so I can kick some ass."

"Are you having trouble in school?"

"Yes, but not just school, you never know what is out there you know, anyone can come out the blue and attack me."

"Don't worry about what's out there. You just have to be tough and you'll get by... just like dad would tell me. I was getting bullied in school until he man-up and stand up for myself."

"You got bullied in school? Really big brother?"

He sighed then said— "Yeah."

"Wow... I never knew. I would get bullied too about my hair..."

"Hmm."—Narrken looked at his little sister then she perplexedly asked— *"What?"*

He handed her a heliotropium flower that has mechanical square vase that's four cubic inches. *"Take this."*— *"A flower? How am I supposed to defend myself with this?"*

"Its beautiful though, right?"

"Yes, it is very beautiful… and purple."

He tittered then said— "Yes, purple like your hair."

She chuckled then said— "Wow, how thoughtful."

"And its not just any flower Tajay."

"Oh yeah?"

"Yeah… it has a sharp end at the bottom. Press that button."

"Oook?" She blankly asked as she touched the bottom then the miniature square vase released a ten-inch knife. "Woah… that's a big knife…"

"Yes, but don't use it in school though only use it for a bigger peril… in school you use your fists and beat the hell out of those kids who make fun of your hair."

"I could also talk back to them."

"Yes, that too but fists are more affective."

She instantly paused and stared at the lake as if she seen something unusual then turned her head to the right.

"NARRKEN!" She shouted repeatedly getting up from the edge of the boardwalk. She turned her head left and right then she sniveled realizing he's gone. As she strolled from the edge, her face expressed sadness complying with loneliness. Vividly, her right-hand trembled gripping the flower with the blade still released and pondering on where her brother went.

<u>*Present time, year 2322, in Mike's truck—*</u>

Tajaymae woke up breathing heavily and looked around her perceived that it was only a dream. Nack, Ki-Yale and Mr. Turd were asleep, she sat back then slowly closed her eyes.

It's 9:30pm and Mike is driving seventy miles per hour on a fifty-five mile per hour highway, Newmans Highway with barely any police and vehicles around. Mike turning a corner—*Sccrreeeetchh!* Dynamically, He pulled the hand break and concurrently stepped on the breaks, the kind of breaks that ceases instantly going high speeds while everyone in seat belt harnesses pushed an inch forward, the seat belt harnesses then put everyone back in place in seconds waking up Tajaymae but Ki-Yale is still sleeping.

"What happened!?" Nack became awake then yelped.

"Yeah. What the hell is going on?" Tajaymae awake and startled.

"I sa... saw some dude lying down in the street! Al... I almost freaking hit em'!"

Mike quickly unbuckled his harness and opened his driver butterfly door that lifts and reclines in the mini truck's rooftop. Tajaymae and Nack look at each other puzzled and did the same. Mike walked up to the boy and looked over him.

"Looks like he's hurt, he probably got ran over." Nack said.

Nack and Tajaymae walked up a closer behind Mike and saw the young man.

"This loo'... this looks like hit and run."

"Let me wake up Ki." Tajaymae said strolling towards the right passenger side of Mike's air truck.

"The boy looks... looks covered in blood..."

Mike turned around then began walking over to his truck. Without notice, the boy sat up, then revealed a tranquilizer gun from behind him and instantaneously, he shot Mike in the back of his neck. "Oh shit, oh shit!" Nack said.

"What the...." Tajaymae said while she quickly puts her hand on the hood of Mike's air truck.

The boy then aimed the tranquilizer gun at Nack while Mike fell forward onto the Road. Tajaymae absorbed the energy from the air truck, then the air truck lost its power and dropped to the road while Ki-Yale is still sleeping. The boy looked at Tajaymae's direction then she blasted plasma energy out of her hands hitting the boy in the right side of his chest as he tried to dodge but it was too late. The boy fell to the floor, while an angry Tajaymae charged towards the boy then in no time she's on top of the boy punching him in the face with plasma energy on her fists. "Get em Tajay!" Nack encouraged her while Tajaymae is beating the young man. Nack then ran back to Mike's air truck yelling—"Ki-Yale wake up! Wake up Ki!" then abruptly, a blast came out from the trees hitting Tajaymae in the head causing her to drop to the road instantly knocking her out.

"*Where did that shot come from?*" A man revealed himself from the darkness of the trees as Nack panicked and looking back at Ki-Yale. "Aah damn it, Ki-Yale wake up."

<u>An hour and a half later</u>—

Ki-Yale's eyes are opening, his head facing down looking at his hands then he sprung up looking around Mike's empty air truck.

"Where is everyone? So, they just left me in here? Hmm." Ki-Yale rattled as he removed his harness, then he opened the left side front passenger door, stepped outside and saw a house with the lights on with two air vehicles sitting outside the front lawn.

"Whose place is this? It's definitely not the tournament, looks like a personal house." Ki-Yale said as he looked back at Mike's air truck and saw that it's sitting on a lowered ramp hooked to a towing truck. He walked up to the metal slide door of the house and pressed the doorbell button. "Someone is at your doorstep; someone is at your doorstep." Said the door attendant machine.

The metal slide door unlocked itself then instant enlightenment occurred seeing Nack standing inside with a bright smile on his face. "Bro. You finally woke up huh?"

"Where the hell are, we? Why didn't you wake me up?"

"I tried to wake you up, I really did but you were fast asleep and you're like..."

"Oh yeah, I could be pretty heavy to move... now, umm... Who crashes here?"

Ki-Yale looked around the house for a moment then a man appeared out of the kitchen hallway into the living room and said—"Ah, come in, come in, you must be the boy this young man was trying to wake up earlier... He said your name was Netro. Am I right?"

"Yes, my name is Netro."

"Ok, nice to meet you, I'm Vince Harven... I'm a Death Angel."

"A Death Angel... Nack, stand back." Ki-Yale said with a modest voice while he got in front of him and clenched his fists.

"Ki, wait, he's no harm."

"How do you know Nack? He's a freaking Death Angel..."

"Yes, I am but I'm no threat to you and your friend I promise."

"Hmm, I heard myths about a few still being around and I'm guessing you are one of them. All you guys do is kill."

"We have a thirst to kill but we can control it, just like how Jahzin Yoko did around 40 years back."

Crime scene at the Little Tree Ville Police Department—

Forensics team and Gel Hev Bomb Squad are gathering all possible evidence while officers help clean up the mess.

"Looks like this Garrett guy infiltrated with an undetectable explosive and blew himself up along with Detective Holloway." Detective Charlie Jacobs said.

"This is a nightmare." Officer Bun Coleman said, one of Detective Holloway's friend.

"I know, he was great Detective." Charlie said as Bun nodded his head then he said—

"We need to take action, take down Sagan and defend this village."

"Action is already taking place as we speak."

"Mayor Tyson!" Charlie said.

"In the flesh baby." Tyson said holding his hand out for a handshake.

"I'm Detective Charlie Jacobs, nice to meet you." Charlie said as he firmly shook his hand. "Yes, likewise."

"I'm Officer Bun Coleman. It's an honor to meet you sir."

"What are you doing here?" Charlie asked.

"I'm here to check on this incident, Detective Holloway was a friend of mine."

"Ah... I guess he's cool with a lot of people... This has to be the work of Sagan." Charlie said.

"It is I believe but I have someone that's working on his capture."

"Military?"— "Way more than military, something like a super weapon."

"Is that so?"— "Yes, this is for sure the one to face him and whatever technology he possesses."

"Good, he needs to get captured and face the death penalty. Let's just hope your weapon emanates through with a good job."

"Oh, I believe he will." Tyson said as looks to the right side of the hallway.

"Luka Shale Jr. was here also, with his wife and daughter."

"Mr. Shale Jr.? I heard about his second daughter."

"Yeah he thinks her suicide was improbable."

Back at the Kafmora family house—

"The trauma has clouded your mind my son. It's events like this make you see all sorts of things."

Neecho shook his head trying to believe that it was hoax from his vison but to him he's sure that he saw his abducted son in the Mini-Mart. Neecho then sighed with a facial utterance that gave his father the urge to speak again.

"We don't know for sure where he may be, he could be on another planet. We don't know but we must continue to grow, all of us will never forget him but now there's a bigger threat we have to be prepared for because it's coming, and we don't know how powerful it may be."

"I need to cherish the moments I have with my family before things get even worse." Neecho said then he took his eyes away from his father and glared at the moon rise above the horizon— "Am I the first one you told about this?" "Yes, I haven't told anyone else…"

"Ok, I should be the only one for now… Just keep that attentive outlook for now."

"I actually love to hear your aphorism about remaining focused."

"Hmm', the things of which I speak is most helpful my son."

As Neecho required more answers he gets the gut feeling not to tell his wife or anyone else that he saw Narrken which is the only lead from since he got abducted. His father believed that it's best to keep his disturbances a mystery and aim towards the ultimatum which will carry out the fate of all existence.

An hour has passed by and Demi is laid up on the bed while Neecho is half naked with his knees planted on the near edge of the bed. He looked at her with admiration after they spoke about the events occurring in LTV. He is just glad that she is safe and not harmed by the plague or anything at that moment.

"So, you wanted to tell me something…" She mentioned.

"Yes, I wanted to tell you… I wanted to tell you that . ."

He paused while ogling deeply into her eyes with a rapid heartbeat and sweat trickling down his cheeks. His face grew pensive as he looked away, fighting himself from the inside to build up his confidence to inform his wife something he should have said days ago.

"You ok Neecho?"

"I just . . . I just had to take a second to sit down and grasp how lucky I am . . . I'm absolutely lucky . . . to have such a beautiful, inspiring, loving and caring wife."

She raised her left eyebrow then blushed and chuckled— "Well, you've gotten all mushy lately, ever since you came back."

"Hm', maybe it counts for something." He said leaning over to her as the mechanical cushion bed marginally sank. "Maybe you're right."

He gave her a peck on her lips then she continued to speak— "I guess it ain't so bad now that most of the kids are gone and we only have Oji right now."

"We got a little extra time of me and you." Neecho said then he kissed her on her lips then slowly made his way down her stomach. "I still hope they are safe though." Demi said as she began holding his head.

"Mmm', no worries baby. They can hmmmm', handle themselves." Neecho said then went in between her legs and kissed her thighs. The pleasures blossomed, her toes curled, a common reaction to his marvelous effort. "Hmmmmm'. Ok… ok. Haaaah."

"Hey, Oji got something to eat right?"

"Yes, yes, yes! I made something for him, now just go back down. You—don't—ever stop!" Demi excitedly said as Neecho smiled and went down on her again.

Unknown residence in Crouton Village—

"We got into accident, Mike saw a boy lying down and he span out of control and we thought he hit the boy, but the boy played us and shot Mike…" Nack said.

"What you mean he shot Mike?! . . . Where is he?! Who shot him?!" Ki-Yale spluttered.

"It was my trouble making son, but your boy Mike is ok. He is resting in the room upstairs." Vince said.

"Yeah, he better be alright. Where is he? And where is my sister, Tajaymae?"

"Yes, Mike the healthy autistic young man. He's safe, sleeping upstairs ever since he got knocked out and your sister is with my son in the living room. I had to take her out with my tranquilizer rifle because she was beating the freaking breaks off him. Ah' man what a strong kid!"

"Rifle? So, you shot my sister?"

"Yes, but it was a sedative only to knock her out. She's right over here."

Ki-Yale followed Vince and he revealed Tajaymae sleeping on the couch while his son being unconscious on another couch across from her.

"That's my idiot son Max. The troublemaker but we are cool here no grave harm done."

"Let me see Mike."

"Ok this way…"—Vince got on his hyper elevator with Ki-Yale to the next floor and reveals that Mike sleeping in Max's bedroom upstairs.

"I let your friend take Max's bedroom, just one of my punishments I'm giving my son. I was going to let your sister stay with him, but she decided to stay on the couch."

"Ok, now we have to leave. Where's Mr. Turd?"

"He left… he said he'll meet up with you again."

"Aah—I see…"

"I hear you guys are heading to the Crouton Village Tournament and that's not too far from here. Actually, this is Crouton Village you guys are in right now…."

"I see, so we're close then."

"Yes. It seems you guys will fit in with other contestants. … Especially with your sister having that weird looking ability…"

"Yes, that's called Netron Plasma. She can absorb any electrical energy from any substance even species that run electricity in their systems."

"And I'm guessing this is abnormal powers obtained from the government? Cause I haven't seen any Mega Humans like this."

"It's alien but not like the Brain Suckers and not government secret either." Nack said.

"Yeah she's half human and half Netron like me."

"Netron huh? Alright! I do see that tiny 'N' in that transparent octagon on your chest, so I guess that's your symbol. What are your powers like?"

"It's a diamond… and my powers, you'll see in the tournament what I can do. That's if you're attending."

"Yeah, I'm going but not fighting and I'm guessing you absorb energy too, but I'll wait and see. My son will be entering as well but seeing as he got beaten by a girl, I'd rather him to be on your side."

"You want him to be with us after he attacked us? Nah, we'll pass on that."

"It wasn't any grave harm done. It's just my son being an idiot."

"More like hungry for blood. The more they kill the more they get stronger for a certain time period." Nack mentioned.

"Yeah, that's how you Death Angels work. You kill, enjoy it and get stronger."

"Yes, that is absolutely but we could control that thirst and not let it get to us."

"Hmm, I don't know how many people he killed and neither do I know about you but I accept truth not conspiracy."

"C'mon kid, you don't have to worry. We are not going to kill none of you—if we wanted to, we would have don't it."

"Your son wanted to, and he failed."

"Just relax… and chill… you have to fight tomorrow so you should get some sleep… or, seeing that you did that already, you can stay up and watch holographic TV... At least you don't have to pay for a hotel room, right?"

"Yeah, I'll stay up and keep an eye on things." Ki-Yale said as he sat down on the couch.

"I'll stay up with you Ki."

"You can get some sleep Nack."

Vince chuckled then asked—

"You ever heard of the lyric…? 'Sleep is the cousin of death'?"

"Nasir Jones." Ki-Yale responded.

"Yes… and that's just something I always remember before going to bed."

"Hm." Ki-Yale vaguely uttered as Vince walked into another room.

"He doesn't seem a little off to you Nack?"

"Aah well besides shooting your sister…"

"Nack, it's not just that but all of these nice gestures and bringing strangers in."

"Hey, as long as you're still present, he won't do anything."

"Hm, yeah, I just need to focus on capturing Sagan and maybe I could get answers on where Narrken is."

"Yeah, Sagan is certainly an option for obtaining answers about your brother and it's respectable that you're doing all of this... helping the village, you're pretty much helping the world at this point."

LTV Mayor's Office—

Mayor Tyson, blood-flecked eyes, his goatee was well shaped and timeworn face walked up to the window looking over his village. He guzzles the disrespect that Sagan brought upon it once more. "I see you still have love for the village."

A familiar voice he hadn't heard in years, it just couldn't be real. He turned around and there she was standing in the middle of the office and looking right him. "I'm sorry sir, I let her in without notice." Preston said.

SIXTEEN

Year 2320—Gel Hev, GTC room on the 19th floor. (Grainian Tech Corporation)—

Glass swords used in combat, a skill in which users call themselves Apaki Warriors who mostly practice the art of swordsmanship, mastering the use of all swords, daggers, knives and many more that was ever used in history. The glass weapons are shaped by the nanochip technology made by Robert Cashmere also known as *Rob Cash* in the year 2258. Robert obtained parts of the technology from recent classified scientific equipment then he miraculously solved the Grainian mathematical equations and put together the proper sequence to rapidly create Grainian glass before any other scientist could. With his brilliant creative mind, he purposely molded the nanochip technology to create Grainian glass swords instead of just a piece of glass. He later constructed anti heat gloves that can withstand over two thousand degrees Celsius and can withstand the pressures when a user grips the sharp glass without acquiring a single cut on the hand.

The glove can also shoot small sharp glass the size of a bullet that launches as fast as 1200 feet per second. The nanochip is inserted into the middle of the hands then it fuses with the flesh, regardless of the layers of skin covering the nanochip, the glass can still be produced with the layers of skin interfering with the process. The nanochip technology gathers body heat and converting it into to temperatures up to seventeen thousand degrees Celsius. The nanochip produces the Grainian sand and contains the heat while melting together several minerals until the glass projects through the hands. The heat can then be surged through the glass while the hand contracts the least heat and the edges of the blade obtains the most heat.

The radiance can be everlasting as the Grainian glass can be regenerated throughout the ongoing heat. To disarm the sword, the user needs to flick his or her pinky and automatically, the glass will shatter into pieces. This could be dangerous without a glove and sometimes doesn't always comply which is one of the reasons why a glove is needed. There are also other ways to disarm it with the glove just by pressing a button or even pressing a button on their clothing. Despite the making of the amazing technology the government didn't see any use for it shortly after the New World Order and ceased its progression, hence that the technology was stolen and built by a bandit.

With the given license, the scientist by the name Erik Sarafian later took upon the challenge to prolong the nanochip technology to create glasslike objects other than glass swords. Erik also believed that it has potential to be a marvelous weapon in combat therefore he decided to moderate it by adding another nanochip into the cerebellum which is in the back of the brain sending telepathic signals to the nanochip in the user's hand. This nanochip was discovered as Grainian Tech harvested from planet Grain. With the mind now being intact with the nanochip in the hand, swords could then be made sharper and denser with more detail, more realistic and stylish with words in different languages imprinted in the Grainian glass blade. The government oversaw that he disobeyed instructions to only create objects other than glass swords. They acknowledged the work he had done and took his scientific ideas and broke bread allowing the technology to be in the military and then eventually civilians harnessed it. He later created the name for this combat skill which is called *Apaki Jermayin* which stands for "Glass Thermal" in Armenian and *Apaki Warriors* could sometimes be called "Apaki Martik" and the plural saying is "Apaki Martiknery". Erik also created better gloves in which the user can shoot the glass at faster speeds and can deflect incoming objects as fast as bullets. He called these gloves the "Apaki Tech Gloves".

Dojos and clans with different symbols depending where their origins began, all over the solar system practice the art of Apaki Jermayin wielding all types of swords, like Katanas, Claymores, Rapiers, Cutlasses, Long Swords and many more. Later the Apaki Warriors called the Grainian glass swords 'Apaki Swords' or adding the word 'Apaki' to the type of sword that they release, for instance, 'Apaki Cutlass', 'Apaki Claymore', 'Apaki Katana'.

"For years with sleepless nights trying to fulfill my legacy passed down from my father and relying on shared wisdom to create remarkable, outstanding technology to keep this city alive. Behold and feast your eyes, on the 'Apex Nanochip', specially made for the ones that wield Apaki Swords." Luka Shale Jr. said.

"Please elaborate on your project Luka. We would be glad to hear more." Said one businessman with a thick British accent.

"Yes well, as you know Apaki Tech has gloves that makes the sword look more like a sword when it's drawn and can even shoot as if it's a firearm. Now check this out… What if we have gloves that can control and create glass from a distance like say, three yards to ten yards?"

"Like a long ass sword?" Another businessman probed as he chuckled.

"No but to create glass from inside the bodies of the enemies."

"Th-that would be instantly lethal."

"Yes, and just imagine the massive booms in the stock market for such a technology."

"Hm, I like it, but we'll have to only work with military for now."

"Oh absolutely…" Luka said as he got interrupted.

"Aaah! I just can't forget the creation you made with the aah—male enhancers. Yeah, the ahh'! The ones that actually make your cock bigger, make your ass fatter and make your pussy squirt like it's a fucking waterfall—fascinating invention if I must add."

"Yes sir, they were."

"I'm sure you made millions with what scientists fail for years to accomplish with those bogus inventions and besides the lawsuits you had to endure. You sir need to stick with that… This ahh', Apex Nanochip is a weapon and weaponry aren't your best profitable move right now, especially if you owe over millions of dollars to the company that technically loaned you the beautiful Ferrari you parked outside and other things you bought."

"Listen, that money will be paid back I just need more time… This invention will do me wonders I'm telling you—military and Apaki Warriors will love this…"

"I've seen this move before Luka and you know I don't care if the invention was really yours that you made—if you fail to pay back your loan and other loans that you owe by the end of the year... You're the man that will be fucked in the ass—literally. If you catch my drift."

"Like I said, my debts will be paid."

Eastside, Little Tree Ville—

"Lexington, I have your ticket." Kumar said an Indian nineteen-year-old boy driving a hybrid air vehicle up on a highway that's 170ft in the air.

"I hope this isn't a sham and these so called five-star massages better be accommodating." Lexington said, a French eighteen-year-old boy from the underwater City of Atlantis.

"Bro, I'm telling you, you're going to love this. The most talented hands in LTV! I'm talking cocktail drinks with a three-dimensional theater with tangible images, all types of glorifying snacks and all the women are gorgeous!" Kumar said.

"Let me see that ticket." Said Hanae, a Japanese seventeen-year-old girl. She aggressively grabbed the ticket from Lexington then looked at it.

Kumar parked his air vehicle at the massage parlor. The municipal parking lot has a high-tech automated system designed to incinerate ninety nine percent of failure while constantly operating twenty-four seven. Vehicles would first hover over a conveyor belt then the retractable wheels are placed onto the belt as the belt brings it into the parking spot which is a self-operated lift machine. The wheels are attached with anti-theft system and an electrical barrier around the parking spot. This municipal parking lot has twenty-seven floors.

"Hm, looks legit."

"Yeah got it for a steal too. Vacation couldn't be more unbelievable." Kumar emphasizing his sentence.

"Better just be women putting their so called professional talented magical hands on me." Lexington said.

"Don't worry. We pick and choose who we want." Kumar said.

"I just want a massage… I don't care who or what machine that's doing the job." Hanae said.

As they walk in the building Kumar gets a call. "What's up Sensei?"

"I need you three at the residence." Alroy said.

"Aah. We just left the residence."

"Yes, and I need you back."

"Hmm', but we have massages to do."

"Ok, finish that, then you come home."

"Ok Sensei." Kumar grunted as he hung up the call then looked at Hanae and Lexington.

<u>*Later at the LTV Apaki Warrior Dojo*</u>—

"Ooh shit its Xack, my boy. What's up bro? Long time no see." Kumar said. "Xack!" Lexington blurted.

"Yeah man what's up, it feels like ages." Xack Machida said as they did pound hugs, greeting each other. "Hell yeah." Kumar said.

"Reunited?" Xack added. "Reunited and it feels sooo' good!" Lexington Quoting a classic song by *Peaches and Herb.*

Fang Machida walked in with Adelia Woods then Alroy said— "Woah Fang! What's up man?!"

"Alroy! It's been forever man." Fang said hugging Alroy.

"Who is that? A daughter I didn't know about?"

"Nah that's my son's girlfriend, Adelia."

"Oh really? Hello Adelia, I like your headband." Alroy said.

"Well, thank you Sensei, I love this headband. I wear it almost every day." She chuckled wearing her favorite burgundy headband that displays the Crouton Village Apaki Warrior symbol. "Please call me Alroy, unless you want my training… Trust me, you don't want my training."

"I'm sure I don't… Fang's training is already enough."

Fang and Alroy both laughed while Adelia chuckled.

"Fang. How is Misses Machida?" Alroy asked.

"Oh, you know, fine as always."

"Good, good. It's really good to keep a woman around you know. C'mon, let's get some grub."

A few hours later after sundown around 9pm in the large back yard, Xack and Kumar are practicing with wooden swords. They seem to be evenly matched then Xack made one false move giving Kumar a chance to strike. He struck him in the stomach resulting Xack to fall on the ground backward then Alroy called the fight off.

"Hm, Kumar you've gotten way better than before." Xack said.

"It's all cause of my training Xack." Alroy said.

"Here use this. Well, not now but in the future, you might need it. It's *Luka Shale Tech* very useful." Fang said handing his son contact lenses. These contact lenses made his sclera turn blue and pupils turn into a small sword pointing down which is the Crouton Village Apaki Warrior symbol. These contacts make the user see the enemy's vital weak points.

"I see how you do Fang; you give your students more gadgets and not make them use their skills to the limit. An Apaki Warrior should rely on the traditional art of sword fighting."

"Hm, Xack has potential and would do almost anything for victory especially in a deadly situation."

Tranquility drifted around them, family and friends relishing a time well spent. Alroy lightly chuckled while he looked at Fang and Fang looked back—

Unpredictably, a flash of darkness appeared representing a charitable nightmare for Alroy. Kumar was induced by a large steel horn while he was pricked in the head. Implausible sightings causing hallucinations, both Fang and Alroy assumed it was just a mirage, but it wasn't. Hanae had gotten impaled in the chest with another large steel horn going right through to the back of her body.

With drastic movement, Alroy screamed at Kumar while he wobbled and his forehead bursting out a pool of blood as Xack and Fang drew their Apaki Katanas.

Lexington gasped as he heard the screaming from his Sensei then ran out to the backyard.

"Kumar! Hanae!" He yelled.

Alroy stood over Kumar and Hanae as his hands were shaking, his fingers were spread out and his body is in a pool of sweat, contemplating on what had just happened.

An enormous muscular Rhino appeared standing upright like a human in between a large Shinto torii gate with six metal horns from his head to his back with one horn that's 123cm long in his forehead. His fingers are close to human fingers and it seems to be wearing an all metal armor with mechanical substances and artillery linked to its body. His right eye had a red scope and he carried a large steal 'Odachi' sword. The Rhino stepped closer then spoke with an extremely deep voice and strong Japanese accent— "My name is Azuma, I'm a Rhino Samurai cyborg, and Mega Animal!"

"What is the meaning of this?! Why are you here?!" Fang queried.

"Isn't it obvious? I come to murder you all—specially requested by Dr. Rogue Sagan."

Adelia ran outside next to Lexington as soon as she saw Azuma, she drew her Apaki Katana.

"No, my apprentice!!" Alroy gushed as his student Kumar is down, he sworn to protect his students with his life now one of his best is mauled by one struck to the head.

"Hm, how unfortunate." Azuma sneered as he released his large Samurai sword.

"You'll pay for this!" Alroy shouted as he drastically got up from his knees then drew his Apaki Katana.

Azuma charging at them while Fang ran to the left side and Xack ran to the right attempting to emit attacks from both sides. Alroy charged at Azuma head on then Lexington stepped behind Alroy. Azuma swung his large heavy Odachi sword then Alroy uses his Apaki Katana and blocked it. Adelia shot a few pieces of sharp heated glass from the generated glass sphere hovering over her hand hitting Azuma in the arm. Azuma unfazed by Adelia's attacks because of his heavy steal armor as Fang and Xack from different directions hitting Azuma with their Apaki Katana but it only shattered them as the glass rapidly fell to the ground. Lexington used his acrobatic skills and power he has in his legs to jump, do a front flip then landing on top of Azuma. The Rhino Samurai then tried to stab him in the back while oscillating at Alroy. Alroy walked backwards as Adelia started charging at Azuma then one of his large metal horns was instantly released from his head then the metal horn pierced Lexington in the stomach.

"No!!" Fang retaliated while Adelia jumped and did a front flip with her Apaki Katana in the air ready to slice Azuma but he back handed her to the ground.

"Aaahh'." Alroy screamed as the rage surged though him then precipitously, he aggressively charged at Azuma preparing to cut open his stomach. Alroy swung his heated glass sword then Azuma used his strength and broke the sword to pieces. Alroy generated a new sword from his hand but it was too late as Azuma struck him in the shoulder as the blade ran deeper unto his chest.

Azuma turned around then recognized Fang and Xack.

"Good you're using the contact lenses to find his weak points." Fang said.

Azuma puts his head down allowing his metal horn that's attached to his forehead to be in front of him then he charged at Xack and Fang as Fang got in front of his son and allowing Azuma to be focused on him. His metal horn carved open Fang's chest while Xack jumped from behind his father then released heated glass pieces from his hand hitting Azuma in the eyes. Azuma is then blinded as Xack tried to stab him in the neck but Azuma used his shoulder left pad and blocked the attack.

Adelia understood what Xack was doing then she quickly ran up to Azuma then released heated glass pieces hitting his armor then pranced seven feet in the air and stabbed him in the temple.

Azuma stood motionless with Adelia's Apaki Katana went right through his head with blood dripping down. He falls forward right in front of Xack and Fang as Fang held his chest then he removed his hand and saw blood dripping from the gash.

"Are you alright father?"

"Yeah… I'll be ok, it's just a cut." He said then he witnessed his old friend Alroy and his students lying down on the ground. He shook his head with a gasp of breath then looked at Adelia which in result took Xack's attention off his father.

He rushed over to her displaying distress. "Adelia…"

She blinked slowly and raised her eyebrows as if a flash of light was shining onto her. "I'm fine Xack but…" She said then took a glimpse at Alroy and his students.

<u>*Present time in year 2322*</u>—

It's the next day and Xack sat by his girlfriend's bedside at the LTV Hospital gazing at her. He stood up and held her favorite burgundy headband that was removed by the physicians to undergo operation on her freely then glared at it. He reminisces about the times he had with her, growing together and going through the toughest of situations. He blinked and buttoned his bottom lip then lifted her hand and kept holding it as he rubbed her fingers. Remembering the past, he lifted her shirt and saw a long scar on the right side of her stomach.

He crushed the bottom end of the shirt then gently puts it back down covering the long scar. "When will this fight end?"

Remaining by Adelia's bedside, sulking over her condition, gripping his fist and fighting the tears but he just couldn't handle it as tears sprung from his eyes.

"You're strong, fearless, a true Apaki Warrior and always will be—I'm going to take down Sagan and Push even if it means joining that tournament."

Xack stood up with a pause for a few seconds then he gradually puts back her favorite burgundy headband around her head. He looked at her one last time then exited the room and saw the physician that woke him up. "Is everything alright Xack?"

"Yes."

"Good, now you need some rest."

"No, I have places to go. How is the plague out there?"

"It died down a bit but still you should..." The doctor said and got interrupted by Xack— "No, you keep her safe. When she wakes up, tell her I'm at the tournament in Crouton Village. Thanks for everything doctor..."

"No problem Xack . . . I will for you"

"Thank you doctor...."— "You're welcome and... it's Damian. Doctor Damian."

"Doctor Damian... I must go now." Xack said while he sauntered around him.

Dr. Damian turned his body around prompting himself to look at Xack stepping away.

Back in year 2320, Luka Shale Tech & Co. Cargo Station—

Shipment arrival from Asia to Gigantica City Bay. Gigantica customs search and inspection which generally takes thirty minutes for the process to occur. The employees were finished with their thorough search and inspection. Joe Stenson, the head of his armed security company that is profited by Luka Shale Tech & Co. instructed his team to transfer the trailers to the tractor unit. A masked man on top of a building looking at Joe and his team, he crouches down and proceeded down the ladder. "I'll be back, I'm gonna get a latte from the office." Joe said. "Alright boss."

The alarm sets off and Joe heard the assault rifle shots.

"Arm your weapons! Stay here and safeguard the containers! Status report. What's going on over there?"

The short-masked man utilized an Apaki Katana in each hand cutting through his opponents which were the guards. "Sir, it's an Apaki Warrior in a mask!"

"I'm on my way! Hold your ground."

The masked man blocking each bullet and shooting heated glass cutting through the bodies of the guards with effortlessness. Joe arrived with red veins in on his sclera and his pupils became small as he revealed three chains equipped with a baseball sized flail ball at each end out from his high-tech forearm guards. "I wonder why an Apaki Warrior is interfering with Luka Shale's business."

"You got something that now belongs to me." Said the masked man.

"Oh really. Let me introduce myself… My name is the Kleaner with a 'K' and you're not getting past me."

"The Kleaner huh?"

"I borrowed the 'K' from Kill and switched the letters… What you get?"

"It sounds like you had a lot of time on your hands." The masked man ran towards Joe and jumped twenty feet in the air. Joe swung his chains then launched it at his challenger's face. The masked man then shot heated glass shards at him, but Joe blocked the attacks rapidly then ripped the mask off and which revealed himself as a young man with double eye patches that blocked his sight.

"Hmm, you're just a kid. Who the fuck is you boy?!"

"My name is Push Monaghan and you're a Death Angel of course—hm', I don't even move that fast with a weapon."

"Yes, my skin, flesh and bones are partially altered into rubber which allows me to be lighter and block your shots easier. Hmm', those eye patches… I'm assuming that you already knew I was a Death Angel."

"Yes, that's correct. I would be a fool to not come prepared against you."

"You seem like quite the smart one but still not smart enough."

"Please, don't think you have the advantage here. I fight blind folded all the time."

Joe laughed loudly then said—

"Trying to bullshit a bullshitter' huh? Ok then, if you say so!"

Joe ran towards Push then began to swing his chains at him like a windmill. Push blocked the attacks and swung his Apaki Katana back at him. After one minute of combat Push got cut with the flail ball ripping open his chest plate. "I'm dissecting your armor, piece by piece and still no hits on me."

"I realize that you moron!" Push responded while swinging uncontrollably but it's not enough. Joe continued to do his worst while smiling and enjoying the sweet moments of triumph then unexpectedly, something heavy dropped from behind Joe. He immediately turned around and there he is— Azuma the cyborg Rhino Samurai with a blind fold around his eyes.

"Hello mother fucker!" He said as he swung his large Odachi sword then Joe blocked it.

"Azuma? This is my fight… Back off!" Push said as Azuma rapidly steps back while Joe swings at him.

"Hey Kleaner, turn your ass around."

He turned around instantly then Push grabbed the chains with both hands then yanks it towards him. Push kicked Joe in the face and quickly let's go of one right hand twisting his body sideways, then he perforated him deeply in the left shoulder. Joe gasped for air as blood squirted out of his shoulder then he falls on his knees.

Joe never thought today would be the day would that he dies so sudden. He breifly thought about the past as he looked to the sky and preparing himself for the final blow. Push moved as quick as he can, he aimed his left open palm at his face then created one shard of sharp heated glass from the generated glass sphere hovering over his hand which then went right through Joe's head allowing him to lean backwards. He then fell frontwards as Push smiled and kicked his body like he's a piece of trash on the ground causing him to face upward again.

"Never interfere in my fights Azuma."

"Ha! It looked like you were losing."

The guards comprehended that they cannot communicate with their boss and lost signal through radio frequency. Running through the trailers, they witnessed their comrades mangled to death. "Shit! Joe is down."

"You got the rest of this? The authorities will be here in the next five."

"Yeah, I got it. You go do your thing but just to let you know—Fang and his group combined—are like me times two."

"Hhfm, no one is stopping this Samurai!"

"Hm, good."

SEVENTEEN

Neecho and Demi depicting unconditional love, its nothing too special though, they met then it was chemistry. Demi, she took a crystal not caring that it would harm her just so she can breed for Neecho, who is a different species. In year 2304, Neecho is Twenty years of age, his body is muscular and toned. He has a *high fade quiff* haircut and always likes to keep a clean facial shave. To most women, he seems to be a young attractive Caucasian man. Almost any girl couldn't resist him being in his prime ages and that's when things completely changed for him.

In a gym called "Gem's Floating Gym" located in Gigantica City, the building literally floats twenty feet in the air and it's being held up by anti-gravity plates. Neecho worked overtime as a trainer for a senior citizen lady named Betsy Cambridge at age sixty-six. She tried to keep in shape by staying healthy and protecting her pride by never taking any Mega Human serums or any Mega Human microchips, she's just pure human.

"Now you're going to lift the ball upward then throw it up to a quarter to the top of the wall then catch the ball then bend on your knees again in a squatting position." Neecho giving Betsy squat and reach instructions with a fitness ball under a high-tech mat machine that records your workout and assist you when you start to feel the burn.

"Wow this looks hard." Betsy chuckling.

"Yes, it's hard but it's worth it. Hard work pays off and you'll love the results when you're done."

"Oh boy you are so right! Perfect saying for why you're doing overtime." Betsy said as she goes on the high-tech mat machine.

"Yeeaah but it's not just the money Betsy. I want to see you succeed, I want to bring out the impressive potential you have. You say you want another day and here you go another day. I'll even do seven days a week if you like."

"Hmm, you're the only trainer that's so energetic, so trustworthy for me and this intense exotic attraction gives me motivation." Betsy prattled while doing her squats and reaches.

"Hm… go all the way down making your legs a ninety-degree angle and your butt should be out."

"Ok, I guess that's two reps."

"Yes, c'mon, you'll get it… Yes, now that's how you do it."

"You need to meet my daughter. She just lost her trainer because of one unfortunate event that happened back in…" Betsy said and being interrupted.

"I already met her… I mean…" He stuttered. "Oh, you met her already?"

"Well… yeah we met a few weeks ago. She has children around my age."

"Yes, four beautiful girls. All of them are a lot of fun Neecho. Great energy and so is yours… Heeww'… Ok that's it, break…" Betsy being overwhelmed by the training.

"Good job now take a breather then two more sets. Ok?"

Betsy chuckled then said— "Please, don't be so gentle with me."

"As you wish Betsy." Neecho said then slightly tilted his down.

"You know what Neecho? We all need to hang out with you. I think you will love our valuable time together."

Sided with two roommates William Raghavan, a young Indian male college exchange student and Melvin Russell, a young Caucasian male college student.

"Ok, so you're like a 'Mc. Luvin" times a million! 'Neecho Mc. Luvin"… Like what the fuck man!" William said in an Indian accent.

"Oh no he's like the lost Porno God from the 21st Century… this dude even got with Arabic women." Melvin said.

"C'mon guys… you think I'm making this shit up? It's literally like pussy being thrown at me."

"Yeah man, this is the third orgy this week! I mean you've pretty much banged the whole women's side of the family…"

"The freaking mom, the freaking four daughters plus the freaking hot grandma…" William added.

"Let's not forget, the freaking lesbian couple that you claimed you banged." Melvin said.

"Trust me that was real, I even showed you the video… With my face in it. How could you still not believe it? I ain't got time to edit videos man."

"Dude. Does your cock ever get tired out man?" Melvin asked.

"Hey man, I'm just a young guy with stamina and the will to go on."

"Bullshit, I'm about to find those prescription pills you pick up every two, three, six months."

Neecho laughed then said— "It ain't pills William."

"Yeah, whatever man. I wish I was you right now. You get all the biddies, you work at a place where you love to work at. Plus, you have like the coolest dad in the world, General Nealo. Dude kicks ass and I heard he never failed a mission."

Neecho chuckled then asked— "Whatever man. We going out tonight?"

"I gotta finish this homework man. I'm far behind this week." Melvin said.

"Hey. I'll do it for you bro, no worries." Neecho insisted.

"Nah man. I keep making you do my homework and it's not right. I actually gotta' learn this shit."

An awkward hiatus from all three of them for ten seconds looking at each other, then William and Neecho sniggered.

"Aw man. I never knew I would actually see the day you say that!" William said.

"Look. If you're really serious about what you're saying right now. I applaud you but I'll do this last one and you do the rest by yourself. Ok?"

"Alright…" Melvin mumbled.

"Now we gotta get going to Main Street."

"Just this last one but I'm serious about this guys, I'm ready do all this myself you know. I gotta learn this shit!"

"Ok yeah, whatever, now let's get ready!" William said.

Later that night thirty minutes to 6pm in Main Street Gigantica, which is the longest street in the world running about (1,987 mi) long which is 3,197.767 kilometers. This street has transit that lets people travel from country to country in just fifteen to thirty minutes using the express one-way air bus that goes at vast speeds. Neecho and his two roommates decided they wanted to go to Puerto Rico to party at a night club.

They were all fast asleep taking their little nap and Neecho woke up then said— "Bro… Where the hell are we going?"

"Check your GPS. We should be on the air bus to Puerto Rico."

"Oh shit…" Melvin exclaimed.

"What?" William concerned.

"We took the air bus going to Africa."

"Just great!"

"How did this happen?" Neecho confused.

"I don't know I could have sworn we were on the right bus." Melvin said.

"There should be some party spots out there." William said.

"Yeah, with a whole bunch of filthy rich folks." Neecho said.

"It shouldn't be all bad." William said.

"Shouldn't be all bad? All of their shit is expensive as fuck!" Melvin complained.

"Hey maybe one of us can meet a rich girl and be cool with her you know… Next thing you know she's buying us all drinks."

"That's not how it works William!" Neecho blurted.

"Alright Neecho. We'll see after your pockets run dry by the second you walk in."

"What time is it now in Africa?"

"It's like 2am."

"*Hello everyone, this is your captain speaking and welcome to Durban, South Africa! Please remain in your seats with your seat belts fastened and wait for the pilot to set the yellow light which is above your seating area indicating you can exit the air bus. Have a great night and enjoy your stay.*"

The Okeke residence, Tanzania, East Africa

Omari Okeke, father of Demi and Atsu Okeke, sat in his favorite chair looking at a picture of his deceased wife. He puts the picture down then looked to the wall across from him and see his beloved children and wonder to himself about the things he would do to keep them safe. As he contemplates some more, his son arrived from work as a waiter at a restaurant and he hollered— "Papa, I'm home."

"What's up Atsu? How was work?"

"Good, I made a ton of tips."

"As I always say, save your money."

"I know Papa. I know."

"Good."

"Is Demi here?"

"No, she doesn't come over today."

"Oh yeah it's Friday. She always goes out on Fridays…"

"She needs to save her money too. Always going out every week. No good."

"Well said papa."

Atsu got a glass of water then walked to his room and called his friend through his ten-dimensional communication device. *"Aaye' Atsu!?"*

"What's up bro? What's the plan?"

<u>Nightclub in Africa</u>—

The DJ is playing some classic African music from centuries ago while young adults are dancing and having a good time. A young woman is grinding on Neecho while William and Melvin are dancing with two girls.

"Now this is what you call a party!" William yelled.

"Yeah! This place never fails!!" Neecho spoke loudly.

"Actually, enjoying yourself Melvin?!" William asked.

"Oh yeah bro!" Melvin said.

Moments later Neecho went outside to smoke a joint with a small glass of vodka in his hand leaning on the edge of the long local balcony. He puts the glass of vodka to his head with his head halfway facing the sky, he then realized a woman like figure walking by him. Immediately after she walked by, Neecho finally felt the alcohol coursing through his system. He puts his drink down on the railing extremely hard not knowing he used his Netron strength breaking the glass and leaving a small dent in the railing. A couple that was about nine feet away from him understood what he did and he just smiled at them then halfway waved his hand. He paused then he immediately turned around to the left where the woman walked by.

There she was the most beautiful young African woman he had ever seen. Her curves resembled boundless spirals wearing a fitted red one-piece silk dress that stopped over her knees revealing her gorgeous glowing legs, wearing black leather sandal finished with black straps and laser cut leaves detailed high heels and a high-tech golden watch. Curly and long hair with a face that could be on a billion-dollar bill with just little eye shadow and a perfect Cupid's bow from her red lipstick. As the sweat began to drip down the sides of his face and his eyelids being wide open in utter shock and lost for words while the young woman awkwardly looked at him then said— "Umm… what the fuck…?"

"Aahh'." He said nervously.

"Um… Hi. You ok?"

"Yeah, I'm good. I'm good. I was just… It was an accident." Neecho stuttered.

"Yeah no shit! How is your hand like not bleeding right now? And that dent. Was that there before?"

Neecho looked back at the couple as they went back to kissing permitted him a more normalized feeling about this situation.

"Yeah, ah yeah, it was there."

"Ok, well stop drinking, I think that's enough for you."

"No, it's not that I'm tipsy. It's well… Ah, you are like very… Aah…"

"Very aah? You got like a speech disorder or something?"

"No, no it's not that."

"It's ok, I don't judge. We all have some kind of disorder and we all are different… it's just part of being human. As long as you're alive and well and living life like what you're doing now. That's what truly counts." She preached.

"No, it's just that I'm… I'm…"

"High as fuck! Yeah, that's what it is—it's a party so aren't we all… Well, I'm not really super high, just buzzed… Can I take a hit?"

"Oh, you want… I… I ran out of battery."

"Oh, it got you right here."She said pulling out her empty electric blunt out of her high-tech purse then she took the battery out.

"Thanks…" He smiled and said as the lady gives him the battery.

Neecho exchanged the battery then gave the lady a pull. "Oh shit! This is strong!"

"The second pull is going to have you…" He said as she took the second hit with ease, then he said— "Ok, you're actually doing well. You know you're smoking the finest and strongest weed in all of Gigantica."

"Well, I happen to smoked them all." The young lady said as she took her forth hit.

"You can kill it if you want."

"Oh sorry, it's just so good…"

"No, no—I wasn't being sarcastic. Take it, I got aplenty more where that came from."

"Ooh ok. You're into the greens heavy huh?"

"Nah, it's just for the party you know."

"Well, you gave this awesome smoke so why not I buy you a drink since you broke that one."

"Oh no, it's cool it's just me being clumsy."

"Nooo! I want to… C'mon." She insisted then signaled Neecho with her hand to go the bar.

"Ok, fine." Neecho said as he follows the lady to the bar.

"Hmm, let me guess you were drinking vodka. Right?"

"Yeah. How did you know?"

"Just a guess. Now how's about a shot of Gold Baron?"

"Oh, that's even better."

"I knew it, you just look like the type of guy that enjoys whisky."

"Well, you read people well."

"Two shots of Gold Baron please." She ordered as she sat on a hover chair.

"Hope you can handle this." He challenged her while he sat next to her.

"I can, trust me… I can handle this. So, what's your name anyway?"

"I'm Neecho, Neecho Kafmora."

"Neecho Kafmora... very interesting name. Where does Kafmora originate from?"

"Hm', well, um… my name is Gigantican... my ancestors were affected by the Grainians vs. Humans war in which their last names were erased from any identification system and so they choose new a last name... How about you?"

"Hmm, I see… that makes sense. Well, my name is Demi Okeke and I'm from here, South Africa… Born and raised."

"Oh, I love Africa, it's like paradise over here. This is actually my third time here, the last time I was here was for vacation and I must say it's absolutely impressive but it's just so expensive."

"I definitely agree on that; this country is the most luxurious compared to most places around the Solar System. You're on vacation now?"

"No, I'm just here to party tonight. I'm not a serious party boy though, just occasionally."

She nodded her head in approval then asked—

"What do you do Neecho? On a day to day basis?"

"Well, I'm a student studying *Pharm.D* at Pearl Star Academy and I'm a fitness instructor at the 'Gem's Floating Gym' in Gigantica City."

"Nice! You're into the medical field and you make sure everyone's in shape like you."

"Yeah, ahem' . . . It's all about technique, doing the proper exorcizes and right eating habits. Lots of protein too ya' know."

"Hmm, you do look like a hunk and it takes the right skills."

"Why, thank you Demi. So, what do you do?"

"Right now, I'm a model and I'm entering a contest for the Gigantica Beauty Pageant."

"Woah... Really?"

"Yeah. What, you don't think I belong?"

"No, no . . . I mean yes, you belong but I mean no I don't think that you don't belong... Ok look... I'm going to come clean here... I think..." Neecho prattled then got interrupted by her phone.

"Whoop', I gotta take this . . . Wassup' babe?"

"*Hey. What's up baby! Thought you were gonna call me about twenty minutes ago.*" Said a man through a holographic message coming from the waist of her dress.

"Yeah... sorry, I just met this drunk guy that smashed his hand with his drinking glass and luckily he didn't get hurt."

"*Drunk guy huh? Then you gonna take him back to your place.*"

"Oh, shut up! My place is your place you idiot!"

"*Maybe hide him underneath the sofa so I won't notice.*"

"Yeah. That's exactly what I'll do, you thot."

"*Do what you gotta do baby, just remember I'm not here. Free apartment for yourself for another hour.*"

"Yeah, whatever. Why did you say another hour?"

"*Cause I'm coming home Demi. I finally quit this dump of a job.*"

"What? Now that's something I wanna' hear… but what did you settle for?"

"*I'll tell you when you get home… you can bring your friend too. We can do dick rubs while you watch.*"

"Um. What!?"

"*Just playing. You know I'm Just playing… come home baby.*"

"Ok. I hope you didn't leave because I gave you the three K' last week."

"*No, I told you, I needed it for a gift I'm buying for my niece. The Fairy Tale Tree House.*"

"Ok, whatever… I'll be home soon." Demi said then she hung up with the hologram going back into her watch.

"Who's that?"

"That was my goofy boyfriend, he always likes to joke around like that. Sorry, I gotta go. I'll see you around at the gym… Ah Neecho."

"Oh ok. I guess I'll see you around Demi…" Neecho said as she walked away then he mumbled in a low voice— "You have a boyfriend…"

Neecho walked with wonders, going back on the main floor and saw his friends at the bar with a few young ladies. Melvin began to speak loudly because of the music and said.

"Hey bro. How was that smoke break?!"

"It was good man." Neecho replied.

"Come here and check this out. I gotta put my boy *Neecho Mc. Luvin'* on with one of these African beauties cause right now there's these two bad ones at the left. You see them?" William said.

"Yeah. Yeah I see them."

"Alright good. I'll come in and say something, then you sneak up out of the blue and do ya thing like we always do man."

"Aaah. Listen William, I'm not feeling it right now man. I got something else on my mind…"

"Other than pussy? Oh man, that dank must have hit you hard!"

"Nah man, I'm serious! It's another girl man . . . Look bro, I gotta go."

"Another girl huh?"

Demi riding an Uber driving home and the Uber was an Android operated automated air vehicle with all types of high-tech features.

"Yes, yes, next week. Oh yeah of course. Yeah… I have that dress… Oh you're talking about the… Oh no that's like half a million dollars! How am I supposed to make half a million in one week then buy the dress? That's crazy, c'mon! . . . Ok! Ok! I'll see what I can do. I want this so bad and I will not give up achieving it!" Demi speaking to a pageant promoter on her compatible earphone as her Uber driver dropped her home.

She pays the driver then went inside and saw her boyfriend Chase Olsen signing paperwork. They had a conversation for fifteen minutes about leaving his job that he hated it so much and talked about his new progressions of being in the Gigantica Military. Demi was thrilled for her boyfriend and his choice; he has been waiting for this moment for a long time and he finally succeeded. Demi and Chase then instantly made out passionately.

"Hey. I'm going to freshen up a bit then I'll come see you." Demi said.

"Alright babe. Don't leave me waiting." Chase smiled and said.

Thirty minutes later Demi came back and saw Chase unconscious on the bed. She shook her head in disappointment and turned the lights off.

Neecho is back at a hotel and he decided to speak through telepathy with his father who is at his office in an army base.

"I'm feeling this girl a lot Dad. She's so beautiful and she seems like an outgoing girl. I feel she may be the one."

"She may be the one huh?"

"Yeah, we Netrons hardly feel this much anxiety but… Why was I so nervous when I first started to talk to her?"

"It's a girl that you like a lot correct? Liking a young lady that you think is the one absolutely for you… you don't want to mess it up by not saying the right thing or making the wrong moves. You think the outcome will be a negative one instead of thinking it would come out successful. Remember, people fear what they don't know but we as Netrons overcome that fear by simply picturing the right possible outcome."

"You're right. This whole thing isn't going to work though."

"Why you say that?"

"She's in a relationship."

"Oooh, well. She is young, correct?"

"Yeah…"

"Maybe she isn't in an all that serious of a relationship. You can still try… Be there for her when her BF isn't. Then overtime she will come right to you, develop a strong connection with something that she never had… Be real with her and this will all turn into true love and love could be dangerous especially when it's powerful. It's actually one of our strengths as a Netron and is also one our emotional weaknesses like humans or any species that comply with love."

"Should I tell her who I really am?"

"Like I said be real with her. If she doesn't like it… She isn't for you son. Oh, and aah' make sure you erase her memory if you show her and she isn't feeling it, just to avoid her trying to tell the entire world."

"Hmm'."

"Just saying son."

<u>Later in the morning around 8am—</u>

Atsu woke up for work as he stepped out the house door and saw his older sister leaning on the railing.

"What's up punk?"

"Oh, look who it is. Thought you were coming over last night but then I realized yesterday was Friday."

"Yes, that's when I party, party."

"I wish I wasn't living with Papa like you."

"It will happen just save your money and when you do leave Papa make sure you come visit every now and then."

"I know sis, he says the same thing."

Moments later walking down an alleyway shortcut to the hyper speed train station.

"Yo Atsu!" One teenaged boy said with a group of teenagers.

"Oh no not him again." Atsu said.

"Who is that?" Demi asked.

"Trouble…"

"Aye Atsu! What happen to my lunch?"

"C'mon Kojo, it's not school today."

"It doesn't matter bitch! I want my lunch! I told you every time I see you give me something."

"Hey, you don't call my brother a bitch."

"Who's this? Your sister?"

"Yeah." Atsu muttered.

"Oh, she's hot man." Kojo said.

"Let me get some of her Kojo." Another teenaged boy said.

"I'm sure lil' Atsu here won't mind." Kojo said.

"Back off." Atsu said as he stood in front of his older sister

"Oh, you wanna get tough Atsu?!" Kojo taunted as he pulled out a knife.

Atsu stood bravely and remained in front of his sister and then all of a sudden—

"You heard the boy… back off." A man with a black mask said standing on top on of a large eighteen feet tall dumpster.

"Oh and… Who the fuck are you?"

"The one who is going to kick your sorry ass if you don't listen to what the boy said."

"Ok, kick my sorry ass! I wanna see you do that."

"Alright… It would be my pleasure."

The man in the black mask jumped and flipped with agility from the edge onto the ground next to the teenagers. Kojo ran up to him and swung his knife then the man in the black mask slapped his hand to the right causing his whole body to twist halfway. Two other teens ran from different directions and swung their fists at him but couldn't land a single punch. The man in the black mask then used his fingers to push both teens backwards at the same time causing them to fall on their buttocks. Kojo turned around and tried to stab him again while another teen tried to do the same. The man lifted both of their arms up then used his finger to push them back. Kojo held his balance then tried to land a punch again but missed pointlessly. Then, without much effort, the masked man quickly punched Kojo in the face knocking him out.

"Oh, shit Kojo!" One of the teens said.

"Yo man we' out." Said another teen.

"We can't just leave Kojo."

"Man fuck him! Let's go."

"That's what I'm talking about. Yeah run, run away you punks!" Atsu cheered walking behind the teens running away.

"Wow." Demi being perplexed watching the bus run away.

"Hey, thanks man . . . Where did he go?" Atsu looking behind him then Demi does the same but realized only Kojo's unconscious body is on the ground.

"I wonder who that guy was." Demi pondered.

EIGHTEEN

<u>*Two days later at Gem's Floating Gym*</u>—

"Ok, another set. Come on you got this." Neecho said.

"Ok, ok I got this. Aagh!" Said a man doing bench presses.

Minutes after the man finished his last set Neecho turned his head to the left. His pupils were instantly as large as a pizza pie inside of a pizza box.

Demi Okeke across the gym executing squats as he approaches her from behind.

He licked his lips as he thought of something to say then said—

"Oh, I never seen you before. You must be new."

She instantly turns around and her heart began to bloat as if it's about to pop then smiled and cheerfully said— "Neecho! Heeey!"

"Demi, you're here and you, remembered my name. Wow, I'm Impressed."

"Well, I actually looked your name up because ahem'— you know—I think its kind of sounds familiar... aaand' I found out that you're the General's son of the Gigantica Army."

"Well, yes—yes I am. Wait... you actually looked my name up?"

"Yeess', I did and you're full of surprises."

"I can say the same for you, looking me up." He said as Demi blushed then said—

"Agh'… I just was bored…"

"I guess we do a lot when we're bored."

She continued her squats then said—

"So, am I doing this right 'Mr. Trainer'?"

"Oh, you're doing fine actually. You're no amateur that's for sure."

"I do this at least once or twice a week but today I really needed to just ease my mind a little. Too much going on right now."

"What's going on? If you don't mind me asking." Neecho being curious as he saw her in a depressed state.

"I need to make half a million to buy a dress for the beauty pageant. I mean they tell me last minute… I should have expected this."

"Damn, a half a mill… For a dress!? Oh man, only the top models will do that." Neecho yelped.

"That's what I wanna be, a top model… but right now I feel like… that won't even happen."

Neecho assumed that Demi is feeling gloomy about her current situation and then he asked—

"Hm, what's your bank?"

"I'm with the LSP Bank. Why do you ask?"—L.S.P is short for Love Serving the People.

"Ok. You mind if I show you something?"

"What is this 'something' that you speak of?" She confusingly asked.

"Come with me to lunch and I'll show you."

Hopinton Diner, Gigantica City—

Moments later Neecho and Demi are at a diner both eating grilled pork chops with corn on the cob, mash potatoes and drinking a glass of water. Demi is on her holographic cellular device that has a web browser opening the LSP Bank website.

"Okay, go into your bank account and check it. I won't look at your password." Neecho said.

"Umm. Ok."

Demi puts her password in and gets into her account.

"Oh! What the… How did I get a million dollars in my account? How did? . . . This isn't real. Did you do this?"

"Well, you can say that…"

"No way is this real man, I hope this is not a scam. That is a long prison time."

"It's not a scam it's all yours now, straight from a money machine with your codes and computerized paperwork all done."

"Wait… Like how did you do this? What's going on?"

"Look at the water in your glass."

"What?"

Neecho used his mind to elevate the water out of the glass and authorized everyone else's mind in the diner to gravitate their attention away from Demi and Neecho's seating area.

"Oh shit… Dude, are you making that water move?!" Demi completely astonished.

"Sshh, keep your voice down and yes I am…" Neecho whispered.

"Woah…" Demi said strongly focused at the water.

"I'm moving it with my mind."

"So that's how you got the money in my account? With your freaking mind?"

"Yes, from a money machine with no traces, it's like you booked an appointment with the 'Special Financial Needs Center' online and got your money right away."

"You keep saying your money but… Hm, look, I love that you're helping me out, I really do but whatever this freaky magic shit is, I don't need it. I rather earn the money. You know? Actually work for it."

"It's not magic. I'm not your ordinary human and I'm not a Mega Human or their descendants either. I'm an extraterrestrial being from another planet far from this solar system."

"Ookaaay... Guess what?"

"What?"

"I was born a man…"

"What?!"

"Sshh', I'm just fucking with you… just like how you're doing with me." She said.

He laughed loudly then said— "No, no, I'm not fucking with you at all Demi. I can show you more if you want but I'm telling the absolute truth. Also… You can't tell anyone. Please."

"Ok I won't… I guess… Hm, just put the money back where it belongs. I'm going to earn it on my own without just getting free money."

"Hmm, you were suggesting free money before with the government not giving you any because it's not a valid reasonable cause based off their criteria…"

"Yeah, you're right I was but when I get it like how you did, I don't feel like a true champion. I need to work hard for this Neecho. The easy way out is for chumps and people who are just not capable."

"Hmm, I so agree on that."

"Now, take that money out!"

"Look at your account…" Neecho said then Demi checked her bank account through her wristwatch.

"Woah… It's all gone, back to my original money. Everything exactly as it was…" Demi amazed.

"And you have a long way to go Demi…"

"Yes, that means I need to get moving then."

Neecho and William just arrived after meeting up at the baseball field while Melvin is still in class. Neecho is sitting on his bed across from him informing him with unexpected news.

"Yo, I'm not getting what you mean by 'quitting the game' Neecho! Please electorate on that."

"Well, I'm quitting the game. How else can I explain? I'm leaving, sayonara, adios... No more banging these women."

"Ok, I need to meet this girl you like so much."

"This 'like' might turn into love real soon. I mean she surprises me every time I'm with her."

"Aye man just be careful. Don't get your heart broken. That shit hurts like a mother fucker and I know from experience."

"Yeah Willie? How do you know? You never fell in love."

"No but I witnessed it—it's like a man's castle made out of all solid brick crumbling down on him."

"Hm, I'll take my chances—staying under my castle."

Apartment room in Gigantica City—

"How's the baby doing girl?!" Demi said.

"He's doing great. He's getting bigger, giving me a bigger bump and just making me look fat." Said Tiara one of Demi's friends on the communication device, a spoiled rich girl from planet Neptune.

"But you're still sexy, beautiful and sweet and you'll always be." Demi encouraged her.

"Aw Demi! This is why I love it when I talk to you, sometimes I regret one-night stands with guys. I should have known I was pregnant from the beginning—I don't even know who this baby is."

"That's why they have DNA tests… Don't worry they'll find out who the baby father is and hopefully he's a man about it."

"Yeah."

"I'm proud of you though, keeping the baby and no abortions. You go girl!"

"I guess the bright side here is a new life…"

"That's the spirit! —Hey, I got this gift for Chase. I should be saving up, but I must do this. It took him a while to get approved you know."

"Well, congrats to him. Does he even know that you need a half a million?"

"Nah he doesn't know…"

"Why don't you tell him to help you?"

"Hmm, I don't want him to stress out over a damn dress."

"What?! That's not just any damn dress. It's one of your dreams to be a top model."

"Yeah, you're right Tiara…" Demi said as she walked in the bedroom and sat down on the bed.

"Hmm'. So, what is this you gotta tell me so bad?" Tiara asked

"It's a little weird… When I tell you you're not going to believe a word."

"Ok, I've heard of lot of weird shit. Ok? Just let me hear it."

"Ok, you're going to be freaked out, but I met this guy at a club in Gigantica City. It's a beautiful spot that has this view you would cry just by looking over the beautiful city. The guy broke his glass of vodka with his left hand and I could've sworn he dented the railing too, but I didn't see it happen completely. His hand… His hand didn't even have a scratch on it… at first, I knew he broke the glass cause' he looked at me walking by I was just so baffled by his hand not being cut from that glass, like what a lucky dude. I met him again Yesterday at the Gem's Floating Gym…" Demi said as she gets up playing with her hair then randomly looked in the drawer where her boyfriend keeps his belongings.

"Gem's Floating Gym huh? So many sexy guys there… Hmm, sorry keep going."

"Yeah, so I met him again at this gym and I told him about what my little issue about getting this dress then he showed me…" Demi said then paused.

"Yeah. He showed you what?" Tiara asked then continued— "Demi?"

"I'm going to call you back…" Demi vaguely said.

"Is everything alright…?" Tiara said as Demi hung up.

"You son of a bitch!" Demi lashed out as she looked at Chase and Tiara in a thirty-four-minute-long video from a mini tablet in his drawer. It showed Chase and Tiara performing sexual activities without any protection. She immediately broke down in tears and smashed her holographic communication device in the wall. Her mind was clouded by emotion as she then began breaking random objects and throwing them across the room in expressing her anger.

Its six AM in the morning at Gem's Floating Gym and Neecho is coming to open the gym. He saw a few *early birds* waiting to do their exercises and there she was again, Demi in the middle of the horde. Neecho said good morning to everyone while he walks up to Demi and recognized her arm has a band aid wrapping around her lower arm.

"Woah. You're here… and very early… What happen to your arm?!"

"I cut myself…"

"What? Why?!"

"I didn't do it on purpose." She said with watery eyes and overall verbal expression of sadness on her face.

"Woah. What's wrong?" He queried as Demi shook her head and looked as if she is about to bawl. Then he began to open the gym doors and said— "Ok, come on."

Two days later at Gem's Floating Gym—

Demi and Neecho are in the gym office and Demi began explaining everything to him.

"That's is so fucked up. I mean I'm not going to lie to you I did a few similar things in the past but at least I wasn't in a relationship to begin with."

"Yeah… You didn't do none of that mojo to make this happen right?"

"What do you mean?"

"Your powers! You didn't use them to put all of this stress on me, right?!"

"Nooo Demi! I wouldn't do that. —Hey… Didn't you say your friend was six months and that video is literally about six months and a half ago?"

"Yeah, I guess. What if you planned this way before? I mean I know you like me, so you did this to try and get me… Well, now here I am Neecho."

"You just don't wanna believe it that this happened, don't you? Look, I wouldn't do that to you or anyone and yes, I do like you, but I play it by the rules. I gave it a shot although you have a man but if you refused, I would have gone on my merry way. There would be others that I hope I could find… like you… which would probably be impossible." Neecho interpreted.

"Hm, I guess… It's just so messed up… They did it raw like they purposely wanted to stab me in the back. I mean my best friend! Like how could she…? I should have seen this coming and my mom read him from the get-go before she died and he's all bad news. He never truly cared for me, only for himself. Should've listened to her…"

"Sorry to hear that…"— "Its ok… heart failure was the cause… we been together for almost a year now and it's been two months since her death… Damn he ain't shit! I thought he was a real man!"

"Hm, it's going to be tough with moving on but you gotta take it one step at a time and focus on your goals… Like winning that beauty pageant."

"Yeah but I only have four days left to buy that dress."

"Well, let's get a move on! Can't just sit here now."

"How am I going to make half a million in five days?"

"I was doing some research and I came up with something…"

"What's that?"

"Magic… People haven't seen magic as an entertainment since the 21st century!"

"Yeah with all this bazar technology."

"Let's give the people some dope old school magic, in our own style."

Dorm Room, Pearl Star Academy

Neecho sends Demi to his dorm room to stay there because she moved out with all her things out of her boyfriend's apartment. The next day they perform their magic tricks after hours of planning. There's always a story behind every magic trick and in history magicians have done magical stunts and tricks that leave people asking if it's real. Well, this is the same operation that Neecho and Demi is doing. Neecho plans to use his Netron powers as Demi would wear a sexy gymnastic outfit performing some dangerous stunts and trust Neecho not to kill her by accident. Demi wanted to enter the pageant so badly she doesn't care how she does it to make the money that she needs, as long as she worked for it. Neecho later gathered all types of equipment for a magic show for the public.

Four days has passed, Demi and Neecho racked up thirty-eight thousand dollars and a couple change.

"One more day left, and this is the day I should be getting that dress."

"Hm, take my money Demi, you earned it."

"No… What?! No! Why are you always being like this? So, generous to me?"

"Because well… the way I see you do these dangerous tricks was good enough and proves you really want to win this. I think you deserve my generosity Demi and I want to be there for you when no one is."

"Hmm, be there for me… I heard this before Neecho."

"Well, let's make this the last time you hear that."

Demi got closer to Neecho then looked him in his eyes and kisses him on the cheek.

"Well, I'm down to get with someone better but for now it will just have to wait."

Chase is opening his apartment door with a censor recognizing his left eye and thumb. This is the same technology used to safeguard special military equipment back in the 21st century. He walked in his apartment and saw all his belonging thrown and trashed all around. He panicked thinking a burglar broke in and deliberately trashed his place. He didn't have any concern for Demi as he rushed to his safe where he kept all his money and thirty thousand dollars' worth of jewelry. He opened the safe and everything was all there and never tampered with. Chase wondered who could've done this and called for Demi's name. He eventually got concerned about her because she didn't answer her calls for days. He then saw a recorded USB chip on the kitchen floor next a small a computer device with a paused video. He played the video and saw the sex tape he and Tiara made. Once he saw this, he had a feeling Demi also saw it—so he plugged in the recorded message.

"YOU'RE AN ASSHOLE! NO! Let me say it better... YOU ARE, A FUCKING ASSHOLE! I hope you and your stupid bitch felt good about yourselves and raise that baby in Tiara's stomach. You should have the money to do so cause' you saved up and plus the money I gave you. Should have known, it was to pay for Tiara all along! I mean that bitch don't even have a job, that bitch never worked a day in her life! Just take money from the government like a lazy bum! Yet she still took money from your sorry ass... My money! You have the nerve to bang my best friend! My best friend! How could you?!I wanted to hurt that bitch so bad too, but I realized the child is already there, the damage, it's already done, and I got better things to do. I don't want to waste any more time Chase. Goodbye and I never want to see your trifling ass again! You ain't shit! And I don't wanna see that two-timing hoe either!"

After Chase heard the recorded message, he stood motionless with a confused look on his face and at shock because Demi found out about his affair. He shook his head in denial and fell back on the wall.

<u>*At the Gigantica Beauty Pageant of 2304*</u>—

"It's been a tough one tonight and it's difficult for us to decide at this point but there has to be one winner, right?!" Judge number one announced.

There are four judges and all four must reveal who is the winner of this pageant. Every model is assigned different dresses that cost a lot but in the end the winner will become a super model and get a prize of ten million dollars with agencies working for the winner. Plus, a golden statue of the first Gigantica Super Model "Maritsa Julia Finely". This is a good way to push one's modeling career to great heights.

"Ok and the winner is..." Said the second judge.

"Demi Okeke!! The new Gigantica Super Model of 2304!" Said the fourth judge.

The crowd is cheering and the model to her left is in disbelief because she was getting rooted by the crowd the most. Demi was slightly behind her making the crowd go crazy. Demi is also in disbelief and started tearing up a little then looked at Neecho. Neecho bobbled his head up and down then Demi released some confidence and starts to walk forward to the host.

"How do you feel Demi?"

"I feel… I feel great!! To think I wouldn't accomplish this now look… I would just like to thank God for blessing me with this and I couldn't do this without Neecho. Thank you so much." Demi said while looking at Neecho.

She does one more walk down the walkway wearing a simpler outfit, a black one-piece with pumps, she steps up to the edge with her hands on her hips as she lifts her head up high with fierce confidence.

<u>*Dorm Room 76, Pearl Star Academy*</u>

Demi triumphed and now comfortable at Neecho's dorm room and his cotenants are all out partying. Demi is so excited to win that she is aroused and started passionately making out ever since they got on the cab ride to the dorm. Both quickly taking each other's clothes off then Neecho paused for bit and grabbed a condom then moments later—

"Woah!! I never had a guy made me cum so hard! You truly aren't human!"

"Well yes, I am not human as I told you before."

"Now I sort of believe it."

"I never had an orgasm like this before either its different…"

"Hm, wanna do it again?" Demi asked with a flirting face.

Neecho pulled Demi down to the bed and instantly they are at it again going two more rounds. They both later felt surprisingly satisfied with their sexual performance and decided to just relax. Demi is on the left side from Neecho while he has his arms around her lying in bed in the dorm room.

"Should have gotten a hotel. What time does your roommates come back?"

"It depends it could be really late like five or even seven o' clock. These guys love to party all the way through the night."

"Some serious party heads."

"Yep, young party fiends."

"Can I ask you something Neecho?"

"You can ask me anything."

"Okay, I don't know. It just crossed my mind but… Okay, I shouldn't be asking this but…"

"Nooo. Go ahead ask me."

"Okay um… So um… Did you rig the pageant with your mind? You know like use your mind to make the judges say that I win?"

Neecho kept quiet for ten seconds and looked up at the ceiling.

"Um are you going to answer?"

"Ah well…"

"Oh my god! Well what?" Demi asked while positioning her body upward and looking at Neecho.

"Well… Yeah… Yes, I used my mind."

She looked at him with her eyelids wide open then yelled— "Oh c'mon Neecho! Why?!!"

"I don't know I read the judges minds and I could hear what they were whispering, and it was the girl next you that really won. I just had the judges change their mind… You were going to be second place." Neecho said positioning his body upward.

"That's cheating Neecho! I don't want to freaking cheat!" Demi bickered getting out of the bed.

"I saw how hard you worked and…"

"No! No! No! I could have tried again next year it's ok. Second place isn't what I wanted but I can learn from that and become even better! Were you even going to tell me this Neecho?"

"Yes, I was when it's the right time to…" Neecho said and being interrupted.

"The right time?! This is so messed up… After we done fucked—thinking… Thinking you was real with me!"

"Look. Demi I'm…" Neecho said being interjected.

"I need you to change everything. If it's true that I was second place, then let me be second and let the other bitch get the first place. If she was really the one, then let it be. I don't care how you do it, but I need it done now!"

"Ok, its little tricky doing that but…"

"Just change it!"

"I'm doing it now."

"Oh my god! I'm going crazy. Aaah… I'm going crazy… Mind control and all this crazy shit!" Demi panicked and hallucinated.

Neecho used his mind to instantly make Demi as second place, the judges, even the audience forgets everything, and it only took Neecho about sixty seconds to get that done. His mind has a solid photographic memory of every person in the in audience by remembering just only a few faces tracking down the faces he saw and used their minds and sight to track down any other face that Neecho didn't see. Neecho might have left out some other people but it'll have to do. Demi's golden statue turned into bronze statue which is the second-place prize and her money changed to five million dollars right in front of her eyes.

The money is revealed through her mini high-tech holographic computer device.

"Okay, it looks like you did it."

"Yes, I changed everything. All the videos recorded was altered using computer software making it seem like you won it in second place with anyone ever finding out. There might be a few people I don't get to change their minds…"

"I'm fine if it's just the judges and the models. They are the most important."

"Ok, now can you please forgive me?"

As he begged for forgiveness, he walked closer to her.

"I need to go." She said.

Without hesitation, her anger significantly expressed as she walked out the dorm room and vigorously slamming the door.

William and Melvin were just outside about to open the door and saw Demi walking past them being upset.

"Woah, she's pissed…" Melvin said as Neecho walked to the door.

"You told her your body count didn't you bro?" William asked Neecho.

"No Willy… I screwed up worse than that…" Neecho said beholding Demi walking away down the hall.

Gem's Floating Gym—

It's the next day and Neecho sat in the office taking his break then his manager strolled in and said.

"Hey man! Why so down today? It's spreading a bad vibe around here. You're usually so lively. What is it? Girl problems?"

"Yeah you can say that." Neecho answered.

"It should be no problem with you man…"

"Nah… I messed up man."

"Hm, love now a days is just becoming immoral all over again. Couples cheating, lying and all out doing the wrong things. I realized though, about most relationships, the powerful ones stick together no matter what. If you two truly love each other… Or maybe like each other. Well with you, I don't see falling in love anytime soon…"

"Why you say that?"

"Well Neecho, the way I see you with a new broad everyday… Well, except for today a few days ago… This girl got your game thrown off."

"I wanna be out the game this one. No more games… She's perfect for me."

"Ok maybe I was wrong. It looks like you could be finding love soon. You just must go find her and tell her how you feel. What she does that makes you want to change your ways."

"You're right. That's exactly what I should do."

Tiara's apartment, Gigantica City—

"Have you mmmm'… heard from mmm'…? Demi lately?"

"Don't worry about her."

Chase is at Tiara's place making out as Chase slowly moved his hands to the clips and took her brassiere off revealing her B cup sized breasts.

"Wait . . . this is way too kinky. You're going to fuck me while I'm pregnant?"

"Hey. There's first time for everything Tiara."

"Oh wow, you're so weird… Ok… ok just be gentle I never done this before."

"I got you baby—Hmm—no worries—Hmm."

Outside of the apartment building it appears to be a person wearing all black with a black mask sneaking inside the back onto the boiler room. Chase and Tiara prepared to have intercourse and the unusual person found a short cut to Tiara apartment room as if the person lived there before. The person pulled out an illegal Fed gun from his pocket, an old Glock 19 from the 21st century and cocks it. The person slowly walked in the empty hallway toward the apartment room and avoiding security cameras holding the gun in a different angle from the camera. The person reached the apartment room door where Chase and Tiara are then another unknown person's hand came across the masked person's mouth. Gripping the masked person's mouth tightly without any screams or any apparent noise.

The security guard in the office that watches the recording tapes didn't see the masked person in all black at all even when the masked person broke in through the boiler room. It's like they weren't there.

"Please… please, don't do this." Whispered the second masked person.

"Hmmmmrrrrr'."The masked person struggled to speak.

Within seconds they're out on the rooftop. "Aah. Uh… What the…?"

"You smell like alcohol… What were you about to do?"

The masked person turned around then instantly said— "It's you… the guy that knocked out my brother's bully."

"Yes." The second masked person said as he took his mask off.

"Neecho?!"

"Yes, it's me. What are you doing with an illegal Fed gun Demi?!"

She decided to take the mask off in shock to see Neecho finding her and ending up in the roof unbelievably fast.

"How did you know it's me? How did you find me?! How did we even get up here so fast!?" Demi confused.

"It's my abilities but, let's focus in the true matter at hand here. You were going to kill them?"

Demi hesitated then gawked at Neecho quietly for about thirty seconds with a one tear drop coming from here right eye.

"Yes. I was going to shoot that pathetic piece of shit Chase but not Tiara because of the baby. At first I wasn't going to do it when I found out but now my mind is made up."

"This is not like you, you're better than this Demi."

"I won five million dollars and I still can't find happiness after what they did."

"I know it's bad, but you have to keep this in the past and move on."

"And move on where?! What place am I going? Huh? Every time I try that, things are just messed up… Aaagh'. What am I doing? I'm talking to an alien or some Mega Human freak with some freakish freaking powers."

"Remember, I said I will always be there for you and look at me now? I'm here to stop you from doing something stupid. Maybe you should rethink about moving on with someone. A certain someone that keeps true to his word."

"Hmm, yeah well, I'm still upset with you Neecho! Using your mind or whatever to make me win!"

"Yes, I was wrong and I'm sorry Demi. I should have let you get second place without interfering and that won't happen again I promise just like how I promise to be there for you."

"Hm', ok, fiiiine... I accept your apology…"

"Now, that gun should be tossed, and you should celebrate because in my eyes you won being the most beautiful woman in the universe."

"Whatever." Demi said as she turned sideways from him.

Neecho uses his mind and took the gun out of her hand and formed it into a rose, then a chocolate heart box.

Demi slightly chuckled but still triggered by what Neecho did and said— "What is this? Valentine's Day?"

Neecho stared at her for a few seconds then he formed a Golden statue of Demi with writings. This made it seem as if it's some sorcery, but it was only his mind and, on the bottom, it announces—

"The Most Beautiful Woman in the Universe and All Time Winner of All Pageants—Demi Okeke."

"Woah…" Demi said then smirked.

"Demi, what I'm saying isn't bullshit. Since that first night I met you I couldn't even speak right, I was so nervous and intimidated by your beauty but I knew beauty shouldn't be the only thing that I should look for so I play by the book and see what you're about. That night you seemed like a chill, fun girl to hang with and you seem so much of a perfect human being at first but you have flaws and no one is perfect which makes you even more beautiful."

She turned her head from him looking downward expressing contempt—

"Hmph', doesn't seem like you accept my flaws when you sabotaged the pageant."

"I do accept them . . . you made me act as my true self every time we're around each other... When I saw such a gloomy face, I had to use my abilities to empathize, so I filled your bank account and you refused it. I never seen one so generous, honorable and take on a challenge by code. I was inspired by the way you instantly did that, even with the pageant you wanted to win by doing so the right way and not be a fraud. I understand now, I know it was wrong that I sabotaged the pageant and winning the right way is what truly makes you pleased."

She looked back at him while marginally tilting her head downward.

"I'm glad you see it like this Neecho, I like you a lot and I see a really good person in you. I just hope I don't get hurt again like with Chase."

"I'm not Chase and I was selfish using my unwise excessive courtesy just so you can be with me. But at least I can own up to that fault."

She slanted her head down and simpered at him revealing her dimples then he continued— "I'm ready, I'm ready for the next step with commitment. I want you to be my girl... then maybe in the future... have my babies."

Demi chuckled then said— "You want me to have your what?!"

He laughed then said— "Sorry, that came out wrong, I'm still a little juvenile and immature."

Demi gently puts down the golden statue then moved closer to Neecho then precipitously hugged him.

They both stared at each other then slowly French kissed. "Hmm... You know what? Let's try this again and see how this goes."

"Good, there's a lot weirder shit I need to tell you."— "I bet you do."

"And don't lose that statue, its pure gold."

"Um is it really?"

"Yes . . . You don't believe me, don't you?"

"Hm, nah."

NINETEEN

"Sir? Hello? Sir?" The overnight lady bartender said then looked at her manager.

"Just blow that thing." Said the El Tally Sal Bar & Lounge manager as the bartender puts the horn to her mouth.

She blew the horn and immediately Mr. Turd woke up swinging his arms rocking his body back and forth.

"WAAAGH!! . . . Huh? Uh . . . Sorry, I had a bad dream."

"Sir, you've slept in."

"It's a twenty-four-hour bar no?"

"Yes, but it's not a place where you sleep sir."

"Wait, let me catch my sanity. This dream I just had been getting to me."

"Sir."

"I'm so sorry, my name is Dunkin Turd. How long was I sleeping?"

"For about an hour."

"Hmm. I just wanna say . . . Oh this hang over is beginning to" He paused then continued— "It's been a pleasure drinking some of the finest shots in Crouton Village. That's what the bartender told me last night. Well, earlier this morning I should say... You know, I feel like this place need more men. Too many hot women especially women like you. I'm just fucking with you, let it be like this more women no other cocks but mine! AAAGH! That's what the dream was about! I, Mr. Turd and all the sexy bartender babes . . . Attack of the Cum Dumpsters! No wait . . . It was Attack of the Poontangs."

"Attack, of the Poontangs...?"

"Yes, that was a movie on the internet made back in the 21st century. Ah man people were so creative back then; it was so repulsive! Freaking talking vaginas with teeth trying to devour some cocks! Then the freaking dominatrix! WOOOH! They did a fantastic job."

"Uum' . . ." The lady bartender said as Mr. Turd got up wobbling on his feet.

"Sorry, let me get the hell out of here. I got to accompany my friend's grandson. Ooooh, the granddad, he doesn't really talk to me anymore. Well, I just haven't seen him in a long time, but his grandson does though. He's a brave kid, he's going to fight in the Crouton Village tournament… Um... Do you know what direction that is? I'm pretty sure he's their already."

"Yes. You go straight on road thirty-six and keep on this road until you meet the roundabout. After that, you will see an entrance to the tournament on the left."

<u>*The Harven Residence*</u>—

It's the next morning at Vince's house. Ki-Yale stood up all night looking through the walls with his Netron vision, waiting for Vince or his son Max to do something of the unordinary or something that would jeopardize his sister and his two friends, but nothing happened. Nack fell asleep while Ki-Yale's protective behavior maneuvered. He woke up Nack then went into the living room and woke up Tajaymae. The TV broadcasted the National Gigantica news channel. As he stood there folding his arms, being acquisitive to whatever conspiracies or crisis of the world.

"This is NG News at 6am! I'm Julia Sanders"— *"And this is Brock McMann."*

"Tragic week as the beautiful village in Gel Hev known as Little Tree Ville met unfortunate evens as a deadly virus called the Genchi created by Dr. Rogue Sagan was spread throughout the village which triggered a plague and the trees to grow rapidly in size, up to over three hundred feet—also resulting of one hundred and fifty three infected residents in Little Tree Ville hospitalized then later pronounced dead, sixty five unable to make it to the hospital and a total of ninety one residents dead outside of the village. Hospitals where filled with infected patients and doctors are working around the clock to keep things stable. Law enforcement are still uncertain of how the virus got into the village and investigating every possible motive."

Ki-Yale turned the TV volume down then asked— "You alright Tajay?"

"Hm? Yeah, I'm good… You're finally up…"— "And I don't like it here."— "Yeah, I knew you wouldn't. Hm… What time is it?" Tajaymae asked with a moaning crackling voice.

"It's time to go, get ready."

"Ok, I'll get my shower... you should too, that's if you did already."

"Don't need to, this suit cleanses my body from any germs and whatever that may contaminate it."— "I see..."

Ki-Yale went upstairs then gently opened Max's room door to wake up Mike but saw that he's already awake. "You okay bro?" Ki-Yale concerned. He's now disenchanted after falling asleep and feeling useless when hearing that his sister and friends got attacked. All he needs now is a modernistic closure to get rid of his distraught feeling.

"Ye'… yeah I'm good, I'm just trying to fi'… figure out how the hell I get from al'… almost running some kid over to an unknown room." Mike answered being unaware on what happened to him. "Good, as long as you're okay Mike."

Moments later—Vince is outside smoking an e-cigarette while his son mows his lawn with machines without the help of androids, just straight human muscle. Ki-Yale, Nack, Mike and Tajaymae walked outside and Vince saw them.

"Oh, good morning everyone." Vince chirped.

"Yeah, good morning." Ki-Yale hissed.

"Thank you for the making us stay overnight." Nack bared gratitude.

"Its cool man, it's the least I can do. Did you sleep last night Netro?" Vince asked.

Ki-Yale kept silent and looked at him for ten seconds then said— "Nah… but I'm good. My body doesn't get tired after one night of no sleep."

"It figures and you're the seriously protective one, you wouldn't even let the lack of sleep lose your focus on the perils."

Max with bruises around his face and arms from Tajaymae pulverizing him glimpsed at Ki-Yale then looked at Mike and Tajaymae then looked back at the machine he was working with.

"Heh'… hey kid. You alright? Tha'… the last time I remember you, wa'… was that you were on the road unconscious."

"Then he attacked you and leaving you unconscious as soon as you turned your back." Tajaymae said.

"Hm, rea'… really?"

"My son here was pretending to be unconscious so he could trick you yesterday. I don't know why but he caught you with a tranquilizer gun." Vince said then he looked at his son for five seconds. "Apologize son."

Max stood completely silent while blatantly looking at Ki-Yale and Mike.

"Now go-ahead son, say it."

"I'm sorry, I'm sorry that I hit you with a tranquilizer gun."

"Hey, apology accepted . . . Next time, I won't be off guard again."

"Let's go." Ki-Yale said.

Ki-Yale and the rest went in Mike's truck and drove onward to the Tournament.

City of Atlantis Criminal Court—

Judge Ernie Phillips imposing justice, as Detective Victoria Bailey and partner Detective Waldo Fleming worked on the Chloe Torbino rape case in which Fabian Torbino pled guilty since he knew he was caught in the act by police officers with precise evidence. It was an early trial mostly because Fabian pled guilty and only wants what's pending for him. Dorimzy participated as a witness to the crime and Chloe as the victim testified then soon after Judge Phillips made his final ruling while Tony, Nicole and Chloe sat on the side lines—

"I have identified characteristics of Fabian Torbino in which determines the sentence. As the court found, the jury found, the conviction of rape in the first degree which is a class 'A' felony and tremendously cruel. The crime inflicted absolute horror amongst his family and leaving emotional scars from her own flesh and blood which hurts the most and more than the physicality of the crime . . . I hear by find Fabian Torbino . . . guilty and sentence him to life without parole, accompanied by torture."

Sentencing to life with torture meaning victims, family or friends of the victims can torture the criminal. This kind of severe sentencing was launched as part of the New

World Order inflicting more fear for individuals making them think twice before committing the most vile and horrendous crimes. It's not mandatory that the criminal gets tortured but usually the victims take advantage and have the felon suffer for the rest of their lives. Chloe didn't want to see him again after appearing in court but Nicole, she took advantage.

Fabian Torbino is now located in Gigantica Maximum Penitentiary. His cell is about 31 length and width with a floor area of about 1000 square feet, he's strapped to a reclining bed and the Prison Persecutors will feed him food and drinks, underneath the bed there is a bucket that collects his waste. If so that the felon does not consume, he will be injected with a sustenance filled syringe that produces nourishment inside his stomach. The Prison Persecutors do not persecute for religious or political beliefs, ethnic or racial origin, gender identity, or sexual orientation but to inflict the punishment and oppressive treatment on felons who is sentenced with torture.

"It's—just—spectacular! —How you still have that same look on your face ever since I confronted you. I'm truly amazed." Nicole said dressed in all white buttoned up lab coat and helmet. Fabian reclined up on the bed with a high-tech mouth mask strapped around his mouth. She paused then looked at one of the Prison Persecutors and said— "So, I can do whatever I want with him correct?"

"Yes, whatever you think is justified Mrs. Torbino."

"I don't approve of that surname anymore."

"Sorry about that ma'am."

"It's okay, I'm not the only one that has to deal with the shame and humiliation. The one who is truly scarred with that surname isn't here to do this, so you get the next best thing." Nicole said as she picked up the unsoiled needle nose pliers then crouched down to his feet.

"It's time you get a pedicure Fabian . . . after all, you're gonna have to look good for me throughout this session . . . starting from the bottom up of course." She continued then slowly puts the needle nose pliers to her ex-husband's big toenail.

"Mmmmm'…" Fabian squealed under the mouth mask as she pulled his big toenail.

He squeaked under his mouth mask as she yanked his big toe nail off completely. His blood gushed out onto Nicole's helmet. She leaned back, then picked up a rag and wiped the blood off for few seconds. Fabian whimpered, panting while his eyelids are wide open from the excruciating pain then she smiled and said— "Oh, screaming already? We're just getting started and look at that—nine more toenails to go."

<u>The Kafmora Residence</u>—

Nealo in a usual meditative state in the training room. Complete silence as he took a deep breath concentrating then something alarmed him from the Netron Book of Edu. He opened his eyes while ascending his body then landed on his feet. He gradually walked up to the crystallized book then opened it.

Instantly it glowed, shinning bright light in his face. He touched it then closed his eyes and immediately, visions appear in his mind again. He saw the same face like before with pale decaying skin and deep cut marks on its cheeks. Nealo's body fidgeted as he saw more occurrence—the ground is lifting and breaking apart as trees rapidly moving down back in the ground as grass bloomed with flowers emerging. The sun is getting brighter reflecting on the plants, then blazing fire erupted, burning the lawn and the blaze got higher beyond his imagination.

"Granddad!!"

"OH! —ah hey… What's up Oji…?" Nealo blurted after his grandson startling him.

"Are you ok? I said your name three times and you don't answer"

"I'm ok, it's ok, I was just daydreaming and I 'didn't answer'. 'You didn't answer'—not 'don't answer'." He corrected him.

"Oh, right Granddad."

"What brings you up so early?"

"I'm hungry…"

"There's nothing in the fridge?"

"No all the breakfast is out. Mom asked if you can please get some breakfast for me."

"Hm, Really? You like bacon egg and cheese?"

"Yeah, I love that Granddad. You never seen me eat, don't you? You're always meditating in the morning."

"Yeah it's the way of exercising the mind, polishing my willpower."

"Hm, will—power?"

"Yes, now look, I have the bacon egg and cheese with croissant down here in my fridge, it's the last one. I'll give it to you so you can give it to the cooking android. Set it on sandwich and it'll make it for you once you place the bacon egg and cheese in the canister. Here…"

Nealo handed him the bacon, egg and cheese with a croissant then Oji said—

"I eat then we order more food online?"

"Yes, my grandson that we will do."

<u>*Crouton Village Tournament entry*</u>—

"Thuh'… there it is guys, the Crouton Village Tournament. One of thuh'… the most dangerous places in the world that's been overrun by Dr. Sagan." Mike said.

"This place is huge!" Tajaymae said.

"Hell yeah." Nack said.

"Ok, now I guh'… gotta find parking, it's free."

"Yeah, I see the sign, free parking for participants. Ain't that something?" Ki-Yale added.

Mike drove up to a clerk then underway a conversation— "Wah'… what's up? We're participants."

"Ok, go through that tunnel straight ahead, park your vehicle and then proceed to the check in area." The clerk instructed as he gave Mike a ticket.

"Ok thank you sir." The scanning machine scanned Mike's truck using laser technology as it moves inside the tunnel on a conveyor belt. "Very old school… gi'… giving me a ticket and shit."

"Maybe it's just extra precautions." Nack said.

"Ex'… extra precautions my ass."

Mike parked his air truck then they all entered the hallway passing the entrance. Ki-Yale went to the bathroom to use the stall which has full body barriers for privacy equipped with automatic flush and cleaning system. It also has built in air fresheners powered by batteries with unlimited lasting time. He finished urinating then turned to the left then unexpectedly, he saw Dunkin Turd standing frontwards with his head tilted to the right and looking at him. "Oh Ki-Yale! There you are."

"What's up Mr. Turd?" Ki-Yale showed an annoyed face.

"My homie man, how was it over that residence? Weird ol' fam' huh?" Mr. Turd asked while reaching out to give him a handshake. "Yeah . . . I didn't wash my hands yet."

"Oh yeah, can't have no alien urine touching me now . . . Probably contaminated."

Ki-Yale gave him a straight face then they proceeded over to Tajaymae and Mike.

"Oh shit! It's Mr. Shit . . . I mean Turd." Tajaymae taunted.

"Oh yes, *'it's a me Mario'* . . . I mean Dunkin!"

"No, you're not worthy of such a Nintendo classic." Nack said as they all entered the main check in area.

Ki-Yale chortled then Tajaymae spoke—

"Wow, just look at all these fighters."

"Ye'… yup, it's all types oh'… of people here."

"Woah, look who it is."

Ki-Yale turned around and saw a familiar face, the Apaki Warrior, Xack Machida.

"Aayy', Xack, you're here."

"Of course, I'm here and I see you actually came to the tournament. Now the world gets to see that power of yours."

"Is everything alright with you? I heard about the eastern section in LTV."

He thought of Adelia then said— "Yeah, uh… yeah, everything is cool. I have my dad over there and I spoke to him around seven am. Nothing for me worry about."

"Let me introduce my friends Nack the one getting us checked in over there, this is Mike and my little sister Tajaymae."

"Ahem." Mr. Turd said.

"Oh, and ah, this is Dunkin Turd. You remember him, right?"

"Yes, yes I remember him."

"Hello again nice to meet you." Mr. Turd said putting his hand out to Xack.

"Nice to meet you guys. I didn't bring any friends just this little guy I found, and my name is Xack."

They shook hands then Xack revealed a baby coyote from his side pouch.

"Nice tuh'… nice to meet you man, any friend of Ne'… Netro is a friend of ours."

"Woah!" Tajaymae gasped— "Is that a baby fox?" Ki-Yale asked.

"No, she's a coyote, I found her before I left LTV."

"Oh my gosh, she's so cute!" Tajaymae howled.

"The virus didn't affect her?" Ki-Yale asked.

"I guess not, my guess is that she could be a Mega Animal."

"Can I hold her?"—"Yeah sure."

Squealing from the baby coyote as he handed her over in Tajaymae's arms.

"Looks like she doesn't like Tajaymae already." Ki-Yale chuckled. "Shut up Ki, she's just shy... Aw you're so cute baby."

"Alright guys I got all of us in. I'm not fighting though; I'll just be the support for you guys." Nack appearing from the check in area.

"Hm, we weren't expecting you to fight anyway." Ki-Yale said while he smirked.

"Hey I can fight... It's just that, you know... I have no crazy powers and gadgets like you guys."

"It's cool Nack, being weak is ok, you are the brains though." Tajaymae said as she handed over the baby coyote back to Xack.

"Yeah brains over brawn but, I'm not weak. Ok!?"

"Hey Nack, this is Xack by the way, the one that got attacked by another Apaki Warrior back home."

"Oh yes I remember you mentioning that. Hey, nice to meet you... our names rhyme." Nack said as they shook hands. "Yes likewise."

"Yeah... Yeah that corny stuff. Now let's get to fighting." Tajaymae said slapping her right fist.

Ki-Yale looked to the side of him from his sister, then his heart began to beat uncontrollably. His pupils expanded, beholding a tan skin girl who seems to be around his age, trapping his attention span. She had long dyed cherry red hair girl with a plain all white lace-up asymmetrical club dress, sandals that has 3.25-inch heels, two gold bracelets on her right arm and a gold choker on her neck. She caught Ki-Yale looking but he never took his eyes off of her. He gave a shy smirk while the cute red-haired girl gave a smile back, showing teeth then walked away confidently and enjoying the attention.

"C'mon Ki, stop looking at that cute chick. She's out of your league."

"Aaah whatever, there's no such thing as out of your league Nack."

"Ha! Yeah, as if you can pull that."

Nealo and Oji are both walking in the woods along a pathway from to the supermarket. The trees around them were still bigger in height reaching slightly over three hundred thousand feet tall. The virus is slightly still roaming in the air as the white glowing particles are seen up close with the naked eye. Nealo and Oji are invulnerable to the virus because of their Netron DNA, their cells correspond with the virus much more differently than humans.

"Why are we going shopping Granddad? We could have ordered everything at home and have androids deliver our groceries."

"Yeah but sometimes we need the walk you know."

"Hm, the trees are so big Granddad! It's usually small."

"Yes, it's the virus making this happen."

"So, we aren't effected by viruses in the air?"

"No, my grandson . . . If you were you wouldn't be walking with me for fifteen minutes without coughing. You worry too much."

"Mommy said viruses kill people…"

"Yes, but you wouldn't be one of those people because your body is different. You're immune to earth's viruses. Even though you are half human and half alien, the Netron

DNA in which you have subdues most of the human DNA."

"Immune? What's that?"

"That means you can't get effected by a virus."

"Oh immune… Immune. I like that word!"

"Hm, here we are. I wonder if it's open now, I actually forgot to check before heading out." Nealo said as he walked towards the supermarket entrance.

"Yes, it's open!"

"Oh, good . . . Hm, they probably wouldn't allow us in without a plague suit."

"Oh, we need one of those lame looking suits."

"Hm, unfortunately it seems so."

"Then, we have to turn back!"

"No not necessarily, I have a trick that makes them all think we have on plague suits."

"Oh, really granddad?!"

"Yes, just follow me and don't wonder off. We'll get our groceries with no sweat."

Little Tree Ville Hospital—

Dr. Damian showing another doctor all the victims that were infected on a screen in one of the office rooms.

"At first they came in like wildfire, my doctors were working overtime, following quarantine protocol, keeping everything sanitized as possible and we had to substitute Androids to perform treatments and as you know, most people don't trust Androids at a hospital." Dr. Damian said.

"Hm, I bet it was a mess."

"Yes, it was. The anti-viral pathway entrance was breached. The virus transmitted through the air, children were vastly diagnosed before they got inside the main facility, most of them didn't make it. Although we were prepared with the cure—we still couldn't save everyone."

"You tried your best . . . The Mad Doctor's evil ways has surged around this world for too long."

"This supposed to be the era of ultimate sustained life, the era of ultimate peace."

"The world was renewed after an apocalypse, people realized we needed a new system and a new way of living but if this continues there won't be much left to live for."

TWENTY

<u>*Crouton Village Tournament*</u>—

"What sec'… what section ar'… are we Nack?"

"Section seven."

Ki-Yale dawdled behind everyone as they all proceed through the hallway to the inside of the arena. As they entered, they saw a large crowd of people, mostly teenagers chanting stridently— *"MURDER MURDER, KILL KILL"* repeatedly as Ki-Yale became condemned by the chant. Fighters are in different sections all around the ring where they sit down or stand waiting to be called to partake in the next fight.

"Yo! Don't ever touch me!" One fighter bickered quickly after he got accidentally bumped.

"Wait... You talking to me bro?!" Asked the fighter that accidentally bumped him.

"Yeah you bitch! Who else?"

"So, I'm a bitch huh?"

"Yeah you a straight up bitch! Go suck a dick and kiss my Jolly Rancher ass! Bitch!"

"Alright, we'll see how you talk to me, after I kill you."

"Man, these guys are like beasts in the jungle." Mr. Turd said.

"Hey fighters, come this way!" One of the tournament employees said leading them onto their post then asked. "It's three fighters plus support, right?"

"Yes, but Xack and Mr. Turd here is with us." Ki-Yale said.

"Ok, as long as you guys are ok with it." The employee said.

"Hey Ki, its Max." Nack said.

"Yeah, I see him and his dad too."

"Who's that?" Xack asked.

"Some duh'… Some dude that knocked me ou'… Knocked me out, with a tranquilizer gun."

"He's a Death Angel and so is his father. It's just shady to me, they attack us then he hospitalized us." Ki-Yale said.

"You could've done something but all you did was sleep in the car brother."

"Yeah it's sort of hard to wake me up when I'm sleeping…"

"The whole thing was just so unordinary…"

"You're right Mr. Turd, it was." Ki-Yale said.

"Hmm, there he is, that delinquent."

The baby coyote slobbered on Xack's face as he glared in another direction.

"Who?" Ki-Yale asked confusingly.

"Push…"

"Ah, the guy I blasted with my lightning . . . Hmph, that's all yours Xack."

"Let's just hope so."

"Who'… who's he to you? Seems li'… like you don't like him very much."

"He's an asshole that's working for Sagan and I believe he did something a while back…"

"What he might have done exactly?" Ki-Yale asked.

"I didn't see for myself, but I believe he was part of the Apaki Warriors working for Sagan that murdered my camp from the Apaki Warrior region in this very village you see here today. The family and friends that I had were all gone. All the children, the infants, the pregnant women, all the innocent lives. None of the people in my camp ever been in a real fight to the death before, all they wanted was to learn self-defense against an attacker until real attackers came and most of them froze up because they were rookies. I was one of the few apprentices that truly mastered the art of sword fighting at the time, but I wasn't there to protect them and my father who is the sensei wasn't there either.”

“Hmmm...” Ki-Yale slurred with an upsetting facial expression.

“He's also responsible for the virus in LTV. Sagan made the order, but Push was the one that did the dirty work… I saw him loading up chemical tanks in which was injected into the trees, the ground and the air which I believe was the Genchi virus inside those tanks.” Xack said.

“Hm and since the Genchi can attach itself to almost anything for long periods of time he uses it to combine with gas so he could spread I in the air faster.” Nack said.

“Now I remember that ugly tattooed face, he was the teen boy that was in the plague suit with a see-through helmet. So, you did know who he was Ki.” Tajaymae recalled while Ki-Yale revealed his staid face.

“No, I had a hunch, like I told you before sis, it's plenty of people with tats on their face but I'm not surprised that it's him nonetheless…”

“Hmm, not to mention the rain. Sagan must've waited for the rain, so the trees get some moisture to help them grow quicker.” Nack implied.

“Xack, I really hope you kick his ass before I do.” Tajaymae said.

“All right everyone! How are you doing today? This is your host Majesty Jackson! This week we have approximately fifty fighters and that's the thoroughgoing for this month. Now, this is Death Week authorized by the supreme government of Gigantica and yes Crouton Village is part of Gel Hev which is an island owned by Gigantica. Contestants will have the option to kill and I know you guys want to see that go down the most. Weapons are also allowed in this tournament, so if you didn't bring a weapon that you really needed… Well, I feel sorry for ya'! Ok fighters, this is the last chance to forfeit and we can substitute your place, or you can just be in the fight and survive. So, anyone?"

Twenty seconds of silence as he stood on a round eleven feet wide hover floor, looking around the tournament but no one stood up to leave.

"Okay, once you say the words 'I forfeit' while in the ring, security will come and get you. But it's best to forfeit now so we don't have to go through all that fucking blood just to get you out."

Ten more seconds of silence and still no one leaves.

"Alright, ok folks, let's get this show on the road!"

"Guess we should have attended next week instead." Ki-Yale said.

"Thah'… that guy is just talking. I… It's Death Week, every week."

"Wish all of you good luck." Xack said.

"This is gonna get wild!" Mr. Turd said.

"Oook everyone! Today we will start off with… Hmm'…" Majesty said as he checked his raffle machine— "The Poker playing badass. The one with a gamble… Loaded Ace versus the Death Angel… Max Harven! Now these Death Angels ain't nothing to be fucked with but Loaded Ace always got something up his sleeves."

Loaded Ace or as his peers call him 'Lo'. He's a twenty-four-year-old young man from Crouton Village that comes to the tournament to practice his lethal techniques and working part time as a bounty hunter. He has a rifle that shoots thin sharp metal playing cards to his enemy's bodies, then paralyzes them and slowly drains the water that the body contains which will result in fatigue, loss of physical energy. Sometimes the cards stick to his enemies, the exhaustion allows him to attack while his enemies are down. Max is twenty-two years old with a folding and detachable axe that was found from Emperor Bullbourne's Anatomy sword, the 'Sword of Grain'.

Max stared at his father as if he wanted a command from him— "Go ahead son."

With a bruised face from Tajaymae, his sclera had veins sprouting up to his pupils as he walked into the ring while Loaded Ace does the same. A cage from the ceiling slowly comes down onto the ring edges as both fighters started slowly walking around in circles from each other. Max expressed his staid face with his hands down while Loaded Ace was walking around with a rifle that shoots his playing cards strapped to his right arm. "All right fighters!! Are your ready!?! Let the fight commence!!"

"You're just another inexperienced Death Angel, so that means you're going to die!" Loaded Ace blurted.

"Yeah, you're right, I am sort of inexperienced, but I'll assure you that I won't lose to you!" Max said as he took his Axe from behind his back.

Without further ado, Max charging at Lo with both of his hands on the axe and ready to cut him open. Lo moved swiftly and shooting his playing cards at him. Max hits away the cards and eventually Max made it closer to Lo. Lo surprisingly hit Max in the left arm with a playing card the same arm in which he is holding his axe.

"Agh." Max said with his axe aiming at Lo but it seems like he can't move his arm. He looked at his arm with a confused facial expression. His mind was lost from the technique he just did and said—

"What the hell did you do?"

"I paralyzed your arm and you should feel your energy draining. Hmm, for you Death Angel, I'm going all out."

"Hmmph..." Vince muttered.

Lo shot more playing cards at Max hitting his stomach, legs, his other arm and neck which made him paralyzed from the neck to his feet. Max's physique is beginning to wobble as the water in his body is being drained. Lo then began punching Max in the face several times causing him to bleed from his nose. Then Lo punched Max in the chest and stomach multiple times as fast as he can. "Agh', agh', agh'!" Max expressed pain.

The audience is chanting and screaming— *'MURDER MURDER, KILL KILL"* while Lo hits him blow after blow.

"Yeah!" Then someone in the audience yelled— "Beat his ass!!"

"He's getting his ass beat again." Tajaymae said.

"As if you weren't enough ass whooping for him." Nack said.

"He gotta have something to stop him." Ki-Yale said.

"Agh', agh', agh', agh'!" Max continued to receive punches from Lo.

Vince squinted with slight worry that his son is about to die. Max clenches his axe tightly then progressively a small bright white glowing orb appeared in midair behind Lo. The orb hovered over everyone as it rises higher, then the audience became completely silent, ceased all noise and loud chanting.

"Agh, agh, agh."

Lo realizes the audience stopped making noise completely and stopped punching him then wondered— "Hm, why everyone is so quiet...?"

Ki-Yale panicked as he looked around seeing that everyone is quiet with their eyes being all white with no pupils, absolutely spaced out while staring at the orb. He saw that his sister was also affected so he waved his hand in front of her face then said— "Sis?"

Lo realized that the audience is looking at something behind him then he turned around. At that precise moment he began to freeze like the others, no movement, just staring straight into the orb. Most of the audience began walking out of their seats and headed straight towards the orb. Even Tajaymae, Nack, Mike and Xack did the same moving towards the orb.

"Tajay… Nack… guys don't go up there…"

"Take him out son..." Vince softly spoke as he is immune to the orb's mind control because he is too a Death Angel.

"Hmph, it's time I show you my paralysis."

The orb resided in the air above Lo then it rapidly dropped down onto him while everyone that got affected by the Orb started moving fast with the orb. As the orb controlled everyone's movements, it collided with Lo's head then gradually sunk in past his flesh.

Everyone suddenly back to normal and wondering why they got out of their seats. The audience and everyone went back to their originals spots and still wondering how and why they even got to a different position. Some had already covered their eyes with blindfolds because they understood that the Death Angel had the ability called the 'Tantu Orb'.

Loaded Ace remained on the ground as Max walked up to him. "Ok folks! Looks like we got a winner!! The Death Angel… Max Harven!" Majesty announced.

"Is Loaded knocked out oorrr'...?" Tajaymae asked.

"No, its an enchantment ability used only by Death Angels, the orb wipes out one's spirit once it touches the lifeform which results in death in spirit, but the body remains alive. His body is now paralyzed, Max now has the choice to either undo the paralysis or keep the body in this state until it is completely rotted away from lack of nourishment. Max also have the choice to return his soul back to his body. Once the spirit abandons the body, the spirit is then trapped in the Death Angel's orb until the Death Angel dies the spirits will roam free but without a body. For him to activate it he just needs Tektonium metal which is what that axe is made of."

"The org can also collect as many souls as it pleases depending on how strong the Death Angel is, and these don't nessisarly have to be inside a body to be collected. It's a very fascinating but messed up." Nack said.

Max looked at Ki-Yale for a few seconds then walked out the ring back to his Dad.

"Hmm, well . . . I wasn't effected by the orb."

"Y-y-you weren't?" Mike confused.

"Yeah, come to think of it, you were in the same spot at our post while we were walking back to it." Xack surprised.

"It's your suit, isn't it?" Nack asked.

"Yes, my suit had already downloaded his technique way before he even thought of using it and gave me knowledge of the attack."

"So, you're like a Death Angel now?" Tajaymae asked.

"Yeah, you can say that. I didn't just download his technique, I made it to be at its peak. Whatever abilities he can't do yet, I can do."

"Nice." Tajaymae said.

"Yeah but. I don't like the ideas of being a Death Angel with the thirst to kill and all."

"Do you feel that thirst?" Nack asked.

"Nah, I got rid of the thirst but if I was to even keep that ability of the thirst to kill, I would have controlled it with ease. Thanks to the suit."

"So, wait, you can copy powers as well and perfect them completely?" Xack asked.

"Yes, and not just powers, I can download anything, take shape or form of any person or thing, except for the Opposites."

"Whoa…" Mike perplexed.

"That's incredible . . . So, you can even copy Apaki technology?"

"Yep."

"Brother, you get all of the attention."

"Ha, cause my powers are cooler than yours."

"Aaah shut up Ki!"

Medics came onto the ring and took Loaded's body up then brings him to a room where they keep dead bodies. "You think he will revive him?"

"I doubt it Netro… Death Angels rarely do that, collecting souls is another way for them to get more powerful in every way." Xack noted.

"I just hope he doesn't do that again. That was so weird!" Tajaymae said.

"I ab'… I absolutely agree, it mah'… It makes my head spin!"

"Well, it's been a fun ride with Loaded he's been participating in this arena for six consecutive months, it's a shame to see him go. Anyways, neeext' up! We have a new fighter from Little Tree Ville. I don't know what his powers are, but he seems like the lil' dude got some shit to kick. His name is…. Netro! Netro, please step in the ring."

Ki-Yale looked at everyone on his side then Mike smiled and said— "Tha'… that's you boy!"

"Kick some ass brother." Tajaymae encouraged him.

"Hey, if you have to take someone's life just do it quick." Xack advised but got interrupted.

"Nah don't worry about me, I don't kill humans, so that means I won't kill, and you shouldn't either." Ki-Yale said as he walked up on the ring.

"Boooooo!" Roared the audience.

"He looks fragile... skinny ass kid!" Said one guy in the crowd.

Ki-Yale then notices the cherry red haired girl from earlier as she smiled at him and he gave a little smirk back to her.

"For his contestant, he's a skilled enchantment user... the wooden spike releasing bad ass... Beaks! . . . Beaks please step onto the ring. Now Beaks is a regular contestant, he's been fighting in this arena for almost a year now going eight months strong."

Beaks walked up on stage while the audience is chairing him on. Beaks is twenty years of age is known for his long nose making him look like a bird which is why he calls himself beaks. He utilizes enchantment which allows him to grow sharp wooden spikes like objects from his body then shoot them at his opponents and he is also part Sila Human.

"I'm going to tear you apart scrawny looking boy!" Beaks said as he grew his wooden spikes.

"Hmm, I want you to come at me with the best you've got!"

"Ha, I don't think you want my best kid."

"Hm, trust me do your best . . . You're gonna' need it."

"What you just say you little punk!?"

Intensity in the air as Majesty intervened.

"The trash talk is heavy folks! Alright fighters!! Are you ready?!! Let the fight commence!!"

<u>*Little Tree Ville hospital*</u>—

Doctor Damian is treating Pamela Shale and her daughter Kathleen after being in stable condition from the explosion back at the police station.

"Just minor cuts and bruises, no sign of radiation or virus detected, so that's good."

"So, we should be good to go?" Pamela asked while picking up her belongings.

"Yes, just be careful outside. I know you took the vaccine, but the air is still contaminated, it's fading away but slightly still contaminated."

"I should be fine" She said.

"Hey Luka . . . I'm truly sorry for your loss . . . She was a great patient of mine."

"Hm, thank you. She tells wonderful things about you doctor; this is one of the reasons why I still attend to you."

"Thank you doctor." Kathleen expressed gratitude while walking behind her mother.

"You're welcome and please if there is any you need... Don't hesitate reach me."

Pamela and Kathleen left the room then walked down the hospital aisle on the seventh floor. Luka Shale Jr. looked at his wife sitting in the bench in the waiting area next to the elevator.

"I knew you would take the elevator. Are you all alright?"

"Yeah we're fine, it's nothing Dad."

"Nothing you say . . . Hmmph . . . There was a suicide bombing in the same building and all you say is 'It's nothing Dad'." Luka said.

"Yeah, we survived with nothing not but scratches, it's nothing. It was a suicide, oh, what a coincidence."

"Hm."

Luka stared at his daughter for a few seconds fathomed everything that's been happening lately is affecting her in some way. It's not surprising for him as Luka himself has taken things to heart but chooses to show strong emotion. He relied on his faith in the lord Jesus Christ who is the Son of God, he is a fellow believer of Catholicism. He remained a sound mind despite the awful things revolving around him.

"Our father will not fail us Kathleen, no matter the situation we must be keep the faith."

"Keep the faith huh? I say our faith wasn't doing anything Dad . . . Maybe God has left us."

"No, God has a place for us..." He said and got interrupted.

"Dad please, I don't want to hear anymore."

Pamela showed no emotion, staring at Luka as she presses the elevator button, she blinked three times then the elevator arrived within seconds. As Pamela remained quiet on the elevator Luka looked at her while Kathleen kept her fixation of being on her phone.

"Pamela, if it's something you want to say. Say it, I can't stand the no talking faze."

"Well at this moment you're gonna have stand for it." She responded.

Kathleen with a staid face, her head straight looking at the elevator glass door as it goes down to the first floor.

"Hm, Pam . . . It's just one step at a time, we will get through this."

Kathleen then looked at her mother and held her hand. Pamela slowly turned her head to her daughter seeing that her eyes had tears ready to burst. Clutching her daughter tightly then she hugged her as the tears dropped down Kathleen's neck. Kathleen then puts her arms around her mother then began to weep as well as Luka stared at them with his chin up.

Back on the seventh floor Dr. Damian spoke with his trusted assistant as they walk down the aisle— "Her vitals are critical. I'm not sure what happened."

Dr. Damian opened the door with his access key that opened any door in the premises.

"Doctor! She's going into shock!!"

"Ok . . . Use full power." Dr. Damian demanded.

No response from Adelia Woods as doctors around her use the defibrillator machine trying their best to keep her up. The electrocardiograph showed flat lines as Dr. Damian's eyelids are wide open and revealing a nauseated state— "Hey I'm not losing her. I made a promise."

"But doctor…"

"DO IT AGAIN!"

Nealo and his grandson are finished with their shopping and proceeded to the pay station.

"That would be one hundred and thirty-six dollars." Said the android.

"Ok."

The I.D scanner machine scanned his face and got a discount because his credit along with being a previous general of the Gigantica Army.

"Ten dollars, hm,'… help with these groceries my grandson." He said while Oji looked in another direction. He snapped his fingers close to his ear and got his attention.

"Oh." He said grabbing a few bags then they proceed to walk out the exit.

As soon as Nealo stepped out the door behind Oji, he recognized the trees aren't the same.

"What the… now it's back to normal. The trees are small again!"

"Woah, Granddad—the trees!"

Nealo looked at his grandson with a look as if he suspects something of him then he asked— "Was this you Oji?"

"What do you mean Granddad?"

"Did you do all of this? . . .Changed the trees back to normal?"

"I don't know…"

"I think you did. The ones changed are the ones in the pathway we walked and if you look to your left and your right further down, those trees are still tall."

Oji looked at his grandfather with his eyes wide open and said—

"So, I have powers like Ki-Yale?"

"Not exactly like Ki-Yale—something different . . . Let's put these abilities of yours to good use."

TWENTY-ONE

The Mad Doctor, altering from place to place thinking two steps ahead of the military and law enforcement. Different hideouts throughout the solar system, the bigger the area the better for one to hide. Many believe concealing in anyway is a sign of mortality meaning you have to hide to protect what you have or what you are. Being in the face of your enemy shows that you have raw power but, in this case, not having raw power is not a primary factor for Sagan as he plays a chess game with humanity, behind unknown areas.

Dr. Rogue Sagan with a coffee mug filled with hot coffee walking through his beautiful garden with all sorts of beautiful plants such as blushing bromeliads, orchids, angel wing begonias, periwinkles and a lot more. He walked up to a waterfall with his right hand out touching the water. He looks down on the water and suddenly, a masked man which almost looked like a ninja, but it was just an assassin with two hook swords appeared from behind. He underestimated Dr. Sagan, as he quickly turned around and splashed the hot coffee in his face. The attacker had a mask, but his eyes were uncovered. The assassin swung out of balance and missed his target then Dr. Sagan revealed his signature weapon 'Ronda' and shot the assassin in the head. The needle went right through his skull while the assassin swung his last swung with his hook sword. Dr. Sagan stood motionless while the assassin went closer with his hook sword ready to slice him then stopped and stood still then his cranium exploded in front of Sagan causing brain particles to scatter all over his face. "Hmm', Rojohn sent you. Didn't he?"

<u>Shale Residence</u>—

"So where exactly did you look for Melissa?"

"Her room, the living room, kitchen, the bathroom, basement…"

"Sister's room?"

"Yes, everywhere."

"Everywhere? Every area in the house . . . Can you pinpoint them out for me please?" Detective Charlie Jacobs said.

"Why ask about the whereabouts?"

"Well right now I should be asking the questions but to answer your question this is an ongoing investigation and I need every detail because of possible speculation that it's not a suicide."

"So, you're implying that it's indeed a murder?"

"Suspect... Not yet implying." He said as he scans the towels with a device in the bathroom.

He then went outside to the barn while Pamela stood inside, he analyzed the outside of the barn yard then lifted the caution tape and entered the barn. Then he used a special device as part of the forensics that analyzes the barn for any clues he can decipher. Fingerprints were revealed as the Shale family but that's their barn, they're supposed to leave fingerprints. No other prints were found as he took a good look at the area where Melissa died and still saw that murder was not the cause of death.

Demi and Nealo partaking in a conversation whereas Oji played with his action figures.

"So, you think he can control nature?"

"Yeah the plants, the ground I'm not particularly sure though but today we will find out." Nealo said as he walked up to his grandson.

"Ok my grandson, it's time."

"Ok grandpa." Oji said as he gently puts down his toys stood up facing his Grandfather.

"I need you to concentrate, you did your powers by fault but now you just need to master them."

"That's how Ki-Yale learned his powers right?"

"Yeah some of it but the right way is to focus and command your power."

Oji turned around to the garden then held his two hands out and he closes his eyes trying to change the size of the trees around him. His hands begin to shake while nothing is happening for about one minute. He looked back at his grandfather then said— "Nothing is happening…"

"Hm, it's because you're not focusing don't look back just focus your mind to command your power... Focus on the multicellular organisms—the fungi in the trees. Focus and harness your power. . . Then after that…."

Oji slowly puts his hands back in front of him holding it out then closed his eyes once more obeying his grandfather and said to himself— "Focus . . . Focus . . . Focus."

"Unleash your power Oji! Unleash it!"

Mayor Tyson staring at who seems to be a ghost or just an illusion, but she was real. Stacey Roberts is right in front of him again.

"I thought you were dead, after that day when…"

"But here I am still alive. You're doing a fine job as Mayor, living your dream…"

"Well, it's a crisis going on now but I'm handling it."

"Good, handling things is what we all should do… I handled my obsessive ways and escaped death."

"So, you indeed went back to him? And I suppose you didn't tell him at first."

"Yes, which is why there were bounties after me for years but now I'm safe within a new name."

"A new name huh?"

"Even you, I can't inform."

"Occupied with the secret agency I presume?"

"Hm', I would love for us to…"

"I don't Stacey, or should I call you 'unknown name'."

"Stacey is fine for now."

"Hm', ever since then I haven't done another relationship."

"Well, you and I… You were the most adjoining to me than any other man. Even though I had an addiction, you stood by me."

"Until I had enough."

"All I could think about was sex… all I wanted was sex at least five times a day, somedays even more… I was a nymphomaniac on a whole new level."

"Yeah…"

"Although… I haven't seen you for years, I just want to make up for my mistakes… There're so many questions that needs to be answered, so many concerns and so many things to catch up on."

He looks at her with a bit of disfavor in his face as she took a deep breath then changed the subject— "How is Mike doing?"

"He's at this tournament in Crouton Village."

"You mean the one that…?"

"Yes."

She squinted her eyes and thought about the dangers of that tournament.

"That could be his life." She said.

"He can handle himself. He's benevolent but he ain't no pushover, plus I created a weapon for him that will surely put him through most situations."

Crouton Village Tournament—

Dunkin Turd left the section to get something to eat and stumbled onto some teenagers.

"Let me get an aaaa'… Get an aaaaa'…"

"C'mon man, hurry up!"

"Hey patience. Ok? Didn't your parents ever teach you that?"

"Yeah and they taught me that you need to hurry the hell up."

"Sir. What would you like?"

"Ok, let me get a double cheeseburger. . .. No, no forget that… Let me get an aaaaa…"

"Dude c'mon man! Just order something already."

"Ok, ok! Let me get a taco with teriyaki chicken, lettuce, onions, sweet peppers and bacon with a medium drink."

"Finally, after millions of years!"

"How much?"

"That will be eleven dollars and thirty-five cents."

"Ok, I can pay that." Mr. Turd's face was scanned for payment then he continued— "Should have just had multiple cashiers here and maybe get an android cashier system. It's so old schools here."

"Yeah, yeah. Now step aside so I could do my order."

Mr. Turd went to the waiting area for his order them received it within a minute.

"Wow, you guys really live up to the name fast food."

The crowd all shouted— "Kill the new kid!!" Repeatedly. Beaks charged at Ki-Yale as he released a twelve-inch sharp wooden spike from his hand then held it. Beaks then swung at the side of Ki-Yale's face as he stood motionless and didn't even flinch. Beaks sliced his face leaving an open cut then briskly punctured Ki-Yale in the neck with little blood flowing down his neck.

"Ooh shit!" Mike surprised as Beaks pulled out his wooden spike.

"Why the hell didn't he move?" Xack asked as Nack smiled.

"Ye'… your best friend just got sli'… sliced and stabbed in the neck… and you're just smiling…?"

"No worries Mike…"

"I'm more surprised he didn't say 'I got the heart of a lion' in this fight." Tajaymae mocking her brother.

"What?!"

"He's fine Xack, just watch." Tajaymae said.

Ki-Yale wearing his Netron Suit originally weighs about 460lbs and his suit can add more weight as to also reduce more weight to his body if so needed. His suit enables his skin and the suit itself to be softer than usual which is like human skin.

With little blood flowing down Ki-Yale's neck, Beaks swung again then Ki-Yale caught his spike while his face and neck healed rapidly.

"What the fuck?!" Beaks said after he saw Ki-Yale's face healing. Beaks struggled as he tries to pull his spike from Ki-Yale's hands but couldn't budge. Ki-Yale then head-butts him in the face allowing him to fall back backwards a couple feet with his head leaned back. "Agh…"—Beaks in pain.

"Woah, so he can heal himself too…" Xack said.

"Yes, he has that healing factor." Nack said.

"You got a tough head their kid, I need more muscle for you." Beaks said as he grew three inches of muscle on his arms, body, neck and legs.

"Hmmph." Ki-Yale muffled as he puts his hands up in orthodox boxing stance.

Beaks revealed more wooden spikes on his fists then charged at Ki-Yale and swung his left arm. Ki-Yale then dodged it swiftly by stepping back and then he took a slow swing back at him. Beaks blocked it with his arm, but he still gets pushed back a little about six feet back.

Beaks and Ki-Yale began brawling like two heavy weight boxers in the ring, Beaks is taller, but he crouches down while quickly throwing his fists and giving Ki-Yale a beat down. Ki-Yale finally seemed to feel a little worn out, he looked at Beaks for a few seconds then said—

"Hmm. Is that the best you can do?"

"Ha. You're fucking bluffing right kid? Look at you. I'm kicking your ass and you're getting tired then you say— 'Is that the best you can do?'."

"I was testing out your strength and it's just not good enough for me. Might as well end this now."

Ki-Yale's eyes generated electricity then Beaks became astonished— "What the…"

"You lose." He said then blasted his electric beam using a small percentage of power enough to knock Beaks down and put a very small electrical current around his body. The electrical current increases all throughout his body which cause him to knock out. "Woah…" Said the audience.

The red head girl ogled at Ki-Yale with a surprised look on her face. Push on sidelines also looked at him with a mini camera devise embedded to his shirt. Beaks is now on the floor while Electricity is flowing around his body.

"He won . . . Well, of course..." Xack said slightly surprised and relieved.

"Ye'... Yeah you ain't seen him in action? C'mon he's an alie... an alien from another planet and he's going to bring in the Mad Doctor be'... behind bars where he belongs—don't let that be known to the wrong people though." Mike said to Xack.

"Hm', he needs more than just bars."

Ki-Yale walked up to Beaks and looked down on him as Ki-Yale only being about five feet tall and Beaks being an adult at six feet tall.

"Kill him! Kill him!" Said the audience shouting at Ki-Yale.

"You have the choice to kill him... Or not." Majesty said.

"No, I don't kill my fellow humans. A knockout is good enough."

"All right folks, Netro chooses not to kill and Beaks will see another day. Let me just go and check him out." Majesty said.

"Booooo!"—The audience all angry and screamed at Ki-Yale.

He notices the cherry red haired girl from earlier at the register room and kept looking at each other while Majesty walked in the ring to check on Beaks.

"He has a pulse and still alive. Let's get a medic and security pick him up." Majesty said.

Ki-Yale kept looking at his new crush then she smiled and waved at him as he walked off the ring.

"Hey kid!" Majesty hollered.

"What's up?" Ki-Yale answered.

"You're good . . . I like that power you have, I never seen that fucking lightning move before—It came right out of your eyes. How did you obtain that?!"

"It's classified for now sir."

"Ok, that's cool. Probably some illegal invention. I like your modesty also but you're going to have to kill one of these fighters. The crowd, they paid their hard-earned money to see things like that."

"No, not happening. It's just my code."

Majesty stared at Ki-Yale as he walked away back to his section.

"Tha'...! That was crazy! Tha'... that lightning and all that!" Mike said.

"Yeah, you almost fried his ass." Nack said.

"Just one of my powers and I used a percentage that would only take him out without killing."

"These people want to see you kill more than a clean knock out but it's still entertaining." Xack said.

"Ok, ok folks! Next fight will be Ron the Don versus Killa Carlisa!" Majesty announced.

In the tournament cafeteria Mr. Turd finished eating his food while the same teenagers are observing him.

"Who's mans is this? He looks like a schmuck."

"Let's play a prank on him bro."

"Yeah, let's fuck with him a bit."

"But how are we going to do that?"

"Yeeaah. How are we doing that?"

"Stink bomb you idiots."

"Oh yeah that's a good one but . . . Where are we going to get a stink bomb?"

"I have the stink bomb."

"Oh shit, so let's throw it at him."

"It's in my room though."

"Damn he's about to leave."

"Ok let's take something from him then lead him to my room and boom! Stink bomb!"

"Yeeeaah'. I like that."

Unknown household in Little Tree Ville—

Henry Luciano, unharmed and standing in front of his mirror buttoning his shirt. The room is dark with only a few dimmed lights on.

He ogled at himself for a minute then he realized he wasn't the only one in the room.

"Its fancy meeting you here… demon."

"Yes likewise." The demon said with a strong deep and beastly voice.

The spirit has the exact same face as the one projected through Nealo's visuals. Henry unfazed by its appearance beside him, naked but only revealing his chest up. With overweening utterance, he smiled at the demon in the superbly clear mirror.

"It looks like your getting accustomed to Earth…" The demon spoke without any lips just speaking telepathically and looking at another man standing ten feet behind Henry. The man wore a hood over his head and a cloak covering his entire body.

The demon persisted—

"Wasting time is what I see of it."

Henry snickered then said—

"I know who you are demon and you don't scare me."

"I see… I figured you do…"

"Yes, and you resemble the boy so well… I'm guessing you choose to invest in him?"

"Well, I can predict the many possibilities of the future and I see it's looking pretty upsetting for him."

"And that's what you love… the rage. You absorb it like a sponge."

The demon growled at Henry with as his severed cheeks lifted with its nose and his eyebrows were down to the glare of its pupils and dark sclera.

"Why not possess the entire family? Hmm? Just tell me what your plans truly are, and I won't annihilate you."

The demon stood silent for ten seconds then responded—

"Annihilate me? We'll have to see about that."

Henry chuckled some more then said—

"I accept your challenge demon… let's see who kills who."

"Keep talking like that child and you will know what's good for you… and when I say child, I mean you are still a child underneath that ugly human body."

"Twenty-five years of living… I consider myself grown and still far older than you."

The demon shouted then growled then said—

"We'll see who kills who... your Royal Highness."

The demon vanished in front of Henry while he continued to look at the mirror. The demon had upset Henry spoke to another being in his head.

"You said you knew its true name my lord?"

"Yes, but that isn't really important… keeping this low profile isn't my speed but I've learned a lot so far being distant from home."

"Yes, the perks of being a variable within society."

"It's soon time that I make my move."

"I think it's a little early for you my lord."

Henry chuckled then said—

"I've waited too long. I already possess the key to profound supremacy."

"Yes, but remember the Demon of Evolution…"

"He's just a child and he's only going after on thing."

"Which is why he concerns me."

"Yes, but it's worth the risk to let him do what he pleases. Besides, I'm more conning than all of them... Hmm, I say it's time I make my move."

A Local Diner in Little Tree Ville—

Later at mid-day, Henry Luciano is eating his meal while the android waitress appeared with a second drink for him and one for Luka Shale Jr. Luka sat across from him with nothing to eat, the tragic events affecting his eating habits, slowly rendering him physically and mentally.

Henry looked at him with complete silence then said— "Things can go right but things can go left at any time. The right side of the road is the safest and the left side isn't so safe you know."

"But either way that road is to be followed in the same direction right or left. As long I get to my destination."

"Hmm, I'm sorry about your loss Luka. Things like this will sneak up on you."

"Yeah and I still believe someone murdered her."

"The Mad Doctor's work?"

"Maybe but I never did anything to get back at him ever since the theft two years ago."

"Because you're smart not to do something like that."

"Hm…"

"So, you wanna hear about the sales?"

"Yeah. What's the update?"

"So far three hundred 'K' in sales revenue and it continues to increase."

"Good . . . that's good Luka."

Luka glanced at him in silence with slightly fastened lips then Henry said— "It's on its way to millions I guess, I'm just surprised it takes this long."

"I guess it takes time, it's a great invention with great potential and I see a bright future with it."

"I agree . . . a toast to your father's invention."

Henry held up his drink as Luka looked at him then smiled as he does the same.

TWENTY-TWO

Crouton Village Tournament—

Push in a room by himself calling Sagan through a holographic projector with extremely advanced graphics as if Dr. Sagan is actually there in the room with him. These holographic projectors are like the _FaceTime_ of the 24th century. "What is it that you want Push?"

"I have something to show you. It should be uploading on your side right now."

Push sent him a video of Ki-Yale fighting Beaks which brings more questions about his abilities.

"Hm, Is he immortal?"

"It's just a theory but I think it's that suit. At first bullets were bouncing off of him and now he actually got cut with blood leaking then… Then he regenerated its remarkable .. . Maybe, just maybe we can get that suit." Push being a little concerned.

"I think that suit is a part of him Push."

"Then this is a very grim difficulty for us."

"Problems can be solved Push. Problems can be solved."

Dr. Sagan logged off the call then two of Push's comrades appeared through the door following two young ladies, Collin Robinson and Guss Clarks walked in with rolled up blunts.

"Yooo'. I got some goodies for you man." Guss said.

"Goodies? Oh perfect, pass that. Just what I need right now." Push said as Guss passed him a blunt.

"C'mon baby . . . It doesn't blow itself now." Guss said as one of the ladies got her knees and unbuckled his pants.

"You're an asshole Guss."

"They love it Push!"

"Hey. You saw that Netro kid out there man? I never seen some shit like that before." Collin said then blew smoke into the other girl's mouth.

"Yeah he looks like a wimp but he's a different breed." Push added then puffed smoke.

"Fucking dude, shoots lightning out of his eyes!" Guss said.

"Yeah man crazy shit." Collin said.

"He ain't a killer like me but he's definitely powerful… check this out." Push boasted as he lifted his shirt showing his strike wound from Ki-Yale's lightning.

"Oh, shit what happened bro?!"

"I got hit by Netro man!" Push answered Collin.

"Oooh shit!" Guss and Collin spoke at the same time while Push nods his head up and down.

"Yeah, with all that power he got he chooses not to kill. What a little chump."

Ki-Yale relocated from the fighting taking place in the tournament, he levitated in the air then landed on the roof of his assigned tournament dorm room sharing with Nack, Mike and Tajaymae. Lying down and gazing into the sky, comprehending how large the clouds are. He utilizes more vision up to an altitude of 38,000 feet and saw aircrafts moving in orderly fashion thousands of miles away. He smiled admiring the technology that humans created, how remarkable and sturdy the airplanes are. He heard movement behind him and his fists instantly glowed ready use his Loose Cannon then turned around and got up.

"Whoa there! It's just me your Father!" Neecho said in his Netron Suit appearing randomly out of the blue and Ki-Yale being surprised to see his father.

"Dad?!"— "In the flesh!"

"You didn't have to sneak up on me like that…"

"I wouldn't just put it that way… I call it a test, to see if those ears are working and your reflex and…"

"And you just want to annoy me."

"That too. Can I join you?"

"You don't need to ask that Pop."

Ki-Yale ogled at his father he sat next to him.

"This is the first time I'm seeing you in that suit and even when I first discovered my suit, I saw Granddad's suit for the first time. Why didn't you or Granddad tell me about it sooner?"

"Well for one, you look really good in that suit. Like a true soldier."— "Thank you."

"And two, we didn't tell you because well, we thought it wasn't necessary. We figured its best you find out on your own and the suit will appear to you when the time is right."

"So, the time is right three years after my brother got taken?"

"Well I say the right time, I mean the time when you diminish most of your fears. The suit has a thirst for bravery from a soldier with the heart to fight."

"So, it's having a feast right now?" He asked staring at his black chrome gloves.

"Yes, you're partially catching onto it. I bet that Granddad told you that if you deactivate your suit your wounds will not appear on your body because it regenerates. Right?"

"Yeah he did…"— "Yes but did he tell you that the suit can affect your body if you stay for a long time with it on?"

"No, he didn't. But how so?"

"The suit comes with a cost. Let's say you decide to equip yourself with the suit for the rest of your life and never change back… the nurtures of your body will become frail. Do that, then disarm your suit, you can possibly die. This is because our armor is made from the Zenith crystal. The Zenith crystal can be sort of an infection that feast on energy. Wearing the suit, you can live forever but deactivating after those long years could be devastating. This is why Netrons take breaks then immediately return to the battlefield."

"I see, not only does it feast off my bravery, it relinquishes my actual body slowly."

"Yes, but don't worry, any serious damage would only happen if you don't train your body often without the suit."

Ki-Yale slightly nodded his head then looked up to the sky again.

"Fascinating, isn't it son? We have our special creations and so does the beings on this planet. You should always be grateful that you're half human and half Netron."

"Yeah… umm—absolutely."—A hazy response from Ki-Yale then he stared at the sky again.

"In history this planet had been evolving for centuries. Millions of years back technology wasn't even a thing until man made it. Now it's used everywhere, every single thing is run by technology. It's just a matter of time that tech takes over."

"Like an apocalypse of machines trying to take over the world. I've seen plenty movies like this."

"Yes, but I don't think that would happen. It would be nice to have someone that can actually take on any threat though."

"Hm… and be a leader."

"Yeeah'… that's just how a prince thinks, being a king, a ruler, it isn't a walk in the park though . . . It's more than just restoring order, it's more than just fortification, or getting a queen and making children..."

Ki-Yale expressed a face of misperception regarding what his father had said then he asked— "Then… what's it all about Dad? Responsibility? I'm pretty sure you said this before."

"It's making the right decisions son."

"Yeeaah, you and your little motivational talks. Why are you truly here Dad? You know I can handle myself."

"Yes, you can but never forget Narrken and what happened to him. You're still a kid, powerful amongst the humans but I fear a greater threat is among us."

"Hm, Narrken… You remember that slogan I always say?"

"Yes. How can I forget…? 'I got the heart of a lion'."

"He's the one that told me that slogan. It was originally his and he told me to use one every time I get scared or when I'm not brave enough to make a decision."

Neecho stood quiet for a minute then said—

"Hm', that sounds like something he would make up. He always played the tough one ever since I told him to be after he got bullied in school."

"Really? He never told me about that."

"Yes, two older boys in their early teens picked on him after school for a month straight until he got fed up of it. He didn't do anything rational instead he told me, and I encouraged him to fight back but don't overdo it, just show them you're not to be messed with. After that, he never mentioned the bullying again."

Ki-Yale turned his head to the left away from his father with his left eyebrow up as if he had a theory.

"What's up?" Neecho being curious.

"Narrken didn't have a suit as well. I guess he was actually scared of something."

Ki-Yale arrived at the table where Mike, Nack, Tajaymae and Xack were all eating then stared at the floor contemplating. His head then lifted upward, observing the live footage of the fights progressing in the arena that is revealed on the TV screens on the wall and ceiling in the cafe.

"This stuff is good." Mike said while eating vigorously on some lobster, side of roast shrimp and cooked corn on the cob and mash potatoes.

"Yeah, this food is awesome."—Tajaymae agreeing with Mike.

"Hey, Ki. You're not going to eat that?" Nack asked.

"No… I mean, yeah… I'm just thinking about something." He vacillated.

"Aaand' what's it that you're thinking about? Care to share?" Tajaymae being nosey.

Ki-Yale raised his left eyebrow responding to his sister then turns his head to Nack and there she was, the girl with the cherry red hair gradually sat next to Nack across from Ki-Yale.

"Hey aah… your name is Netro… Correct?" She asked in a strong Hispanic accent.

"Hey, yeah that, that's right…" Ki-Yale being shy.

"I'm Litzy… Litzy de la Rose."

He goggled at her, noticing they had the same eye color as she puts her hand out for him to shake it.

"Ah… nice to meet you… um… Litzy." He stammered while shaking her hand then took a glimpse at Nack while he gave a smile.

"Hope I'm not interrupting…" Her strong accent expressed a rich and subtle approach causing the males at the table to be extra nice. "No, no you're not." Nack said.

"Nuh'… no interruption here ma'am." Mike said.

"I agree on that." Xack added.

"Cool, well, Netro... you're like so cool, with all that lightning impending out of your eyes and that healing factor you got! It's so astonishing." She jabbered.

"Yeah, my powers are..." He said and got interrupted.

"Fucking awesome! —Like, where are you from? What's your origin? Are there more like you?" She asked excessively.

"You wanna know his dick size too?"

"Tajaymae! Sorry, that's my sister..."

"It's cool. Hmm, sister huh? I'm guessing her powers are similar."

"Yeah similar but not the same, let me introduce everyone here. That's Nack sitting next to you, next to him is Mike."

"Hey." Mike and Nack spoke at the same time.

"This guy next to me is Xack."

"What's up young one?" Xack greeted.

"It's nice to meet you all."

"Now it's certainly a lot of questions you want answers to."

"Oh yeah, a lot."

"Well, I'm from Little Tree Ville, I'm a half-breed extraterrestrial being, half human and half Netron and yes there are more like me."

"Wow... So, you're talking about like an alien?" Litzy confused as she looked at Ki-Yale's friends and sister.

"Yes, an alien... Is that a little too much for you?" Tajaymae tested.

"No, it's just kind of weird but at the same time so believable because aliens actually exist based on our history with the Grainians . . . So, you're not a Mega Human but like a half-breed alien from this planet called Netron? Your parents named you after the planet?"

"Yeah something like that, Netro is the rightful name given to the current leader of their planet, my planet."

"Woah… a leader of an entire planet!" She gasped as she nodded her head.

"Now she's even more interested." Tajaymae added.

"It's a lot to explain but what about you. Where are you from? What's your powers?"

"I'm a mixed breed myself I'm part Italian, Dominican and French and I'm from the Great Welkin City, you know, one of those cities up in the sky."

"Wow that is mixed." Ki-Yale intrigued.

"Now, to answer your question about my powers… well, you have to find out when I'm fighting."

"Element of surprise. Hmm, very useful." Xack said.

"Her a… her abilities probably ca... probably can kick all of our asses, whatever it is."

"I don't think I'm that strong, but we'll see." Litzy said giving Ki-Yale a smile then got up and walked away.

"I guess we will see."

"Hm, I guess we will see." Nack taunted Ki-Yale.

"Shh'… she's a cutie... be'… be'… better make a move before Nack here does."

Ki-Yale raised his eyebrows at Mike then Nack said—"Ha, naaah' that's all for Ki."

"I se'… I see how you look at her too man. Yuh'… you younglings gonna' ha'… gonna have to learn that even your best friend can steal your girl."

"No! That's bro code violation man." Nack said.

<u>*Gigantica National Prison*</u>—

Correction Officers with rifles fully uniformed stood guard at each entrance and exit. In a barricaded canteen, Rojohn, the thug that got beat up by Ki-Yale back at the warehouse in Little Tree Ville is now incarcerated speaking with his guys. It's been incredulous for him, contemplating on how he got in this situation and still being demented. "This is bullshit! I was going to be powerful, deadly, adding some fire… Like serious fire power to my team but this fucking kid comes out of nowhere!"

"Some kind of set up if you ask me." An inmate said sitting right side from Rojohn.

"Yeah by Dr. Sagan. That hypocritical faggot all of his fucking crew, just a bunch of faggots!"

"We need to get em back but it's all up to you Rojohn. Are you sure you're up to this?"

"Yeah, I want him to know what I'm about…"

"Ok I'm down but… How suppose we do that?"

"We still got an outside crew, playing it smart, attacking him when he's vulnerable."

"I hear that man has never slipped up. All his facilities are protected and well thought out." Said the inmate sitting right side from Rojohn.

"Well, we just gotta' hit him harder than what he's protecting himself with."

"And what are your proposals Rojohn?"

"Well, I'll use my outside source and if that fails, then the kid with the black and white suit would have to do the job."

"The kid huh?"

<u>*Crouton Village Tournament*</u>—

Majesty speaking with his colleagues in a large office room while a substitute host is hosting the fights.

"This Netro kid, he's a freaking wimp but still so powerful. I never seen anything like it." Majesty said.

"It could be some new technology that the little rascal stole." Said one colleague.

"Nah he seemed very perceptive, he doesn't wanna kill knowing his power is great. He can shoot lightning from his freaking eyes. I mean with that kind of power; you can dominate the world."

"Yeah but I guess that's not like him."

"Well at least he's still entertaining, which gives my audience a good show."

"These people still wanna see lives being taken away, that's the primary reason they are here and that's what they paid for, but this kid is unfortunately the one that don't wanna kill."

"Unless we let him. Provoke his guts until he losses it."

"Hmm… I think I know where you're going with this."

Ki-Yale, Mike, Nack, Tajaymae and Xack went back to their station.

"Alright everyone. Next fight we have a special someone… The Mayor's son of Little Tree Ville."

Instantly the crowd cheered after hearing Majesty say— "Mike Roland!"

The crowd got louder at each end of his sentences— "He calls himself a savage! A real cold-hearted killer! That's right, he'll go up against Gallico!"

The crowd continued to cheer after he announced the contestants.

"Oh, shit that's you Mike, go show them what that device does." Nack encouraged.

Mike smiled then looked at Ki-Yale.

"No killing." Ki-Yale demanding with a voice full of pity.

"Al'… alright Dad." Mike spoke sarcastically.

Mike ambled up on stage as Gallico does the same while the cages slowly went down.

Majesty launched the fight saying— "Alright fighters . . . Let the fight commence!"

Tyson Roland is explaining his project to a group of government patrons willing to purchase it when it goes into marketing in the future. He pressed the switch on the desk which brought up a screen slider that shows touchable holographic images in the center of the desk.

"This device is basically a bracelet, a weapon that go against any Mega Human. During my previous time attending Linden College of Technical Robotics, I had to deal with a lot pressure and also dealing with a lot of stress just to later overcome my dreams of doing inventions. What you are looking at here is the Gazen Weapon!"

"Gazen Weapon you say? Please elaborate more." Said one of the patrons.

"Well, first you simply have to… place the weapon on your left arm. This weapon doesn't require injections, it'll just latch on then you press your buttons. Now why I call it the 'Gazen Weapon' is because of its unique power to produce one glasslike animal that surrounds the user except for birds of course because it won't be able to fly so well, it'll be too heavy."

"So, you're saying that device allows the user's mind to create any graphical beast surrounding the body then the user acts as a pilot?" Asked one of the patrons.

"Yes, that's exactly what it is."

"Impressive…" Said one of the patrons.

"Whatever animal you want it to be the user has to think of it and the chip that's inside the weapon is only programed to form animals."

Tyson continued to explain while some of the patrons wrote down the details to then soon after everyone stood quiet for about fifteen seconds.

"The source of power is similar to Apaki Jermayin Tech?" Asked another patron.

"Yes sir, Apaki Warrior Tech. It projects the same glass substance as the swords that appears from their hands during battle."

"Now how does these glass animals move around? It's harnessed from Apaki Tech but its animals we're talking about here not swords."

"Well it's liquid sand that was created by enchantment, this type of liquid sand is called Gazen inherited from planet Grain..."

"Gazen Sand... hm, now I see."

"That's right... Gazen Sand plays a big role with this weapon. This sand is an advanced way of creating glass which moves freely as if it were soft tissue though some pieces of glass will break then reform itself." Tyson said.

"Yes... Military Apaki Soldiers were the first to utilize this sand and they do it so well that they can create almost anything made from glass. This is what's used to create the barriers around cities as well. Now the glass being around the body is different."

"There will be a suit that transfers from the weapon to the body for protection as well."

"Very thoughtful Tyson..."

"Hmm, nowadays building weapons is more of a hobby."

"Now demonstrate this ability for us, please Mr. Roland."

"Absolutely."

Current Time, Crouton Village Tournament—

Gallico slowly stepped closer to Mike with a huge grin on his face with his hands behind his back.

"I'm going to rip your black ass apart and your father, the Mayor... he's black, isn't he?"

"Yes... my father is black bu'... but I was born with white skin color. Suh'... so what?!"

"It's in your blood... you're still a stupid piece of shit black! One that I'm going to murder!!! It's going to be fun!"

"You are... you are an imbecile."

"Ha! I love this place I can taunt people with racist comments and not get arrested for it."

"Why do yuh'... Why do you have to bring race into this? You're jus'... you're just trash brining up... bringing up poi'... pointless racism from the 21st century."

"What are you? A stutter-mouth? Or are you just trembling?! Ha! C'mon let's fight blackie!"

Gallico pulled out an illegal Fed gun from behind his back, a Pal 1500 pistol that suspiciously holds 21 rounds of 9mm bullets then the crowd instantly boos Gallico.

"Wow folks Gallico is getting straight to the point with bullets and yes in this arena guns are allowed as I stated before any weapon is allowed. This is a Death Week, but it seems you guys hate guns because it's quick and easy, no real entertainment here." Majesty said.

"He's an asshole." Ki-Yale said.

"Yeah a boring one at best using a damn pistol." Xack said.

"That too but I'm talking mainly about his racism."

"Racism?!" Tajaymae baffled

"Yeah, I heard him call Mike a piece of shit black."

"Oh no, that's at least one year in prison under Gigantica Laws using such a hideous speech." Nack said.

"Should've pull'... should've pulled that gun out . . . twenty minutes later into the fight of me kicking your ass and give thuh'... give the people a show."

"Ha! Kick my ass? Fuck the people! Fuck a show! I just wanna merk' some shit."

"Of course, . . . of course you do."

Mike quickly moved to the left while Gallico fired his gun. The shots missed Mike then instantly he pressed a button on the Gazen Weapon on his arm. Mike then transformed into a large clear glasslike Bear that's twice Mike's size around his body. Everyone from the crowd wowed as Gallico paused.

"Woah, I never seen this before." Xack said.

"You ain't seen nothing yet." Ki-Yale said.

"That graphic projector seemed similar to the Apaki Sword, except, it's only a portion of glass." Xack said.

"He better kick his pitiful racist ass." Tajaymae said.

Gallico kept shooting at Mike but the bullets only pierce projected glass skin.Mike growled at Gallico and ambled towards Gallico with his Bearlike legs. Gallico then said—"Man, fuck this!" Then dropped his gun.

Gallico stepping backwards while Mike ran towards him and cornered him. Mike then did a bear stand being about seven feet tall and sliced Gallico's face three times with his claws and then knocking him out with one slap.

"Well done." Tajaymae amused while Ki-Yale gave a stern face at Mike on the ring and Xack nodding his head up and down.

"Ok folks. It looks like we have a winner. Mike Roland!"

"Tha'… that was a breeze." Mike said as he walked down the platform back to the section.

"Interesting invention..." Xack said.

"Compli'… Compliments to my father."

"He isn't dead though, right?"

"If he mah'… makes it to tuh'… the hospital on time… yeah."

Ki-Yale stared at Mike hoping for a better answer.

"I di'... I didn't hit him enough for him to die bah'… bah'… but just get knocked out . . . If he doesn't get to a medic, he could ble… could leed out from the glass cuts. They'll figure it out nuh'… no worries."

"Hm, I hope so Mike."

Androids delivering food to the audience fueling the smell of hotdog, chestnuts and hamburgers. "Aaalriiight' eeeveryone'! This next fight, we have the first female fight of the day."

The arena shook as the crowd cheered for the fight that's about to go down as Majesty continued— "We have Litzy de la Rose versus… Tajaymae Kafmora!"

"Wow, I guess you're up sis."

"Go ge'… get em Tajay."

Tajaymae blushed at Mike as he smiled at her.

The leaves are moving in different direction while a massive amount of pollen began to reveal itself into the air. The splendor of restoration, Demi gulped at Nealo while he stared at his grandson. "You got this Oji . . . The whole village will be back to normal."

"Hm." Demi mumbled transporting her attention back at her son.

Oji holding both hands out as the sweat dripped down his neck because of the nervousness hoping not to fail. He focuses like what his grandpa said as his eyelids are squeezed shut then suddenly, all the trees around him begin to slowly morph back to their original size being small again. As citizens walk around the village detected what's happening and smiles revealed from face to face. Screams of joy all around Little Tree Ville as the signature is back to normal.

Oji opened his eyes then began to smile and looked at his hands. Nealo walked up behind him then said— "I knew you can do it."

"Oji..." Demi called him then he looked back at his mother.

"You're amazing." She acknowledged him.

Jody Field Cemetery in Jody Field, Gel Hev—

Multiple burials were held because of the tragedies that the Genchi had caused onto Little Tree Ville and a few areas outside of the village. Melissa's body, lying in an open coffin with red and white sympathy flowers formed as a cross and pictures of her surrounding the coffin. Her entire body seemed vastly pale mostly because of the mild effects of the Genchi. The minister is conducting the funeral as the Shale family members and the Taylor family members from all over the country attending the funeral, school mates and even her crush Jace Terry crowding over Melissa's deceased body. Jace stared at the girl he once fantasized to be with, the girl he never got to take out on a first date. Pamela sitting down hugging her husband with uncontrollable tears falling down her flushed cheeks. He hugged tighter with his arms around her shoulder then rubbed her upper arm up and down.

She slowly looked at everyone around her as one police officer observed her from behind the family members.

"We gather here today to mourn our fellow beloved Melissa Shale." The minister said.

"I would like something to say . . . I would like something to say!" Pamela stood up and said.

"What's that?" The minister asked.

"I don't know... I . . ." She muttered then looked around her once more with more tears dripping down her cheeks.

"You alright?"

Complete silence from Pamela as Luka looked concerned about her and stood up to bring her back into her chair.

"Hey . . . It's ok, it's ok hun'."

"No . . .no Luka . . . I . . . I . . . I killed Melissa."

TWENTY-THREE

The Great Welkin City—Created in year 2268 and once was the Grand Manan Island. This is the first ever city to exist in the sky and it's right above The Atlantic Ocean close to Gigantica floating around 40,000 feet in the air. The Gigantica Government gathered a huge body of land around 28.2 square miles and placed heavy tanks which are called 'anti-gravity plates' in the ground that hovers and also linked with compressed air. These tanks thrust the land upward to the sky until it reaches around 40,000 feet. There are approximately forty-six tanks the size of a baseball field which is around 250 – 400 feet in distance. The tanks all around underneath the city is what keeps the city up in the sky and if those tanks get dismantled the entire city will fall drastically because of the weight of the city and gravity of the Earth. These tanks are examined every week as the people live in the sky and yes that may sound a little off since a certain altitude can affect the way a human breathes, bad weather and closer to the sun. Consequently, man created a barrier, a similar Grainian Tech barrier used on all the planets that's in Earth's solar system. Using heated laser technology, these barriers are see-through comparable to glass, it does not get impacted by bad weather, the sun and it also contains air so that people can breathe. Airplanes and other aircrafts such as flying vehicles fly around daily.

Therefore, the sky systems, international airports, air transport systems and the Air Force communicate often to make sure things are good to go. One false command, direction or distraction can result in billions of dollars of damage and possible deaths. Nonetheless, there has been no reported malfunctions ever since the Great Welkin City was born.

Year 2321, Litzy de la Rose, living in an apartment building in a project housing in what looks like luxury compared to the 21st century's apartment projects in New York City or Chicago. She had just finished painting her short nails with peach nail polish and lets them dry while listening to music.

Litzy started messing with her jewelry then opened her mechanical box that's on her dresser. In this storage contraption was a choker and three necklaces that she adores very much.

"Litzy! I have one of your friends here that wants to see you." Litzy's mother Kayla de la Rose talking through a speaker that connects from the living room to her room.

Although Litzy is listening to her tunes, the music will stop once her mother speaks with a voice recognizing system. Litzy's father had deserted her mother for another woman about one year ago and they never talked ever since, not even a stop by to say hello or a phone call. They both kept their composure though and tried their best to make things seemed like it never happened.

"Who the hell could that be? Ok I'm coming."

Litzy opened the front door and saw a boy that has a crush on her for about a year now and he consistently tried to get with her after many denials.

"Oh, it's you again."

"Hey, Litzy. How you been? I got these flowers you…"

"No." She said then slammed the door in his face.

"Hey, that was rude."

"Yeah, I know but he deserved it."

"Why you say that?"

"He likes to beat up on girls and I don't like all that violence, especially on us girls."

"Now that's not right. Did he hit you?!"

"No Mom but he hit my friend at school. He got suspended and he wants to get with me—that's what I heard but I'm just like hell no, he sucks!"

"Good, I like that you turned him down and think that violence is no good. Especially against girls and even grown women too. A man is not a man if they go around hitting ladies like that—always keep that in your head."

"Well I don't like to fight but I would hit him back if he had hit me."

"Hmm."

"I would even hit Dad in the face, oh, I mean Ethan if he ever…"

"Litzy . . . what I tell you about mentioning him."

"Sorry but... Is he ever going to come back?"

"No . . . He's a fuck boy! He's a 'grade A' asshole and those the kinds that don't stick around Litzy. He goes for the big tits, fat ass and gold-digging cunts. I just wish that broad he's with is a man so that he kills himself."

"Hmm…"

"Ok, maybe not kill himself but look at you, a fatherless daughter with intentions of violence."

"Well I have to express my feelings somehow."

"Yes, but not with violence..."

"I feel a lecture about getting job is about come on."

"Yes, you're not too young for a part time. Don't be like those kids who believe androids should be doing all of the labor."

"Labor is a better fit for androids not me, but I'll consider a hobby or a sport to occupy my time."

The crowd screamed making their rumbling noise while Tajaymae and Litzy got into their fighting stance. Tajaymae has a watch that has a power source of 4000 watts which would give her enough power to stay in a fight for about an hour. Tajaymae drained the phone with her plasma sludge before heading up on the ring.

Tajaymae keeps it simple, wearing jeans, a shirt and sneakers. Her hair is tied up into a ponytail while Litzy's hair is untied.

"Look who it is… I was hoping I get to slap a hoe." Tajaymae said.

"Hm, it seems like I get hate from certain girls all the time. It's nothing new, your shit talking goes right through me." Litzy said.

"And so, will my foot... when it goes up your hinny."

"Wo'… wow, she… she's a bit of a shit talker. I mean I noticed this before beh'… but man, it's like she's getting more crea… creative each time she speaks."

"Oh, you don't even know the half of it." Ki-Yale said.

"Ok ladies… you ready? Ok… Let the fight commence!"

Litzy had her hands up in boxing style while Tajaymae ran at her full speed then jumped three feet in the air with her fists ready to punch her.

"C'mon, let's see what you got." Litzy said.

Tajaymae landed a punch to her guarded right arm then grabbed Litzy's guarded left arm. With a tight grip, she pulled her while still having her left hand into a fist.

"Oh, I got a lot!"

Litzy grabbed her opponent's shoulder real tight while she moved to the left. Tajaymae instantly saw an opening then punched Litzy in the face with a remarkable right hook.

"Agh'!"

Litzy stood firm and absorbed it then she did a counter strike kicking her in the stomach. Tajaymae then caught her leg with the same right hand she punched her with.

"Get off my leg!"

Tajaymae swung her around then hurled her about five feet across the ring causing her to land on her left arm shielding her rib cage from injury then quickly body rolls until she stood up with her hands up in boxing style. "Hm', damn lil girl, you're strong but you're gonna need more than strength to win."

"Aagh'!" Tajaymae yelled running towards Litzy.

Tajaymae swung at her as Litzy dodged every punch with her body.

"Stand still!"— "Ha, you're too slow."

Tajaymae made fists, spreads her arms out leaped six feet in the air then planted her feet on Litzy's chest which caused her to fall backwards on the floor. Tajaymae now on top of her, while fists were meeting Litzy's arms that's covering her face. Her rapid punches fueled the crowd causing more exhilaration. "Yeeah', beat her ass!" One guy in the croud cheered.

"Yup, Tajay's got her." Nack said. — "She... she's a brawler."

Ki-Yale took a glimpse at Mike with his left eyebrow up then brought his attention back at the fighting stage.

"Looks like Tajaymae got Litzy stuck down there." Majesty said.

Tajaymae kept on punching but Litzy kept her arms defending her face blocking every punch she lands.

"Move your arms already!"

Litzy smirked then used her two legs to hold Tajaymae's body and tossed her off resulting Tajaymae's body to face upward in midair about four feet. She landed flat on her back about five feet from Litzy. With hoarded fatigue, Litzy quickly stood up then Tajaymae said— "Ok, no more playing."

"What the hell is that?! Looks like some purple slime coming from Tajaymae's hands." Majesty said.

Her eyes glowed a fiery purple as her plasma sludge began to form into a clear sphere that has another sphere inside which is connected to the center of her halfway opened palm. The inside sphere began to emit electrical filaments just like a *Plasma Globe*.

"What the hell is that?!"

"This is the first ability my granddad taught me, the Netron Plasma Star."

"Woah…"

Tajaymae opended her palm completely and blasted her spherical attack which went about 1,200mph onto Litzy's chest as she fell backwards.

"Ugh!"

Tajaymae moved in closer to her and created another plasma sludge. Litzy had determination in her as she held her chest enduring the burning sensation and slowly gets up.

"Oh, you want more, huh?"

Tajaymae blasted another Netron Plasma Star then Litzy quickly got her left hand up as a reaction to block it from hitting her face.

The Netron Plasma got in contact with her arm which had her gold bracelets equipped. One of her bracelets had gotten drained of electricity which made the bracelet dismantled itself.

"Ugh! My Jewelry!"

"It drains whatever electrical stuff you got going on there. I should give you a stronger dose, so I get those electrolytes in your body… You're lucky I'm only using a low percentage." Tajaymae said as she gathered more plasma sludge.

"Wow, this must be akward for you Ki, the girl you like is fighting your sister." Nack said.

"Yeah it is, and I hope it doesn't get too gruesome."

Litzy flicked the plasma off her and suddenly, her jewelry began to release itself and stood in midair around her.

"Hmm'?" Tajaymae puzzled while raising her left eyebrow.

Litzy's jewelry moved quickly towards Tajaymae as she blasted her plasma at the airborne jewelry hitting only two, but the rest went around the shots then got clamped onto Tajaymae. Litzy has a total of three hundred jewelry but in this tournament, she brought around twenty-three jewelry to this fight. She had worn two bracelets on each arm, a choker, two leg bracelets and two necklaces, four bracelets on each of her wrists and four bracelets on each of her legs.

The choker went around Tajaymae's neck, the two leg bracelets went around both Tajaymae's legs.

"Get this stupid jewelry off of me!"

Two of the bracelets that was spiraling and soaring towards her had gotten drained of electrical power which seemed to be resulted in a malfunction. The other two arm bracelets that went on Tajaymae's arms and the two necklaces that went around her neck seemed to have gotten zapped by plasma as small amount of smoke came from the jewelry.

"Wooah' folks! Things just got real. We all know how Litzy do things." Majesty said as the crowd goes wild.

"What is Majesty talking about?" Ki-Yale asked.

"I… I have no idea."

Tajaymae stood stationary while Litzy slowly walked up to her.

Ki-Yale's inner detective was exposed on his face as he squeezed his eyelids and being in a confused state.

"What did you do to me? I can't move."

"Yes, you can." Litzy said.

A new outlandish experience for Tajaymae as she hits herself in the face, stomach, legs with her fists and elbows. Brutal hits after hits making herself look like a mockery to the crowd.

"Why is she hitting herself?!" Ki-Yale asked showing apprehension.

"It must be that jewelry. Litzy's jewelry can be detached from her then attached to her enemies which allowed them to attack themselves." Nack said.

"Woah! Looks like Tajaymae is in a bad situation here. You know what they say your worst enemy is yourself! In this case it's a big problem." Majesty said.

"But I drained the energy in the tech…" Tajaymae said.

"True but I have Tektonium metal covering the motherboards and the backup wiring. Once I inject the jewelry in your body, I gain control of your nervous system."

Tajaymae kept on hitting herself and started to crumble.

"Please make it stop!" Tajaymae yelled.

"Not so tough now huh?"

"NO! I'm the toughest one here! I'm not giving up!" Tajaymae said as she kept hitting herself.

Tajaymae got up and tried to go closer to Litzy but then she hits herself even faster and harder.

"Damn it Tajay." Ki-Yale said as he looked at his sister brutally beating herself up.

Tajaymae struck herself in the head with an impact that is loud enough for the audience to hear then suddenly, she fell and ceased all movement.

"Woooaaah'!" Said the audience.

"That's a hard-hit folks… aaand' she's down!"

The arena became the Krakatoa when it's erupted the way the audience chanted— *'MURDER MURDER, KILL KILL''.*

Ki-Yale divulging fret in his eyes as he opened the small door that connects to the border of the area of their section that they stood around. He slowly moved a little closer to the ring while Litzy looked at Ki-Yale then she said— "I'm going to forfeit."

"What?! You can end her right now! You got her pinned down!" Majesty said as Tajaymae started to move.

"Naaah, she had enough." Litzy said then she walked off the ring and the jewelry came off of Tajaymae and followed Litzy in midair.

The audience chanted in anger— "Booooooo'!"

"Just end that bitch. C'mon this is some bullshit!" Said one person in the crowd.

"That was wack'!" Said another person.

"Ok, ok folks, ok folks."—Majesty on the mic then he called the medic to clean up Tajaymae.

Ki-Yale looked at Litzy with relief while shaking his head in sanction and smiled then decided to go up on the ring as the medic is walking to her direction. "We got it kid!"

"No, she's my sister . . . I got it!"

<u>*The tournament housing*</u>—

"This thing smells like straight booty-hole!"

"I know it's the Vile Stink Bomb. This thing would make you smell for a whole week or even more."

"Oh, hell yeah! He's about to get it."

In the hallway of the housing, Mr. Turd chased down one of the teenagers that took his hat that he left on the table.

"Damn it… come back here kid!"

"Should have never leave your belongings out like that…"

"Give … me … back … my … hat!"

"I'm coming around the corner guys." The teen radioed his friends.

"Ok, get ready to throw that thing and make sure it touches his skin."

"Do it now!"

"Ok throw it."

The teen threw the stink bombs hitting Mr. Turd in the neck and instantly the putrid slime dripped down his chest. "AAAGH! What is this?"

"Stiiiink' booomb'!" The mischievous teen walked to the room door then said— "Here's your ugly ass hat. I already got better ones."

Mr. Turd took his hat then looked down at himself. "So, it's just a prank huh?"

"Yeah we're just fucking with ya."

"So how long is this gonna stay on me?"

"Just wash it off you'll be fine."

"You should have seen your face... 'Give me back my hat, give me back my hat!'." The teen mocking him then walked in the room.

"You guys are just crazy playing these pranks on me."

"Hey, we're just having fun. Now we got shit to do so, see you never." The teen said as he closes the door.

"Damn kids."

<u>*Gigantica Maximum Penitentiary*</u>—

Nicole Torbino looking at Fabian as he is badly beaten, his right cheek looked puffy, his upper left corner of his eye is purple with blood dripping down his face. His other eye is covered with swelling from his eyelid, his lips has a large slit in the middle from a blade. Scars all around his body from a spiked bat and all his toenails are ripped off his toes. She walked up closer to him touching his bottom lip with one finger and said—

"Look at that, we give you an opening for your mouth for you to speak and still not a damn word from you . . . No apology…"

Fabian brought his head down slowly then Nicole said—

"No keep that head up! . . . I said, keep your fucking head up!"

He kept his head down which aggravated her some more.

"What's even worse is that, you probably thought what you did was right . . . Ha', you probably think I'm a sadist now… yeah . . ."

Distraught expressed through her voice as she shook her head left to right.

"Hmph'. . . You wanna keep your mouth shut? Well, so be it."

She strapped his head tightly to the headrest then picked up a sowing kit and takes out a needle then she smoothly laced the needle as the Prison Persecutor strapped Fabian's face with extra straps so that his head doesn't move around. She plugged the stringed needle to the right side of his lips and moved the needle right through upward. He groaned and tried to struggle but he cannot move an inch as she goes in and out of his lips with the threaded needle over and over until she stitched his mouth together.

"You probably were going to tell your daughter to be keep quiet. Hm, now here we are . . . Ok, ok . . . I'm done for the day . . . I'll be back for experiments to see how well a grown man's body can sustain a massive beating from his ex-wife!"

At the Torbino residence—

A male therapist sat around a table conducting the first session and trying his best to convey a positive energy speaking with Tony, as his older sister Chloe and younger brother Dorimzy sat next to each other. Chloe sat quietly ever since the therapy session began and wished to not speak about anything.

"I see that she looks healthy which is good, but does she eat regularly?"

"Yes, I've seen her eat very often, whenever she can. Our food supply here is endless."

"Good, how is her sleep process? Does she wake up early? Does she stay in the room all day?"

"She sleeps but from what I observed; she goes to bed around ten o'clock. Usually she hits the bed late at night and now she sleeps in the living room. . . I guess, she doesn't really want to go back in her room."

"Yes, yes… I see . . . Chloe…"

"No fucking questions…"

"Ok… but I'm your therapist now, I'm here to get you back on track…"

"Get me back on track?"

"Yes, I know this was a horrible thing to happen to you but I'm here to help."

"You know what… fuck you and your shitty help! Tss'… You know what I need you to do? Is all of you therapist fucks to get the hell out of my fucking life and go make your money somewhere else!" Chloe seethed as she stood up then walked away from the table.

. . .

"It's fine. I get these reactions from cases like this all the time. It just takes time, that's all, then she'll comply." The therapist said then continued—

"Now Dorimzy. You are a remarkable young man and you did the right thing when your sister needed someone. How do you feel now?"

Dorimzy with a straight face staring blankly at the therapist and not answering his question for ten seconds. "Ok…"

"He's not much of a talker. Very smart in school though."

"Oh really? Is he a Super Genius? What grade is he in?"

"Yeah umm, he's in Pre-K… He's a—aah late bloomer but those grades are springing up fast." Tony said as he faked his smile.

"Hm, I see."

TWENTY-FOUR

Crouton Village—

Later into the night after the first day of Crouton Village Tournament Death Week. Majesty is throwing a house party in a large Mansion. The party consisted of teenagers around the ages of eighteen to nineteen and adults in their twenties. In the 24th century, the legal age to drink and smoke ranges from ages seventeen to twenty-one depending on the country or region.

"Thi'… this party is bumping!" Mike said nodding his head to the music.

"Yeah I guess!"Xack spoke loudly.

"Le'… let me see if I could ge'… get me one of these girls! Tha'… they love autistic guys who embraces their mental condition."

"You should have got with Tajaymae!" Xack joking around.

"Wha-. What you talking about, sh'… she's like thirteen years old man!"

"She has the hots for you man! She's part alien so maybe the age limits are different on their planet!"

"Yo! I don't wanna hea'… hear this pedophilia talk from you!"

"I'm just messing with you man!" Xack said then he laughed.

He paused after looking to the left then said— "Yo look it's that Death Angel Max!"

"Aye Max, co'... come through man!" Mike waved at him.

"Hey what's up?" Max greeted them after walking closer.

"Thuh'... this kid right here is... uh' is a bad seed man." Mike spoke jokingly.

Max smiled then Xack asked— "How'd you get in here man? Death Angels aren't allowed!"

"Yeah I got my ways, I did the bouncers a favor." Max said as he showed Xack and Mike some pills and a small piece of paper.

"Woah. That's ecstasy and acid!" Mike surprised.

"Just gotta have the right stuff!" Max said.

"Nice." Xack said.

"Hook me up man. You want!?" Mike asking Xack.

"No man I'm good." Xack denying the drugs.

"Ah man, c'mon man! Turn up!"

"No!"

"Alright, more for me. How much do I owe you?"

"It's on the house man—no charge—a gift from me being an asshole and shooting you yesterday."

Xack squinted at Max while Mike took the drugs in his hands then puts it in his pocket.

"Duh'... dope, now let's go ah... and snatch some buh'... some bitches!"

"Hey, I'm attracted to men!"

"Se'... say what?!" Mike surprised— "Yeah. I'm a homosexual!"

"Ok shit, you... you never seem to me ah'... like the gay type!"

"Yeah, I get that a lot."—Max showing pictures of him and his boyfriend kissing lips to lips.

"Ok well… Let's go snatch some beh'… some bitches… to fuck and du… and dudes to... Ok, that didn't sound too right but… you get my point, beh'… bitches for me an... and dudes for you."

"No, no, no snatching of anyone cause I ain't trying to cheat. I'll be like you Xack and just chill or dance." Max said.

"Aye... I respect it!" Mike said.

<u>The arena's medical room</u>—

"Wow there is nothing to watch on here Tajay. All the networks are junk at this time, I'll put it on the news." Ki-Yale said.

"Hmmm." She grunted.

"Ah no news?"

"Just get me some freaking water."

"Hey, you did well out there. You're still the toughest one in the arena."

"Yeah but I lost, I should've beaten her face. I mean she is so pretty, prettier than me."

"Ha! That's why you don't like her so much because you think she is prettier than you. Jealousy is no good Tajay, especially if you want to beat another girl for it."

"I guess."

"Well she forfeited. So technically you won."

"Yeah because I was losing so bad and she could have killed me."

"But… but she didn't."

"Just go get me water please…"

"I got you." He said as he walked out the room and closed the door.

He closed the sliding door then suddenly— "Is she ok?" Litzy concerned.

"Woah! —Umm—yeah, she's fine. Her plasma, it heals her injuries pretty quickly."

"I'm sorry about that. I wasn't expecting to fight her."

"It's cool, I just wasn't expecting her to actually get beat up. And it's a lot of amazing powers I have never seen before. Well it's not just powers mostly inventions."

"Still couldn't beat what you can do… Like you're so slender but technically strong as a Sila Human. Hm… are you really an alien? Or part alien?" Litzy investigated as Ki-Yale began walking.

"Yes, I'm actually quite stronger… I know it's kind of hard to believe, especially when the government don't have me locked up somewhere. I may look human but I'm not fully human, I was born through a crystal that was inside my mama's stomach, the crystal also provided a cocoon for me to reside in. The Pinnacle, they made us based off humans so either I would look more like a human…"

As Litzy walked with Ki-Yale she interfered then asked— "Wait? The Pinnacle?"

"Yeah, they're a higher level of species that creates galaxies, planets and species that reside in them. It's funny how they can create but can't destroy their own creations. Some higher species they are."

"Hm."

"Yeah so I'm very different from humans. I also don't have a belly button…" He said revealing his stomach which doesn't have a belly button.

"Wow, you're not kidding."

"I even defecate and urinate different."

"Uummm'… Really?"

"Yeah, I poop green without any stench and pee clear like water."

She chuckled then said.

"What?! Green?! Uh, so gross... You look so serious saying all this too! You know peeing clear water means that you just drink too much water."

"I know but I don't need to live off water nor do I need to live off food as much as humans need to. Water is good for you as it is for me, but I just don't need to drink it as much. Yeah, it's all weird but it's all true."

His suit allows nourishment without taking action to consume. Without his suit, however, has limits to how long he can survive without sustenance but it's a longer undertaking than humans.

"Oook, ok. Can I see something?" Litzy asked and stopped walking.

"See what?" Ki-Yale asked as he also stopped walking.

"An experiment." Litzy said as her two bracelets came off and went on his left arm.

Ki-Yale just glared at the bracelets on his left arm then looked at Litzy. The bracelets started to sock itself then blew up emitting a tiny explosion.

"I knew it... it's that suit that's giving you all these abilities!"

"Yeah, you're right it is. How'd you figure?"

"I don't know... it's a wild guess. I mean I never seen a suit like that and... When I look closely it almost looks like it's alive." She said.

"How does your jewelry make your opponent attack themselves?" Ki-Yale asked.

"Well, this is an invention I made when I was fourteen which was last year. These jewels have nanobots that can connect to the veins, nervous system, the bone marrow structure and the brain which allows me to control a person's body movements. There is also a mini microchip inserted inside my brain. I had it inserted it with a device that drills through my skull onto the brain. Here is the scar, it makes me look like a freaking Frankenstein."

"A very cute Frankenstein."

Litzy blushed as she lifted her hair showing Ki-Yale her scar behind her ear.

"Woah! Ok, it seems so dreadful!"

"I was under some severe anesthesia." She said.

Ki-Yale slowly nodded his head then Litzy continued— "I can also take the jewels off without using my hands… I may be a super genius but I'm still in high school."

"Yeah but you still made an amazing creation. Illegal but amazing—hmm—this should be military weaponry. You could make a lot of money but don't say that you made the invention already just show the blueprints." Ki-Yale expressing encouragement towards Litzy.

"Yeah, agreed but I did that already, I've turned down many offers because there are still some tweaks I need to work on as you can see. I consider myself doing this independently though—after I get this legalized although I've used it in the tournament with cameras all around." Litzy said taking off the damaged bracelets and looking at Ki-Yale's arm then makes her way to Ki-Yale's chest as she touches him.

"You're very observant." He said as he smiled awkwardly.

"Sorry."

"No, it's cool, my suit is sort like a person, but it doesn't talk with a language. It talks to me by feelings. The suit is also sort of indestructible and I can change my skin to be soft or unbreakable, but curtain attacks wouldn't matter." He continued to smile as Litzy with an obvious blush looked up at him.

"So aahh'. What else can you do…?" She paused then added— "Prince?"

"Ever been airborne without a vehicle aircraft or even a parachute?" He asked.

"No. What do you mean?" Litzy confused as Ki-Yale grabbed her hand and grinned at her.

He then took off the ground gently and kept his attention on her. "What the...?" As he ascended higher, Litzy looked at his feet. She was amazed by raising both eyebrows, her eyelids wide open and gasped then Ki-Yale took off into the sky about three hundred feet with her. "Oh shhit'!! What the...?! You can fly?!" Litzy in utter shock and hugging him tightly.

"Yep." He phlegmatically said.

<u>The Torbino residence</u>—

Dorimzy sat in his wheelchair without any straps holding him down as he looked outside of his room window then progressively, his mother creeped by the open room door.

She looked at him for a moment then said— "Ever since that day you never been strapped back to that bed."

Complete silence from Dorimzy as his mother continued— "It's just astonishing how you escaped with only one arm and no legs. It's amazing to see what I'm creating in from of my eyes."

She slowly walked closer behind him. "I know you understand everything that went down that day. I know you understand the pain your sister is going through. The evil of men . . . I want you to become better than him. Following under his footsteps would be an abomination to this family."

She leaned on the dresser and looked at the floor then she turned her head to him. He still stared at the window as if he's looking through a dark abyss.

"I know one day, you'll be better than anyone. The power you will hold will be unimaginable . . . You'll banish the wicked and their sinful ways. Dorimzy my son, one day people will look up to you like a God!"

Dorimzy's hands began to shake while he glared angrily at the window. She slowly reached her hand towards his shoulders then abruptly, he hastily turned his head towards his mother with rage of blazing fire in his eyes, showing the face of a very young vexed Grinch.

At this moment Nicole knew he didn't want her around him. She puts her chin up high as she looks at him then he turned the direction of his head back to the window and looked outside. She fixed her clothes then turned around and slowly walked to the door. She instantaneously stopped and looked back as he relentlessly glared at the window then she walked out his room with slight distress on her face.

In the skies of Crouton Village—

Litzy never been in the air like this so open, without any barriers around her body, in an aircraft, no equipment to make her float, just raw air and wind hitting her face.

"Wow! This is so beautiful… This village… Hmm, but I miss my home. I don't want to fight all the time you know. Home is where I really want to be." Litzy said as Ki-Yale flew her around going eighty miles per hour around Crouton Village.

"So why don't you just stop fighting?"

"I ran away from home."

"You ran away from home?"

"Yes, my mom contacted police then a search party out for me for weeks until they found out I was involved in this tournament. My mom doesn't like that I fight, and she said never to come back if I continued in the tournament. As you can see, I didn't listen, and fighting grew on me but family and being home looking at my posters… I came to realize, all that is way better right now."

"You ran away to fight in a tournament just for the sake of fighting…"

"You make it sound so wrong."

"Well, I had an older brother that ran away and I never seen him since. Running away may feel like it's the right thing to do but it's not, it leaves your family members traumatized. My parents hated that I wanted to do this fighting thing too and eventually they let me go. I'm pretty sure your mom will forgive you and I bet she misses you a lot."

"I know, I did something stupid but she doesn't want me back, she even compared me to my dad."

"I guess your dad wasn't so pleasant."

"Yeah, he left my mom for another woman, I guess he wanted something else. Now… now she hates me, I don't know if I could go back."

"Trust me no matter how much drama you and your mom has I'm sure she misses you a lot and wants to see you again just like me who misses my brother who ran away all because of some royal eternal prophecy."

"Hmm, I'm guessing one of you had to become prince."

"Yes, you're right, good guess. He's the first born so it would make more sense but it was that was chosen."

. . .

Litzy glared and smirked at him then she started to reach for his upper arm and Ki-Yale recognized she wanted to be held a different way, so he slowed down. Down to about forty miles per hour then reached to grab her other arm and made her get on his back.

"Put your arms around my neck and please . . . Hang tight!" He said as she puts her arm around Ki-Yale's neck then Ki-Yale flew faster going about one hundred miles per hour and higher into the sky going about five thousand feet then stopped midair.

"It's my city! Oh man I haven't seen it since . . . It's... It's so freaking beautiful I miss it so much!" Litzy said smiling as her eye started to water.

. . .

"Let this be a motivation for you to forget this fighting, get back home and make things right with your mom… Family is everything." Ki-Yale encouraged her then he continued—

"Aaand let's get down before you get altitude sickness."

"Oh yeah, I don't want that now…"

Later, Ki-Yale went back at the tournament and returned Litzy back to her room in the fighter's housing building.

"Thanks for giving me that awesome ride… In the sky." Litzy said as she looked awkwardly at Ki-Yale then he did the same. She hugged him for ten seconds then slowly let's go and saw Ki-Yale smiling shyly at her.

"I guess I'll see you tomorrow."

"Yes, goodbye Netro."

<u>*House party*</u>—

Xack walked out the party on the balcony to look at the village by himself through the huge backyard of the mansion.

"Crouton Village, it's so beautiful at night…" Push randomly loomed next to Xack.

Xack slowly looked to his left then kept silent

"Some places just never leave us laddie."

"You got nerve stepping up here."

"You got nerve stepping in this tournament . . . Aye', we got something in common... We both got balls."

"Yeah well… We'll see who lives longer."

"Yeah, dangerous living usually doesn't live that long…"

"What is the meaning of your tattoo on your face?"

"My life is an endless maze Xackie boy…"

"Hm', creative… You got Apaki Warrior abilities. What region are you originally from?" Xack asked.

"Hm, surprised you don't remember me Xack, we met way before LTV."

Xack squinted at him trying to remember then Push said—

"I'm from the Crouton Village Apaki Warrior region. I was in the same class as you back when I was eight years of age and I guess you were about seven years of age. I remember going through intense training, busting my ass just to capture a flag. I remember jumping over tires until your legs bleed then I had to walk home six miles… Well, because I wanted to but I remember one day coming home and hearing a news about my mother and father are actually blood brother and sister. What a news for me that was right?" Push explaining as Xack raised his eyebrows and looked in disgust.

"Anyway, I moved on from that class then got into another training facility." Push continued.

"Yeah owned by my dad's backstabbing friend I suppose."

"Yes, the only secondary Apaki Warrior dojo in Crouton Village."

"Hm." Xack muttered.

"Nine years later this village was under attack by Dr. Sagan. He had a vicious group, I guess he paid them off or they didn't really have a choice. I fought my best and held my own, but I got ambushed and they took me in. Sagan liked the way I carried myself, so he offers me to live and work for him and…."

"You said yes… Hmm', I would have let him kill me." Xack said.

"No… I said no. That's where I fucked up . . . He killed my parents, with no hesitation, he had me barricaded in a cell and overtime I just, wanted for it to stop . . . All the torture, grief and guilt. So, I just . . . Worked for him."

"Why don't you just kill that asshole? I've seen your skill and you're close to a level three."

"Nah, he can't be touched. I've seen many Apaki Warriors… Stronger, more skilled than me try but they ended up dead. It's like he knows every move that they would make. I have nothing else to protect, he took it all . . . So, I'll just advance my life without a purpose."

"It doesn't have to be like that. We both can stop him!"

"That's what the other Apaki Warriors said . . . Before they were slaughtered." Push said as he walked away then suddenly stopped and continued— "By the way Xack . . . I was helping Sagan's men attack your father's dojo and your people. Oy', it was grand I tell ya' . . . I probably butchered your mother . . . I don't know, I was slicing so many people I don't even remember."

Xack with heavy breathing making his fists shake as he looked at him with a bit of rage in his eyes then Push walked away again and said— "I was your enemy long time ago . . . bitch!"

Ki-Yale deactivated his suit and now wearing simple house clothes as he sat on his hover chair speaking to Nack.

"Hey, so what's the smile all about man? You got a new girl?"

"Yeah like I ever had one in the first place."

"Is it that girl Litzy? Did you at least try to talk to her on the low?"

"She came by to see Tajaymae. Good thing I was there maybe Tajaymae would have tried to fight her again."

"Yeah, your sister doesn't take defeat so well . . . Why is Tajaymae still there? She can heal herself with her plasma, right?"

"Yeah but she wants that 'hospitalized treatment'."

"Oh of course. So how did it go? What did you tell her?"

"I told her my sis was ok, then I gave her a little air ride."

"Ooh shit! You took her in the sky? That's a good move man, that's how the heroes get em." Nack said.

"I guess. Well, she surprised me too, she's a super genius and those jewelry she has makes her opponents attack themselves. She created them herself and had someone drill a chip in her brain."

"Hm, a little crazy if you asked me… But I bet you can handle that." Nack said as he tapped him on the shoulder.

"I guess."

"That someone must have used a similar needle from a Mega Human soldier suit and the chip is what controls the jewels . . . Hm, impressive."

"Yeah, I took her back to her dorm room and she gave me a hug."

"Niiice' bro, some progress!" He then Ki-Yale started calling his mother.

"Mom!" Ki-Yale hollered.

"What's up baby? Is everything ok?"

"Yeah, I'm fine over here, just hanging out with Nack."

"Nice, I just had a talk with Tajaymae…"

"Is that Ki-Yale! Yo bro!" Oji shouted with gusto.

"What's up little punk?" Ki-Yale hollered.

"Ha! Guess what happened to me today?"

"You finally grew some balls?"

"Ha, you think you're so funny… Hm, I have powers Ki-Yale!"

"You have powers?"

"Nice." Nack added.

"Yeah I can control the ground, the trees, plants and 'poe-len'."

"That's pollen son, pollen."

"Pollen, oh yeah pollen... Sorry Mom."

"Ha! He said 'poe-len'." Nack chuckled.

"Woah, really? So, you have Zeal powers like Tajay but a different kind?"

"Yeah I made the trees little again."

"Oh bro! That's so awesome!"

"Nice. You restored the original look of our village!" Nack said with enthusiasm.

"Yeah I'm cool, I'm cool." Oji said doing a fist-pump.

"No don't do that again... Not cool."

"Not cool?"

"Yeah the fist-pump Oji... that was poorly done and wasn't executed properly."

"Whatever Ki-Yale..." He said then Mike busted in the door with two eighteen-year-old girls.

"Woah." Ki-Yale surprised.

"Oh..." Nack said.

"Wha'... what's good y'all." Mike said as he walked up the stairs to his assigned room with the two girls.

"Now we see who is getting some real action." Nack said.

"Is that girls I hear Ki?" Demi asked.

"It's not me Mom."

"Oooh' I wish I was him right now." Nack said.

Mike went to his assigned room with the two young ladies then locked the door, as one of them took her shirt off having no bra is underneath. He stared at her perky breasts with a large smile on his face. "Thuh'... this is so awesome!"

"Yes, and you deserve it." The young lady spoke in her sexy tone as she grabbed his crotch then the other girl also took her shirt off showing that she has no bra underneath as well.

The house party—

It's 3am and the bouncer that obtained the acid strips from Max went to the restroom to consume them. Moments later, the bouncer went to the restroom again. He looked at the mirror because he felt something was up ever since he took the acid which he shouldn't have in the first place. Everything became blurry for him as he squints his eyelids and began to wobble. The bouncer leaned on the sink and looked at the mirror again. He lifted his head up glaring at the ceiling then instantaneously… he fell onto the restroom floor.

TWENTY-FIVE

In year 2311, Crouton Village was one of the wealthiest villages in Gigantica alongside Little Tree Ville, Kaolin Village, Hail Rhode Village and many more. The people in Crouton Village are mostly Mega Humans that are civil and doesn't cause any destruction. Its 1:36am at night and a Caucasian man named Morris in his late 20s shouted—

"Yo hurry the fuck up!"

"I'm driving the fastest I can and maneuvering this bitch!" Fang Machida said.

Fang is also in his late 20s and has the same thick Asian accent.

"The fuck man! They're gaining on us." Morris said while the authorities chases them.

Fang Machida driving a sports air vehicle soaring in high speeds above Crouton Village. "Driver pull over now!" The officer talking through a radio that connects to any vehicle's radio in their police vehicle.

Usually the police can stop a moving car in pursuit by just the click of a button connecting the wiring of the car but this car was tampered with and the mechanics had been altered so the police won't stop them easily.

"Fuck the cops!" Morris responded to the radio message from the officer.

Fang drove under a small tunnel that collects garbage bins from the housing and empty the bins then returns it.

"You try'na get us sanitized?"

"Shut up! We ain't garbage, I know what I'm doing... watch me."

"I really hope you do." Morris said as he shot at the police out of the window.

Fang extended the vehicle's speed into the air about 15,000 feet within seconds.

"They're pushing it." The officer said.

"Follow through." The second officer said then extended their speed as well pursuing them.

"Eject button Morris!"

"What?!"

Morris hesitated to press the eject button, so Fang did it for him then Fang did it for himself. As they both ejected from the vehicle, the vehicle became deserted while the police were going hyper speed behind it.

"Oh shit!" Both the officers yelped.

The police have an emergency eject system that ejects when a sudden collision is about to occur. Both officers got ejected moments before the police car collided into the Fang's car.

"Aah! Those bastards!"

The officers still got affected by the blast and one officer's parachute was damaged, but the second officer caught him in time before gravity took him. Fang and Morris got down safely to the ground on a building.

"What the fuck man! You always pulling these fucking stunts."

"Yeah but we got those fucking pigs!" Fang said as both went downstairs through the emergency stairs unto the ally way.

They dashed around the corner with heavy breathing as if they're running a marathon then unexpectedly, their adrenaline rush ended. Approximately thirty police officers with six Mega Animal dogs, a couple shields planted on the road and two SWAT armored trucks contributed as a roadblock across from the dead end.

"Put your hands where I can see them! Now!" The police commander said.

"Awe shit man! These guys are good!" Morris said then dropped his illegal fed rifle called the 'Mad Man X'.

"Fuck!" Fang blurted as they put their hands up in the air.

Fang and Morris in a dark questioning room with two small lights on the ceiling.

"You guys done fucked up man." The detective said being on the right from Fang and Morris.

"You done got fucked in the ass!" The second detective said.

"Man, you got fucked so bad the doctor said not even a truck load of lube could save you!" The detective said on the right.

"Man, just put me in a cell already. I don't wanna hear this shit." Morris said.

"A cell huh? So, guys could butt fuck you some more!" The detective on the right said.

"Where're not in the 21st century anymore." Fang said.

"Well, believe it or not we can arrange that for you." The second detective on the left said.

"Man, fuck you." Morris said.

"Hm, ok. What we got here? . . . Charged with possession of an illegal deadly weapon. Charged with assault and attempted murder on two police officers with an illegal deadly weapon. Charged with high speed police chase, charged with resisting arrest and charged with possible contraband offense... Wow! Ain't it such a beautiful day?"

Morris shook his head while Fang looks towards the ground.

"Hm, . . . We'll make an acceptation for you."

"What's that?" Morris asked.

"You tell me where Lorenzo is collecting his shipment from…"

"What's the catch here?" Morris inquired.

"One of you guys go free. That's us showing you some leniency."

"Aah!—Fuck this… and this shady ass police bullshit!" Fang argued with his strong Japanese accent.

"Think about this now." The detective on the left said.

It's complete silence for ten seconds then Morris said—"Let me stay Fang and you go."

"What?! Hell no. We both go down together."

"You got a whole Village of little Apaki Warriors to build… a family… And I ain't got shit!"

"No. I can't man."—"Yes you can."

"Tick, tock… Time is ticking..." The detective on the right said.

"Ok. It's final, I'll tell you but first... let Fang go." Morris said as Fang looks at him and shaking his head in denial then he said—"I can't believe you're going through with this."

"Ok, two officers are coming in right now to take his ass out of here."

Two officers came inside the dark room and aggressively removed Fang as he tried to remain still with little fight, refusing to leave and blaring 'no' repeatedly.

Unknown area—

A stunning large mansion with plenty of women walking around and some guards at every entrance. Three men are at the bar next to the kitchen and dining area and one of them said—

"Yo Mark, show him that video of Krarrell Vadagore. Shit's crazy man."

"Oh yeah, yeah. Check this shit out."

Mark opened his holographic phone from his clothes and shows his friend a video of a woman being tied down around a group of guys.

"Is this a porno? A gang bang from a hundred fucking years ago?"

"Yeah until Krarrell switched the script on em' with his little vendetta… Just watch man."

"Oh shit! Is he going to do what I think he's going to do?"

"Yup he's going to shove that chainsaw right up her cooch!"

"Keep watching! This is where it gets nasty!"—The video showed a man 'Krarrell Vadagore', inserting a chainsaw in a young woman's vagina as blood and body parts splashed all over him, then left her there to bleed.

"That thing went right up to her cooch man, right up to the stomach man. Holy shit! That dude was a savage!"

"Man, I would have chopped his dick off man."

"Chopped his dick off? You wouldn't even dare step to that dude if he was alive today."

"Well, he dead now and he ain't shit."

"Nah man, that dude is awesome!"

In the massage room Lorenzo and his henchman is receiving the usual significant massage they get every weekend.

"A little more up to the left." Lorenzo said in his Hispanic accent as a lady massage therapist treats his back.

"This is awesome sir. Thank you for this." The henchman said.

"Yes, it is and since you're my trusted and best henchman, I give the most absolute best treatment."

"Hm, a little more to the right yeah… yeah, that's good…"

"Sir…"—another henchman arrived through the entrance.

"This better be good Mark."

"Morris is locked up."

"Really? And who told you this?"

"Incarcerated insider."

"Really? We have one of those?"

"Um, yes sir."

"Ok Mark. You're my new most trusted henchman, good job."

"What?"

"Now kill my previous trusted henchman for me, there can only be one."

"But sir…"

"Or you can keep your rightful place as just a henchman …"

The regular trusted henchman got up from the massage bed then picked up his illegal Fed gun but it was too late for him and he took a bullet in the face as the massage ladies screamed out loud.

"Good job Mark—my new trusted henchman . . . Get back to work my babies and Mark, lay down, get a massage from these lovely ladies."

Lorenzo got up from his massage bed and stretched his back as his bones cracked.

"Ah yes that was good . . . Don't worry I'll get that cleaned up but first I have to go see the real cleaner."

Lorenzo walked through his hallway then saw a few young women sitting and socializing.

"I'll get a piece of you later baby and you too... yeeaah', you love me being rich…"

He entered an elevator that goes all the way down to the basement. He walked up to a scientist and mechanic then said— "Hm, how is he holding up?" Lorenzo asked as he looked up at a young man's body lying down on a machine.

"Good sir it's just the blood transfusion is a slow process with him."

"Well, only six percent of blood was left in him and Joe will do anything to get him back. Including asking for old friends."

"Why don't he just revive him?"

"He doesn't know how… Joe is a low-class Death Angel. He's a party boy like me and perhaps forgot his son was here."

<u>Gigantica Army Base—</u>

General Nealo Kafmora of the Gigantica Army at age sixty-three, looking at a surveillance video where Dr. Sagan commuting countless acts of murder in Benila Hospital. Nealo is with his army of Mega Human Primes, he mentioned when they found Tyson reveling himself and explained how he ran away from the Roland family's house that was burnt down. Dr. Sagan achieved Mega Human Prime abilities and his favorite ability is Apaki Jermayin, he uses a Gladiator sword as his choice of generated glass instead of Katanas.

"This is him being physical huh?" Nealo asked.

"Yes sir, he carries a great deal of abilities."

"We can still take him."

"Yes, we can sir, but he has the leverage with his Genchi virus."

"That smoke in the air, it's not from a fire isn't it?"

"No that's the Genchi. The virus we believe was made from unknown technology that he has in his possession. The same unknown tech that he uses to utilize ninety percent of the androids across the solar system… even military androids."

"And that ten percent are just the ones that are impossible to hack."

"Exactly… he has a high arsenal."

"He has no gas mask on…"

"And he walked through it without coughing, no signs of fatigue . . . He's immune to it."

"He vaccinated himself before doing all this?"

"No . . . even if he vaccinated himself before all of this, he still would be infected overtime with a massive amount of the Genchi in the air to do so."

"So, what makes him so immune? Has he become a Death Angel?"

"Yes, I'm afraid so…"

"Hm, without these attributes . . . He wouldn't be the so-called Mad Doctor of the 24th century." Nealo said as he folded his arms around his back and squeezed his eyelids at the screen.

"He's very erratic, he even fused his cells with the cells of liquid Tektonium metal which makes him similar to project Kleaner but only for a limited time due to inconsistent configuration."

"I'm guessing enchantment paved the way for him."

"Yes, the Tektonium metal is supposedly the strongest metal in the universe but we found a liquid form of this metal from planet Grain and the liquid form is literally like water. If not softer than water."

"He could use the liquid as a barrier, the same barrier we use to cover the Earth but we use the magnetic Grainian technology to make the metal solid so that wouldn't make sense . . . the metal on his cell would become solid."

"It's enchantment, he's got accesst to enchantment that creates a barrier to protect himself from the virus."

"Or just maybe… maybe his enchantment ability is to create the Genchi and utilize it as his weapon."

One couple in a room getting busy. Stacey Roberts the same young Caucasian lady who presumed to be a companion for Mayor Tyson but in this year she's in her early twenties shouting with exhilaration— "Yeah! Nut on my face!"

"But… you got all that pretty makeup on."

"Fuck the makeup bae', just nut on my face!"

"Ok, ok, I'm cumming . . . I'm cumming!"

Just as Paul was about to climax, he heard a huge knocking and someone stridently uttered— "Hello!"

"Ah fuck! Who the fuck is that!?" He uttered with frustration.

"Damn it Paul, I thought you said no one would be coming here at this time."

"Yes, I did say that." The person continued knocking and being loud, as Paul went to the door. It was Fang returning home to his training center with a large group of Apaki Warrior children outside.

"The fuck… Oh—ah—hello . . . Fang. How are you? —Back so soon!" Paul jabbered.

"What's going on? Why you take so long to answer? Hmm? You got kids out here waiting for training!" Fang furiously confronted him.

"Wait but today is…"— "Monday."

"Oh shit!"

"Language around the kids Paul."

"These little dweebs say cuss words all the time."

"Oh really?" Fang said as he walked inside the dojo.

Xack Machida the son of Fang Machida, at age seven walking behind him and so did the rest of the children. Push Monaghan was also there as one of the students at age eight, at the back of the crowd of children. A total of eighty Apaki Warrior progenies in training that attended to the dojo.

Stacey appeared from the room and spoke in an angry sarcastic voice— "Oh, so no one's coming over today right?"

"This is what you were doing Paul?" Fang tensely asked.

"Well, I wouldn't call her a 'this'."

Fang shook his head while the children were behind him smiling. "Paul's in trouble now." Said one of the children.

Later, in Fang's office, Paul and Fang are having a sit down. "So how was that little trip to Spain?" Paul asked.

"Great, until I get into some shit." Fang answered.

"What happened?"

"Remember Morris from high school?"

"Morris… Oh yeah you mean Morris the squirrel. I remember that dude." Remembering Morris by his nick name from high school because his face looked similar to a squirrel.

"Well we met up in Spain at the airport, we got back to Gigantica City without any trouble with Gigantica customs and he started rambling about him carrying some heavy weight for a guy named Lorenzo. As soon as we hit the streets we got ran by cops."

"Carrying weight?"

"It's an illegal Fed gun called the Mad Man X, a rifle that's both semi-auto and full-auto. It creates multiple calibers up to a 50 caliber bullets and has a self-reloading system that reloads within ten seconds. The gun shoots one hundred rounds per second and it will automatically cease fire after it senses that it's about to overheat and cools it down within thirty seconds then it will be free to fire again.

It can also shoot beams, it's one of those high-tech automated guns that's worth a fortune."

"Wow, almost sound like a set up to me but… What happened? Did you get caught and how are you even here right after fucking with stolen military tech. The Feds don't play with that shit."

"They captured us then offered one of us to be free for Intel on Lorenzo."

"Oh, shit you ratted on that dude Lorenzo, didn't you? I mean is Lorenzo a bad dude or you shouldn't be worried about him? Right?" Paul concerned.

"No, I didn't rat but Morris did. That's why I'm here and I don't know who Lorenzo is or how he works."

"Well you shouldn't worry about it then."

"Yeah and guess what?"

"Umm… what?"

"You're fired…" Fang sternly said.

Paul, Fang's best friend got *the other end of the stick* because his lack of training the progenies and this isn't the first time, he did it. It seemed that he lacks responsibility, keeping a promise and had almost put the children in danger of accidentally burning down Fang's previous dojo. Paul then later opened a dojo for himself resulting in building up tension with Fang. Fang is now looked at as an enemy which eventually Paul got in contact with Lorenzo's crew and informed them that Fang and Morris ratted him out.

<u>*At the Gigantica Embassy*</u>—

President of the United States—Jacob Homan, Vice President Amber Lynn and the Gigantica council all sat around a large table discussing the many crimes that are being made during that year. Most of them revolved around the world of Sagan, crime rate is beginning to spring up as if it was the 21st century all over again but they are trying their best to prevent such things from happening and keep the world safe as possible.

"Crime is rising and adding to a string of crimes each year. Highest crime now is murder and rape."

"We suspect such madness be administered by this time. Our highest President, President Moore Jr. has finalized the impeachment of Gerald Quito. Now I'm here to reconsolidate and unify our country."

"Mister President . . . Here are the videos of the tragic events in Odisha, India—El Salto, Mexico—Kenya, Africa."

The video revealed bombings and the Genchi virus surfacing all around the world. Up close video of people mutating, coughing up blood and their veins start to appear on their skin.

"There's a lot more where that came from."

"I don't wanna see anymore…"

"I agree this evil has to be stopped at all cost."

"We have General Nealo with the Gigantica Army, he stopped many foes without failure. He stopped one of our most feared secret extraterrestrial mission on the Bazonious nation and their enemy fleet."

"The Bazonious. One of the threats that are left untold and that mission should remain banned to the public . . . Another major crisis worldwide and the solar system would erupt, citizens didn't want to perceive about another alien attack beginning to rise."

"That General Nealo . . . He's more than a Mega Human Prime . . . He used more than what we expect to take down the enemy vessel, it's remarkable."

"Yes. This proves we humans can descend to greater heights."

"Indeed."

"Our primary focus now, is Sagan. This is one of the most notorious criminals of all time. History repeating itself, the only thing now is to grant full force and execution to the Mad Doctor at all costs. Meeting dismissed."

"Yes, Mister President."

Year 2312—

"Are all the codes and passwords elapsed yet?"— General Nealo of the Gigantica Army.

"The computer reports ninety six percent sir." Said Vixen, Secondary command bypassing passwords for the enemy machinery using special bypass equipment used by the Special Ops teams.

"Ok, by the time we arrive it should be a hundred percent." Nealo said.

"I just want to say something sir."

"And what's that Vixen?"

"You're looking good as always. I don't know how you do it, being so healthy."

"Thank you, Vixen. You're looking good as usual..." Nealo said then traffic control spoke through the radio at the military air base in Great Welkin City.

"Sky Dream, ready to deploy sir!"

"This is team 109 and we have coordinates to the unknown site in Spain where Lorenzo is residing. I've stepped in as highest command of the capture and criminal flush out of the fugitive, Lorenzo De La Hoya. Ok team, all settled in?"

"Yes sir."

"Deploy."

Unknown Area—

"Look at this shit go man!" Lorenzo said as he shot an assault rifle in his shooting room.

"AR-15, old school shit man, oouu' let me try boss."

"Be careful with my baby man."

Lorenzo walked out the room as gun shots begin to burst.

"I need another massage. Hm, but first let me see how that snapper is cooking…"

Lorenzo walked through his hallway on his way to the kitchen as he passes some young women.

"Looking good baby."

Nealo and his special ops team had arrived at the location and immediately sets their positions using well practiced stealth skills. Special equipment was set in motion to tap into microphones and speakers inside the mansion.

"Let me see the microphone." Nealo said holding his hand out.

One of his soldiers gave him the microphone then he instantly announced—

"Lorenzo, we have this place surrounded. Show your face and surrender now or face the consequences!"

"Shit! —Yo Papi Lorenzo! It looks like the feds outside man, oh shit, no that's military." Said one Latina lady.

"What?! How the fuck they find us?!" Lorenzo said as he looked outside the window.

"Shit! That's General Nealo! Fuck! Aah fuck! Everyone get ready. This not going to look pretty." Lorenzo shouting and rushing to his armory.

Lorenzo and his crew gather all the weapons and gear then get in defensive positions. Nealo uses his hand signals to move in then he separated his route from Vixen as she proceeded through a different direction. Nealo went through the back while Vixen and seven other soldiers went through the front busting open the door with a large door ram.

The soldiers tactically went inside then instantly Lorenzo's crew and the soldiers started exchanging gun fire. Team 109 had better gear and survived the shots while most of Lorenzo's crew is shot dead.

Nealo puts his assault rifle to his back and took his knife out, he can end Lorenzo's crew easily, but he doesn't show his true power around humans, so he acts as if he is just a top notch Mega Human Prime soldier. Nealo spotted some of Lorenzo's crew as he puts his fists up in a fighting stance.

"Get that son of bitch!" One of the crew members said.

They began charging at Nealo then he dodged the first swing by ducking downward then impaled one combatant in the neck with heated laser beam knife.

The second one shot at him but Nealo used the guy that he stabbed as a shield then took his rifle and shot the rest of the attackers. Nealo continued to the back and spotted Lorenzo trying to escape on a boat. Nealo quickly pull out his pistol then shot the boat's engine five times. Nealo saw the boat slowing down then suddenly, Lorenzo jumped in the water and began to swim. Nealo uses his athletics and quickly jumped in the water to go after Lorenzo.

Nealo swum amazingly fast as if he was a professional swimmer at reasonable speed going ten miles per hour. Nealo could go faster but chooses not to and eventually he caught up to him then Lorenzo started to shoot. A 9mm bullet caught in Nealo's shoulder but Nealo never stopped then he grabbed Lorenzo then they started to swing at each over.

"No! I can't go down yet!"

"Just give up, there's no point."

"No!"

Lorenzo began punching Nealo but he was unfazed and effortlessly won the little brawl and knocked Lorenzo out cold.

Thirty minutes later, team 109 gathered all of the arsenal, drugs and all sorts of illegal items until they stumble upon the decreased young man lying down in a machine barely keeping his flesh and bones alive.

"Bring him in. The Gigantica government will deal with him now." Nealo ordered.

The Crouton Village Apaki Warrior Dojo—

Fang Machida, his wife Yaeko Machida born as Yaeko Onishi, a Japanese lady from Gigantica. Their son Xack Machida and plenty other young students sit around a large table eating a ton of food as if it was Thanksgiving.

"Hey, that was my chicken leg!" Said a student boy.

"Mine now!" Said the other young boy who took the chicken leg.

"Ok guys don't fight for the food now. Plenty more where that came from."

"But I want a chicken leg."

Yaeko gazed at Fang then said—

"Ok, I'll get one for you." Yaeko walked into the kitchen to grab a chicken leg on the counter where all the cooked food is.

The doorbell rang and Fang went to go answer it.

"Hello?"

"Hello, Fang. Do you remember me?" It was the same Detective that let him off for giving up Intel.

"Yes, how could I forget your face? What brings you here Detective?"

"Well I come to inform that Lorenzo was captured. There is no need for any more protection here. I know you asked for protection because you felt ratting or snitching whatever you call it, will get you in trouble with outlaws."

"No, I want the protection to prolong, I feel there is still someone out there for me."

"Hmm, well you can't have it for long you know. We'll eventually have to call it off soon."

"Yeah, you're right but mostly for the children and family you know."

"Yes, I know… Well, we can authorize protection for a few more months. We do believe Lorenzo is working for a bigger crime organization. We're not sure what it is yet, but we'll keep everything in good shape and that includes you, your dojo and this village."

Gigantica National Prison—

"You have a visitor… Papi Lorenzo." Jokingly said a prison guard.

"Ta' . . .Chill man, only the bitches call me that."

He later walked into the visiting room then unexpectedly, he saw a little boy that looked about seven years of age calling him over to sit with him at one of the tables.

"Oou', over here sir." Said the little boy.

"Who are you kid? Do I know you?" Lorenzo bewildered as he walked closer.

"No but you know why I'm here."

"No, I don't. How you even get in here? Don't you need a parent with you? Damn, I hope you ain't my child. I ain't trying to be a father fuck that!" Lorenzo said as he sat down across from him.

"No, I'm not your son."

"Well, who sent you?"

"Hmm . . . you're a bad man. You failed, you failed to do what you're told. I'm here to punish you." The little boy whispered.

"I failed? What are you talking about?"

"You know exactly what I'm talking about." He whispered some more.

"Oh fuck…. No! No, no, no. It was out of nowhere, I swear, I don't how they found me. Look kid, don't say his name! He told you to say his name, right?" Lorenzo raised his voice as the guards looked at him indicating that he is behaving out of line.

The little boy squeezed his eyelids and said— "Yeah and he told me once I do that, you will be dealt with and I walk away freely like magic." The little boy said as one guard approached them.

"Magic? No kid, you don't understand! You won't walk at all! Please, don't say his name!"

"Lorenzo! Pipe down, or else we'll take you back to your cell. Understood?!" The prison guard strictly said.

"Yes, please, take me back! Quick!" Lorenzo intensely said as he dramatically gets up from his chair.

"Ha! I don't think so."

"What?! . . . NO! . . . DON'T SAY THE WORDS!" Lorenzo shouted then instantaneously; the little boy yelled at him saying—

"THE MAD DOCTOR!"

Instantly, an explosion emitted from the little boy, the blast was enough to kill Lorenzo, the young boy, the guards, other prisoners and visitors around them in the entire room.

TWENTY-SIX

Kelvin Guerrero, a successful preschool teacher who teaches at Albacore Preschool in the City of Atlantis. Sitting down at his desk while his classmates do a quiz on math then unpredictably, the principal walked in— "May I speak with Dorimzy Torbino?" Principal Annie Palen asked.

"Absolutely principal Palen." Kelvin said as he gets up to assist Dorimzy on his wheelchair.

"No that's fine I got it." Annie said as she walked over to him and grabbed his wheelchair.

"How are you today Dorimzy?"

No answer from Dorimzy, he kept silent with a solemn face as she wheeled him out of the classroom.

Moments later in the principal's office. One lady of the board of education and two Detectives are with Dorimzy while Annie stood on the side.

"Hello Dorimzy, my name is Shania Clark."

"And my name is Detective Victoria Bailey. My partner here is Detective Waldo Fleming."

"We recognize an exponential growth in your quiz scores and suspect that you're in the incorrect grade."

Dorimzy squinted at Shania and then she said—

"Now I would like you to please take a few tests to determine what grade you truly belong. Now, this is nothing to be scared about its just tests."

Dorimzy stayed quiet without a single word out of his mouth as Shania hands him a difficult grade three test sheet. He looked at the test then looked back at Shania.

Present Time at the LTV Police Precinct—

"I feel like everything is falling apart Henry."

"This feeling for you. It must feel like a somber cavernous bite in your neck."

"It's worse than that man. It's like... I can't describe it right now man."

"It's ok…"

"Luka Shale Jr... How are you sir?" Detective Charlie greeted as he approaches them.

"I'm alright... So, what's the verdict?"

"As of right now, there isn't any traces of DNA or any other hard evidence that supports the claims of your wife killing your daughter so going up in court with nothing is pointless."

"Hmm . . . So?"

"So, we recommend therapy. . . Or even a center for her to recover. Our thesis revealed a possible severe psychological trauma."

Luka buttons his lips and slowly shakes his head then looked at Henry for a moment. He then stood up and fixed his buttoned up slim blue cotton sateen blazer. "Alright . . . Where is she? Can I see her?"

"Yes, right this way sir."

Henry stood up as well then followed him walking towards a window where Pamela is in a room by herself staring at the wall. Her eyelids are wide open and her eyebrows lifted without a blink as Luka slightly tilted his head up with grief in his face.

Henry patted his shoulder then buttons his lips and looked down to the left.

"C'mon, let's go." Luka muttered.

Luka and Henry walked outside as his Butler Marvin Dalton opened the door to his all black air limousine.

<u>*Crouton Village Tournament*</u>—

The second day of the Death Week at the Crouton Village Tournament, everyone is talking in the audience at once then Majesty started to speak.

"Ok folks, did everyone have fun last night?!"

The crowd began to get loud with excitement for about a minute then Majesty spoke over the noise.

"Yes, I agree last night was fun but unfortunately, one of the bouncers are in critical condition in the hospital. Doctors reported that he took something toxic now normally this doesn't happen, but anything can happen around here so let's keep it positive and I wish everyone good fortune."

The crowd quiets down a bit with minimal speaking around the arena once they heard the news of the bouncer and Mike said—

"Ha, keep it positive he said."

"Fucking asshole! Hey you ok man? That stuff he gave you last night, it didn't affect you right?" Xack being concerned.

"Nah, I'm good. I'm good."

Mike glared at Max with his father across the arena while Ki-Yale, Tajaymae and Nack appeared.

Ki-Yale looked at Litzy across the arena then she started to blush then waved at him.

"Oooh shit, you are really making moves bro. I see you!" Nack said.

"W-whoa, yuh'… you making moves on Litzy? Nice bro!"

"Ah guys relax." Ki-Yale said.

"He'… hey, I like the new cut buh'… by the way bro." Mike complimented Ki-Yale's fade haircut with five inches of hair on the top.

"Thanks, my hair grows fast so I gotta keep a good trim."

"Tha'… that dating life could co'… comes with a lot of headaches you know."

"Yeah, my dad says the same thing." He said then laughed.

"So, Xack what's her name huh?"

"Oh aah… I call her Yaeko… That's my late mother's name."

"Oh, your mother past, sorry to hear that."

"It was two years ago along with most of Crouton village, all because… Of Sagan."

"Damn… Sagan, he's just always bad news." Nack said.

"He ju'… just dos'… doesn't stop."

Everyone stood silent for twenty seconds then Nack said—

"Hey Ki, tell em' what your little brother did."

"What did he do?" Tajaymae said.

"Oh yeah, so, my lil' bro Oji got his powers."

"Nice, so, he can do the abilities that you do?" Xack asked.

"No, it's different, its Zeal powers like Tajay except it's not plasma but it's controlling the ground and the plants that grow from it."

"Like controlling things of nature." Xack said.

"My Zeal power is still better." Tajaymae bragged.

"Well Tajay, did you change the trees back to normal?"

"No…"

"Well that's what Oji did, it's already on the news."

"Wha'… What? Nuh'… no way!" Mike perplexed.

"Incredible." Xack said.

"Yeah, just rub it in Ki."

"Aye, I'm just saying Tajay. I gotta give the credit where it's due."

Majesty picked up his microphone preparing his next announcement then seconds later he said— "Ok everyone! Today is a little different! Yes, the first Apaki Warrior fight of the Death Week!"

The audience started to get loud again as they screamed with excitement.

"First we will have Xack Machida... versus . . . Push Monaghan!!" Majesty said as the audience continued to get loud.

Xack instantly looked at Push while Push smiled deviously and locked fists with his friends then walked up on the arena.

"Finally." Xack said then looked at Ki-Yale and nods his head then Ki-Yale nods back.

He handed over the baby coyote to Tajaymae then strode on the arena to face Push.

"Oy', would you look at that? The little fuck boy finally gets to fight me."

"Hmm, says the one being controlled like a poppet."

"Well let's get this over with shall we."

"Fighters are you ready?! Let the fight commence!!"

The grace of two warriors showcased no fear circling the arena as Xack revealed his Apaki Katana out of his right hand and so did Push.

"Well, don't you have a face to slice? Don't be scared now..." Push taunted him.

Xack charging at Push with both hands on his Apaki Katana and made the first swing. Push bent his back and dodges it then Xack quickly gets into a defense position while at the same time, Push swung his Apaki Katana hitting Xack's Apaki Katana.

"Agh, you still fight like a novice Xackie boy!"

Push and Xack kept striking each other's swords as the nearly indestructible glass crackled from the impacts.

"Aagh! Shut up!"

Xack responded then jumped back then fired heated glass from the generated glass sphere hovering over his left hand onto Push's shoulder. Push abruptly held his shoulder then smiled, he then released another Apaki Katana out of his left hand then opened both palms allowing the glass swords to hover over them.

Push stood in the opposite direction towards him as he held his two arms out and spreading his palms while his Apaki Katanas swung like a windmill. Push grabbed his two swords then puts his hands up in a boxing posture with the swords facing down. Xack charged at Push and Xack lifts his Apaki Katana, gripping with two hands to slice Push's face but Push rapidly twists his body all around in circles hitting Xack's Apaki Katana.

'No, I can't lose! I won't lose!' Xack thought as he's holding his own but eventually his Apaki Katana is dismantled as glass shatters.

Push stopped backwards to Xack and Xack instantly released a new Apaki Katana in his right hand and released another in his left hand. Xack began to swing as Push used defensive techniques and swung his Apaki Katana relentlessly while facing his back to Xack.

"Are you seriously gonna' fight like that?!"

Back in 2320—

Dr. Rogue Sagan, standing by his art on the wall and observing the little details as he is speaking to Push about how he saw the world. There are a few dead bodies sliced up from Push with blood stains all over the office room, on the walls, the desks, the doors, the newly vacuumed carpet floor, even some blood made it up to the ceiling.

"Life is made of positives and negatives and it's all a balance, without negatives, there wouldn't be a positive. The leaders around the globe came together and insisted that everyone should be pure of heart . . . ever since we won the war with the Grainians. The New World Order... hmm... people just wanted peace, endless peace but there is no such thing. Way before the new world order people lived in poverty, some were poor and now everyone has dollars in their bank account because the government wants no one to live poor like that again. Now it's just the oil companies, with a wide body of technology for humans to accustom to mostly without failures and assist them in any way possible. We have other planets that connect to Earth so that people can now reside on them and NASA is looking to go beyond the solar system. Back in the 20th and 21st century, people predicted days like this thinking we will live amongst bigger and better living. Mega Humans that can literally abolish most of mankind . . .. hmm', let's focus on my point here Push . . . the tribulations, the thirst for conflict, will never be disabled no matter how much money, power, intellect you feed the peace and no matter how much contributions for better living—we as humans, we as a planet and we as a universe will always commit and feel the wrath of the wicked!"

"Then I must choose on how I should live my life."

"Choose wisely but in this case, you don't really have a choice."

Gigantica Army Base 76, Year 2320—

Luka Shale Jr., Henry Luciano and Super Genius scientist Miranda Harris are analyzing the current state of an African American young man named Malik Stenson, the son of Joe Stenson.

Luka looked at Miranda and asked— "Don't you think keeping the bullet hole in his head exposed like that is a little too graphic?"

"Hm, I don't know Luka, I'm sure he wouldn't be out looking for pretty women."

"True but based on what you said earlier, he can still perform in the bedroom . . . So, an appropriate look would be nice occasionally."

"Yes, I said that, but I'll be surprised any lady would want to consider a man such as Mr. Stenson."

Luka shook his head with approval of what she said then Henry commented—

"All of this is . . . very intriguing to say the least."

"I agree Henry . . . after years of attempts to operate on 'Project Kleaner'. Joe has finally come to a decision to put him in the Gigantica Army." Luka said as he types on the glass keyboard.

"Yes, the first ever Cadaver Soldier." Henry said.

An operation team of Super Genius Scientists are all active on the project as they extract the full Tektonium metal exoskeleton from the large container with advanced machinery.

They place the exoskeleton in front of the deceased body as they melt the ice that's keeping his body stable for nine years.

Vapors coming from the melted ice and immediately the exoskeleton is placed on the deceased body. The exoskeleton emits a two degree Celsius which is thirty-six-degree Fahrenheit as it injects millions of extremely long and thin needles all-round the body for possible future movement.

Lately they insert small Tektonian Crystals which gives him his enchantment abilities. The Tektonian Crystals emits extremely strong magnetic field around the Tektonium metal which keeps the metal in place.

"We'll put the commanding chip in tomorrow, then, we'll witness his true entity and what he can do."

Luka and Henry walked out the cell block facility unto the bridge that leads to the exit.

"Misses Harris, she's one of a kind Henry."

"You like what you see huh?"

"I was going to ask you that question."

"Oh well. She's a smart woman and very beautiful I'd say."

"Agreed but notice I said Misses."

"Hm—hm." Henry chuckled.

<u>*Present time at the Crouton Village tournament*</u>—

"Woah folks, it looks like Push got some skills fighting backwards!"

"C'mon Xack. He's toying with you!" Ki-Yale yelled.

On the other side of the arena Guss and Collin believing in his friend as they cheered him on.

"Ha! Look at this guy, Push got this in the bag." Guss said.

"Yeah but the fight isn't over yet." Collin said.

Xack finally struck Push in the back with his heated glass sword leaving a large cut resulting in stunning pain.

"Aagh." Push reacted.

"C'mon enough playing around Push!"

Push instantly upset turning around and began swinging again. He finally struck Xack in the face leaving a small sliced mark. Despite the attack, Xack kept swinging while Push continued to land direct hits, slowly slicing the side of his body. Then, both Xack and Push briskly shot each other with heated glass in the legs, chest and arms.

"I finally got you Push!"

As the sharp heated glass all went right though them, both were knocked down by with blood leaking all around the arena. As the crowd awed by the gory attacks, Push stood up then ran towards Xack with the little stamina he has left. He hovered over him, ready to finally end the fool Sagan ordered to do weeks ago. Lifting his heated glass sword but suddenly, he felt utter fatigue and wobbling, losing his balance. The crowd sat silently, waiting for an outcome then he fell next to him.

"Woah folks it looks like Push couldn't finish the job. He's too beat up." Majesty announced.

"Good, let it stay that way." Ki-Yale said.

"C'mon medic, let's go, clean it up. The fight's over." Majesty said while the audience screamed out of joy then asked— "You guys are loving this Apaki fight huh?"

"It's either one fighter gets killed or both gets beat to a bloody pulp is when they really wanna cheer." Nack said.

"Sagan ma'… made them this way… they lo'… they love to see blood." Mike said as he slowly shook his head.

Little Tree Ville—

"So, he did all that to the trees huh?" Neecho asked walking with his wife down a pathway through the woods.

"Yeah just look at them, the air . . . It's clear like how it was before . . . It's like the plague never happen." Demi said.

"Ki-Yale and Tajaymae learning their powers so early then Oji . . ."

"It still isn't complete without Narrken."

"He isn't here to witness all of this but, I still believe that day will come where all four of our children are back together and also with us… and not out of our site."

"Right now, they're three of them out of our site."

"We made that decision because we believe Ki and Tajay can handle things, but I still keep a photographic memory of their life force. Narrken's life force just isn't revealing itself."

"Sensing his life force is one thing but seeing it with your own eyes is another. I believe he's still out there alive and I just want to get my baby back."

Luka sat around his desk in Luka Shale Tech & Co. main building as one of his associates brings him old files from the Gigantica City Police Department.

"Thank you for that."

He opened the old file and looked at it carefully for a moment then he puts his hand around his mouth. He couldn't believe it, right under his nose the entire time. The enemy was his close friend, he shook his head in anguish then he receives an alert through his wristwatch. He touches the button and instantly the hologram of his daughter Kathleen appeared. He looked at his associate and gives him the look for him to leave the office. The associate stepped out immediately and Kathleen said in a slight dragging voice—

"Hey, Dad."

"Hey, what's up Kathleen?"

"How did it go?"

"Hm, authorities said it could just be the trauma and besides, there's no evidence that supports her claims."

"So, she didn't do it?"

"Apparently, I guess not."

"Well. What do you think Dad?"

"What do you mean?"

"I mean. Do you think she did it for real?" Kathleen said as her eyes start to water.

He paused then shook his head and said— "Listen, it makes total sense, no evidence shows that she did it..."

She interrupted him and said— "Yeah but you said it yourself that Melissa wasn't self-inflicted."

"I know what I said Kathleen, but this is your mom we're talking about here. Ok? She said what she said but her daughter that she loved so dearly died cause of that stupid plague. Only God knows what she was going through, and this is just part of the aftermath."

"I don't know what to think anymore Dad. My head isn't in the right place right now."

She tried effortlessly not to weep then Luka said— "Hey baby, just, just get home. We'll talk about it some more when I get home. Ok?"

"Dad, I'm not coming home tonight. I'll be at Chloe's house."

"Ok . . . How's it going with Chloe?"

"She is barely hanging on to sanity but… but so am I . . ."

"She needs your support; you both need some support so be there and support each other. Tell her I said to be strong . . . Times now are changing; history is repeating itself all over again."

"Ok Dad, I'll speak to you later."

"Ok hun, talk to you later. I love you."

"Love you too Dad."

She hung up and Luka looked at the old files again then takes a deep breath.

<u>*Albacore Preschool, Atlantis City*</u>—

Dorimzy completed all eleven grade tests now he is on a twelfth-grade level Math, English, Science and History test as he contemplates and challenges the difficulty of the questions. In minutes he finished the test, Shania gradually looked at the two Detectives then looked at the principal then picks up the test.

Dorimzy staring at Shania with a stern, unfazed face and still no word coming out of his mouth.

She puts the test question in the grading slot and the scores came out as an outstanding hundred with every question answered correctly.

"Dorimzy . . . It shows on your record that you weren't born as a super genius. Is there something you need to tell us?"

Dorimzy's face gets even more serious as it started to turn red with his veins showing in his head and breathing heavily. Shania stared at him in fear with apprehension in her eyes and swallowing a piece of her own saliva.

"The police are at your door! The police are at your door!" The automated recognizing door system spoke.

"I wonder what happen? —Yeah . . . I'm coming! I'm coming!" Nicole shouting.

She opened the door and saw Detective Victoria and Detective Waldo.

"Nicole Torbino, you're under arrest for injecting Mega Human substance inside a minor without consent of the Gigantica government. You have the right to remain silent. Anything you say can and will be used against you in the court of law."

"Wait… What?!" Nicole dumbfounded as the Detective continued— "You have the right to have an attorney present during questioning. If you cannot afford an attorney, one will be appointed for you."

With disappointment and guilt on her face already thinking about prison and how she would handle it. She never got arrested and this experience to her it feels like a total hell. Chloe rushed to the front only to see that her mother is getting hand cuffed. "Mom?! What happened?!"

Tony also came to front and instantly alarmed— "Mom?" At that moment Nicole knew she has to sacrifice the impression that everything would be alright.

"It's ok . . . I'll fight this . . . its ok. Take care of your older sister Tony. You're the younger one but your growing up as a man . . . I love you son. Be a man and Chloe stay strong . . . you're a strong girl and always will be. I love you baby."

"Ok, time to go."

"Wait . . . What was the crime that she did?!"

"Dosing your brother with illegal Mega Human substance and he's a minor. This could be a ten-year prison sentence." Victoria said as one officer brought Nicole to the police vehicle.

Four other officers appeared then Detective Waldo said—

"This house is now a crime scene and will be searched for further evidence."

"Under what jurisdiction? Can you do that? Can they do that sis?"

"Yes, we can and we are going to have arrest you both."

"Oh fuck no. Where is our brother Dorimzy?!" Chloe shouted.

"At the station . . . Now, just cooperate with us."

<u>*Little Tree Ville Catholic Church*</u>—

Luka Shale Jr. sat on the front bench facing the altar with his hands together and took a deep breath closing his eyes for about fifteen seconds.

He opened his eyes and looked up at the golden statue of Jesus Christ on the cross on the top level of the wall.

"It's been a while since you came here Junior." Pastor Cadre Gilliam said.

"Hm', you're the only one I know that calls me that."

"It's the Lord that truly favors that name."

"The Lord. . . The Lord has forsaken me."

"You been away too long that you have forgotten the scripture. Hebrews 13 verse 5 'Never will I leave you; never will I forsake you'. He will never forsake us because His Son was forsaken in our place."

"I may not have been in holy grounds for long but, I've kept my faith in the Lord ever since I found him. My trust for God will never be eradicated yet the things happing around me led me to distress, nothing but sorrow."

"Then you must replenish with more scriptures, the things happening around us is part of life. We are in a sinner's world and to be free from all sin we must repent. Continue to love him and keep the good faith no matter how terrible the things may seem, God has a place for you at the end my brother. Hatred and anger, that's just the work of Satan."

"What about my children? What if they don't accept the word of the Lord?"

"Even the path of righteousness can be broken, though the Lord works in mysterious ways and one way that is most popular, is that he forgives. Give your children more time and if the time is already up, judgement will occur."

Luka looked down with a frozen face for a few seconds then looked back at the statue up on the wall over the altar.

The Harris residence, Year 2320—

Miranda Harris had just arrived home and saw her husband Dane Harris in the garage working on a coffee dispenser. She smiled then asked— "When are you ever going to finish that so-called project?"

"I can't rush perfection Miranda and this so-called project keeps me going just like your so-called project."

"Hey I told you not to speak of my work. You never know…"

"Never know the place could be bugged?"

"I'm just saying. This is confidential and you know Gigantica administrations that deal with this kind of stuff is really strict about it."

"Maybe you never should have told me."

"Hey, you're the one that wanted trust in our marriage no matter what."

"Yes, and I don't regret wanting that, but trust is what truly makes us whole . . . Don't worry though Hun, being scared all the time isn't good."

"Even if I'm scared or it's just in my head, precaution can be useful."

She gave a quick peck on her husband's lips then walked out the garage into the living room.

<u>*Crouton Village Tournament*</u>—

Xack is being carried on a stretcher by medics heading to the ER.

"He's going through shock!" Said one medic.

"What's hap'...? What happened to him?" Mike asked walking briskly with the medics.

"He's lost a lot of blood during that fight!" Said the medic.

"Lis'... listen... you better put him back in shape! Duh'... don't let him die!"

"He's not going to die, we promise! Now, please stay back!" One medic said then they ran away with Xack.

"He's going to be alright. They got it." Ki-Yale said arriving with his sister behind Mike then Mike then looked at him.

"Hey, uh. Mike, Majesty is calling you to the stage." Tajaymae said.

"Ok... Ok... I ne'... I need to take my medicine! — Uh... Oh no. I forgot that I don't have... I left it back home!" Mike said holding his head.

"Hold on, you don't have to fight, I'll tell them you forfeit." Ki-Yale said.

"Nuh'...! No, I want to fight tuh'… I want to fight for my village!"

Tajaymae looked at her brother then he said—

"It's not worth it. Let me fight in your place."

"Nuh'… no I don't want to come ho'... home as a failure to my Dad. I… I've always been a failure; I need to make my father proud."

"You're not a failure Mike…"

"Nuh'… no you don't undeh'… understand."

"Ok maybe I don't but fighting out there in this condition won't do anything."

"Oh, that's what you think Netro? Well I'll show you; I'll show everyone that I'm not a piece of work."

Mike upsettingly walked pass him towards the arena as Tajaymae gloomily gazed at him.

"I guess this fight is for him…" Ki-Yale said then raised his left eyebrow at his sister. "You know he's too old for you right?"

"What are you talking about? No, no. What?" She quickly replied as she blushed.

"Don't act like you don't like Mike…"

"Whatever… I wanted to give Yaeko back to Xack." She said as she revealed Xack's baby coyote in a baby carrying pouch for animals.

"Just take care of her until he recovers."

"Oh, I will absolutely do that."

Litzy appeared from the entrance. "Litzy…" He said.

"Hey. Is everyone ok? Is your friend ok?"

"Yeah, he's ok. Look at you, coming to check up on me and my friend."

"Yeah, of course… Hey Tajaymae… Woah… Y-your wounds healed already…"

"Hi…" She responded as she walked away to the entrance.

"Wow, guess she's still mad…"

"Yeah she gets like that."

"I have something to show you."

"What's that?"

"I was kind of bored and well… I made this…" Litzy said as she revealed a short golden neckless that has an "N" emblem like the symbol on Ki-Yale's chest and shows it to him.

He gasped then asked— "Wow… This is so cool. You made this in one day?"

"Yes."

"Woah! I wanna wear it." He said as Litzy started to blush.

She opened the neckless hook then puts gently the neckless around his neck.

"Well, I have the equipment in my room that helps me, and I've been doing is for a while now…"

She paused while her arms are remained around Ki-Yale's neck. Both gazed into each other's eyes as her face blushed like a bright red apple. At this moment they knew a feeling that they had never felt before had emerged.

"Sorry, I'm staring at you too much." She said while she immediately let's go off him.

"It's ok, I was doing the same as well. I'm aaa… I'm a little tired."

"Yeah um'… me too… kind of went to bed late." She said being in her fig leaf position as they began walking to the hallway door. Ki-Yale ogled at his new necklace then looked at her with a shy approval and nodding his head.

<u>*The Shale residence*</u>—

Luka has arrived at his residence as the automatic door recognized him. He walked in the main entrance and the door closed itself.

He looked around the house and sighted nil but the living room and the insignificant ounce of darkness as the light from the outside reflected on the windows. No Pamela and no Kathleen in spectacle, then the thought of his late daughter Melissa finally led him to tears. The lights automatically turned on as he walked to the kitchen and refiled the kettle with water then turned it on. He grabbed the logs of wood in the closet then went back to the living room to throw them in the fireplace.

The only warmth he has now, inhaling one of his electronic cigarettes and looking at the old files he got earlier at his office. Contemplating to himself as the vapors exhaled from his mouth then he paused. Impulsively, he threw the files in the fireplace then watched it all burn.

The Harris residence, Year 2320—

Dane Harris alone in his domain while his wife Miranda Harris is out doing overtime at work. Weeks had passed by as she complained about her work not being done yet and it's of at most importance that she gets it done.

He's in his room reading a book then he seemed to be taking a break from it as he puts the book down and grabbed the bookmark. He closes the book then he said—
"TV on."

The TV on the wall instantly turned on then eagerly, he's skipping through stations. He finally found the station he likes then smiled as his favorite show comes on.

Without conscious decision, he looked to the left of him and saw his middle drawer slightly open. Out of curiosity, Dane moves closer resulting him to get out of bed. The closer he gets a figure revealed itself.

456

He finally reached to the drawer and an eyeball looked right at him through the opening, his face in utter confusion, condemnation and discomfort noticing that the eye seemed so familiar. As he slowly opened the drawer he instantly gasped for air and there she was, his wife Miranda. Her head decapitated with both of her eyelids wide open as if she was left agitated before her death. Only a piece of her arm that seemed to be chewed up by an animal with extremely sharp teeth and blood had leaked all over his clothes.

Dane screamed out loudly and uncontrollably then instantly backed away out of fear after seeing such a horror.

Crouton Village Tournament—

"Ok folks, just waiting on Mike to make it to the stage. Thank you, Taw Hoffman, for being patient." Majesty said.

"No problem. You know, these little chumps just scared now you know. He's probably saying his little prayers before he gets up here."

The audience chanted— "Taw kills them all!"

"Ok! Uh… Ok! I'm here!" Mike said as he arrives on the stage.

"Good. Get on up here Mike! You'll go up against Taw the strongest Sila Human in Crouton Village and the best fighter here because well, he never lost a fight." Majesty bragged.

"Never lost a fight huh." Nack said as Ki-Yale and Tajaymae arrived at their section.

"Everything good with Xack?" Nack asked.

"Yeah, he'll be fine." Ki-Yale said.

"Well Mike's up next and his opponent is big news."

Tension in the air as Mike and Taw are facing each other on the arena ring all prepared to fight.

TWENTY-SEVEN

Gigantica Army Base 76, year 2320, armed soldiers posted on different positions around the premises guarding important weaponry. The entire base is protected by electrical wired fences as the first gate opens. The driver, private Phillips and Captain Chelsea in a truck pulled up to the clerk.

"Phillips . . . Captain."

The clerk opened the second gate then the soldier drives his lady Captain through the main entrance then parked. They both get out and the lady captain said—

"Phillips. Take a position and stand guard I can handle myself from here. We're in the safe house now . . . I'll be in the office.

"Yes Captain."

A peculiar phenomenon occurring within the large hazy Cell Block 16 without notice of any operatives. This is also used as an operation room which is kept below ten degrees Celsius. The deceased body of Malik Stenson equipped with an exoskeleton all around his presumed dead body, moving his fingers then suddenly, his eyes began to open. His pupils became diminutive and his sclera revealed red veins burgeoning up to his pupils. At this very moment, Malik Stenson knew he was finally awake.

"Hm, this should be interesting." Mr. Turd said being in the opposite side from Ki-Yale and the others.

"Hey, guy…"

"Mike is so focused."

"Hey, guy…! Dude!"

"Me?"

"Yeah you. You took a shower last night fam'? Or do you even take showers at all?"

"What do you mean? Of course, I took a shower . . . Wait a minute… It's those boys."

"Nah I don't think you showered fam'. You smell like straight ass! You smell like you ate ass all night!"

Mr. Turd smelled his armpits then said—

"Yeah, it's bad but I showered! It's just that some group of kids were messing with me with that Vile Stink Bomb."

"The Vile Stink Bomb? Oh, shit homie, that shit doesn't come off for like a week! No matter how much you shower."

"No! No! No! Those freaking kids!"

Mr. Turd got up from his seat then accidentally bumping into the seated audience causing them to lean back and hold their nose. He slowly walked to the exit and said—

"Damn it! Hmmmmm… I need to get this smell off me."

Loud shouting from the audience as Taw and Mike on the arena fighting stage.

"This is my fighter? Huh?"

"Yeah I'm thuh'… I'm the one that's goi'… going to break you!"

"Excuse me?! I haven't seen you fight; I've been too busy playing those classical videos games from the 21st century but you should know what I can do already, there's no excuse for you to talk like that."

"I can tah… I can talk… any… I can talk anyway I want to."

"Ok stutter mouth."

"I'm gon'… I'm going to end . . . your streak!"

"Ha' kid, that's what they all say!"

"No! No mo'… no more failures!"

"Ok fighteeerrrs'! Are you ready?!…." Majesty announced.

"No more failures…"—Mike repeatedly thought.

<u>*In year 2311, 6:10am an older model house in Little Tree Ville*</u>.

"Aaah! Baaby' yes! Yes Baby! Fuck this pussy! Don't stop baby!!" Stacey Roberts screamed as Dr. Rogue Sagan is on top of her pressing her legs up to her stomach.

"Aah. You like that?!"

The bed shook from the hardcore sex as Sagan thrusting as hard as he can. He looked in her eyes and kissed her then he softly bit her lips. Her toes curled as he looked up to the wall and grunted while he continued to pump her then suddenly, he climaxed and shouted—

"AAAGH! AAAAGH!"

Moments later—

Sagan prepared a quick breakfast meal and served it to Stacey with a light smirk on his face.

"There's a reason why I made this for you."

"Oh really?"

"Yeah you have something special, something no other woman has."

"And what's that?"

"Some good fucking walls."

She smiled at him and said—

"I guess that's hard to find out here."

"Yes, and I'm very lucky to have you."

She paused and blushed then said—

"I'm very lucky to have you too."

"I'm still surprised you even came home with me."

"I know, with all that allegedly a killer thing . . . You know allegedly or allegations doesn't mean you really killed anyone."

"What if I did?"

She paused and stared at him for about five seconds then said—

"Hm, even if you did . . . I know somewhere in your heart... there is still some good left."

"Hmm, yes... Some good sex..."

She smiled at him again then said—

"Hm, which makes me wonder Doctor.... Why does your treatment always work?"

"Well, let's just say I'm an expert on sex. I've even banged guys before."

Stacey kept a smile on her face then said—

"Oook'... Really?"

"Yep, I admit it . . . I'm a man that goes both ways."

"Ook well... If fucking guys makes you this good in bed with women, then... keep doing what you do." She said while smiling.

He stared at her then seconds later she bit her lips and moved in for a kiss. Her phone that's built in her clothes vibrated awakening her attention. "Damn, I gotta go."

"Emergency? Duty calls?"

Stacey gave Sagan a quick peck on his lips then she quickly grabbed her clothes and said—

"Yeah, it's an urgent family thing."

"Ok."

"I'll call you later."

She walked out his room while he looked behind her back with a blank stare.

<u>Roland Residence</u>—

Screaming and throwing from a younger Mike Roland at age six. His autism is harder to control at a young age and he seemed be to upset.

"NO! I waaant'!" Mike yelled being vexed as he threw a battery at his father.

"C'mon Mike stop throwing stuff." Tyson said.

"Maaaa!?!?!"

Mike then ran into the second living room hitting himself on his hips with both hands in a fist then hits himself on his legs. Mike fell and kept hitting himself then grabbed a small glass vase then threw it at the wall.

"Where are you? —I need you here, like right now." *Tyson speaking to a local friend who's a therapist and lives next door through a communication cube.*

He goes back in the room with Tyson and moments later the friend arrived and pinned down Mike to keep him calm.

"I'll go clean up the room. You got this?"

"Yeah, I got it."

Mike is finally calm, and Tyson's friend began to settle him down on a cheer.

"What was he upset about?" *The friend asked.*

"I guess he wanted his mom."

"Your mom is at work Mike. You know she has to go to work."

"She hasn't been home since yesterday morning. Mike gets up at 7am and my girlfriend leaves at 5am and gets back for 3pm but she told me she has overtime and still hasn't been back yet. It's almost mid-day"

"You called her?"

"Yeah but no answer."

"Hm."

"Maa'! Mamaaaa'!"

"Hey. How's running for Mayor going?" *The friend changing the subject trying to make everything seem ok.*

"It's a raffle with tons people with political beliefs so it's all up to the decision with the people you know."

The front door started to open sliding quickly then closes. Tyson then walked to the front— "Oh... Where the hell were you?" Tyson angrily asked.

"I had overtime, I told you this." Stacey Roberts argued.

"And your phone?"

"Ma! Maamy'!" Mike said in a loud voice running to his mother, Stacey.

Later—

Tyson, Stacey and Mike sitting around the dinner table as Mike chewed vigorously on his food. Everyone is having Pork chops, rice and beans with some vegetables.

"You haven't touched your food Tyson."

"You haven't told me where you were last night and why you didn't answer your phone."

"I'm sorry... My phone was on airplane mode..."

"That right there . . . Is Bullshit."

"What you mean?! Look I can't use my phone at work..." Stacey said and being intervened again.

"Bullshit . . . A whole lot of fucking bullshit!" Tyson said as Mike lifted his shoulder and his head gets closer to it and with his eyebrows lifted, slightly looking at Tyson, implementing that he is getting scared.

"Really. In front of Mike?!"

"Oh, you care now."

"What are you talking about?!"

"Look . . . I'm not hungry anymore." Tyson said as he threw the fork at his plate then got up out of his hover chair then walked away from the table.

Two hours later—

Stacey was outside the front yard smoking an e-cig then began to walk back inside. She walked to Mike's room and saw that Mike is sleeping then heads upstairs to the bedroom.

"Hey." Stacey said as she walked over to sit next to Tyson.

"Hey." Tyson responded with a low muttering voice.

Stacey began to slowly put her hands around Tyson's arm then slowly goes does down to his hands.

"I'm sorry I didn't call it was all my fault and it won't happen again."

Tyson then looked at his girlfriend as he shook his head up and down.

"I love you baby. You're the only one that ever been there for me. Even when I was down to nothing."

"I love you too Tyson and I will never leave you no matter what."

Tyson began to move in for a kiss and so did Stacey. They French kissed as he slowly touching her waist then moved his hand down to her leg.

<u>The next day at school—</u>

Mike is drawing a man wearing armor with flames around his body and a sword in his hand riding on a horse with flames around the horse as well.

As he focuses on his sketch, a chubby young boy at age six named Jeffery walked up to him and said—

"Hey little bitch."

"I'm dra'… I'm drawing… Eh."

"You drawing 'Eh'?" Jeffery mocking Mike.

"He talks like he got a dick in his mouth." Brad said another young boy.

Everyone in class started to laugh after Brad made a comment on Mike's speech impediment due to his autism. The teacher stepped out the classroom moments before Jeffery started to bother him.

"Fu'… fuck you beh'… you bitch!"

"What you just say?!" Brad asked while everyone in class is instigating what Mike said.

"Yo beat his punk ass! I'll help you!" Jeffery said as he pushes Mike off his cheer.

"C'mon! Beat his ass. Can't let him talk to you like that!" Jeffery said.

Brad seemed hesitant to hit Mike but seconds later uses his foot and stomped on Mike's arm, then his face.

Mike managed to get up after Brad stopped then grabbed a book and threw it at Brad. Brad Ducks then Mike yelled random words and grabbed another book then threw it across the room.

Mike expressed a lot of anger throwing his drawings and supplies on his desk. Mike then began throwing pens and pencils around the room in different directions.

The students started to duck and scream as the teacher entered the room and saw Mike having a temper tantrum. The teacher quickly held him down to the floor trying to tame him, but he was still swinging his arms around and hitting the teacher.

<u>*Shale Residence—*</u>

Luka Shale is on the phone speaking to a soldier on an all glass screen—

"The video is gruesome sir, it was like a slaughter house in those hallways. It was like he was enjoying it."

"Yes, I remember it like it was yesterday."

"Good thing I wasn't there."

"Yes soldier, good thing you wasn't."

"You could still be responsible for this."

"That's what they say after two years of pending investigation."

"Yes, Luka they still want someone to blame."

"Well, if the Feds want to keep doing the case with me involved fine but it'll still be a dead end."

"I agree sir."

"What could have possessed him to do all of that? Sure, he has Death Angel DNA but…"

<u>*Year 2320 at the Gigantica Army Base 76—*</u>

The alarm is triggered, and guns shots are being fired in the facility.

"This is Captain Chelsea! We are under attack! I repeat! We are under attack and taking heavy fire! Multiple soldiers down!"

Malik walked through the hallways as the sound of metal hitting the metal floors from his exoskeleton shoes. Soldiers fire their heat ray weapons and regular guns, but Malik was unfazed by the shots as the Tektonium exoskeleton that he wears deflected them. He grabbed a pistol from one of the dead soldiers and used it to fire back shooting two soldiers in the body. The metal around his arm opened and started deflecting bullets and beams again as parts of his exoskeleton is detached and used as large knives. Malik reaping his gore as he cuts open a Soldier's throat then stabbed another in the eye and decapitated him. As the blood slushed out, he picked up the beheaded soldier's head and carries it. Malik ran to the exit and saw a group of soldiers ready to fire their guns at him. He held the beheaded soldier's head by the helmet in front of him and threw it at the soldiers as a distraction then he jumped sixteen feet in the air and landed in the middle of the group of soldiers with Captain Chelsea. Malik instantly cuts and gutted all of them piece by piece then minutes later he mutilates the rest as the soldiers screamed barbarically.

Captain Chelsea backed up while aiming her assault rifle at him then said—

"What the fuck are you? How are you alive?"

No words from Malik as he gets closer to Captain Chelsea as she pulls the trigger, but no bullets came out of the assault rifle then she said—.

"All my men… All of them murdered…"

She dropped her assault rifle and draws her pistol as the Malik detached another sharp piece of his exoskeleton on his right arm and slowly aims it at her.

"Fuck this…" She said as she aimed the pistol to her head then pulled the trigger.

A loud sound from the gun fire as the blood busted out from the left side of her cranium.

Malik just stared at her with a staid face then used his sharp piece of metal and repeatedly chops her neck until her head is eventually detached with a piece of her neck bone connected. He held up her head by tightly grabbing her hair then walked down to the exit metal fence.

<u>*Present time, 2322 in Crouton Village Tournament*</u>—

Mike and Taw are circling each other as they prepared to make the first move.

"Hmm, you seem sure of yourself. Do you really hold enough power to defeat me?"

"Hm. I keep my word." Mike vouched.

Taw slowly blinked with a large grin then said—

"I'm not just an ordinary Sila Human you know. It's a lot of skill to get where I'm at now."

"Hm." Mike unfazed by his words.

"You will feel the wrath of a Prime Human."Taw bragged.

"So, this Taw guy… Is he really a Prime Human?" Ki-Yale asked.

"Checking right now Ki…" Nack said as he searched the Internet for information then continued—

"Yes, look at this fighter's profile here…. He's a Sila Human, he was ranked Prime Human two years ago when he was sixteen. His father trained him since a toddler." Nack said looking at his holographic computer device.

"Hmm, I never seen a Prime Human up close." Ki-Yale fascinated.

"Well there is a very few Prime Humans here. Taw is just the more advanced one… Maybe in the next year he would be a Mega Human Prime."

"Prime or no prime… Mike's got this…"

"Hm, I agree Mike's weapon is double the strength of any animal."

Mike uses his Gazen Weapon and changed into a large glass Gorilla he roars then moved with the projected glass animal surrounding his body. His roar sounded exactly like an Ape as Mike charged at Taw standing in a defensive position.

<u>Year 2311—</u>

"You know we have to suspend you too, right?" Said the Principal.

"But he called me a bitch!" Brad said.

"True but you made fun of his autism. Which is not very nice, you two are suspended and you will be assigned to a class to teach you guys some respect. Now leave." Said the Principal as Jeffery and Brad walked by Mike, Tyson and Stacey.

Mike has a bandage around his eye from the stomps to the face from Brad.

"Glad to see the parents for Mike is here, it's a shame whoever raised those kids haven't showed up. Probably embarrassed and waiting outside." Said the Principal.

"So, my son is not in trouble, right?" Tyson worried.

"No. But don't you think he will need something better than being here?" Asked the Principal.

"What do you mean?" Tyson asked.

"I mean… He needs to be in child services…"

"No, that's not happening!"

"Why? I mean he's fine where he's at." Stacey argued.

"This isn't the first time he had outburst like today. He threw sharp objects around the classroom. Could have poked an eye out, plus heavy books, repeatedly hitting the teacher... It's a lot more to name what he does with these outbursts. It's all in the record book and I'm sure this isn't your first visit here."

"This is bullshit!" Stacey yelled.

"I see where he gets the foul language from."

"There has to be another way. A class or after school program!" Tyson mentioned.

"We don't provide anger management and it's mandatory that he goes to child services. We can no longer tolerate this. I'm sorry."

Outside of the school entrance Tyson shook his head then looked at Mike looking down on his hands.

"Aye man. Hurry up with your Sunday!" Malone said sitting in vehicle across the street.

"I'm coming bro, I'm coming." Derrick said.

"Oh, shit Derrick! There she is!"

"Oh, shit!"

Malone and Derrick is in the car looking at Stacey, Tyson and Mike walking out of the school building.

"Ooh who is that next to her? And that little bastard looks like her a little bit.

"Let me use this scanner the Feds use." Malone said as he smiled.

"Always got the gadgets and shit."

"It's the boss man, he hooks us up all the time."

"Us? You mean you."

"Shut up! Don't be jealous Derrick... Woah, check this out. That's her kid man his father looks just like that dude. Kid's name is Mike Roland and father's name is Tyson Roland."

"Ooh we getting paid extra for this!"

"What you mean?"

"Bro.... Tyson Roland. That's his brother!"

"He should have been in child services a long time with those outbursts. The principal was looking out for us the whole time, but he just got tired of it..." Tyson said.

"Tyson." She hailed.

"Yeah?" He answered.

"I have something to tell you." Stacey vaguely said as Tyson looked puzzled to what she is about to say.

"Ok, tell me when we get home."

<u>*Present time at the Tournament—*</u>

Mike jumped and landed on Taw using the glass projected Gorilla arms. Taw in defense mode blocks the attack with is arms then Mike removed Taw's arms away and smashes his face. Mike then picks him up and threw him across the fighting ring then Taw grabbed a grip of the fighting ring pavement and looked up at Mike.

"Hm, all glass huh? And this gorilla seemed stronger than a regular one. I know because wrestled with one."

"Thuh'… the weapon provides mah'… more strength than the average gorilla, pluh'… plus my body and unfortunately you'll have to get a few glass pieces in your skin."

"Amazing… amazing creation… I don't mind some glass… cuts and bruises ain't nothing to me. I ain't no punk! . . . Did you make it yourself?"

"Hmm'… no mah'… my father did."

"Nice, you should be dominating the world with that weapon. Use it against all those bullies you had. I'm pretty sure you had bullies in your life. Having autism as a kid seems to have that effect. I know because I have a relative that has autism."

"Ye… yeah, I always had bullies before I introduced to this weapon… but I… I don't want it to be for bullies except one…"

"Oh—I think I know which bully you're talking about."

<u>*Year 2311—*</u>

"I can't fucking believe this shit!! You fucked the fucking Principal, some piece of shit cook from a fucking piece of shit restaurant!! Some weird sword fighting guy and on top of that, my... My brother?! This is some sleazy shit!" Tyson bickered walking in circles, waving his hands and Stacey looked ashamed while Mike is right outside the room hearing the conversation.

"I didn't know he was your brother at first..."

"I can't believe you... he's a fucking mass murderer Stacey. You know that right?! And on top of that you been swapping each other's junk."

"Yeah, I know... I."

"You know what? I don't even want to hear it from you anymore. Please just leave, you caused enough headache for me. You can say goodbye to Mike before you leave."

"But look, let's work this out..."

"No Stacey, No. I'm done with this shit. Please just leave."

"No, please!"

"STACEY!!" He blurted as she looked at him with a bit of tears running down her cheeks then he continued—

"I really don't want to say it again..."

Stacey looked down and shook her head then walked out the room door. She saw Mike and walked up to him and kisses him while she sobbed.

"Hmm'... Moh'...!" Mike struggled to say call to his mother until it was too late as Stacey walked out the door.

Stacey is at the bus station and decided to make a call through her wristwatch. It was Dr. Rogue Sagan and despite the investigations surrounding him he still answered the call.

"Hello?"

"Hey. I... I don't know where else to go."

"What happen? You can always drop by, I'm here."

Moments later—

Tyson is in the living room by himself looking at the wall. He shook his head thinking about what he found out earlier. He tries to get his mind off it as he picked up the blueprints for the Gazen Weapon. He gawps at it for moment then the holographic projecting phone rings.

"Hello, Tyson Roland residence."

"Yes, hello Tyson. This is the Board of Little Tree Ville. How are you today?"

"I'm great. How are you?"

"I'm great myself, you were selected from a raffle to be the new Mayor of Little Tree Ville." Said the office man.

"Woah! What!?" Tyson yelled excitingly.

"Congratulations sir!"

"I can't believe this."

"Yes, your office is ready in LTV, we just need for you to attend Gigantica City Hall to fill out some paperwork then we will announce it to the public. You can also make your first speech tonight. Is there anything you would like us to do starting from now?"

"Yes, please... I need my son out of child services."

"Sure, uh we'll see what we can do."

"Please... Thank you."

<u>Crouton Village tournament—</u>

Mike attacked Taw as a giant glass Buffalo aiming for the body. Taw then quickly converted to a defense position with two arms together and blocked the attack as he is pushed back about ten feet with his feet still planted on the platform. Mike changed into a large forty feet long Anaconda then wrapped the body around Taw and started squeezing him tightly.

"You se'... you see, this weapon was truly ma'... made for me as a gift. Nuh'... not for destruction... buh'... but for protection and most importantly a certain someone! Muh'... my dad knew wha'... what was out there for me."

"Aagh! You know, your dad truly gave that weapon to the perfect user… Aagh… a user who isn't going to fold easily because of the pessimism that surrounds him… very inspirational. Although, I just have this feeling your father gave this weapon to you to divert you from the fact he still can't give you back your mother." Taw said while slowly being crushed by the large glass Anaconda and his skin being pierced by sharp fragments of glass.

"He har… he hardly mentions Mom an… and I understand why he doesn't, but I haven't seen her since. No visits, no calls, no traces of anything today buh'… but he seems has some forgiveness now. It's just that we bo… both believe she isn't alive."

"Hmm', messing with Sagan can have almost anyone disappear easily."

Year 2311—

"Now, the start of a new society, a new campaign, a new lifetime together… Little Tree Ville… Will continue to be a spectacular village! After countless hours of finding the perfect fit for a new Mayor we perceived it was worth every minute. Being Mayor is not just leadership but honor, integrity, bravery, not afraid to take on any situation! We decided that this man would be a great fit. Yes, and this man goes by name, Tyson Roland!" Said the council man.

The Little Tree Ville citizens are chairing as Tyson gets on the podium.

Present time in the Atlantis Police Precinct—

Kathleen gets a call from Chloe then she rushed right away to see her.

"What is this? Why is Chloe here?"

"She may or may not be involved in a crime and we need her here for investigation purposes."

"What crime is this?"

"Dosing a minor with illegal substance."

"No, that's not her. You don't know if she is a part of that!"

"Well, we'll just have to find out for ourselves. Don't we?"

Gigantica Army Base 76—

"I remember it like it was yesterday… All those men murdered by that Death Angel!" Captain Jenkins said with anger.

"That project was a failure." Luka expressed doubt.

"No, I say it was a success the only thing is that he was revived but he has the exoskeleton that is fastened to his brain. If we can put the commander chip inside, we will have full control of him." Henry mentioned as all three men walked down the hallway to the operation room.

Captain Jenkins opened the door with his keycard and said—

"Deja-vu Luka?"

"Yes, yes. I can't forget the day I had the hopes and dreams that someday my father's exoskeleton will become on top again."

"Well, without competition there wouldn't be the true excitement . . . The raw feeling of becoming the best."

"This is why I like you around Henry, you give that extra push you know."

"Well that's what a friend does."

"As much as I hate to say this, we need him back on our side. I haven't heard anything from him, but he could be a part of the daily killings." Captain Jenkins said as he types on the glass keyboard commanding the machinery to pick up one of the exoskeletons.

"He's not making an appearance anytime soon but for now we should focus on the Motogon."

Luka gazed at Henry for a moment then said—

"Yes, we certainly do…"

Present time Gel Hev, the Shale residence

Luka Shale Jr. sipped his hot tea and looked up to the giant painting of his father on the ceiling.

"No one said that I was going to fail you father… So why should I stop now, I always have plans, I always had a solution. I cannot break down, no not now."

He continued to ignore his emotions and stood up from his seat then walked to the living room closet and goes to the end of the closet. He stooped down and touched the lower area of the wall then suddenly, the wall pushed itself back as if it's a secret door. The wall is pushed all the back giving him room to walk through to the darkness. He walked past the threshold and the wall closes with naught but complete darkness then he simply touched a button on his left forearm sleeve to turn the lights on.

The brightness bloomed instantaneously revealing the large room with mechanical equipment all around. He walked towards a body pod used for air displacement plethysmography, then he types in the code to open it.

Luka slightly chuckled then said—

"The new Kleaner… from the moment I saw you at my doorstep, I knew I haven't failed what I started. Your predecessor wanted you to succeed as a descendant just like how my father wanted me to be. Hmm, your father died guarding the thing that would make this world crumble... the Motogon. I've been deceived by the one I call, friend, a so-called friend who is truly responsible for taking the item.

And it's not just any item, its unknown power source found by Henry . . . Luciano . . . or maybe…" He paused for a moment reacting to a thought, a conspiracy in which he hoped isn't real.

"No way… maybe he's just . . ."

He paused again being frightened and reacting to his theory then continued.

"He's just another threat against humanity."

TWENTY-EIGHT

Year 2312, Gigantica City—

"Ever since I began my duties as Mayor, I was pushing for more androids to detect any illegal fed guns. Even inside people's houses the android police will detect an illegal fed gun and a person without a SS microchip they will act accordingly to defend those residents. If federal facilities have them so can the people of Gigantica have them in their houses."

"Soon that bill will be signed by the POTW and have every house in the solar system equipped with such technology." Preston said walking with Mayor Tyson to the burnt down Roland residence while security is behind them.

"Yeah, and that tech will reduce the crime rate even more."

"It's been a while since you been here, I presume."

"It's time I let go of this place and make it another home for someone else. I'll take care of the rebuilding process..."

"I'll be glad to help sir."

"Yes, thank you Preston..."

Tyson then shook his head and continued— *"His father is responsible for this mess. I feel that if Kevin hadn't come into our lives this would have never happened. Am I wrong for blaming Kevin?"*

"He didn't know of his father's origin... I'm sure he never even imagined this would've happen to your family as you did."

"No… he should've never come into our lives! Sometimes I just wish I was burnt away along with my parents, but I guess I had the strength to escape, I barely moved to the window in time with a gunshot wound in my leg."

"Yes, luckily you survived and now you're well. This is an opportunity for you to continue the Roland legacy…"

"With a damn exoskeleton keeping me standing but if this is how I'm going to make sure Mike becomes a success then so be it."

<u>The Kafmora residence, present time</u>—

"Turn of events occurred in the village, the trees are back to normal." Said the news anchor.

The LTV News Channel revealed live footage of the remarkable change as the News reporters interviewed the citizens—

"I can't believe it! I thought all hope was lost with this village."

"Would you say this was a miracle sir?"

"To me, this looks like God is on our side."

"Look at that Oji, you brought joy and happiness upon the village." Demi encouraged her son.

"Yeah but…"

"But what?"

"But no one saw me do it."

"Your grandfather and I did, that's two. Besides you don't wanna be seen with these abilities right now."

"But, I wanna be like Ki-Yale going around saving people in a Netron Suit."

"I know but you don't have a Netron Suit right now. You'll probably have to wait a little longer until you're older."

"That's not fair."

"I don't know how it works but maybe you're too young Oji. Ki-Yale got his suit at fourteen and you're eight years old now."

"I wanna get a Netron suuuiit'!" Oji whined.

"I know baby. It's nice that you want to help people with your powers but first you must master it. It takes a lot of time and God knows how powerful you would be but for now it's too dangerous going around being a hero. I still think it's unsafe for Ki-Yale and Tajaymae to be out there. Especially Tajaymae…"

"She doesn't have a Netron Suit."

"Exactly, which is why it's unsafe for her, but she knows how to handle herself."

"Well . . . I need to practice so I can become a pro and then I'll become a superhero!" Oji said as he smiled looking at his mother.

She smiled back at him as he ran playfully back into the house.

. . .

"Something's not right… everything is a mystery at this point. Why would the book show me such illusions? I figured out the Zeal abilities for my grandson but…"

Nealo looking at the mirror in the bathroom, leaning over the sink and leaving water to run after washing his face. Being deep in his thoughts, he kept his focus on the strange entity that encountered him.

"Ever since I touched the Book of Edu, I've been seeing these visions… what are these visions?!"

He held his forehead with his right hand then rubbed his fingertips downward and stopped in between his eyebrows. Targeting his pressure point he rubbed some more and tilting his head down, taking his eyes off of the mirror.

"Whatever it…" Nealo thought while tilting his head back up to look at the mirror. He quickly backed away, goggling at the face once again.

The bathroom lights were instantly off, divulging absolute darkness, no windows to let in outside light. The entire mirror was dark as well, as if there was another dimension through it, only showing a face. There was no glow to its pale skin as the anger and thirst for a soul expressed from its white pupils and dark sclera.

"It's you again..." He said while standing his guard. Both of his fists activated his Loose Cannons as it idled with a ringing sound, charging and ready to fire.

Its severed cheeks lifted along with its nose, growling and revealing more anger as if it wants to attack Nealo.

"Are you... some kind of spirit? . . . You have no lips... you can't speak, can't you?"

It screeched as loud as it can with its lower teeth being inches away from its upper teeth. Nealo walked backwards and slightly collided onto the wall behind him as the image disappeared.

He sighed while disarming his Loose Cannons and looked down at his trembling hands.

"*I... I never been this terrified since... I faced an Opposite for the first time when I was younger...*"

<u>*Crouton Village Tournament*</u>—

Mr. Turd is in one of the restrooms outside the arena as he looked at his face and said—

"Damn kids, at least I'm still handsome. Yeah, look at that handsome fellow! Yeah!"

Another man stood beside him as he began to wash his hands then encountered the miasma coming from Mr. Turd with a drastic whiff.

"Holy shit man! What is that awful smell?!"

The man couldn't stand to sniff anymore as he quickly left the restroom leaving Mr. Turd embarrassed then he walked outside the restroom. He began looking at his hands, sniffing his armpits and clothes as he walked to a bench then he heard a lady's voice saying—

"Hey, leave me alone!"

"Come here bitch!"

He quickly turned around and saw a lady about to get mugged by two men then he kept his attention on the occurring incident and speed walked to the lady and the two men.

"Hey leave her alone!" He shouted.

"Oh, you wanna be a hero huh?" One of the two men said walking up to Mr. Turd.

"Yeah a brave one." Mr. Turd said as he puts his hands on his hips and points his chest out.

"Ooh! What the fuck is that smell?! Dude!"

The second man walked up to Mr. Turd then said—

"Oh shit! You right man! This guy stinks! Let's get out of here man."

"Yeah! You better run! I don't play these games you fake thugs!"

He looked back at the lady then asked—

"Are you ok ma'am?"

"Yeah, yeah, I'm ok just stay back a couple feet please." The lady said as she covered her nose.

"Oh sorry, some group of kids played a prank on me and…"

"It's ok . . . You just need to get cleaned up . . . Come with me."

Tournament Medical Facility—

Loaded Ace laid down in the hospital bed as two physicians spoke about his recent fate.

"So, his soul is disappeared huh?"

"Yeah and he's paralyzed. It's categorically zilch we can do here, he doesn't even have family according to the background check results."

"We can send him to the military."

"True or the Mad Doctor could have him. After all, he is the one that led him here."

"That's probably a better idea. He probably would've had our asses doing something like that."

As one of the physicians picked up several documents while the other looked at the screen materialized from the projector around his arm then suddenly, the cardiac monitor began to function indicating that there is a heartbeat. Both physicians gasped as they turned around and saw Loaded.

"Is he?"

"Max revived him…"

Inside the arena—

"Taw seems to be trapped in Mike's giant snake binding!" Majesty said.

"That's it for that guy." Nack said.

"He got cocky and didn't muscle up before now look at the position he's in and he supposed to be the best fighter here. Ha! I don't think so." Tajaymae said.

Mike squeezed Taw tighter, then Taw started to smile then Mike with his giant snake felt his grip slowly becoming loose. Taw's muscle mass began to increase all around his body, ripping parts of his shirt but he has special pants and shoes that expands when he gets bigger to a certain size. The muscles are slowly pushing off the giant glass snake and his skin became tougher than usual.

"Em'… impossible. I have the gri'… the grip of a Green Anaconda bah'… but quadruple the strength! How?"

"Grragh'… this is… only… forty percent. Aagh!" Taw said pushing away the giant snake around his body then jumped and did a backflip away from Mike.

"Woah! He got out folks!" Majesty said.

The crowd instantly cheering after seeing what Taw did.

"He's strong for sure and that's only forty percent." Ki-Yale said.

"How do you know?" Nack asked.

"I heard him say it."

"Even under all this noise from the crowd?"

"Yep."

Mike was unarmed and Taw's muscles were two times bigger all around his body, but they were still a few grazes from the glass penetrating his skin.

"That was a good massage Mike, it gets the muscles moving smoothly." Taw said as he chuckled.

"Geh'… guess I need to go harder."

"Oh, please if you will. I need a good workout."

<u>*Tournament Men's Locker Room*</u>—

Max changed his outfit in the locker room as his father appeared from the entrance and had a short conversation.

"You're sure that he took the drugs?" Vince asked.

"Yes, I gave it to him." Max said.

"Well, I'm surprised he's still moving for the fight."

"Well, everyone's different."

"You're right son… Everyone is different."

Vince then left the locker room while Max stared at the side of where his father was standing then unexpectedly, seven ladies came inside with eyewear technology built to be ineffective to Max's Tantu Orb.

"This is the men's locker room…"

The lady in the front named Sally stood across from him and said—

"Oh, we know Max . . . we know."

One of the ladies fires an illegal Fed gun that only shoots high tech handcuffs that connect when clamped to both hands. Either to the back or the front with a magnetic pull. This time the handcuffs connect both hands to the back. Max struggling to break the cuffs off of his hands and gasped—

"What is this? Who are you!?!"

"My name is Sally and you know who we are. Or should I say you know who we work for."

Max continued to struggle trying to get out of the cuffs as Sally walked up to Max.

"I want to know why Mike is still alive. Hmm? Why isn't Netro going up against Taw?" Sally inquired.

Unknown Area—

In the Mad Doctor's room, painting on the wall that he created with his own hands harvested from human remains. The stench around the room represents a foul personality. Dr. Sagan sat in his favorite hover chair and asked—

"A turn of events huh?"

"Maybe the military thought of a way to reduce the effects on the trees." His lady servant said.

"Hm, but to make them small again is very odd. They would have to grow them from scratch but instead it happened within an hour."

"Hm, indeed unusual sir."

"I'm going to ask you something and you need to be clear with me."

"Ok, what's the question sir?"

"This question is very important . . . Do you think I will be alive for the rest of eternity?"

"Aaum'..."

"Go ahead, answer the question."

"Well . . .To be honest no, you're human like me we aren't immortal."

"Hm, exactly. I'm a human, a mortal that takes advantage of other mortals. It's always like that no matter how you beg…"—Dr. Sagan breathes heavily as he makes a fist and looked at his paintings.

"I'm sure it's not going to be soon."

"What's going to be soon?!"

"Your death sir…"

"Oh yes, yes. Sorry, I dozed off for a second there."

"It's ok. I know your history and it's messed up what your father did."

"Hm, I have one more question for you . . . What would you do after I'm dead? And how would you feel? . . . Well, that's two questions…"

"Aaum…" The lady servant confused as he looked at her with a somber face.

"Speak the truth now."

"Ok well . . . I would be pleased."

"Pleased?"

"Yes, I would be pleased with the perkiest smile on my face when you're dead. I would be celebrating with screams of joy and drinking vodka by myself because all of my family members you ki…" The lady servant paused then she broke down in tears.

"That's what I like to see… I like to see the unembellished truth. We can't just talk to each other without the veracity in the air…"

The lady servant continued to bawl then he said—

"I did that to your family right? And you know all this what I did, it was me that single handedly murdered your family with an Apaki Katana in Russia two years ago. I wanted to spread my reign of terror with the Genchi by my side."

She looked at him with a bitter look on her face as if she wanted to strike him down right now.

"I loved every minute of it and yet you come here to work for me."

"Yes… Keep my friends close and my enemies closer."

"Oh, smart words… Your friends are in the Gigantica Military correct?"

She stood quiet and glared at him.

"Well, I was informed of this already, they would've busted open that door a long time ago. They said not to contact them at all after going through security screening and step foot on this place with a blind fold on correct?"

She looked at him surprisingly and he continued—

"The General thought I would slip up but clearly she's wrong and left you as a hostage . . . And now I will grant you a new status from a hostage."

She slowly walked backwards as he walked closer to her then swiftly, an android came up behind her then stabbed her in the back with its sharp metal finger on its hand. The android aggressively ripped out her entire spine causing her insides to egress.

"Hm, I could've gotten that myself, but you did a good job… so, good job."

He sat back down on his favorite chair then smiled with his eyes closed.

<u>Mayor Tyson's Office</u>

"Regime agent David Hahn of the Clandestine Extraterrestrial Unit wants to see you sir."

"The CEU? Of course, bring the fellow in."

Tyson drunk his cappuccino from a coffee cup and looking at an all glass touch screen tablet. He puts his coffee cup back on the cup holder that's connected to mechanical arm coming from the ceiling.

"Hello Mr. Hahn."

"Hello Mayor Tyson. How are you today?"

"I'm doing fine. Now, I know you didn't come here to ask me how I'm doing."

"Yes, but you know why I'm here."

"Netro."

"Yes, and I will like to ask you a few questions about the boy, as you know, outsiders are dwelling amongst us."

"Ok go ahead I have nothing to hide."

"How old is he?"

"Fourteen years old."

"You know, it's just weird that you have an alien by your side like it's how it's weird your son's name is Mike and your name is Tyson. *Mike Tyson…* together you guys are like the legendary boxer."

"You figured out the meaning of my son's name, bravo…"

"What I'm trying to say is… Why is an alien with you and not with us?"

"I don't know the boy came to me. Said he wanted to help capture Dr. Sagan and turn him in. He uses his powers to be a hero you know, not terrorize the world with it."

"Heroics… You think heroics will linger with a child with that power?"

"Well, he's on our side right now…"

"Yes, but I've seen him in action—a man sent me videos of him helping the police officers in the plague. He didn't have a mask, but we couldn't identify him anywhere through Social Security. I also saw video of him flying around Little Tree Ville, I guess he thinks no one will catch him and video of him in the Crouton Village Tournament."

"He's getting close to Sagan."

"He got sliced in the face and his throat slit wide open . . ."

"Is he?!" Tyson concerned.

"No, the kid's alive. His neck and face regenerated. I don't know how that happen but it happened."

"It's his suit. It enhances his abilities and I guess it gives him regeneration."

"Hm, how can we obtain a suit like that?" Mr. Hahn asked.

"I don't know but, suits like that would benefit us in many ways." Tyson answered.

"I don't think the kid is alien like he said. He looks human as a human should, I think maybe it's just the suit that's alien."

"Maybe you're right Mr. Hahn."

"What if I say you try and retrieve the suit for us? We will reward you something large, large enough that you would even resign as Mayor."

"No money in the world would make me resign as Mayor right now, especially when the Mad Doctor is still a fugitive and that request, I'll have to pass on."

"Pass you say? It could be easy; you find out what's his weakness and I'm pretty sure he has a weakness . . . Then simply take his suit."

"That might take a long time to find out."

"No. It wouldn't take too long. Let him come here, follow him to his home then listen . . . Listen until you find the golden ticket."

"Smart plan but aren't you supposed to be doing all that?"

"We will be but you're already close to him and has the opportunity to get closer to him."

"I will think about it."

"Please, think about it Mr. Mayor, this could be possibly the most power we humans can possess. Defending the Earth from whatever is out there with suits like that . . . The future, is in your hands."

<u>Eastern Sentry Space Station</u>—

Henry Luciano sat in the middle of the conference room with the space station captain and the team of officers.

Without a word from any of them as they stare at each other without a blink, Henry sipped his glass of wine then said—

"It's time we do this world a favor, humans will all change into better beings and be prepared for any outsiders under my control . . . I must say captain, life on earth is very unordinary now isn't it?"

Complete silence from the team as a servant Android comes in with a plate of baked chicken and mashed potatoes then Henry continued to speak—

"No let's not say unordinary, let's put another word . . . Chaotic—the way you see it is the way I see it."

He cuts the chicken then took a piece of it and puts it in his mouth. He chewed the piece of chicken then sips his glass of wine.

"Very simple meal but it's cooked really good." He said as he puts his right hand in his inside blazer pocket and takes out a very small crystal that is the size of a ladybug in the tip of his fingers.

He held the crystal up to his face and asked— "Do you know what this is?"

Still no word, no movement just complete silence from the team as Henry looked at the captain.

"That right here . . . Is the future of existence as we know it." The captain said in a monotone voice.

"Yes, you are absolutely right. What I hold here is the key to outstanding leverage."

Henry smiled as he puts back the crystal in his inside blazer pocket and said—

"Sorry, I just can't leave that thing alone, it's like a toy for me."

The Kafmora residence—

"Their powers are growing earlier than us; this is truly a new era of Netrons" Nealo said.

"The era where we will succeed." Neecho said.

"It's still going to be a tough fight my son…"

"Yes… was there any Zeal Netrons on planet Netron?" Neecho asked as he picked up the Netron Book of Edu.

"I haven't seen any from what I remember when I was a kid, but my mother found the crystals right before she sent me to Earth with the crystals as well. I'm sure she revealed most of it to the Netron Army."

"Hm, as the days go by, I wonder what's out there for us. The book even had a new page."

"Oh really… let me see . . .. Ah… prepare yourself for what's coming…"

"We've been prepared so far."

"Hm, sometimes prep isn't guaranteed victory."

"Yeah, that is true…."

"Hmm, I've witnessed something when I came in contact with the book and this was before I seen the visions of the trees, the grass and the ground moving… It was a face, a face with its sclera all black and white pupils. I didn't actually see the full face though because it was dark, but his checks had deep cuts, enough to see the inside of its face and it . . . I just can't describe it."

"Is it worse than the Opposites?"

"I'm afraid it might be… it's been haunting me ever since. I also seen a vision of it before I touched the book… It's like, it wants to be freed from some sort of intangible prison."

"Hm… Whatever it is father… I believe we can handle it"

"I hope so…"

"You once told me, that no matter how frightening or how hopeless a situation may look… It's always a way to solve it."

"I'm glad I told you that son, it's good to have this conscious by our side..."

"Well, we have no choice if Ki-Yale dies we all die, including the rest of the Netrons and our planet."

"We still have Tajaymae and Oji... The book will most likely choose one of them if that was to happen."

"But they're Zeal..." Neecho being confused.

"Yes, but remember my son, they have Royalty in their blood."

"Yes. How could I forget...? Well, enough of the 'ifs', we will prevail, and I know it." Neecho spoke with confidence.

Kelly, the lady that Mr. Turd helped from thugs trying to rob her. She introduced him to a special soap that eliminates most smells even Vile Stink Bombs.

Moments later Mr. Turd came out of the shower and said—

"Thank you very much . . . You hardly see anyone this generous—lending me your bath."

"It's fine. You stood up for me, I hardly see anyone doing that around here in Crouton."

She walked closer to him then her face suddenly looked disturbed.

"Wow. What kind of Vile Stink Bomb did they use?"

"The smell... It's still there?"

"Yes, unfortunately..."

"Damn, this sucks!" He said as he looked to th floor with anger then continued—

"You sure? You aren't trying to prank me?"

"Um can you even smell yourself?"

"I guess my nose got used to it over time..."

"Wow that's bad..."

"Damn . . . I'm sorry . . . I really appreciate the time you have given me but, now I must dig deep and do some research on it. I know a Super Genius, maybe he can help."

"You're welcome. It's the least I can do, and I wish you luck." She said as she covers her nostrils and mouth.

"I'll be around..."

"Yep... take care."

"I guess I'll see you . . . When I aah', get this fixed."

"Yeah. We'll see each other sometime. Good luck."

"Number?"

"No... Oh yeah. I'll see you around, no worries." She said trying to avoid his question.

"Yes. I'll see you." He said as he walked out the room awkwardly.

"Yep, yep. Ok, alright now..." She said as the sliding door closes.

Mr. Turd leaned on the wall and looked up to the ceiling then said— "Damn it."

He thought. *Damn I'm just a stink man. A freaking mighty stink man...*"

He paused then said—

"Hm."

<u>*Inside the arena*</u>—

Max's father Vince is looking around the arena in guilt and thinking about his son as he took a deep breath.

"You had your fun. Now, it's my turn." Taw said pumping his muscles up more allowing his shirt to fully rip off. Taw's veins began to expose through his skin as they turned vivid blue all around his body and is now at sixty percent.

"Oh, yea he's dead now, that's sixty percent." Said one guy in the crowd.

Taw started running at Mike as a large twenty feet high African Elephant merged around Mike's body.

"C'mon Mike!" Tajaymae cheered.

Taw jumped then punches Mike as a giant Elephant several times. Mike is in defense position with loud punches from Taw pushing back Mike as the crowd went wild.

"What you wanna be when you get older Mike? Huh? What you want to be?"

"Wei'… weird question… to... ask me right now… In a fight!" Mike said holding his own as Taw continued punching.

"So, what, just answer the question… I love a good convo when I'm beating the shit out of someone."

"Ta'. . . a powerful leader… I wanna be a powerful leader." Mike proudly said.

"A powerful leader? Like your Dad?"

"Ye'… yeah you can say that."

"Well he ain't incredibly powerful, I mean let's face it. He's the Mayor of LTV… He ain't no President of the World."

"Heh'… he still has responsibilities tuh'... to protect the village and all the people in it."

"Well, it looks like he's doing a bad job at it! That virus floated around LTV, making trees bigger and shit… everyone dying… ha!"

<u>*Tournament Men's Locker Room*</u>—

"I don't know! He should be dead! But apparently he's still here!" Max shouted as he squirmed to left to grab his axe.

"You gave him the wrong dose of drugs and instead gave it to the bouncer, just a horrible job done."

Max paused and looked at Sally then he said— "Why come at me? Why just make Majesty rig the raffle."

"True but it was simple orders and you know the Mad Doctor doesn't like when people don't follow what he said. Especially the simple orders and... he told me to get at you! Soooo... Rita, Nikki, hold him down on the bench." Sally said as two other ladies begin walking up to Max.

Max immediately touches his weapon equipped with the Tektonian Crystal and summons his Tantu Orb.

"That's not going to work kid!" Sally said pointing at her enhanced eyewear then kicked Max's axe off the bench.

Max slowly started to lose momentum because of his Tantu Orb once released then disarmed he becomes fatigue.

"I hear you don't like pussy . . . Yeah, you want some cock! You love cock and the first thing you got was cock!" Sally taunted Max then she aggressively pulled his pants down.

"No! What are you doing?!" Max shouted as the two ladies suppressed him down to the bench.

"Hmm, you're gonna love this!" Sally uttered and looking over his head.

"No! No pleeaase'!"

"Now this is how you'd drug someone and take advantage!" Sally said as she gives Max an enhanced sexual stimulant drug so he can get erect.

"No wait, please don't do this. I'm in a relationship with a man!!" Max petrified as Sally pulled down his underwear.

She robustly licked her lips as she looked at him up and down.

"Ha! Where's your man now huh? —Hmm, I'm gonna make you love this pussy!"

Mike pushes back Taw a couple inches then Taw began to find his grip and picked up Mike that's has a large elephant surrounding his body.

"What? How could he be this strong all of a sudden?" Mike thought.

He held him up fo a moment and screamed barbarically then slammed him to the arena floor. Taw rapidly slammed him again and again until Mike finally broke out of his glass pragmatic animal. Mike quickly merges with a 1,340 pound eight feet tall glass Tiger.

"Oh, you wanna get broken again huh?"

"Le… lets se… let's see how . . . you handle a Tiger!"

"Mike's still standing firm! He certainly has heart." Nack said.

"Mike has heart for sure he's going to beat this guy; I know he can." Tajaymae said.

"Yeah, Taw needs to be knocked out with something hard."

Mike is in disbelief to what Taw can do but still puts up a fight. Mike swung his paws and Taw blocked the attack with his arm. Mike then opened his jaws and chomps on Taw's head. Taw then tighten up his muscles and puts his two arms underneath the large 1,370-pound Tiger. Taw slowly picked up the Tiger surrounding Mike then threw him to his back slamming him to the arena floor as if the fight was a *'WWE'* wrestling match.

"Woah folks! Looks like Mike got hit hard that time!" Majesty speaking on the microphone.

"Damn… and that's sixty percent of strength." Nack said.

"Hmm, my brother can kick his ass."

"Agreed." Nack said as Ki-Yale looked at them then he said—.

"Looks like Mike isn't really standing a chance here guys."

"Brother, how can you doubt our boy Mike? He got this… I hope."

Mike's pragmatic glass animal is broken again as he laid on the arena floor. He slowly gets up as Taw strode towards him.

"You are a true fighter Mike. You don't back down and that's what it's all about. Never giving up and it seems that device is in the way of me tearing you apart." Taw said as Mike chuckled.

Taw puts his hands behind his back reaching in his pants back pocket.

Vince decided to walk off his section and heads towards the locker room to see his son. The seven ladies walked away from the locker room in the walkway as Vince walked pass them then went inside the locker room and saw Max completely naked with blood on the locker room floor.

"Oh son. What happened?" Vince asked as Max looked up at his father.

Inside the arena, Taw ominously staring at Mike.

"What is he reaching for…?" Ki-Yale concerned.

"Whah'… what? You just going to stand there an'… and just look at me?!" Mike bickered as he reached to switch into another animal.

Suddenly, Taw took his right hand from his pant pocket and fired a device that seemed to be a small metal spray bottle. The bottle fired a small pellet hitting Mike. Being unaware of this technology, the small pellet melted onto his skin. "Hm? Whah'… what's this?"

"Your death."

Mike instantly caught on fire into a large flame that surrounded his entire body. Mike screamed in pain as the blaze erupted higher and harsh fumes ruptured all around his body.

"Oh no!" Ki-Yale in utter shock.

TWENTY-NINE

Yesterday morning in Gigantica City, on the subway express train going two hundred miles per hour inside a tunnel only for a train to pass by and not even a construction worker could be in this tunnel while this train is in service. Tyson Roland is sitting in the middle of the train with first class hospitality. He arrived at his stop and saw the Gigantica Embassy through a giant glass that connects to the train's stop. His communication device alerted Tyson then he answered it.

"Netro. What's up kid? How's it going?" Tyson hailed viewing at Ki-Yale's hologram.

"Not much, so far so good… Well, a little accident occurred."

"Yeah? What accident?"

"A stranger that was a teenager happen to be on the street knocked out and Mike thought he ran him over but that wasn't the case. The teen deliberately laid down on the street to make it seem that way. So, then Mike, my best friend and my sister went to check it out then the teen started attacking them. I was fast asleep…"

"Attacking? Wait is my son okay?" Tyson fretted and interrupting Ki-Yale.

"Yes, he is fine. He was just knocked out."

"Hmm, okay good."

"So, my sister beat up the teen then the teen's father arrived and shot my sis with a tranquilizer. Then he took everyone to his house including me, but they couldn't move me because I'm a little on the

heavy side and I was fast asleep, so I was left in Mike's truck. I woke up then got inside the house and I saw my best friend. The father of the teen then appeared explaining to me that his son was just a mischievous kid."

"They attacked you all then took you in? Hm, this doesn't sound right."

"I had the same reaction and get this, they are both Death Angels."

"Death Angels being nice huh?"

"Yeah apparently."

"You need to be careful, you promised me you'll take care of my son kid!"

"I know, I will sir."

"And how the hell did you sleep all through all that?" Tyson said as he walked into the Gigantica Embassy.

"I tend to go into deep sleep and it's very hard for me to come out of it."

<u>The Harven residence—</u>

Vince is in the hallway ease dropping on Ki-Yale's conversation with Tyson. Ki-Yale used his Netron vision and saw that he was on the other side of the wall in the hallway. Vince doesn't know of Ki-Yale's extramundane ability to see through anything. Ki-Yale stared at him with a serious facial utterance and his eyes squinting.

<u>Present time at the Crouton Village Tournament—</u>

"Alright… alright it's time for a new hero to be born. Yesss'… this side of me has been bottled up for too long! Yes, I'm strong, yes, I'm powerful and I'm worthy! It's time I banish all the thugs of this world." Mr. Turd said as walked up the mirror in the restroom.

He grabbed one of his red used sheets from his dorm room and tied it around his back to make it look like it's a cape.

A teenage boy covering his mouth and nostrils, looked at him then said—

"C'mon man. You ever heard of a shower?"

"Yes, but it's not to disturb the peace with this smell, it's to help citizens of Crouton Village!"

"Whaaat'?"

"With this gifted power, I will deliver goodness on onto do-gooders. I'm not just an ordinary man . . . I'm the MIGHTY STINK MAN!!"

The young man glared at him as if he is crazy.

"Dude, you need some help. Get help please."

"I'm the Mighty Stink Man! I don't need help, I help others." He said as he walked closer to the boy.

The teenaged boy backed up then quickly walked out the restroom.

"Hm, ok. It's time I go help some do-gooders." He said as he walked out the restroom.

Suddenly, he heard loud and heavy noise from the crowd in the arena as he walked down the aisle then said— "Something must be going down… It's time for me to make an appearance!"

The arena—

"Aaaaaggh'!" Mike screaming in agony from the combustible pellet. He fell to the platform as the flames continue to burst out uncontrollably and expands.

"Woah folks! It looks like Taw got him with an incendiary flame pallet!" Majesty spoke over the microphone.

Tajaymae is at lost for words with her mouth open for a moment.

"No! No! No!" Ki-Yale said as he looked around the arena then continued—.

"Fire extinguisher! Fire extinguisher! There it is."

He tried to locate a fire extinguisher using his Netron Vision as he quickly ran from his section going eighty miles per hour and grabbed the fire extinguisher in the hallway then ran back in the same speed up to the arena cage. Ki-Yale puts down the extinguisher then touched the cage as it immediately shocks him, but the electricity is not affecting him in any way because of his Netron Suit.

"No Mike! This is bad! Really bad!" Nack said while Tajaymae's eyelids are wide open and her pupils became minuscule with has her hands covering her mouth.

Ki-Yale miraculously bends the cage bars into an opening for him to go on stage.

"What the…?" Majesty perplexed.

"What the…"Taw said as Ki-Yale walked up to Mike and started using the fire extinguisher, but the fire is still lit.

Ki-Yale kept on spraying vigorously but still the fire blazed around Mike. Ki-Yale then blew wind from his mouth but it's still insufficient to take out the fire as the blazes ascended even more and the crowd booing Ki-Yale and telling him to get off stage. He blew even more but the colder the fire gets the more it erupts.

"Get all of the security."—Majesty talking to his assistant.

"Stop this now! Or you better get to a hundred percent because I'm going to beat the shit out of you!" Ki-Yale uttered angrily.

"Ha! You're impressive, I've seen your work on the arena but I ain't doing shit kid." Taw responded.

Not the words Ki-Yale wanted to hear as he immediately ran going about sixty miles per hour towards Taw and brutally punched him in his stomach.

"Aaghh! Aagh!"—Taw in immense pain while holding his stomach.

"STOP THIS NOW!!" Ki-Yale punched him again in the stomach even harder with blood gushing out of Taw's mouth.

"Aaaghh'! I . . . can't..."

Ki-Yale looked at Taw with the look of rage in his eyes then turned around to look at Mike on the arena floor as the flames are still lit around his body.

"Oh shit! Taw is down just by two punches." Said one man in the crowd talking to his friend while the rest of the crowd is screaming around him. Taw stumbles more to the floor and said—

"It's all . . . Dr. Sagan . . . he made me do it . . . if I didn't do this . . . severe consequences would have . . . happened to my family."—Taw struggled to speak.

Ki-Yale ran up to Mike and blows some more wind from his mouth, but it was already too late. The fire slowly began to quiet down while the crowd started throwing food and drinks all around the arena.

"No! No! What is going on?!!" Majesty vexing as the crowd got on a rampage causing a massive food fight and fist fights.

The cages are slowly going back up to the ceiling while Ki-Yale stared at Mike as his body has no movement, just a burnt to skeleton with a bit of flesh, lots of smoke and ashes started to build up.

Ki-Yale still kept some hope in his heart as he gets closer to Mike then checked for life while his body is still extremely hot, and Ki-Yale not faded by the heat because of his Netron Suit. He didn't feel any pulse as he pressed on Mike's neck then pressed harder for a pulse then instantly—

Mike's entire body turned into ashes.

"C'mon it's time for us to go." Vince said.

Max sat down on the bench trying to get back his sanity, but nothing can change what just happened to him. He stared at the ground as his father walked up to him.

Max with the look of vengeance on his face paused for a moment then said—

"Did you know?"

Vince stared at Max as Max stared at the locker room floor.

"What you are talking about son?"

"Don't son me! Don't you dare! Alright?! Those ladies came in here right after you left. I guess it wasn't suspicious that ladies are just walking right up in the men's locker room!"

"Listen. Dr. Sagan he threatened…" Vince said being interrupted while touching Max's shoulder.

"Get the fuck! Off me!! I thought you of all people…. My father, my own father . . . I don't want to ever speak to you again!" Max shouted as he pushed off his father and stormed out the locker room as Vince depicted a guilty look on his face.

"Sagan said he wasn't going to kill you just something minor… What? What the hell did they do to you?"

Oji invited his two friends Jake and Cory over play a virtual board game called "Nation of the Unknown Beasts" This game allows them to make one choice between over fifty different monsters and fight each other. If one loses, they can get another monster but after the third loss you are out of the game. Oji was down to his last monster and had high hopes of winning but at the last second, he lost to a lucky shot.

"Heyyy! That's not fair! I had you!"

"No that was fair and square Oji. A loss is a loss." Cory said.

Oji is the youngest of the group being only eight years old and his two friends are nine years old.

"Mmmrrr'… this sucks, you're always cheating."

"I'm not!"

"Is too!"

"I'm not!"

"Is too!"

"I'm not!"—Oji and his friend Cory argued over the game then Jake said— "Ok guys, let's just do a rematch."

"No." Oji declined.

"Oji's just a sore loser."

"I'm not a sore looser!"

"Ok, ok guys let's just work on an agreement."

"Like a truce?" Cory asked.

"Yes. Like a truce. Whoever wins the next battle has to shut up for a whole week well, not shut up completely but just not complaining."

"Ta' I'm down as long as Oji ain't scared."

"Hey, I don't complain I'm just saying the truth."

"The truth? Yeah right!"

"You know it is!"

"Aaagh, just do the rematch already."

<u>The Gigantica Embassy</u>—

LTV Mayor Tyson participated in a private meeting with the congress, Gigantica House of Representatives.

"You know he is a dangerous man. Outstandingly he outsmarted the government. The elite Gigantica Mega Human Prime army. The most powerful team of soldiers in this solar system and you send someone who is supposedly an alien." Said one congress man.

"Netro is unbelievably the one to do the job. He is more powerful than a Mega Human Prime." Tyson said.

"So, you say. But your son?"

"What about my son?"

"You send your son out there to face the most feared man of this century?" Asked a lady of the congress.

"I assure you my son is fine. Sending him out there is my concern and he's older now and he wants to honor his village."

The Tournament—

Taw flat on the arena floor with his stomach internally bleeding and his mouth bleeding a pool of blood while a security team running up to the fighting ring to pick him up. Ki-Yale stared at the floor where Mike was alive just moments ago. The rest of the security team are focused on calming down the crowd while guards went after Ki-Yale. With his reflexes, he punched one of the guards that tried to hit him in the face and sent him flying out of the platform and hitting a wall with his back. Ki-Yale turned to another guard and the guard instantly got scared, Ki-Yale then turned his head to Majesty then quickly ran up to him going eighty miles per hour. Ki-Yale immediately held Majesty's neck and brought him up to fifteen feet into the air.

"Where is Sagan hiding!?!" Ki-Yale asked in an angry tone.

Litzy ran from her section to Ki-Yale as Tajaymae did the same towards Ki-Yale then Nack started running behind Tajaymae.

"I don't know!" Majesty said as he was barely breathing.

"I'm not playing anymore games!! WHERE IS HE HIDING!?!"—Ki-Yale interrogated Majesty.

"No Ki-Yale! Don't do it!" Tajaymae shouting.

"C'mon Ki. It's not worth it!" Nack shouts.

"Ki? Ki-Yale?" Litzy confused.

"Ki-Yale, that's his human name. I guess he didn't tell you." Nack said.

. . .

"I need answers!" Ki-Yale demanded.

"I don't know where he's hiding. All I do is host this tournament and if I don't, I'm screwed… I'm so sorry…. please… don't kill me." Majesty pleaded as he cried.

"Ki-Yale!" Tajaymae yelled.

He brought Majesty down to six feet then dropped him then Majesty started coughing reacting to him being choked.

The alarm was triggered throughout the arena, the hospital that is next door and the dorm rooms then crowd is going wild. Push was in his hospital room lying in the bed as he heard people outside being loud with their voices and irregular footstep noises.

"Aah… What the hell is going on?" Push asked himself.

Xack was also in his hospitalized room with bandages covering up his stitches from the brutal cuts that Push gave him. Xack fidgeted as he reclined his back on the bed and started to groan because of the noise outside of his room.

Push, damaged from his fight with also a couple stitches being covered by bandages, slowly walks up to the sliding door and opened it. As soon as he opened the automated sliding door, he saw some teens running around sabotaging the hospital objects in the hallway.

Outside of the tournament—

Max exited the tournament building and saw it was raining but still went on ahead to the deserted eating area. The tables had a thirty feet long awning. He went underneath the awning to keep himself dry from the rain then immediately called his lover Tommy through his holographic cell phone cube.

The first ring didn't go through then he did it again then suddenly, he picks up the call.

"Aye! What's up smooth boy?"

"Hey . . ."

"What happened? Why you look so sad?"

"I got... you not gonna' like what I'm about to tell you."

"C'mon Max. Tell me, it shouldn't be that bad."

"No . . . It's bad Tommy, very bad."

"Max? Don't be childish now."— ". . . I got raped."

"You got what?!!"

"Yeah..." Max said as tears filled his eyes.

Tommy beheld him for a moment with a single word just showcasing misperception on his face. "This has to be some type of prank, right?!"

"No! It's not Tommy!"

"Oh no. That shit ain't right!!" Tommy said as Max continued to weep some more.

"What the fuck man. Who did that to you and is the authorities on this?!"

"It was a group of ladies, they pinned me down and dosed me with a pill then they took turns and I... and I didn't tell anyone..."

"What the fuck dude?! You must report this! What the fuck man!"

"I can't do anything about it..."

"What?! No, I'm going to call the cops! Since you're too scared, that's fine."

"No! No! Don't call the cops Tommy!"

"Why? They will be on your side!"

"Because it's Sagan Ok. It was Sagan that ordered the ladies to do it. Ok? Don't call the freaking cops!"

"I can't believe this..."

"It's for your own safety . . . Tommy, look, I'm already putting you in danger telling you this."

"Oh man, fuck Sagan. What? He has an army?"

"He's tangled with the army plenty of times. Don't you watch the news?"

"The news is bullshit."

"Listen, Tommy. For your own safety . . . Don't call the authorities, please. He'll find a way to kill you sooner than you think. He's always one step ahead of the system."

"No Max... this isn't right."

"Tommy." Max said as he shook his head and looked down at the ground then continued—

"We need to take a break. Ok?"

"What?"

"I'm going through a lot right now and I just need to recover."

"Ok. I'm here to be by your side Max. I'll call out from work right now and come over there. I'm here for you Max."

"I'm sorry Tommy. It's better like this . . . I'm so sorry."

Max hung up with tears dripping down his cheeks, he lifted his hand up towards his face as it shivered. He placed his hand on his mouth contemplating on what he just did then his phone rings and it was Tommy.

He stared at the phone and shook his head then cancels the incoming call. He looked up to the sky as pigeons fly by.

"Let's do some damage guys!" Said a teenaged boy erratically appearing out from the building.

"Yeah everyone's going berserk in that bitch! Let's do the same outside." Said the second teen boy.

"Yeah!"

THIRTY

Crouton Village Tournament—

"I can't believe this kid! Man handling me like that. A freaking fourteen-year-old kid."

"He is pretty strong sir . . . Definitely scared the shit out of me punching Taw like that and Taw is like the strongest one here."

"I know but at least the Mad Doctor's got what he wanted . . . Mike Roland's death."

. . .

"You still got your ass handed to you." Shelton Renzo said, one of Dr. Sagan's assistants, wearing old military gear with a high-tech circle glasses that has yellow lenses. He creates robotics, human machinery and cyborgs for Sagan.

The two men were startled when Shelton said something behind them and instantly turned around. One had an illegal fed pistol in his hand, and one had none.

Shelton with an illegal pistol of his own quickly shot the one on the left in the chest then moved to the left side to dodge the bullet from the guy on the right. Seconds after, Shelton shot the second man also hitting him in the chest.

"Looks like your guys are a little shaken up by this kid."

"Same goes for you walking around with a pistol. What are you doing here?"

"Sorry. Is this a bad time?"

"Yes, well, not really . . . If it's a message you have to tell me then I'm all ears."

"Nah I'm just here to drop by and say hello. Things are going to be in effect real soon, he has plans you know"

"Hm." Majesty said as he glares at him.

"Let's go before authorities arrive in here."

<u>*The Kafmora residence*</u>—

Oji and Cory had just finished the rematch of another game of "Nation of the Unknown Beasts" and Oji lost again.

"Aah, well, would you look at that I won again. I told you Oji… I'm just too nice in this game."

"Yeah whatever, I still think you cheated Cory."

"Hey, you agree that the loser can't complaining for a week. Right Jake?"

"Yes. No complaints for a week."

"Yeah no complaints loser! Hey, is there anything good you can do?"

"Shut up…" Oji spoke under his breath.

"You said something?"

"I'm good at something ok!"

"Oh really? Like what?"

"C'mon Cory. Stop being an asshole." Jake said.

"I'll show you. I'll show both of you!" Oji said as he walked up to his window.

"What are you doing?"

"Just watch me." Oji said then he rests his hand on the window.

Outside of the window is a plant called Coleus. It sat in a wide plant pot that's on a mounted iron shelf.

He closed his eyes as he concentrated on trying to make the plants grow.

"Uumm'…" Cory said.

"I don't know…" Jake said raising his shoulders.

Oji stands at his window for thirty seconds and nothing seems to be happening. He opens eyes and saw the plants still in its regular form.

"Hey Oji. What the hell are you doing?"

"I'm trying to make the plants grow. Ok? I have powers!"

"You have powers? Ha! What like a Mega Human?"

"No, I'm different than a Mega Human."

"Yeah no shit! Mega Humans don't make plants move just by standing by it." Cory said than laughed.

"No, you don't understand. You see those trees outside? I did all of that I made the trees small again."

Cory continued to laugh then looked at Jake and said—

"He must be on drugs. Right?"

"I'm telling you I have awesome powers!" Oji said being frustrated.

"Ha! You're a weakling. You don't possess the great power like me."

"What?" Jake said.

"I'm just playing along…"

"You're mocking me, aren't you?"

"Well, maybe just a little. You know, maybe I actually truly have these amazing powers and be an imaginary wizard!"

"A wizard? No, no, I'm half alien."

"An alien huh?"

"Yes, but I'm part human, part alien . . . Ok, I'll try again and show you my powers."

Oji turned back around facing the plants and puts his hand on the window. He focused on making the plants grow and thirty seconds later still nothing happened.

"Ok, it's time for us to bounce Oji."

"No wait…"

"Sorry man I got duty calls from home."

"Mama's boy…"

"Shut up Jake!"

"Well I gotta go myself. Good luck on trying to make plants glow by standing in front of it." Jake said as he followed Cory out of Oji's room

"But guys I have…" Oji said sadly and disappointed.

<u>*Outside of the Tournament*</u>—

"Yo bro! Take this shit!" Said one of crowd members giving his friend a Juice Sprayer that sprays Fruit Punch as if it was connected to a fire truck.

The two crowd members sprayed the juice all over the running crowd coming their way.

"I'll take the right side around the corner. You stay on this side."

"Alright. Do your thing."

The teenager began to run around the corner to the right then about a dozen policemen appeared.

"Oh shit!"

"Drop your weapon!"

"It's not a weapon it's a juice sprayer!"

"I don't care what it is. Drop it!"

"Nah, fuck that!"

The crowd members came from around the left side then one crowd member said—

"Blast em'!"

The crowd sprayed the Fruit Punch then the policeman switched his suit to a different firearm.

"Fire your needle guns! No Tasers!"

The policemen got sprayed but didn't move because of how heavy they are with the police suits. The crowd members kept spraying the juice sprayer and then suddenly, the needles are fired hitting the crowd members. The crowd members' instantly loose fatigue then fell to the ground.

"Put cuffs on em'!"

The police suits have unlimited steel handcuff supply that the suit creates. The handcuffs are fired from the suit then switches to circle around the hands and connects to each other looking like handcuffs. This is the same technology to create certain metal in an instant.

"Ok, for now just use the tranquilizer and try to refrain from killing anyone."

"Yes sir!"

The policemen then went around the arena seizing as much as they can, reducing the rampage going around the tournament.

The arena—

"Woah everyone is going crazy." Mr. Turd said.

The audience is going rampant throwing food and all sorts of hazardous items leaving each other in critical condition.

"All of this is insane. Hmm. I wonder where Ki-Yale and the gang are right now."

The Tournament infirmary—

Ki-Yale holding bits of Mike's burnt Gazen Weapon, Nack, Tajaymae making both fists and Litzy with her arms folded walked down the hallway in the hospital going to Xack's room to call Mayor Tyson where it's a lot quieter.

"You see his room, right?" Tajaymae asked walking with Yaeko in the baby pouch.

"Yeah. Over here."

Ki-Yale opened the door and saw Xack lying in bed with oodles of bandages and wraps around his body.

"What you guys doing here? What's going on outside?"
Xack asked with a hoarse voice.

"The members are going wild and here is the place to be
right now..." Nack said.

"Yeah but, what's going on out there?"

Litzy still has her arms folded while Tajaymae had tears
falling down her cheeks and Nack shook his head. The
appearances on all their faces caught the attention of Xack
even more.

"Netro?" Xack asked.

Everyone kept silent for a moment then Ki-Yale said—

"Mike is... He's...."

"What? You guys are fucking with me, right?"

Ki-Yale with a puffed-up face looked at Xack and shook
his head.

"What?! I don't believe you..." Xack said as Tajaymae
walked over to him and handed over Yaeko.

"We have to call his dad." Nack said with a sad mellow
voice.

Ki-Yale opened his Netron Suit around his wrist and
began to look for the Mayor's contact info in his wristwatch
then paused.

"No way. How did this happen?" Xack queried.

"This fighter named Taw uased a fire pellet." Nack said.

"Hmm, Taw isn't the weapon type."

"Aaagh! Damn it! Damn it! Damn it!" Ki-Yale barked
with dramatic emphasis on his words, his body against the
wall crouching down with Mike's burnt weapon still in his
hand. Litzy slowly approached Ki-Yale rubbing his upper
back then gave him a hug.

"Max... he planted some kind of laced acid into the
bouncer..." Xack said.

"Max is responsible for that?" Nack confounded.

"Yes, he is but I don't think that's what he intended. He
gave Mike the drug too... I mean what does that bouncer

have related to Max? It's a theory, but I think that laced acid was supposed to be for Mike." Xack said.

"That whole thing with Max attacking us and Vince attacking Tajaymae then took us in was possibly all planned. Maybe Vince and Max expected a fight then took us in to say Max was just being a pest. 'Oh Sorry! Forgive us, take our hospitality, please and let's be friends' so they could give Mike the laced drug." Nack said mocking Vince and Max.

"Well, that failed until Taw did a cheap ass move." Tajaymae said.

"Fire pellet you said right? Hm, that's the Devil Soldier tech used in the military. Ki-Yale, you would've needed to carve the pellet out of Mike's skin." Xack said

Ki-Yale expressed a flabbergasted look on his face since he did not know of such information until now and neither did the others. Everyone else were speechless as well, wishing they knew of such knowledge. They can't seem to grasp this entire moment of disbelief. Xack continued to speak—

"Hey, Netro . . . It's not your fault. We all must keep a level head and get through this together. I lost friends myself and even my mother all because of the Mad Doctor . . . He's going to get what coming to him, I promise."

Nack noticed two contact lenses on the small light brown wooden dresser then asked—

"Those contacts... are they Shale Tech?"

"Yes, they reveal the vital weak points of the bodies I see. I didn't use them in which I should have, especially against Push."

Nack walks up to it and examined it.

"Can I take it home with me? I think I can alter it for you and add more features to it."

"Yeah, you can do that. The more the merrier."

Xack got out of his bed then he began to walk to the room exit.

"You're still hurt. Where are you going?" Nack queried.

"No, I'm good, trust me I've been in plenty Apaki fights before, with heated glass piercing me. It's nothing, plus they were all flesh wounds."

Ki-Yale took a glimpse at Xack leaving the room then slowly nods his head.

Moments later—

Ki-Yale walked out the building with Litzy and rest behind. Ki-Yale stopped then stood in one spot. He clenched his fists, intensely gazing at the eastern direction, detecting something he should have detected a long time ago.

"Are you ok?" Litzy asked.

"Yeah. I'm—fine… I'm fine." He said.

"Ok. Let's go."

Unknown Area—

Dr. Rogue Sagan relaxes in his large bedroom with a movie theatre screen, glasses of wine, bottles of champagne, Chardonnay, mimosa, a large plate of lobster and fried shrimp with corn on the cob and green beans.

The bed is a king size bed with robotic extensions handing Dr. Sagan's food to his mouth. This is the Mad Doctor's bedroom, a luxurious room with lots of space.

On the large screen, it shows live video footage of the arena.

He smiled then said— "Now this is what I like to see, this is what I call entertainment."

The Kafmora residence—

Oji is by himself in his room looking at a multidimensional picture projected through a mechanical cube of his oldest brother Narrken. Oji was five years old when Narrken ran away and got abducted by an unknown assailant and he only remembered the little moments he witnessed with his older brother. He kept the picture of him in his room on the wall, every morning he would wake up and every night before he goes to bed, he looks at the picture just to keep the little memories that he had with him.

He puts the picture down then walked up to the window and stares at his Coleus plants on the outside. He raised his hand then placed it on the window, he closed his eyes and tried to focus on moving the plant itself.

In just twenty seconds later the Coleus plants began to move slowly upward. His eyes are still closed and focused on releasing his power. He finally opened it, the Coleus plant bloomed and became twelve inches longer.

He gasped as he stepped back one step after he witnessed his success by commanding his power and fulfilled his desire.

"Tragic day for Mayor Tyson as his son was burnt to death in a tournament by a Prime Human, Sila Human and fighter… Taw Hoffman. No arrests were made due to tournament guild lines of Death Week where fighters can murder each other. These guild lines are protected by Crouton Village from a negotiation with Dr. Sagan just a few years ago." Said the news anchor.

Ki-Yale and his grandfather are in the training room at their domain looking at the news. Nealo caught a glimpse at Ki-Yale siting down on a chair and saw he's upset with his fists quivering and breathing heavily.

"This was bound to happen . . . Sagan is outstandingly smart. Many have died while I was in the military. He had no trace after his killings, it's messed up and I know you're thinking you've messed up...." Nealo said and being intervened.

"I made a promise to Mayor Tyson..." Ki-Yale said then continued—

"I made a promise to myself. I vow to protect my team at all costs and Sagan still managed to murder plenty of my soldiers."

"Is taking a human's life who doesn't have a heart, a sense of goodness, purity . . . Is it justified for us to do so?"

"Murder on a human or any other species by a Netron royalty is a big move ..." Nealo said and being interrupted.

"You killed some of the worst criminals. You don't have to lie to me, I know... I know that you took matters into your own hands and dealt with the situation by taking a life."

"Yes, I took matters into my own hands by taking a life, but it was necessary."

"That's a complete violation of the Netron Law and I should arrange for you some kind of... chastisement."

"Hm, I would accept the consequences my grandson, but I did it because I had no other choice."

"How about, actually revealing ourselves..."

"You know our premeditation was not to reveal ourselves . . . The Opposites were after us trying to prevent a new coming royalty from being born at all costs. I wasn't my best when I arrived here but my mother, Queen Tella, didn't have any other suggestions. She could have sent me to another planet, but it was Earth because we could fit in easily. We look like humans and Earth... Earth has evil roaming around just like other planets and that's what mother failed to understand. She made this law about not killing any humans but never knew that the Opposites aren't the only ones with no hearts."

The rampage that went down right after Ki-Yale hit Taw in the stomach is now being cleaned up. The crowd couldn't believe that Taw was defeated a mere child in under a minute, they believed Taw should always be the victorious one and that whole thing was rigged. Plus, the fact that Taw used a weapon against Mike and not his muscles as usual. Taw has a motive to never use a weapon just utter brute strength and that's the kind of fighter the crowd loved.

At the hospital in Crouton Village Tournament, Shelton walked down the hallway to Push's room and then opened the door.

"It's time to go Push, Sagan awaits you."

"Hm', I have not yet recovered."

"That's why I'm here to help you young one. Now . . . Can you walk?"

Little Tree Ville, Gel Hev—

Silence among the people of Little Tree Ville surrounding the outside of Mayor Tyson Roland's office.

"They're all supporting you sir." Preston said, Tyson's assistant.

Tyson sat in on a hover chair looking at pictures of his son as Preston stared at the pictures then Tyson said—

"Preston, I want you to leave . . . I want to be alone . . . Please."

"Oh, ok sir. Just call me if you need to anything." Preston said as he leaves the office.

Tyson slowly got up from his seat then looked outside the window and saw the people of LTV surrounding his office with signs, flowers and candles in support of the death of his sons. Some of the signs said—

"Sorry for your loss", "Stay strong for Mike", "Gone but not forgotten", "Long Live Mike Roland" and many more.

Even Mr. Turd is back in LTV and participated in supporting the Mayor after he found out the devastating news. Standing with the crowd, he held up a giant sign—

The sign reads— "SAGAN MUST DIE!"

<u>*Gigantica National Prison*</u>—

Rojohn and his prison goons sitting around a table discussing recent events.

"You haven't eaten in days Rojohn. What's going on?" One prisoner concerned.

"I told you I ain't eating that food fam'. Sagan knows I lowkey sent a hit-man for him and I'm pretty sure Sagan took him out."

"So, you think he poisoned your food or got a hit on you?" Asked another prisoner.

"Yeah fam', that's exactly what I think."

"Well, he'll be dealing with another burden on his hands now." Said another prisoner.

"Yeah? What's that?" Rojohn inquired.

"What? You didn't hear? Sagan got Tyson's boy Mike Roland killed and now check the fucked-up part about this... Tyson is Sagan's non-biological brother."

"Yeah, that's right, Sagan was adopted... Damn, what a cold-hearted scum bag."

"Yep. He was adopted and went under the name Kevin Roland."

"Shit... I've seen that kid around Little Tree Ville, he had autism disorder. He chastised his own brother that he grew up with as a child." Rojohn said as he shook his head.

"Well, the kid is gone now, burnt to ashes."

"So, what is Tyson going to do about it fam? I mean Sagan is nowhere to be found and I'm pretty sure he has an army built and ready for what's to come for him."

"Yeah. There's no search party for him out there yet. Well, that's what the news said…"

Xack arrived and walked up to the front desk receptionist.

"Hi."

"Hello sir. How may I help you?"

"My name is Xack Machida. I'm here to see Adelia Woods. Is she well as yet? I haven't gotten a call from her or the doctors. I called too but no answer."

"Ok. . . ."

The receptionist paused while looking at the screen then looked back at Xack. Her eyes quickly went left to right and left to right then looked back and picked up the phone.

"Dr. Damien can you please come to the front desk to see Xack Machida."

The doctor arrived pushing through the double doors then he looked at him with sorrow on his face and immediately, Xack knew what happened just by the look on the doctor's face.

"We tried everything. We tried everything Xack but…"

"No don't tell me this! C'mon this isn't real!"

"I'm sorry Xack but . . . She didn't make it."

Little Tree Ville—

On a store roof top, three blocks from the Mayor's Office. Litzy and Ki-Yale watched over the crowd of people gathering around the office with military squadrons guarding the building.

"Wow, my mind was all messed up. I never experienced any schizophrenia or any mind tricks for that matter."

"But you're ok though, right?"

"Yeah, the same question goes for you. Are you ok?"

"Yeah… I'm ok…" Ki-Yale gave a hesitated reply.

Litzy looked at him for five seconds trying to bring out his true feelings

"No. No I'm not ok. I promised him I keep him safe and now look what happened..." Ki-Yale said as he shook his head.

"It's not your fault." She said while touching his arm.

"If I would have known Taw would do something like that, I wouldn't have let him go up against him."

"None of us knew that Taw would do that, and Mike was a true fighter, he had a lot of heart and he died being a brave soul."

"No. I promised to protect Mike and take down Sagan. I'm still at square one! I'm no hero Litzy. I let the Mayor down and I let Little Tree Ville down. I can't do this anymore…"

"Stop beating yourself up like this. So, what if you're still at square one. You keep going and never give up…." She said touching his chin then he looked away from her

"Look. I'll help you take down this Mad Doctor asshole! Just me and you. If anyone else wants to help, then I would be much obliged."

"No, I can't let anyone else get hurt or killed."

"Well, you are strong enough to take him on by yourself. That's fine if you do that but, just don't give up."

"I… I know where he is."

"What?"

"I know where Sagan is… when we were leaving the tournament to get back to Little Tree Ville, I was just thinking about something while looking in the eastern direction and I saw an island approximately four hundred miles from Crouton Village. I looked deeper into it and there he was Sagan lying in bed just chilling while deaths are being controlled by him."

"Umm. How did you see Sagan in an island seven miles away from Crouton Village?"

"I have this ability where I can see from a long distance and also see though things similar to X-Rays. It's called Netron vision."

"So, you're saying you have X-Ray vision and enhanced human sight? Like when the doctors would install micro pupils inside your pupils to see further."

"Yea you can say that but it's more advanced."

"Nice! So, you can see what's underneath my clothes huh?"

"Ah um… no, I haven't been doing that at all, I respect your boundaries." He said with a blush.

"Good, you're not a pervert."

"Of course not."

"Good, and we're definitely not doing the nasty."

"The nasty?"

"Yeah you know like um… like… sex." She whispered on the word 'sex'.

"Ooooh… like fornicating?" He asked as he smiled.

"Yeah, like the hanky-panky."

He laughed as Litzy continued to lighten the mood by changing the subject then asked—

"So, should I call you Ki-Yale now or should I continue to call you Netro?"

"Well, I love it when you say Netro with that cool accent."

She giggled then said—

"Of course, you do."

"Ki-Yale is ok too but, only when I don't have on my Netron Suit, or you can call me Ki-Yale when no one knows my human name while I'm in my suit."

"Ok I guess it makes sense. I bet you prefer Netro, I mean, it's actually your real name."

"I do prefer that name because it means a lot to me, of someday becoming a king…"

"Wow a king, hmm'. I wonder who your queen is going to be…" Litzy said as she smiled.

"Umm… I … umm I don't." He nervously said while smiling.

"You're smiling harder than twenty minutes ago… I love making you smile."

He blushed and looked away then she asked—

"So is Netro going after Sagan once more?"

Ki-Yale puts on a serious face again and paused for about five seconds then took a deep breath.

"So…?"

"I don't wanna' do anything else to be honest with you."

"What?!"

"That's it I'm done…"

"C'mon! You can't quit! You can't just throw in the towel!"

"I don't know… I just… I just need some time to myself and figure this out."

"Hmmm, ok."

He gave Litzy a hug then said—

"I'll see you later." He slightly turned his body to the left then she grabbed his arm.

"Wait…" She said as she gazed at him with her arms around his neck.

He raised his left eyebrow projecting a conjecturing facial expression then she began to reach in for a kiss. He froze and unexpectedly gasping for air while goggling at her closed eyelids. He closed his eyes as he felt his lips against hers.

"Whoa…" He wheezed enduring his first kiss from the girl he likes.

Revealing a sensitive smirk, Ki-Yale thought of playing it cool and turned around once again but this time he had full confidence with his chest out. Litzy grinned at his change of mood as he flew away at high speeds.

Mayor Tyson with a serious facial expression and watching outside his window then randomly, he saw Ki-Yale flying away as the crowd outside of his office continued to support him.

"Hey everyone! Listen up!" Mr. Turd shouted.

The supporting crowd looked at him strangely but stood quiet.

"This cannot be anymore! The murder! The criminal activities residing in our world! This has to stop. The General of the Gigantica Army is there. The most powerful army out of all of our nations, with their large guns and armory. People are dying for nonentity and the people is all we've got. So, let's let em' know what needs to happen to the Mad Doctor! C'mon say it with me! . . . Sagan must die . . . C'mon say it! Sagan must die!"

A few people in the crowd with their fists in the air began chanting— "SAGAN MUST DIE! SAGAN MUST DIE!" Repeatedly.

Suddenly, the whole crowd began to say the words attracting the attention of Mayor Tyson and the soldiers guarding the Mayor's office.

The Kafmora residence—

Its sundown and Neecho, Demi, Tajaymae, Oji and Nealo are all at the dinner table waiting on Ki-Yale to come to the table so everyone can start eating. Ki-Yale entered from the living room then walked towards the table.

"Come on Ki, challenge your feast." Neecho said.

Oji looked at Ki-Yale while he goes to sit down at his original seating.

"Hey big head! That leg is mine. I called it before everyone, mine I say!"

"You can have it this time Oji. I'm not going to make it disappear like some magic trick like every time." Ki-Yale said as he smiled.

Neecho smiled at Ki-Yale then said— "Ok family! — Dig in!"

Everyone began to eat as Tajaymae grabbed some salad then Demi said—

"Oh, my daughter loves the healthy stuff."

"Yes, the greens keep me strong."

Demi shook her head up and down as she smiled at her daughter then smiled at Ki-Yale then asked—

"How's the mash potatoes Ki?"

"It's great Mom. You always make the best food."

"Awe, thank you my son."

An hour later Ki-Yale went on the balcony in his Netron Suit with his pet lion looking at the stars and listening to Hip Hop. The family's Air Basketball court is planted to the ground and has the option to levitate to the sky. Titus growled lightly as Neecho loomed behind him then stood next to his son. He turned to the left and saw his father looking at stars then looked back upward.

"Listening to music is a way for me to escape my troubles." Ki-Yale said as he turned the volume down.

"I do the same all the time son. I listen to the golden age of Hip Hop."

"Aah, 90s Hip Hop."

"Yeah, I love all eras but that's my favorite. I would catch a vibe and look really far into space looking for Netron, although I don't know exactly what it looks like but it's supposedly the biggest planet in the universe and it's like . . . Really, really, really far away."

"That's exactly what I was doing Dad."

"How far did you look this time?"

"I can sort of see the Earth's barrier and that's about it. I can't see any further."

"Well I can see the Moon perfectly, the satellite hovering over it and a little more beyond that. You should be able to see more when you get older. You're developing your abilities quicker than we thought." Neecho said as he looked at his son and perceiving that he is a little sorrowful.

"Do you remember when I bought Titus for your 10th birthday? Your first pet?"

Ki-Yale puts his hand on Titus's head and rubs him.

"Yeah I remember. You introduced him to me on this very balcony…"

Year 2318—

"Hmm, oh, I almost forgot." Neecho said then he left the balcony then returned in twenty seconds.

"Look what I got."

"Woah! Is that ah?"

"Yes, it's a baby lion, a cub . . . It's a little late but it's your birthday gift."

"What?! I love lions! Can I pet it?!" Ki-Yale asked keenly as he looks closely at the cub.

"Yeah man, he's yours!"

Ki-Yale slowly took the baby cub in his arms then said— "Heart of a lion."

"If you got a heart like that… Hm, then you got the heart to raise him."

"Wow . . . .He's already chewing on my arm. Hmm, I don't know what to call him …" Ki-Yale said as he lifted his new pet lion over his head.

"Be careful with him, before he pees on you."

"Hmm, I'm going to call him, hmm…. Titus."

"Titus, I like it… It's Roman for 'Title of Honor'."

*"Yes, you are correct Father." Ki-Yale responded while Titus is
playing on his neck and shoulder.*

Present time—

"Hm, your slogan Ki-Yale…"— "My slogan?"

"Yes. Do you know what that means?"

"It means to go up against anyone and anything with no
fear no matter how big that thing or being is… that's my
view of it."

"That is true, fight and protect what's yours but that
slogan has many meanings to it. One in particular I like is
never surrender… Having heart to me is giving your all."

Ki-Yale nods his head in agreement to what his father is
saying then Neecho continued—

"Now this applies to what you did earlier to a girlfriend
I suppose you have?"

"What are talking about?"

"You know, don't lie now son."

"How did you even know this? Did Tajaymae tell you?
Hmm, but I didn't tell Tajaymae I was with Litzy today."

"Oh, her name is Litzy… Cute name."

"Hm, I agree."

"Tajaymae didn't tell me anything... if that's what you're
thinking."

"Soooo'... How did you know?" Ki-Yale asked.

"I can read your mind son." Neecho answered.

"You can read… My mind?! Well of course, I was just
thinking that Tajay told you about…" He said as Neecho
interrupts.

"Yes, you haven't developed telepathic and telekinesis
abilities yet. It's difficult to learn at a young age, I assure
you… Sorry I went into your private space in your head but
you look so saddened lately I just wanted to see what's
eating you up besides the death of your friend."

"It's ok Dad… Have you been reading my mind before?"

"This is the first time I ever read your mind and went along with a message; you know freestyle."

Ki-Yale moved his head up and down some more then his father continued—

"Look, you need to pull yourself together. Being a quitter isn't going to benefit you on reaching your goals."

"Yes sir, I know."

"Good." Neecho said then began to walk away.

"Since you went in my head. You must know now, deep down what I really want to do to him. Right?"

He turned around to look at Ki-Yale then said—

"Yes, and you're Netro Two… you make the decision, the right one." He said then began to walk to the door to get back inside the house.

Ki-Yale jumped over the balcony and landed on the Air Basketball court. He ran to the basketball that was left lying around. He picked it up and operated the court to levitate.

"Hey Dad."

"Yes, my son."

"You ready for another 'L'?"

Neecho turned around again with his left eyebrow raised, staring at him inanely for few seconds then nods his head with a smirk.

"I feel a good game will keep my mind at ease for a little…" Ki-Yale continued.

"All right, let's go, I'm gonna' need some lunch money tomorrow anyway." He jested then Ki-Yale smiled in a competitive way.

"Ha, you got jokes Dad!"

THIRTY-ONE

Jarrach City, Pollasun on planet Mars. Alexis Cobar, a twenty-two years old young Australian lady that grew up in Gigantica City then relocated on Mars to attend college in Jarrach City, Pollasun and studied for her master's degree in Social Work. Alexis and her Caucasian friend Patricia went to a night club and this club seemed to be the most active club in the city that night. People in their twenties partied as if it's their last while upstairs had a lounge where people chill and enjoy the view. This club is called "Lax's Party Pack" and "Lax" is for short saying. It's 'Throwback Friday Night' and the DJ is playing old music of different genres from the 20th and 21st century.

"Ok, this is officially turning up! I never been to one of these parties! I just love the idea of rewinding the old school music!" Alexis said dancing with Patricia.

"Yeah I told you this would be dope!"

"Hey, let's go upstairs and get a bottle." She said as she grabbed her friend's hand.

"Ok let's go, lead the way."

They both walked upstairs to the bartender and asked for a bottle of wine with two glasses. Patricia turned her head and beheld a handsome young man in his early twenties who looked like he could be Italian with long straight black hair and about twenty long strands of blood red hair coming from the middle of his scalp. He is wearing a full black silk tuxedo with black shoes, black leather gloves, black shirt with a red bow tie and red handkerchief.

"Woah, look at that guy." Patricia said being a little tipsy from drinking earlier.

"I see him. Looks like some pretty boy."

"A pretty boy I would love to eat like a cannibal! Then ride his face!!"

"You're a crazy bitch. You know that?"

"That's why you should go talk to him. I'm too crazy for anybody."

"I never do the first move."

"So, do I but for this guy he is worth the first move baby. He looks like one of those… 'Must conversate then go on a date' kind of guys. "

"Hm, well, let's see if he can conversate… then if I'm not successful then I'll let your crazy ass give it a try." Alexis said as she approached the young man.

"Hello. Um… hey… How are you tonight?" She nervously asked.

"Hey! I'm doing fine… just enjoying this lovely night. Thank you for asking…"

"Ok, great… bye."

Her nervousness drove herself away after he spoke in such a fancy and polite manner. The man stopped her with a smirk and said— "Wait. Don't you wanna' know my name?"

"Um yeah… I do…"

The handsome man reached his hand out to her as she blushed then he said—

"Please. Have a seat with me, don't be shy . . .My name is Henry . . .. Henry Luciano. What's your name?"

She sat down slowly gaining comfort with a bright smile on her face then said—

"Alexis Cobar."

Fang Machida served his two local customers as they stared at Xack Machida sitting by himself and contemplating on the loss of his beloved. He barely said a word ever since he arrived back at his home except for breaking the news to Fang leaving him grieving. Adelia was left a stray when Sagan being responsible for murdering her adoptive parents in Crouton Village resulting in Fang to take the place as a parent more than the roll of a sensei. Fang blamed Xack for this tragedy as he disobeyed his father by going after Sagan. Now all Xack had was thirst for blood in his eyes with just a burgundy headband and a body to bury. Funeral plans were set in only a few days along with friends attending.

"He's been this way ever since he came back home."

"It must be hard for him, just look at him. He's broken."

Xack looked at his five-inch tattoo that says "Adelia" on his right arm which he had recently gotten before her death. Yaeko rubbed his right hand as he squeezed his eyelids and gazing at the baby coyote then began to ponder.

<u>Little Tree Ville, five months back</u>—

Adelia in her apartment with an open space where she practices with a woodened sword. Apaki Jermayin means a lot to her as it does Xack and becoming better every day is the primary goal for her. Xack was expected to return to her apartment after he recently left to Gigantica City to run special errands which would take an entire day.

As she swung the wooden sword, she heard the automated door saying— "Xack Machida is here, Xack Machida is here."

"Back here already in two hours? He must have forgot something." She said as she rushed to the door.

She opened the automated door then suddenly she saw a deep well of horror as Xack's right arm is cut wide open and bleeding excessively. She yelped then he started to fall on top of her as he tried to control his balance. She grabbed him immediately and brought him to the wall. With little time to think she called a first aid android that's affixed to the living room wall.

"What happened Xack?"

"Adel, agh'… I don't know. I was walking down a pathway then, mmph'. Suddenly, I got shot by several shards of heated glass… I… pulled them out before I came back here."

"It looked like they went deep… Damn it Xack, it seems like he keeps sending Apaki Warriors just to toy with you."

"Yeah and I couldn't get a visual of the warrior that attacked me."

"Were you followed?"

"No, I made sure of it and even took a different route."

Within seconds the android arrived to assist her then she noticed there isn't enough wrap to stop the bleeding entirely. She grabbed the bottle of alcohol then took off her favorite burgundy headband. She poured the alcohol on the headband then wrapped it around on the higher area of his wound.

Xack fidgeted then the android professed that Xack needs serious attention and began to alert the 911 emergency call.

"No! No hospitals." He said then immediately the android ceased the call then Adelia said—

"No hospitals?"

"No, not this time."

"Trying to be like me huh…?"

"Hm', something like that. I just, rather not deal with any law enforcement for this one."

"I'll call my neighbor; she has a way better kit than mines."

"Haagh'!" He slightly howled as he looked at the hideous wound.

She touched her holographic ultraportable that appeared from her watch.

"Your headband..."

"It's ok... It's you over my headband any day Xack..."

He brightly smiled at what she had said then she continued—
"I've seen this before, but I need more cloth, this wrap is just not enough."

<u>*Present time*</u>—

As Xack remained on the chair and stared at his beloved's headband he squeezed his eyes then suddenly, he slowly crushed it with both hands at each end. He took a deep breath then lifted the headband and bent his head forward then slowly wrapped the headband on his forehead just like how Adelia use to wear it.

He stood up as his father and the two customers watched him then he sauntered across the bar. He exited his father's bar then immediately Fang walked to the exit then opened the door and said—

"You're going back out, there aren't you?"

Xack stopped with his back turned

"Yes father." He said as the door closed behind his father.

"I'm sorry for the way I spoke to you last night."

Xack maintained his posture while his back turned to his father as silence arose from Xack for a few seconds then Fang continued—

"Normally I would say it's too dangerous, but I can't stop you. So, I just hope you get rid of the ones responsible for her death."

"Father. I want you to look after Yaeko for me while I'm gone."

"Well, of course my son."

"It seems as if Push owned her but must have left her a stray. When I come back, I'm going to be taking care of her. I know Adel would have don't the same."

<u>Great Welkin City</u>—

Litzy de la Rose on a hyper train arriving at the last stop then as soon as she exited the train along with her belongings, she smelled the air then said—

"Home sweet home."

Moments later—

She walked up to a house door and ringed the bell.

"Your daughter is outside! Your daughter is outside!" The automated door detector system said.

In a matter of seconds Kayla de la Rose opened the door. Both froze, just staring at each other. Heart beating from their chests, beholding at what was once dearest in every way.

"Oh, my baby!" She spoke in Spanish as she bends down to her height and hugged her.

"Mom!"

Kayla looked at her in the eyes then asked— "Litzy. Why do you do all these crazy things?"

"I'm… I'm sorry Mama."

An hour later Kayla prepared some food for her daughter and they continued speaking in Spanish about everything.

"So how was this tournament you loved so dearly?"

"I don't love it anymore. Things are just so crazy . . . The fighting, it's not for me right now."

"Was it ever for you? Ever since you made that weapon you think you're invincible and wanna' fight everybody in the world. Especially guys…"

535

"Speaking of invincible… There's this boy…"

"A boy?"

"Yeah, ah he's a friend… I ah' met him at the tournament."

"Oh really? A friend you say… What's his name? Is he cute?"

Litzy began to blush right after the question that her mother asked.

"His name is Netro and he's handsome but Mom, I'm not talking about looks here. I'm talking about power; his powers are amazing. He said he's half alien, he's like super strong and can fly. He took me into the sky Mom! It was so beautiful seeing the village and Welkin City up high."

"Wow, he took you to the sky huh? Kind of putting you in danger don't you think?"

"Yeah but I held on very tight, plus he wouldn't let me fall."

"I still think you were in danger being so high up like that."

"Well I'm still here Mom."

"Yes, and I thank God for that . . . So what else happened?"

"Well he had a sister and she had powers too. I guess she can absorb electrical energy."

"I see."

"I had to fight her though…"

"And?"

"I won. I've beaten her with my jewelry."

"Was it a bad beating?"

"No, she remarkably healed herself."

"Healed herself?"

"Yeah with her own powers. I guess the plasma that collects the energy healed her wounds and at the same time her body consumes the energy."

"Wow . . ."

"Yeah it's crazy. When I saw her the next day it's like she never got into a fight . . . Anyway, it was a lot of things that went down but the most devastating thing was…"

"What?"

"Someone's demise, the Mayor's son Mike Roland."

"Oh, yes, I saw on the news last night. Poor guy must be going through a lot with the loss of his son."

"Yeah, Netro wasn't too happy about it. His rage attacking the killer who is supposed to be the strongest fighter made the entire stadium go wild."

"This is why I don't want you fighting." Kayla said then a tear plunged from the right side of her eye.

Litzy relishing this long-awaited moment, staring at her mother as she looked back at her and whipped her tears with a mother's touch. Litzy stood up then walked over to her to give a hug.

"Hey Mom." She said as her mother looked up at her in response then she leaned over and hugged her.

<u>*Little Tree Ville, Gel Hev*</u>—

One week apart from Mike's death. Early in the AM around 6o-clock Nealo is teaching his grandson a new ability. Ki-Yale pays attention to detail as he wore his Netron Suit and floating fifteen feet in the air.

"The 'Big Bang Wipeout' is practically a bomb emoting electromagnetic radiation which is made up of inferred rays that generate a lot of heat. This can cause damage to the cells of any species, from radio waves to gamma rays and possibly beyond which can damage more than just cells— depending on how powerful you are. . .. Alright, I'm going to use about five percent of power to give you an idea of what it looks like when you detonate the bomb." Nealo said floating fifteen feet in the air.

"Ok now here is the bomb." Nealo continued creating a small light circle of energy. Nealo puts his fists together then uses them to hover parallel and apart from the energy.

"With about five percent of power I can control it and not detonate it as yet."

Ki-Yale listening and looking at his grandpa performing the new power as Nealo continued— "The energy is in between your fists. Now you just slam your fists together and say . . . big bang wipeout."

Nealo creates a ball of energy that explosion stood around his body.

"I'm controlling the energy from the bomb before it explodes. If I want to, I can put more power into the energy until I can't control it then it detonates!"

Ki-Yale had an amazed look on his face while his grandpa reduces the energy back into a small glowing energy ball with his fist in the same position.

"Now you try it." Nealo said while the energy disappears in his hands.

"Now that's really effective. Ok, let's see."

Ki-Yale began to put his fists together about five inches apart while concentrating for the glowing energy ball to appear in between his fists. About three minutes had passed by and still noting appeared in between his fists.

"C'mon Ki."

"I'm trying but nothing is…" Ki-Yale said pausing his sentence while a small glowing energy which is the bomb, appears in between his fists.

"Woah!"

"There you go, that's it."

"Wow… I can feel the pressure from the energy pushing my fists away!" Ki-Yale said while he tries to keep his fists together.

"Now you got to control it, remember the energy comes from the core. Put enough energy that you can control from your core into the bomb then detonate it by slamming your fists together."

"Ok. Here goes."

The bomb in between Ki-Yale's fists grew an inch bigger while Ki-Yale's arms are shaking and slightly pushing away from the bomb. He slowly pushed his fists back in closer to the bomb and then slams his fists together ultimately detonating it.

"Big! Bang! Wipeout!" Ki-Yale said as an explosion erupts from his body. Ki-Yale lost the energy and failed to keep it around after detonating.

"That looks like about ten percent of what I did, and you didn't keep your bomb active for long like I did so that means the ten percent of energy for me, you can't control it . . . That's what you must work on but overall, you did it. The 'Big Bang Wipeout', very effective in a serious fight. Use it."

"Nice. I feel a little fatigue and ten percent is nothing for you huh."

"Yeah, you'll feel fatigue the first time ever perform this attack, but the Netron Suit will recover in the next couple seconds then you should be able keep performing this attack without fatigue, just keep practicing. I can control up to ninety percent of my Big Bang Wipeout, controlling it allows me to keep the energy blast effective for long periods of time without losing the energy and I can also move around with it, like walking, running, flying around with it. All I must do is keep that bomb in-between my fists. Ninety percent for me is like a giant ball of energy. Now just keep in mind that practice makes perfection and later try to perform it without saying the words."

"Yeah, I'll get this attack down pact!"

"Yes. Now a little fun fact about the Loose Cannon I didn't mention to you yet."

"What's that?"

Nealo's right fists and lower arm that has black gloves from his Netron Suit started to glow a reddish yellow.

"I taught you to shoot the Loose Cannon one round of power blast at a time. When the particles hit the target, those particles explode which is very lethal." Nealo said aiming his fists in the air then fired his Loose Cannon rapidly then continued to speak—

"But it can be more lethal… Instead of just shooting slow… you can also fire rapidly like an assault rifle."

"Aah exciting… I always thought about that but never really done it…"

Ki-Yale aimed his right fist in the air then shoots his Loose Cannon rapidly just like his grandpa did.

"Yeeaah'… this is what I'm talking about!"

"Very easy to do. Also, very effective in a fight also because those beams still expand when hitting a target even though you're firing rapidly."

"Nice… now I just need to master reading minds. Have you ever read my mind Granddad?"

"No, I haven't. It's a form of respect not to do so but in battle it's ok because you can figure out your enemy's attacks before they do it. Plus, mind control and also controlling anything with your mind… even matter, time, space and so on... It takes a long time to master."

"That must be the advanced level powers for advanced Netrons."

"Yes, they are. I'm guessing your dad did that to you."

"Yeah he did… snooping through my private space."

"I'm sure it was for a good cause."

"Yeah I guess it was."

<u>*Great Welkin City*</u>—

Kayla woke up hearing noises downstairs then she attended to the noise and saw her daughter gathering her belongings.

"Good morning my sunshine."

"Good morning Mom."

"Ah. What are you doing?"

"Getting ready…"

"To go where?"

"To go help someone."

"You mean that boy. You're going to fight again aren't you?"

Litzy still packing her things and didn't answer her.

"Hey. I'm talking to you."

"Yes, Mom I'm going to fight again."

"I can't believe you. Don't you ever learn?"

"Yes, I've learned that I have a purpose now and that's to help others."

"Help others? Since when you want to help others?"

"I'm done with that mentality Mom."

"Wow, you've changed . . . Helping others… does this include strangers?"

"Yes, including strangers that has to struggle with Sagan's underground control."

"Being nice to strangers… I don't believe in your bullshit."

"No Mom, this is really me. I want to make a difference by using my skills to do what's right!"

"Now you just want to cover up the faults you've done. You're selfish Litzy, you didn't have a care in the world about what I may think when you left me."

"Mom, I'm sorr…" Litzy said as she got interrupted.

"That tournament in Crouton only flattered your vanity to think you need to fight all the time."

Litzy stood quiet and looked awake for a few seconds then said—

"I know now running away was wrong and I can't take back what I did…. I just want to continue to prove to you that I'm not a failure."

"Failure? Hmm, you're not that at all baby. You're my life and you're all I've got; I don't know what I'll do if I lose you for good. You understand what I'm saying Litzy?"

"Yeah." She replied as she slowly nodded her head.

"You don't have to prove anything to me or to anyone else just do what is best for you and with respect for your family."

Litzy receiving lectures as she pierced her lips and nods her head. The look on her mother's face revealing that she's struggling to let her go out again.

"Ok. Mom, I will."

"Well, whatever it is you're going to do with that boy, just please be safe and get back here safely." Kayla said as her daughter looked back at her then walked to the door. Litzy stopped and stared at the door.

Kayla stood with a confused face on why her daughter stopped so suddenly. Litzy turned around then ran up to her and hugged her.

Kayla with her arms down and still with a confused face then realized that what she said really paid off for her relationship with Litzy. She puts her arms around Litzy's back and hugged her tightly.

THIRTY-TWO

Soldiers of the U.S. Mega Human Prime Army are lined up outside of the Mayor's office while the citizens crowd around it. Corporal Maya Gatson, standing by the entrance witnessing Mayor Tyson suffering a devastating loss as he sat in his chair looking out the window.

"How are you feeling sir?" Preston asked.

"Taking it a day at a time."

"Hm, are you sure you want to do a speech?"

"Yes Preston. I'm sure."

"A boy here by the name of Netro wants to speak with you." Said the security operator.

Tyson didn't respond for a few seconds.

"Sir? I have a boy here…"

"Yeah… bring him in." He said while he continuously stared at the window.

Ki-Yale went on the elevator as he contemplated about what to say and how to react around the Mayor. Seconds later he reached the Mayor's office then opened the door. He stepped pass the threshold and immediately its complete silence from everyone for a few seconds then Ki-Yale said—

"Hello Preston."

"Netro…" Preston answered him.

"Hello… Mayor Tyson." Ki-Yale nebulously said.

Tyson didn't respond to Ki-Yale then everyone kept completely silence again for a few seconds. Ki-Yale expressed a bit of nervousness then said—

"I came to… I came to…" He said nervously looking to the floor then got interrupted.

"To what? Stutter and mock my son's autism? . . . What is it that you want kid?"

"No. I…" Ki-Yale said as the room became cloudier and hazier for him.

"You promised me! You fucking promised me… THAT YOU WOULD KEEP HIM SAFE AND ALIVE!!" Tyson bawled as he got out of his seat facing Ki-Yale then walked a closer to him.

Preston began to express sorrow on his face witnessing Tyson going through numerous emotions.

"I know." Ki-Yale vaguely replied.

Tyson shook his head left and right as he squeezed his eyes then said—

"You know? Did you really? Cause if you knew, he wouldn't be dead today . . . All is left, is his truck and a fucking burnt weapon that I created. Everything else... is just ashes… I don't know if I should blame myself for the lack of protection in the weapon. I should've known better to mix enchantment and technology."

He grieved then continued— "Sagan… he went after Taw's parents and had them killed, even though Taw did his dirty work on my son."

"What?" Ki-Yale surprised.

"Look at this." Tyson said showing Ki-Yale videos through a hologram. This video contains news articles and footage about Taw's parents being murdered.

"I can't ever forgive Taw, but I don't fully condone that aftermath. This man, he killed hundreds of people including the deaths linked to him. Making orders to people to do his dirty work while he hides like a coward! Unfortunately, he… He was my non-biological brother. He was there with me when his real father slaughtered our parents. Ever since then he wasn't the same. I was pronounced dead because of the fire and no trace of me but I managed to escape before the fire erupted completely. I was lucky with only a few burns. —I hid myself for some time from everyone, including family then I decide to show my face… I'm sure he knew of my existence because the info had surfaced all over the news and I try to have meet ups with him, but I guess he thinks I would set him up. After a while I distinguished hatred coming from him, unknown death threats to me and my son, murdering some of my family members that worked in Benila Hospital . . ."

"It wasn't his fault that happened to your parents, his father was just a psycho."

"Hm, yes but then his psychopathic father made him who he is today."

"I know where Sagan is. I found the location when I was leaving the tournament."

"You know where Sagan is…? So why didn't you go after him?!" Tyson argued.

"I found out right before I left to come back here. I don't know at the time I felt on the verge to giving up but now I'm ready for him." Ki-Yale said.

"Whew, that was bad… sorry I had two much eggs earlier…" Colonel Vixen said as she casually exited the restroom then looked at Ki-Yale and he looked back.

"You must be Netro."

"Yes, that's me."

"My name is Colonel Vixen of the Gigantica Army."

"It's a pleasure to meet you Colonel."

"Yes likewise. I've been looking for you and the Mayor's Office is the first place I chose. I hear you have these abilities far greater than any Mega Human and I've seen the videos but I'm a little skeptical of what you can do."

"Let me see your gun." Ki-Yale said to Corporal Maya.

"Um…" She looked at Colonel Vixen then she nodded her head in acceptance.

"Ok." Maya handed him her pistol then he puts it to his right thigh. "Woah! What are you doing kid?!"

Without any hesitation, making his skin soft, he pulled the trigger shooting himself as his right thigh to disperse immense amount of blood. Corporal Maya and Colonel Vixen is in complete shock and lost for words as he turned his head at Maya handing back her pistol. "Thank you."

Instantly his Netron suit regenerated his wound. "Sorry about all the blood."

"It's ok, I'll get an android to clean it up." Preston said.

"Wow, I guess the videos are true." Colonel Vixen said. "Amazing." Corporal Maya said.

"How is this possible?"

"My suit gives me these special regeneration abilities and not of any technology."

"I see. Is it magic?"

"No, it's far beyond that."

"Hm', now what's important here is the execution of the Mad Doctor. You now have the rights for you to do so signed off by President Moore Jr." Colonel Vixen said depicting a hologram of the signed documents.

Ki-Yale shook his head left and right as Vixen continued to reveal numerous graphic videos.

"I know you have doubt in your heart to take a life but if you work with us, we can rid this world from corruption once more. He's trying to make everything a spitting image of the 21st century. His illegal oil trade operations, excessive contraband of illegal weapons surpassing the system of safeguarding the human race. The murders of innocent children, women and men making this world a shithole, year by year it increases. The riots occurring globally, he won't stop until he's dead, even if we incarcerate him, he has a widespread of connections to set him free immediately before trial and we all know he'll be getting the death penalty. He is the largest kingpin performing illegal technology, weapons and oil trades thus far..."

"That's enough, I don't want to see any more of that video."

"Listen kid… you're powerful, like nothing I have ever seen before so your help shouldn't be a problem for us. Now Vixen, a special team should go after him, preferably yours. I also want you and Netro to go to his location and bring him to me. Matter fact… I don't even want to see his face anymore. Especially up close, because if I do . . . My time as Mayor would instantly be expired."

"You can help us to bring him in Netro. It won't make much of a difference, as soon after he faces the Jury, he gets the death penalty on the same day." Vixen said.

"Mister Mayor and General . . . You don't need your team or army to put their lives on the line much longer. More will just die, and I know they would die fighting for peace and justice. . .. I'm sure it's always been like that but, I will put an end to this . . . I promise…"

"No more promises kid. Just do it!" Tyson said.

"Yes, sir and General I won't let you down."

Ki-Yale began to walk towards the exit then stopped then looked back.

Tyson nods his head showing approval then Ki-Yale exited the office. Tyson walks back to his seat and looks out the window.

Moments later—

Ki-Yale flying to the gate of Little Tree Ville to travel towards Crouton Village where the island Sagan is residing nearby.

"Yeoo'!" Nack hollered.

Ki-Yale recognized Nack's voice calling to him. He turned to the voice and saw him near the Little Tree Ville gates next to the entry booth. "What? Nack? Tajaymae? Xack? Litzy? What you all doing here?"

"Hey Netro." Litzy said standing next to an air vehicle.

"What's going on?" Ki-Yale confused.

"We're coming with you!" Xack said while wearing Adelia's favorite headband.

"I knew you were going to fly by here, so we waited from two hours ago after your grandpa told us you were going after Sagan. So, I informed Tajaymae, Xack and Litzy. Now you got back up." Nack said.

"My grandpa told you I was going after Sagan? Wow. Why would he do that? I told him I'm going alone... I don't need back up. I can..." He said being interrupted.

"I was the one that told them." Litzy said.

"What?" Ki-Yale muddled.

"Umm." Nack said.

"Yeah, she was the one, Nack here just wanted to make up a different story." Tajaymae said.

"Litzy. I can handle this myself . . . guys, I can handle this myself you all know that."

"Yes, we know you can, but we want to help anyway." Xack said.

"What about your wounds?" Ki-Yale asked.

"I'm good man. I got stitches and patched them up and I'm moving quite well."

"Nack, you have smarts with many educational aspects but what physical traits do you have when it comes to a fight?"

"Well, I have my hyper beam shotgun right here." He said revealing his firearm out from the air vehicle.

Ki-Yale looked at Nack with a blank stare then he nods his head vaguely. He then looked to Litzy and she smiled at him. He took a deep breath, contemplating on what to say next.

"Ok… ok you can tag along but please be careful."

"Sagan is one who should be careful." Tajaymae said.

"Hm, are you and Litzy ok now?" Ki-Yale being concerned.

"Yeah I'm over it. I lost but next time I will kick her ass in a fight but for now we are allies."

"Good." Ki-Yale said with a smile then gently landed on his feet next to Litzy. She stared at him with her left eyebrow up and a smirk while walking behind his back then hugged him. "Let's go airborne." She said.

He responded with a blush then ascended into the air.

"Hey, I can always carry all of you."

"Umm no brother, not with those butter fingers." Tajaymae said as she gets in the air vehicle.

"What? I don't have butter fingers."

"Lead the way Netro." Xack said.

"Hey, I like your headband by the way." Ki-Yale acknowledged.

"Thank you Netro. It's from a special someone, now please, let's go." He said trying not to show any melancholy.

"I see… Okay then, follow me!"

He began to propel himself in the air then flew in the direction toward Crouton Village which is about 180 square miles from Little Tree Ville while Nack, Tajaymae and Xack began to follow Ki-Yale in an air vehicle.

Unknown Area—

In a large laboratory, Shelton Renzo stepped in after the automated sliding door closes.

"Fusing your cells again?"

"No not yet Shelton but when it's time to move out, I'll be needing it."

"How about proceeding with a contraption that produces liquid Tektonium?"

"The military surprisingly had beaten me to it two years ago and I still haven't gotten the technician and scientist that can do the job. Apparently, the project went loose, and the scientist is deceased."

"Hm, well, the next move of you coming out of hiding will have the military thinking they have the upper hand."

"They can think that, but they should know better not to underestimate me."

"Especially Colonel Vixen, she is now a just simple fly you can swap at any time."

"Yes, but for now she is of great importance to me."

"Hm', I'm amazed how a woman like her could dig her nose into things. She's top rank now and already in over her head."

"She will provide for me, I use to be able roam freely now I have to make orders while I stay here. That's going to change real soon."

Shelton became quiet for a moment as Sagan across the laboratory refilling his needles with his back turned to him.

"Hm, can I ask you something sir?"

"You just asked me…"— "Yes I did, well, ahehm'. I never see you prolong the process of saving your memory and possibly transfer it…"

"Yes, I already know what you're going to ask but some questions should be left unasked and unanswered."

"As you wish…"

Thirty minutes later, Ki-Yale soaring through the sky, passing Crouton Village then descending towards the water.

The sun glistening its light as he perceives the far ocean ahead. Litzy witnessed the beauty around her, everything seemed so clean and well taken care of. The world now being at a peek level where mankind lives in environmental augmentations.

"Wow, this is like the best experience I ever had."

"That's how I felt when I first started flying."

"This is the only thing blinding my fears right now."

"You're scared?"

"To be honest with you… yeah I'm scared."

"Don't be scared… you know I'll always protect you."

She chuckled then said—

"I can protect myself don't worry about me Netro… it's just that… you're going up against Sagan and from what I know he's very unpredictable."

"Yeah, this is a big mission, but I believe I can take care of him."

"Well, what about you? Are at least scared?"

"Hm, ever since my brother was abducted, I try to challenge my fears and in order for me to challenge anything . . . So, I guess you can say that I am scared but I know I can't be because if I am then things won't be the same."

"Hm,' . . .. You think that Sagan has your brother?"

"Well, from what I've known with Sagan is that he keeps captive of anyone and use them. Its long a shot but the only way to know is meeting him face to face."

She became quiet, anticipating his decisions.

"There it is."— "Where? Wait… I forgot your eyes are different from mines."

"Yeah, it's invisible and undetected. I'm sure plenty ships and planes pass by, then they end up disappearing."

"Invisibility tech is definitely illegal outside of military use and I've heard over the news of disappearing transports…"

"Yeah, like another Bermuda Triangle."

"Maybe a wormhole in the ocean."

"Hmm', maybe…" Ki-Yale said then stopped in midair and twisted his body around.

"Hey, did they keep up with me?"

Litzy's body still pressed against his back. Her arms were around his chest, poking her head out from the left side of his shoulders and squeezing her eyes then said— "I can see them, a little far behind but I can see them."

"Yes, so can I, we'll sneak in from here."

"Hm, how should we sneak in?"

"I'm looking for an opening right now, all I see I possible traps and land mines." Ki-Yale said using his Netron vision.

They waited for the rest then a few minutes later Xack arrived next to Ki-Yale and Litzy. "What's the move?" Xack asked.

"I'm looking for a way in but all I see is traps all around."

"We just need to bust in the front door!" Tajaymae said.

"That's not very smart, being stealthy is way more accomplishable." Nack said.

"We got incoming . . . looks like androids." Ki-Yale alerted everyone.

"I guess they are invisible like the island because I don't see them!" Tajaymae said.

Seconds later the androids disabled their invisibility as more appeared from underwater and heading straight towards Ki-Yale using their thrusters.

"I had a feeling we reached somewhere in his radar." Litzy said.

"I got this." Ki-Yale said as he places Litzy on the air vehicle.

"It's a whole gang coming through guys!" Xack said.

"Now I see them!" Tajaymae said.

"We all see them now." Nack said as Ki-Yale moved in towards the fifteen androids that appeared.

The androids started shooting at Ki-Yale as he dodges every shot then he moved in closer to the androids while they surrounded him. All the androids that surrounded him quickly move in then attached themselves onto Ki-Yale.

"Ok we need to help him." Litzy said.

"Nah we need to move in on that island. My brother got this."

"Yeah, she's right. Ki's way is too much for them, let's use these contacts for the invisible island. It's the Shale Tech lenses you had, I modified them and made enough for all of us." Nack said giving everyone eye high tech contacts lenses.

"Very fascinating Nack." Xack said as he put on the contacts and so did everyone else.

"Yeah, it's time I be convenient for the team."

"So, this is illegal then."

"Well, I didn't look into that but I'm sure using illegal gadgets to stop Sagan is worth it."

"I agree… that must be the island about two miles ahead." Xack said as he drove the air vehicle closer to the island. In just under five minutes later they arrived on the island then parked the vehicle. They exited the vehicle then began to move in.

Ki-Yale seemed to be trapped with the androids all attached to him then he shouted— "Big… Bang… Wipeout!!"

The explosion came from Ki-Yale's body with his fists pressed together.

"Woah… What was that?" Nack asked.

"It's Netro!" Litzy said.

"He's ok. An explosion wouldn't stop him." Tajaymae said.

"Let's go and be careful of land mines." Xack said.

Ki-Yale's energy which looked like a large ball from the Big Bang Wipeout is surrounding him and it seemed that he can control it now only using twenty percent. The androids seemed to be all destroyed from the explosion. Some fell into the water, some just were just obliterated and destroyed to pieces. Ki-Yale realized of what he had done leaving a smile in his face then he began to fly towards the island.

<u>Little Tree Ville</u>—

In the backyard, Neecho sat on a chair with a cup of coffee in front of him on the round table looking at his garden. All of sudden a tiny centipede crawled on the side of the table. Neecho seen the insect as it slowly crawled closer to the edge of the table. He gently puts his hand next to it then the centipede stopped in front of his fingers. After seconds of no movement from the insect he puts his fingers facing up closer to it. The centipede began to move once more as Neecho stood still. The centipede gradually crawled onto Neecho's fingers then he smiled as the insect's legs tickled him. Suddenly, he heard footsteps as Nealo walked from the door then he sat around the round table and looked at him.

"I still remember when I saw Ken at the Mini-Mart. That image isn't leaving my head."

"It was just a vision, a reflection of the anguish that you're experiencing."

"We should've let you train them earlier… It was my fault, for letting them believe it wasn't necessary."

"You thought we were in a time of peace. No one never actually bothered us until that day. Even I believed it wasn't necessary."

"Hm, Ki-Yale shouldn't be out there."

"You think he's going to take a life?"

"Perhaps he's following in your footsteps."

"A son mostly follows in their father's footsteps, especially when the father is there for him."

"So, you're saying, he isn't going to do it?"

"Yes, I believe so and finding out you killed a man two years ago would perhaps change his perspective . . . So, it's best you continue to keep it on the hush."

"And shroud him with lies?"

"He never asked you if you killed anyone now, didn't he?"

"No but if he actually does ask that question."

"Look, he's gonna' have to make those decisions as a king anyway."

"As a king… not a prince and he's still very young."

"I'm just saying son but even at that age on Netron, they have to protect themselves from the evils. Evils meaning not just Dragoons but the evils all over the universe. Truthfully, we Netrons don't have mercy for the wicked."

"Even Humans…"

"My son… when my mother sent me here, I thought us Netrons had expanded on another planet and had a habit of forgetting they are only humans here. I've watched televised recordings of the iniquities in the past before their *New World Order* and I think to myself… The new world will be rendered of the wicked, but it still surges. I found it when I joined their military, the murder, the rape, the slavery it's all just like the Opposites."

Neecho took a glimpse at his father then looked at his garden once again.

"The inevitable cycle of the universe." Nealo continued.

Neecho played with the centipede allowing it to crawl all around his hand then he lets it go freely. Seconds later, he took a long sip of his coffee then said—

"I know we agreed not to bring this up again but what I did was uncalled for…"

Nealo sat silently then Neecho continued—

"I shot your comrade and it was wrong…"

"Yes, I know son, but you didn't actually shoot her, remember my suit can see through illusions. Right after I figured out it was you and not Scheel, I saw everything, it remained as an illusion for everyone else for a while though. I'm pretty sure they thought it was enchantment."

"I know that you figured that out but what I really want to tell you is… I never killed Sergeant Roscoe Scheel."

Nealo looked at him with confused face as he continued–

"One of his own just so happened to shoot him the same way you would've shot him. The shooter on the left was the one that shot him, then tried to flee—right before you came along. He didn't see me, only you and Maya did which made it awkward that you were pointing at the wall from the shooter's perspective and it was I that made your comrade survive with a miraculous recovery."

"So…? So, it just so happened that one of his own men shot him?"

"Believe it or not father. I didn't kill that man."

"Why tell me this now?"

"I figured this is the right time."

"Hm, it was utterly extreme of you Neecho and out of character to act in such a manner just to prove a point."

"Truthfully… I wanted to see the look on your face, to see that you were proud of me . . . It's evident that you weren't before I made your mission look like a hoax and my little stunt didn't even go as planned." Neecho said feeling a bit of contempt.

. . . .

"Hm… but I am proud of you son, I always was. You grew up to be a good father, you successfully brought the second Netro to life and on top of that, you successfully brought more Netron royalties, Prince Oji, Princess Tajaymae and…" Nealo said then paused.

"No . . . You always wanted me to be like you Father, you know, follow in your footsteps. You wanted me to be a soldier just like you, you hated that I wanted to just live life, being with beautiful girls and just having fun . . . You said… On planet Netron you had no choice but to be a soldier because Grandma Tella forced you. Right? She wanted you to be skilled in combat and carry to out one mission, to come to Earth. Well, now that I'm on Earth I do have a choice."

"Good, that's good son. You made a choice and that's why I'm proud of you. I gave you the initiative to do whatever you want including the things I desire you to do . . . This is what a father does while his son is advancing to be a prosperous Netron . . . In the end, you still became a manifestation of victories."

Unknown Area—

Xack, Nack, Litzy and Tajaymae arrived on the island and quickly they ran into the large bamboo trees then they reenacted some basic stealth moves they saw from movies.

"Sir. I have intruders! It looks like they exceeded the grade one defense level and on they are on the island as I speak." Shelton said.

"Well take them out!"

"Yes sir."

"Shelton."

"Yes sir?"

"Let Push help you!"

Ki-Yale landed on the island and started running forward onto the woods going about eighty miles per hour.

"Hold on, stop. Don't move." Xack said in front.

Xack stopped then drew an Apaki Sword from his right hand while Nack held his shotgun and pointed it at the large shrubs.

"What happened?" Litzy said putting up her fists and looking around.

"I heard something." Xack said.

"Hmm." Nack said.

"Don't worry, I got your back." Tajaymae said to Nack while she started collecting electrical energy from her communication device.

Complete silence for a few seconds then unexpectedly four androids switched to visible mode and appeared in a circle around them.

"How come we didn't see them Nack?!" Tajaymae said.

"It appears that the androids have an advanced analyzing ability and used that ability to subdue our contacts lenses."

"Ok, I hope the contacts doesn't explode in our eyes..." Tajaymae said.

"No that won't happen and even if that was to happen, the contacts lenses have a barrier that blocks the damaged circuits that would emit microscopic electrical currents."

"Great Nack, you're freaking awesome!"

"Thank you... I guess its one killer android for each."

"Yep or maybe more. Now everyone be on your guard, let's hit them from different directions." Xack said.

Xack started running to the opposite direction from the android while it followed him. Litzy did the same. While Tajaymae grabbed Nack then said—

"Stay with me Nack. I'll take on mine and the android for you."

"You're taking on both at a time?!" Nack said.

"Yeah. A little exercise is good." Tajaymae said.

The android gunning after Xack started analyzing him and noticed that he's an Apaki Warrior. The android quickly released an Apaki Katana like Xack's as another android arrived on the left side.

Xack stopped then turned around and vigorously threw his sword at the android with the katana. The android used the Apaki Katana in defense position then broke Xack's sword in two shattering it into pieces.

"I need a tougher sword." Xack said as he instantly created a new sword and making it denser.

The glass is then ignited with heat then he quickly ran towards the android. The android to the left released a cannon in-between its stomach then charged the cannon's beam. Xack immediately threw his new Apaki Katana at the cannon allowing it to malfunction. The armed android with the cannon on its stomach fired the blast aiming at Xack to kill him but it instead exploded while the android with the Apaki Katana ran towards Xack. Without any time to think he created another Apaki Katana in his right hand then blocked the android strike with its Apaki Katana. Xack then out maneuvered it swiftly getting behind the android's back. With the little time he had to create another glass sword he instead created over a dozen shards of heated glass and fired them onto the android's back

The android facing Litzy is analyzing her body then differentiated her jewelry which are high tech similar to military tech and highly hazardous. The android doesn't know for sure what the jewels can do yet, so it released two laser beam guns from its body. Litzy quickly detached her golden choker and two bracelets. Within seconds, the jewels quickly moved towards the android and the android shot both bracelets damaging them. The choker maneuvered its way around the laser beam shots and attached itself onto the android.

"Hmm, let's see what happens now." Litzy said with a smirk while the android immediately ceased fire and stood still.

Nack used evasive maneuvers as the android pursuing after Nack aimed at him with laser gun ready to fire. He jumped then turned around and shot the android in the abdomen with his shotgun.

Tajaymae absorbing energy from the android that is supposedly wanted to kill her.

"Almost done!" Tajaymae said.

Seconds later, she finished gaining power from her attacking Android and quickly fires a Netron Plasma Star from her hand consequently decapitating the android.

"Woah. That's more power than usual these android things hold a lot of juice!"

"Yes, now get em' Tajay!" Nack felt relieved as he blasted another android.

Push with his two fiendish coyotes Ryker and Beatrix along with Shelton exiting through the gateway bridge onto the woods where the combat is held.

"Right over here!" Push said.

Push walked up to on top of a large rock and saw Xack behind it fighting an android.

"An Apaki Warrior?" Shelton said.

"Yes, and he's the one that made me get these stitches on my body."

The two coyotes instantly galloped towards Xack and both pounced about ten feet in the air from a five feet rock.

"Agh! Agh!" Xack yelled fiercely as he sliced the android in half causing it to explode.

Beatrix landed on Xack's left shoulder from the back then bit him while Ryker bit him on the upper left arm.

Xack immediately impaled Ryker in the stomach then ripped out its innards.

"Ryker!" Beatrix shouted while jumping off then circled him while Xack is in a primate stance watching the coyote's movements preparing for him to strike.

"You can talk?"

"Yes, and I'm going to eat you alive!"

 "My creation!"

"Relax Shelton. They're plenty more where that came from."

"Yes, they are!" Shelton said as he presses a button ordering over a hundred more androids entering from the ground up in the woods.

"What the…" Xack said.

"Oh shit…" Litzy said and Tajaymae smiles.

"Hello Xackie boy!" Push said.

"Push… Should have known with these coyotes you'll be here."

"Yes, and I'm going to bring your dead body to the Mad Doctor."

Beatrix finally preceded with an attack jumping about six feet then Xack immediately gouged her throat open. Ryker bleeding out while he stared at his partner bleeding out as well. She ogled back at him then shuts her eyes and breathing her last breath. Xack killed two animals forced to fight without any true honor but only to protect their children from Push.

"These animals were forced to do your bidding . . . I have no choice but to end them."

"Ah Xackie boy, look at you out for blood and killing my pets... now you'll pay."

Suddenly, out of the sky, Ki-Yale threw an android he had got in physical contact with down to the ground. On the sidelines, another android analyzed his strength and concluded that he was a Sila Human at Mega Human Prime level.

"What?! It's that Netro kid!" Push said.

"That must be the boy you were talking about. He doesn't look so scary..."

"Don't be fooled by his appearance lad . . . He's stronger than he looks."

"I'm glad to see you again!" Xack said to Ki-Yale.

"Let's take them out." He said while his suit downloaded Xack's ability and released a heated glass katana from his hand, but his sword had a black handle.

"I'm still amazed on how your suit can download Apaki Jermayin abilities."

"Yep, I downloaded the entire three pieces of apparatus in your body... There's even more to what I can do." He said as he smirked.

"Now that's awesome!"

"Kill them all." Shelton said.

"Leave Xack to me!! His life is mine." Push ordered as he ran towards Xack with his Apaki Katana drawn.

<u>*Little Tree Ville Mayor's Office*</u>—

"I was selfish, only wanting Sagan for myself to handle... so bad that I even let my son go after him. But he wanted to anyway. I guess now, it's best only sending the kid to take him on."

"Yes . . . I could've ordered my troops to set a tracking device on him or maybe his suit would've disarmed it, so maybe I would've had troops follow him using powerful military vehicles . . . This is our best opportunity Tyson . . . meaning me and you."

"And you're trying to say?"

"What I'm trying to say that... the real reason why I came up here with Maya and check for bugs in this office as soon as I got in, is because he's one step ahead and I have to think one step ahead."

"You left your troops outside because one of them could be working for him."

"No, not one Tyson... but the entire Gigantica Army is corrupt. I don't know how he did it but he did it. The man has control of practically everything."

"The entire? That means you too."

"My computerized communication devices armory and weapons, even radios had been tapped so I tampered with it. I'm pretty sure he knows by now and if not, he'll know sooner than I think."

"He's very persistent, I think he already knows."

"I just betrayed him . . . The difference between me and these troops you see out there is that I have real vengeance for him. I'm just hoping that he fails because if not me and my family will suffer a dreadful fate by the end of this day."

THIRTY-THREE

Ki-Yale made sure of it that no one trailed him. He reviewed his surrounding of any cohorts, especially from the Gigantica Army.

Standing on the edge of a cliff, an unknown man in a high level Gigantica City police uniform observing everything. His helmet covered his face and its mechanical lenses zoomed in on the combat.

"Now fly android!" Litzy commanded, being in control of the android that tried to kill her.

Her jewels have the option to take control of both humans and robotics. The jewels are affixed to every wiring under Litzy's command using the chip in her cerebellum similar to Apaki Jermayin technology. Litzy on the android's back flying towards five other androids and despite the other androids in the way they fired their weapons at her. The android under Litzy's command dodged all the shots. She hid herself behind the android and the five other androids ceased fire then attempted to implement another attack. The android being controlled by Litzy shot at the other androids destroying three of them. The other two fathomed the friendly fire and could not utilize the self-destruct system on the deserted android as Litzy disabled it. They began to fire grenades at her then immediately she initiated an evasive maneuver and dodged the explosives.

Her android flew her down to a lower level which was about 20ft in the air while the two androids chased after her. The android with Litzy stood airborne, turned around and shot one with a beam allowing the android to fall and explode.

Litzy with her sagacious habit realized one more android is coming at her in full speed. She then jumped off of her android while the attacking android that's going full speed crashing into each other. Litzy hits the grassy terrain then body rolled from the impact of the explosion. Litzy stopped rolling and laid on her stomach with dirt on her face then she looked up and saw about eight other androids surrounding her.

"How many are these guys?!"

Tajaymae also surrounded by a dozen androids as she smiled with a lust for power in her eyes. She stood still while the dozen androids engaged her then suddenly, she eked out her striking strength and pulverized them with her plasma.

"Yeaah', agh! Agh!" Tajaymae said while punching and single handedly ripping apart every android.

At the same time, she attacked them and gained more power, adding physical strength, durability and speed.

"She is getting stronger every time she attacks them. Yes, go Tajaymae!" Nack cheered.

Nack heard a robotic sound behind him then he slowly turned around, looked up then saw an android ready to engage.

"Oh shiiit'!" Nack blurted while he tried to shoot it, but the android deactivated the shotgun with its built-in defense system.

Tajaymae saw that he needs assistance, so she blasted her Netron Plasma Star at the android's chest.

Nack turned his head back to her direction then smiled as she smiled back.

Ki-Yale fought most androids already but then shortly after, about thirty androids surrounded him.

"What?" He gasped while using an Apaki Katana slicing a few androids in pieces.

Ki-Yale tackled one android then cuts the torso in half and used his Loose Cannon dismantling more androids.

"It's like he has an endless army!" He said.

The fight between Xack and Push began to undergo a ruthless Apaki Warrior fight as Xack screamed with his Apaki Katana colliding with his.

"Ha. I see a lot of anger in you Xack!" Push strikes his katana back at Xack.

"You gave me a long string of calamities." Xack dodging Push's attacks.

"Don't tell me you just figured that out now."

"AAGH! Should have killed when I had the chance."

"Yes, but that Netro kid stopped you with his perceptive words." Push said then tittered.

"Well I'm not letting that happen again!!" He yelled.

"Such fire! You didn't have this before at the tournament. I guess the murder of Mike got you over the edge now."

"No… It was more than just Mike's death."

"It's your mother isn't it…?"

"Yes, and the many people you've killed… including Adelia."

"Adelia? I don't recall."

"Hmmph', they're both gone now, in a better place but where you're going isn't going to be so nice."

"You mean hell? Ha'! I don't mind going there."

Ki-Yale continued to fight the androids as they grew in numbers. He then realized that it's an endless amount of them approaching each time he destroys a certain number of them at once.

"There has to be a source for these androids, I can't just fight these tin cans for the rest of my life." Ki-Yale said then searched around using his Netron vision to find something that may stop the androids.

"Woah! That must be it!" He continued.

"Why you stopped fighting boy. You got tired?" Shelton spoke to himself under his breath while looking at Ki-Yale.

Ki-Yale heard what he said then turned around to look at him. He smiled at Shelton then quickly ran off instantly going a hundred miles per hour.

"Yeah, run away kid."

"Nack!" Ki-Yale hollered.

"Woah! Ki-Yale." Nack said as Tajaymae prolonged her fight with the androids.

"I know a way you can stop these things all together."

"How?" Nack asked desperately.

"Shelton has a machine that creates unlimited supply of androids within seconds in some control room."

"Aah'... I figured there was source like that."

"Yeah and I want to take you there so you can disable it. My suit can help do it but I can't take all the shine."

"Oh, you wanna' give me some glory especially when I don't have much fire power."

"Yes, that's exactly what it is Nack."

"Ha! Ok, bring me to it."

Ki-Yale picked up Nack with his arms and said.

"Sorry to man handle you like this."

"It's cool I guess."

Ki-Yale instantly ran a four hundred miles per hour.

"Woah!" Nack said surprised at Ki-Yale's speed running fast.

"There it is!" Ki-Yale said as he puts down Nack.

Nack immediately entered inside the automated control room.

"Now to find Sagan."

<u>The Kafmora residence</u>—

Neecho and Nealo prolonged their conversation about Ki-Yale and Tajaymae while being out in a secluded area. Neecho feeling worrisome as Demi entered the backyard and asked—

"Hey, have you seen Tajaymae?"

"No aah'…" Neecho said then looked at his father then continued—

"She's out with Ki-Yale."

"Ok they're out but… Where are they? The location."

"I'm not too sure of the location but Ki-Yale is at it again hunting down Sagan."

"Hm', Tajay shouldn't be out there and Ki-Yale, he's so relentless, especially after his friend got murdered by these awful people." She said.

"I agree on Tajay, her suit didn't appear on her body as yet so it's still risky, but Ki-Yale will look after her."

"Yes, he will and it's about time Sagan get what's coming to him." Nealo said.

"Is he going to…?" Demi concerned.

"No, I doubt it. Ki-Yale isn't going to make a move like that right now."

"Good, because he's only fourteen years old, he shouldn't have to endure that so early." She said.

"I'm still wary about this whole thing." Nealo said.

"No need to fret, I'm connected to them. I know the exact dangers that may occur before it occurs." Neecho said.

"And so am I but we must never underestimate the unknown possibilities."

"Demi, I need to tell you something."

She sighed then said—

"Go ahead Neecho."

"Ok, the night before I came home, I saw something… Something I wish I didn't encounter."

"And what's that?"

"Narrken."

"What?" She gasped.

"I saw a clear vision of him in a Mini-Mart but he was evading me. I tried to get a hold of him, but he vanished before I could even get close."

"And you're telling me this now…"

"I know I was trying to figure out what I really saw."

"Well then… Did you figure it out? Or did you just end up figuring out that he had a mother too?" She debated.

"I'm sorry Demi… It just spooked me that's all."

"We should be able to figure things out together Neecho and this is something serious… Maybe it was something messing with your mind."

"Or someone." Nealo added.

"My dad is experiencing visions as well."

"Yeah, it just happens out of the blue now. I don't even have to touch the book to see it anymore."

"Ok, now you're seeing visions too?"

"Yeah, this is constant…"

"Don't worry about it Demi and you too my son, I'll be ok."

"Don't worry?! No, I'm definitely worried! This is Narrken we're talking about here… what if it really was him and not a vision? . . . Huh?"

"I don't know baby I could've sworn it was him but it's . . . it's complicated."

"Complicated?" She said with an uneasy voice then continued— "This needs to be resolved. Narrken is out there and I want him back it's way too long without him."

Neecho kept quiet as she got up and walked back in the house.

After several days of astonishing intimacy an unusually young Henry Luciano and Alexis Cobar met once again, and it seems like the mutual taste for each other bloomed. As music played at medium volume he sat in her bed while Alexis sat on a hover chair that levitated to the ceiling. She moved closer to her bookshelf that's affixed to the wall as he stared at her then he laughed—

"What's making you so amused?" She asked.

"Nothing, nothing."

"No tell me, you just busted out laughing… Don't tell me you're going insane now."

"No, I'm sane. It's just that you remind me of a friend of mine who did the same thing you're doing right now except you didn't fall yet."

"Wow, you're so bad and immature. Laughing at a possible accident."

"But you love the bad immature side of me."

She chortled then grabbed the book that she wanted.

"What book is that now?" He asked.

"It's the first book my Uncle has ever given me and first book I ever read. That's when I developed a hobby." Alexis said as she hovered closer to him.

"He did a good thing. If he hadn't given you a book you probably wouldn't be so well spoken."

"Yes, and if your parents hadn't had made you, I wouldn't be with the sexiest man on Earth."

"Well my parents were very ambitious when it comes to… creating me."

"Especially with all that success." She admired.

He stood up while she remained in the hover chair and gazed into her eyes.

She smiled and said—

"Oh, I know that look too well."

"That means I'm doing something right." He said as he grabbed her by the waist and kissed her.

Alexis puts her arms around his neck then suddenly, he picked her up with his miraculous strength.

"Still can't get over how strong you are Henry." She said.

"This is what the gym does, and I don't take those Sila Human microchips either just straight regular muscle."

She grinned at him then he kisses her again while he held her body up to his abdomen. He spun her around then slumped over her bed then took his shirt off. As they made out aggressively, he subdued her to the bed then slowly kissed her neck. She quickly undressed her top before Henry made his way down to her large breasts then kissed her stomach. He gradually unbuckled his belt, unfastened his pants then took her sweatpants off then kissed her thighs teasing her as he kissed around her clitoris. At that very moment she began to release her breath as he continued to perform his marvelous sexual chemistry.

"I knew you would love that baby." He said as he went back to kissing her lips.

Henry made his way inside her thrusting his hips slowly as if he's moving to the music while she puts her arms around his back. She then turned his body to the right and pushes him close to the edge of the bed then went on top of him.

Alexis then caressed his brawny chest then made her way down to his abs. He bites his lips while she rode him steadily and enjoying every move she made.

<u>*The invisible island*</u>—

Litzy substantially back on another flying android being controlled by her mind and her jewels. She significantly had control of a few more androids behind her in the air following her to wherever she pleases to go.

"Woah! This is not happening right now." Litzy said as she saw over a hundred androids appearing in the sky.

"Oh yeah, this is my kind of party right here!" Tajaymae said looking up into the sky and seeing all those androids.

Dr. Sagan relaxed, sitting upright complimenting one of his associates Masha. A Russian young lady in her early twenties that was massaging his shoulders as he scrutinized one of his recent paintings harvested from human remains then she said—

"Thank you sir."

"Hm, you really have some skills Masha. Way better than the machines." He continued.

Ki-Yale began to hover four feet from the floor through the bridge gateway then he detected four guards armed and ready to shoot.

"Hold it right there."

"Why work for this guy huh?"

"Don't move. Stay where you are!"

"No can't do that." Ki-Yale said then stepped one foot closer.

"Fire!"

The guards all fired their guns at Ki-Yale, hitting him in the body with bullets but the shots didn't pierce him. Ki-Yale walked up to them then he demanded—

"Move."

"Agh! What kind of…?" Said one guard trembling.

Another guard went behind Ki-Yale and hits him in the back of the head but that hit didn't faze Ki-Yale. The guard started screaming in pain and said—

"What?! He's like a solid brick wall! Aagh!"

Ki-Yale walked right pass the guards.

"We should stop him."

"No man. Let him go… Maybe the Mad Doctor is finally finished after all."

Ki-Yale kept hovering then heard a small explosion from the guards. He turned around and saw all four guards blown up to pieces which came from the inside of their stomachs. Ki-Yale squinting his eyes realizing Sagan planted those bombs inside them as a repercussion when they don't follow orders without informing them. Ki-Yale gritted his fists, feeling as if he's the one to blame because he can see far more than humans but didn't even see that they were explosives in their stomachs. Either way, there wouldn't be much he could have done to get rid of them.

"No more, this has to stop."

Ki-Yale beheld Sagan upstairs in a room then instantaneously, he decided to break through the ceiling walls to the hallway. He walked up the entrance then bent the metal in half with his strength. "Oh!" Mesha responding to the sudden noise.

"Leave now! It's only me and him." Ki-Yale said with rage in his eyes, finally being in the presence of his enemy.

"Who the…?" Dr. Sagan alarmed and looking at Ki-Yale.

"Sagan." Ki-Yale said with a straight face.

Xack and Push went blow for blow from delivering their versatile swordsmanship, utilizing their Apaki Jermayin skills as they lacerated each other in many areas of their bodies.

"You think you're going to win this fight?!"

"Best believe it Xack! I'm going to slice you in half and then some!"

"You shouldn't even be fighting me. Sagan is behind this whole thing, controlling you like a puppet!"

"Sagan is the enemy I agree but he made me who I am today."

"Yeah, a worthless dog! You brought tragedies to my family and Adel . . . You really are a piece of…" Xack said while holding back tears them shook his head.

"Go ahead… Say it!"

"Hm, aagh!" Xack grunted while attacking him.

. . .

Tajaymae attacking all the androids in the air and delivering strength from her leg muscles she developed from the electrical current. She hurdled from one of the tree branches onto an android then leaped from android to android and destroying each one thus getting stronger. Litzy also assisting her and controlling a few of the androids with her jewels then she said—

"Woah Tajaymae! Why didn't I see this side of you at the tournament?!"

"I didn't have a lot of juice to feed off from like right now and right now I love it!! My plasma power is like my second stomach" Tajaymae said.

"Hm, I see."

Nack in the automated control room swiftly hacked into the system to shut down all the androids but later had slight trouble because the system was all advanced.

"Woah. This is like high level military tech. I never interfered with something like this before. Hmm, but it's still worth a try… I have to stop this!"

"There is a breach in the main control system!"—The security system alerting Shelton.

"What?! Must be that damn Netro kid. No wonder he ran away smiling at me."

Dr. Rogue Sagan gazing at Ki-Yale as he grabbed his lady servant by the wrist after she listened to Ki-Yale and started to leave. He pulled her in from of him half blocking Ki-Yale's view as Sagan cracked a smile. Masha looked back at him portraying intolerance with his extremely tight grip. Precipitously, Ki-Yale noticed he had planted a five-inch hunting knife in his hand instantly he began to charge his Loose Cannon but it was too late.

"No..." Ki-Yale grunted as Dr. Sagan stabbed his assistant in the spleen.

She screamed as Dr. Sagan jammed the knife in some more then twisted it fueling Ki-Yale's anger causing him to activate his 'Lightning KO'. He then kicked her to floor with the knife deep inside then he said—

"You must be that kid that was interfering with my plans."

"I wouldn't just call it interfering." He said as he walked up to Masha and held her up.

"Well, I succeeded in many areas."

"There's a ton of questions to why you did those things." He said then disengaged his 'Lightning KO'.

"Yes... yes, the murder of countless families, the murder of Mike, the murder of those people in Little Tree Ville and the ones fighting for their life in a hospital. This is just adding to the things that I've done before."

"Mike... he was the son of Mayor Tyson... your brother!"

"NO! HE WAS NOT! . . ." He lashed out then began to pant— "He should've been dead, somehow, he managed to escape the blaze then got the nerve to stay incognito. Tyson was possibly on Venus with his aunt the whole time while I had to deal with the aftermath."

"He had to deal with the aftermath as well..."

"Yes, and he blamed me as soon as my blood father revealed himself. I could see it in his eyes, the way he looked at me."

"But still, why so much hate? Why be so messed up? Things could've gone another way."

"People in this world do fucked up things kid and it's a never-ending cycle… You should know this."

"Oh yeah, I know this for sure."

"Your powers… Push first told me about it and to me these powers almost speak of immortality and then again he tells me you could be an alien. I didn't believe it at first, but I saw you perform some of these powers and I'm impressed. I want to know everything of these powers you possess."

Ki-Yale picked up Masha and held her in his arms then brought her out to the side of the wall away from Sagan then he said—

"I am part alien and I wouldn't say immortal. I believe I could be, but I still don't know the peak of my power yet . . . I'm a lot more powerful than a Mega Human Prime and I could destroy this whole island if I wanted to."

"Hmm… You're bluffing kid… Well you did burst through the walls like it's nothing. I still don't believe you can destroy a whole island."

"But I can. It would take a few minutes or so, but I sure can."

"That would be amazing, very amazing… You should work for me kid, show the world what you're capable of and without holding back. I'm not your real enemy… the real enemy is all of this putrid world."

"And why would I work for you?" Ki-Yale asked as he stepped closer to him.

"You don't see the truth here don't you Netro. You just don't see what the world is."

Ki-Yale looked at him then looked to the floor.

"Hmm. You know if you die here… I will easily find where you live and kill your mother, your father, General Nealo, Tajaymae and Oji… Your friends and the rest of Little Tree Ville… just with one shot!"

"How did you…?" Ki-Yale being utterly confused.

"I figured out your name... It's Ki-Yale, when I heard the police recordings after you've beaten my men to the ground. I didn't know who you were when you said your name, but I researched it and when I found you it was an unbearable. My head was spinning like never before and I couldn't comply that you were the same person but . . .."

"But?"

"Someone informed me of it and freed my mind."

"Someone informed you?"

"Yes, but that person isn't of you concern right now. It's me that you should focus on as your peril and all I need is one shot Netro, one shot!"

He changes his face to a more serious look as Sagan continued—

"Hmm, I know what you're thinking. Yes, I am... I am a piece of shit but not everyone is born a villain or a hero. The things that I have experienced when I was younger. If you were in my shoes... If you had ever functioned as my soul and seen what I saw..."

"Hm... I know... I know about of the catastrophes that your parents endured, and I know it must be hard to stomach what you witnessed."

"Then you should know that all the tragedies that I commit is still meager."

"You're insane... all those people you murdered including the ones connected to you! All that was just unnecessary death. You went for revenge and it was successful, I could almost say it was justified but the others..."

"You're a nifty kid but you still don't know how this world works. Humans live with love, lust and hatred. Love is what you start your life with, as a child you could be living life with happiness until one day, one minute, one moment and your heart is completely broken! Some may live their life not having to experience and never feel that way… So, it was my duty to become an infamy and make everyone suffer and feel the same way I felt! It's only fair Netro. I think of it as doing this world a favor."

"A favor huh?"

"Yes…" He said then smirked.

"You saw how I bonded with Mike then took it upon yourself to make me feel like how you feel knowing I have powers that can cause a lot of destruction… I'm not so easy to turn like you Sagan, I know to believe in justice… even if it means to take a life."

"Hmm… Let me introduce you to someone… her name is Ronda." Dr. Sagan said walking to get his firearm that shoots needles with all type of contaminants combined.

Ki-Yale looked at Sagan with disgust as he loads his weapon.

"I knew that beings like you were on this planet way before you revealed yourself to the Mayor. I knew way before you were born, I knew they were extraterrestrial beings still among us. After the Grainians and planet Grain, I just had that gut feeling."

"I have one question, which I really wanted to ask you."

"You can ask me anything child."

Ki-Yale paused and looked away from Dr. Sagan for a few seconds then looked back at him then begin to ask— "Did you take my brother…? Narrken?"

"Hm." He responded.

"Did you?!"

"I don't recall such a name."

"So… so, you don't know who that is?"

"Sorry to disappoint you but no, never heard of him. Was he abducted?"

"Yes… When I was seven."

"That's three years now, he's probably dead by now. I hope you're not still looking for him because if you are, then you're just wasting your time."

Ki-Yale with a staid face didn't speak for a moment while he took in Sagan's negative words.

"Hm', you know Sagan, your soul… it's completely lost and devoured by immortality."

"Correct, that's exactly what I am. Everything I did Netro, I enjoyed every bit of it, especially the murders . . . I have a collection you see, if you look at my paintings. I made the beauty of death rendered as art on these canvases."

Ki-Yale shook his head showing condemnation then Sagan continued—

"Hmm, now let's see if those videos of that I saw were true." Dr. Sagan said then suddenly, he shot six needles hitting Ki-Yale in the body and one in his right eye.

Ki-Yale unfazed as his Netron Suit does its work as he stared at Dr. Sagan with a staid face then slowly took out the needles one by one out of his body and dropping them on the floor. Revealing more of his power, he crushed the last needle which he took out of his right eye as it regenerates rapidly.

"Incredible… you should be infected and mutating by now!"

"I heard about this on the news plenty of times… the Genchi, these syringes that injects different types of diseases and infections onto the human body in which causes mutation or just instant death but me on the other hand…" He said as he walked backwards further away from Dr. Sagan.

Ki-Yale puts his right hand into a fist then continued to speak—

"I've seen you terrorize the world for a long time now. I never actually believed it, I thought it was just conspiracies that the media created to falsely show that there are still devious people such as yourself residing in this century.

Even when my granddad stepped forward to put a stop to you, I was lost by thinking everything is undiluted."

"Yes, Nealo, I bet he's an alien like you that explains why he is so agile and still so skilled as if he's still twenty years of age, especially a few years back. I wanted to murder him so badly, but I failed miserably."

"He's still the same moving person. He made moves to stop you, but you were hiding like a coward. We sort of hid ourselves as well only to conceal our abilities until I decided, I won't hide anymore . . . I revealed myself and now I'm here with you . . . When my brother was taken, I felt helpless because I couldn't stop the abductor... how pitiful and I'm a prince and one day I'll be a king of an entire planet. At first, I didn't know what that means for me exactly but now I understand, and I know what I must do."

"Hmm and here you are turning me in."

"No..."

"Hmm?"

"I'm not here to turn you in Sagan . . . I'm here to kill you."

Dr. Rogue Sagan without a word, beheld him for a few seconds then laughed and said—

"You don't have that kind of stomach kid! I've seen and heard how you are. You don't even like to think about killing a human."

"Yes, but there's no coming back from what I've witnessed." He inferred as he puts his right arm back and made his muscles, skin and entire body completely solid.

His arm shaped a ten-inch dent in the steal wall behind him just by putting his arm back, not even touching the wall.

Sagan began to step backward a bit as he is staggered with one eyebrow up then he started to hold his gun 'Ronda' aiming at him with both of his hands gripping it assuredly tight.

"Kid... there's one thing I will trade anything for."

"And what's that?"

"Is to speak with my mom and dad once more and tell them that... that I'm sorry... I'm sorry they had to be killed because of something so absurd. It's very shameful to even think that I was related to the Sagan family, but I had to embrace it, it's the only way for me to live on and accept everything."

Ki-Yale looked to the floor for a few seconds then looked at him again then said— "It wasn't your fault, and I'm sure if they were to somehow return from the dead, they would've never blamed you for what happened to them."

Sagan chuckled then said— "Mom and Dad coming back to life... that would've been something."

"Goodbye Sagan."

Ki-Yale glared at Sagan with a somber face while Dr. Sagan kept pointed his firearm 'Ronda' at him. Sagan then fired six more shots resulting the needles to break against his chest and face as if the needles hit a solid brick wall.

With no further hesitation, Ki-Yale ran twenty miles per hour towards Sagan with his right arm still pushed back preparing to punch him. Ki-Yale levitated and gets close to Sagan looking at each other face to face, then suddenly, he punched him in his face. The hit from Ki-Yale instantly impacted his brain, shattering his skull and his neck bone impacted as well. Blood viciously exploding from his mouth with his head turned to the right.

The impact from the punch also created a loud sound wave shattering the windows, glass doors and leaving a few dents in the steal walls. Saga kept a tight grip on his bio-weapon as he flew back instantaneously, through his broken glass doors that's behind him onto the large balcony, then he ultimately landed into his outdoor pool.

Assured with his decision after going through a dilemma, constructing a move barely any fourteen-year boy would courageously make in this situation. He felt he was different though, a different kind of boy who needed to make this choice. Now he must live with this enactment from this moment on and he's blissful that he's obliged to do so without any consequences. He walked up to the balcony edge and ogling over Sagan, slain by his fist in the outdoor pool full of blood.

THIRTY-FOUR

"No doubt about it. You were trained a little by my father, but you see. My father was way better than his friend that trained you. It took me a while to study your moves, but I can finally dance around you." Xack said as he dodges and blocks every strike Push gave him with his Apaki Katana.

"Ragh'! Ragh'! Stay still!" Push frustrated shooting heated sharp glasslike pieces out of his sword towards Xack.

Xack miraculously blocked all the attacks that Push gave him then he moved forward towards Push while dodging every sharp pieces of Push's sword. Xack quickly swung his Apaki Katana towards Push then paused mid attack to Push's neck.

"Look at that… I could've caught you right there. I don't know Push! I think you're getting sloppy!" He said.

"Shut up!" Push yelled absorbing the embarrassment as he swung rapidly toward Xack but still didn't catch him not even once.

Xack walking backwards and dodging his attacks once again. Feeling overconfident in his moves, Xack backed into a tree behind him and instantly got shot with a heated piece of glass coming from Push's sword. He was aiming for his heart but missed and shot the piece of glass in his left shoulder.

He held his shoulder enduring the pain and brings his head down as Push lifted his Apaki Katana, seeking to decapitate his rival.

"It's time to die!"

With quick thinking, Xack maneuvered to Push's left side of his body then sliced open his stomach causing his guts to burst out.

"Aaah'! Ugh'! Ugh'!" Push in dreaded pain as he looked down on his stomach and saw his insides hanging out.

Push immediately disarmed his glass katana knowing that he's been beaten and held his stomach with blood gushing out rapidly. Push looked at Xack with a surprised and startled expression.

"Yes, that's the look I wanted to see . . . I learned a lot from you Push. You're strong but all I needed was skill, the skills I embodied as an Apaki Warrior. Now, I will cherish this moment and make the world a better place by putting an end to you." Xack paused then continued— "That was for my mother… and this… This is for Adel!"

Suddenly, he aggressively stabbed Push's throat with the heated glass sword connecting upward to his skull. As he abided the long-awaited slaughter, Xack stood vexed while he ogled into his eyes, then he withdrew his Apaki Katana out of him.

Xack kept the face of no remorse as he moved to the side then instantly, Push fell frontward to the ground as the steam came from the severed areas of his body.

Meanwhile—

Ki-Yale went back out in the woods with the assistant that had gotten stabbed, he treated her to a first aid kit wrapping the wound with the knife still inside to slowdown the bleeding. As she is unconscious, he positioned her to sit up straight on a tree to slow the blood flow then he looked upward to the right of him.

Tajaymae on an android's back with her legs wrapped around the thrusters in the back of the android's body. She used her fists and punched open the androids back then collected more power as the android began to malfunction and fall from the sky. Litzy is riding on an android's back that's being controlled by her and she used the android to catch Tajaymae from falling to the ground.

"I see that you can go on fighting these things all day but I'm running out of jewels to use." Litzy said.

"Yeah I'm loving this but I'm beginning to get full and once I'm full I can't consume anymore energy for about two hours unless I use it all on the androids then I'll be able consume more if I want... So basically, this is an endless fight for me." Tajaymae said.

"Well I don't wanna' fight all day. I want to end this and there must be a source for these things. A machine that's creating these things as we speak."

"Yeah but where is it?" Tajaymae said as Litzy ordered the android, she is controlling let her go onto an attacking android.

Tajaymae used her plasma around her hands dismantling up the android into pieces. Litzy got hit by another android then she ordered her android to elude so that the attacking one can chase her. The attacking android indeed chased her around in the air while a few more followed behind it. Tajaymae jumped off Litzy's android falling to the ground then hits a bamboo tree and body rolled down in between three other bamboo trees.

She lastly hits the ground then slowly gets back up unfazed by the impact. Tajaymae smiled as her hands had a purple glow then started running up on a bamboo tree and instantly jumps off into the air catching one of the androids going after Litzy.

Nack in the control room still figuring out how to disarm the machine creating the androids.

"Ok, most of this wiring is unfamiliar but if I can at least find the motherboard… hm." Nack said.

"Boy, you got some nerve fucking with my equipment!" Shelton barked at him while pointing an illegal Fed gun.

"Oh no…" Nack frightened as he looked at Shelton. — "Oh yes. Seems like you must be the brains that your comrades trust to dismantle my invention?"

"Yeah you can put it like that."

"You got brains but, in this case, you need brawn."

With little time to think, he took out a small device that he created. Suddenly, a tiny holographic screen appeared then with just one touch on the screen the gun in Shelton's hand got disarmed.

"No gun, no brawn." Nack said.

"What? What did you do to my firearm? Mmm' no matter… I can still beat your ass kid."

"Not while I'm here."

The unknown man in a Gigantica police uniform spoke then elbowed Shelton in the back of his head and knocking him out.

"Who the hell are you?"

The unknown man opened his automated helmet and instantly Nack goggled.

"Father?"— "Yes my son I'm here."

Missing his father Solomon Yaldara, after parting ways for six months. He ran up to him and hugged him while Solomon thought of almost regretting that he sent him away for school in LTV.

"Dad, I'm so glad to see you."

"So am I son..."— "What are you doing here?"— "Could have asked the same for you, being in this kind of danger. If your mother found out about this, you would be in huge trouble."

"I know but I had to help my friend although he could do it all by himself, I felt that I needed to be a part of Sagan's take down."

"Hmm, I see. Well good thing I followed you and saved your ass."— "How exactly did you follow me?"— "I remembered you spoke about this Netro kid and his powers... well I did some calculations and figured I stood at a certain distance inside a police base up in the skies. I knew if I stood too close to him, he would spot me with his enhanced vision."

"I see, then you waited until Netro reached this island with me on it then landed here."

"Yes, and more authorities should arrive in any minute now... hmm, this must be the control room for the androids." His father said as he handcuffed Shelton.

"Yeah, I would just break everything, but this machine may have a backup system in which the machine would just keep creating more. Plus, this is higher level tech than what I learned in school or even studied at home. Try your suit Dad, maybe it can diagnose the mechanism."

"Hm, let me see what I can do here . . . it's been a while son, solving things together. This moment already brings back memories."

"Yeah Dad... woah'... wait, I think I found something . . . ok, here goes." Nack said with his hand inside the machine. "Shit, be careful son..."

Seconds later, the machine stopped entirely, and the androids are no longer being created.

Litzy using the android she had command over to blast at the other attacking allied androids. Tajaymae impressively jumping from android to android destroying each one then Litzy holding her own until she is seconds away from being ambushed and she is down to just one jewel left and that one jewel is being used for the control of the android she is riding on.

"I'm coming for you Litzy. Hang tight!" Tajaymae yelled.

One of the androids punched Tajaymae in the face allowing her to lose balance while she was on an android. As she falls down heading to the ground again with her arms swinging up and down then suddenly, Ki-Yale grabbed her.

"What's up sis?"

"Brother." Tajaymae said as she smiled luminously.

"Let's stop these droids." Ki-Yale said as he flew towards the android trying to ambush Litzy.

"Drop me on one!"

Ki-Yale dropped his sister on an android then she began to rip them apart. Ki-Yale also destroyed some androids using his 'Loose Cannon' from his right arm hastily as if it were an assault rifle built in his right arm then flew closer to Litzy. Litzy looked back and marveled in her strong Hispanic accent—"Netro."

"Miss me?" He asked as he puts his hand out for Litzy to hold while flying.

"Oh, hell yeah!" She chirped.

"I'm guessing that you're controlling that thing?"

"Yes, thanks to my jewels but I'm running out."

"Ok, I'll take it from here."

Litzy separated her last mechanical jewel from the android and instantly the android is back to normal. Ki-Yale picks up Litzy and used his Loose Cannon to deftly destroy the android.

Tajaymae finished destroying the rest of the androids and falls to the ground again.

"Whelp. I hope I at least land on a few trees again..." Tajaymae said while folding her arms.

Ki-Yale appeared beside her then held his sister up while holding Litzy with his arms. He then saw Nack and his father out the woods near a structure which is the control room then began to land next to them.

"Looks like thats the last of them. You stopped the machine Nack?" Ki-Yale asked.

"Yep, all thanks to me... and a little help from my father."

"Woah, Mr. Yaldara, it's been a long time..."— "Hey what's Ki... aagh' my head! My head! What the hell is going on!?"

Solomon complying with the effects of the Netron Suit because Nack told him that Ki-Yale is Netro. He changed his suit for him to see then changed back to his suit. "Ok, hold on..."— "You ok Dad?"— "Yeah, aagh'... I'm good. That was so weird."

"Yea, it's the suit but, thanks to everyone for helping me here." Ki-Yale expressed gratitude.

"Ha, you could have done it all by yourself but hey, you're welcome." Nack said.

"What happened to Xack?" He asked turning around searching for him then precipitously Xack appeared out of from the scrubs. "You can't just get all the bad guys for yourself man."

Ki-Yale smiled then said— "Xack, there you are, you look completely beat."

"Aagh, yeah but I'm fine, I'm an Apaki Warrior... so butchery is bound to happen."

"Hey ah... Where's Sagan?" Litzy asked.

"Did you knock him out?" Nack asked.

Silence in the air for a moment as Ki-Yale ogled at the ground then looks up at everyone.

"Sagan... Sagan is no more."

"Woah, bro... you...?" Tajaymae asked.

Ki-Yale shook his head up and down and said—

"Yes... I killed Sagan."

"Woah..." Litzy said.

"I never slain anyone before, and it already feels like a nightmare but at the same time I'm . . . I'm actually satisfied..."

"I feel the same way you feel right now but I say it's worth it."— "Push..."— "Yeah, I dealt with him as well..."

"Hmm', in all honesty, I'm glad you made that move kid, it's about time someone stopped him..." Solomon added.

Ki-Yale kept an impassive facial expression while looking at Litzy for a moment then she smiled and nodded her head. He slightly smiled back then Nack asked—

"What about her? Is she ok? She's just been sitting by this tree with her head down."

"That's his assistant that he stabbed."

"I already called for medical assistance." Solomon said— "Good, we need get back to LTV and..." Ki-Yale mentioned then paused and tilted his head to the ground for a second. He then looked up, glaring at the sky for a moment.

"You ok brother?"

"LTV... Oji... Mom . . . He said he can do it in 'one shot'." He quoted what Sagan said to him earlier.

"One shot? What does that mean?" Nack asked.

"The Heaven Bolt!" Ki-Yale gasped.

"The what?" Xack queried.

"Wait, Ki... What about the Heaven Bolt?" Nack asked.

"I think Sagan might be using it..."

"Oh no... that's really not good..." Litzy said.

Ki-Yale looked back up to the sky then lifted himself off the ground and instantly he went six thousand miles per hour in the sky.

The wind blew heavily around them as they put their hands in front of their faces to protect themselves from the oncoming dirt.

The Heaven Bolt is the military space weapon that orbits the Earth. Every planet has it, these guns are the weapons specially designed for attacks inflicted by the Grainians or any other alien race and also used to defend an enemy from entering. The weapon shoots advanced nuclear missiles that can contain different types of warhead identities from previous wars. The missiles can withstand the vacuums of space, the compressed gas in the atmosphere and can be disarmed mid shot when the missile is still in space and not reaching the Earth's gravitational pull. These weapons are mostly used as a last result when such a threat is on the planet itself.

Dr. Rogue Sagan, even when he's defeated his schemes somehow find its way. He wanted to guarantee a never-ending ruin. Speaking with an unknown source and even finding out the partially intangible, Ki-Yale's family. An intelligent mind now imminent to a complete end, his underhanded agonizing soul vanquished from the Earth. His pool filled with his blood that fled from his face. Milder than a severe concussion, this is an injury no man can ever come back from. His deceased body sank to the bottom of the pool as carrion crows stood on top light poles and trees surrounding the pool. 'Ronda' had been cracked when he landed to the bottom initiating a breach. The Genchi had escaped the bio-weapon and effects coursed through his system. Leisurely decaying of his skin, flesh and bones stirring up an appetite. They ponder and wait, until the final corners of his lungs and entire body were yielded by water. His lifeless body escalated to the top, floating along his pool. The carrion crows cooed, cawed, rattled and clacked expressing satisfaction of finally getting the chance to feast on a new dead body.

Eastern Sentry Space Station—

The alarm is going off and alerting all the soldiers inside the facility.

"Sir, it's the big gun. It's scheduled to launch in T-minus three minutes, and we can't... We can't seem to stop it! Someone or something had overridden the system!"

"What?! Then, shut down the breakers!"

"We tried that sir and nothing is happening."

"Sir, even the Earth's shield is open."

"Where is it headed?"

"Gel Hev..."

"Shit... How many percentages in the shot?"

"One hundred percent sir."

"That's enough to wipe out the entire Gel Hev and even more."

"Sir, the Gigantica main base isn't responding. Neither is any of the stations... All airwaves are down connected to this station."

"Shit! Shut everything down!!"

"We're trying everything sir!"

The countdown until missile fire is at one minute as Ki-Yale entered the atmosphere.

The Heaven Bolt, filled with enormous power, a combination of nuclear projectiles and shooting radioactive nuclear beams. Over a million parts were working well, as the agents in the space station hope for a malfunction. Four agents who are specialists strictly for astrodynamics and aeronautical engineering, swiftly situated their space suits to go to the core of the gun to manually disarm it. As the chamber's exit gate took its ordinary time to open and releasing the air.

"Oh no…"

The Heaven Bolt fired its nuclear warhead with a beam following the projectile as Ki-Yale flew through the layers of Earth being unburnt because of his suit being able to adapt to any temperature. The sound waves of the loud fire impacted the agents as they exited the space station too late. The missile entered through the open barrier and the thermosphere then tersely the nuclear warhead collided with Ki-Yale causing a massive explosion. He then underwent an additional impact from the beam that was following the projectile causing another large explosion. The space station previously primed its shield with the engineers who exited were just inside the barricade. Loud sounds with shockwaves expanding, the pressures in a narrow region traveling through a medium and shaking the space station. Brief static came from the computers as the captain bewilderingly gazed at the blast.

"What just happened?" He queried.

"That was fucking close."

No serious harm was done to the station, as the agents rejoiced on behalf of the missile and the beam not reaching the Earth's surface.

<u>*The Kafmora residence—*</u>

"I wish I was over there fighting with Ki-Yale." Oji said as he randomly walked out to the yard.

"I know you do son but what good is it if you don't know how to use your powers properly . . . Yet."

"Mmm'… I guess you're right Dad."

"Now Oji go back inside with your mother so I and your dad can chat in peace."

Oji mocked his grandfather then Nealo continued—
"Raagh'! I'm the giant wale and I'm going to eat you alive!
Raagh'!"

Neecho looked to the side and sensed that something
isn't right. He looked up to the sky and said— "Ki-Yale…"

"Where Dad? I don't see him."

"Stay here with grandpa." Neecho demanded then he
accelerated off the ground while changing into his Netron
Suit.

Ki-Yale descending rapidly from the massive explosion
as Neecho soaring at immense speeds, entering the
atmosphere and saw his son falling out of the large cloud of
smoke. He caught him, realizing that he is unconscious, and
his body is damaged all around. His Netron Suit then slowly
regenerating his wounds, abnormally slower than usual
while his father is bringing him back down to the surface.

"Look at you… playing the hero." Neecho said.

<u>*The next day Machida Bar Little Tree Ville*</u>—

Victory arose, the joy of triumph drifted with the crowd of
customers inside the bar as they all watched the news and
celebrated.

"Today is a new day everyone! As Dr. Rogue Sagan is
found deceased on an invisible island that he had created
along with illegal operatives over the years and was secretly
concealed. His death was said to be inflicted by the
fourteen-year-old half alien boy called 'Netro'. Shortly after,
The Heaven Bolt was launched which leads to the
investigation involved with the captain of the Eastern
Sentry Space Station and any military agents connected to
Sagan."

Xack Machida with wrapped bandages around his body
sitting on a chair next to his father.

"I never knew I would actually see the day." Fang said.

"Because you just never believe he would be stopped."

"True . . . You did a good job son. You and that alien kid. I'm proud of you but trusting an alien around you is not a wise choice." He said as he patted his son's shoulder.

"I know Father but he's harmless and he only fights for a good cause."

"He still murdered a human and at that age tells me things might turn for the worst."

"Hm, . . . we'll see what happens." Xack said then he took a glimpse at Adelia's favorite burgundy headband in his right hand then smiled.

THIRTY-FIVE

Two months later, after the slaying of the Mad Doctor and the death of Mike Roland, wonders erupted wildly about a mere boy who performed such bizarre feats. Little Tree Ville is now back to its regular life. No more contaminants infested around the village, the trees are all diminutive again and still a beautiful place where tourists can adore the scenery. Ki-Yale made a huge impact on his village as the half alien hero who bloomed across the world then the solar system. Even the current P.O.T.W, Blane Nixon Moor Jr. looked at Ki-Yale as a hero and congratulated him on the defeat of Dr. Sagan and rewarded him access to stay on Earth.

Many underground operatives were detained along with the military, law enforcement and many other secretive individuals working for him. Explosive chips that were placed inside the victims of Sagan's unbearable leverage and cunning devious tactics were detached. The unknown bizarre technology was found and handed to the Clandestine Extraterrestrial Unit for examinations. Ever since Ki-Yale made one of the biggest decisions in his life to take another life, he saw the world differently, he saw that it constantly needs a hero not just a ruler but deep down in his heart he feels like he should be the leader of Earth more than a hero because of his nature of becoming a king.

After the death of Dr. Rogue Sagan, people witnessed what Ki-Yale can do through recordings from the security cameras that was specially designed for the invisible island. Even from the audience with camera devices back at the Crouton Village Tournament. Although Ki-Yale displayed clemency at the tournament, some people still look at him as an ultimate threat. An ultimate threat that can wreak havoc amongst the human race, especially after he executed the man most people are afraid of.

Regime operations, Clandestine Extraterrestrial Unit obtaining unknown technology and reviewed recorded surveillance on the invisible island of Ki-Yale and his abilities. With their multidimensional equipment, enhanced megapixel camera and photo editing software rearranging each possibilities of fraudulent recital, but they picked up nothing of such. Dunkin Turd strapped to a hover chair as they asked him questions.

"Several sightings with you and the boy…"

"I don't know what you're chitchatting about…"

"Mister… aah'… Turd… you really should change that name, it's really hard to function with such silly monikers."

"Silly moniker?! My name is very precious to me and I'll carry it till the day I die. My parents named me, and they loved me very much."

"Hm', very passionate… Now, tell me what you know about the boy."

"Well, ok I'll tell you…"

He paused and gawked at the CEU agent.

"Ok go on…"

"Ok, he's a very peculiar one as you can see…"

"Yeah, yeah we know. He says he's partially another being."

"Yes, you see… he isn't really a boy…"

"Hm?"— "Yea, he's actually a woman in a little boy's body and he got…" He said moving closer to agent then whispered— "He's got four rows of three tits. Not two but three man… ain't that crazy."

"Aaalright', you're just fucking around here."

"No, no I'm being for real."

"Yeah ok and I bet he got five dicks too."

"Oh man, as a matter a fact…"— "Ok, I'm done with you." The agent said then proceeded to the exit.

"So, am I gonna' get out of here now?"

"Not till I get some truth out of you.'

Crouton Village—

The asphalt, the terra firma covered now in large bales of snow. It's that time year again in Gel Hev, winter gear and obtaining warmth at any given time. Riding through the sky in an air van Vince Harven with a new purpose. Ever since he lost the trust he had with his son; Vince is now looked at as an enemy. Max hasn't been home ever since the incident. His absence caused suspicion of a possible abduction but that was just to cover the fact that he's scowled with numbed adoration. Autopilot initiated, roving onto the drop zone as the vehicle faces some strong wind.

Arriving at the drop zone, he exited the air van plummeting from about 3,000 feet in the air. A simple notion using his experienced skydiving to release his parachute, formerly paragliding until he landed. Vince pulling out his rifle and sprinting towards the facility were his targets are, Sally and her lady crew.

"Ma'am we have stumbled upon an intruder, a man."

"Bring him in."

Two lady guards brought Vince into Sally's room manacled with stolen police tech. "Oh it's you."

"Here I am…"

She closed her eyes as her crew mused on to why she did that and not knowing that Vince is a Death Angel.

"Yes… here you are, armed… I'm presuming you attempted to throttle upon me and my guards."

"As you can see, I didn't fire a single shot."

"So, you've come to do business?" She asked mockingly.

"Yeah, you can say that, but I have one question for you… Why close your eyes and not inform your little squad to do the same?"

Sally smirked as some of her members suspected him to be a Death Angel and closed their eyes then she said—

"Because I don't give two fucks about these thots…" Some were still confused then she continued— "It's just funny how you would be here when our connections were cut weeks ago."

"Make sure all of your eyes are covered!" One of the guards yelled.

"It's the different principles Sally, you're heartless and stood under his command and I was heartless because I didn't have a choice."

His face in confusion while Vince remained kneeling to the floor and being restrained.

"What are you gonna' do? Kill me? I'm sure it's me you want."

"Yes, you are now the last of the six that raped my son."

"So, it was you that offed my girls…"

Vince smiled then his sclera exposed red veins sprouting to his pupils which had shortened and revealing a half centimeter Tektonian Crystal in his mouth with a strange aura around his body, white flames blazed from his shackled hands.

One guard opened her eyes and was instantly stunned. "Oh shit…"

Another guard opened her eyes and said— "No that's the…"

"Mazemka!" Vince blurted his attack as the bleached flames ruptured through the guards in front of him. The guards in agony as their bones disintegrated, then their flesh and skin liquefied to the floor.

Sally with her eyes still closed aimed her illegal Fed gun at him then abruptly she dropped it. Her eyes changed to an orange color and her skin became pale bearing an unusual appearance. Vince ceased his attack, pondering to himself. *"Did I do that?"*

Her body proceeded to mutate growing and screeching harshly as if she's a wild beast.

"No…" He figured it wasn't his doing and summoned his Tantu Orb and instantly the mutation ceased. Her eyes ogled upon the orb and as she treaded towards it.

"What the hell are you?"

He witnessed an undone transformation of something he had never seen before. She didn't fully transform because she consumed the Tantu Orb. Her body is now lifeless as she tumbled down to the floor.

"If it wasn't for my orb, I would've seen something beastly."

Little Tree Ville, Mayor's Office—

Tyson and Stacey buried what's leftover of their son, the Gazen Weapon. Being within a room once more, sharing each other's presence. Tyson stood by his window witnessing his village being overthrown by snow. She stood beside him with her hands folded.

"It was difficult… it was difficult for me to choose whether I wanted to tell him that you were alive when he was at the tournament or when he comes back home."

He walked to his chair and sat down then continued—

"I still believe he's out there and he's just going to burst through that door at any minute. I should've never let him go… now you didn't even get to see him again…"

He clenched his fists while his body quivered.

"It's not your fault Tyson…"

She placed her hand on his shoulder. "I just wish I get to see him again after those mistakes I made."

The Kafmora residence—

Another family gathering, Demi cooks food to last a week while her children wait for their cousins to arrive.

"Atsu Okeke is at your door, Atsu Okeke is at your door." Said the automated system

Oji ran to the door and opened it.

"Uncle Atsu!! Auntie Uma!!"

"Aaye' lil' guy." Atsu said picking him up. Oji looked over his uncle's shoulder and saw his two cousins, an eleven-year-old boy, Berko Okeke and an eight-year-old girl, Ebele Okeke.

"Berko and Ebele!" He gushed after Atsu puts him down.

"Oji!" Ebele blurted. "It's been a long time Oji." Berko said.

"Hey there young man." Grandpa Omari said standing firm and being at age 52.

"GRANDPA!"

"Oh Atsu, look at you with all this meat in your bones."

"I know, I know I'm getting bloated, after eating your food I'll become an elephant." He said giving his sister a hug.

"Hey Uma."— "Sorry, we're late with the pumpkin pie."

"It's cool, you're all here just in time."

"Uncle and auntie!" Tajaymae said running towards them. "Tajay!"

"Hey, my little purple haired beauty." Uma said.

"Tajay, come say hi to Berko and Ebele." Oji said.

"Now where's your little prince Ki-Yale and Neecho."

"He's on the roof with his girlfriend, I'll go call him and Neecho is with his father in the training room."

Up on the rooftop, Ki-Yale and Litzy sat close to each other while holding hands tightly with fingers interlocked and watching a documentary through a holographic screen projected from their contact lenses. Both had one plate of sliced Lemon Blueberry Yogart Bread. Titus ate a piece of the Yogart Bread as he sits by Ki-Yale who has his left hand resting on the back of his head. The roof top is covered by a round weatherproof barrier with a heating system that's big enough to hold two vehicles and is emitted from a mechanical cube. It also has a heating system and cooling system.

Titus's stomach rumbled then Ki-Yale hands him the rest of the Yogart Bread.

"Does Titus ever do anything besides eat, shit and sleep? He's like a slothful little baby."

Titus roared in response to her comment then Ki-Yale said—

"He was energetic but now he just loves books. He's big now and my mom is more scared of him, especially when he's walking around the house."

"Hmm… That's why you keep him in a cage…"

He kept quiet for a moment then said—

"Hey Litzy…"— "Yes, Netro."

He pressed a button on his long sleeve shirt to pause the projection coming from his contact lenses which made her attention more on him.

"We haven't spoken about what I did to Sagan."

"You stopped him and that's all we been talking about."

"No, I'm talking about what I did to him, I murdered him. I did something I never even dreamed of doing... It happened so fast and... and now I just... I don't feel any remorse."

"I hate to sound like this but... he needed it. He's been causing mayhem for way too long and what you did impacted many lives. Netro... people look at you as a hero now."

"Not everyone, I'm sure they're people out there that's scared of me."

"Well that's good in some way for criminals."

"So, you're saying I should fight crime?"

"Yeah and help bring that crime rate back to a minimum again. You already took down the chief of crime, now to clean up the rest. Well, put them behind bars."

"You're right, it's a lot that needs to be done."

"Especially finding your brother, the one goal you always wanted to accomplish."

"Yeah..."

"Yeah so don't be discouraged, things happen for a reason and this is a good one."

Ki-Yale looked at her and nods his head slowly while giving a light smile.

—In the training room, Neecho and Nealo are boxing once more then Atsu stepped in the room.

"Even till this day it's hard to believe my sister married an actual alien."

"And conceived children as well." Nealo added while hitting the heavy weighted punching bag.

"It's just true love guys, true love."

"That's good, taking on many things, partners acting as one. I remember all the crazy situations you and my sister went through and one thing I could never forget... is that smile she has when she's around you."

Neecho smirked at Atsu responding to his statement then said— "I've seen a difference in the past few weeks though."

"Yes, the move that Ki-Yale made… she doesn't agree as much. It even took me by surprise as well."

"She thinks it's a little too early for him to make decisions like that. I said the same thing, but I read his mind for the first time and… I saw his true thoughts; I saw that he really wanted to put an end to him. I believed that he wouldn't but…"

"But instead he actually did…"

"Yeah, I kind of regret making him go after Sagan."

"Hm, to be honest with you Neecho… I'm glad as the many people out there who dreamed of that day to come."

—

"Ki-Yale! Come down and say hi to your relatives!" Demi spoke through the hologram projecting from his clothes.

"Yes Ma, I'm coming."

<u>*Shale residence, Gel Hev*</u>—

Luka Shale Jr., sat in his living room contemplating, worried about his life and where it's heading. As the weeks passed by, his daughter had moved out, found a new girlfriend and things still hasn't turned out for the better with his wife Pamela. Pamela Shale has been in traumatic phases ever since she confessed to killing her own daughter as doctors try to cure her, but things got worse. Outbursts, tantrums and overall unusual behavior has led her to stay in the Gel Hev Asylum.

Luka contemplated to himself as he recalled a collapse with the marketing of *Apex Nanochip* at the same time he debunked Henry Luciano and his way of living. Secrets were kept with him as he sits free in his home, no law enforcement trying to crack a case with his name in it. Luka thought ahead of almost any failure, but he isn't perfect as grey areas and answers are still unanswered till this day.

He took a pull of his e-cigarette then abruptly, the door rings.

"An unidentified person is at your door." Said the automated security system.

Luka picks up his registered Fed gun and puts it behind his back then walked up the door to open it.

"I've been waiting a while for this Luka… You murdered my wife!!"

"What?"

"I got it from an inside source so don't play games with me. She would tell me everything about the project and the personnel around her. After years I finally came to a decision and found it was you… it was you Luka!"

"Miranda Harris…"

"Yes, and you're going to pay for that!" He said as he released an illegal Fed gun and pointed it at Luka.

"Look I have nothing to do with her murder!"

"That's what they all say… you left her to die in pieces! You fucking ate her alive! You fucking wild anima…"

His sentence was cut short from a bullet that came from behind Luka hitting the man's face in the mask.

Luka turned around and grasped that it was Malik Stenson that had shot him.

"Hm, thanks…"

He turned back around then took off the man's mask after he fell backwards.

"Dane Harris. Unsolved murder of his wife . . . of course he would think it's me and now that the big man is out of the picture… dolts run wild." He paused then said—

"Help me lift him up, I'll have to burn this body."

Luka Shale Tech & Co. Hangar, Gel Hev—

Luka Shale Jr. partaking in a gathering with his associates discussing new ways of underground profit.

"Patience is a virtue."

"Yes, it is Luka but the question I would love to ask is… Are you sure you want to do this?"

"I'm absolutely sure… Everything here would be a fine asset to my name, well, without the authorities involved of course."

"You ain't soft no more Luka, I love this new you man."

"People change…"

"What happened to your right-hand man? Henry?"

"We don't speak anymore. Haven't seen him since Sagan was slain."

"Shit… friends come and go huh?"

"Yes. I agree on that very much…" Luka said as he walked to a large iron cargo container then he continued to speak— "Friends do come and go."

Impulsively, the sound of Tektonium metal exoskeleton from the feet bottom up to the head hits the floor as Malik Stenson walked out from behind the large iron cargo container. He wears a metal headpiece around his forehead covering his bullet hole which contained tiny Tektonian Crystals in the middle that can allow him to activate his enchantment.

"It's the Kleaner..."

"Oh, you know him already."

The men began to fire their guns at Malik, but the bullets didn't faze him as the Tektonium exoskeleton all around his body emits unlimited amount of Tektonium liquid. Malik didn't speak, he just expressed a face with blood lust in his eyes.

With no hesitation using his enchantment, a white colored flame erupted from his hands which is called the 'Mazemka Blaze' or some would call it the 'White Fire'.

This ability that is only used by Death Angels only burns the victim's bones until it becomes nothing and can also be obscure to the naked eye at the user's request. Since the fire only burns a species bones it can travel through anything as if it's a ghost with a certain distance depending how strong the user is.

All of the men's bones were disintegrated with only the flesh and skin left causing their bodies to look like slime.

<u>*Two hours later at LTV Catholic Church*</u> —

Luka arrived with in a limousine and told Malik to stay in the vehicle. His butler opened the door then he got out and fixed his suit jacket. He nods his head then walked inside the church.

"Bless me father for I have sinned . . . this is my first ever confession . . . After years of seeking guidance to a life free from sin. I pray day and night for a better world until I decided to . . .."

"Decided to do what?"

"Give up on the Lord above us, I was once sacred and devotional. Now I've done things to shame him and it's getting worse."

"Whatever sins that you wish to confess, don't hold back, don't be scared to let loose Luka."

"My father . . . my father would always say to me . . . 'The things you do in life will reflect in the future'. As simple as that sounds, he would never stop stressing it to me, telling me that I can't control the future and the things I do now would be in the past. I wasn't into the inventions that he made, I wasn't into the businesslike culture and I was never driven by the thought of being successful. All I ever wanted was a life of happiness until one day he came to me and sat down next to me. He said to me... 'Love is what creates true happiness... not only success with wealth and if happiness is what you don't have now then happiness shall be your only success in life before anything else.' I looked at him then I smiled . . . then he smiled back as if he knew that would be the last time, he smiled at me. I took over the undertaking of fulfilling his success and my success of complete happiness. I promised myself I would do whatever it takes to achieve it, even excluding my beliefs and following false teachings."

"And now you have found a different path?"

"Yes. I've found my own path and I'm sticking to it."

"Following more than one belief isn't going to get you where you truly should go."

"I still only believe in one..."

"Hmm?"

"And that's myself."

Planet Mars—

Approximate year on Earth is 2322, however Mars has a different time frame, which is year 307. Within the neighborhoods of Token City, Mercy, a murder case is being investigated.

"Alexus Cobar, age twenty-six, aiming for a degree in Social Work. From what I've seen here, it looks to be like bite marks from a creature eating pieces of her body all around. Possible forced objects with heat, from my analysis it appears that her insides have melted . . . My hypothesis is that this could be self-inflicted with a vicious dog involved. Hm, her parents were reluctant about suicide but it's mostly the ones that you least expected it from." Detective Flare Kennedy said.

"Nah, this looks more like carborane acid, sulfuric acid or just some kind of fluid that ate her insides. Yes, the lesions were triggered by some sort of fluid eating the flesh, the main damaged area is in the vaginal passage and I'm just blazing out things here... I say it's possibly some sort of acidic sperm cells." Detective Moja Wyser said in his vocal fry tone.

"Acidic sperm cells? . . . Like really? Who comes up with this shit?! And Dude… What the hell you doing here?! This is my case!"

"I analyzed the body first and as you can see; I developed the better possible solutions... C'mon you mixed up suicide with a dog eating her."

"Yeah, whatever . . . You want to share this case? Fine. Let's share this case but I'll assure you it's going to be at my station."

"That's fine, you aren't too far from me."

"Anyway, our killer here was very sloppy usually in this era, we don't get this a lot for a murder, but we still use protocol. Fingerprint… this man goes by the name Henry Luciano lives on 805-566 Gale Street in Seven Tens City, Ranomia."

"You knew that shit all this time huh?"

"You got to waste a little time once in a while you know."

"You're a piece of work Flare. You know that?"

Thirty minutes later—

Henry Luciano in his younger form with the same hairstyle, wearing the same outfit that he met Alexis with. The full black silk tuxedo with black shoes, black gloves black shirt with a red bow tie and red handkerchief. He was at his domain with his hands folded behind his back looking through his window, staring at the beautiful view of Seven Tens City residing in Mercy, Section 41 which is a popular place on Mars.

All of a sudden, his door is alerting him about two detectives outside his doorstep. Henry didn't answer forcing the two detectives to break in. Detective Moja and Detective Flare used a police device wiring the door to open. They became armed with their Fed guns and started aiming inside the hallway looking for Henry.

"Hello?! Is Henry Luciano here?!" Flare probed.

"We just need to talk!" Moja yelled.

"My censor has body movement in the next room to the left. . . Ok now, he could be armed so move wisely."

"Been doing this for a long-time brother." Moja said as both detectives move tactically into the next room then they saw Henry standing at his window and looking outside.

"Hands where we can see em'! Now!"

"Hm." Henry muttered without moving an inch.

"I don't want to say this agai…" Moja said then instantly pausing.

"You alright man…" Flare said noticing that he seemed paralyzed then continued to speak—

"Moja! Yo, Moja!"

Flare waved his hand around his face after he puts his Fed gun down but nothing on Moja's face moved or flinched.

"What did you do to him?!" Flare yelled pointing the Fed gun back at Henry.

Flare's right hand holding the Fed gun moved to the left towards Moja's face.

"What the fuck! W-W-What the fuck is going on? No! Stop this!!"

Rashly, Flare shot Moja in the face as the blood gushed put of the back of his head.

"Aah shit! Moja! Aaagh shit!!"

"Your turn." Henry said.

In an instant, Flare's body exploded into a million pieces leaving loads of blood and insides ruptured out all around the room.

Rapid buzzing sound from an alerting emergency device at the office inside the building.

"We have a Detective in grave danger! I need a crew at the location profited by the alerting system, our neighbor city, Seven Tens City! I'm sure their officers are on it too, but I want no jerking off over there, let's get this done right!" Chief Officer Quentin said.

A police crew gathered their gear and proceeded to the location.

The officers arrive to the location where the Detectives are presumed to be in danger.

"In that house right here. Move in! Move in!" Chief Officer Quentin said as he sends his men inside Henry's house.

"Sir, it seems like we have a homicide. It's very bad in here, undoubtedly a beast."

"Ok keep breaking down the place and see what else you can find."

"Yes sir!"

The house began to shake unusually and objects in the house started to move around rapidly spooking the officers. The house is made out all technology and every machinery are being broken up then all the house parts started to take itself apart.

"What the…" Quentin being alarmed.

The officers, Henry in the middle and the house parts are in the air and immediately everything exploded along with the officers.

"This isn't just a beast this is something worse…"

Henry revealed himself from out of the smoke and instantly, the outside police crew fired their Fed guns at him and walking towards the target. All the bullets and beams just miraculously bounced off him. Henry in his all black silk suit smiled then suddenly, the officers leisurely and strangely ascended into the air while screaming in fear and then their heads exploded.

"Oh shit! I need all units from every region, every possible section! I need all units! We need Mega Human Prime Forces!!"

<u>*Unknown Area*</u>—

In a dark room with red night lights, Terrorgon the King of the Dragoon Spirit World had a conversation with Goonie, who is too a Dragoon and loyal servant of Larthgon. Terrorgon resembled a fiendish demonic figure as his face is painted and barely covering his burned wounds in which he had gotten years ago. Male Dragoons, who are royalty, are usually fifteen feet tall and Terrorgon is considered short with only being seven feet tall. He is muscular with clipped wings, he has dark scales, small sharp teeth coming from his biceps as well as other small sharp teeth coming from his neck, chest, stomach and legs.

His legs stood straight but are like a reptile figure. His face is painted, and his jaws are out by twelve inches like a dog and his fingers have small sharp nails. Terrorgon painted his face because his flesh has been mildly burnt exposing some of his skull. He has a similar look to Terrorgon with severed wings, but he is a little smaller, he's about six feet and six inches tall.

"This apparatus is always needed, for he is not naturally foul like us. His body has denied some of the DNA. Hmm, soon though, it will be victory for us... It all comes with perfect timing; our prince will become victorious and rebel over the Netrons... They will never see this coming, the element of surprise. For years they've been a nuisance, now they will all fall!" Terrorgon said in a heavy beast like voice looking at a body locked inside an automated pod.

"Yes, agreed but our prince had the opportunity a few years ago." Goonie said.

"He was young, he enjoyed the thrill of his energetic youth. Now he's older but much smarter, ready to conquer and be the king he always wanted to be."

"Yes, the younger we are the livelier we get."

"When should I release him?"

"In a few hours he should be ready." Goonie said as he walked away from him.

"Hmm." Terrorgon muttered while observing the body.

Planet Mars—

Alexis Cobar's mother Lisa Cobar riding on an express train heading towards Seven Tens City. Her friend is with her hugging her and supporting her as she cried with drops of tears running down her cheeks. The train stopped as locals looked around and trying to figure out why it stopped. Some thought the train stopped for the tracks to clear on the next stop but usually this express train doesn't stop for things like that. As they wait for the automated system to tell them the reason why the train stopped, an explosion went off in Seven Tens City which is about four blocks away from the train causing everyone to get out of their seats to look.

"Alexis…"

"It's ok Lisa."

"Ok? No, it's not! I want to at least see my daughter one last time and if that explosion is where she's at, then I won't be able to…" She paused then sobbed uncontrollably.

"I'm here for you Lisa… I'm here."

"This is Jet Team Alpha seventeen. Captain Marc Glenvor speaking, we are currently proceeding to execute the target."

The captain of a Jet Team associated with the Gigantica Air Force, one of the strongest Air Force teams in Earth's solar system. The Jet Team Alpha are equipped with body suits that transform into Jets. They are very light which makes them move quickly with power thrusters. These suits never malfunction ever since they were launched. They serve the purpose of dropping Nuclear weapons, to fire rockets, machine guns and heat beams. They also fly with automated jets that has the option to have an agent manually operated from an Air Force base.

In this mission they will not drop a nuke and flush him out just yet. The troops must first evacuate the citizens of Seven Tens City while they will simply test Henry's abilities and try to take him out using smaller fire power and avoid destruction that would cause billions of dollars.

On the ground in the heart of Seven Tens City, Henry on top of a building looked at the city and said—

"Feeble… pathetic species…" Henry scorned the humans and having his hands in his pants pockets.

Flexing his increasing power, he simply flicked his hair and simultaneously buildings broke apart, roads caving in, automobiles were flying out of control.

Citizens are self-exploding all because of Henry's mind. The screams of people in agony and fear, running for their lives as Henry decides to destroy some more with just his mind.

Military drones, androids and tanks are all heading towards Henry.

"Get in formation!" Captain Marc commanded.

The team members had gathered close to him hovering in midair around Henry ready fire their weapons.

Within no time, heat beams were fired hitting Henry and causing explosions all around him.

They stopped shooting and waited a few seconds for the smoke to clear. Suddenly, a dragon appeared from the cloud of smoke on the ground. With its wings flapping in midair, its mouth opened as it charges a radioactive energy. Then in seconds, a heated red beam blasted from its mouth, killing the entire Jet Team. The beam was so hot that the heat waves were surrounding the incoming blast.

"What in the world is that? . . . This is Captain Sonny Bale of the Mars Mega Human Prime forces; a Jet Team Alpha has been dismantled by aaa... by a flying beast... thing. We need support teams from all sectors, now!"

The captain looked at his team then said—

"Alright everyone, let's make our move!"

On the deserted road, just one block away from the target, they began tactically moving in. The Captain is in the front leading the way while two Soldiers are beside him, one on each side.

Another team is also engaging from the other side from Henry then suddenly, the soldiers were being lifted in the air.

"Oh God help us all..."

Another team of Police Officers in speeding air vehicles, moving in towards Henry as they were shooting their guns equipped with fifty caliber bullets. All hits are hitting Henry but nothing seemed to faze him. The soldiers he controlled with his mind are still in the air. He uses them and drastically threw them towards the gun fire.

"Hold your fire! Hold your fire! Those are troops over there!"

As the soldiers continued heading their way Henry stopped them in front of the police officers then Henry used his mind to detonate the C4 equipped in the soldier's armor killing them all and ultimately impacting the officers.

The beast that appeared to be a dragon that was with Henry went flying to the uptown area of the city firing its heated beam that destroyed buildings, overhead trains, roads, bridges and causing a long list of destruction.

"It's time I create more of my children." Henry said as he revealed a small crystal in his hand.

Hyper High School Football practice in Uptown Seven Tens City—

Hyper football requires several high-tech gears that allows players to move quickly and become stronger. The most successful trait of the gear is the helmet which prevents chronic traumatic encephalopathy. A topical day where young players were practicing then unexpectedly—

"Hey look."— "Wooaah'…"— "What the fuck is going on?"

"Those are buildings being destroyed."

"But what could've caused all of that?"

"Look! Maybe that's the reason…" Said one player pointing at a flying creature.

"It's heading this way guys!"

"Fuck this practice. I'm out!"

The players all ran in separate directions as the dragon attacked the field.

"Looks like a freaking . . . large flying demon!"

The players exited to the backyard leading them to hurdle over the bushes. One player accidentally tripped on a stem. His best friend turned around and saw him lying on the ground and paused for about ten second as the boy pleaded for help.

"I'm sorry bro… But I got to save my ass!"

Although he had the chance to save his best friend, he left him there to die and ran off. As he sprinted away his eyes started to change. His iris turned orange and pupils turned pitch black, dark scales began to emerge through his skin. He couldn't control what was happing to his body as he made noise with a beastly screech and ultimately fell victim to the peculiar mutation.

THIRTY-SIX

It's the next day and Ki-Yale Kafmora has been unceasingly receiving stern training from Nealo. His grandfather is the perfect sparring partner. The stronger Ki-Yale gets the more power Nealo uses for intense training. Nonetheless, Ki-Yale would do three to five sets of a hundred sit-ups, a hundred pushups, a hundred one handed pushups for each arm, fifty dips, fifty pull ups, everyday then he jogs and runs around Little Tree Ville which is thirty-two miles square miles in area. He does that for two hours straight for his cardio without stopping. He ended the trained an hour ago and now getting ready to head out along with his mother to a new home.

"Mom! Mom!" He shouted with short 3-5-inch dreadlocks dangling with his head.

"What?! What?!" Demi replied poking her head out of the bathroom with her hair covered.

"I got one hair strand on my chin Mom! I'm a man!"

"You ain't no man yet boy! You need to have a full beard then we can talk business."

"Yeah, I guess but it's a start... but hey, look what I found!" Ki-Yale said with a bright smile showing his mother his pet lion's baby tooth.

"That's nice son. Now I must finish getting ready. We're meeting with the real estate agent today."

"Yes. I know but what I really, really, reeaally' wanted to show you... is this. You were looking for it forever." Ki-Yale said while showing his mother a 2x4 picture of a high-tech frame.

"That's me and Narrken." Demi said recognizing a picture that Narrken sketched when he was three years of age of himself and his mom.

"Yeah. I was just snooping around, and I found it buried in the ground in the backyard."

"The drawing... it's still so detailed... I never forget the day he came home showing me this and I ignored it like it was nothing. Thank you, my son." Demi said giving her son a kiss on his forehead then wrapped her arms around him tightly.

He looked at her with a smile projecting his innocent face then she continued—

"And I won't ignore whatever you have to say to me. I'll be there to answer your questions."

Ki-Yale stood quiet for moment while looking at the floor then said—

"Well, I have one question."

"What's that?"

"Did you think... what I did was justified? . . . Taking a life?"

Demi's hands are still affixed to his shoulders while ogling at his focused eyes. She slightly tucked her bottom lip while conveying her dimples and looked away to the left for a few seconds then looked at him again.

"Hm, what you did Ki-Yale... what you did... it was noble... and rather acceptable."

He raised his eyebrows in disbelief to what his mother just said.

"I wish it wasn't you that made that decision, but it's already done. It could've been worse and truthfully the world is better without that kind of negativity coming from one man."

Ki-Yale nodded his head gradually then said—

"I really don't have any remorse about it. It's just that... I don't want to let you down because of the choices I make."

"I'm not going to like every decision you make but overall, I am proud of you and what will make me even more proud… is that you'll grow up to be a man and a Netron that has values that are intelligible to you."

He smiled and adored the moment of acceptance from his mother as she smiled back at him, fueling their profound relationship and comfort.

"For now, you're just a teen and phases are happening as we speak."

"Yeeaaah', I know Mom."

"Like hormones, puberty..."

"I know Mom."

"And getting aroused and sex and..."

"Mom."

"And girls."

"Mom, please."

"And I hope you keep Litzy, she's smart and has a bright future ahead of her. I don't wanna' see you with no raggedy hoes!"

"Moooom'!" He said as Titus roared behind him.

The mountains of Gigantica City—

A recently renovated and seemingly attractive large house located on a mountain which is mounted on the sides. It is firmly built and Neecho wanted to check it out right away as he already got most of everyone's things on a large cargo vehicle because he was so sure that this is the place for his family.

"Now on our way down the hall we have the bedroom complex with six bedrooms all on one floor." The real estate agent said.

"All of this is beautiful. Well put together . . . I'll take it." Neecho said.

"What?! Would you like to see the upstairs?"

"It's ok I already seen every… I mean I already seen everything that I mostly like about the place plus no rodents I presume."

"This is Gigantica my friend. The home of technology paradise, it's not the same as Gel Hev."

"Hm, you know Gel Hev is owned by Gigantica right?"

"Ah… How would you like to pay sir? Cash or credit?" He inquired as Neecho smirked at him.

Moments later—

"What did we miss?" Demi queried entering the household while Neecho finished signing the documents.

"I bought the place."

"Really?! Without me looking around. Do you even know what's behind the walls?"

"Yea. I saw everything."

"But we didn't decide together Neecho. You know like mutual decision. What you think the kids will say? And Nealo?"

"Woah this is nice! It's so spacious!" Ki-Yale amazed.

"Oouu'… I like this Dad. Now this is what I'm talking about." Oji said.

"Nice, not bad, not bad." Tajaymae said.

"Yep this is perfect Neecho. I love it already." Nealo said walking inside the new domain with Tajaymae and Oji.

Demi looked at her husband then said—

"Well ok… The place isn't so bad after all."

"Especially that view." Neecho said pointing to the large window in the living room.

The large windows revealed an impressive angle view of the city.

"I'm going to miss Gel Hev though." He continued.

Demi walked up to her husband and rubs his back while he puts his right arm about her neck. "I'm going to miss it too and every time I say it's hard to move on but here, we are moving on." She said.

"Bad things have happened but, this is good right now. We don't know what to expect next, but we will handle it, as a family."

In the evening—

Everyone proceeded to feast at the dinner table while Ki-Yale went out in his Netron Suit flying around Gigantica City then went to go meet up with his now girlfriend Litzy. She upgraded her high-tech jewelry asking them to attack faster which results more fatal attacks and makes her go airborne and hover. Litzy flying four thousand feet in the air going about two hundred miles per hour while Ki-Yale creeped up behind her and said—

"You're in an unauthorized military airspace. Please turn your aircraft around immediately or we will have to take action!" Ki-Yale mocked by changing his voice to talk just like a radio from a military base.

"What?! Oh wow, you're a goof ball!"

"Yes, and here I am once again."

"Oooh' look, it's the key to my heart!"

"Oh, that was horrible…"

"C'mon that wasn't clever? Like your name is Ki because it's pronounced like key…"

"I know but blaaah'!"

"Whatever. How's your new place?"

He sighed then said—

"It's not so bad… I really like it but… it isn't like Little Tree Ville."

"Aaw', you miss it. Don't you?"

"Yeah but not as much as I miss you."

He gets closer to Litzy in midair as she blushed and stood still facing him with her hands folded.

"Hm, what are you doing? Do I know you?" She joked.

"After this dance you're going to wish you know me."

"Dance?"— "Yeeaah, I'm gonna' put my hips into it. C'mon let's dance in midair!"

She chuckled then said—

"Dance in midair?"— "Yeeaah."

"This is one of your weird moments I see. Ok, let's try it. Let's see if you got moves."

"C'mon, you know I'm the one."

She giggled then said— "With that confidence I can already tell you probably used your Netron suit and copied some of the best dancers in the world."

While being in midair, they held hands facing each other about two feet apart. Ki-Yale began moving his feet as if he was on solid ground. Litzy looked confused to how he's moving, stepping back and forth and rocking his hips but she's virtually astonished.

"Wow, this is actually happening."

She began to do the same and smiled being surprised that she can move like him. And now they're dancing Bachata to old music from the 20th century playing through small speakers on Litzy's mechanical clothing.

"Maybe I did but I'm doing well though right…?" He asked while smiling at her.

She shook her head in sanction and smiled back at him as they danced as if they've been doing it for years. "Yeah, this is pretty fun Netro!"

Ki-Yale spun her around with slight force until they are face to face again. Ogling at each other, he continued to dance as she followed with a precise rhythm. Both moving so well that they forgot that their movements were limited even if they were good at Bachata you still need to be on a surface. Litzy unexpectedly made one incorrect step which threw Ki-Yale off then she landed her head in his chest. He chuckled while she could hear his heartbeat pounding smoothly then faster as she hugged him. She laughed and brought her head up to his face. "You're very talented dancing in midair." He said.

"Yeah and you're good too."

He remembered something and pulled out a gold neckless out from his Netron Suit that he's been wearing around his neck. "Wow… you still have that thing?"

"It's not just a thing Litzy, it's the first gift you ever made me."

She blushed at him and tried not smile. He continued to lighten up the mood by acknowledging her talents.

"Plus, it has my symbol on it that's been hand forged by you… How can I ever get rid of this?"

He placed his left arm around her waist as she pressed her body against his, sealing the deal for a passionate kiss is all he's thinking of right now.

"*Ki-Yale!*"—Said a familiar voice in his head.

"Who said that?" He questioned the voice.

He still had his body pressed against hers, looking around but no one else is there.

"Was that you Litzy? You have such a manly voice all of a sudden…"

"Umm...?" She jumbled.

"*It's me your granddad!*"

"Aah… Granddad? Are you inside my head?"

"Wow, the perks of dating a half alien."

"*Yes, my grandson. I'm communicating with you telepathically and we have a serious problem.*"

He instantly flew back to his home while holding Litzy. Although Litzy achieved the ability to fly, she isn't fast enough to keep up with Ki-Yale. He arrived at the new Kafmora domain in Gigantica City. He entered inside and saw everyone watching the news on a wide holographic TV in the large living room.

"Hey Litzy." Demi greeted.

"Litzy." Tajaymae also greeted.

"Hey. What's up everyone?" She replied.

"Bad news, that's what's up." Oji added.

"Yeah, in Seven Tens City on planet Mars." Neecho said.

"Seven Tens City is going up in ruins by what appears to be a man in an all-black silk tuxedo. We don't know how he is doing it, but it appears that he is controlling anyone and anything around him. The Mega Human Prime Forces are there now trying their best to stop him!" Said the news anchor.

"Definitely not a Mega Human Prime but..." Tajaymae said.

"But? But what?" Ki-Yale asked.

"He's so beautiful!"

"What?!" Neecho staggered.

"I'm sorry but he's just too handsome. Devious but handsome."

"Oook' Tajaymae . . . Ki-Yale, he's not a Mega Human Prime . . . that's your opposite." Nealo implied.

Ki-Yale held a serious face looking at everyone then asked—

"How do you know?"

"Judging by the way he controls those Dragons, I'm pretty sure he's royalty."

"But he looks humanlike…"

"Yes, because he has a similar suit to ours."

"The Intercosmic Suit…" Neecho said.

"The… Intercosmic Suit?" Ki-Yale bewilderedly asked.

"His predecessor, Larthgon and our predecessor Netro One used the Crystal of Zenith to Intercosmic Crystals which is what our suits are made of. Netro One utilized these crystals to create Netron Suits combining it with our DNA so that it's a natural ability for to activate the suits at any given time. The Intercosmic Crystals can be used as suits as well but instead it's not shared with our DNA. An Intercomic Crystal can only be used once, so once a lifeform removes it from their bodies the crystal will no longer exist. The Netron Army calls it the Synthetic Netron Suit. Now… now it seems that the Opposites utilizes these crystals for their armor." Nealo said.

"Woah… not good."

"Well... we should go stop him."

"Yes Tajay, but he is very strong. Going out there now will put you guys race at risk." Neecho said.

The news station continued— *"This just in, it appears to be creatures, terrorizing Gigantica City we don't know where they come from, but they look as if they may have something to do with that man in the tuxedo. Here is a closer look on them now. Lauren?"*

"Yes, this is Lauren Stellar reporting live, as you can see here, flying monsters terrorizing Gigantica City and shooting what it seems to be radioactive beams out of their mouths. Still no information on how they came about, but we already have multiple casualties and more lives are at stake here."

"What the hell are those?!" Demi astounded.

"Those are Dragoons aren't they Granddad?" Ki-Yale inquired.

"Yes, I can't ever forget the way those creatures look."

"He's causing all of this destruction and my duty . . . My duty is to protect the humans from the Opposites."

"Yes, that's true but you have to play this smart."

"Hm."

"Listen to your grandpa son." Demi said.

"Yes. The best action right now is inaction and prep." Neecho said.

"Ki come with me." Nealo said.

Ki-Yale followed Nealo to a giant room the size of six football fields with machinery underneath the basement which is below the mountain.

"This room here is our new training room. It's compatible with standard holographic features by operation from the mainframes over here. This is used as a playroom for Mega Humans with whatever scenery they want. The walls, ceiling and floor are compatible with indestructible substance that can withstand most of our attacks at hundred percent. I'll modify it in the future but for now this is what we got."

"Ok now what you got to show me really?"

"Well, it seems that you still want to face your opposite. So, the only way you can really defeat him is using the 'Death Gun' and using psychokinesis."

"You said my mind isn't strong enough yet for mind control."

"Your mind is strong enough now, but you just need to master it."

"Ok then teach me Granddad and explain this aaah'… Death Gun."

"The Death Gun is a natural Netron armament used by all Netrons. It is used for one shot kills, if it just touches you in any way, anywhere on your body, it kills your opponent in an instant. If the Death Gun bullet touches anyone or anything else other than the locked target the bullet won't destroy it. The bullet terminates only the target, if the bullet was to miss the target… which it wouldn't, then the bullet does nothing. The Death bullet is actually an Intercosmic virus and in fact the deadliest virus in all of existence that infects your opponent instantly when shot."

"Woah…"

"The destruction of your opponent or thing will be destroyed depending on how powerful the Death bullet was. The Death bullet is effective based on how much power you put into it, the bullet has the tiniest cells that infect anything and anyone including Dragoons. The infection literally eats everything that exists on your body all the way to your tiniest cell, your molecule, atom… And you get the rest. You can even target and shoot at space or even the air, it can penetrate anything, and the Death Gun will eliminate it depending how strong the Netron is."

"Oook'… powerful stuff… very powerful stuff. How do I activate it?"

"To activate it for an ordinary rookie Netron like yourself… he or she has to say "Death Gun" until you fully mastered the power and shoot it without saying a word. A Netron's left or right hand must be shaped like a pistol in order for it to shoot."

"Like so?" He asked shaping hand like gun pointing out his index finger and thumb facing up.

"No, the index and middle finger must be joined together pointing at the opponent or thing or whatever. As for the ring finger, pinky and the thumb . . . The ring finger and pinky should be closed and the thumb acts as a hammer. When the hammer is cocked which the thumb is down you are charging the gun putting extra power into it. When you lift your thumb and hear a 'click' that means it's ready to fire.

"Woah, it's like the real thing…"

"Sort of… the power in a Death Gun is equivalent to the current power you possess in your body, which is your core and if you want you can reduce such power. So, when you charge it, you're putting whatever power you have into it plus the power you already possess that's equivalent to it… After you fire it, it comes back to your regular power that the gun had at first. The thumb must be lifted, facing up to the sky, ceiling, et cetera… For the gun to fire. You can shoot it any amount of times without feeling any fatigue. You need to think of what or who you want to shoot for it to lock on target and even though the target moves the bullet will follow."

"I guess it has recoil too."

"Oh, yes it does my grandson… Now the safety will be fully controlled by the user, so they should be careful and always be aware of their thumb in any situation. Now aim like so . . . put your arm straight... A bullet will appear, and you don't have to think of a target just fire blank shots."

"Death Gun! Ok . . . I'm aiming but not firing… Death Gun! . . . This is getting difficult..." Ki-Yale frustrated.

"A bullet didn't appear yet Ki-Yale."— "Now concentrate and harness the Death bullet."

He closed his eyes while Nealo continued to talk putting pressure on his concentration.

"A way to stop the Death Gun's bullet is shooting another bullet that is equivalent or stronger than that user who also used the Death Gun and possibly deflect it right back to that user."

"I see…"

"The Death bullet can move up to boundless speeds as it corresponds with a possessor's ability to go light speed or even faster or just the speed of sound or slower. It's possible for one to dodge the bullet but the bullet will instantly set a new direction and eventually land on the target even if the target dodged the bullet for the rest of their lives."

A four-inch black ovoid with red energy surrounding it appeared in front of his hand emitting a buzzing idle. The black ovoid reduced its size to half of an inch and resembling a pellet. "Open your eyes, your Death bullet has emerged."— "Woah…"— "Now shoot it."

"Death Gun!" He yelled.

A loud pistol sound effect emitted from Ki-Yale's hand while firing his first shot. Echoes hurdled across the room drastically. His face became refined with all smiles as he achieved his new ability.

"Nice, I mastered it!"

"Good. Now keep practicing and fire some blank shots."

"Alright." Ki-Yale said as he kept on firing.

"Now here are more details… An advanced possessor of the Death Gun can aim at a target but can land a shot on a different target instead hence what I said about target lock. Even if the target tries to dodge or get away from the bullet, the bullet will still eventually hit. It's possible that the person or thing may be too strong and can just take the bullet without getting damaged but if you shoot multiple death bullets at once, just maybe that very strong enemy can be damaged or even destroyed."

"Death Gun! Death Gun! Ha, this is so addicting… such immense power… all in one hand!"

"Yes, a very effective ability… you also have to very be careful about your surroundings when you shoot because it's loud enough to pop a human's ear drum."

"Yeah, it is pretty loud."

"The more powerful the possessor and the gun, the more loudly it gets. If you had enough mind power, you can suppress the sound or maybe you can protect people's ears from the powerful sound waves. Remember now, the Death Gun can kill anyone and anything as long as the possessor is stronger than the target." Nealo said while Ki-Yale kept firing.

"I'm getting this down pact."

"You actually should've learned this a little sooner."

Ki-Yale stopped shooting while glaring at his grandfather then fully turned to him and said—

"Yeah . . . well... What about Ken? You ever think maybe if you would've taught him this, he would be here today?"

"You're right but the Death Gun is treated just like how humans treat guns for young children at a certain age, unrestrictedly. They give some super genius's a pass but still risky giving a young mind this kind of power."

"Hm, yeah I guess safety and responsibilities first."

"Look, right now we have to focus in you defeating the Opposites . . . Now, the power of the mind, this is simply called the Netron mind. This can be used wearing the Netron Suit or without it. Now you're going to activate the muscles of your Netron mind, I have this piece of paper, all you have to do is lift the paper up with your mind just by looking at it and thinking that the paper is going to lift... very simple."

"Yeah very simple Granddad." Ki-Yale said then he began to try and lift the paper with his mind.

"Focus and remember your previous training."

"I am but it's not working." He said then closed his eyes.

"No don't close your eyes. Look at the paper... You need vision transitioning to eidetic memory so you can perform this power. When your mind gets more powerful you really don't need sight but now you do. Just think about all the atoms, molecules, solid cells, fibers and the overall paper itself to simply... lift."

Ki-Yale is looking at the paper for literally five minutes straight concentrating hard on moving that piece of paper.

"Hmmmrrrr'." Ki-Yale being irritated.

Moments later the paper began to slowly lift from the floor. The paper is then up to Nealo's face and Nealo smiles at his grandson then said–

"Good, now this still isn't enough to take down your Opposite, but it can be enough to resist his mind control a little then throw dirt in his eyes and fire the Death Gun. Easy tactic, you just need to make sure he least expected it." Nealo said.

"Throw dirt in his eyes? That's not going to do much if he has the ability to use his other four senses."

"It's just a figure of speech."

Moments later, Ki-Yale is back upstairs with his family.

"You guys better be careful. I'm still skeptical of you going Tajaymae." Demi said.

"Mom, I can handle myself. Plus, I have my Zeal Netron Armor now..." Tajaymae said then she changes into her Zeal Netron Suit.

She recently developed her suit within the two months and ever since then she has been getting rigorous training from her grandpa which made her plasma more effective and she is more skilled than before. While wearing the suit, she cannot download other effects into her suit and she's still only able to perform Netron Plasma skills but they're more effective now. Litzy and Demi already went through the identity phase of recognizing Tajaymae. Her eyes are now fiery purple again because her suit is activated.

"You're staying here right?" Ki-Yale asked Litzy.

"Yeah. I don't think I'll match up at all to that guy or even those alien dragons."

"I'm coming too." Oji said then smiled showing his green braces.

"No, you're not." Demi responded.

"Oh, c'mon Mom."

"Don't c'mon Mom me. Alright? You don't even have a Netron Suit yet."

"Well now, I wouldn't say that." Oji said.

"Really?" Neecho asked.

"Check me out." He said as he changed into his Zeal Netron Suit, which is green, black and white. For the first time he revealed his armor to his family and he's feeling relieved to do so.

"Ok, I didn't see this coming." Ki-Yale said.

"I didn't either." Tajaymae added.

"Ha, my suit even made my braces disappear, so it won't get in the way of a fight! Oh yeah I'm definitely going now."

"Umm, who are you?" Litzy asked while being unaware for his presence.

"Change back and do it again Oji." Ki-Yale said.

"Oh yeah." Oji said as he phases back his regular clothes then phases back into his suit for Litzy to recognize him.

"I'm officially a Turf Netron!" Oji being appreciating his Zeal powers.

"Oji, you haven't trained much ever since you got your powers, didn't you?"

"No, I haven't Granddad but I'm pretty good…" Oji said as he got interrupted.

"Then you don't stand a chance. You only use your powers in non-combat situations and not enough sparring sessions. So, you? Going up against them? . . . I'm afraid that's a no, you can at least stay here and defend you mother." Nealo said.

"Alright, whatever." Oji upsettingly said and changed back to his regular clothes then immediately going back to his room.

"Ok, I have to go now." Ki-Yale hugged his mother, Litzy and giving her a quick smooch.

He then walked up to his father and granddad.

"Now this is just a reminder, if the royal eternal prophecy was to be broken by death meaning…" Nealo said.

"Meaning if I, Oji and Tajay dies… every Netron dies."

"Only your mom, girlfriend and Titus here will be the ones left… That's not so pretty." Nealo said.

"Enough about this 'if you die' stuff. You two are gonna' get things done and come back here alive! You hear me?"

"Yes Mom." Tajaymae and Ki-Yale answered.

"And play it smart."

"So, both of you are going to stay and help the military defend the Earth from the Opposites?" Ki-Yale asked.

"Yes, this is you and Tajaymae's fight. More so towards you but she's your back." Neecho said.

Ki-Yale looked at his sister then Neecho said—

"The second I see you guys losing badly over there, I'll come in and get both of you." Neecho said.

"Now remember the game plan. Clean and simple, he won't see it coming. Even if he knows about your attacks which more likely he does but he might not know that you can use them. He's attacking you at this age because now he isn't an easy kill. He wants to have fun, that's where you come in, use that enjoyment to get to his head and take him out."

"Yes sir."

"Now go, I'll help my father for a bit then I'll take the space bus after you, then meet you over there."

Nealo shook his head at his son in approval to the plan then instantly, he felt a sting of pain in his head.

He closed his eyes and grunted while holding his forehead with his right hand. "You alright father?!"

"Huh? It's you again? What the hell do you want?! Why don't you tell me?" Nealo thought.

"The time is near... I WILL SOON HAVE NETRO'S BODY!!"

The pain went away as he looked at everyone in the room. "You ok Granddad?" Ki-Yale concerned.

"It must be those visions again..." Neecho thought.

THIRTY-SEVEN

Seven Tens City, Ranomia, Mars—

Henry with his hands in his pockets walking down the destruction that he caused just by using his mind.

Thousands of soldiers went towards Henry and tried to take him out but failed. One soldier running towards Henry with an Apaki knife recording his words while being in battle—

"I'm in Seven Ten City, Mercy. Section 41. I'm pinned down by this monster. I have a family at home with two kids. Man, I just wish I was home with them right now . . . Please, if anyone gets this recording please tell my family I love them dearly. I love them sooo' much but… but I'm a soldier and I'll die protecting the human race and most importantly . . . I will die for my family!!! Aaahh'!!"

Henry is still walking and isn't giving any attention to the soldier. The soldier then hits him in the face with his heated glass knife thinking it would cut right through him, but the heated glass knife shattered into pieces.

"What the fuck are you?"

Henry smiled and used his mind to make the soldier explode right in front of him. The soldier's body parts were in tiny pieces and blood splashed all over Henry.

More military forces arrived while Henry is just too powerful for them to handle throwing back the bombs that the military launched. He sent them flying into a few buildings allowing them to fall and crumble. With people still residing in these buildings and the overall metropolitan areas, every human he sees he kills with no remorse. Survival seemed to be little to none.

"This is unbelievable everyone! It looks like history is repeating itself with destruction from an unidentified being . . . Sorry, this just in. The man you see there is named Henry Luciano, he has zero family members and information about his parents stays a mystery. We don't know what will happen next but right now we need someone who can take him down and we have no choice but to hope for Netro to appear and take this monster down." Said the News anchor watching the scenery of Henry from four miles away through a small hovering android.

<u>Torbino Residence in Atlantis City—</u>

Chloe Torbino and Tony Torbino were suspected of involvement of injecting illegal substance to a minor but Dorimzy didn't say anything of it. The main culprit Nicole Torbino was convicted of all counts and the court sentenced her to ten years in Gigantica National Prison. Tony loved his mother dearly and blamed Dorimzy for speaking with the police. Tension was growing between the two which instigated an argument to occur within the household involving Chloe until Tony decided that he should leave them both and depart on his own. Alterations were conveyed and he was never heard from since.

Chloe never saw the same animosity he has for Dorimzy and thought it was the right thing that he did by informing the police. Dorimzy Torbino's mind had progressed in many ways making him surpass the average Super Genius intellect and now obtained enough knowledge to take on an advanced University. He indeed took on a University in Gigantica for a PhD degree in Political Science and surpassed Ki-Yale Kafmora by being the first ever Super Genius to attend college before reaching age ten which turned heads all around the world. Although Ki-Yale didn't attend college and instead took an exam in which he passed easily, it still counted as attending college because he most likely attended for twelve hours to take the Central IQ Test and obtained a certificate in *Mega Human Advanced Intelligence*. Despite the awful things happening in Chloe's life she had her brother Dorimzy who took his time in making sure she remains secure. Witnessing family fall apart and even distancing herself from friends, she left school and decided to join the Gigantica Space Corps in which she seeks enlightenment and a steadfast life. She already underwent stern training which she passed remarkably and now she is allowed to go on missions.

Dorimzy entered the dining room in a hover chair devoted to the floor's mechanical automated system which allowing him to move without falling off due to his inability to walk. After traveling inside the house's elevator, a closet constructed within the walls making it shift, it opened like a drawer allowing him to choose whichever sweater he desires to wear.

"Hey Dorimzy, what's up." Chloe said sitting down and eating her breakfast.

"Hey Chloe, just getting some food then I'm going outside for a bit."

"So, I guess no school today?"

"No, no school."

"Why not?"

"I don't need to."

"Umm…. Want to explain why you don't need to?"

"I encounter the exams on Friday and it's not required for me to attend the institute just to study for that particular exam."

"Yeah but what about the new things to learn? I'm pretty sure that they have new material for the next week plus the homework."

"Material? The only educational material I'll get is the professor's incompetence and that homework that they issue is just simple utter nonsense."

Chloe stood quiet then he said—

"Pardon my profanity sister, it's hard to settle with my philosophy on quantifiable challenges . . .I'll go tomorrow . . . I promise."

An urgent call from one of the space station military defense bases, hologram projection of an agent who contacted her. Chloe is a Private on her first leave and is now needed right away. With little hesitation, she readied her possessions and tells Dorimzy goodbye.

"You have everything available for you so just stay put here." She instructed. "How grim is this mission?"

"Tune into the newscast and you'll find out. All broadcasts are live right now."

"Are you going to come back?"— "I'm not sure..."— "But you've just returned yesterday, and we didn't even get to hang out yet. I sought to do that today, with you... now... now I'll be alone once again... I'm always ending up being alone."

Seeing the melancholy illustrated around her little brother, nearly resembling a full-grown cheetah without its legs.

"Hm', Dorimzy, I can't promise you I'll be back because if I do that and I don't come back... it'll break your heart even more than it should."

She gets closer and stooped in front of him, sister to brother. His vexation wreaked from his face and turned his head marginally to the left. "But I can promise you this… you're not going to be alone forever and someday you will be the greatest phenomenon this planet has ever seen. Just keep following your dreams."

With no reluctance, she hugged him tightly as if it's the last hug she will ever give him.

"I'm going to miss you."

His head remained slightly away from Chloe then brought his attention back to her. "I'm going to miss you too."

"Now can you promise me… to follow your dreams?"

"Yes. I promise Sis… for you. I will make you proud."

<u>Space Station</u>—

Ki-Yale and his sister walking onto a public hyper-speed cargo bus going to Mars which will only take four hours to get there. This transportation is typically called the 'Space Bus' which is only three hundred and fifty dollars round trip which is considered a small amount of currency in the 24th century.

"Space buses traveling to Mars are shut down." Said the computer in an intercom at the space station.

"Hey, we need a ride to Mars ASAP."

"Kid… Didn't you hear the intercom? We don't have any buses going to, to Mars… Woah, wait a minute, it's you… Aah, Netro!" Said the worker at the station booth identifying him.

"Yeah. You think you can give us a ride? You know I'm needed over there."

"Absolutely. Let me call in my manager."

Ki-Yale and Tajaymae is now on the space bus going to hyper speed to Mars. Ki-Yale can fly and breathe in space to Mars but with his current state, it will take him about twenty-eight days and that's not enough time. The bell on the bus rings then the intercom is offering hospitality to Ki-Yale and Tajaymae.

Suddenly—

"Tajaymae, Ki-Yale!" Oji said in his Netron Suit.

"What the…" Ki-Yale said.

"Oji?!" Tajaymae muddled.

"You're wondering how I got in here… Well, I did tactical movements you know. I morphed myself into the ground, camouflaging my way into the bus."

"Shit." Nealo said seeing through Ki-Yale's eyes.

"What happened? You see something?" Demi being fretful.

"Yes, it's Oji. But how the…?" Neecho said.

"What happened to Oji?"

"He's… he's on the space bus to Mars with Ki-Yale and Tajaymae." Nealo said.

"WHAT!?"

The Machida residence Little Tree Ville—

Xack at age twenty-two at his home in LTV being geared up with his armor as his father walked in the living room and asked— "Where are you going Xack?"

"To fight those monsters."

"To fight the monsters!? C'mon son… enough of this."

"I can't just sit here and watch TV while the world goes under fire."

"True . . . But it would be most wise to send the pawns out and figure out strategies to take them down…"

"Pawns Dad? Really?"

"Hey unless you want to go out there and fight and die instead of staying low, figuring out the strengths and weaknesses of these monsters. Plus, I don't think heated glass swords is enough."

"Ok you could be right here, but I hate the fact that I could be a convenience helping authorities."

"What are you? Some kind of superhero? You stay here and stand your ground. Defend your home first. When you're gone who is here to protect your old man?"

"Hmmph'… fine. I'll stay but if those creatures reach over here then I have no choice but to defend what we have."

Four hours later, high ranked military forces from Earth, Pluto, Venus, Saturn, Neptune, Uranus, Mercury and Jupiter with giant spaceships arriving to Mars's atmosphere and sending smaller ships into Mars filled with Mega Human Prime soldiers ready for combat and take down Henry.

"Wooow, look at all these spaceships!" Oji being astonished.

"Space Bus 227 you are in violation of war zone atmosphere. Please return the bus back to Earth." Said the military guard speaking to the captain of the bus.

"I have Netro here on the Bus."

"Ok it's time to move." Ki-Yale said as he opens the steal bolted door with his strength and exiting the space bus with Tajaymae and Oji holding them.

The alarm went off because air is escaping the bus, Ki-Yale closed back the steal bolted door with his strength bending it together. Ki-Yale then grabbed his brother and sister with his arm bringing them down to the Mars Space Bus Station which is connected onto the invisible barrier surrounding all of Mars.

"Woah. It's Netro… What should we do sir?"
"Let him in." Said the commander.

Moments later, mid-day in Ranomia, Mars.

"Can you find him?" Tajaymae asking Ki-Yale.

"Yeah over here."

"Ok let's go." Oji said walking in the direction his brother pointed along with Tajaymae.

"Yeah . . . you stay here and search for survivors." Ki-Yale whispered directed then without notice, he instantly ran off the building.

"What?" Tajaymae confused. His siblings turned around and all they witnessed was Ki-Yale flying Mach 3 speed to Seven Tens City.

"What the…" Tajaymae said.

"He left us! Aagh', c'mon bro!" Oji being vexed.

"Mmmrrr'… he really doesn't think we can manage fighting with him."

"*Good, let them do the cleanup.*" Nealo thought witnessing what Ki-Yale did through his eyes. Neecho smiled while Demi observed her husband and father in law as if she's the odd one out.

"I wish I knew what you guys are seeing…"

"Demi, close your eyes and reopen them." Neecho said.

"Woah... Is this my son's eyes?"

"Yes, and you can hear everything as well."

Ki-Yale endeavoring to fight his Opposite alone. He witnessed crumbled buildings as the dark smoke from burnt metal, stone and lumber. He could smell the destruction as he reduced his velocity flying over the ruined Seven Tens City looking at the people in need of assistance. Ki-Yale landed down next to the horde of helpless survivors and realized they are speaking German.

"What happened to him?" Ki-Yale probed using his Netron Suit allowing him to translate in German.

"He injured his leg!" The lady said in German language.

"Who are you to him?"

"I'm his mother. Please help him I don't know what to do, please!"

"Ok it seems that his leg is dislocated. Ok what's his name? How old is he?"

"Danny and he's ten." She said. "Ok Danny listen this is going to hurt a lot. Ok? I'm going to put your leg back in place. Now stay still."

"No. No. NO! NAAOO MOMMY! NAOO! AAGH!" Danny paranoid and enduring his pain.

Ki-Yale puts he leg back to normal, but it seems that Danny is extremely scared. So, frightened he goes into shock.

"Oh no! My baby!!" Danny's mother said.

"Damn…" Ki-Yale said as he looked around for something metal and found a metal pipe. He then used his lightning from his eyes and puts small amount of electrical current onto the pipe enough to revive him.

"Hhaaggh'…" Danny releasing his breath.

"Danny! Oh, my baby." Danny's mom gasped then Ki-Yale looks at them and smiled.

"Thank you so much Netro. Thank you so much." Danny's mother said.

"You're welcome. Now I need to bring you to safer grounds."

Ki-Yale grabbed Danny and his mother to a safer spot in Seven Tens City where some survivors are held with police officers.

<u>*The Kafmora residence, Gigantica City*</u>—

"Wow… Ki-Yale look at you. Good job baby!" Demi being proud.

Neecho chuckled then she continued—

"I still can't believe Oji! I'm proud of one and disappointed in the other. Honestly, I don't know what to feel right now."

"Well, our son wants to help. We can't stop him now; he's already gone with them."

"It's time we go my son, let's help this city and the rest of the Earth." Nealo said as he changed into his Netron Suit.

"Right, let's get it done." Neecho said as he also changed into his Netron Suit.

"Hey, be careful out there."

"Be careful in here too . . . Litzy."

"Yes sir."

"You can contact us through your mind . . . We are connected, just say my name or my father's name and we will respond. Once I leave for Mars though it's just my dad here on Earth."

"I will." Litzy promised.

"I'll be fine baby." Demi said.

"Oh yeah, make sure to feed Titus. You can have the maid android help you, I'm pretty sure Ki-Yale didn't give him dinner yet."

"Sure, I'll do that."

"Don't worry, he's harmless."

Unremitting scenes of bravery displayed by humans, like fireworks, sparks bursting from their strong hearts and never giving up on their race no matter how difficult the enemy is. Gigantica Military has the strongest forces in the solar system, and everyone together is even stronger. The Jet Fighters, a special team of Gigantica Air Force soldiers with special flight suits that transform into miniature Jet airplanes. A team of five arrived on Mars heading straight towards Henry Luciano to drop an air strike targeted by satellite space stations orbiting Mars.

"This is Jet Fighter One, fifteen minutes until air strike on the target."

New minuscule drones recording live broadcastings of Henry on the sidelines as the news anchor speaks in another location.

"*Ok. It seems this guy has whipped out all the military that tried to take him down. It's not looking too good for this city… uh… wait… It's Netro! Netro just arrived! The young boy from Little Tree Ville!*" Said one female reporter.

After three minutes of searching around in the sky and Ki-Yale found his Opposite and immediately fired a Loose Cannon blast hitting his chest.

He landed on a crumbled building as Henry is unfazed after he took the Loose Cannon like it was nothing. "*That barely did any damage.*" He thought then said–

"You must be my opposite."

"Opposite? I don't know what you're talking about." Henry said while flicking his hair.

"Don't play games, I know it's you . . . You're the Prince of Dragoons and you finally revealed yourself."

"Ha! Prince of Dragoons huh? And I thought I was crazy."

Ki-Yale looked at Henry with his left eyebrow up then asked—

"Then who are you?"

"Hmm . . . alright, alright, I'll come clean . . . My name is Dragazell, the Dragoon Prince."

"Dragazell . . ."

"Yes, I'm your opposite." He said while he grinned.

"We knew it from the time you revealed your power . . . this power you possess it's not of any human for sure… Why attack all these people? It's me you really want."

"Because it's fun… been doing this for a long time now, all the missing people. No one knows where they went… Some think the children just ran away because of depression and seeking a better place but actually… they faced unfortunate events. You should know this by now, what my nature is and besides, I haven't had a good mate in quite a long time! I met a fulfilling woman and she insists that we should make love. So, I went along with it and her insides couldn't handle it."

"You're disgusting… you're telling me all this just to make me upset... aren't you?" He asked as Dragazell ignored his question and looked at him with a grin then said—

"We Dragoons and you Netrons are too much for the human females you know."

"You're an asshole."

Dragazell laughed loudly and uncontrollably then said—

"Finally, I get to meet you again Netro." He said as he sneered.

"Again? What do mean again?"

"Oh, don't tell me you forgot the day I made one of the most glorious moves ever."

"What are you referring to?"

"My son…" Neecho said witnessing what's happening through Ki-Yale's eyes and ears.

"Narrken… you're responsible for my brother!"

Dragazell chortled then sarcastically asked— "You figured that all out on your own?"

"WHERE IS HE?!"

"He's right behind you."

THIRTY-EIGHT

General Mewsin, currently the head of the Mars National Space Guard is in a Space War Ship hovering over Mars with his soldiers.

"Looks like Netro is handling this now sir." Soldier Chip said.

"Let's see what will happen. We don't know for sure if Netro can beat this guy." General Mewsin said.

"We should go down and help him sir."

"No, we help our species first. Let them fight to the death… call in Team Nine. I need you down there now and help any civilians, any survivors."

"Yes sir."

Team nine, now on a special a rescue mission to get everyone away to a safe haven and away from the fight.

Little Tree Ville, year 2319—

After long moments of searching for his big brother he finally found him. Ki-Yale ogled at him sitting in the bridge railing as if his favorite food was displayed on a table all just for him. Narrken didn't know of Ki-Yale's presence as he kept his focus on the water under him. It was time for Ki-Yale to make his move and speak to him, maybe he could cheer him up.

"Narr..." He just couldn't finish his name as his heart stopped. His eyes were wide open witnessing a petrifying moment.

A masked assailant dressed in all black quickly grabbed Narrken off the bridge railing then ran off into the trees. Narrken seemed completely unconscious when the assailant grabbed him. No vehicles passed by on the bridge, no one airborne, no one walked by to witness what was happening... it was only Ki-Yale.

"NO! No no no no! Dad! Grandpa! Someone's taking Narrken!"

Ki-Yale is after the masked abductor, but the masked abductor was too fast for him. Ki-Yale stopped and breathed heavily.

"NARRKEN!"

Ki-Yale held his right fist towards the abductor who seemed to be further ahead beyond the small trees.

"Loose Cannon! C'mon . . . Loose Cannon!"

He tried to shoot at the abductor, but it wasn't enough. His Loose Cannon failed to shoot out of his hand, only bits of radiation came out.

"Damn it! I'm still too weak! NARRKEN!"

"Ki-Yale! What happened to Narrken!?" Neecho said as he arrived in the speed of sound along with Nealo.

"Someone in a masked knocked out Narrken and took him away!"

"What!?"

"Use your vision Neecho."

Nealo began looking around and so did Neecho. They both went to the skies for a better view and looked all around the village.

Neecho began breathing heavily as he continued to search around the sky. "Don't panic my son..."

"Don't panic?! What do you mean don't panic! I can't find him anywhere!"

"I'm sorry... I'm just trying to keep you calm."

"Calm?!" Neecho began to breathe heavily some more then looked at his father with absolute fret in his eyes.

Hours later—

"What do you mean you can't find him?!" Demi yelled.
"We looked around the entire village and even further beyond that and still nothing." Neecho said.
"This can't be happening to me. My baby..."
"He's strong and smart. I'm sure he can handle himself... I'll look again first thing in the morning."
"Hm, you better find him Neecho! I want my son back..."

<u>*The Kafmora residence Gigantica City*</u>—

Nealo and Neecho was on the verge to leave the house but something alerted them. Something they could not believe.

Through a telepathic connection and astral projection using Ki-Yale's eyes, Nealo and Neecho saw what's happening on planet Mars. Ki-Yale looked behind him and there he is, his long-lost brother, Narrken all grown up from the last time he was with Ki-Yale. Narrken is now fifteen years old and he doesn't look so exultant to see Ki-Yale.

"MY SON!"

"What happened?! Let me see again Neecho." Demi alarmed.

"I have to go! I have to go to Mars now... Father, can you handle the Opposites on your own?" Neecho said then he starts to move towards the door.

"Yes, from what I've seen on the television, these Opposites are like Cadet Soldiers on their planet, but I'll expect the unexpected."

"Hm..."

"Whah... what happened to Ki-Yale? Tell me." Demi concerned and Litzy as well. "Is Netro all right?!"

"It's not Ki-Yale he's talking about..."

"What?!"

Seven Tens City, Ranomia, Mars—

The sun's brightness beaming across his face as he stared upon the one, he's been searching for, for the last three years.

"Tsk, tsk, tsk, well look who it is." Narrken said then chuckled as he leaned his head to the left. He's one inch taller than Ki-Yale, has an ectomorph body type with short black hair but with strands of red hair partially throughout which almost resembled polka dots and his left eye is the same as Dragazell's eyes.

"Brother! . . . You're alive!" Ki-Yale lashed out while moving closer to his brother. His spirits lifted far into the heavens after all the trauma and wishing to be with him once again. It seems like it's finally a dream that became true. "I always knew you were alive Narrken..."

"And you aren't dead yet..."

Ki-Yale chuckled in response and said—

"Hm. What did he do to you? Your left eye...."

"I simply showed him my intentions to kill you and he agreed with it." Dragazell said.

"I wasn't talking to you . . . I'm talking to my brother..."

"Oooh, I'm sorry..."

"That isn't true... Right?"

"Oh, but Ki-Yale, it's absolutely true... I want to see you burn into the ground!" Narrken uttered walking up close to him.

"But you have Netron blood. How does he make you this way?"

He ignored his question then said—

"Yes… I'm part Dragoon now and it feels good. This power is amazing, I could now harness Dragoon DNA and perform their powers without being weakened."

"No way…"

Without any warning, Narrken quickly backhanded Ki-Yale in the face sending him flying onto a large pile of broken-down building rubble. Ki-Yale broke through the rubble then he quickly regained momentum and stopped five feet in midair.

Narrken briskly moved towards his brother and stopped.

"Ken . . . you let this happen . . . didn't you!?"

"Hmm." Narrken mumbled while charging his Loose Cannon then fired it.

Ki-Yale blocked it with his left hand then Narrken shoots a few more. Ki-Yale blocked most of his shots then got hit in the face with just one causing his head to lean backward in a 180-degree angle.

"Been waiting for this for a long-time brother!" Narrken said then smirked deviously.

"I… I've finally found you Ken… and I'm glad for this but I just never would've imagined you would be fighting alongside with the Opposites."

<u>*Downtown Seven Tens City*</u>—

Tajaymae and Oji are helping survivors around the city in whatever way they can, but they are still disappointed that their brother left them.

"Man, this sucks Tajay, I wanted to be out there fighting with Ki."

"Yeah me too, I guess he wanted no one to get in his way."

"Get in his way? We would have been a team taking that monster down!" Oji argued.

"True but he could have caught us off guard and then Ki has to worry about saving us."

"Hmm, whatever."

"At least we can fight off some of the Opposites flying around and firing that beam thing out of their mouths."

"Where are they anyway?"

"Must have went off to another city after they finished with this one."

"Well, let's go find them sis!"

A few minutes later after they gradually moved through the abandon area Tajaymae noticed an unusual tall man in a cloak standing on top of a building.

"Hm, why is that man up there? It's too dangerous." Tajaymae said.

"I don't know, probably on drugs."

"I'm going to go check what's going on." She said as she ran up the building.

She reached the top and saw the man in an all-black long coat facing away from her looking at what it appears to be Ki-Yale, Narrken and Dragazell talking.

"Woah. It looks like Ki and that man... Who...? Who is the other kid next to him?" Tajaymae thought.

She can't see as well as most regular Netrons, but she could be creative with her plasma if she wanted to.

"Sir, are you ok?"

The man turned his head in Tajaymae's direction, and it was a Dragoon with a painted face. Tajaymae and Oji were completely startled to see such a hideous looking creature as they stepped back a few feet.

"Woah, you definitely aren't human!

"Hmm, I must be the ugliest thing you have ever seen."

"Oh yeah, you are so right about that one."

"Hmm, I never seen this type of suit before, but you do have a Netron Symbol..." Terrorgon said and being interrupted— "I'm a Zeal Netron." She said.

"Zeal you say? You must possess abilities from the crystals… Hmm' I'm positive Queen Tella did this."

Tajaymae raised her eyebrow and asked, "Who are you?"

"I'm Terrorgon, King of the Dragoon Spirit World."

The Eastern International Space Station—

Neecho effortlessly departed on a space bus heading straight to Mars. Neecho manipulated the captain of the space bus by messing with his mind.

"All this time… the Prince of Dragoons took my son… I have to talk to him and get him back on our side." Neecho thought.

At Gigantica City University—

Nack watching his best friend on TV and so is his college friends as they are on lock down due to the destruction in the city. Nack is now in college studying for master's degree in engineering physics pursuing an engineering career.

"Uh oh. It looks like Netro is going to get his ass beat."

"Nah he can't, he needs to win so we can live."

"Hey no worries, I've seen this kid do all sorts of crazy shit. He's like unstoppable. Haven't you seen the online videos?"

"What you think Nack?" One of his friends calling him but no response.

"Hey, Nack? . . . Nack?

"Woah that looks like his brother…" Nack thought remembering old pictures of Narrken as he stared at the TV.

"Aaagh!" Screams came from a student who is behind them.

"What's wrong with that kid?"

"You ok man?" Nack concerned.

"No, something is wrong with me, I don't feel good..."

Suddenly, the student began to turn as black scales developed around his body. His mouth began to stretch forward as his iris became orange, his black pupils rotated vertically and became thin.

"Oh shit! It's one of those beasts!"

He started to grow in size causing everyone to panic.

"EVERYONE, GET OUT!!"

Students ran in every direction as the mutated boy blasts its heated beams. Fire erupted around the campus and walls tumbled down as Nack ran through the hallway.

"Oh no, oh no!" Nack being frightened.

Students getting disintegrated by the beams right in front of him which made him undergo more fear.

He entered the staircase then unfortunately, he tripped and knocked himself out cold.

The dragon lost its purpose, flapping its wings and broke through the walls then flew away to cause more destruction on the city following the rest.

Gigantica City—

Litzy downstairs next to Titus opening his large cage talking with her mother in Spanish through a holographic generator.

"Litzy. Are you ok!?"

"Yes Mama."

"You sure? With all of those monsters flying around and destroying Gigantica City, I'm worried about you."

"Yes, I'm fine Mama. I'm on the Southside of the city they are attacking the north side right now."

"Ok good. I don't know what I'll do if something happens to you."

"Nothing will happen to me. Are you ok? This madness is worldwide and on other planets too."

"I'm ok baby. No signs of the monsters in Welkin City."

"Good. I'll call you back later ok?"

"Love you baby."

"I love you too Mama." Litzy said then she began to open Titus's large cell.

"My son… my son is still alive…" Demi said with some tears of joy running down her round cheeks.

"Yeah but that's not the Ken we know, he's on the wrong side, he should be fighting with us." Nealo said.

"What did that bastard do to him?" Demi asked.

"To be honest… I don't know but I just heard him say he is part Dragoon."

"No no…" She said as her eyes start to water a bit.

"Look Demi I have to stop these Opposites in the City. I can't stay any longer."

"I'll look after her." Litzy said coming up the stairs bringing Titus out of his cage.

Nealo shook his head up and down then instantly, he left the house. He reached the sky hovering over the city and immediately he saw the dragons using his Netron Vision and they are about fifteen miles away from him.

<u>*Seven Tens City, Ranomia, Mars—*</u>

"Can't believe you would betray us like this!"

"Betrayal?! I can say the same for you, the old man and father!" Narrken argued while rapidly shooting his Loose Cannon at him while Ki-Yale puts his two arms like an "X" protecting his face.

Using his impressive speed, Narrken miraculously appeared in front of his brother and elbows him in the cheek.

"How did we defile you?! It was the book—the book was the one that made the final decision!"

"Shut up!!" Narrken said then he punched Ki-Yale in the face sending him into a building than said—

"Do me a favor brother and fight back!! I want your death to be honorable, then I'm going after Oji and Tajay. The book would have no choice but to choose me to be Netro."

"Hm… so that's what you truly want brother?"

"Oh yes…"

"I'm still shocked that you forget the companionship we had. We were a family!"

"That's all in the past . . . The time is now Ki-Yale! The time is now."

"No, I looked up to you Ken! This can't be you, I refuse to believe it!"

"Well then, I'll give you something to believe brother!" Narrken said as he charged another Loose Cannon at him with his right fist. Ki-Yale still kept hope, trusting that his brother would be by his side again.

"Wait… you remember the slogan . . .?"

Narrken growled with his left hand on his right forearm and continued to look at him furiously with rage in his eyes as his brother pleaded with him.

"I got heart…"

"Don't you, dare say it!"

"I got the heart of a lion . . . You remember that? You taught me that when you first said it and ever since then I've been using that same slogan…"

Narrken puts his fist up aiming at his brother then started to charge his Loose Cannon adding some more power into his ability.

Ki-Yale puts his hands up then his brother blasted him with his Loose Cannon which exploded on impact causing him to fall back into a building breaking through the walls then landing on a concrete pillar.

Additional explosions occurred from other particles that came from Narrken's Loose Cannon which had impacted other collapsed structures.

Narrken recharged his Loose Cannon and got ready to shoot at Ki-Yale again but unexpectedly, his father appeared in front of him.

"What the…" Narrken stunned.

"My son…" Neecho said.

He appeared to be a bit surprised with his eyelids wide open and then instantly, he began to glare at his father.

"Not so happy to see your father?"

"No but what would satisfy me though, is erasing you from my sight."

"We all know that's not what you want."

"No that's exactly what I want. I'm counting on it…"

"You were held against your will and you had no other choice but to do what they say… Now I'm here now… Come back on our side, we all can help Ki-Yale defeat this evil together."

"You're here now but where were you back when they kidnapped me."

"What was I supposed to do Ken?! You went off running then your brother went after you . . . There was no trace, you need to believe me, we were looking countless days for you…"

"Until you gave up!"

"There was one point, after three years we just presumed you were dead… but we still kept on looking for you. It was your brother that returned hope, he couldn't bear that conjecture!"

"Hm', dead? But here I am ready to kill you… And it's you I really want. Ki-Yale is for the Dragoon Prince." Narrken said as he goes closer to Neecho and glared at him then suddenly…

He punched his father in his face.

"No… My son…" Neecho thought enduring the impact and witnessing the rage impending from him.

"Been waiting a long time for this day father!"

A horde of survivors witnessed Ki-Yale getting slammed into a building and they're wondering if he's ok. Boulders started to move and instantly Ki-Yale throws the boulder off of him. Ki-Yale flew up to the sky then looked at the horde and nods his head. People are cheering then he immediately started flying back to the action.

Ki-Yale stopped and witnessed his father facing Narrken. Now it's time to focus on taking out his Opposite.

The Dragoon Prince, still in his tuxedo flies up to Ki-Yale in the air and said—

"What a nice way to see your brother again." Dragazell said as he turned his head and looked down at the fight.

Ki-Yale saw an opening to strike. He clenched his fists, tilted back his right arm while gritting his teeth then soared towards him to punch him in the side of his head.

Immediately, Dragazell stopped Ki-Yale's body with his mind.

"Oh no, not the face!" Dragazell bantered then he turned his head towards him and smiled deviously.

"Granddad! I can't move!" He said speaking to his grandfather through telepathy.

"You have to keep fighting and resist it."

"Speaking to your grandfather telepathically I see…. Hm', poor guy, he's going to witness all of this bloodshed through your eyes."

"We'll see about that."

Dragazell smirked then said—

"Now, this outfit doesn't look right while killing you. Let me use something more cultural."

His clothes quickly shape shifted back to its original form. The suit resembles Ki-Yale's suit with black and white coloring all over, but the black lining is spiked. His dark chrome shoes, gloves, belt and shoulder pads has spiked lining patterns while everything else is pearl white.

"Oh no… the Intercosmic Suit…" Ki-Yale thought.

"Yes, my grandson… that's was what I was afraid of. It's similar to your suit as it can perform the same powers your suit gives you and the natural Netron powers. Even if he is the opposite species of Netrons, he can still perform them all because of the Intercosmic Suit. He has the healing factor, he can be practically impenetrable, shape shift, downloading other species abilities and do lots more."

"Damn it, this really isn't going to be easy."

"Hmm… you should join me Netro, rule this planet and rule the universe! We can enslave the humans together and execute whoever that declines… We will be kings amongst kings!! I'll even spare your species. Now what do you say child? Join me."

Ki-Yale remained silent for a moment as he ogled at the ground then said—

"That's exactly what a prince wants, to be a ruler but to enslave and commit meaningless murder? . . . It ain't my style."

"Ha! I knew you were going to say that. Maybe you need to take a human's life just for the fun of it and see that it isn't so bad after all!"

Dragazell continuously in control of Ki-Yale's entire body as he made Ki-Yale put his arm up in a direction where a group of people are.

"Wait… What are you doing?" Ki-Yale panicked.

Dragazell smiled while Ki-Yale's Loose Cannon began to charge up.

"Oh no…" Nealo wheezed in his mind.

"What is he doing?" Tajaymae asked as Oji appeared out of the concrete of the building rooftop. "Hm?" Oji queried.

"It's Ki… he seems to be controlled by his opposite and he's about to shoot those people."

"Ok let's stop him sis before it's too late!"

"Let's go!" Tajaymae said moving towards them then immediately she stopped and so did Oji.

"Yo . . . Tajay . . . I can barely move!"

"Me neither!"

"Because I'm in control now." Terrorgon chuckling with a feel of dominance.

He has telekinesis abilities and also can take control of any spirit that is less powerful than him then gain power from the species spiritual energy.

"Something isn't right with Tajaymae and Oji. I can't find them anywhere, I lost connection with them." Nealo said.

"*Woah. It looks like Netro is pointing his left arm towards the ground... It seems that there's a group of people over there!*" Said the news reporter.

"This can't be happening." Demi said— "Netro." Litzy added.

Ki-Yale charged his Loose Cannon, his fists and lower arm shook with a bright orange glow.

"Stop this now!! Please!!"

"A ruler doesn't beg..."

"Grrraaahh'!" Ki-Yale blurted struggling to control his arm as it shudders a bit off target.

"Woah... you have some resistance!"

Dragazell then puts more pressure into his control as Ki-Yale's arm is aimed at the small crowd on the ground again then he smiled at him.

"Run!! Everyone, get out the way!!" He screamed at the crowd.

The citizens heard Ki-Yale shouting at them as they began to run in a different direction.

"Oh no." Neecho said looking at Ki-Yale.

Neecho began to fly up to him but instantly he gets a hit from Narrken sending him into a crumbled building.

Dragazell still in control then suddenly, Ki-Yale fired his Loose Cannon towards the people. In seconds the Cannon shot hits the area and expands along the surface with explosions from each particle.

"No!" Tajaymae shouted as she is shocked at what Ki-Yale did.

"Looks like you killed a few people there… Netro." Dragazell said chuckling and stopped controlling him.

"Aaaggh'!!" Hastily, Ki-Yale soared towards Dragazell while being ready to punch him but instantly, he stopped Ki-Yale with is his mind again.

"C'mon, fight me! Forget all this mind control abilities and Fight me!"

Dragazell chuckled then said—

"We are fighting, this is the battle . . . You just don't know how to do mind control like me."

"That's not fair!"

"Ha I'm a Dragoon… we don't play fair!"

"I can't believe it everyone… It looks like… It looks like Netro fired at a group of people!" The news reporter said.

—At the Mars Northern Space Station.

"Never trust a fucking Alien. One of the first rules of the military . . . Ok we need to proceed with evacs. It looks like Netro is not on our side anymore." General Mewsin said.

"Team Nine is on it sir." Chip said.

"They need to be on it faster. People are in danger!"

The Kafmora residence—

"No, no my baby!" Demi overwhelmed
Nealo flying to the location of the dragons terrorizing the city as Demi spoke to him through her mind.

"*Nealo… Whyyy? Why did he do that?!*"

"*His opposite was controlling him… Through his mind.*" Nealo replied.

"Oh my God. This has to stop! All those people… C'mon Ki, you can beat his ass." Demi said.

"He's got this I feel it." Litzy said.

"*Narrken needs to stop the act and get on Ki-Yale's side. I know there is some good in him.*" Nealo said.

"*Yes, Narrken. Is there any way you can talk to him or can you let me talk to him?*" Demi said.

"*I could do both those things, but his mind is blocking me from doing so.*" Nealo said.

<u>*Planet Mars*</u>—

"I find it hard to believe you are fighting with the Opposites. I thought you were stronger than this son… You got succumbed when they took you past their threshold… I guess you are feeble minded as you look."

"Hmm… Feeble? I evolved! I'm still stronger than Ki-Yale and damn sure stronger than you!"

"Yes, I see you have grown healthy… except for your eye. What did they do to you son?"

"I'm even better now… all because . . . they made me . . . part Dragoon!"

"No…"

Neecho uttered a dumbfounded look on his face. He couldn't believe it, his own son possessed by the nemesis. "You're lying…"

"Lying? Ha! . . . I bred hatred for you father… You encouraged me to be a ruler! You uplifted my spirits, guiding me to be a flourishing man and Netron . . . and then . . . And then you announced that bullshit!"

"Son… It's all the Book of Edu. The book chooses whoever it felt that deserved to be Netro Two. I felt you were the one all along because of how brave you were, ambitious, taking action more than Ki ever did but the only thing you were missing, was being humble. The book oversaw every move you make and since you and Ki are half human and half Netron it's difficult for the book to decide…"

"I don't want to hear it anymore. I've yearned for this day to come father and now I'm going to kill you!"

"And what's that going to accomplish?! What will your mother think of you? Your granddad… Your sister? Everyone else. They all still believe in you Narrken, prince or not."

"No! Mother? Haha'! I'm going to kill her too and everyone else!"

"But . . . That's your mother . . . Your mother that birthed you Narrken."

"DIE!! ALL OF YOU!" He shouted while rushing towards Neecho.

"*Woah . . . He's completely gone…*" Nealo thought.

Dragazell is still in control of Ki-Yale as he approached him and stared at him in a devious manor then said—

"Hm, you want to brawl Netro? Ok, let's brawl."

THIRTY-NINE

"Man, it's chaos on the Red Planet. Who are those guys? Aliens?" Said a man at a bar on planet Mercury drinking a Jack Daniels shot mixed with Coca Cola.

"Yeeaah. This happens so much it's just normal now, its ok and our solar system isn't in shambles. Alright? These guys are gonna' fight themselves to death. I mean it looks like they're gonna' do more damage to Mars than themselves but hey, we can rebuild." Said another man.

"Yeah all that money going down the drain and more money to rebuild. Man, do you hear yourself? Rebuilding . . . That shit ain't easy and they ain't gonna' make the engineers keep building the machinery and robotics just to make the construction worker's lives easy. The shit just ain't easy." Said the man drinking another mixed shot.

"Man let them get some work to do instead of being lazy. Hell, I'll go there myself and sign up for a job. I used to do construction a while back, it's a lot of Sila Humans in the job too."

"I don't know man. I don't think we will have any jobs soon cause this fight here looks like the end of worlds."

"Maaan' you just sauced up."

"Yo, look at this fool man. Coming in here again after we embarrassed em' yesterday."

"Aaah', keep ya' head this way, I don't want him over here."

The man walked in and sat next to the two men.

"Aayye'. What's up man? Long time no see?"

"Long time no see?! If you don't get your corny ass out of here."

"Or what?! You gonna' fight me? You gonna' kill me?" He said as he pulled out a knife.

"Yo chill guys… it ain't that serious."

"You ain't gonna stab me man, just get out of here… aagh…" The man said as he got stabbed one time in the stomach. "Yeah, fuck you! Die!"

He continued to stab him repeatedly as his friend tried to stop him. Immense amount of blood revealed on his shirt and instantly his friend punched the man in the face. The bartender and the rest of the people inside stood up and all looked at the man. "Woah, this dude is crazy."

He stood there then groaned looking down on the floor.

"Gragh… ok, I don't feel good."

Suddenly, he looked up then his iris turned orange and his black slit pupils became vertical just like both of Dragazell's and Narrken's left iris. His skin started to mutate all around into dark brown scales, his body started to grow bigger up to thirty feet tall. Everyone looking at him with fear in their eyes as a large beastlike figure with wings appeared.

Customers and employees were terrified, screaming in fear and running for cover. The bar was large enough for the mutated man to fit in without breaking the ceiling. He roared and emitted a large blood red beam with heat surging around the bar instantaneously killing anything in the creature's path.

Gigantica City—

Nealo met the dragons and fought a few of them using his impressive Netron combat skills. He took the time save anyone who seems to be in danger but as soon as he saves someone a dragon shoots a beam from a distance killing others around him. The news stations recorded him during the fights using miniature drones and people all over doesn't recognize him as General Nealo.

<u>Mid-day on Mars</u>—

Terrorgon in control of Tajaymae and Oji letting them fight each other. Terrorgon doesn't know their powers much at best but since he can also read minds, he finds info on how their powers work. Tajaymae gained power from a nearby electrical substance while Oji covers his fists with rocks. Tajaymae ran towards her brother then rigidly punched him in his face while Oji solidly hits back using his fists.

"Aagh! No Tajay, stop!"

"I can't!"

"Yeees', kill each other for me."

<u>Safe Zone in Seven Tens City</u>—

"Captain Fletcher here from Team nine. We gathered as much civilians as we can into Pod One. They will be transferred on the Military Spaceship in twenty-five minutes. Engineers are making sure everything is intact and ready for lift off sir." Said Captain Fletcher broadcasting to General Mewsin.

"Excellent work Team Nine. I'll see you guys when you're back up here."

Dragazell and Ki-Yale are finally going at it in combat but Dragazell seemed to have the advantage of brutal power—

"This is what you want kid! A fight!" Dragazell said.

"I'm going to take you down!" Ki-Yale yelled as he heads toward him. His teeth gritted with his right arm curled back and ready to punch him. Too late to give in now, Dragazell's power seemed greater but he isn't planning to give up. Ki-Yale swung at his face but couldn't land a single blow as Dragazell dodged every swing. Dragazell then moved at the speed of sound punching Ki-Yale in the stomach causing him to lose his breath.

"Aagh!" Ki-Yale in agony.

Seconds later the Netron Suit regenerates the wound and revives him from the pain.

"That punch wasn't even my best, c'mon kid, you aren't ready for my true power."

"Aaah'!" Ki-Yale barbarically while he attacked Dragazell with his 'Lightning KO' with loud lightning sound.

Dragazell made fists and puts his arms up like an "X" defending himself from Ki-Yale's attack. He puts more power into the lightning then suddenly Dragazell deflects the lightning causing him to stop shooting.

"My turn."

Dragazell immediately opened his mouth then a heated beam is discharged onto Ki-Yale's entire body. He had his guard up enduring the impact and falling backwards about sixty feet.

He stopped the blast as smoke surrounded Ki-Yale's body.

"Aagh!. . . It stings!" He blurted in anguish as his entire body is slightly burned.

Dragazell chuckling, relishing the way Ki-Yale's being unaware of his power.

"What's this, my suit isn't regenerating fast as usual."

"That's the 'Chronic Beam' which contains radiation and . . . Dragon's Blood."

"*Dragon's Blood… Granddad talked about this before.*" Ki-Yale thought.

"*Yes, that's right my grandson! You need to be careful don't let him attack your heart! . . . C'mon Ki. You just need one hit of the Death Gun…*"

"I heard about this before. I'm not scared of your disgusting blood! Bring whatever you got!"

"Hmm… Let me show you my foul and raw Dragon's Blood." He said as he made two fists and instantly blood started rushing down his arms then he added—

"Here's a taste."

His skin turned utterly pale as his blood began leak from the pores of his skin downward all around his body. He then gathered his blood in his right hand as if its slime then twitted his right arm to the left and pointed with his fingers down.

"I call this the 'Dragon's Blood Bath'…. this Intercosmic Suit allows me to form the blood and extract it limitlessly initiating me to create lethal attacks."

He twisted his hand upwards as he flicked his blood at Ki-Yale. The blood became densely sharp and traveled faster than the speed of sound hitting Ki-Yale in the face, neck, chest and stomach.

The blood instantly rendered him with nothing but pain as it rapidly surges through the Netron Suit. Ki-Yale screamed in agony with his eyelids wide open exposing a distressed expression. His anxiety progressed as the blood went in contact with his chrome "N" symbol which is at the identical spot where his heart is.

"Your heart is fragile against my blood. Pure Dragon's Blood from Dragoon royalty . . . This is your terminal weakness Netro. The Dragon's Blood enters your bloodstreams eating away your blood cells rapidly until there is no more blood cells left. You think you'll survive this fight? Think again! You think that your father is going to come and get you when thinks get dark!? Think again! You think you're going to leave this planet alive? Ha'! You know what I'm going to say…"

"Damn it Ki! I told you to not get hit with that and look what happened . . . Damn it… I guess that attack was too fast for him." Nealo thought.

Narrken and Neecho is blasting each other with their 'Loose Cannon' then Neecho decides to fly away from Narrken forcing the fight into a chase.

"Why run-away Dad? Huh?" Narrken questioned his father while trying to assault him with his 'Loose Cannon'.

Neecho then decides to fly to a higher altitude then his fists started to glow the color blue then a blue energy ball appeared in front of Neecho's chest. Neecho instantly turned around and detonated his 'Big Bang Wipeout' as soon as Narrken ran up to Neecho with a loud explosion from his 'Big Bang Wipeout'. Moments later a cloud of smoke appeared around Neecho while Narrken didn't fall back from the impact and seemed to be inside the cloud of smoke.

Ki-Yale and Dragazell ogled at the cloud of smoke then Dragazell said—

"Would you look at that prince? Your family killing each other and you're over here helpless."

"You bastard!"

"I absolutely agree. It's a shame this don't happen sooner. I fired the missile toward LTV where your family reside, and it was enough."

"You were behind that?"

"Yes… well, the Mad Doctor and I were acquaintances."

"It makes sense now… the source… was you. That's why he knew my family so effortlessly."

"Yes, and I sabotaged the Heaven Bolt with my blood, that's why you were so weak when you got shot with the missile. I'm surprised you survived."

"I didn't wake up until the next day… my father said it was the radiation, but my suit should have adapted to it."

"I guess your father had a hunch but didn't inform you."

"I'm sure it was to protect me."

"Yes, but here you are, unprotected from me murdering you and getting what I want."

"No, I will not give up!" He yelled as he charged at Dragazell in midair.

Dragazell kept his hands behind his back as Ki-Yale gets closer to him then landed multiple punches. He was unfazed by Ki-Yale's punches, but Ki-Yale was reluctant to lose. Dragazell used little effort and substantially stopped one punch with his forearm then said—

"You're slowing down and getting weaker. I can feel it in your punch."

Ki-Yale instantly kneed Dragazell in the jaw with his left knee then caught a hold of Dragazell's neck with his left hand and screamed— "Agh! It's time to end this! . . . Death Gun!"

Using his right hand as a hand gesture, mimicking a pistol pointing at Dragazell. A loud gunshot noise occurred with sound waves reaching across the city as he significantly shot him in the face.

<u>*Gigantica City*</u>—

Demi, Litzy and Titus were watching the holographic TV and saw what Ki-Yale did to his Opposite.

 . . .

"Did he? Did he win?" Demi probed.

"I never seen that move before." Litzy said.

"It's called the Death Gun. An extremely dangerous attack and that should put him down." Nealo speaking to Litzy and Demi telepathically.

"Hmm . . . Good." Litzy thought.

"It's about freaking time!" Demi said.

"Yes… I always knew he had it in him. There's more to Ki-Yale's power, he just needed to release it."

Nealo had just finished his fight with a few dragons tearing them apart like it's nothing but he experienced a little fatigue as the dragons use their Chronic Beams at him weakening him. He retreated to an alleyway behind a building then shouted— "Yes! He got him! I knew he can do it…"

<u>*Little Tree Ville*</u>—

"Woah… that thing . . .It went right through the guy's head . . . Hey Xack come here, you got to see this."

"What happened?" Xack said as he walked from the hallway.

"It looks like you don't have to go anywhere after all."

Xack rewinding the livestream and stood quietly with his eyelids wide open and his pupils became small.

"Hmm, looks like its over." Fang said.

"Woahh'…"

"Good thing this news station permits live graphic content."

"Yeah mostly if it's something unusual like this . . . I knew Netro had this in the bag. He always does."

"He's remarkable for sure."

<u>*Planet Mars, Seven Tens City*</u>—

The cloud of smoke is beginning to clear up after Neecho uses his uncontrollable 'Big Bang Wipeout'. It appeared that

Narrken survived the explosion and was right next to Neecho with both of his fist on his chest.

"You're not even damaged..." Neecho said.

"Now that's the spirit but use more power next time." Narrken said charging his 'Loose Cannon' then fired it sending Neecho down a lower altitude.

"I-I did it. I actually I did..." Ki-Yale paused as his hand is still around Dragazell's neck believing that he defeated him but Dragazell moved back his head then smiled at Ki-Yale deviously.

"What?!"

"That Death Gun was weak!"

Dragazell cunningly got a hold of Ki-Yale by the neck then said— "My turn."

Dragazell started rapidly hitting Ki-Yale with powerful punches and at the same time choking him. Ki-Yale's suit instantly adapted to the little air he's getting then charges up his Lightning KO.

He smiled as he uses his Dragon's Blood turning it into densely sharp substance and flicks it into Ki-Yale's eyes. The blood went right through both of his eyes blinding him as the particles of his eyes gushed out with blood. Dragazell then let's go of him as Ki-Yale is holding his eyes and screaming.

Dragazell began to add more brutality and used his blood as a sword slicing Ki-Yale lacerating his entire body.

Gigantica City—

"Damn it. Thought he had that!" Nealo said.

"That attack wasn't strong enough." Litzy said.

"Oooh my baby, c'mon keep fighting and don't give up!" Demi said then she contacted Nealo through her mind.

"*Yes Demi.*"

"Where is Tajaymae and Oji? Are they alright?" Demi asked.

"I can't track them down I don't know what happened to them, but my suit still senses their life forces." Nealo said.

"What?! That means they're in danger!" Demi said.

"Yes, but I'm sure they're handling themselves."

"No something's up…"

Nealo ran into more dragons causing him to lose the connection then she said—

"Litzy . . . We need to go to Mars."

"What?! No, we can't. We're safer here."

"Damn it, I knew I shouldn't let Tajaymae go fight and that boy Oji sneaking behind my back. Aagh! Narrken needs to get his shit together and stop fighting his father like that!!" Demi yelled.

Planet Mars—

Dragazell began brutally beating Ki-Yale senselessly with his Dragon's Blood then the Dragoon Prince formed his blood into thousands of sharp separated pieces and constantly throwing them at Ki-Yale. Despite the brutal beating, Ki-Yale continuously held his own and used a few tricks of his sleeve like the 'Big Bang Wipeout' but that wasn't strong enough, he used the Tantu Orb used by the Death Angels but Dragazell wasn't suppressed by the orb so Ki-Yale loses momentum and the orb misfired causing it to disappear. He even used Apaki Warrior's 'Apaki Sword' forming a katana to continuously cut Dragazell but it still wasn't enough. Everything he tried just misfired like it's nothing for his opponent. Ki-Yale even had the chance to use Tajaymae's plasma abilities but it's still not effective.

It seemed like all of Humanity is doomed.

Ki-Yale's symbol is now badly damaged, and he is extremely fatigue. He's bled all over with open flesh wounds, deep cuts and contusion and taking him a long time to regenerate because of the Dragon's Blood.

"Now you look so tasteless Netro! This is what happens when you brawl with me. Power for Power and in the end I become victorious."

"AAAGH!" Ki-Yale bawled in pain from the brutal attacks Dragazell gave him.

"Hm, if I had known that you would become Netro I wouldn't have taken your brother, but perhaps such move would be a failure because you're just so weak compared to him."

Ki-Yale had ongoing pain and suffering as the blood dripped down his forehead onto his damaged eyes and it's so much blood that he doesn't even know whose it is.

"I even gathered some warriors of mine to go up against you and this planet. Well it's not a total waste at least… At least I will conquer this galaxy with Dragoons residing then I'll conquer everything else in existence."

"These Opposites… How did you get them here?"

"Hmm, it's very simple . . . The Motogon."

A few miles away—

Narrken and Neecho are still fighting, blow for blow. Narrken was persistent having the upper hand and Neecho was slowing down by the minute but he can't die by just getting hit with Narrken's physical attacks even though he's stronger. This is because of Neecho's Netron Suit, it has to be a certain deadly attack.

In midair, punches and kicks rapidly hitting each other as most of the hits from Neecho are missing the target. Narrken dodged his attacks multiple times then he elbowed his father causing him to fly down right into a large library and smashed through a large concrete pillar. He followed him bursting through the walls and landing on the floor. He saw his father kneeling on one leg struggling to get up.

"We can go on forever or you can just knock me out cold."

"Knock you out cold father? Ha!"

"Or you can just kill me like you said you would."

"Hm, I'm enjoying this to be utterly frank with you."

"Ok. Let's be real now . . . You don't want to kill me, but you do want to express that anger towards me…"

"Trust me. I want to kill you." Narrken said putting his right hand mimicking a pistol facing upward then a black round bullet appeared with a red electricity surrounding it.

"Well… well, come on then… kill me." Neecho said as he finally gets up with little stamina returning to him.

Just like how Narrken pictured it, his father being weak and unsustainable compared to him. At that moment, he knew it was time to execute his father.

<u>*Planet Mars*</u>—

Ki-Yale's eyes began to clear up slowly as his Netron Armor tried its best to heal his wounds quickly but Dragazell's blood is feasting on his cells rapidly.

"Marvelous isn't it? It's only controlled by a royal Dragoon such as myself. It's a crystal claimed by my great grandfather Larthgon. The *Dragoon Crystal of Race* which is under my control turns any species into Dragoons… permanently. If their hearts are wicked and I must say Earth has showed me that they all belong to me. The Motogon progresses their impurity and if they conceal their true personality the Motogon will simply bring out the evil in these humans… then my children are born."

"No!"

"Netro . .. I'm a true ruler, unlike you . . . You want to rule without showing your wrath. Killing Sagan wasn't enough you should've showed millions no mercy then they'll be afraid of you . . . Hmm, either way I would've intervened and snatch your throne."

"If given the chance I'd be glad to rule over all humans but killing them senselessly isn't the way. I murdered one of their own because he was a congruence of how you Dragoons are."

Dragazell laughed deviously then said—

"Feast your eyes Netro! Observe the rising of my new nation!!"

Dragazell revealed the Motogon Crystal with his telekinesis and he brought it to Ki-Yale's face. He looked at it deeply and saw humans on Earth turning into Dragoons miraculously.

<u>*Solar System Wide News Station in Gigantica City*</u>—

The news reporters ordered their miniature androids to move in closer to record a clearer sound of Ki-Yale and Dragazell speaking.

"Ok, we are live on the air and the monster seems to be talking about humans changing into these creatures and from what we overheard is that the people that do evil things are the ones that turns... and... and they won't turn back into a human!"

<u>*Gigantica Maximum Penitentiary*</u>—

Fabian Torbino is in his large cell strapped down to a reclined bed sitting upward. He is by himself; his lips are stitched together tightly; his right eye is stitched, and scars are all around him. He opened his left eye, his iris turned orange and his black slit pupils became vertical. Then instantly, he started to mutate as dark grey scales started to appear all around his skin. Fabian groans as the stitches on his lips and right eye began to rip open causing his skin to tear separately and bleed. His entire body began to reveal dark scales and he grew exponentially allowing him to be free from his straps.

The alarm suddenly turns on causing the entire facility to be on lock down. Fabian turned into a thirty-foot-tall Dragoon with wings on his back. He roared alerting the guards, they arrive and see the monster standing at the door ready to burn everything in its path to pieces and that's what he did. Fabian charged his 'Chronic Beam' and blasted the officers in the hallway. The Chronic Beam is an energy blast that practically contains Dragon's Blood mixed with radiation. The more powerful the Dragoon, the more heat it emits, this heat can even surpass the sun's temperature.

"This is the Gigantica City News reporting live with an urgent emergency. We believe the alien on Mars has permanently transformed people into what seems to be alien dragons."

"This is Neptune World News reporting live with an urgent emergency. We are under attack by wild flying monsters. They're are destroying cities in a matter of minutes with beams coming out of their mouths."

"This is Neptune World News reporting live with an urgent emergency. We are under attack by wild flying monster. They're are destroying cities in a matter of minutes with beams coming out of their mouths."

"Neptune World News reporting live with an update. As you can see here the dragons are flying around shooting heated beams out of their mouths destroying everything in sight. Uh . . . Oh my God! One is coming over here right now! Take cover! Take cover!"

"Stop this Dragazell… This, all this, it doesn't have to be this way!"

"Look around you Netro… c'mon take a look."

Ki-Yale turned his head to the left and saw what hated to see, more destruction, more death. At this point, all he can do is watch. Maybe if he leaves his enemy to stop the beasts but it wouldn't make sense. He has to face the core of the complication.

"Look at the evil surging through… Humans . . . The humans are just as evil as us Dragoons."

Dragazell's terror reigns as every planet is now under attack throughout the entire solar system.

FOURTY

Little Tree Ville, year 2314, the Kafmora family are all in their domain doing their regular routine. Demi is sleeping upstairs and undergoing recovery after giving birth to Oji and he's now a few days old. Neecho bought many supplies along with supplies from the baby shower, everyone at the house is supporting her. The baby is finally home, and kids adores the newborn especially Tajaymae.

"Ooh, look at that smiley face! Who loves to smile? Ooh you do! Blub' blub' bluh'!" Tajaymae being goofy and keeping Oji happy. Oji was a tiny premature baby and he's very playful.

"Ok now Tajaymae. Leave your brother alone and come help your other two brothers with this 'Welcome to the Family' Cake." Neecho said.

"Be steady bro." Narrken said holding the cake.

"Oh my… this so hard to accomplish." Ki-Yale said dressing the Cake with icing spread technology.

"It's ok Ki just move it up a little . . . gently now…"

He tried his best to get the Cake dressed on correctly then suddenly he made a mistake and put too much icing on the top left of the Cake.

"Oh, Ki you clumsy goof."

"Damn I almost had it."

"It's ok. We can fix that!"

Tajaymae used her imaginative skills and decorated over the mistake that Ki-Yale made just in time for Demi's awakening.

"Woah!! Is that for Oji?!" Demi asked after her two sons brought the finished can upstairs to Demi's large room. Tajaymae brought Oji upstairs while Neecho brought up some dinner plates. Nealo is right behind them.

"Ok family. It seems like we're having dinner up here, in mommy's room." Neecho said.

"Well. As long as my stomach is filled up, I'm ok with it." Nealo said.

—*An hour later Neecho asked Narrken to tag along with him to the training room. Nealo was already there as usual. They trained for an hour and a half then decided to stop.*

"Alright. Anything besides my strength? I know there's like some power that makes us turn into a Werewolf!"

"Ken… Turning into Werewolves are not one of our natural powers…" Nealo said.

"Damn."

"Hey. We're giving you training more than Ki because we think you are the one. We feel that you could be the prince." Neecho said.

"I guess, I'll keep training some more."

"No, we're finished for now… Get your brother Ki. We're going on a ride around the village."

"But Dad, I wanna' keep training…"

"We'll train when you get back, I promise. Now let's go."

—*A few minutes later Neecho is giving Narrken and Ki-Yale a ride over the woods of LTV in his new Tesla he bought about two weeks ago.*

"Woah, this thing is fast! You got to let me drive Dad!" Narrken said as Neecho goes 110mph at 80ft in the air.

"You don't have your license yet kid." Neecho said.

"You enjoying this Ki?"

"Aaah', yeah sort of." Ki-Yale being scared.

"You're always shook man. You need to toughen up and loosen up a bit. Enjoy the life on the edge." Narrken said.

"Oh man… I'm trying Ken. I'm trying." Ki-Yale said tightly gripping the seats.

"It's ok to be scared Ki. I was just like you at that age, but I overcome my fears and that helped me become the man I am today. It's a process you just have to go through." Neecho said then suddenly—

"Oh crap, police lights." Neecho said.

"Oh, you're in trouble Dad..." Narrken said.

"Oh no." Ki-Yale fretting.

"Hey Dad, we should ditch them."

"No Ken. That'll just make it worse." Neecho said.

A police car pulls over Neecho in midair then the officer gets out a hovered towards the vehicle in his hover shoes.

"How are you today officer?"

"How am I today?! Ah I'm great. How bout' yourself sir...? How are you today?" The officer responded in a sarcastic voice.

"I'm doing great myself officer just giving my kids a ride."

"Oh man... You got kids in the back too? Wow, this must be a wonderful day for you and me. Ain't it?"

"Well... I... I guess."

"Man 'F' the cops!" Narrken yelled.

"C'mon Ken." Whispered Ki-Yale.

Neecho turned around and looks at Narrken then said— "Really?"

"Hey, I said 'F'. I didn't say the full word. This is what they use to say back in the 21st century . . . The cops were so corrupt back then."

The officer sighs then said— "License and registration."

"Sorry about that. That one's the troublemaker and that one's actually a stable kid..." Neecho said looking for his license and registration.

The officer's technology quickly analyzed Neecho's information and background.

"Ok Neecho Kafmora son of General Nealo Kafmora. I'm going to have to give you a ticket for speeding you were going over a hundred in a thirty mile per hour zone. I also have to charge you for endangering kids. No good man, I love that your father is the head of *the Gigantica Army, fighting for the human race and all but this ain't gonna' fly."*

"These kids… Trust me when I say they aren't in danger; they aren't in danger but alright officer. I'll go with what you say."

"Yeah these kids ain't in danger huh… And I didn't wipe my ass this morning, so I guess we both did something today that we both are gonna' regret." Said the police officer.

The officer went back to his vehicle then came back and changed his mind and didn't give Neecho a ticket because Neecho used mind control. The police officer walked back in his car went the opposite direction while Neecho started to drive again.

"Ok that was weird, dude just changed his mind all of a sudden." Narrken said.

"Hey, some officers just like the fact your Granddad is the General of the Gigantica Army."

"This is fun Dad . . . we got to do this again. What do you say Ki-Yale?"

"Umm. How about No."

"Pussy." Narrken whispering to Ki-Yale.

"I heard that Narrken."

<u>*Present time on Mars*</u>—

"We used to be family . . . me and you… Ki-Yale, Tajaymae, Oji, your mother and your granddad… This is not you Narrken. This isn't the Netron way."

"The Netron way . . . I never wanted this Father but Dragazell showed me the way. The real way not this ridiculous Netron way you speak of, all of it father… is bullshit!"

"You're blinded Ken… The Dragoon Prince . . . He's disgraceful, a tyrant to the universe and a being full of evil! How can you be this naive?"

Narrken looked at his father with anger in his eyes as Neecho provoked him with talking. This feeling of his own son, his first born tormented by the enemy's forgery, fed him nothing but hate.

A few miles away, the battle continues as Ki-Yale's life seemed to be coming to an end.

Dragazell continued to repeatedly beat Ki-Yale senseless with no mercy whatsoever. He is fond with every blow he gives him. Ki-Yale's face is being pounded with punches, taking any hit his enemy dished him and in no shape to fight back.

Dragazell finally stopped and held him by the throat with his telekinesis.

"Maybe I shall make you meet your ultimate fate right now Netro . . . you're boring me."

"Hm... just go ahead and kill me . . . I failed but I know I tried my best fighting for my planet."

"Look at you, being a quitter... you're weak and not fit to be a king. You filthy pathetic Netron."

Ki-Yale pants while receiving punitive words.

"You failed and also your planet will be conquered once you are destroyed."

"Conquered?"

"Yes, and I'll make them my slaves. Hm', unless you made an offspring already? Hmm did you?"

"No . . . but if I was to die, my brother Ken will take my place then take the throne as king."

"Hm... and you think your brother can rule a whole planet of pure righteousness after he betrayed you? If the Netrons found any knowledge of that... What king would he have been? . . . Well, essentially he would still have to be, so that your species and your planet wouldn't become obsolete."

"This fight between me and him . . . It was all a plot from the beginning..."

"You're thinking . . . you're getting close to the truth."

"How did you make Narrken with pure Netron royalty in his blood give into the Motogon?"

"It took a while with the torture and lament pain he endured but it was hatred that led him to be consumed by the Motogon. It is true that Netrons cannot be consumed, however, he is part human after all."

Dragazell grinned at him, enjoying his triumph and at this point, Ki-Yale could barely stand with his suit completely damaged. His black gorget is completely ripped apart along with his shoulder pads and the rest of his garment.

"You truly are a descendant of Larthgon…"

He chuckled then responded— "Yes I am the tyranny that my great grandfather passed down and I truly wanted you to see that. Netro we are destined for this. Our ancestors originated this war and we shall finish it…"

Ki-Yale still couldn't stand up straight, but he maintained his courage.

"Yeah, you're right. So… so let's finish it!"

Dragazell sneered then said—

"Hmm, yes but there has to be something . . . something I can taunt you with and have a little more fun."

Colonel Vixen and the Mega Human Prime Army are gathering their weapons, armor and loading the vehicles.

Corporal Maya Gatson stepped in the office while Vixen stood by the window watching at her troops. Maya Gatson, the same soldier that apparently got shot in her stomach by Neecho impersonating Sergeant Roscoe Scheel. She was in critical condition but later recuperated, it was like her wounds where never there as some believed that Sergeant Roscoe used enchantment all along. Regardless of the many combats, she stood firm and persistent to serve under the continental Gigantica Army.

"General Zion will be joining us on the battlefield... that is how we know this is going to be the toughest fight ever."

"How are we even going to beat this Colonel?"

"That's one of the toughest questions you ever asked me."

"And you're the toughest one I know to answer it."

"Hm."

"We understand the reason for the creatures. They're possibly humans that were permanently transformed into them."

"We could set up a barrier and contain them and exterminate from the inside but then again some of the evacs may turn as well."

"Everything is a risk at this point. What's the status of the droids and evacs?"

"Droid Soldiers are on the front lines in every city and assisting local police. It's approximately fifteen to thirty minutes till all citizens evacuate to the safe houses."

"Good. We're going to need the area clear of civilians when we arrive on the battlefield . . . Gigantica is crumbling down to rubble. Hm, it wouldn't even matter for them to conceal when one can just turn unintentionally . . . Even one of us could turn but I'm sure I have my soldiers in line."

She walked up the railing then looked over the bridge, staring at the vessels and contemplating then she said—

"This may all seem like the end, but we've been there before with an alien invasion and we prevailed. It's time we put away fear and go in full force. We do it as one nation, we're going to rid this solar system from the vastly evil that roams."

Three dozen Opposites are attacking downtown while police officers are taking cover fire. Suddenly, Nealo appeared about two thousand feet in the air and immediately fired his Loose Cannon penetrating one Dragoon in the stomach.

Three Dragoons saw that Nealo is a threat then they approach him and started firing their Chronic Beams. He immediately uses his Big Bang Wipeout energy as a shield for just twenty seconds while the Dragoons continuously blast their beams.

Three more Dragoons appeared preparing to attack Nealo as he held his own. Sharply, he detonated his Big Bang Wipeout and ended up eradicating the six Dragoons that we're trying to attack him.

Colonel Vixen and the U.S. Mega Human Prime Army which were roughly four thousand soldiers are finally on the scene as the Droid Army are the first to go out on the front lines.

"Ok now we set up a perimeter and drop the steel shields about two thousand yards from the targets. Every soldier must have an android guarding them at all times."

Terrorgon amused with laughter remaining control over Tajaymae and Oji.

"This is fascinating! Look at you two, fighting to the death, I love it"

"I'm so sorry brother. I just can't resist his control!"

"Me neither . . . there . . . has to be . . . a way to resist his control!"

Terrorgon chuckled some more then said— "You don't have the power to resist my control."

—The battle between father and son continued as one provoked the other.

"Shut up! Shut up! Shuut' uup'!!" Narrken frustrated.

"You don't know what I'm seeing right now . . . I just see the same arrogant brat from back when he was younger."

Narrken equipped with his Death Gun kept his aim at his father.

"You still haven't bloomed yet... c'mon Ken by now you would be a remarkable Netron... making better decisions than this, instead wasting your precious youth with these foul creatures. You are half human so I can argue that... you aren't even a man yet, with this, behavior you displayed . . . I'm disappointed son... the life of a Dragoon... it's an absolute unbearable life and that's not you son."

"I told you... to shut up!!" He seethed as Neecho walked closer.

"Listen . . . please, son . . . just come back . . . come back to the life we use to have. I don't care about what happened today or how many humans you killed, if you did... I just want you back . . . Son, I love you and I missed you a lot. We missed you a lot, every day I wish you were back with us for at least one more day."

The wind blew against Neecho's body as he shook his head with stifled tears tumbling from his eyes.

"I get that you're angry... it's ok to be angry... I'm sorry son, I'm so sorry. I'm going to be a better father to you and not mislead you into something like this ever again..."

Narrken frustrated with his plea while he glared deeply at his father with anger overflowing from his face.

"Please Ken, just come ba..."

Gigantica City—

Extraterrestrial mutated Dragoons were airborne firing their Chronic Beams upon the city as Nealo defends it. Fighting the Dragoons with all his might depicting raw strength then suddenly, he discovered an odd feeling with his son.

"*Neecho! His life force is draining rapidly . . .that attack . . . What was it?*"

Nealo being startled seeing through Neecho's eyes. "Damn it!"

Anxious to know what's truly going on, he quickly evacuates the scene flying the speed of sound towards the International Space Station to take a space bus.

<u>*Little Tree Ville, Year 2314—*</u>

Ki-Yale and his older brother Narrken with amateur boxing gear sparring in the backyard practicing their boxing techniques.

"Why do you always gotta' move away like a punk Ki-Yale?"

"Because you hit too hard Ken! Ok I'm so done with this!"

"Hey, you need to toughen up and never quit! Quitting is for losers."

"I'm trying but I'm just not tough enough Ken."

"Not tough enough? C'mon Ki, we have Mega Human strength and Dad said in the future we will become stronger. Just imagine being stronger than a Mega Human Prime."

"I guess that would be awesome."

"Hell yeah it will, just think about it… being tough and strong gets you through almost anything, especially those criminals."

"Oh yeah. Definitely don't want anyone to rob me."

"Or even worse man, it's so much crazy people out there. Especially with that Mad Doctor."

"He's not real, he's a gimmick just to scare people."

"What? He's real as he gets Ki but he's lightweight. I could knock him out easy!"

"Well, I wanna' be just like Dad! He said that he was just like me when he was my age and look at him, he's like freaking strong."

"No, I wanna' be like Dad! You're Grandpa."

"Hmm, ok… I guess I'll be Grandpa, he's a General."

"Yeah but Dad is like the…" Narrken said as he abruptly got interjected by Neecho arriving outside the backyard.

"What you guys doing?"

"Dad!" Narrken shouted as he ran towards him with his arms out.

"Woah…" Neecho said as his son hugged him around his legs then he continued—

"Ok, I haven't got a hug like this in a while."

"I'm just happy to see you. You've been so cool lately and I realized how great it is to have such a wonderful father like you."

Neecho lifted Narrken then said—

"Hey, I hope this is not turning into some kind of bribe."

"Absolutely not Dad." He said then laughed

Neecho looked at Ki-Yale as he looked away from his father chuckling and being awkwardly shy.

"Hey, you want a hug too?"

"No… Hm, I gotta' be tough."

"Hahaha!" Narrken laughed.

"I know Ken probably told you to be tough but you're still very young and it's ok to have a soft side. Hugs aren't so bad, especially when you're alive, appreciating life and family that's there for you when no one is."

"You're right Dad." Ki-Yale said as he ran up to his father and hugged his leg.

<u>Present time 2pm on Mars—</u>

"NAAAOO!" Ki-Yale screamed aggressively.

Dragazell with astonishing speed, blasted Neecho with a sharp Dragon's Blood attack that pierced right through his heart and causing it to fall out through his back. Neecho's heart is halfway split in half and landed on the library floor with a four-inch hole in the chest and a six-inch hole in his back with tons of blood gushing out of Neecho's body. He stood still barely breathing, traumatized and looked down on his chest as he touched his open wound.

Narrken with his eyelids wide open, his pupils became minuscule and still pointing his Death Gun at his father while Neecho gazed at him. His father tried to speak with the little bit of breath he has left but the words could not come out.

Just minutes away from the library where Ki-Yale witnessed his father getting shot down. Still badly hurt from the beating, he struggled to walk towards his father. His eyes were still partially damaged, and his sight was nil but a slight blur.

Ki-Yale entered the library focusing on his father, he doesn't even care that he walks pass his Opposite and then he yelled— "DAD!! C'mon . . . This can't be happening!"

The echoes streamed through the large library from his bawling as Neecho lost absolute fatigue then abruptly . . . he fell down to the ground with is head facing Ki-Yale.

"*No . . . My son . . .*" Nealo worried while being airborne through the atmosphere.

"*Woah everyone. It seems Henry Luciano attacked another man right in the chest, and it seems like he's not getting up any time soon.*" Said the news reporter talking through the android that hovers over the fight.

Demi gazing at the TV with a shocked look on her face. Her aspiration defended her heart moving close to the high-tech big screen TV.

"C'mon baby get up... C'mon Neecho... What are you doing?"

Demi knew of the effects the Dragon's Blood but denied the actuality of what had happened. Litzy lost for words and spell bounded by the unbelievable grief.

"C'MON! GET UP! No . . . I SAID GET UP!"

She fell to her knees and hits her thighs while Litzy rushed to her and tries to help her up.

"NO! My husband… no, no. No!" Demi mourned as her eyes start to water.

Litzy traumatized, slowly walked towards Demi then gave her a hug.

The abandoned Library on Mars—

It was ocular trauma for him, so unbearable to see. He just couldn't believe it, his father lying down and unresponsive.

"Dad… Dad get up… Please…!" Ki-Yale shaking his body keenly for him to rise again.

Narrken with an astonished look on his face discharged his Death Gun.

"Grandpa! I don't know what to do… Dad, he's not getting up! His eyes are open put he's just not moving… He's not moving!" He spoke telepathically with tears coming down his cheeks.

"I know, my suit, it doesn't feel his life force anymore."—Nealo responded.

"Dad…" He continued to whimper, holding up his father with his left arm embracing his body and his right arm around his neck.

—Terrorgon minutes away on the rooftop with a grin acknowledging Dragazell.

"Hm, our prince… A savage as usual…"

Ki-Yale knelt and tightly hugging his father then he touched his own chest. He pierced his hands through, digging his fingers into his own flesh. "AAAGHH!!"

Narrken with a look of confusion on his face, wondering why his brother would do such a thing to himself. Ki-Yale pulled his sternum upward allowing his rib cage to crack open as he endured pain and snapped it in half. An opening was now available for his heart with his ribs sticking outward past his skin. His bone tissue was already fragile from battle which made it even easier to break. He then grabbed hold of his heart, little time to think while seconds go by, no movement and no breath. No sign of life from his father whatsoever.

Ki-Yale ripped his own heart out with just the veins and nerves still attached like melted plastic stretching and oozing from his body.

Narrken became more alarmed as he saw his brother trying to replace his heart into his father's chest.

"Ki-Yale! My grandson, it's already too late. You're just going to get yourself killed... If you take your heart out with all of that Dragon's Blood leaking around your chest... You will die!"

"But my father, I can't just let him die! . . . hffmp' . . . Narrken! Do something! This is your father!"

Narrken beheld Ki-Yale with a face of guilt then looked over to Dragazell.

"He was mine for the taking!"

"Yes, he was but you weren't going to kill him." Dragazell implied then smirked and shook his head.

"All of you Netrons are just pitiful filth that roams the universe, such waste of life. This is why I'll be the victor! You think this is bad? Hmm'? . . . When I'm done with you Netro, I'm going straight for your planet!"

Ki-Yale heard Dragazell's words repeatedly in his head as his entire body shook. He looked back at his fallen father and all he saw was the Dragon's Blood creating steam all throughout his body. Comparable to the Death Gun the blood acts like a virus rapidly expanding throughout the bloodstreams, decomposing the cells away and replacing his blood with Dragazell's. At this point, not even telekinesis could save him.

Blood salivated from his heart, as it beats rapidly while holding it by his chest. Both of Ki-Yale's entire eye structures altered to an all-black abyss as his brother became disconcerted of his strange presence. The aura around him began to shift, the dirt ascended from the library floor alerting the Dragoon Prince.

"Hm?"

His body began to move peculiarly as his heart slowly become intact again with two large lumps appearing from behind his back.

"*Nealo….*"

The odious spirit calling upon his name once again with a grim and morose tone.

"*Nealo...*"

The demon grabbed Nealo's attention by continuously droning his name.

"*It's that voice again.*"

A veteran of war amongst the human race now startled by the being that's constantly haunting him. His armor seemed to be powerless against the demon and his thoughts clutched within its telepathic cluster.

"*Where am I?*"

"*My world, the world of evolution!*"

Nealo no longer has vision of the space craft. All he sees is an unknown peculiar realm.

Nothing but darkness until it finally appeared in front of him. It's that menacing face again, resembling a one of a kind fiend.

"*I have much more to show you… and many mysteries to reveal.*"

"*You're after Ki-Yale. Why?*"

"*He's part of the mystery. He's a special Netron and I'd be a fool to not take advantage.*"

All that's running through Ki-Yale's mind is that his father is gone and never to be seen alive again. His father's life, Dragazell took that away from him and his family.

"How can this occur so hastily? I didn't even get the chance to properly say goodbye to my son and now, a demon is plotting on my grandson."

"And the stage is set Nealo, now let me demonstrate"

The demon was phlegmatic with its intentions, abiding with patience until this very moment.

"All I need now from Netro... is to let loose and you'll see a glimpse of what I can provide to you all."

A sudden deep change in Ki-Yale's voice as he screamed in pain. Nothing but emptiness had swallowed him whole.

He growled as he got up and lightly dropped his dead father on the floor then looked at him with one last tear drop.

"What . . . the . . . fuck...?" Dragazell confused along with Narrken. "Hm?"

All of Ki-Yale's injuries were rapidly regenerating including his heart as his body slightly matured and adding four inches of muscle all around. Instantly, the two lumps converted into extra arms from each end of his side back, gashes appeared while his cheeks started to split open and it seemed as if it was carved. His sclera in both of his eyes remained pitch black but his irises and pupils became colorless.

"Ki-Yale? . . . Ki-Yale!" Nealo with fraught and unable to reach his grandson telepathically then continued— *"I can't communicate with him. What the hell is going on!?"*

"Hm... What do we have here? You're all healed up with a... new... look..."

A golden crystal emerged from Ki-Yale's forehead while his lips and cheeks became ripped skin showing his full teeth with an overall unusual new look. He remained in the same spot, facing his father. He growled then turned his head towards his brother once more.

Narrken frightened, beholding an entity that seems menacing to his eyes. He stepped back a few feet on the partially broken-down wall as Ki-Yale stared at him with deep rage in his eyes then he howled loudly expressing complete anger. He positioned his body in a primal stance as Dragazell squeezed his eyelids then said—

"Whatever you transformed into still isn't enough to beat..."

Within a millisecond, Ki-Yale turned around and got close to Dragazell and now being face to face. Dragazell remained still with goggling eyes and being stunned at how fast he moved. Ki-Yale then back handed his face with his regular left hand. The hit was so unyielding that the air itself was shaking from the impact as the concrete began to leave small fractures and windows began to shatter. Loud sound waves emitted from the impact and reached past ten miles.

"It appears that Netro... mutated into some kind of... into something I'm not sure of!" The news reporter speaking from a space station.

Ki-Yale screeched harshly with absolute beastly vexation while his Netron Suit completely grew back on his body. Expressing more anger, he blasted his Loose Cannon with his extra right fist, creating a large hole in Dragazell's chest thus causing him to have a hard time breathing.

Dragazell remains in midair then began to fall and loose fatigue then suddenly, Ki-Yale recognized something's strange progressing with Tajaymae and Oji. He immediately moved in the speed of light then arrived at Terrorgon's location facing him.

"W-Wha-What...?" Terrorgon stuttered.

The news reporter observing through in the small hovering android realized Ki-Yale disappeared then noticed that he relocated to the top of a building in the south direction.

"What the hell is that? Holy ####! Excuse my language but I never seen such a hideous looking thing."

"Don't come any closer or I'll eat their souls!" The devious mind of Terrorgon threatening Ki-Yale and trying to draw him back from attacking him.

Within seconds, Ki-Yale used his left hand and forms it like a pistol then a Death bullet appeared in front of his hand activating the Death Gun.

Terrorgon immediately began to tense up realizing that he cannot move a muscle.

"What's going on?! I can't move! . . . No, he's controlling me... He's controlling every single fiber in my body. He has complete control..." Terrorgon thought.

Without any hesitation, Ki-Yale fired an exceedingly loud Death Gun with a decibel meter of two hundred and forty as the sound increased. It was so loud and heavy that the sound waves traveled about twenty miles away breaking building windows.

Terrorgon instantly lost control of Tajaymae and Oji then their ear drums started to bleed from the Death Gun's sound.

Ki-Yale didn't have to say "Death Gun" because in this form he miraculously mastered the entire attack through sheer muscle memory and he also doesn't have to say the words in his mind.

Terrorgon has a three-inch hole in his forehead and the back of his head had his brain particles ruptured out displaying a twelve-inch-wide hole. Terrorgon then immediately fell backwards onto the rooftop floor with tons of blood rapidly spilling from his head.

Oji and Tajaymae's Netron Suits were in effect as their damaged ringing ear drums regenerated. Oji, with his hands covering his ears and gawking at his brother while Tajaymae did the same.

"Ki is that you?" Tajaymae asked while Oji is slowly panting.

With his hand still imitating a pistol, he stared at his brother and sister then moved the speed of light back to Dragazell. Ki-Yale hovers over him once again and growled. He noticed he was unable to speak fluently, touching his severed mouth. With quick thinking, he used his Netron Suit and formed back his lips with his ripped skin remaining.

Ki-Yale spoke with a deeper voice than before along with a serious stance— "Now it's your turn Dragazell."

Dragazell in shock at what his opposite did which made him wonder of the new potential he enthralled.

"Terrorgon…"

FOURTY-ONE

In the Gel Hev Asylum, Pamela Shale had finished taking her medication with injections and pills as a part of her psychotherapy. Psychiatrists then tied her up firmly in her room where she resided by herself. She was never the same ever since her confession of killing her own daughter. With little to non-evidence the system decided that she needed help and Luka agreed to it. Sadly, this led to the distance from family causing distress amongst Luka and Kathleen. It is presumed that no one knows of the real truth behind Melissa's death and Luka never believed it was a suicide, he believed it was an actual murder.

Pamela sat quietly as the belts around her were strapped tight. She hasn't spoken since her the funeral, only screaming agony, it was as if she was possessed by an unknown force.

She continued to sit quietly for a few more minutes as her arms started to jitter a bit. Her eyebrows lifted and her eyelids were wide open as if she saw something, something she didn't want to see then her arm shook along with her entire body. The machines came to a conclusion that there was discomfort coming from Pamela then psychiatrists came in the room with a remarkable respond time. Both of her iris color began changing into an orange color. Her skin began to develop dark scales and her body mutating with a high-pitched scream.

"Shit! Sound the alarm… This is not a drill!"

Planet Mars—

Terrorgon effortlessly murdered in cold blood. Truthfully, Terrorgon is slightly more powerful than Dragazell and Terrorgon being his teacher teaching him everything he knows. Now the tables have turned, Dragazell couldn't believe it how drastically his enemy increased his powers. Dragazell didn't just kill Ki-Yale's father but awaken the maximum power within him.

The Prince of Dragoons, making eye contact with Ki-Yale while he's still in his blood bath form with a stench barely anyone can endure. Ki-Yale's gashes formed itself back as he touched it and realized what happened to his mouth again.

"Hm', this… this must be your inner power… your Evo form but the mutation isn't under your full control." He said slowly moving towards Ki-Yale, making a fist and bending his arm.

Dragazell grunted and punched him in the face as the impact from the punch creating a loud noise with wind traveling his direction moving Ki-Yale's hair but his body didn't move a single inch.

Dragazell speechless and in utter shock as Ki-Yale being unfazed by the powerful punch.

He disregarded the hit then continued to strike Ki-Yale as he activated his Dragon's Blood Bath and puts more power into every hit but still, nothing was effective.

He stopped with the look of confusion and wondering why he's so incapacitated compared to the Netron Prince.Ki-Yale began to use his telepathic ability to speak while looking at all of his four hands.

"I'm a lot stronger somehow . . . What is this Evo form?"

"Hm... you don't know huh? . . . If you look in the mirror and see what you look like you wouldn't believe that you're the same person."

Ki-Yale utilizes his telekinesis and picked up a broken mirror that he easily found from the rubble. The mirror now in front of his face, his eyebrows lifted looking at the drastic change. He removed his lips once more to witness what he looks like whole.

His eyes are now clinched to his new appearance. He already had a vast distaste for this new look, but he quickly accepted it and screeched lividly as the mirror broke apart in pieces.

"Look at you, buried in fury and you just can't help yourself but to just be angry right now... That's exactly what the spirit wants."

"The spirit?"

"Yes, just by the look of that crystal on your forehead and those gashes, you're most certainly consumed by the Demon of Evolution."

"The Demon of . . . Evolution?"

"That's correct, it has the ability to possess multiple entities at the same time. As many as it wants, there's no limit to how much it can possess. It feeds off rage and haunts your loved ones for the fun of it, but it grants the hosts full power in exchange for rage."

Ki-Yale kept ogling at his hands then Dragazell continued—

"It makes you evolve into a form that brings out your maximum power, causing you to mutate as a partial image of what the demon resembles. I've learned this a while back when I was on my planet. Somehow, it's fused with you Netrons like a parasite, now you all have been relying on this demon for power . . . Hm, I could make my suit copy this power but consuming so much anger isn't really my style."

"Yes, the suit would've been the only thing to protect you from the demon but unfortunately the demon made its move beforehand… and from what I've heard this evil spirit was originated from your planet. You Netrons aren't so undiluted after all."

Ki-Yale removed his sights from his enemy and looked to the left. He closed his eyes, contemplating about the evils that surrounds him. Even his own planet, his own species that were sworn to be pure of heart are infested with foulness.

Ki-Yale looks at his hands once more and made fists, thinking about what's to come next. He molded his lips behind his ripped skin once more—

"Hm, if this demon will help me kill you... then, I'll be happy to remain like this."

Dragazell chuckled then said—

"Let's see how long this will help you. A demon shouldn't be trusted."

With no more idling, Ki-Yale began to release his undying pain out on Dragazell.

Moving at the speed of light Ki-Yale punched him using his upper arms and kicks all to his body and face as his other two arms hits him in the body. Every hit was unimaginably powerful, loud and creating impact that broke the sound barrier. Dragazell instantly in pain after just fifty hits every half second.

Without Ki-Yale's mind control holding Dragazell at his will, he would've been flying miles away after every hit.

Ki-Yale then used his two left arms and gave him one strike causing him to fly backwards going over seven thousand miles per hour. The punch has an energy of almost two hundred quadrillion joules, which is about forty megatons of *TNT*. Dragazell unable to control himself smashing into deserted buildings and Ki-Yale caught him by his hair. Ki-Yale immediately stopped Dragazell with his telekinesis then he pummeled his head into a building window then smashes his head into the building concrete creating impacted cavities.

With no time to react Dragazell is enduring the worst beating of his life. Dragazell in pain as the Intercosmic Suit is reforming his wounds but every time it regenerates, Ki-Yale's saw to it that he gets unbearably thrashed.

Litzy is lost for words and watching the holographic TV and continued to support Demi as the mechanical news reporters are focused on Ki-Yale beating Dragazell to a pulp.

"This cannot be happening…" Demi paused and still in disbelief that her husband is dead then continued—

"I have to get over to Mars! My baby needs me…I have to… I have to!" Demi panicked with a drop of hope left in her heart that Neecho is still alive although she saw him getting murdered on a livestream.

"But it's too dangerous…"

"No."

Demi rushed to the door and opened it.

"Ok then, well, I'm coming with you."

Litzy being unafraid of Titus, grabbed his collar then she followed Demi out the door to the front yard. Seconds after Demi walked outside to her vehicle, she saw heaps of Dragoons causing destruction.

Titus started to roar uncontrollably.

"Its ok boy, it's ok." Litzy said.

Suddenly a Dragoon appeared from below the platform flapping its wings as Titus immediately got in from of Litzy and Demi.

"Oh shit!" Litzy said as she quickly grabbed her jewelry from her pockets.

Titus roared then ran to the left side of the dragon as it fired a blast. Titus used its quickness and agility then jumps up on the dragon's neck and holds on using its sharp teeth.

Titus revealed its claws from its paws then repeatedly stabbed its neck and showing his brute strength then dragged the dragon down slowly as it screamed in pain.

"Woah…"— "This is new…" Demi and Litzy surprised.

Titus stood up right like a human and turned around looking at them then spoke in an extremely deep voice—

"Let's head to Mars."

"Y-you can talk?!" Litzy surprisingly asked.

"Wow, I guess reading those books paid off."

Suddenly, another dragon appeared as Demi and Litzy were motionless as if they saw the most terrifying thing hovering right in front of them.

"What out!"

The dragon then blasted its beam at Demi's car as she was shoved away from the heat by Litzy just in time before the blast hit the vehicle. Titus crouched down like a primate and looked at the dragon.

Litzy flung her jewelry at the dragon as it didn't defend itself because of it being confused of what the jewels can do.

Her jewels attached itself to the dragon's wings and head.

"Come to me you destructive beast, you're mine now!"

Nealo amongst the atmosphere, immediately soaring Mach 6 speed towards his family.

"Woah… Ki-Yale, he like, changed!" Oji said.

"Oji… It's… It's Dad, in that library! He's down!" Tajaymae said realizing her father is down on the ground next to an unknown boy which is Narrken.

Tajaymae leaped off the building plummeting eighteen stories down then she hits the ground firmly then she continued towards her father. Oji moved into the building concrete morphing into it until he made it down to the ground then following his sister.

"You're going to pay for what you done!" Ki-Yale raged with his deeply changed voice.

"You should just kill me now—Aagh."

"No, I want you to suffer first and humiliate you like how you did to me."

Ki-Yale created an Apaki Katana igniting it with fumes duplicating the Apaki Jermayin technology and it is ten times more solid than before then instantly cuts Dragazell's hair off on the left side of his head, including the scalp itself.

He gave a bright smile enjoying his opposite having bald spots with blood dripping down his head. While the bad haircut amused him Dragazell created his Chronic Beam after opening his mouth. He blasted the beam hitting Ki-Yale's face as the heated blood covered his face completely then suddenly… he shook his head to remove some of the blood and revealing not even a scratch or bruise just his unusual mutated face.

Ki-Yale looked at him as the blood began to levitate around him despite the blood being his weakness, he overpowered it and used his mind to extract it from his face. Dragazell slightly trembled realizing no matter what attack he does—they're not effective.

Library in Seven Tens City—

Narrken still in shock as he strode towards his father with a face full of guilt looking down at his dead body.

"Dad!" Tajaymae said running towards her him with Oji behind her.

"Woah. Sis who is that next to him?!"

"I don't know but he needs to back off!" Tajaymae making a fist full of purple plasma sludge and gathering some electrical energy from the library building's power source.

She aimed at Narrken without knowledge of her abducted brother being present with his head turned slightly to the left.

"Move away from my father!" Tajaymae yelled as she fired a strong dose of her Netron Plasma Star at him.

Narrken felt the sting from her plasma then instantly his head turned to her.

"Hm . . . Tajaymae? —Oji?"

"Na. . . Narrken…" She stuttered.

"No way." Oji surprised.

"Get away from them Narrken!" Nealo demanded appearing through the crumbled wall.

"Grandfather."

"Don't Grandfather me . . . I said get away now . . . Don't let me have to say it again."

With a slightly shamed look Narrken's face, he levitates and looked back as he moves through the broken-down wall. Then seconds later he instantly flew away from the library going about a thousand miles per hour.

"Grandpa… Why?"

"He's the one that led to this happening to my son… He betrayed us . . . A total disappointment."

Tajaymae looked at Narrken's exited direction then dropped down to the library floor looking at her father and tears instantly fell down her cheeks.

Oji is in shock and lost for words as he gawked at his father's deceased body without a blink in his eyes.

Nealo trod next his son and his two grandchildren.

"Was it Narrken?!" Oji angrily asked.

"No, it was Dragazell. Your brother's opposite."

Tajaymae shook her head immediately then began to grieve then Nealo waked closer to his son and crouched down.

"I know what you're both thinking right now... But your brother Ki has it under control. Ki is a lot stronger than he was before."

"But we . . . We can't die! The Netron Suit, it wouldn't allow it!" Tajaymae barely talked as her weeping succumbed her speech then continued—

"It's the Dragon's Blood—their blood, it can vastly penetrate the suit."

She breathed heavily as Nealo closed his son's eyes and Oji still looking upset, holding his fists tightly as if he wants to hit something.

As the rage began to build up, her eyes were wide open and bloodshot red from the tears. The library floor suddenly got dismantled as it encountered her knuckles.

"This is bullshit! This bullshit!!" She repeatedly shouted.

Tajaymae instantly gets up then vigorously walked to the broken-down wall.

"Tajay. Where are you going?"

She didn't answer ignoring her grandfather and stepped on the ruble ready to exit the building.

Immediately Nealo hugged her from behind after she began to run away. She tried to let go of the crutches of her grandfather, but he was too strong.

"Please don't . . . My granddaughter, you will only get in your brother's way and get yourself killed."

She turned around and looked at her deceased father once again as Oji is kneeling next to him mourning his death then immediately, she began to bawl.

General Mewsin ordered his troops again to pick up some more survivors along the southern area of Seven Tens City. Captain Fletcher reviewing his tactics to the team—

"Ok, let's make this quick and easy. Connect the bridges and have the civilians cross in an orderly fashion. We don't have to rush this completely but just make it neat, we don't want any fatal accidents. I need troops to stand guard by the exit and entrance. The survivors are on a thirty-story building. The first five floors are bolted, and they are on the sixth, seventh, eighth, ninth and tenth floor. I have a group entering the top floor right now checking for any lost souls up there... Let's move out, save some lives and make this a success."

Dragazell holding his own against Ki-Yale as he encountered more brutal attacks. He got hit in the chest flying backwards going around fifteen thousand miles per hour without any control of himself to stop. Then Ki-Yale used his impressive speed to quickly grab a hold of Dragazell by his neck ultimately chocking him and aiming his Death Gun at him.

"You truly want to keep humans protected, don't you? —Aagh." Dragazell asked barely breathing then he reached his hand out pointing in the south direction.

Civilians began crossing advanced mechanical bridges powered by high tech operating machinery onto the rescue ships then the bridges began to collapse unpredictably.

"Sir we have a very serious situation!!"

"What is it?" Captain Fletcher asked.

"The bridges are malfunctioning and seems to be breaking apart!"

"What?!"

Civilians screaming in fear bumping into each other then began to rush across the bridge. Some of the survivors managed to reach in the rescue cargo ship but precipitously, one of the bridges dismantled itself causing people to fall instantly.

Ki-Yale looked in the southern direction realizing what Dragazell has done as the rest of the bridges began to collapse.

He moved beyond the speed of light and immediately arriving to the scene leaving Dragazell by himself. Ki-Yale used his mind to get a hold of stragglers from falling. The other falling people screamed and panicked not realizing they were being held up by Ki-Yale's mind. Then he continued to use telekinesis to recreate the bridges.

<u>*Space Station*</u>—

After camouflaging their way to the station using the dragon to fly them there. Demi, Litzy and Titus reached the entrance.

"What do you mean I can't get on?! I have a husband in need of my help and possibly my children. So, if you can let me in, that would be well appreciated!" Demi said.

"Sorry ma'am, I can't give a ride. All space ways to Mars are closed right now. No private or public space vehicles aloud." Said the man at the space station booth.

"Where're going to be in big trouble for this but..." Litzy said using her jewelry to take control of the man's arms.

The man opened the gate for Demi and Litzy to go on the space bus then they began to run towards a space bus.

"Hold it right there! Don't touch that alarm... Or I'll have my pet lion rip you apart!" Demi threatened the security guard.

The guard immediately obeyed her and asked— "What do you want?"

"A ride to Mars…. now." Litzy demanded.

"Hm, ok but not in a bus. I'll use my security patrol car. Space Cops usually don't stop me."

"Most of them would have been fighting off those dragons anyway." Demi said.

"Hey, as long as it's fast enough." Litzy said.

"Oh yeah, this little thing can be pretty quick."

Planet Mars—

Dragazell floating in the air and feeling pain and contemplated to himself on what had just happened. He looked up at the west side space bus station orbiting Mars and the barrier then he began to fly towards the space bus station. Although he is hurt, he can still move slightly decent.

"Woah where is he going?" Asked the mechanical news reporter and not being able to keep up with him using the small drones.

Mars Space Bus Station—

Two security guards in the entry booth on the west side of the station speaking about the recent events.

"Man shit! I can't believe I'm still working here. I just got a call from my husband at home, so everything is good over there, but I still think things are going for the worst." The lady guard said.

"You think this is the end of humanity? People are turning into destructive creatures universally . . . It's just endless chaos." The male guard said.

"I don't know man as long as my family is ok, they're living in an underground anti-nuke safe house on Venus but after I seen that kid beating the crab out of that guy and I'm pretty sure he is responsible for all this. If he's dead, then all of this will stop."

"Well both of them needs to die or get this conflict away from our homes."

"Yeah I agree but only for Netro's death."

"What? . . . Woah shit!! Shit!! It's that fucking guy! Draw your gun!"

Dragazell took full control of their bodies and broke both guard's necks then went inside the station to use a space bus. He saw a few guards approaching then he instantly broke their bones with his mind leaving them no time to react to sound the alarm. Another guard in the security office saw what was going on and immediately sounded the alarm and having metal doors close pathway to the space buses. Dragazell uses his mind and struggled simultaneously but seconds later he opened the steal barriers giving him access to the space bus. He gets into a space bus and uses his mind to control a driver to travel to Earth.

"Is everything ok Captain?" General Mewsin concerned.

"Yes sir, apparently the bridges failed but Netro came along . . . Everyone is ok." Captain Fletcher said.

"Hm, bridge failure huh… How does this happen?"

"I'm not sure sir. There was no attack on us from anywhere but my possible theory, it could be some type of special mechanical tampering charges that was set on the bridges. No explosives, they just collapse."

"I see… we will have to run a full thorough scan of the entire system but they're all safe thanks to Netro, but I still don't trust him."

"What should I do to him sir?"

"Take him out."

Ki-Yale recreated the bridges putting them back piece by piece and allowing people to finish crossing and placing a few survivors that he controlled with his mind onto the rescue ship. Moments later everyone is on the rescue cargo ship and Captain Fletcher made sure the building is evacuated. He then made his way to the entrance of the rescue cargo ship looking at Ki-Yale with a bit of fear because of his mutated face. He looked back squinting his eyes at Fletcher as he held his gun in firing position ready to shoot Ki-Yale.

He turned his head to the sky, used his senses and found that Dragazell isn't on Mars anymore. He looked back at Fletcher who's still pointing his rifle at him, Ki-Yale screamed in rage and instantly moved in the speed of light back to the library where his deceased father is.

"Ki-Yale…" Nealo said while his grandson walked closer to him and then looked at Tajaymae and Oji.

"I assure you all . . . his death will not be in vain . . . I will avenge my father's death . . . Our father's death."

Nealo stunned to see Ki-Yale like this, the exact look that was haunting him is now right in front of him. Lack of knowledge for what may happen next to his grandson, he pondered on his peculiar mutation.

"That's the… that's the same face from the Book of Edu… the same look that's been haunting me! Hm, his skin seems decayed… What is this form? It doesn't look too pure, but it seems that, he's controlling it."

Dragazell used his telepathic powers and ordered the captain of the bus to go into hyper drive allowing the bus to proceed with interstellar travel.

Within minutes the space bus made it the Earth's Eastern International Space Station which is attached to the barrier gate. The gate has an auto system that lets in the space busses according with the captain. He used his mind and ordered the captain to drive the space bus with full speed towards Great Welkin City where there are possibly remaining survivors. The city's shields were down which made a clear path for him to land onto the buildings. The captain's body is completely subdued by Dragazell's control with his eyelids wide open and without a blink.

He smiled, knowing what would happen next and in no time the space bus collided into the city causing yet another building crumbled to rubble with possible casualties.

The Dragoon Prince then exited the crashed space bus, his suit nearly back to normal and some power is returning to him after the brutal attacks from his sworn enemy. He went airborne then a few police officers appeared from the shuttles. The police officers are opening fire on him realizing he is the leader of the monsters destroying everything.

Dragazell used his mind to instantly shatter apart the officers by making their bodies explode as dragons flew around him then he said—

"My species, unleash your terror and take over this planet!"

Planet Mars—

Ki-Yale lifted himself off the ground then broke the sound barrier going Mach 40 passing through high altitudes then hits the atmosphere. His body began to burn from the atmospheric pressure then regenerated miraculously. After flying and phasing through the barrier then flying all the way through passing the thermosphere, he began to go faster hitting light speeds then proceeded even faster heading towards Earth.

Great Welkin City—

The Dragoon Prince hovered in the sky once again and looked to the right with his enhanced vision and saw his dragons being killed by Colonel Vixen, the powerful U.S. Mega Human Prime Army and the U.S. Marines in Gigantica City.

The embodiment of vast endless evil that's parallel with his vitality. He quickly flew towards the city within minutes and landed with a dozen dragons behind his back uttering a loud prolonged sound with vile aggression.

"Colonel . . . It's their leader..." Corporal Maya said.

"No…"

"Shit! What do we do?"

"Coloenl . . . Colonel . . ."

. . . Still no response. Vixen knew from the start what she was getting into and now she faces the heart of the beasts.

"Everyone!! Aim your weapons!!"

Her army in the crumbled city all aimed their guns at Dragazell while he just looked at them with a straight face.

Colonel Vixen took a deep breath and planted her feet firmly to the ground.

"This is an army of strong soldiers. But are we making a stupid decision? It's my call, all of this falls on me! If these men and women die, it would be all because of me! No! We stay and fight! We are strong soldiers! This monster already murdered most of the population! How would we look like, running like cowards?! The world depends on us now!"

"Fire!!"

Heat beams and bullets all went towards Dragazell and his mutated human Dragoons. Most of the shots landed on him and the rest were stopped in midair with his mind protecting the Dragoons.

"Unbelievable . . . All of the shots didn't even faze him." Vixen said then continued—

"All right . . . Reload! We're not going to give up!"

"I… I can't move…" One soldier said.

"What?"

"Me neither." Another soldier said then the rest said the same as tension roams the air Vixen opened her eyes wide open and looked at Dragazell then she said—

"I can't move . . . I can't move either."

Dragazell in his stance clenching his fist, with slightly bent arms and showing a scowling face of a predator ready to strike back.

"It's been a pleasure fighting with all of you. You are all brave men and women fighting for the human race! We all came into to this force knowing one important thing, is if we fight together . . . We die together!!" Vixen spoke with an oration of patriotic words.

"It's been pleasure fighting with you too General . . . You're a woman of honor and bravery."

Vixen smiled then said—

"I have a picture of my wife in my pocket. I didn't even look at it before I came out here to fight. My conscious was telling me that this would just be another victory, but I was foolish, and I should have known better . . . I guess I was too scared to face this unbelievable reality."

Dragazell puffed his cheeks as if he sucked in air and leaned back, puffing out his chest then instantly fired his Chronic Beam out of his mouth.

"Goodbye everyone."

The heat from the beam burning anything and anyone in its surroundings, melting metal and concrete of the buildings. Disintegrating everything in its path, as it travels through the air at Mach 10 speed until it ultimately impacted them. The soldiers screamed revealing their inner barbaric ways and expressing their patriotism as the beam approaches them. Seconds after the beam landed, a massive explosion was emitted from the impact leading to the obliteration of the entire army.

Dragazell smirked showing some of his sharp teeth then ordered the mutated human dragons with his mind to destroy the main power core holding up Great Welkin City where millions of survivors are still alive. All the engines underneath the city slowly beginning to shut down from the damages from the creatures and will eventually cease causing the floating city to fall.

Meanwhile—

The Northern Sentry Space Station on guard for any opposing threat heading towards Earth. Agents stood and watched the news anchor speak the dreadful update.

"It's a tragic moment today as it gets even worse. A large crater with clouds of smoke is seen here as Colonel Vixen and her combatants were killed today in Gigantica City by a single blow from Henry Luciano's unusual beam. It was said that the General brought approximately four thousand soldiers to fight with her against the invasion. It seems that humanity is lost as the invasion is drastically increasing… We will continue to do a broadcast but please everyone, do not panic. We will get through this… We did so in the past."

The captain of the space station observed the horrid actions on Earth. — "That's insane… a whole army with one blow."

The fear of extinction is blooming rapidly while his hands shivered.

"Captain there's a breach in the east side of the Earth's barrier!" Said one worker.

In just one minute which is faster than a space bus, after traveling hyper drive from Mars, Ki-Yale slowed down then orbits Earth. He miraculously found Dragazell with his sight. As he hovered over the Earth's barrier, the alarm was triggered at that very minute activating the Heaven Bolt.

"Hm, someone's in a place they shouldn't be… Hm, If I'm not mistaken that could be the alien boy coming from planet Mars."

"Shut down the Beam?"

"Yes, shut it down."

Ki-Yale phased through the Earth's barrier which is made from Tektonium metal and Tektonian Crystals that has magnetic components.

Ki-Yale arrived at Dragazell's location after traveling light speed towards him then he realized Great Welkin City is falling rapidly. In a matter of seconds, Ki-Yale is underneath the city looking upward as he is ready to use his unbelievable strength.

Out of all four arms, he puts up one arm which is his left arm and began to grip the very center of Great Welkin City. Ki-Yale's muscles on his left arm grew another three inches trying to hold the city with no strain. The city began to fall slower then moments later it completely stood motionless as he held it in place and gaining absolute balance. With only one hundred and twenty feet from the ground, he began to lift it up.

As Ki-Yale miraculously balanced and pushed the city back up to its rightful place he lets go of the city causing it to fall for a few seconds. Then he instantly used his telekinesis to hold up the city putting back the damaged pieces of the engines back together and recreating the obliterated wreckages.

Dragazell was astounded by what he can do as he backed up from him realizing to himself that he is just no match for him. The Dragoon Prince refused to accept failure as he sends his dragons to attack him.

Ki-Yale just stood firm and unfazed in the same area as he ceased the dragons from attacking him with just his mind. He realized that the engines are back and running then he flew up over the city then he observed the destruction Dragazell and the dragons had caused when he crash landed on the west side.

More dragons were coming towards him with full force, he contested them all using an Apaki Katana gutting and mutilating each one. His lightning from his eyes are much powerful than before striking three large dragons at once. The dragon's spill their lethal blood on him but still unfazed as he is too strong making his weakness hard to penetrate his Netron Suit.

Ki-Yale landed on top of a crumbled building and blasted a Netron Plasma Star easily killing a dragon instantly then unexpectedly, another dragon had devoured him as he enters the esophagus, he then makes two fists and aligning it together in front of his chest preparing to launch his Big Bang Wipeout. Energy emitted from his fists pressing against each other as he finally reaches the stomach. The dragon screamed for victory believing that it killed Netro but then a slap of fists came from inside its stomach.

Ki-Yale detonating the Big Bang Wipeout causing a fatal explosion killing the dragon and four more surrounding dragons.

He defeated most of them but there was still more heading his way coming at him from miles away from the northern direction.

He looked for the Dragoon Prince for a moment only to find him hiding and being quick-witted recovering from his lacerations with the Intercosmic Suit.

Momentarily... after moving the speed of light, he reaches to Dragazell's location and is now facing him again.

"That speed…"

Dragazell is still alarmed by how powerful Ki-Yale has become, it seems like he's now staring at death in the face and contemplating how this will end.

"The things I was told about you Opposites are true. You have no regard for innocent life… Why turn all of them into many of your own?"

"These species are worthless just like you Netrons… I'll grant all of them the power they need to overthrow the universe! . . . It's only right that I do so…"

Dragazell chortled then continued—

"Why fight for them Netro? You think these are innocent species? Look at them… the same dragons you see there… Those are the same humans with devious hearts… Hearts of pure evil . . . The Motogon, I've been using this crystal for years now, simply depicting their true side and turn them into what they should have been a long time ago in their boring lives."

"No…" He said with a heavy voice as he moves closer to him.

"Yes Netro, after being compelled by the crystal, they then commit senseless murder, rape and many other foul things. Even if you just think of something foul… hmm… Then eventually those ones will turn. The Motogon will imbibe them all! Yes! These species will be all mine!"

"Sagan… you created him…"

"Hm, no I didn't… that man was already gone way before I started using this crystal. Yes! The crystal only fueled his wicked heart…! That goes to show you, what these species truly are . . . I was even occupied with him sharing information, clandestinely and discretely. I helped paved the way… the military, the Heaven Bolt, the overall corruption stimulating back to how it should be with the mass murders and other irrational crimes. I've been plotting till this day, although you killed him, it still didn't even come close to the main source of my deeds."

"No . . . everyone, is not like him and there are still innocent people out there who deserves to live and not be conquered by your awful sense of dictatorship."

"Hmm, foolish Netron."

"This won't go down, not while I'm alive... I will see to it that your terror reigns no more!" He blurted then palmed his entire face. His fingernails grew two inches long underneath his black crystalized glove.

Ki-Yale with vengeance in his eyes, expressed raw anger and squeezed his enemy's head.

"Before you were telling me I'm weak, now you run away like a coward... Fix your face, you look like a mess."

Dragazell in pain as his entire head is crushed with his eyeballs slightly draped out of his eye sockets, his brain particles started to gush out and blood splashed out repeatedly.

He released his squashed head from his hand then used his telekinesis to carry Dragazell with him as he flew light speed into the sky on a 38,000 altitude away from any sky city and possible aircraft traffic. Large clouds slowly shifted by as Ki-Yale unleashes more fury on Dragazell repeatedly punching him in the face and body. Loud sounds from impact of each punch then he ceased and flew backwards. He lifted all four arms and clenching fists, pointing at his opponent then activated with his Loose Cannons.

Nealo decided to leave Mars by utilizing his Netron Suit to form himself as the galaxy surrounding Earth then molded himself back to his original form right in front of the Earth's barrier gate. Using this technique allows him to reach to Earth as fast Ki-Yale when he was moving through space. This is another method to travel out of space using the suit's way of forming itself and the user into different things.

"Whatever Ki-Yale transformed into, could be a potential threat after he deals with his opposite. Let's just hope that's not the case."

<u>In the sky, slightly above the clouds</u>—

After blasting him repeatedly, Ki-Yale puts his right hand up and shaped it like a pistol then a Death bullet appeared in from his hand pointing straight a Dragazell's head. The time is now to end his sworn rival.

"I only met you today, but it feels like I knew you my whole life after you took my brother away from me."

He continued to speak expressing his vengeance through words—

"My grandfather and my father warned me about you Dragoons since the day I was informed that I'm part of another race from a different planet . . . You are the definition of pure evil and even if you die today evil still roams the universe, that's ok because it's my duty to wipe you all out! If evil isn't there, then I'm close to being useless."

His thumb is then raised upward, allowing the Death Gun being ready to fire as Dragazell is paralyzed by Ki-Yale's mind and had no words to say.

"From this day forward… I will never forgive you! I will never partner with you on domination! I will never…"

He paused as he felt sudden stiffness throughout his body.

His grisly face began to somber; his additional arms were beginning to return inside his body then he slowly leaned backward with his eyelids gradually closing. The paralysis became ineffective while Dragazell's face is slowly regenerating with enough flesh for him to smile and looked down at Ki-Yale's body being pulled in towards the ground by earth's gravity.

Ki-Yale unhurriedly changes back into his regular form with deep cuts, large bruises and abrasion all around his body with his symbol being damaged like before.

"That Evo form was draining your body as soon as you transformed! The power you unleashed on me here wasn't the same as back on Mars. Every hit was getting weaker and weaker. My blood was still affecting you making you obtain this power only for a short time. Goonie told me about this maximum power that you Netrons have . . . I just never imagined you would actually unveil it." Dragazell said following Ki-Yale as he falls rapidly.

Ki-Yale hits the ground hard and rolled on top of his face. He slowly tries to get up using his only two arms. Dragazell reached the ground and propels his leg onto Ki-Yale's stomach kicking him about twenty-five feet away as the impact of the kick made him body roll again—this time he landed on the side of his body in the direction of his opposite.

Ki-Yale's vision is momentarily blurry then his sight became clear, seeing Dragazell floating and smiling at him.

His smile reveled his sharp dragon teeth reflecting victory knowing Ki-Yale is going to die.

"Hmm… no more Evo Netro…"

FOURTY-TWO

A secluded locked down barricaded residence on Gel Hev Hills, two friends are with their family members went outside to the balcony and saw dragons terrorizing Gel Hev with people running in fear. Joe and Francis spoke about the events not realizing at any moment things can go wrong.

"We're like the coolest dudes ever! We're having a party here while we watch those aliens take over the world."

"Aah, shut up Francis! We chilling and that's it, forget everybody else!"

"I'm just saying man!"

"Hey, you heard what the news said earlier about having good hearts. Only the pure evil will transform."

"You really believe in all that crap man?"

"Yeah… I guess…"

"C'mon, those monsters you see man, they're from the freaking military. They're possibly loose projects or something."

"Yeeaah, now that makes more sense. You're so smart bro."

"Hell yeah I'm smart."

"But what if it really is like how the news say it is."

"C'mon now…"

"We can find out right now."

"Where are you going?"

Francis didn't answer as he went into his room then grabbed a sniper rifle.

"Whoah', whoah', whoah'! What you doing? I thought you changed those ways."

"Ooh I did but I just want to see something…"

"Put the gun down Francis! You said you weren't going to kill anyone anymore."

"True but this is an opportunity, the world is ending and plus I've never gotten caught using this sniper when I was working for Sagan."

"Oh, shit bro… your eyes man! What's up with your eyes!?"

<u>Planet Mars</u>—

Litzy's jewels manipulated the driver as the vessel orbits the space station. The automated exit system attached the vessel to the bridge and prepared for departure.

"Ok how are we getting past these tin-can soldiers?" Demi queried.

"We fight them…"

"I like your style Titus." Litzy said.

"But first we move in using stealth." Titus said.

"Woah. Who did all of this?" Litzy alarmed as they saw the dead bodies committed by Dragazell.

"I don't know but I hope that person or thing ain't here."

As they walk closer to the android facing the barrier gate Titus puts his hand over Litzy and Demi.

"Let me…" Titus bravely said as he ran towards one of the androids that has its back turned then smashed its body in half with one blow to the back.

Titus stopped and realized none of them are responding to the attack.

"They must be offline." Demi said.

"Yeah . . . maybe the one that did all of this, dismantled their motherboards with some-type of hacking system." Litzy said.

"Ok let's take a shuttle."

"I'm driving."

"You sure about that?" Demi asked.

"Yeah… Well it's bigger than a car but I've driven before…"

"No. Let me drive." Demi insists.

"Hmm… Ok."

<u>Earth—</u>

The sun is rising as the skies began to lose its darkness, Dragazell gently lands on the ground and slowly started walking towards Ki-Yale.

"Granddad!" He hollered in his mind.

"Hm, now you want to talk to me. What's going on? Wait, never mind I can see through your eyes again… What happened? How are you down? You should be destroying him!!"

"I was but I lost momentum. It seems that his blood from before I changed was still weakening my regular form and it was effecting me this whole time…"

"Damn it Ki! . . . Listen, I'm flying over right now but for now fight with all you got . . . I'll always be the one that plays the hard ass and being soft isn't my specialty but now is good as any other time . . . my grandson . . . I never said this to my son, nor did I say it you and I know I should have way before but…"

"I know . . . I already know you do Granddad and I love you too but I'm not going to make him win!"

"Ki-Yale…"

The Opposites are still inflicting their wrath tearing down cities with their beams. Most of the Special Forces are down and the other locations are too busy with their own crisis of human mutated dragon attacks. Ki-Yale with his feeble legs slowly tried to stand up and raised his right arms aiming his Death Gun at Dragazell. Fortified without fear, he uses he left hand to hold his right arm, his thumb is placed downward to charging the gun and using nothing but hope.

<u>*The Kafmora residence Year 2314—*</u>

"You think you got what it takes Ki-Yale! You ain't got what it takes to overpower me!" Narrken *said with an action figure of the legendary Jahzin Yoko.*

"Yes, I do my name is Ki-Yale the Emperor of the Grainians yeah! My power is much greater! I have the Sword of Grain that revives the dead. Graaaaah'!" Ki-Yale *blurted with an action figure in his hands.*

"No, Jahzin Yoko will not lose to you evil alien! Graaah'! With my Twin Swords of Ketsueki I will banish them all. AAAGH'!"

"Grraagh'."

"Wow... You guys really love your presents."

"Yes Mom, thank you very much and Merry Christmas." Narrken *said as he kissed her on the cheek.*

"You're the best Mom! Merry Christmas." Ki-Yale *said then gave her a kiss on the cheek.*

"You're both welcome, I love you boys."

"Now time for my present!" Tajaymae *said as she opened her first Christmas present.*

She ripped open the gift wrap and immediately she recognized the gift then said—

"Oooooh'... Mom! Mom!"

"Yes Tajay..."

"You got me a pretend castle set!"

"Yes, you like it?"

"Yes, Mommy I love it! This is the one I wanted! It's a portable folding set that folds within thirty seconds with all the royal dolls and

horses and the great hall! Oh, thank you Mommy!" She said as she gets up to hug her mother.

"You're welcome baby, you're my little princess and I love you. Now open the rest of your presents."

"Wait... I have to give my presents out too . . . Look at you, stealing all the glory." Neecho said.

"Ha, you're the one that said ladies first." Demi said then Neecho continued—

"Let's take turns...."

"Fine..."

"Hm, ok, the first present is for each one of you. Oji over here wouldn't understand what I would be telling him but for now it's mostly for you 'Three Musketeers'. Now the present will be opened right here..."

"Oh, so the present, it's like a secret to a bigger present."

"Yeah, you can say that Ken..." Nealo said.

"Now, does anyone know what the secret is?"

"We get our driver's license."

"Nope, too young Ki-Yale."

"New video games.

"It's way more than video games Ken."

"Ice Cream and chocolate covered strawberries!"

"No Tajay, we just finish having that."

"Ok, ok, ok...It's a pet dog!"

"No but, I didn't know you like dogs Ki-Yale."

"It's an antique android soldier from Grandpa's army base!" Tajay guessed.

"Nope."

"Ok... I know, I know..."

"And what's that Ken?"

"I . . . Don't . . . Know."

"Ha, he gives up!"

"Well. Do you know Ki?"

"Aaah'... Nope I give up too."

"None of you guys got it correct but I'll tell you."

. . .

Complete silence as their children desperately waiting to hear what their father is about to say.

"Alright . . . the secret is . . . you four, are all part aliens."

<u>*Present time Gigantica—*</u>

"Now look at you. You're just as weak like the humans . . . after all this you think you can…" Dragazell said and unexpectedly—

A Death Gun was fired by Nealo hitting Dragazell in the chest causing him to lean forward enduring the impact. Then immediately, Nealo moved as fast as he can, punching him in the back of the head then sprung in front of Ki-Yale to guard him. Dragazell being unfazed and smiled then said—

"Oh look, it's the old man."

"Hm, it looks like that form has worn off..." He thought while observing his grandson.

"Keep your eyes on me…" Dragazell said then tittered and used his telekinesis to hold Nealo in the air. He moved closer to him with immense speed then repeatedly punched him in the face. "Filthy Netron!"

"Damn it, he's still too strong. I could download the density of the universe into my fists then strike him or even download it into my Loose Cannon… but... He'll just counter it by doing the same or just regenerate… and on top of that everything would be destroyed from the impact."

Despite the pain he underwent from the Dragoon Prince, Nealo spoke telepathically to Ki-Yale. — *"My grandson… You cannot give up. Use the Death Gun… Take him out! . . . The Motogon is also inside his body… target him and the Motogon when you shoot."*

"Granddad!"

The unfortunate events lingered unceasingly, even the hope of survival tumbled. His grandfather arrived to fight alongside with him but it's still not enough. He had the supremacy, the advantage, such divine leverage just a few minutes ago but now the face of failure remains in front of his enemy.

"No, I should've killed him sooner when I had that power . . . I never knew of such power until I unlocked it then and it felt so breathtaking harnessing it and implementing my anger with it. The rage I had towards him, I had so much rage! I wanted to enjoy every minute of it but… I let my emotions cloud my judgment."

Dragazell kept beating Nealo, pummeling him into the ground. As Nealo's fatigue overwhelmed him, he wobbled and took a knee to the stomach causing him to feel absolute agony. With more strength than before, Dragazell punched him in the face and breaking his jaw.

"No, Granddad… not him too!"

Nealo fell flat on the ground without any movement. Dragazell released his control on him and saw that he wasn't his primary target at this moment then turned his head concerning Ki-Yale.

Unable to stand, Ki-Yale watched as Dragazell with a scheming smirk walked towards him.

"This can't be happening. I had the advantage! It's… it's all over…"

"Stop giving up already Ki-Yale!"

"But Granddad…"

"No, we're… we're not finished here… we never give up!" Nealo spoke with lethargy.

Dragazell stopped walking and didn't look back as Nealo slowly stood up, he then implied—

"I see you really want revenge after I killed your son."

"And revenge from me as well…"

A Loose Cannon beam appeared from behind Dragazell knocking him down to his knees. Dragazell twisted his head all the way around while his body was still in the same position as if he was made of rubber then growled showing his vastly sharp teeth and his overall inner Dragoon.

"Ken?" Ki-Yale being dumbfounded.

Planet Mars—

As Demi, Litzy and Titus flying to Seven Tens City, they unpredictably witnessed three dragons on a rooftop eating one of their own for a meal. Demi soared past them thus alerting two of the three triggering them to follow behind.

"Shit, I guess that dragon isn't enough for these two." Demi said

"Damn, they're fast." Litzy said.

"No, we're just running out of fuel."

"Oh… That's not good."

As the shuttle slowed down it loses flight and began falling as the dragons continue to follow.

"Ok, emergency landing . . . Everyone hang on!"

The shuttle hits a crumbled building rooftop then sliding off into another crumbled building causing them to have a rough landing. Minor injuries as the shuttle's left side is caved in with airbags all around. The ceiling automatically opened sensing the crash landing that occurred and the emergency doors immediately opened.

"Is everyone alright?!" Demi concerned.

"Yeah I'm fine…" Litzy answered.

Titus slowly stood up then suddenly, the two dragons appeared over the open roof of the shuttle.

The dragons prepared themselves to fire their beams then a swift plasma attack hits one on the left side of its neck causing the beast to drop instantly.

Oji appeared surrounding his body with solid stone then repeatedly hits the second dragon in the mouth. The dragon collapsed while Oji unleashing his brutal hits breaking the dragon's jaw. He then grew a large six-foot-long spine plant that has sharp edges and pointed top with thorns around his right arm, then punctured the dragon in the throat ultimately skewering the six-foot spine plant all the way in.

"Woah… this is new…" Litzy said.

"Mom?!"

"Tajay… Oji…"

"Oh, you're both ok…" Demi said as Tajaymae rushed to give her a hug.

"Mom…" Oji said as he also gave her a hug.

"Litzy . . . Hey is that Titus standing up?"

"Yeah, he can stand up like a human, I guess it's the Mega Animal serum."

"Ah of course…"

"Ok now where's your father?"

Gigantica—

The first born appeared with a whole new determination and now that's to terminate the Dragoon Prince.

"What?! You dare to defy me? After all I've done for you child…"

"To you . . . I'm just a filthy Netron, you were never looking out for me . . . And on top of that, you murdered my father!"

"You wanted to murder him! . . . Until you hesitated, somehow you disobeyed the Motogon. It must be because you are part human... Either way Narrken, I did you a favor."

"No . . . I hated that putrid prophecy but taking my father's life wasn't yours to take!"

"Ok well, he's already dealt with, and I don't regret what I did."

Seconds after Dragazell's last comment, Narrken flew at high speed towards him punching him in the face then swiftly, Nealo came from behind and punched Dragazell in the right side of his stomach.

"Narrken . . . My grandson . . . Now this is the Narrken I want to see . . . I guess the power of family isn't something to take lightly . . . Yes, this is what it supposed to be! We all have to stick together and remain as one, a Kafmora . . . a royal family!"

<u>*Planet Venus, Sentry Space Station*</u>—

All of Earth and the planets in its solar system are taking extreme action as Mega Human Prime forces all around tried to fight the unstoppable creatures. Operatives preparing to do the first missile fire on an empty city ordered by President of the World, President Blane Nixon Moore Jr. Extreme measures is now taking into place as survivors are evacuating into rescue vessels and may be kept putter space to be clear of nuclear fallout. Despite there might be survivors left, the highest leader is now launching full force after hearing Colonel Vixen and the Mega Human Prime Army is wiped out with only a few teams left in Southern Gigantica City.

"Arm the Heaven Bolt."

"Yes sir . . . the weapon is armed, and the target is now set for Orpana, the gun will fire in approximately thirty minutes."

"This is the first time ever doing such an extreme flush."

"Well sir, we need to save our human race, doing whatever it takes."

<u>*Unknown underground area*</u>—

The President is with his family and being held in an underground facility in a private location that only he and few construction workers knew about. The automated door system locked and bolted shut which only Blane has the code to open and close it. David Moore and Anna Moore were playing chess while their little adopted baby brother Haden is in his crib.

"Hey, it's your turn."

"Oh sorry, I was a little dazed there…" Anna said.

"Don't tell me you're nervous about this whole thing."

"Why wouldn't I be… this is end of time as we know it brother."

First Lady Alicia Moore, Blane's wife is with him in the next room speaking about everything that's going on.

"Are you sure this is the safest place to for us?" She asked.

"Yes, I'm sure. This is the only place I know that will survive a nuclear war and feasibly more than that." He said.

"It's better than nothing but all of those people are in a horrific nightmare while we sit here."

"I made sure National Guards worldwide and other planets are gathering all the survivors but these monstrosities, they just keep rising. Maybe… soon we will have to make a truce with their leader . . .Hm, even if we don't that, I'm sure the leader will want us to all change into them."

"Surrender? That isn't like you."

"Yes, but this invasion is worse than the last one. I wasn't in office at the time but trust me, I observed it from the recordings."

"Maybe you're right… this is the worse than the last and it's only been about sixteen hours…"

"Yes, the Grainian invasion took years and with the help of Jahzin we ended them. I only have one more shot at this and that's firing the Heaven Bolt."

"But the monsters are on our planets… not in space. What if there's still survivors?"

"The National Guards are equipped with some of the best technologies on finding survivors. I hate to say this but… if there's any left . . . Alicia, sacrifices must be made. I don't want this to happen as much as you do but every planet has a big gun and it's time, we use them."

"But…" She said as something unexpectedly alarmed them.

Their son screamed out loud and woke up Haden. Immediately they react and ran to the next room that the children are in.

"What the… How did it get in here?!" He said looking at David blocking his little brother, protecting him from getting hurt.

"No . . . It's . . . Its Anna!"

Seven Tens City, Ranomia, Mars—

Just a few blocks away, after finding their mother that crash landed on a crumbled building. Tajaymae and Oji watched her sob irrepressibly until the tears from her eyes is drained. Sadness on everyone's faces seeing the hurt that Dragazell caused as Demi laid her body down on her side next to Neecho and facing him on the dusty floor. Together forever with longevity, that element is now broken. A being that could live up to five hundred years promised to always be there for her. She leaned over to him and being halfway on top, touched his face, feeling his sharp cheek bones one more time. All she can endure now is Neecho's deceased body by her side as she slightly lifted him up and hugged him tightly.

Everyone currently ignoring the dragons causing havocs and roaring outside the library. Tajaymae walked up to her and Demi finally let loose. She shed her tears uncontrollably knowing that it was true that he was murdered in cold blood.

Tajaymae is lost for words on what to say as her mind is completely frozen. Oji began to look at the floor as Litzy rubbed his back and nods her head as he looked at her.

Oji immediately started to snivel as his face shivered up then Litzy hugged him as Titus stared at them.

"My father…" Titus said.

"Your father?" Litzy confused.

"Yes. Did he win the fight yet? With that monster that did this?"

"Oh, you mean Netro is your father… Make sense since he raised you… Well I don't know. The last time we saw him he was on TV beating the crab out of his Opposite."

"Perhaps he may need our help Litzy."

"I don't know Titus, but I have a feeling he got this in the bag."

"I hope you're right, this madness has to stop now."

Gigantica—

"Look at this world it's showing its true colors… it's… it's so dark! The ones who didn't transform is gonna fight and surrender then will have no choice but to serve me!"

"Yeah, then you'll kill them because they didn't transform into dragons."

"Trust issues Narrken… trust issues."

Dragazell chuckled and endured some fatigue but momentarily he stood firm again catching one of Narrken's right arm with his left hand then caught Nealo's left arm with his right hand.

Narrken then shot him in the chest with his Death Gun causing Dragazell to slightly bleed from the wound but still unfazed as he used his telekinesis to make Narrken fall back about thirty feet while Nealo also shot his Death Gun at him in the right cheek.

The Death bullet entered through and exiting Dragazell's left cheek then he used his Dragon's Blood on his right hand to form a falchion sword stabbing Nealo's chest close to his heart then he used his mind to propel him backwards about two hundred feet.

"Granddad…" Narrken fretted as he unloaded four shots unto Dragazell.

His body moved backward from each shot, the first shot landed against his chest, one shot in his neck and one to his shoulder.

Ki-Yale watched the fight as he is weakened with his hand still lifted ready to fire his Death Gun.

"You're still slowly recovering from my brother's earlier attacks which means there's a chance."

"Oh, that's what you think… but I'm still powerful than you."

Dragazell opened his mouth then instantly a three-inch ovoid of energy appeared activating his Chronic Beam then blasted it towards Narrken.

Dragazell focused on attacking Narrken, as Nealo appeared from the right side striking him with his right fist but Dragazell still unfazed by his attacks. The Dragoon Prince used his mind a held his entire body at his will preparing to put another falchion sword created with his blood into his chest.

Ki-Yale with his hand still lifted and Narrken looked at him recognizing he is traumatized with the battle taking place.

"Take the shot Ki-Yale… take the shot!" Narrken speaking to his brother telepathically as Dragazell targets him.

He stood frozen as his rage bloomed then reminisced about his father…

<u>The Kafmora residence 2322</u>—

"I used to look really far into space looking for planet Netron although I don't know exactly what it looks like but it's supposedly the biggest planet in the universe and it's like . . . Really, really, really far away."

"That's exactly what I was doing."

"How far did you look this time?"

"I can sort of see the Earth's barrier and that's about it. I can't see any further."

"Well I can see the Moon perfectly, the satellite hovering over it and a little more beyond that. You should be able to see more when you get older. You're developing your abilities quicker than we thought."

"Do you remember when I bought Titus for your 10th birthday? Your first pet?"

"Yeah I remember. You introduced him to me on this very balcony..."

"Hmm, oh I almost forgot." Neecho said then he left the rooftop then returned in twenty seconds.

"Look what I got."

"Woah! Is that ah?"

"Yes, it's a baby male lion, a cub . . . It's a little late but it's your birthday gift."

"What?! I love lions! Can I pet him?!"

"Yeah man, he's yours!"

"Heart of a lion."

"If you got a heart like that... Hm, then you got the heart to raise him."

"Wow . . .He's already chewing on my arm. Hmm, I don't know what to call him ..."

"Be careful with him son, before he pees on you."

"Hmm', I'm going to call him, hmm'.... Titus."

"Titus, I like it... It's Roman for 'Title of Honor'."

"Yes, you are correct Father."

"Hm, your slogan Ki-Yale..."— "My slogan?"

"Yes. Do you know what that means?"

"It means to go up against anyone and anything with no fear no matter how big that thing or being is... that's my view of it."

"Yes, that is true, but that slogan has many meanings to it. One in particular that I like, is never giving up. Having heart to me is giving your all, fight and protect what's yours."

<u>*Crouton Village Tournament housing roof top 2322—*</u>

"It would be good to have someone that can actually take on any threat."

"Hm... and be a leader."

"That's just how a prince thinks. Being a king, a leader, a ruler, it isn't a walk in the park though . . . It's more than just restoring order, it's more than just protection, or getting a queen and making children..."

"Then... What's it all about Dad? Responsibility? I'm pretty sure you said this before."

"It's making the right decisions son."

<u>*Present time—*</u>

Dragazell slowly piercing Nealo while holding Narrken's neck and strangling him with his mind.

"You kidnapped my brother and you took my father's life! Now you expect me to stand here and let you cause havoc to the rest of the universe? No! I can't lose! One day, I'm going to be... the King of Netron and maintain peace!"

Dragazell walking slowly towards his sworn enemy with his right hand out and his fingers clutched together. His blood pouring down his palm, ready to strike, ready gut him piece by piece.

Ki-Yale's heart pounding against his sternum, sweat began to trickle down entire face then he felt the breeze pulling his hair to the right. The memories had come back to haunt him and now all he sees in front of him was the target on Dragazell's forehead.

"DEATH GUN!"

FOURTY-THREE

Planet Venus, Western Space Station—

"Fire!"

The Heaven Bolt of Venus launched a radioactive beam at hundred percent traveling about 30,000 mph towards Orpana, a country that's well known. The mutated human dragons were reported to be destroying cities in Orpana and the survivors had already deserted the areas. Within minutes the radioactive beam touched the ground and instantly causing a massive explosion. The crackling of the flames bursting through the ground as the large dark smoke appeared in the sky. The mutated human dragons scorching into oblivion as some try to fly away, but the flames caught up them in time. Screaming of pain, suffering and agony meeting the taste of their own medicine.

Northern Sentry Space Station—

Chloe Torbino, keener, stronger and brave in the heart fighting against a mutated human dragon. They don't know how it got inside the space station but all they knew was to safeguard important equipment. She sat behind a machine with a fellow soldier taking cover.

"Hey, take this."

"You are giving me an e-cig?"

"Yeah, this could be your last vape... might as well enjoy it."

She remained silent as his hand held the e-cigarette out to her.

"Come on, it's fresh cannabis santal."

"Ok, I'll take a pull..."

"Good shit, right?" He chuckled.

"Yeah, now let's get in there."

Some agents were hesitant and wanted to leave in escape pods, but the captain would not allow it. The space station was on lock down as the mutated human dragon blasted his heated beam across the facility. Bodies mutilated by vast beams, but the walls were impenetrable because it was Tektonium metal. The creature went wild noticing that it is stuck within the station and could not escape. Their artilleries could not tame the dragon as Chloe ran up to it and kept blasting her firearm onto its legs. After witnessing her comrades fall from the beast, awoken her rage leading her to do the extreme.

"Captain!?"

"Chloe get out of there!!"

The time to end this was now, the captain opened the gate releasing the air from the station as the creature is sucked in the chamber.

Gigantica City—

The sound barrier cracked as the bullet traveled the speed of light hitting the Dragoon Prince in the forehead. The Death Gun is equivalent to the user's strength and their Netron Suit where it's omnipresent, even uniting with the multi-universe and so forth. Although Dragazell seemed to be still a bit stronger than the three, he is still weakened from the battle with Ki-Yale's Evo form. The clash of both

Netron suits, yes, the Intercosmic Suit is like an actual Netron Suit, but it does not have Netron DNA and it's impervious to Dragon's Blood. He can't die by just sheer powerful brutal hits; he needs to be slain by a Death bullet.

As he leaned back, oodles of blood gushed out from the back of his head and his blood leaked from the bullet hole. Some of his brain particles spouted out his skull as well and his knees conveyed fatigue causing him to kneel. He brought his head back glaring at Ki-Yale walking towards him.

At that moment the Prince of Dragoons knew he was defeated.

Narrken staggered as Nealo fell to ground free from his enemy's mind control. Exhaustion from all three of them formerly being belligerent in battle of absolute gore. Ki-Yale being the most fatigue wobbled forward to his sworn enemy. His Death bullet went right through him and landed on the ground. The bullet has lost its purpose and fainted away like dust blown by waft.

The last thing he saw was Netro bobbing towards him.

"You filthy… filthy Netron…"

The infection is rapidly eating away Dragazell's corpse as Ki-Yale looked over his lifeless body. Finally, in front of him, Ki-Yale's arms still damaged nonetheless slowly positioned his hand up halfway pointing at him. All he can think about now is victory and one final blow as if the Death Gun wasn't enough.

He flicked his middle finger at him, casting down his abhorrence for Dragazell. One last strike, just to let out the anger, Ki-Yale then punched Dragazell in the jaw with his right fist making him fall sideways to the ground. Ki-Yale stumbled beside him as Nealo moved at approximately 400mph and caught him before he hits the ground. As Dragazell's body laid down on the right side, his long hair now covered his face and his entire remains slowly disintegrating into nothingness, devouring the completion of the virus.

"You did it my grandson, you kept pushing..."

Nealo turned his head to Narrken and stared at him for a few seconds then nods his head. He squinted his eyes as he elevated from the ground, he turned his head to the left with a slightly disturbed facial utterance, then looked at Ki-Yale being unresponsive once more.

The millions of dragons, which were once humans, mutated into such violent beings and never to be human again are now falling instantly. All the dragons began to perish falling into the buildings, into the oceans and even neutralized when attempting to attack another human. As the Motogon is finally shattered, the malicious deity power that surged throughout the solar system for years is now ceased.

~~ONE MONTH LATER~~

<u>Relief Hospital in Gel Hev</u>—

"Luka Shale Jr.? Hello, Luka?!"

His eyelids slowly lifted, his sight blurred and only seeing a figure that appears to be a man, then he saw clearly seconds after.

"Hello sir, you were in a coma after we found you and your friend. Ah, he didn't speak at all but the military came and they said that they have ownership. When I came to get him to hand him over to them, he was gone."

"No, I aagh', I have to go find him."

"No sir, you have to rest. Your fellow survivor here is wanted for several murders. Hm, it's strange that he didn't transform though."

"His exoskeleton is Tektonium metal injected into him and fused with his cells guarding the cellular structures so it will prevent that from happening."

"Ah I see . . . very interesting, that's probably one of the reasons why the military wants him back."

Luka observed the windows on the left of him and saw armed combatants in the hallway guarding the room then asked—

"Where's my daughter and my butler?

"I'm… I'm so sorry sir…"

"No . . .Oh no..."— "She didn't make it and neither did your butler…."

"NO! NO! DON'T SAY THAT!" Tears suddenly welling in his eyes as he held his head with his two hands and stirring it left and right enduring the devastating news.

"I'm so sorry sir, investigators had found that a one of the flying beasts disintegrated them when they arrived at the Gel Hev Asylum to see their mom once more."

Luka lashed out in agony knowing his family is now gone leaving him all alone with nothing but pain and suffering. The doctor gazed at him, witnessing such a damaged man but more had to be said. He knew if he didn't tell Luka the full details, he wouldn't accept himself as being a good person.

"Luka…" He paused then continued— "Investigators believe… the alien creature was indeed your wife, Pamela."

~~THREE MONTHS LATER~~

Humanity had just encountered another cataclysmic invasion, and this was by far the worst one yet. After the ruin of properties and countless lives lost, humans once again began rebuilding. Ki-Yale hasn't heard from Nack Yaldara ever since the attacks but before he went looking for his best friend, he had to fulfill some sort of closure from the devastating ordeal as his father's life was taken away from him. Ki-Yale's Death Gun apparently wiped out Dragazell's body from existence along with the Motogon and his Dragon's Blood. Neecho's armor has become nonfunctional and therefore cannot regenerate him.

It was the most difficult thing for the Kafmora family to confirm but a proper funeral was done. His body was buried the same week that Dragazell was killed. Non-vase bouquet of white roses covering his wound as his body is lying face up in a coffin. Neecho's Netron Suit became defective and lost its abilities leaving him with just a regular Netron body. Although Dragazell's blood was targeted by Ki-Yale's Death Gun and is now gone completely, Neecho's suit lost its purpose prior to Dragazell's death. This could've saved Neecho's life sooner, but it was too late. Since his suit is now nonfunctional, humans can see him without disruption in the mind. Ki-Yale, Demi and her family from Africa who miraculously survived the horrors from Dragazell attended the funeral with old friends, Nealo, Tajaymae, Oji, Titus, Litzy and her mother were surrounding Neecho as he goes down into the dirt.

Remembering the cherished moments as he walked closer to the large monument tombstone and ogled open his name. He slowly puts his hand on the engraved letters.

"I'm going to miss you father…"

Narrken didn't show his face ever since Dragazell was killed but however, he attended the funeral on the sidelines watching without anyone knowing anything of it.

Nealo walked closer to Ki-Yale and joined his presence.

"Neecho wasn't a soldier like me, he doesn't get into a lot of fights but that day he put his life on the line to just get his son back and I will never forget his bravery."

"And so, will I…"

Ki-Yale, Nealo Tajaymae and Oji helped rebuild the cities and assisted the government in many ways, but Ki Yale still has to stand trial in the large court room.

Thurgood Marshall United States Courthouse—

"Your honor, it was mind control from my opposite, Dragazell. He had full control of my powers and forced me to shoot at these people. It truly wasn't my intentions… I just... I just wasn't strong enough to stop it." He said as he faced the lady Judge.

Five civilians were in critical condition which caused Ki-Yale to be convicted of attempted murder and public endangerment. Some happened to encounter shattered arms, some in hover chairs with fragmented legs and fragmented necks which later resulted in a sequence of unbearable emotions. One man had acquired prosthetic arms and legs and nothing but sorrow to the court room.

Ki-Yale in his Netron Suit, displaying his tapered dark Caesar haircut with fades on the sides and handcuffs weren't on him because authorities believed it was pointless to have them.

The jury of twelve individuals found Ki-Yale to be guilty of the crimes and now the judge wants to speak with him before doing the sentencing.

"Do you know how many people have died because of this invasion?"

"Over eight hundred thousand and over six thousand unknown lives who are still not yet found."

"And counting… the final report of the deaths and missing lives are not even finished yet. All because of that war you brought upon our home with that fiendish creature, Henry."

"His real name is Dragazell and I..."

"Draga… whatever his name is! This would never had happened if you aliens stay away from our home in the first place! . . . You murdered someone before. Correct?"

"Yes, your honor."

"Dr. Rogue Sagan... Although the President of the World issued the license to take him out and we all thank you for that, but it was still murder... Perhaps you thought one isn't enough?"

"No, your honor. We Netrons are full of righteousness, honorable, ethnical and murder is not what we ultimately prefer to solve every situation but if it's a nation of species, a life form presenting pure evil . . . a final decision of execution is required."

"The methods of a Netron to me is ideal, however, you are half human. Correct?"

"Yes, your honor."

"You said those traits are of a Netron but yet you are half human. Well, I'm a human myself and I know from experience, I've seen the vilest evil of human hearts step on the same platform you're on right now."

"Your honor, I've developed a new ability over the last three months, and I would like to display it to you."

Police officers lined up on the side and at the back of the court room seemed awfully nervous after what he had said then one of them with is hand on his holster said to the other—

"Be prepared to fire at will."

"You're going to display your new ability and kill us all?"

"No, your honor, it's beneficial for the victims. Please let me reveal it to you."

"Ok, proceed."

Ki-Yale walked over to the casualties then said—

"Hello, as you already know my name is Netro and what is your name?"

"Fuck you!"

"Ok I deserve that . . . Would you like your arm to be restored?"

The victim with his broken arm wrapped in a cast looked at him strangely and chuckled then said—

"Oh, so you're going to get my arm to move again? It's disconnected you fucking asshole!"

Ki-Yale held his palm out hovering over the victim's broken arm as officers aimed their guns at him. Despite the officers, Ki-Yale closed his eyes concentrating his ability.

"Lay down your weapons! Please, lay down your weapons…" The judge said.

Ki-Yale used his telekinesis as he focused on every cell, every fiber down to the very molecule and atoms in the victim's severed arm. Within five minutes his arms regrew entirely as people in the seating area were all amazed. The victim was utterly stunned and lost for words then joyfully screamed with his eyes wide open looking at his new arm.

The judge was astonished herself as she is lost for words with her eyebrows down and her mouth slightly open. Ki-Yale walked to the next victim with disjointed legs and sitting on a hover chair.

"Now for your two damaged legs."

After complete focus, the victim's shattered bones were restored in just under five minutes. The male victim got out of his hover chair gasping and couldn't believe that he can walk again.

"Remarkable."

"I am truly sorry for what I've done and what you had to go through."

"Apologies accepted man… Thank you Netro."

Ki-Yale walked over to the other casualties as they were still in utter shock at what he did.

"You seize to amaze me Netro." Litzy said.

"That was impressive Netro but unfortunately I still have to issue a sentence."

"I'm ok with that your honor."

"But he undid the damages as you can see!" Tajaymae yelled.

"Tajay…" Ki-Yale said with hollow tone.

"Wait, I don't wanna' press charges anymore!" The first victim said.

"You didn't press charges in the first place. The deadly action captured on live TV caught the attention of law enforcement before you were even hospitalized. Even if you press charges or not, he still has to face the consequences."

Ki-Yale finished with the other three then walked to the last one.

"No thanks, I'm good man… I'll stick with the prosthetics." He said as he lost his composure.

"Are you sure?"

"Yeah man I'm good, I'm getting used to this arm already anyway. Thank you."

"He still gets a sentence… This isn't right she let him perform all of this healing in front of her…"

"It's ok Mom." Ki-Yale spoke to his mom telepathically.

"Now, I'll give you a reduced sentence after what I've just seen but as you know you still will be prosecuted."

"Thank you, your honor, I understand."

"We the jury, hear by find the defended, Netro Two guilty of attempted murder, public endangerment that endangered billions of lives and must serve a sentence of five years in Gigantica City Federal Prison."

"What?! Five years?!" Demi lashed out as she stood up.

"Brother…" Oji said.

"No… that's bullshit!" Tajaymae blurted and stood up as well.

"No this isn't right!" Demi protested then proceeds to reach Nealo through linked telepathy— *"Nealo! Nealo! Can you hear me?"*

"Yes yes, I can hear you Demi… It's ok Demi… we can always visit him and I'm sure he would endure reasonable treatment." Nealo responded from an unknown area.

"It's not ok Nealo! Can't you like manipulate the judge to change her mind and make everyone forget?"

"Yes, I can but this is what Ki-Yale wants."

"No that's five years of his life wasted!"

"He wants to show everyone that even though he is extremely powerful with all sorts of abilities, he still faces the consequences of the law."

Litzy seemed saddened as she shook her head left to right.

Ki-Yale turned around and smiled at everyone before two officers began to escort him and still didn't situate any handcuffs.

He stopped and said his goodbyes as Litzy immediately stood up then gave him a hug and a kiss on the lips. Demi walked by Litzy, squeezing in between her and the bench, then hugged her son with the tightest grip she ever done in her life.

"Ok time to go." One male officer said.

"Wait!" Tajaymae and Oji hollered at the same time then Ki-Yale hugged his two siblings.

"Come on, let's go!"

"Alright." Ki-Yale replying to the male officer as he followed him to the exit.

"Are you sure this is truly best for Ki-Yale? . . . Nealo? . . . Nealo? Can you hear me?"

<u>Gel Hev, Little Tree Ville—</u>

Winter days are still here but the sun is shining bright as ever. Nealo walked on the slushy road onto a familiar place, the bridge over the waterfall. The bridge in which his first grandson allegedly disappeared.

"Narrken…"

He saw a spitting image of him and it's so real he could touch him.

"No!" Narrken said with a deeper and monstrous voice than how he usually speaks.

"Wait… that voice…"

"Yes, you know who I am."

"You aren't Narrken… you're that demon."

Chuckles coming from the evil spirit as Nealo looked confused.

"You lured me here… Who are you? Why don't you tell me your real name?"

"Patience Nealo… In due time, you'll know my name… I have to accomplish a few things first."

"Well, atleast tell me why you lured me here."

"You wanted answers… you want to know if it's true that Narrken possesses half Netron and Dragoon DNA which is quiet amusing."

"We aren't compatible with the opposites. So how does Narrken possess such DNA and still be alive?"

"He had a lot to endure."

"I'm sure he did…"

"Hmm, let me show you a memory."

"A memory?"

<u>*Unknown Area in the past*</u>—

In a dark room with red night lights Dragazell in his older Henry Luciano form along with Terrogon and Goonie stood in front of Narrken as he was strapped down inside an automated pod. Narrken was screaming on top of his lungs enduring the most pain. This machinery was specially designed by Goonie to graft on Narrken's body injecting thousands of needles filled with Dragon's Blood all around.

"Are you sure this is going to work Goonie?"

"Yes, I'm positive… what I'm using is Tektonium liquid along with its crystals. This machine is designed to counter the blood while it's fusing with the Netron cells. It will take some time though; it takes years but as long as he stays on this machine."

"This better work Goonie."

"My lord, I promise you it will."

"Goonie is always a technological genius no matter what planet he's on."

"Narrken will join us now and since he will have our blood his hatred for the prince would be even greater."

"Well, he's overcome all of the hatred."

"I don't think so Nealo, he hasn't seen you guys ever since Dragazell was killed… maybe he still wants to…"

"Nah… once a Netron is always a Netron."

"Hm, you might want to reconsider what you just said… don't tell me you forgot about me and my abilities…"

"So, you've got what you wanted from Ki-Yale . . . rage… and still I wonder why you feed on something so trivial, it's very bewildering."

"Nealo, you should be wondering why I brought you here. I'm the Demon of Evolution. I'm connected with the past, present and future."

"The Demom of Evolution… I'm sure that's not your real name but, what are you saying? Everything that has happened you were already aware of?"

"Yes, even when I said Netro will be mine I knew it will be guaranteed such a thing would happen but… I only got a small portion of his rage and I couldn't control him. In fact, he is the only Netron that seemed hard for me to control."

"Well, he's only partially a Netron… Why only target us? Why not the Dragoons? They're as evil as ever."

"Yes, that would be a powerful combination but the Netrons and I are a powerful combination as well.

However, true rage comes from broken love and Dragoons… they don't have any love amongst them to begin with."

"Yeah, that makes sense."

"I can witness the forthcoming of more than a million possibilities of how things could play out and only one thing would happen as time goes by. Well, let's just say that I failed for now... but for the next time… Netro Two could be fully embraced on my clutches."

"I don't see how you can rule an entire planet with only being driven by anger. It would just be destruction along the way."

"It's already being destroyed as we speak… just take a look for yourself."

In an instant, the entire scenery had changed as Nealo's question was answered.

"This… this is Planet Netron . . . You transferred me here?"

"Well, I wouldn't say that I brought you here..."

Nealo focused on what was in front of him. Everything seems so real that he had to make sure it is. He bends his left knee to the ground then touched the soil and grabs a handful of rock particles.

"It's usually glistening…"

"Look over there Nealo…"

He walked closer to the edge of the cliff and looked over the large land.

"All of this destruction . . . this, this can't be..."

"It was me that transported you here."

It was a familiar voice right behind him, a voice he heard when he used to reside on Planet Netron.

Nealo turned around and there she was.

"Welcome back… Nealo, Royal Son of Netro One."

-TO BE CONTINUED-

ACKNOWLEDGEMENTS

First and foremost this is my first book ever written and I was self-taught. It was surely a lot of work and I believe my work in the future would be more draining but I wouldn't have done it if it wasn't for the push that my family and friends gave me. Overall, it was fun writing this book and that's what counts the most.

I would like to express my special thanks to everyone for their support and I would like to thank Dorian Moore for creating the name "The Pinnacle".

I'm also appreciative for all of the many creations from the masterminds of the science fiction and fantasy works. I had many influences and some were Dragon Ball Z, Yu Yu Hakusho, Stars Wars: Episode III – Revenge of the Sith, The Terminator, The Dark Knight and many more.

I would also like to thank Eight Little Pages for doing a fantastic job on the artwork and overall book design inside and out.

Last and most importantly I'm grateful for my actions of finally deciding to let the world see my imagination. This story has been inside my mind ever since I was eleven years old and now I'm in my twenties. It's always good to see progress especially in oneself.

www.ingramcontent.com/pod-product-compliance
Lightning Source LLC
Chambersburg PA
CBHW020904110726
47900CB00001B/9